British & American
Literature and Culture in English Films

英美影视
文学与文化

主　编　胡　贞
副主编　吴玲娟　卢　佼　刘青青

WUHAN UNIVERSITY PRESS
武汉大学出版社

图书在版编目(CIP)数据

英美影视文学与文化/胡贞主编．—武汉：武汉大学出版社，2018.4(2024.1 重印)
ISBN 978-7-307-19888-3

Ⅰ.英…　Ⅱ.胡…　Ⅲ.①影视艺术—文学研究—英国　②影视艺术—文学研究—美国　③影视艺术—文化—研究—英国　④影视艺术—文化—研究—美国　Ⅳ.①I106.35　②J905

中国版本图书馆 CIP 数据核字(2017)第 307645 号

责任编辑:谢群英　　责任校对:李孟潇　　版式设计:马　佳

出版发行：**武汉大学出版社**　(430072　武昌　珞珈山)
(电子邮箱：cbs22@ whu.edu.cn　网址：www.wdp. com.cn)
印刷:武汉邮科印务有限公司
开本:787×1092　1/16　印张:28.25　字数:471 千字　插页:1
版次:2018 年 4 月第 1 版　2024 年 1 月第 3 次印刷
ISBN 978-7-307-19888-3　定价:79. 00 元

前　言

影视作品是现代科学技术与艺术相结合的产物，通过画面、声音、蒙太奇、故事情节等形式来传达与表现，是一种以视觉符号为主的、直观的传播形式，是当代最具影响力的大众传播媒介之一。作为综合艺术的影视作品在汲取艺术养料丰富自身综合特质方面，与文学、文化密切融合。影视作品借鉴文学作品中的叙事和抒情手法，鲜明塑造人物性格，形成新的综合艺术特质；另一方面，影视作品更为直观地体现异国生活方式、社会价值、道德标准等表层和深层的文化特质，因此，影视鉴赏成为有效提升文学素养、了解异国文化的有效途径之一。

在大学开设英美影视相关课程有利于学生了解西方文学与文化的发展概况，更有利于加深他们对英语国家的政治、经济、社会、文化等方面的认识和了解，从而在文学和文化两个层面上更好地掌握英语这门语言。作为上海第二工业大学拓展类大学英语课程和通识课程，“英美影视文学与文化”已完成上海市教委重点课程的建设工作，初步形成自身特色，广受学生好评。本书拟作为该课程的重要后续成果，以飨读者。

本教程在内容上包含三大模块：英美影视基础知识、英美文学与影视作品、英美文化与影视作品。其中，英美影视基础知识包含影视发展概览、影视语言、影视经典作品等章节；英美文学与影视作品包含英国文学概览、影视作品中的英国文学、美国文学概览、影视作品中的美国文学等章节；英美文化与影视作品包含历史、宗教、教育、科技、社会等主题的影视作品，凸显英美文化精髓。

本书在编写过程中得到了上海第二工业大学科研处、教务处的大力支持；校级培育学科“外国语言文学”负责人张军教授给予了编写指导；文理学部《英美影视文学与文化》课程建设小组全体成员承担了繁重的编写任务；冯亚民先生提供技术协助，我们在此一并表示感谢。

由于编者水平有限，书中难免有错误和不当之处，恳请读者批评指正。

编　者

2018 年 1 月

目 录

Module One

English Film Outlook

Unit 1
English Film History

The history of film cannot be credited to one individual as an oversimplification of any history often tries to do. Each inventor added to the progress of other inventors, culminating in progress for the entire art and industry.

The history of World Cinema, to a certain degree, is a history of American Cinema, with Hollywood interacting with a range of national and transnational cinemas, from German Expressionism to Hollywood and Chinese films. The American film industry has dominated all others in last and this century.

American cinema (often referred to as Hollywood) has had a far-reaching influence on cinema of the world since the early 20th century. Its history is separated into four main periods according to this book: the early period, the classical Hollywood period, the new and post-classical period, and the contemporary period.

1. Early Cinema

The cinema did not emerge as a form of mass consumption until its technology evolved from the initial "peepshow" format to the point where images were projected on a screen in a darkened theater. The Early Cinema Period started from 1830s to 1920s.

1.1 Birth of Motion Pictures

A recorded instance of photographs capturing and reproducing motion was a series of photographs of a running horse by Eadweard Muybridge (1830-1904), an American photographer. He made a pioneering series of photographs on glass plates, using twenty separate cameras placed in a row, in order to show precisely how a horse ran. Muybridge's accomplishment led inventors everywhere to attempt to make similar devices that would capture such motion.

Horse Jumping (circa 1877), sequential photographs by Eadweard Muybridge

In the United States, Thomas A. Edison (1847-1931) was among the first to produce such a device, the Kinetoscope. He completed with his assistant Dickson the design of an electrically controlled camera, the Kinetograph, and a peep-show machine called the Kinetoscope, giving viewers the thrill and novelty of perceiving life-like movements of vaudeville performers and boxing exhibitions. The Kinetoscope was patented in 1891 and heard by an entrepreneur named Norman Raff two years later. Under Edison's name and Raff's manufacture, the first Kinotoscope parlor opened in 1894.

Edison was one of the determining figures for the early development of motion pictures as an industry, while his French competitors, the Lumiere Brothers, had taken the lead due to their ability to project motion pictures in front of an audience. Louis Lumiere (1864-1948) invented the Cinematograph upon Edison's design of the Kinetoscope. It combined moving images with front projection using intermittent movement. In contrast to early Edison's large and cumbersome Kinetograph, the camera was portable, lightweight, and thus free from studio restrictions for easy outdoor use as a cinematic recorder of "actualities" of life. The Lumiere Brothers had his new Cinematograph exhibited in public for the first time in Paris in December, 1895. The immediate successes of the exhibition won the enthusiastic support and wonder of the public and made 1895 the official birth year of the cinema as we know it today.

1.2 Headquarters to Hollywood

Competition in film industry was fierce because of the temptingly high profit. In 1908, Edison formed the Patents Company, allied with nine other leading companies including Vitagraph, Selig, Biograph, etc., claiming 16 patent rights. The Company strangled all those companies not allied with them. By 1910, it had monopolized the production, distribution and exhibition in America. To free from its monopoly, independent producers left the filming centers of New York and Chicago and filmed in Hollywood, a little village several miles away from downtown Los Angeles. D. W. Griffith shifted his filming place to Hollywood and there he made hundreds of films and gathered a favorable number of outstanding actors.

After the Treaty of Versailles was signed in 1919, which formally ended World War I, the American film industry permanently relocated its production headquarters to Hollywood. It grew and prospered there between 1920 and 1929. The population in Hollywood had grown from 5,000 by 1910 to 36,000 by 1920, and it would be 157,000 by 1930. The major movie studios (around twenty) were located in Hollywood, among which, there were the "Big Three" (Paramount, Metro-Goldwyn-Mayer and First National) and smaller studios like Warner Bros., Fox and Universal, etc. In 1924, the Big Three Studios consolidated their film production and distribution companies by acquiring their own theatre chains. Zukor's Paramount Pictures absorbed a number of smaller companies. Lois Mayer and Sam Goldwyn created MGM as the production arm for Loew's theatre chain. First National depended on independent producers to supply films to its movie houses.

American film production gradually completed its transformation in 1920s from director-centered system into producer-centered mode. Hence came into being the "star system". Things in Hollywood became scandalous when rumors spread on "the sins of Hollywood" which included accusations of depravity, sexual license and amorality among Hollywood stars. News of alleged rape and murder of leading actors and directors such as Fatty Arbuckle and William Desmond Taylor became headlines on various newspapers. Fearing huge economic losses resulting from the scandals, Hollywood decided to take measures to establish and maintain the highest possible moral and artistic standards in film production. In 1922, Hollywood founded the Motion Picture Producers and Distributors of America (MPPDA) and made the famous Hays Code under the host of Will Hays, which aimed to cast out the amoral plots, dialogues and scenes when censoring films.

1.3 Early Directors

Films shot in documentary style from 1895 to 1905 were not edited. Like the Lumiere films, they "rendered the world as it is" in their presentation of news stories of the day. Meanwhile, the development of fantasy films by Georges Melies, with "in-film", stop-motion editing, enabled some directors to create "magic realism" for their fictional narratives. These films recreated the world according to the filmmaker's imagination. Both tendencies influenced other directors in film production as the demand to tell simple narratives held the interest of the audience and helped them identify with characters in the filmed events.

1.3.1 Edwin S. Porter (1870-1941)

Born	April 21, 1870 Connellsville, Pennsylvania, the United States
Died	April 30, 1941 New York City, the United States
Occupation	Film director, film producer
Years active	1899-1915

Filmography: *Jack and the Beanstalk* (1902), *The Life of an American Fireman* (1902), *The Great Train Robbery* (1903), *The Kleptomaniac* (1905), *Life of a Cowboy* (1906), *Rescued from an Eagle's Nest* (1908), and *The Prisoner of Zenda* (1913)

To profit, moviemakers turned to dramatic stories. Though the growth of this genre was slow, some dramatic films proved exceptionally popular. Edison hired Edwin S. Porter as projectionist and director when his new studio was built in New York. Porter directed two important films, *The Life of an American Fireman* (1902) and *The Great Train Robbery* (1903), which proved to be a complete revolution for the narrative structure of motion pictures.

Porter built his short film narratives from the sensational stories carried by daily newspapers and skillfully reconstructed these stories into one-shot films showing one continuous action from beginning to end staged without a moving camera. His skill in reconstructing the actions of major characters had been revealed in films like *Capture of the Biddle Brothers* (1902) and *Fun in a Bakery Shop* (1902). When directing *Jack and the Beanstalk* (1902), Porter imitated the structure of theatrical story-telling that French director Georges Melies had improved. And he playfully experimented and capitalized on the essential connection between documentary films shot in real time and studio scenes shot within a theatrical space. Therefore, he managed to expand the linear narrative with the introduction of simultaneous actions through cross-cutting one scene with a different one. His cutting back and forth from one scene to another developed tension or suspense within the narrative.

In Porter's *The Life of an American Fireman*, this editing technique was utilized to heighten the dramatic effect of the last-minute rescue. At the start of the film, the first shots show the thoughts of a fireman through a "balloon", borrowed from comic strips. The fireman imagines his family in a fire; the film then cuts to a close-up of a fire alarm and a hand pulling the alarm. Documentary footage follows of fire fighters answering the alarm. Porter then combines these scenes with staged events of firemen entering the building by ladder and parallel shots of the dramatic rescue of the woman and child trapped inside the burning building. In some versions of the film the editing of the rescue scenes shows intercutting from the exterior arrival of the firemen at the building to the interior room where fire men break down the door, creating a new narrative dimension.

In 1903, Porter made *The Great Train Robbery*, which took a few more steps in evolving a film grammar. This film is one reel of action, violence, frontier humor, special effects (a very effective matte shot of a train passing as seen through a stationhouse window), and, as a final fillip, a full-screen close-up of a bandit firing his pistol at the audience. Porter's camera angles tend to emphasize the realism of the exteriors. In fourteen scenes, he told a complicated (at that time) story and told it visually and vividly, with virtually no titles. *The Great Train Robbery* was not only the most famous film produced by Edison studios; it was also the single most famous American movie until it was displaced twelve years later by *The Birth of a Nation*. *The Great Train Robbery* made Porter the leading filmmaker of his day.

1. 3. 2 David Wark Griffith (1875-1948)

Born	January 22, 1875 Kentucky, the United States
Died	July 23, 1948 California, the United States
Occupation	Film director, film producer
Years active	1908-1931

Filmography: *The Musketeers of Pig Alley* (1912), *The Girl and Her Trust* (1912), *Judith of Bethulia* (1913), *The Birth of a Nation* (1915), *Intolerance* (1916), *Hearts of the World* (1918), *Broken Blossoms* (1919), *True Heart Susie* (1919), *Way Down East* (1920), *Orphans of the Storm* (1921), *America* (1924), *Isn't Life Wonderful* (1924), *Sally of the Sawdust* (1925), *The Sorrows of Satan* (1926), *Abraham Lincoln* (1930), *One Million B. C.* (1940)

Labeled as the "father of the American cinema", David Wark Griffith (1875-1948) was the first American director who established the cultural significance of motion pictures. Griffith's cinematic practices influenced all future filmmaking and directly revolutionized the impact of motion pictures upon audiences to become the foremost cultural art form of the 20th century.

From 1908 to 1913, Griffith made some 485 films, mainly one- and two-reel films for Biograph Studios in New York. He showed interests in headline stories about the courage of single, young women caught in the dynamics of city life and a world of street crime and corruption. Many of these films highlighted themes relating to an assault on values and moral wisdom. Griffith focused on sharp contrasts in the melodramatic adventures in his early films, from *A Corner in Wheat* (1909), *The Lonedale Operator* (1911), to *The Musketeers of Pig Alley* (1912) and including his biblical drama *Judith of Bethulia* (1913).

Griffith's filmmaking apprenticeship at Biograph Studio perfected his talent for transforming sentimental melodramas into exciting and suspenseful film narratives. It was during this period that Griffith developed a film language to help him tell his narratives cinematically. He developed a complex use of parallel editing and innovative acting techniques. The major film techniques he created to manipulate screen times and space included innovative camera placement movement, dramatic interior lighting, and parallel or cross-cutting that enhanced the dramatic tensions within the scene. His *The Sands of Dee* contained sixty-eight scenes when a half dozen competing firms used only from eleven to forty-six in their films.

Griffith's achievements in these years were not merely technical. Technique served his employment of principles of narration in the Hollywood Cinema, and his passion for the gesture and the moment that would reveal a human soul. In *The Mothering Heart* (1913), he let the heroine Lillian Gish thrash madly at the bush around her to reveal the seething emotion of a woman overcome by her child's death, by destroying the strong green life around her.

The peak of his directing career came with the films he made between 1915 and 1920, among which, *The Birth of a Nation* (1915), *Intolerance* (1916), *Hearts of the World* (1918), *Broken Blossoms* (1919), and *Way Down East* (1920) are the most memorable ones.

There are several starting points for cinema, but it was Griffith's *The Birth of a Nation* that fired the starting gun for the American cinema. *The Birth of a Nation* proved a firestorm success. An investment of less than $110,000, the film produced returns of 10 to 14 million dollars, which affirmed that the cinema was commercially a sleeping giant newly sprung to its feet.

Thomas Dixon's novel and later successful stage play *The Clansman* gave Griffith the material he needed to connect his own ideological message with this epic film narrative, *The Birth of a Nation*. Covering the war year and the turbulent Reconstruction period, this three-hour-long masterpiece reveals a full view of the history of the Civil War and its aftermath as reflected by two families, the Stonemans of the North and the Camerons of the South. The eldest Cameron son founds a racist organization known as the White Knights, or Ku Klux Klan, and makes the streets of the defeated South safe from the ravage of wild-eyed Negroes and white carpetbaggers.

Because of the racist politics in the film, Griffith was faced with public outrage from liberals and black American organizations such as the National Association for the Advancement of Colored People (NAACP). *The Birth of a Nation* was denounced and boycotted in various northern American cities. Within the American debate, Griffith achieved his goal. He brought the power of the film to the middle class, and persuaded them that movies could not only appeal to the emotions of a wider audience, but that films also could reconstruct and reinforce certain cultural values and beliefs of that audience.

Griffith decided to produce a film of epic scope to strike back and overwhelm his critics. He took eighteen months to make *Intolerance* (1916). Moving far beyond what even he had done, he refused the easy alternative of telling the four stories of the film one by one. Rather, he chose to tell them concurrently and alternatively. In other words, he cross-cut from exposition of one story to that of another, from development to development, and breathtakingly, from climax to climax. The film was three hours and ten minutes long. It failed, forcing Griffith to spend the rest of his professional life backtracking. However, many theories have been advanced for the financial failure of *Intolerance*. They range from the film being ahead of its time to audiences not being able to follow the plot.

Anyhow, Griffith's reputation rests with *The Birth of a Nation* and *Intolerance*. One is a racist defense of a pre-Civil-War Southern life-style, the other a plea for universal understanding. Griffith seems to be a tradition-bound bigot in the former, crusading liberal in latter. Yet these two epics share some characteristics. They both imply that history serves best as a chaotic background for a fictional drama of separation and unification.

Griffith moved away from Hollywood and returned to New York to direct a number of feature films from 1919 to 1931, among which, *Broken Blossoms* (1919), *Way Down East* (1920), *Orphans of the Storm* (1921), *The White Rose* (1923) and *Isn't Life Wonderful* (1924) thematically attempt to depict their heroines overcoming the ordeals of racial intolerance and strife in one form or another and to triumph over the shortcomings of life itself. However, Griffith framed each film within his older melodramas, offering the audience a "shallow sentimentality" that was deemed by critics as old-fashioned and biased. Yet with *Isn't Life Wonderful*, Griffith shot the film in Germany using "actualities" or found locations for most of the documentary filming. At the end of the silent period in 1927 Griffith's artistic methods were considered too extravagant for financial backing. He attempted two sound films, *Abraham Lincoln* (1930) and *The Struggle* (1931). Each film was found wanting an audience, but *The Struggle* appeared to be more than a fictional story since it conveyed Griffith's own battle with the demons of alcohol.

1.4 Early Actors

1.4.1 Charlie Chaplin (1889-1977)

Born	April 16, 1889 London, United Kingdom
Died	December 25, 1977 Vaud, Switzerland
Occupation	Actor, comedian, film director, film producer, screenwriter, editor, composer
Years active	1899-1976

Best Films: *The Tramp* (1915), *Easy Street* (1917), *The Immigrant* (1917), *A Dog's Life* (1918), *The Kid* (1921), *The Gold Rush* (1925), *The Circus* (1928), *City Lights* (1931), *Modern Times* (1936), *The Great Dictator* (1940), *Limelight* (1952), *A King in New York* (1957)

Charlie Chaplin is considered one of the most important figures in the film industry and the film world. As a great comic actor and filmmaker, he rose to fame in the silent film era and became a worldwide icon through his screen persona "the Tramp". His career spanned more than 75 years, from a child close to his death at the age of 88.

Raised in London, Chaplin's childhood was featured with poverty and hardship. Chaplin started performing from a young age, touring music halls and later working as a stage actor and comedian. At 19 he went to Hollywood and made his first appearances in 1914. He soon developed the Tramp persona and formed a large fan base. What's more, Chaplin directed his films from an early stage, and continued to hone his craft as he moved to the different corporations. By 1918, he had become one of the most famous men in the world.

In 1919, Chaplin co-founded the distribution company United Artists, which gave him complete control over his films. His first feature-length picture was *The Kid* (1921), followed by *A Woman of Paris* (1923), *The Gold Rush* (1925), and *The Circus* (1928). He refused to make sound films in the 1930s, instead, producing *City Lights* (1931) and *Modern Times* (1936) without dialogue. Chaplin became increasingly political and his next film, *The Great Dictator* (1940) satirized Adolf Hitler. The decade of 1940s was marked with controversy for Chaplin, and his popularity declined rapidly. He was accused of communist sympathies. An FBI investigation was opened on Chaplin, and he was eventually forced to leave the United States and settle in Switzerland. He abandoned the Tramp for his later films.

Unlike most filmmakers, Chaplin dominated almost every aspect of his filming and did every job like writing, directing, producing, editing, scoring and starring in his films. More importantly, Chaplin developed a unique method of filmmaking. Until he began making spoken dialogue films with *The Great Dictator*, he never shot from a completed script. If he thought he was out of ideas on what to do with the story, he would often choose to take a break from the shoot which could last for days, while keeping the studio ready for when he felt inspired again. Chaplin usually spent much longer time on the development and production of his films than most other filmmakers at the time because Chaplin was a perfectionist. His films are characterized by slapstick combined with pathos, and often feature the Tramp struggling against adversity. Many contain social and political themes, as well as autobiographical elements.

Chaplin liked conventional camera angles and only used close-ups to highlight emotional scenes, and usually preferred a static, "stage-like" camera setting where the scenes were portrayed as if set on a stage. Chaplin depicted social outcasts and the poor in a sympathetic light in his films from early on. His silent films usually focused on the Tramp's plight in poverty and his run-ins with the law, but also explored controversial topics, such as immigration, illegitimacy and drug use. Although this can be seen as social commentary, Chaplin's films did not contain overt political themes or messages until later on his career in the 1930s. *Modern Times* (1936), which portrayed factory workers in dismal conditions, was viewed the first of his films by critics to contain an anti-capitalist message, although Chaplin denied the film being political in any way. However, his next films, *The Great Dictator* (1940), a parody on Adolf Hitler and Benito Mussolini that ended in a dramatic speech criticizing the blind following of patriotic nationalism, as well as his first European film *A King in New York* (1957), were more clearly political and caused controversy.

In 1972, Chaplin received an Honorary Academy Award for his incalculable effect in making motion pictures the art form of 20th century which brought a high regard for himself and a renewed appreciation for his work, with *The Gold Rush*, *City Lights*, *Modern Times*, and *The Great*

Dictator often ranked among the greatest films of all time.

Chaplin's legacy lies in his unequaled influence as a filmmaker together with the image of the Tramp. Unique and indelible, the Tramp is considered one of the most iconic images in cinema; and it's recognizable to people who have never seen a Chaplin film, and in places where his films are never shown. No other comedian could match his worldwide impact. Chaplin's films with the Tramp contain greatly eloquent and richly comedic expressions of the human spirit in film history.

As one of the founding members of United Artists, Chaplin also played a role in the development of the film industry. Although UA never became a major company like MGM or Paramount Pictures, the idea that filmmakers could produce their own films was ahead of its time. Today, several of Chaplin's films are still regarded as classics and among the greatest ever made. Books about Chaplin continue to be published regularly, and he is a popular subject for media scholars and film archivists.

1.4.2 Buster Keaton (1895-1966)

Born	October 4, 1895 Piqua, Kansas, the United States
Died	February 1, 1966 Woodland Hills, California
Occupation	Actor, comedian, film director, film producer, screenwriter, stunt performer
Years active	1920s

Best Films: *One Week* (1920), *The Playhouse* (1921), *Cops* (1922), *The Electric House* (1922), *Sherlock J.* (1924), *The General* (1926), *The Cameraman* (1928)

Buster Keaton was best known for his silent films, in which his trademark was physical comedy with a consistently stoic, deadpan expression, earning him the nickname "The Great Stone Face." Critic Roger Ebert wrote of Keaton's "extraordinary period from 1920 to 1929, when he worked without interruption on a series of films that make him, arguably, the greatest actor-director in the history of the movies". His career declined afterward with a dispiriting loss of his artistic independence when he was hired by Metro-Goldwyn-Mayer and he descended into alcoholism, ruining his family life. He recovered in the 1940s, remarried, and revived his career to a degree as an honored comic performer for the rest of his life, earning an Academy Honorary Award in 1959.

He was hired as a co-star and gag man, making his first appearance in *The Butcher Boy*. In 1920, *The Saphead* was released, in which Keaton had his first starring role in a full-length feature. It was based on a successful play. Keaton was recommended to take the role for the remake five years later, since the film was to have a comic slant. Then Keaton moved to full-length features.

Film critic David Thomson after described Keaton's style of comedy: "Buster plainly is a man inclined towards a belief in nothing but mathematics and absurdity ... like a number that has always been searching for the right equation. Look at his face—as beautiful but as inhuman as a butterfly—and you see that utter failure to identify sentiment."

Keaton signed with Metro-Goldwyn-Mayer in 1928, a business decision that he would later call the worst of his life. He realized too late that the studio system MGM represented would severely limit his creative input. For instance, the studio refused his request to make his early project, *Spite Marriage*, as a sound film and after the studio converted, he was obliged to adhere to dialogue-laden scripts. However, MGM did allow Keaton some creative participation on his last originally developed/written silent film *The Cameraman*.

2. Classical Hollywood Cinema

Classical Hollywood cinema or the classical Hollywood narrative, are terms used in film history which designate both a visual and sound style for making motion pictures and a mode of production used in the American film industry between 1927 and 1963. This period is often referred to as the "golden age of Hollywood". An identifiable cinematic form emerged during this period called classical Hollywood style.

2.1 Silent Films to Sound Films

It was decades after the first known public exhibition of projected sound films took place in Paris in 1900 that sound motion pictures were made commercially practical. The coming of sound required three phases of change: invention, innovation, and diffusion. The transformation took place between 1926 and 1930. First, apparatuses were developed to record and synchronize sound and image with a quality and tone suitable for presentation to large audiences. Then, companies had to figure out how to market sound films to the public. Finally, the major movie companies had to decide to accept the new technology and substitute it for the standardized silent film.

During the golden age of Hollywood, which lasted from the end of the silent era in American cinema in the late 1920s to the early 1960s, films were prolifically issued by the Hollywood studios. The start of the golden age was arguably when *The Jazz Singer* was released in 1927 and increased box-office profits for films as sound was introduced to feature films.

It seems that sound film replaced the silent film overnight. In 1925 silent filmmaking was the standard while merely five years later, Hollywood produced only sound films. The introduction of a sound track to complement the film image was accomplished by the development of Vitaphone by

Warner Bros, which is the leading brand of sound-on-disc technology. In the fall of 1926, Warners released its first feature, *Don Juan*, a costume romance starring John Barrymore. By this time Vitaphone had successfully synchronized a sound-on-disc recording mechanically with the film projector. This technological innovation followed Harry Warner's decision to provide an orchestral sound track to attract audiences to movie houses outside the larger urban centers. With the release of *The Jazz Singer* in 1927, Warner Bros. created a tremendous audience response to this film. Sound-on-film, however, would soon become the standard for talking pictures. By the fall of 1928, when Warner Bros. completed its soundstages in Hollywood, it made the first all-talking feature, *The Lights of New York*, and released a second Jolson film, *The Singing Fool* (1928), an "all-talking, all-singing, all-dancing" musical feature film that was also a box-office hit.

Paramount and MGM, realizing the tremendous gains acquired by Warners, began to quickly convert their studios to soundstages. In 1929, both studios entered the sound era on solid financial footing, but both still had to withstand an attempted takeover by William Fox. The Fox Film, Corporation — Warner Bros.' only one true competitor — adapted a version of AT&T's pioneering technology of loudspeaker and sound amplifier, to record sound-on-film. Warners' Vitaphone system of sound-on-disc soon gave way to the superior sound-on-film system. In the 1930s, Fox's Movietone sound-on-film system became the industry standard in America.

2.2 New Film Genres in 1930s

Now motion pictures needed to invent a new branch of dubbing and subtitling to allow sound films into foreign markets. With this problem in mind, Paramount and MGM experimented with multilingual feature films. Both Josef von Sternberg's *The Blue Angel with Marlene Dietrich*, and *Clarence Brown's Anna Christie* (1930) starring Greta Garbo, were made in English-German Versions. Yet these film productions were a costly solution.

Instead, during the 1930s, Hollywood invested and created hundreds of popular feature films annually, which mainly fell into 3 categories: Musicals, Gangster Pictures, Screwball Comedies. They were new and very popular, and would help bridge the language gap while retaining their dominance in the European film market.

2.2.1 Musicals

Ernst Lubitsch (1892-1947) of Paramount, a German director who came to Hollywood in 1921, created the first musical to be conceived in film terms. He styled light operetta plots into fashionable bedroom farces in *The Love Parade* (1929), *The Smiling Lieutenant* (1931) and *The Merry Widow* (1934). Warner Bros. experimented with the revue format, borrowing heavily from Broadway hits that featured musical song and dance acts. *Gold Diggers of Broadway* (1929) followed Warners' success with Jolson in Lloyd Bacon's *The Singing Fool*. Most musical numbers were staged within the film narrative as if they were part of a performance before and audience.

And there appeared two great innovative stylists of the movie musical: Busby Berkeley and Fred Astaire, the former a choreographer and the latter a dancer. Berkeley (1895-1976) first established his style in *42nd Street* (1933), and achieved apotheosis in the musical numbers of *Gold Diggers of 1935* (1935). Fred Astaire (1899-1987) was the opposite of Berkeley. This talented Broadway performer invented the dance musical. Astaire and Ginger Rogers, his most frequent partner in the decade, made nine films for RKO that served as the standard by which dance musicals are judged. When they danced in *Flying Down to Rio* (1933) for RKO Pictures, musical became identified as youth-oriented romances that celebrated lovers' unions through a number of song-and-dance routines.

Walt Disney was the most adventuresome filmmaker who recognized the artistic possibilities of orchestrating animated action with musical rhythms in his first cartoons, *Skeleton Dance* (1928), *Steamboat Willie* (1929) featuring Mickey Mouse. But it was no surprise that filmmakers such as Charlie Chaplin resisted the use of dialogue. Chaplin's two features of the 1930s, *City Lights* and *Modern Times*, both used a synchronized musical soundtrack and special effects but were shot to enhance the pantomimes of the Little Tramp. Chaplin composed the scores for these films and because he had complete artistic and financial control over his work, he was able to make these films without dialogue.

2.2.2 Gangster Films

Gangster films emerged since the silent film era, such as Von Sternberg's *Underworld* (1927) and Lewis Milestone's *The Racket* (1928). And the audible rat-tat-tat of machine guns and the stylized argot of tough guy talk were an electrifying combination with its popularization. The gangster cycle was begun by Mervyn LeRoy's *Little Caesar* (1930) starring Edward G. Robinson, William Wellman's *The Public Enemy* (1931) with James Cagney, and Howard Harks' *Scarface* (1932), starring Paul Muni. All focused on arch criminals who set out to gain wealth power through a deliberate "war" with their enemies. Dialogues and street jargon play important roles in establishing this characterization. The dramas were infused with the excitement of a realistic sound track punctuated by loud machine gun fire, music from furious car chases with screeching auto tires.

These movies defined the parameters of the genre. They were ironic variations on the American success story and a sign of the desperation of the times. In the films, guns and cars are everywhere. Sexual relationships are abnormal, or else women are used as kittle more than receptacles for either passion or rage. Plotlines detail the rise and fall of Catholic immigrants, garrulously rolling over all obstacles to make a grab for that brass ring that was otherwise impossible to reach.

There emerged scores of other gangster films in little more than three years. However, with the public surfeited and newly strengthened censors making loud, threatening noises about the genre's violence, the gangster film became more explicitly moralistic, devoting less time to the glamorous nihilism of the Tony Camontes and more on how they got that way and what to do about it.

Branching out, Gangster pictures introduced a more liberal social perspective that saw environmental causes for the sociopath. Policemen became the new heroes, whereas before they had been either stooges or thugs who were little better than the men they were battling. Socially crusading films like *I am a Fugitive from a Chain Gang* (1933) or *Wellman's Wild Boys of the Road* (1933) showed other aspects of the suffering proletariat. There would still be a few great gangster films — *Angels with Dirty Faces* (1938) and *The Roaring Twenties* (1939).

The gangster provoked a responsive echo in audiences and has held our imagination ever since. Robert Warshow, in his essay "The Gangster as Tragic Hero", hit on the reason of such phenomenon: "The gangster is the man of the city, with the city's language and knowledge, with its queer and dishonest skills and its terrible daring, carrying his life in his hands like a placard, like a club... It is not the real city, but that dangerous and sad city of the imagination which is so much more important, which is the modern world."

2.2.3 Screwball Comedies

Comedy of the 1930s followed to a large degree the environment created by gangster films and musicals of low-class and indecency with snarl, cynicism and a lack of hypocrisy. Mae West (1892-1979) and *The Marx Brothers* led the way of exploding comedy in the face of audience, both embodying a strong disfavor of hypocrisy. Mae West was one of the last actor-managers on Broadway. She wrote most of her films, which are basically devoted to showcasing herself.

The conventions of screwball comedies were a variation on the theme of a world gone mad. Two of the best screwball comedies were *Twentieth Century* (1934) and *Nothing Sacred* (1937), both written by the redoubtable Ben Hecht. *Twentieth Century* is structured as a series of mutual humiliations imposed by two crazies, who base their madness on their employment in the theater. Their love, hate and jealousies are all fictitious pretexts for the contemplation of their own faces simulating various emotions. *Nothing Sacred* is something a little more personal and different. Its hero is a reporter recently exiled to obituaries because he writes a phony story about an oriental potentate who is really a shoeshine boy. Desperate to get back to the big stories he needs to justify his ego, he seizes on Hazel Flagg, who believes herself to be dying of radiation poisoning, misdiagnosed by a drunken doctor, and wants to see New York once before she dies.

The lack of moralizing or sentimentality became reverse conventions. *It Happened One Night* (1934) reveals the roots of the genre's subsequent fade-out, with its homely American types and celebration of down-home values and eccentricities. In 1933, Leo McCarey directed *the Marx Brothers* in Duck Soup, their most overtly surrealistic assault on order and reason; by the time McCarey directed *The Awful Truth* (1937), he was operating on lower octane. The tenets of screwball comedy had been reduced to a few flourishes in a frothy domestic comedy of loyalty and love surviving divorce.

Different from *Twentieth Century* and *Nothing Sacred*, the comedy of *The Awful Truth* (1937) has gone soft at its center. It neatly divides those characters whose feelings are to be taken seriously from those who are butts. This was comedy made to reconcile, not threaten. As critic Andrew Bergman wrote, "These comedies became a means of unifying what had been splintered and divided. Their wackiness cemented social classes and broken marriages." The heartlessness that had been lavished on America by the laws of economics was reflected in the best of its popular art. As the Depression waned, this harshness was being replaced by something more hopeful, something that would be necessary for the taxing years of World War II.

2.3 Directors

2.3.1 Alfred Hitchcock (1899-1980)

Born	August 13, 1899 Leytonstone, England
Died	April 29, 1980 California, United States
Occupation	Film director, film producer
Years active	1921-1976

Filmography: *The Lodger* (1926), *Blackmail* (1929), *Murder!* (1930), *Rich and Strange* (1932), *The Man Who Knew too Much* (1934), *The Thirty-Nine Steps* (1935), *Sabotage* (1936), *Secret Agent* (1936), *Young and Innocent* (1937), *The Lady Vanishes* (1938), *Jamaica Inn* (1939), *Foreign Correspondent* (1940), *Rebecca* (1940) *Mr. and Mrs. Smith* (1941), *Suspicion* (1941), *Saboteur* (1942), *Shadow of a Doubt* (1943), *Lifeboat* (1944), *Spellbound* (1945), *Notorious* (1946), *The Paradine Case* (1947), *Rope* (1948), *Under Capricorn* (1949), *Stage Fright* (1950), *Strangers on a Train* (1951), *I Confess* (1953), *Dial M for Murder* (1954), *Rear Window* (1954), *The Trouble with Harry* (1955), *To Catch a Thief* (1955), *The Man Who Knew too Much* (1956, *remade*), *The Wrong Man* (1956), *Vertigo* (1958), *North by Northwest* (1959), *Psycho* (1960), *The Birds* (1963), *Marnie* (1964), *Torn Curtain* (1966), *Topaz* (1969), *Frenzy* (1972), *Family Plot* (1976)

Alfred Hitchcock is widely recognized as the master of the thriller genre, also a brilliant technician who deftly blended sex, suspense and humor in his films.

Born in England, Hitchcock often described a lonely and sheltered childhood worsened by his obesity. Hitchcock started his filmmaking career in 1919. In 1920, he received a full-time position at a studio designing the titles for silent movies. His rise from title designer to film director took five years.

Hitchcock completed his first film *The Pleasure Garden* (1925) as director. *The Man Who Knows too Much* (1934) established a favorite pattern: an investigation of family relationships within a suspenseful story; it was the only film which was remade by Hitchcock. The film was followed by *The 39 Steps* (1935) and his last British film *Jamaica Inn* (1939). After a successful career in British cinema in both silent films and early talkies, Hitchcock moved to Hollywood in 1939 and made his first Hollywood try *Rebecca* (1940) which was nominated for 11 Oscar awards and awarded Oscar Best Picture. Hitchcock's second American film, *Foreign Correspondent* (1940) was nominated for Oscar Best Picture that year.

In Hollywood, the suspense and the gallows humor that had become Hitchcock's trademark in film continued to appear in his productions. In addition, Hitchcock did extensive location filming to break with Hollywood conventions, e. g. *Shadow of a Doubt* (1943), his personal favorite of all his films. Hitchcock's films during the 1940s were diverse, ranging from the romantic comedy *Mr. & Mrs. Smith* (1941) to the courtroom drama *The Paradine Case* (1947) to the dark and disturbing film noir *Shadow of a Doubt* (1943). *Suspicion* (1941) marked Hitchcock's first film as a producer as well as director. Hitchcock felt uneasy living and working in Hollywood while his country Britain was at war; his concern resulted in a film that overtly supported the British war effort. The film avoided direct references to Nazism, Germany, and Germans to comply with Hollywood's Production Code censorship.

The 1946 film *Notorious* was a huge-box office success and has remained one of Hitchcock's most acclaimed films. It starred Hitchcock regulars Ingrid Bergman and Cary Grant, and features a plot about Nazis, uranium, and South America. His use of uranium as a plot device led to Hitchcock's being briefly under FBI surveillance. In 1948, Hitchcock filmed his first color film *Rope* featuring James Stewart in the leading role, and *Rope* was the first of four films which were cooperation between Stewart and Hitchcock. For *Rope* and *Under Capricorn* (1949), Hitchcock formed a production company with his partner called Transatlantic Pictures, which became inactive after these two unsuccessful pictures.

Undoubtedly, 1950s became peak years in Hitchcock's film career. He worked for Paramount Pictures and Warner Bros. successively and 1954 *Rear Window* and 1958 *Vertigo* were both his masterpieces. Although it is widely considered a classic today, *Vertigo* met with negative reviews and poor box office receipts upon its release. By this time, Hitchcock had filmed in many areas of the United States. He followed *Vertigo* with three more successful films. Two are also recognized as among his best movies: *North by Northwest* (1959) and *Psycho* (1960). The third one was *The Birds* (1963).

Psycho is almost certainly Hitchcock's best-known film. Produced on a constrained budget of $800,000, it was shot in black-and-white on a spare set. The unprecedented violence of the shower scene, the early death of the heroine, the innocent lives extinguished by a disturbed murderer became the defining hallmarks of Hitchcock's new horror movie genre and have been copied by many authors of subsequent horror films. The public loved the film, with lines stretching outside of theatres as people had to wait for the next showing. It broke box-office records in the United States and many other countries. It was the most profitable black-and-white sound film ever made. And it was the most profitable film of Hitchcock's career. Hitchcock's second most profitable was *Family Plot* (1976) and third place was a tie between *Torn Curtain* (1966) and *Frenzy* (1972). Failing health reduced Hitchcock's output during the last two decades of his career. *Family Plot* (1976) was Hitchcock's last film.

Hitchcock directed more than fifty feature films over a career spanning six decades. Often viewed as one of the greatest filmmakers and cultural icons, Hitchcock did more than any director to shape modern cinema, which would be utterly different without him. Hitchcock fashioned for himself a distinctive and recognizable directorial style. He pioneered many techniques in the suspense and psychological thriller genres, exactly, the use of a camera made to move in a way that mimics a person's gaze, forcing viewers to engage in a form of voyeurism. In addition, he framed shots to maximize anxiety, fear, or empathy, and used innovative film editing. His stories often feature fugitives on the run from the law alongside "icy blonde" female characters. Many of Hitchcock's films have twist endings and thrilling plots featuring depictions of violence, murder, and crime. Hitchcock's films also borrow many themes from psychoanalysis and feature strong sexual overtones.

When it comes to awards, Hitchcock was a multiple nominee and winner of a number of prestigious ones, including two Golden Globes, eight Laurel Awards and five lifetime achievement awards. But he had no luck to win Academy awards in spite of his five times nominations for Academy Best Director. In addition to these, Hitchcock received a knighthood in 1980 when he was appointed a Knight Commander of the Most Excellent Order of the British Empire (KBE) by Queen Elizabeth II.

2. 3. 2 Stanley Kubrick (1928-1999)

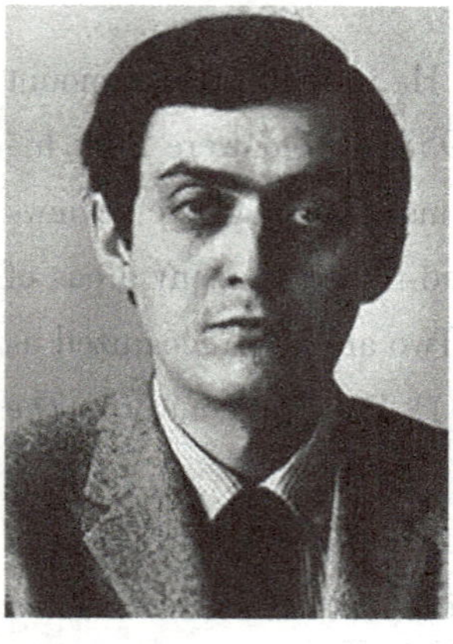

Born	July 26, 1928 New York, United States
Died	March 7, 1999 Hertfordshire, England, United Kingdom
Occupation	Film director, film producer, screenwriter, cinematographer, editor
Years active	1951-1999

Filmography: *Day of the Fight* (1951), *Fear and Desire* (1953), *Killer's Kiss* (1955), *The*

Killing (1956), *Paths of Glory* (1957), *Spartacus* (1960), *Lolita* (1962), *Dr. Strangelove or: How I Learned to Stop Worrying and Love the Bomb* (1964), *2001: A Space Odyssey* (1968), *A Clockwork Orange* (1971), *Barry Lyndon* (1975), *The Shining* (1980), *Full Metal Jacket* (1987), *Eyes Wide Shut* (1999)

Stanley Kubrick was an American film director, screenwriter, producer, cinematographer, and editor. Kubrick made a variety of genres of films, covering war film, crime film, romantic comedy, black comedy, horror, epic and science fiction. He directed, produced and wrote all or part of the screenplays for nearly all his films. His films are featured with a cool, formal visual style, meticulous attention to detail, and a detached, often ironic pessimism.

Stanley Kubrick was bought a camera by his father when he was 13. From then on, he showed great interest in photography. His first film, *The Day of the Fight* (1951), is a short documentary about the boxing world, notable for using reverse tracking shot, later to become one of Kubrick's characteristic camera movements. Inspired by this early success, Kubrick was encouraged to work on others including, *Flying Padre* (1951) and his first color film *The Seafarers* (1953).

His first feature-length film, *Fear and Desire* (1953), dealt with World War II. *The Killing* is Kubrick's first full-length feature film shot with a professional cast and crew. Its non-linear narrative would have a major influence on later directors, including Quentin Tarantino. *The Killing* followed many of the conventions of film noir, in both its plotting and cinematography style, and although the genre peaked in the 1940s, many critics regard this film as one of its best. Not a financial success, it still received good reviews, and brought Kubrick and his producer partner to the attention of Metro-Goldwyn-Mayer.

Kubrick's next effort *Paths of Glory* was his first significant commercial success, and was critically praised and admired within the industry, establishing Kubrick as a major up-and-coming young filmmaker. The film's unsentimental, spare, and unvarnished combat scenes and its raw, black-and-white cinematography was favored by critics.

At age 31 Kubrick directed *Spartacus* which became his largest by far with a cast of over 10,000 and was the most expensive film ever made in America at that time. Despite the on-set troubles, *Spartacus* was a critical and commercial success and established Kubrick as a major director, receiving six Academy Award nominations and winning four.

In 1962, Kubrick moved to England to film *Lolita*, his first attempt at black comedy. *Lolita* was Kubrick's first film to generate controversy because of its provocative story. Stylistically, *Lolita* was a transitional film for Kubrick, marking the turning point from a naturalistic cinema to the surrealism of the later films. Kubrick's next project was another satirical black comedy *Dr. Strangelove or: How I Learned to Stop Worrying and Love the Bomb* (1964) which stirred up much controversy and mixed opinions.

Kubrick's next effort *2001: A Space Odyssey* cost him five years. Upon its release in 1968, the film was said to defy genre convention and was claimed to be unlike any science-fiction movie before it, and different from any of Kubrick's earlier films or stories. It contained ground-breaking special effects designed by Kubrick to give the viewer a dazzling mix of imagination and science, and winning Kubrick his only personal Oscar, an Academy Award for Visual Effects. The film was not an immediate hit among critics. But today, the film is regarded as the greatest and most influential science fiction film ever made as well as the most significant Hollywood breakthrough since *Citizen Kane* (1941), and always included All Time Top 10 lists.

The 1975 film *Barry Lyndon* found a great audience in Europe, particularly in France. Although the film was nominated for seven Academy Awards and won four, more than any other Kubrick film, however, its measured pace and length at three hours put off many American critics and audiences. *The Shining*, released in 1980, was adapted from the novel of the same name by bestselling horror writer Stephen King. The film opened to mixed reviews, but proved a commercial success. Like most Kubrick films, subsequent critical reaction has treated the film more favorably. Among horror movie fans, *The Shining* is a cult classic with memorable scenes.

Kubrick's final film was *Eyes Wide Shut* (1999), starring Tom Cruise and Nicole Kidman as a wealthy Manhattan couple on a sexual odyssey. Kubrick worked 18 hours a day, all the while maintaining complete confidentiality about the film. He sent an unfinished preview copy to the stars and producers a few months before release, but his sudden death on March 7, 1999 came a few days after he finished editing. He never saw the final version released to the public.

Stanley Kubrick made some of the most dazzling films of the 20th century works whose titles alone have come to represent filmmaking at its most astonishing, challenging, and psychologically spellbinding. A true auteur, he was meticulous, formally inventive, and philosophically provocative. Few filmmakers can boast a career that includes the antiwar classic *Paths of Glory* (1957), the controversial *Lolita* (1962), or the disturbing Vietnam war drama *Full Metal Jacket* (1987). Kubrick is regarded as one of the greatest filmmakers of all time. His films, are known for their dazzling and unique cinematography, attention to details to achieve realism and an inspired use of music scores. Kubrick was also noted for being a perfectionist, using painstaking care with scene staging and working closely with his actors.

Many of Kubrick's films broke new ground in cinematography, but interestingly, most of his films were misunderstood and under-appreciated when first released. Then came a dawning recognition that they were masterful works unlike any other films. Film historians and critics consider his films to be among the most important contributions to world cinema in the twentieth century; and Kubrick himself is a legend in every sense of the word, and is one of the most influential, shocking, and well-respected men in the history of film.

2.4 Actors

2.4.1 Humphrey Bogart (1899-1957)

Born	December 25, 1899 New York City, New York, U.S.
Died	January 14, 1957 Los Angeles, California, U.S.
Occupation	Actor
Years active	1921-1956

Best Films: *The Petrified Forest* (1936), *Dead End* (1937), *Angels with Dirty Faces* (1938), *The Roaring Twenties* (1939), *They Drive by Night* (1940), *High Sierra* (1941), *The Maltese Falcon* (1941), *Casablanca* (1942), *Action in the North Atlantic* (1943), *To Have and Have Not* (1944), *The Big Sleep* (1946), *Key Largo* (1948), *The Treasure of the Sierra Madre* (1948), *In a Lonely Place* (1950), *The African Queen* (1952), *Beat the Devil* (1953), *The Barefoot Contessa* (1954), *The Caine Mutiny* (1954), *Sabrina* (1954)

Humphrey Bogart was an American actor and is widely viewed as an American cultural icon. The American Film Institute ranked Bogart as the greatest male star in the history of American cinema in 1999.

Bogart was born on Christmas Day, 1899 in New York City and the Bogarts lived a well-off life. As a youngster, Humphrey and his friends put on theatricals. Bogart's parents hoped he would go on to Yale, but in 1918, Bogart was expelled. Bogart followed his passion for the sea and enlisted in the United States Navy in the spring of 1918 because he had no viable career options. During his naval time, Bogart's character and values developed independently of family influence, and he began to rebel somewhat against their values.

Although Bogart had been raised to believe that acting was not suitable for a gentleman, he enjoyed stage acting. He never took acting lessons, but was persistent and worked steadily at his craft. He appeared in at least seventeen Broadway productions between 1922 and 1935.

Bogart obtained his first real romantic lead in 1942's *Casablanca*, playing Rick Blaine, the hard-pressed expatriate nightclub owner, hiding from the past and negotiating a fine line among Nazis, the French underground, the Vichy prefect and unresolved feelings for his ex-girlfriend. The film was directed by Michael Curtiz and produced by Hal Wallis, and featured Ingrid Bergman. It was reportedly Bogart's idea that Rick Blaine be portrayed as a chess player. In real life Bogart played tournament chess, one division below master level, and often played with crew members and cast off the set.

Casablanca won the 1943 Academy Award for Best Picture. Bogart was nominated for Best Actor in a Leading Role, but lost to his rival. The film vaulted Bogart from fourth place to first in the studio's roster, and by 1946 more than doubling his annual salary to over $460,000, making him the highest paid actor in the world.

Bogart's career was redefined because of the enormous success of *Casablanca*. For the first time, Bogart could be cast successfully as a tough, strong man and as a vulnerable love interest as well. Despite Bogart's elevated standing, he did not yet have a contractual right of script refusal, so he had to play roles in the films with weak scripts such as *Conflict* in 1945. But he successfully turned down God is *My Co-Pilot* (1945).

Bogart cooperated with Katharine Hepburn in the film *The African Queen* in 1952. The *African Queen* was the first technicolor film in which Bogart appeared. He starred in relatively few color films during the rest of his career, which continued for another five years. The role of Charlie Allnutt won Bogart his only Academy Award for Best Actor in a Leading Role in 1951. Bogart himself considered his performance to be the best of his film career.

Throughout his whole life, even after his death, Bogart had gained numerous honors. During his career, Bogart was nominated for several awards including the BAFTA award for best foreign actor in 1952 for *The African Queen* and three Academy Awards. In 1999, the American Film Institute ranked him the Greatest Male Star of All Time.

2.4.2 Clark Gable (1901-1960)

Born	February 1, 1901 Ohio, U.S.
Died	November 16, 1960 California, U.S.
Occupation	Actor
Years active	1923-1960

Best Films: *A Free Soul* (1931), *No Man of Her Own* (1932), *Red Dust* (1932), *Dancing Lady* (1933), *It Happened One Night* (1934), *Manhattan Melodrama* (1934), *Mutiny on the Bounty* (1935), *San Francisco* (1936), *Gone with the Wind* (1939), *Boom Town* (1940), *Mogambo* (1953), *Run Silent, Run Deep* (1958), *The Misfits* (1961)

Clark Gable was regarded as the "King of Hollywood" when he was the leader that made box-office attraction throughout the 1930s. The name Clark Gable remains indelibly associated with the mustachioed image of Rhett Butler in *Gone with the Wind* (1939).

In 1924, Gable went to Hollywood and changed his name to Clark Gable. In 1930, after his impressive appearance in the Los Angeles stage production of *The Last Mile*, Gable was offered a contract with MGM. He acted his first role in a sound picture and received a lot of fan mails as a result of his powerful voice and appearance which aroused the studio's notice. Gable's timing in arriving in Hollywood was good, as MGM was looking to expand its stable of male stars and he was an excellent choice.

At the beginning, Gable mainly played supporting roles. To support his rocketing popularity, MGM frequently paired him with well-established female stars. He built his fame and public visibility in such movies as *A Free Soul* (1931), *Susan Lenox* (*Her Fall and Rise*) (1931) and *Possessed* (1931).

Gable's acting in *Red Dust* (1932) soon made him MGM's most important male star. After the hit *Hold Your Man* (1933), Gable and Jean Harlow began their cooperation in six films together as an enormously popular combination, on-screen and off-screen. Gable was not the first choice to play the lead role in *It Happened One Night* (1934). Gable won the Academy Award for Best Actor for his performance in the film, and the movie itself won the Academy Award for Best Picture. Gable also earned an Academy Award nomination in 1935's *Mutiny on the Bounty*.

Interestingly, Gable was reluctant to play the role in *Gone with the Wind* (1939) which had made him best known for his performance and earned him an Academy Award nomination for Best Actor. Whenever his career would start to fade, a re-release of *Gone with the Wind* would soon revive Gable's popularity, and he continued as a top leading actor for the rest of his life. Thanks in part to MGM's dominance in balloting, Gable was the leading actor in three films that won the Academy Award for Best Picture between 1934 and 1939. *Gone with the Wind* was given theatrical re-releases in 1947, 1954, 1961, 1967 (in a widescreen version), 1971, 1989, and 1998.

In 1955, Gable established a production company and then produced *The King and Four Queens* which was his only production. At this time, producing and acting were too taxing on his health, and he was beginning to manifest a noticeable tremor, particularly in long takes. At 57, Gable finally acknowledged it's time he acted his age.

His following two films were light comedies for Paramount: *But Not for Me* and *It Started in Naples* (his last film in color). The latter one, despite an icy critical reception, was a good box office success and was nominated for an Academy award and two Golden Globes.

Gable's last film was *The Misfits* which was also the final film completed by Monroe. Many critics regarded Gable's performance to be his finest, and Gable agreed after seeing the rough cuts. It was speculated that Gable's physically demanding role in *The Misfits* contributed to his sudden death soon after the filming was completed.

Gable was named the seventh greatest male actor of all time by the American Film Institute.

2.4.3 Gregory Peck (1916-2003)

Born	April 5, 1916, California, U.S.
Died	June 12, 2003 California, U.S.
Occupation	Actor, humanitarian
Years active	1942-2000

Best Films: *The Keys of the Kingdom* (1944), *Spellbound* (1945), *Duel in the Sun* (1946), *The Yearling* (1946), *Gentleman's Agreement* (1947), *Yellow Sky* (1948), *Twelve O'clock High* (1949), *The Gunfighter* (1950), *Captain Horatio Hornblower* (1951), *David and Bathsheba* (1951), *Roman Holiday* (1953), *The Man in the Gray Flannel Suit* (1956), *Moby Dick* (1956), *The Big Country* (1958), *Beloved Infidel* (1959), *On the Beach* (1959), *Pork Chop Hill* (1959), *The Guns of Navarone* (1961), *Cape Fear* (1962), *To Kill a Mockingbird* (1962), *The Omen* (1976), *MacArthur* (1977), *The Boys from Brazil* (1978), *Old Gringo* (1989)

Gregory Peck was one of the world's most popular film stars and an American Academy Award winning actor. He is famous for his performance in the 1962 film *To Kill a Mockingbird*, which earned him the Academy Award for Best Actor.

After graduating from University of California, Berkeley with a BA degree in English, Peck headed to New York City to study stage acting where he lived a tough life. He was often broke and sometimes slept in Central Park. He worked at the 1939 World's Fair and as a tour guide for NBC's television broadcasting.

In 1941 Peck began his stage career when he played the secretary in a production of George Bernard Shaw's play *The Doctor's Dilemma*. Unluckily, the play opened in San Francisco just one week before the attack on Pearl Harbor. In 1942 he made his Broadway debut as the lead in *The Morning Star*. Peck's first film, *Days of Glory*, was released in 1944.

Peck was nominated for the Academy Award for Best Actor five times, four of which came in his first five years of film acting: for *The Keys of the Kingdom* (1944), *The Yearling* (1946), *Gentleman's Agreement* (1947), and *Twelve O'clock High* (1949). *Twelve O'clock High* was the first of many successful war films in which Peck embodied the brave, effective, yet human fighting man.

Peck's other films included *Spellbound* (1945), *The Paradise Case* (1947), *The Gunfighter* (1950), *Moby Dick* (1956), *The Man in the Gray Flannel Suit* (1956), *The Big Country* (1958), *On the Beach* (1959), *The Guns of Navarone* (1961), and *Roman Holiday* (1953), with Audrey Hepburn in her Oscar-winning role. Peck and Hepburn were close friends throughout their life.

Peck finally won the Academy Award with his fifth nomination for his playing a Depression-era lawyer and widowed father in *To Kill a Mockingbird*. Released in 1962 during the height of the US civil rights movement in the South, this film and his role were Peck's favorites.

Different from other actors, Peck was a physically powerful man and was known to make a majority of his own fight scenes, rarely using body or stunt doubles. In the 1980s Peck moved to television. In 1991, Peck acted in the remake of *Cape Fear* directed by Martin Scorsese. After his last prominent film role in *Other People's Money* in 1991, Peck retired from active film-making. During the last few years of his life, Peck traveled the world doing speaking engagements in which he would show clips from his films, reminisce, and take questions from the audience.

In 1998, he came out of retirement. *Moby Dick* was his final performance and won him the Golden Globe for Best Supporting Actor in a Series, Miniseries or Television Film. Peck had been offered the role in the 2005 film *Charlie and the Chocolate Factory*, but died before he could accept it.

Peck had achieved great success as an actor which could be proved by a number of awards and nominations. Besides Academy Awards mentioned above, Peck also won quite a few Golden Globe awards. He won in 1947 for *The Yearling*, in 1963 for *To Kill a Mockingbird*, and in 1999 for the TV miniseries *Moby Dick*. He was nominated in 1978 for *The Boys from Brazil*.

In addition, in 1989 the American Film Institute gave Peck the AFI Life Achievement Award. He received the Crystal Globe award for outstanding artistic contribution to world cinema in 1996. In 1993, Peck was awarded with an Honorary Golden Bear at the 43rd Berlin International Film Festival. In 1998 he was awarded the National Medal of Arts. Particularly, in 1969, US President Lyndon Johnson honored Peck with the Presidential Medal of Freedom, the nation's highest civilian honor.

2.4.4 Katharine Hepburn (1907-2003)

Born	May 12, 1907 Connecticut, USA
Died	June 29, 2003 Connecticut, USA
Occupation	Actress
Years active	1928-1994

Best Films: *A Bill of Divorcement* (1932), *Christopher Strong* (1933), *Little Women* (1933),

Morning Glory (1933), *Alice Adams* (1935), *Sylvia Scarlett* (1936), *Mary of Scotland* (1936), *A Woman Rebels* (1936), *Stage Door* (1937), *Bringing Up Baby* (1938), *Holiday* (1938), *The Philadelphia Story* (1940), *Woman of the Year* (1942), *State of the Union* (1948), *Adam's Rib* (1949), *The African Queen* (1951), *Pat and Mike* (1952), *Summertime* (1955), *The Rainmaker* (1956), *Desk Set* (1957), *Suddenly, Last Summer* (1959), *Long Day's Journey into Night* (1962), *Guess Who's Coming to Dinner* (1967), *The Lion in Winter* (1968), *Rooster Cogburn* (1975), *On Golden Pond* (1981), *Love Affair* (1994)

Katharine Hepburn was a prestigious American actress known for her headstrong independence and spirited personality. As a Hollywood leading lady, Hepburn's career spanned more than 60 years with her involvement in a wide range of genres, from screwball comedy to literary drama. Noticeably, she gained four Academy Awards for Best Actress—an unequaled record for any performer. The characters Hepburn portrayed were often strong, sophisticated but vulnerable inside.

In her childhood, Hepburn was a tomboy. Raised in Connecticut by wealthy, progressive parents, Hepburn was cultivated to exercise freedom of speech and encouraged to think and debate on any topic they wished and was stimulated to fight against barriers she encountered. Hepburn showed great gratitude to her remarkable parents for their upbringing and providing the foundation for her future success. Throughout her life she remained close to her family.

Hepburn started her acting while studying at college. After four years in the theatre, favorable reviews of her work on Broadway brought her to the attention of Hollywood. Her early years were marked with success, including an Academy Award for her third picture, *Morning Glory* (1933). But the following were a series of commercial failures. In 1938 she was labeled "box-office poison". In the 1940s she made contract with Metro-Goldwyn-Mayer where her career began a 25-year screen-partnership with Spencer Tracy in nine productions.

In the latter half of her life, Hepburn challenged herself for regular appearing in Shakespeare stage productions and tackling a range of literary roles. Three more Oscars came for her work in *Guess Who's Coming to Dinner* (1967), *The Lion in Winter* (1968), and *On Golden Pond* (1981). In the 1970s she began appearing in television movies, which became the focus of her career in later life. She remained active into old age, and her final screen appearance was in 1994 at the age of 87. After a period of inactivity and ill-health, Hepburn died in 2003 at the age of 96.

With the independent characters she portrayed and her own unconventional lifestyle, Hepburn came to epitomize the "modern woman" in 20th-century America and helped change perceptions of women. Hepburn famously shunned the Hollywood publicity machine, and refused to conform to society's expectations of women. She was confident, independent and intelligent, providing an image of an outspoken, athletic, assertive woman and wore trousers before it was fashionable for women to do so. She married once, as a young woman, but thereafter lived independently. A 26-year affair with her costar Spencer Tracy was hidden from the public.

Hepburn had enormously influenced fashion where she was a pioneer for wearing trousers at a time when it was radical for a woman to do so. She contributed towards making trousers acceptable for women, as fans began to imitate her clothing. In 1986 she received a lifetime achievement award from the Council of Fashion Designers of America in recognition of the influence she played in women's fashion.

A number of Hepburn's films have become classics of American cinema, with four of her pictures (*The African Queen*, *The Philadelphia Story*, *Bringing Up Baby*, and *Guess Who's Coming to Dinner*) featuring on the American Film Institute's list of the 100 Greatest American Films of all time. *Adam's Rib* and *Woman of the Year* were included in the AFI's list of the Greatest American Comedies. Even her clipped, patrician voice is considered one of the most distinctive in film history.

Hepburn is viewed an important and influential cultural icon. The legacy of Hepburn lies both on screen and off. She is often included in the lists of great women who has changed the world. More than a movie star, Hepburn is the patron saint of the independent American female. In 1999, the American Film Institute named Hepburn the "greatest American screen legend" among females.

2.4.5 Vivien Leigh (1913-1967)

Born	November 5, 1913, British India
Died	July 8, 1967 London, England, UK
Occupation	Actress
Years active	1933-1967

Best Films: *Fire Over England* (1937), *Gone with the Wind* (1939), *Waterloo Bridge* (1940), *That Hamilton Woman* (1941), *Caesar and Cleopatra* (1946), *Anna Karenina* (1948), *A Streetcar Named Desire* (1951), *The Roman Spring of Mrs. Stone* (1961), *Ship of Fools* (1965)

Vivien Leigh was a British stage and film actress. She won two Best Actress Academy Awards for her performances as Scarlett O'Hara in *Gone with the Wind* (1939) and Blanche DuBois in the film version of *A Streetcar Named Desire* (1951). She won a Tony Award for her work in the Broadway version of *Tovarich* (1963).

Leigh made her first stage acting at the age of three for her mother's amateur theatre group. Leigh's film debut came from her friends' suggestion that she take a small role in the film *Things Are Looking Up*. From then on, she took "Vivien Leigh" as her professional name.

After seeing Leigh in *The Mask of Virtue* in 1935, Laurence Olivier and Leigh developed a friendship and began an affair while acting as lovers in *Fire Over England* (1937), but Olivier was still married to another actress. During this period, Leigh read the Margaret Mitchell novel *Gone with the Wind*. Leigh and Olivier began living together, as their respective spouses had each refused to grant either of them a divorce. Under the moral standards and then enforced by the film industry, their relationship had to be kept from public view. Leigh appeared in *A Yank at Oxford* (1938), the first of her films to receive attention in the United States. During production, she developed a reputation for being difficult and unreasonable.

At that time, Hollywood was in the midst of a widely publicized search to find an actress to portray Scarlett O'Hara in David O. Selznick's production of *Gone with the Wind* (1939). Though she was thought "too British", Leigh travelled to Los Angeles to try to convince Selznick that she was Scarlett. Eventually, she secured her role as Scarlett. Filming was not easy for Leigh, for she made clashes with some actors except Clark Gable. *Gone with the Wind* brought Leigh immediate attention and fame and it won 10 Academy Awards including a Best Actress award for Leigh, who also won a New York Film Critics Circle Award for Best Actress

Waterloo Bridge (1940) was popular with audiences and critics though it was planned originally a cooperation between Leigh and Olivier who filmed *That Hamilton Woman* in 1941. The film was popular in the United States and an outstanding success in the Soviet Union. Winston Churchill arranged a screening of the film for a party that included Franklin D. Roosevelt. From then on, the Oliviers remained favorites of Churchill, attending dinners and occasions at his request for the rest of his life.

A Streetcar Named Desire (1951) won glowing reviews for her and she won a second Academy Award for Best Actress, a British Academy of Film and Television Arts (BAFTA) Award for Best British Actress, and a New York Film Critics Circle Award for Best Actress. During her prolific 30-year stage career, she played roles ranging from the heroines of George Bernard Shaw comedies to classic Shakespearean characters such as Cleopatra, Juliet and Lady Macbeth. In 1963, Leigh won a Tony Award for Best Actress in a Musical for her role in *Tovarich*.

For much of her adult life Leigh suffered from bipolar disorder. She earned a reputation for being difficult to work with, and her career suffered periods of inactivity. She suffered recurrent bouts of chronic tuberculosis which ultimately claimed her life at the age of 53.

Leigh was considered one of the most beautiful actresses of her day. But she thought beauty could be a great handicap to some extent. Great beauties are infrequently great actresses — simply because they don't need to be. But Vivien was different who demonstrated those great qualities of an excellent actress. In 1999, the American Film Institute ranked Leigh as the sixteenth greatest female movie star of all time.

2.4.6 Ingrid Bergman (1915-1982)

Born	August 29, 1915 Stockholm, Sweden
Died	August 29, 1982 London, England
Occupation	Actress
Years active	1932-1982

Best Films: *Intermezzo: A Love Story* (1936) *and* (1939), *Dr. Jekyll and Mr. Hyde* (1941), *Casablanca* (1942), *For Whom the Bell Tolls* (1943), *Gaslight* (1944), *The Bells of St. Mary's* (1945), *Saratoga Trunk* (1945), *Spellbound* (1945), *Notorious* (1946), *Joan of Arc* (1948), *Stromboli* (1949), *Under Capricorn* (1949), *Voyage in Italy* (1953), *Anastasia* (1956), *Indiscreet* (1958), *The Inn of the Sixth Happiness* (1958), *The Yellow Rolls Royce* (1964), *Cactus Flower* (1969), *Murder on the Orient Express* (1974), *Autumn Sonata* (1978)

Ingrid Bergman was a Swedish actress and starred in various European and American films. She was a great awards winner, for she received three Academy Awards, two Emmy Awards, and the Tony Award for Best Actress. She is best remembered for her roles in *Casablanca* (1942), a World War II drama co-starring Humphrey Bogart, and in *Notorious* (1946), an Alfred Hitchcock thriller co-starring Cary Grant. She is ranked as the fourth greatest female star of American cinema of all time by the American Film Institute.

In 1932, at the age of 17, Bergman was allowed only one chance to become an actress by entering an acting competition with the Royal Dramatic Theatre in Stockholm. As a result, she received a scholarship to the state-sponsored Royal Dramatic Theatre School. Her first film role after leaving the Royal Dramatic Theatre was a small part in 1935. She later acted in a dozen films in Sweden. Bergman's first acting role in the United States came in *Intermezzo: A Love Story*, an English language remake of her 1936 Swedish film, *Intermezzo*. Bergman expected to complete this film and return home to Sweden because of her inability to speak English and uncertainty about her acceptance by the American audience.

Intermezzo proved an enormous success and thus Bergman became a star. She was unique among Hollywood female stars for she was a tall girl with light brown hair and blue eyes who was painfully shy but friendly, with a warm, straight, quick smile.

In 1942, Bergman co-starred with Humphrey Bogart in the classic film *Casablanca*, which remains her best-known role. However, Bergman did not consider *Casablanca* to be one of her favorite performances. After *Casablanca*, she played the part of Maria in her first color film *For Whom the Bell Tolls* (1943). For the role she received her first Academy Award nomination for

Best Actress. The film was adapted from Ernest Hemingway's novel of the same title. It's said that Hemingway stated that Miss Bergman should play the part rather than any other actress.

In the next year, she won the Academy Award for Best Actress for *Gaslight* (1944). The film was the peak of her Hollywood glory. Bergman next played a nun in *The Bells of St. Mary's* (1945) for which she received her third consecutive nomination for Best Actress. Then Bergman starred in the Alfred Hitchcock films *Spellbound* (1945), *Notorious* (1946), and *Under Capricorn* (1949).

Bergman received another Best Actress nomination for an independent film *Joan of Arc* (1948). The 1959 TV drama *The Turn of the Screw* brought her an Emmy Award for Outstanding Single Performance by an Actress. Bergman became one of the elite actresses to receive three Oscars when she won her third (and first for Best Supporting Actress) for her performance in *Murder on the Orient Express* (1974).

In 1978, Bergman played in Ingmar Bergman's *Autumn Sonata* for which she received her 7th Academy Award nomination and made her final performance on the big screen. In 1979, Bergman hosted the AFI's Life Achievement Award Ceremony for Alfred Hitchcock. In 1982 she starred in a television mini-series, *A Woman Called Golda*, about the late Israeli prime minister Golda Meir. It was to be her final acting role and she was honored posthumously with a second Emmy Award for Best Actress.

Bergman was tall, natural-looking, and intelligent and was regarded by Hollywood as a unique actress who was completely natural in style and without need of makeup. Bergman was also one of the most international stars in the history of entertainment.

2.4.7 Audrey Hepburn (1929-1993)

Born	May 4, 1929 Brussels, Belgium
Died	January 20, 1993 Vaud, Switzerland
Occupation	Actress (1948-1989) Humanitarian (1988-1992)
Years active	1948-1992

Best Films: *Roman Holiday* (1953), *Sabrina* (1954), *War and Peace* (1956), *Funny Face* (1957), *Love in the Afternoon* (1957), *The Nun's Story* (1959), *Breakfast at Tiffany's* (1961), *The Children's Hour* (1961), *Charade* (1963), *My Fair Lady* (1964), *How to Steal a Million* (1966), *Two for the Road* (1967), *Wait Until Dark* (1967), *Robin and Marian* (1976), *Bloodline* (1979), *They All Laughed* (1981), *Always* (1989)

Audrey Hepburn was a British actress who was active during Hollywood's Golden Age.

Labeled as both a film and fashion icon, she was ranked by the American Film Institute as the third greatest female screen legend in the history of American cinema and been placed in the International Best Dressed List Hall of Fame.

In 1948, she appeared for the first time as an air stewardess in an educational travel film. She supported herself with part-time work as a model. Hepburn's relatively tall height of 5 ft 7 in (1.70 m) coupled with her poor nutrition during the war would keep her from becoming a prima ballerina. Therefore, Hepburn decided to pursue acting.

In the Italian-set *Roman Holiday* (1953), Hepburn played her first leading role as Princess Ann who escapes the reins of royalty and falls in love with an American newsman (Gregory Peck). Elizabeth Taylor was the producers' first choice, but director William Wyler was so impressed by Hepburn's screen test that he cast her in the lead. Hepburn garnered critical and commercial acclaim for her portrayal and won unexpectedly Academy Award for Best Actress with her first BAFTA Award for Best British Actress in a Leading Role and Golden Globe Award for Best Actress — Motion Picture Drama.

After her success in *Roman Holiday*, in 1954, she starred in a romantic Cinderella-story comedy *Sabrina* collaborating with Humphrey Bogart. For her performance, she was nominated for the 1954 Academy Award for Best Actress while winning the BAFTA Award for Best Actress in a Leading Role. In the same year. She began another collaboration with actor Mel Ferrer, starring in the fantasy play *Ondine* on Broadway, which contributed to Hepburn's marriage with Ferrer in 1954 in Switzerland. Her performance won her the 1954 Tony Award for Best Performance by a Leading Actress, the same year she won the Academy Award for *Roman Holiday*. Hepburn, therefore, stands as one of three actresses to receive the Academy and Tony Awards for Best Actress in the same year. Hepburn received the Golden Globe for World Film Favorite — Female in 1955.

As one of Hollywood's most popular box-office attractions, she continued to star in a series of successful films during the remainder of the decade. Hepburn's role as Sister Luke in *The Nun's Story* (1959) brought her third Academy Award nomination and earned her a second BAFTA Award. According to some reviews, Hepburn had met her most demanding film role, and she gave her finest performance. She admitted that she gave more time, energy and thought to this than to any of her previous screen performances. Hepburn's portrayal of Sister Luke is regarded as one of the great performances of the screen.

She remains one of the few entertainers to win Grammy and Emmy Awards posthumously. More accurately, Hepburn remains one of few people who have won Academy, Emmy, Grammy, and Tony Awards. Also, Hepburn was the first actress to win an Oscar, a Golden Globe and a BAFTA Award for a single performance: *Roman Holiday in* 1954.

During her late life, Hepburn devoted herself to humanitarian work and was appointed Goodwill Ambassador of UNICEF. Hepburn's legacy as an actress and a personality has endured long after her death. The American Film Institute named Hepburn third among the Greatest

Female Stars of All Time.

3. New Hollywood and Post-classical Cinema

New Hollywood Period started from 1967 to 1976. During the World War II years, to support the war effort for the government, Hollywood directors produced different genre films and the main studios made new combat films to resist psychologically America's enemies. After the war, many socially conscious films were made to examine and question the social and political conditions. Yet the postwar years for the American film industry were plagued by the fear and delusion caused by the Cold War between the United States and the Soviet Union.

The power structure and practices of Hollywood filmmaking were changed by various postwar factors. The major studios had to stop "block bookings" and divest themselves of their theatre holdings. New technical innovations were introduced to meet the challenge and growth of television and to halt the steady decline in movie attendance. The innovations included wide-screen projection with Cinemascope, stereophonic sound, 3-D movies and color. The two decades gave rise to independent producers and directors like Billy Wilder, Fred Zinnemann, John Huston and Alfred Hitchcock, etc. New style of filmmaking and acting were utilized.

Hollywood revival started in the mid-1960s. New cinematic trends from Europe helped Hollywood reemerge as a production center for commercial filmmaking. To offset television dramas and sitcoms, new films broke away from the traditional genre films of Hollywood and began to explore sexual psychological conflicts of offbeat heroes. Producers targeted to the particular interests of the youth culture and younger audiences within urban centers. The new independent cinema and the experimental films introduced new cinematic forms of elliptical construction and controversial depictions of sex, drugs and violence. A new Hollywood cinema arose.

3.1 Technological Innovation

In the postwar years, American film industry struggled to halt the decline of movie audiences. To attract more mature audiences, Hollywood producers managed to produce movies of more adult attitude to the description of social and sexual relationships. Besides better movies, they realized that bigger films with better sights and sounds, especially including three-dimension, longer motion picture spectacles and full color (instead of black-and-white or tinted), were required in the face of competition from television.

A feature film in 3-D was released in 1952. It was *Bwana Devil* by Arch Oboler, a radio mystery writer. With its initial success of the 3-D effect, more directors made 3-D films and got marketed successful. In 1953, Andre de Toth directed a mystery thriller *House of Wax* (which starred Vincent Price). And Jack Arnold Directed *Creature from the Black Logoon* in 1954. But production values did not save these films as a result of commonplace stories with poorly developed characters, as well as the inconvenience of wear special glasses for the stereoscopic 3-D effect.

Warner Bros. introduced its multiple-screen film process, Cinerama, attempting to recreate a three-dimensional depth of vision. The film *This Is Cinerama* (1952) proved a hit with audiences mostly as a novelty, but this wide-screen technique lacked dramatic narratives and its novelty soon wore itself out with the public. Then wide-screen medium of CinemaScope was produced at 20th Century-Fox as a technological breakthrough. In 1953, Fox introduced CinemaScope to audiences with Henry Koster's film *The Robe*, which was adapted from Lloyd Douglas' best-selling novel and starred Richard Burton and Jean Simmons. This film is a blend of earlier DeMille-like fascination with religious spectacle and a display of Roman power, aided by a stereo soundtrack. With the innovation of this wide-screen system, the Biblical epic was widely approved by audiences. Other historical epics were made using CinemaScope's new screen aspect. Among the wide-screen films, westerns with romantic love stories set in foreign places led the parade of hits, like *El Cid* (1961, by Anthony Mann) and *Lawrence of Arabia* (1962, by David Lea). Some musicals also fared well, like *South Pacific* (1958, by Joshua Logan) and *The Sound of Music* (1965, Robert Wise), which starred Julie Andrews.

3.2 Rise of Independent Producers

Movie audiences declined since the early 1950s, in face with television expanding as a powerful competitor. The major Hollywood studios understood they should change their production practices. They freed their employees from long term contracts and rent out their studio properties to former producers and directors. It came to become the norm that the independent producer-director allied with the major studios, to make sure that their independent films could be distributed worldwide.

Such deal making pushed the independent directors to produce commercially sure films since they had to raise money for each film and the studios took a quite considerable portion of their profits.

Billy wilder stopped making films noirs after *Sunset Boulevard* (1950) and *Ace in the Hole* (1951), and began to make romantic comedies like *Sabrina* (1954) and *The Seven Year Itch* (1955). In his subsequent films, like *Love in the Afternoon* (1957) and *Like it Hot* (1959), Wilder expressed his satiric attitude towards the conventions of popular romantic mores. He dealt in most of his romantic comedies with themes concerning American capitalism to sexual lure, casual sex and adultery etc. It was not difficult to understand his intention to convert moral corruption in sexual games.

Attempt was made to internationalize movie making. John Huston(1906-1987), working with a British producer, Sam Spiegel, traveled to Africa to make *The African Queen* (1952) with Humphrey Bogart and Katharine Hepburn. His most successful films are placed in quasi-wartime conditions, like *The Treasure of the Sierra Madre* (1948), *The Asphalt Jungle* (1950), *The Red*

Badge of Courage (1951), with a background of American Civil War. *The African Queen* was also set at the start of World War I. Huston's films are usually about a main character sacrificing his or her life to a powerful obsession or quest. His antiheroic characterization is a deconstruction of the myths of bravery and heroism. After working with John Huston, producer Sam Spiegel teamed with noted British director David Lean (1908-1991). They produced two films adapted from popular novels about war and gained commercial success. One is *The Bridge on the River Kwai* (1957) and the other, *Lawrence of Arabia* (1962). Spiegel gathered international stars from both America and Europe to guarantee his films be distributed worldwide and to secure the box office financing.

The antiestablishment attitude flourished in the mid-1950s as part of the evolving youth culture. It focused upon teenaged gangs, rock "n" roll music, motorcycle gangs and a set of values clearly in rebellion against the conventional wisdom of adult conformity and the status quo. The two leading Hollywood stars who typified teenage idols of rebellion were Marlon Brando and James Dean. In the musical world of rock and roll, it was Elvis Presley. Brando's first movie was *The Men* (1950), directed by Fred Zinnemann (1907-1997). The film deals with a study of paraplegic war veterans frustrated by confinement and impotence in an army hospital. Zinnemann uses documentary techniques to suggest government incompetence that created conflict by testing a man's moral conviction in his fight against an oppressive system. Later Zinnemann directed *High Noon* (1952) as an allegorical western (with references to the McCarthy "witch hunt"). It starred Gary Cooper as a sheriff caught in a moral dilemma with his community when he is called upon to face a band of vengeful outlaws. He cast Burt Lancaster, Montgomery Clift and Frank Sinatra as career soldiers in the Academy Award-winning *From Here to Eternity* (1953), in which Lancaster feels morally charged to defend his men facing the wrath of incompetent officers. Zinnemann, who won his first Academy Award for the 1938 short, *That Others Might Live*, won a third with his film adaptation of Robert Bolt's play, *A Man for All Seasons* (1966), starring Paul Scofield as Sir Thomas More, a man of conscience in the realm of Henry VIII.

Marlon Brando's screen image as a rebel grew with his performance as a revolutionary Mexican outlaw in *Elia Kazan's Viva Zapata*! (1952), and the biker in Lazlo Benedek's *The Wild One* (1953). He played the lead in *Kazans on the Waterfront* (1954), in which as the central character Terry Malloy he takes and unpopular stance and testifies to a crime commission against a mob-ridden labor union, exposing the gangster in control of the waterfront. On the Waterfront earned six Academy Awards, including best picture, best actor and best direction. In *East of Eden* (1955), Kazan directed James Dean as a rebellious son fighting against and authoritarian father. Dean became a teenage icon with his strong angst-ridden performance in *Rebel Without a Cause* (1955), directed by Nicholas Ray, a follower of Kazan.

At the end of the decade, Samuel Bronston became the major independent producer. He worked through MGM to finance a program of epic historical spectacles by selling in advance distribution rights throughout the world. His epic films included *El Cid* (1961), *55 Days at Peking* (1963) and *The Fall of the Roman Empire* (1964). Each film exploited wide-screen images in color with synchronous sound to excite movie audiences. Finally the epic dramatizations reached their pinnacle with Stanley Kubrick's *Spartacus* (1960), and Nicholas Ray's *King of Kings* (1961). Both films told about an open rebellion against the oppressive forces, thematically supporting messages of personal freedom. The two directors were precursors of the antiestablishment directors who produced films in the 1960s in the United States.

3.3 Revival

The 1967-1976 eras constitute one of the richest periods in movie history. The American cinema was undergoing a renaissance in an interesting way in the midst of all violence, corruption, and despair.

The 1960s was a dissociated decade in the American cinema. It began in transition and declining and ended in revival. In the last few years of the decade, the American cinema shifted into a strident direction, generally like American society at that time. Most film critics agreed that the escalation of the war in Vietnam (1959-1975) was the principal reason for this shift in sensibility, which was angry, militant, and harshly critical of the Establishment. And there are other reasons for this shift in sensibility. The 1960s was a prosperous decade for the most part, accompanied by an increasing permissiveness especially among the young. Youth was enjoying the fruits of the sexual revolution and other youthful rebellions like smoking, marijuana and even more dangerous behaviors.

More important was the introduction of the antihero protagonist, who challenged the norms and values of modern industrial society as a misfit, loner or outlaw. From these trends, a new Hollywood cinema arose that responded to the social and political changes in society created by the Civil Rights movement, the assassinations of Robert Kennedy and Martin Luther King, Jr., as well as the student protests against the Vietnam War. Many important films were made in the final three years of the 1960s. Commercial films such as Arthur Penn's *Bonnie and Clyde* (1967), Mike Nichols' *The Graduate* (1967), and Stanley Kubrick's *A Clockwork Orange* (1971) appealed to a new generation of moviegoers by reflecting the spirit of the counter-culture. Each film presents different social accounts of the antihero protagonist during this period of film history — rebels against the American mainstream.

A box-office champion of the decade was Mike Nichols's *The Graduate* (1967). It pushed the actor Dustin Hoffman to become one of the foremost actor-stars of his generation. Young audiences were strongly attracted by the confused hero, who doesn't know what he wants to do with his life. He just knows he doesn't want what his parents and their friends have — an overstuffed yet empty existence. This film presents an acid portrait of the lifeless materialism of the capitalism. Nichols' directorial style in *The Graduate* is clever and witty. The editing is sprinkled with deliberate jump-cuts and leaps in continuity, comically throwing us off guard. The scenes are often accompanied by the sad songs of Simon and Garfunkel, which comment obliquely on the action. The widescreen images are strikingly composed, suggesting a multitude of feelings and ideas through the mise en scene. And like most of Nichols' films, the acting is first-rate, filled with freshly observed details, subtle quiet moments, and brilliant touches of deadpan comedy on the part of Hoffman.

Most film historians point to Arthur Penn's *Bonnie and Clyde* (1967), a gangster film set in the Depression thirties, as the turning point from the old sensibility to the new. This film caused a furious controversy among commentators. Of course, violence was hardly something new in the American cinema. (American movies even in the silent era was said to be divided into two genres: Kiss-Kiss and Bang-Bang.) What was new in Penn's film was the utterly intensity of the violence. Penn has said of his character: "The only people who really interest me are the outcasts from society. My sympathies lie with that person who cannot accommodate himself to society and may have to lose his life to change it." Ideology is a foreign concept to most of them. Their rebellion is instinctive, spontaneous, and usually unfocused.

The earlier 1970s, dominated by the unending war in Vietnam and the Watergate scandals, represent a continuation of the sensibility of the late 1960s. The most important movies of the Vietnam-Watergate era emphasized violence, racial and sexual conflicts, and the moral bankruptcy of public institutions. It was a pessimistic period. For the first time in American film history, movies with downbeat themes became the rule rather than the exception. Some of the key films of the period are *Petulia* (1968), *Five Easy Pieces* (1970), *M * A * S * H* (1970), *Little Big Man* (1970), *Joe* (1970), *A Clockwork Orange* (1971), *The French Connection* (1971), *McCabe and Mrs. Miller* (1971), *Klute* (1971), *Carnal Knowledge* (1971), *Straw Dogs* (1971), *Shaft* (1971), *Cabaret* (1972), *The Godfather* (1972), *Serpico* (1973), *Mean Street* (1973), *Chinatown* (1974), *The Conversation* (1974), *Lenny* (1974), *One Flew Over the Cuckoo's Nest* (1975), *Nashville* (1975), *All the President's Men* (1976), and *Taxi Driver* (1976). Among the films, *Cabaret* is a musical film starring Joel Grey and choreographed and directed Bob Fosse. The controlling metaphor of this musical is taken from the title song: Life is a cabaret. The musical numbers — noisy, flashy, and cynical — comment obliquely on the dramatic episodes, mocking their sentiment and undermining their sincerity.

For the first time in twenty years, film attendance began to rise, not decline. Most of this expanding audience was young and well-educated. American movies also reasserted their dominance on the international scene. Up to 50 percent of the grosses of American films were — and still are — earned abroad. The studios were now controlled mainly by younger men under forty, who became more receptive to innovative projects. Since many of the most profitable films of the period were made on relatively small budgets and even without important stars, studio executives were willing to gamble on new talent and fresh story ideas. An exceptionally large number of young directors made their first shows during this period.

The time-honored conventions of classical cinema were increasingly regarded as old-fashioned and mechanical in the revival period. The new filmmakers tended to prefer loose, episodic structures. Their films were more personal, more like European movies, often with unpredictable and inconclusive endings.

Even the genre films of this era were different from the traditionally conservative ones. They generally reversed or undercut an implied classical ideal in the ironic mode, questioning many of the values of the genre in its classical phase. It can be seen in many films like Bob Fosse's *Cabaret* (1972). As a love story in part like most classical musicals, *Cabaret* ends with the girl procuring an illegal abortion and going her solitary way, too fearful and self-absorbed to commit herself to a permanent relationship, which is very different from the traditional boy-wins-girl finale.

With the loosening of the censorship code in 1968, American movies soon became the freest and frankest in the world on the subject of sex, though sex has always been one of the most popular subjects of cinema in the United States.

By 1972, there were more than 700 theaters in the United States exhibiting only hard-core pornography. Oddly enough, this was not a good period for love stories, and sexual scenes were rarely romantic, often fused with violence like rape scenes.

Another characteristic of the films of this period is their technical and stylistic panache. Of course, American movies have always been among the best crafted in the world, and Hollywood was a consistent leader in advancing the technology of its art. This characteristic was especially true of the French New Wave movies of the 1960s — moves that exerted an enormous influence on the young American directors who came to prominence in the Vietnam-Watergate era.

The new directors were often called as the "whiz kids" for their showy technical tricks. Good examples were Spielberg, Coppola, Lucas, and Scorsese. Even the works of established directors like Peckinpah, Kubrick and Fosse were superbly crafted, with stunning photographic effects, innovative editing techniques. The techniques are often combined simultaneously as in the famous chase sequence of *The French Connection* (1971), starring Gene Hackmann and Marcel Bozzuffi and directed by William Friedkin. The chase sequence of this film is a stylistic tour de force, brilliantly orchestrated to keep audience at the edges of the seats. The editing is punctuated by abrupt jump-cuts and a driving sense of urgency.

3.4 Directors

3.4.1 Francis Ford Coppola (1939-)

Born	April 7, 1939 Detroit, Michigan, United States
Occupation	Film director, film producer, screenwriter
Years active	1962-present

Filmography: *Dementia* 13 (1963), *You're a Big Boy Now* (1966), *Finian's Rainbow* (1968), *The Rain People* (1969), *The Godfather Trilogy*: *The Godfather* (1972), *The Godfather Part II* (1974); *The Conversation* (1974), *Apocalypse Now* (1979), *One from the Heart* (1982), *Rumble Fish* (1983), *The Outsiders* (1983), *The Cotton Club* (1984), *Peggy Sue Got Married* (1986), *Gardens of Stone* (1987), *Tucker*: *The Man and His Dream* (1988), *New York Stories* (1989), *The Godfather Part III* (1990), *Bram Stoker's Dracula* (1992), *Jack* (1996), *The Rainmaker* (1997), *The Virgin Suicides* (1999) (*producer*, *daughter directed*), *Apocalypse Now Redux* (2001), *Youth Without Youth* (2007), *Tetro* (2009)

Francis Ford Coppola is an American film director, producer and screenwriter. In 1970, he won the Oscar for best original screenplay as co-writer of *Patton* (1970). His directorial prominence was cemented with the release in 1972 of *The Godfather* which revolutionized movie-making in the gangster genre and earned praise from both critics and the public before winning three Academy Awards—including his second Oscar (Best Adapted Screenplay, Best Picture, and his first nomination for Best Director. *The Godfather Part II* in 1974 became the first sequel to win the Academy Award for Best Picture. Highly regarded by critics, it brought him three more Academy Awards: Best Adapted Screenplay, Best Director and Best Picture, and made him the second director, after Billy Wilder, to be honored three times for the same film.

While majoring in theater arts in university, he was awarded a scholarship in playwriting which furthered his interest in directing theater despite the disapproval of his father who wanted him to study engineering. After graduating from university in 1959 with a bachelor's degree in Theatre Arts, Coppola enrolled in UCLA Film School for graduate work in film. In 1965, Coppola won the annual Samuel Goldwyn Award for the best screenplay written by a UCLA student. This secured him a job as a scriptwriter. Coppola epitomized a group of filmmakers known as the "New Hollywood" that emerged in the early 1970s with ideas that challenged conventional film-making. The group included Steven Spielberg, Martin Scorsese, Woody Allen and George Lucas.

The release of *The Godfather* in 1972 was a milestone in cinema. The near 3-hour-long epic, which chronicled the saga of the Corleone family, received overwhelmingly positive reviews from critics and fetched Coppola the Academy Award for Best Adapted Screenplay, which he shared with Mario Puzo and two Golden Globe Awards: for Best Director and Best Screenplay.

Coppola shot *The Godfather Part II* parallel to *The Conversation* and it was the last major American motion picture to be filmed in Technicolor. *The Godfather Part II* is ranked as the #1 greatest movie of all time in TV Guide's "50 Best Movies of All Time" and is ranked at #7 on Entertainment Weekly's list of the "100 Greatest Movies of All Time". Coppola was the third director to have two nominations for Best Picture in the same year. Victor Fleming was the first in 1939 with *Gone with the Wind* and *The Wizard of Oz*; Alfred Hitchcock repeated the feat the next year with *Foreign Correspondent* and *Rebecca*. Since Coppola, two other directors have done the same. Coppola, however, is the only one to have produced the pictures.

In 1990, he released the third and final chapter of *The Godfather* Series: *The Godfather Part*

III. While not as critically acclaimed as the first two films, it was still a box-office success, earning revenue of $136 million against a budget of $54 million. *The Godfather Part III* went on to gather 7 Academy Award nominations, including Best Director and Best Picture. The film failed to win any of these awards, the only film in the trilogy to do so.

Up to now, Coppola has obtained a number of honors which prove he has been one of the accomplished and respectable filmmakers. Looking back, in 1991, he was honored with the Berlinale Camera at the Berlin International Film Festival. In 1992, he was awarded a Golden Lion — Honorary Award at the Venice Film Festival. In 1998, the Directors Guild of America honored him with a Lifetime Achievement Award. In 2003, he was awarded a Lifetime Achievement Award at the Denver Film Festival. In 2010, the Academy of Motion Picture Arts and Sciences decided to honor him with the Irving G. Thalberg Memorial Award at the 2nd Governor's Awards in November.

3.4.2 Martin Scorsese (1942-)

Born	November 17, 1942 New York, US
Occupation	Film director, film producer, actor, screenwriter
Years active	1963-present

Filmography: *Who's That Knocking at My Door?* (1968), *Boxcar Bertha* (1972), *Mean Streets* (1973), *Alice Doesn't Live Here Anymore* (1974), *Taxi Driver* (1976), *New York, New York* (1977), *The Last Waltz* (1978), *Raging Bull* (1980), *The King of Comedy* (1983), *After Hours* (1985), *The Color of Money* (1986), *The Last Temptation of Christ* (1988), *GoodFellas* (1990), *Cape Fear* (1991), *The Age of Innocence* (1993), *Casino* (1995), *A Personal Journey with Martin Scorsese through American Movies* (1995) (*documentary*), *Kundun* (1997), *Bringing Out the Dead* (1999), *You Can Count on Me* (2000) (*ex. producer*), *Gangs of New York* (2003), *The Aviator* (2004), *No Direction Home*: *Bob Dylan* (2005), *The Departed* (2006), *Shine a Light* (2008), *Shutter Island* (2009), *Hugo* (2011), *The Wolf of Wallstreet* (2013)

Martin Scorsese is widely regarded as one of the most influential and significant directors of all time directing landmark films such as *Mean Streets* (1973), *Taxi Driver* (1976), *Raging Bull* (1980), *GoodFellas* (1990) and *Casino* (1995).

Part of the New Hollywood wave of filmmaking, he is widely regarded as one of the most significant and influential filmmakers in cinematic history. In 1990, he founded The Film

Foundation, a nonprofit organization dedicated to film preservation. He is a recipient of the AFI Life Achievement Award for his contributions to the cinema, and has won an Academy Award, a Palme d'Or, Cannes Film Festival Best Director Award, Silver Lion, Grammy Award, Emmys, Golden Globes, BAFTAs, and DGA Awards.

It's said that Robert De Niro practically saved Scorsese's life when he persuaded Scorsese to give up his cocaine addiction to make his highly regarded film *Raging Bull*. Scorsese poured his energies into making this violent biopic of middleweight boxing Jake LaMotta. The film is widely viewed as a masterpiece and was voted the greatest film of the 1980s. It received eight Oscar nominations, including Best Picture, Best Actor for Robert De Niro, and Scorsese's first Best Director. In 2007, *Raging Bull* was ranked as the 4th greatest film of all time on the AFI's 100 Years—100 Movies (10th Anniversary Edition) List.

After a decade of mostly mixed results, gangster epic *GoodFellas* (1990) was a return to Scorsese's most confident and fully realized film since *Raging Bull*. De Niro and Joe Pesci in *GoodFellas* offered a virtuoso display of the director's bravura cinematic technique and re-established, enhanced, and consolidated his reputation. The film is widely considered one of the director's greatest achievements. The film was nominated for six Academy Awards, including Best Picture and Best Director, Scorsese earned his third Best Director nomination for *GoodFellas* but again lost to a first-time director, Kevin Costner (*Dances with Wolves*).

Gangs of New York earned Scorsese his first Golden Globe for Best Director. In February 2003, *Gangs of New York* received ten Academy Award nominations, including Best Picture, Best Director, and Best Actor for Daniel Day-Lewis, however it did not win in any category.

The Aviator (2004) was a lavish, large-scale biopic of eccentric aviation pioneer and reunited Scorsese with actor Leonardo DiCaprio. The film received highly positive reviews. The film also met with widespread box-office success and gained Academy recognition. *The Aviator* was nominated for six Golden Globe Awards, it won three, including Best Motion Picture — Drama and Best Actor — Motion Picture Drama. In January 2005, *The Aviator* became the most-nominated film of the 77th Academy Awards nominations, nominated in 11 categories including Best Picture along with a fifth Best Director nomination for Scorsese, yet Scorsese lost again.

Hugo is Scorsese's first 3D film and was released in the US on November 23, 2011. *Hugo* is an adventure drama film. The film has been met with critical acclaim and earned Scorsese his third Golden Globe Award for Best Director. The film was also nominated for eleven Academy Awards, winning five of them and becoming tied with film *The Artist* for the most Academy Awards won by a single film in 2011. *Hugo* also won two BAFTA Awards, among other numerous awards and nominations.

3.4.3 George Lucas (1944-)

Born	May 14, 1944 California, U.S.
Occupation	Director, former chairman & CEO of Lucasfilm
Years active	1967-present

Filmography: *Herbie* (1966), *THX*-1138 (1971), *American Graffiti* (1973), *The Star Wars Trilogy*: *Star Wars* (1977), *The Empire Strikes Back* (1980) (*producer only*), *Return of the Jedi* (1983) (*producer only*); *Raiders of the Lost Ark* (1981) (*producer*), *Indiana Jones and the Temple of Doom* (1984) (*producer*), *Indiana Jones and the Last Crusade* (1989) (*producer*), *Star Wars Episode I*: *The Phantom Menace* (1999), *Star Wars Episode II*: *Attack of the Clones* (2002), *Star Wars Episode III*: *Revenge of the Sith* (2005)

George Lucas is one of the American film industry's most financially successful filmmakers. He founded Lucasfilm Limited as chairman and chief executive before selling it to The Walt Disney Company in 2012. He is widely known as the creator of the space opera franchise *Star Wars*. *Star Wars* quickly became the highest-grossing film of all-time, displaced five years later by Spielberg's *E. T. the Extra-Terrestrial*. Because Lucas exploited merchandising rights wisely, Lucasfilm has earned hundreds of millions of dollars from licensed games, toys, and collectibles created for the franchise.

In 1994, Lucas began work on the screenplay for the prequel *Star Wars Episode I*: *The Phantom Menace*, which would be the first film he had directed in over two decades. *The Phantom Menace* was released in 1999, beginning a new trilogy of *Star Wars* films. Lucas also directed *Star Wars Episode II*: *Attack of the Clones* and *Star Wars Episode III*: *Revenge of the Sith* which were released in 2002 and 2005, respectively. Numerous critics considered these films inferior to the previously released *Star Wars* films, though the prequels were nevertheless huge box-office successes in each of their respective releases. In 2008, he reteamed with Spielberg for *Indiana Jones and the Kingdom of the Crystal Skull*.

Lucas currently serves as executive producer for *Star Wars*: *The Clone Wars*, an animated television series on Cartoon Network, which was preceded by a feature film of the same name. He is also working on a so-far untitled *Star Wars* live-action series. For the film *Red Tails* (2012), Lucas serves as story-writer and executive producer. He also took over direction of reshoots while director Anthony Hemingway worked on other projects. In addition, Lucas is working on his first musical. In January 2012, Lucas announced his retirement from producing large scale blockbuster films and instead re-focusing his career on smaller, independently budgeted features. He did not specify whether or not this would affect his involvement with a fifth installment of the *Indiana Jones* series. With the sale of Lucasfilm to Disney, Lucas is currently Disney's second largest single shareholder after the estate of Steve Jobs. Lucas has pledged to give half of his fortune to charity as part of an effort called The Giving Pledge led by Bill Gates and Warren Buffett to persuade America's richest individuals to donate their financial wealth to charities.

In June 2013, it was reported Lucas will propose establishing a museum, Lucas Cultural Art Museum, to be built near the Golden Gate Bridge in San Francisco. If the proposal is accepted, Lucas' large collection of illustrations and pop art, with an estimated value of more than $1 billion, will be displayed there. According to the report, Lucas will offer to pay the estimated $300 million cost of constructing the museum, will endow it with $400 million when it opens, and eventually add an additional $400 million to its endowment.

The American Film Institute awarded Lucas its Life Achievement Award on June 9, 2005. Lucas was also nominated for four Academy Awards: Best Directing and Writing for *American Graffiti*, and Best Directing and Writing for *Star Wars*. He appeared at the 79th Academy Awards ceremony in 2007 with Steven Spielberg and Francis Ford Coppola to present the Best Director award to their friend Martin Scorsese. During the speech, Spielberg and Coppola talked about the joy of winning an Oscar, making fun of Lucas, who has not won a competitive Oscar. The Science Fiction Hall of Fame inducted Lucas in 2006, its second "Film, Television, and Media" contributor, after Spielberg. The Discovery Channel named him one of the 100 "Greatest Americans" in September 2008. In July 2013, Lucas was awarded the National Medal of Arts by President Barack Obama for his contributions to American cinema.

3. 4. 4 Steven Spielberg (1946-)

Born	December 18, 1946 Ohio, U. S.
Occupation	Filmmaker, businessman
Years active	1963-present

Filmography: *Duel* (1971), *The Sugarland Express* (1974), *Jaws* (1975), *Close Encounters of the Third Kind* (1977), 1941 (1979), *Raiders of the Lost Ark* (1981), *E. T. the Extra-Terrestrial* (1982), *Poltergeist* (1982), *Twilight Zone: The Movie* (1983) (*segment 2*), *Gremlins* (1984) (*producer*), *Indiana Jones and the Temple of Doom* (1984), *Back to the*

Future, *II*, *III* (1985, 1989, 1990) (*executive producer*), *The Color Purple* (1985), *Empire of the Sun* (1987), *Who Framed Roger Rabbit* (1988) (*executive producer*), *Always* (1989), *Indiana Jones and the Last Crusade* (1989), *Hook* (1991), *Jurassic Park* (1993), *Schindler's List* (1993), *Twister* (1996) (*executive producer*), *Amistad* (1997), *The Lost World: Jurassic Park* (1997), *Men in Black* (1997) (*producer*), *Saving Private Ryan* (1998), *A. I.: Artificial Intelligence* (2001), *Jurassic Park III* (2001) (*ex. producer*), *Minority Report* (2002), *Catch Me If You Can* (2002), *The Terminal* (2004), *War of the Worlds* (2005), *Munich* (2005), *Indiana Jones and the Kingdom of the Crystal Skull* (2008), *The Adventures of Tintin* (2011), *War Horse* (2011), *Lincoln* (2012)

Steven Spielberg is considered one of the most popular and influential filmmakers in the history of cinema. Over a career of more than forty years, Spielberg has made a great many films covering various themes and genres. Spielberg's early science-fiction and adventure films were seen as archetypes of modern Hollywood blockbuster filmmaking. In later years, his films began focusing on humanistic issues such as slave trade, war, and terrorism. He is also one of the co-founders of DreamWorks movie studio.

Spielberg was born in Cincinnati, Ohio, to a Jewish family. At age thirteen, Spielberg won a prize for a 40-minute war film he titled *Escape to Nowhere*. In 1963, at age sixteen, Spielberg wrote and directed his first independent film, a 140-minute science fiction adventure called *Firelight*.

Spielberg's debut feature film was *The Sugarland Express*. Spielberg was then offered the director's chair for *Jaws*. It was an enormous hit, winning three Academy Awards (for editing, original score and sound) and grossing more than $470 million worldwide at the box office. It also set the domestic record for box-office gross, leading to what the press described as "Jawsmania".

Spielberg collaborated with *Star Wars* creator and friend George Lucas on an action adventure film *Raiders of the Lost Ark* in 1981, the first of the *Indiana Jones* films. A year later, Spielberg returned to the science fiction genre with *E. T. the Extra-Terrestrial*, which went on to become the top-grossing film of all time. *E. T.* was also nominated for nine Academy Awards including Best Picture and Best Director.

Spielberg's next work *Schindler's List* earned his first Academy Award for Best Director (it also won Best Picture). With the film a huge success at the box office, Spielberg used the profits to set up the Shoah Foundation, a non-profit organization that archives filmed testimony of Holocaust survivors. In 1997, the American Film Institute ranked it among the 10 Greatest American Films ever Made (the 9th) which moved up to the eighth when the list was remade in 2007.

Spielberg won his second Academy Award for his direction of *Saving Private Ryan*. The film's graphic, realistic depiction of combat violence influenced later war films such as *Black Hawk Down* and *Enemy at the Gates*. Later, Spielberg and Tom Hanks produced a TV mini-series based on *Band of Brothers*. The series won a number of awards at the Golden Globes and the Emmys.

Spielberg followed that with *War Horse*, shot in England in the summer of 2010, which received generally positive reviews from critics, and was nominated for six Academy Awards including Best Picture. Spielberg then directed the historical drama film *Lincoln*. Based on the bestseller *Team of Rivals*: *The Political Genius of Abraham Lincoln*, the film covered the final four months of Lincoln's life. Upon release, *Lincoln* received widespread critical acclaim, and was nominated for twelve Academy Awards including Best Picture and Best Director for Spielberg. It won the award for Best Production Design and Day-Lewis won the Academy Award for Best Actor for his portrayal of Lincoln, becoming the first three-time winner in that category as well as the first to win for a performance directed by Spielberg.

Spielberg has garnered numerous honors and awards for acclaiming his great contribution to the film industry including three Academy Awards. He has been nominated for seven Academy Awards for the category of Best Director, winning two of them (*Schindler's List* and *Saving Private Ryan*), and nine of the films he directed were up for the Best Picture Oscar (*Schindler's List* won). In addition, Spielberg received the AFI Life Achievement Award in 1995.

3.5 Actors

3.5.1 Marlon Brando (1924-2004)

Born	April 3, 1924 Nebraska, U. S.
Died	July 1, 2004 California, U. S.
Occupation	Actor
Years active	1945-2001

Best Films: *The Men* (1950), *A Streetcar Named Desire* (1951), *Viva Zapata*! (1952), *Julius Caesar* (1953), *The Wild One* (1953), *On the Waterfront* (1954), *Guys and Dolls* (1955), *Sayonara* (1957), *One-Eyed Jacks* (1961), *The Chase* (1966), *The Godfather* (1972), *Last Tango in Paris* (1972), *Superman*: *The Movie* (1978), *Apocalypse Now* (1979), *A Dry White Season* (1989), *The Freshman* (1990), *Don Juan DeMarco* (1995), *The Island of Dr. Moreau* (1996)

Marlon Brando is a cultural icon whose popularity has lasted for over six decades. He gained national attention in the 1950s, which had a profound effect on the motion picture industry. He is widely acclaimed for bringing a gripping realism to film acting and is generally considered to have been one of the greatest and most influential actors in the film history.

Brando is most prestigious for his Oscar-winning performances in *On the Waterfront* (1954) and in *The Godfather* (1972), together with other impressive performances in *A Streetcar Named Desire* (1951), *Julius Caesar* (1953), *The Wild One* (1953), *Reflections in a Golden Eye* (1967), *Last Tango in Paris* (1972) and *Apocalypse Now* (1979). Brando was also an activist, notably for his supporting African-American Civil-Rights Movement and various American Indian Movements.

The Men (1950) was Brando's first film which was followed by *A Streetcar Named Desire* (1951) that brought initial success and popularity. His iconic portrayal of the rebel motorcycle gang leader in *The Wild One* (1953) was thought to be one of the most famous images in pop culture. Brando won a Best Actor Oscar for his multi-layered performance in *On the Waterfront* (1954). Brando was also nominated for the Oscar for his roles in *Viva Zapata*! (1952), in the 1953 film adaptation of Shakespeare's *Julius Caesar* and in *Sayonara* (1957). During the 1950s, Brando belonged to the group of top money-making stars.

Brando directed and starred in the cult western film *One-Eyed Jacks* released in 1961. After that he delivered a series of box-office failures beginning with the non-success of the 1962 film adaptation of *Mutiny on the Bounty*. The 1960s proved to be a fallow decade for Brando in which he did not star in any commercially successful movie. Then he won his second Academy Award for playing Vito Corleone in Francis Ford Coppola's *The Godfather* (1972), a role which was regarded among his greatest. The film became the most commercially successful film of all time when it was released. The role of Godfather and his Oscar-nominated performance in *Last Tango in Paris* in the same year contributed greatly to revitalizing Brando's career and reestablishing him in the ranks of top box-office stars.

Brando failed to capitalize on the momentum of his revitalized career, taking a long hiatus before appearing in *The Missouri Breaks* (1976). After that, he found contentment to be a highly paid character actor in parts which were glorified cameos in *Superman* (1978) and *The Formula* (1980) before taking a nine-year break from motion pictures. He ended the decade of the 1970s with his controversial performance in another Coppola film, *Apocalypse Now*. The film was a box-office hit for which he was highly paid and helped finance his career break during the 1980s.

Brando was ranked by the American Film Institute as the fourth greatest screen legend among male film stars. Considered to be one of the most important actors in American cinema, Brando, along with Charlie Chaplin and Marilyn Monroe, was one of only three professional actors named by *Time* magazine as one of its 100 People of the 20th Century in 1999. Upon his death in 2004, Brando left an estate valued at $21.6 million. In addition, he was named one of the top-earning dead celebrities in the world by the *Forbes* magazine.

Brando is widely viewed as one of the greatest and most influential actors in the world. Because of his memorable performances and charismatic screen show, he has earned great respect among critics. As a film actor, Brando has achieved unequaled success in his time, for he reinvented acting and revolutionized acting. Brando demonstrates the single greatest performance ever which is so natural, powerful and real. It's known that Stanislavski created "method acting", but it was Brando who showed the world its power. Even according to some critics, the art of screen acting has two chapters—"Before Brando" and "After Brando".

Marlon Brando has become a cultural icon summing up "the road" in all its maverick glory with sporting leather jacket, jeans, and moody glare. His portrayal of the gang leader Johnny Strabler in *The Wild One* has been an iconic image, a symbol of rebelliousness armed with a fashion accessory that includes a Perfecto style motorcycle jacket, a tilted cap, jeans and sunglasses. Johnny's haircut inspired a craze for sideburns, followed by James Dean and Elvis Presley and others. Brando was also a sex idol, one of the earliest in the film world to gain widespread attention, due to his enigmatic and sexy persona and reports of his dalliances and relationships with various major Hollywood celebrities.

3.5.2 Dustin Hoffman (1937-)

Born	August 8, 1937 Los Angeles, California, U. S.
Occupation	Actor
Years active	1960-present

Best Films: *The Graduate* (1967), *Midnight Cowboy* (1969), *Little Big Man* (1970), *Straw Dogs* (1971), *Papillon* (1973), *Lenny* (1974), *Marathon Man* (1976) *All the President's Men* (1976), *Kramer vs. Kramer* (1979), *Tootsie* (1982), *Rain Man* (1988), *Dick Tracy* (1990), *Hook* (1991), *Hero* (1992), *Outbreak* (1995), *Sleepers* (1996), *Wag the Dog* (1997), *Sphere* (1998), *The Messenger: The Story of Joan of Arc* (1999), *Moonlight Mile* (2002), *Confidence* (2003), *Finding Neverland* (2004), *I Heart Huckabees* (2004), *Meet the Fockers* (2004), *Stranger Than Fiction* (2006), *Kung Fu Panda* (2008), *Last Chance Harvey* (2008)

Dustin Hoffman is an American famous Jewish actor who began a career in film, television, and theatre since 1960. His versatile portrayals of antiheroes and vulnerable characters have made him prestigious.

Hoffman played his first major role in *The Graduate*, for which he received an Academy Award nomination for his performance. *The Graduate* was a gigantic box-office hit, making Hoffman a major new star at that time. Mostly thanks to Hoffman's acting, the film received nearly unanimously positive reviews. Hoffman was regarded as a symbol of young actors who broke the mold of the traditional film stars and brought to their roles a new candor, ethnicity, and eagerness to dive deep into complex, even unlikable characters.

Hoffman's next major film was *Midnight Cowboy*, for which Hoffman received his second Oscar nomination and the film won the Best Picture honor. Hoffman continued to appear in major films over the next few years. *Who Is Harry Kellerman and Why Is He Saying Those Terrible Things About Me?* (1971), *Straw Dogs* (also 1971), and *Papillon* (1973) were followed by *Lenny* (1974), for which Hoffman received his third nomination for Best Actor in seven years.

Hoffman's next leading role was in *Kramer vs. Kramer* (1979). Hoffman gained his first Academy Award, and the film also received the Best Picture honor, plus the awards for Best Supporting Actress (Streep) and Director.

In 1984, Hoffman starred in the Broadway revival of the 1949 Arthur Miller play, *Death of a Salesman*, a role he reprised in a TV movie of the same name, for which he won the 1985 Emmy Award in the category of Outstanding Lead Actor in a TV Movie or Miniseries. He also went on to win a Golden Globe for the same performance.

In director Barry Levinson's *Rain Man* (1988), Hoffman's performance gained him his second Academy Award.

Though he was reluctant to perform in an animated film, in 2008, Hoffman had a prominent role as Shifu in the acclaimed film *Kung Fu Panda*, which was praised in part for his comedic chemistry with Jack Black and his character's poignantly complex relationship with the story's villain. He later won the Annie Award for Voice Acting in an Animated Feature for *Kung Fu Panda*. Hoffman reprised his role as Shifu in *Kung Fu Panda II* (2011) *and III* (2016).

Hoffman has been nominated for seven Academy Awards, winning two, thirteen Golden Globes, winning six (including an honorary one) and has won four BAFTAs. Hoffman received the AFI Life Achievement Award in 1999.

3.5.3 Robert De Niro (1943-)

Born	August 17, 1943 New York, U. S.
Occupation	Actor, film director, film producer
Years active	1963-present

Best Films: *Bang the Drum Slowly* (1973), *Mean Streets* (1973), *The Godfather, Part II* (1974), *Taxi Driver* (1976), *The Deer Hunter* (1978), *Raging Bull* (1980), *The King of Comedy* (1983), *Once Upon a Time in America* (1984), *The Untouchables* (1987), *GoodFellas* (1990), *Backdraft* (1991), *Cape Fear* (1991), *A Bronx Tale* (1993), *Mad Dog and Glory*

(1993), *Mary Shelley's Frankenstein* (1994), *Casino* (1995), *Heat* (1995), *Sleepers* (1996), *Wag the Dog* (1997), *Ronin* (1998), *Analyze This* (1999), *Meet the Parents* (2000), *The Score* (2001), *Analyze That* (2002), *Meet the Fockers* (2004), *The Good Shepherd* (2006), *Little Fockers* (2010), *New Year's Eve* (2011), *Silver Linings Playbook* (2012)

Robert De Niro is an American actor, director and producer. De Niro has been widely acclaimed for his outstanding acting and fruitful career which can best be proved by the AFI Life Achievement Award (2003) and the Golden Globe Cecil B. DeMille Award (2010) that De Niro has received.

His first major film roles were in *Bang the Drum Slowly* and *Mean Streets*, both in 1973. His longtime collaboration with director Martin Scorsese began with *Mean Streets*. In 1974, he starred as the young Vito Corleone in *The Godfather Part II*, and he won the Academy Award for Best Supporting Actor. In 1980, he earned an Academy Award for Best Actor for his portrayal of Jake LaMotta in the film *Raging Bull*. He was also nominated for his leading roles in *Taxi Driver* in 1976 and *Cape Fear* in 1991.

Besides, De Niro received Academy Award nominations for Michael Cimino's *The Deer Hunter* (1978), Penny Marshall's *Awakenings* (1990), and David O. Russell's *Silver Linings Playbook* (2012). His portrayal of gangster Jimmy Conway in Scorsese's *GoodFellas* earned him a BAFTA nomination in 1990. In addition, De Niro has earned four nominations for the Golden Globe Award for Best Actor — Motion Picture Musical or Comedy, for his work in *New York, New York* (1977), *Midnight Run* (1988), *Analyze This* (1999), and *Meet the Parents* (2000).

De Niro's brand of method acting includes employing whatever extreme tactic he feels is necessary to elicit the best performance from those with whom he is working. During the filming of *The King of Comedy*, for example, he directed a slew of anti-Semitic epithets at co-star Jerry Lewis in order to enhance and authenticate the anger demonstrated by his onscreen character. In 2009, he was among the five recipients of the Kennedy Center Honors, presented by U. S. President Barack Obama.

3.5.4 Meryl Streep (1949-)

Born	June 22, 1949 New Jersey, U. S.
Occupation	Actress
Years active	1971-present

Best Films: *The Deer Hunter* (1978), *Manhattan* (1979), *Kramer vs. Kramer* (1979), *The*

French Lieutenant's Woman (1981), *Sophie's Choice* (1982), *Silkwood* (1983), *Out of Africa* (1985), *Ironweed* (1987), *A Cry in the Dark* (1988), *Postcards from the Edge* (1990), *Death Becomes Her* (1992), *The River Wild* (1994), *The Bridges of Madison County* (1995), *Marvin's Room* (1996), *One True Thing* (1998), *Music of the Heart* (1999), *Adaptation* (2002), *The Hours* (2002), *The Manchurian Candidate* (2004), *Lemony Snicket's a Series of Unfortunate Events* (2004), *The Devil Wears Prada* (2006), *A Prairie Home Companion* (2006), *Evening* (2007), *Lions for Lambs* (2007), *Doubt* (2008), *Mamma Mia!* (2008), *Julie & Julia* (2009), *Fantastic Mr. Fox* (2009), *It's Complicated* (2009), *The Iron Lady* (2011)

Meryl Streep is an American actress of theater, television, and film. She is widely regarded as one of the most talented actresses of all time. Streep was born and grew up in New Jersey. She received her B. A., in Drama in 1971. She subsequently earned an M. F. A. from the Yale School of Drama. While at Yale, she played a variety of roles onstage.

Julia (1977) was Streep's first feature film in which she played a small but pivotal role during a flashback scene. In 1978, she played a leading role in the television miniseries *Holocaust* as a German woman married to a Jewish artist in Nazi-era Germany. She won the Primetime Emmy Award for Outstanding Lead Actress — Miniseries or a Movie for her performance.

A month later, *The Deer Hunter* (1978) was released and Streep was nominated for the Academy Award for Best Supporting Actress for her performance. Streep drew critical acclaim for her performance in each of her three films released in 1979: the romantic comedy *Manhattan*, the political drama *The Seduction of Joe Tynan* and the family drama, *Kramer vs. Kramer*. Among the awards won for *Kramer vs. Kramer* were the Academy Award and Golden Globe Award for Best Supporting Actress.

Her first leading role came in *The French Lieutenant's Woman* (1981). While many female stars had cultivated a singular identity in their films, Streep was praised for her willingness to play any type of role. Streep was awarded a BAFTA Award for Best Actress in a Leading Role for her work. As the Polish holocaust survivor in *Sophie's Choice* (1982), Streep's emotional dramatic performance and her apparent mastery of a Polish accent drew praise. Among several notable acting awards, Streep won the Academy Award for Best Actress for her performance.

Streep entered the 2000s with Steven Spielberg's science fiction *Artificial Intelligence*. In 2002, she began work on the comedy-drama *Adaptation* (2002), in which she portrayed real-life journalist Susan Orlean. Lauded by critics and viewers alike, the film won Streep her fourth Golden Globe in the Best Supporting Actress category. In the same year, Streep appeared alongside Nicole Kidman and Julianne Moore in *The Hours*. Focusing on three women of different generations whose lives are interconnected by the novel *Mrs. Dalloway* by Virginia Woolf, the film was generally well received and won all three leading actresses a Silver Bear for Best Actress the following year.

Streep was awarded the AFI Life Achievement Award by the Board of Directors of the American Film Institute in 2004. In *The Devil Wears Prada* (2006), Streep portrayed the powerful and demanding fashion magazine editor (and boss of a recent college graduate played by Anne Hathaway), and her performance drew rave reviews from critics and earned her many award nominations, including her record-setting 14th Oscar bid, as well as another Golden Globe. The film became Streep's biggest commercial success.

In 2008, Streep found major commercial success when she starred in *Mamma Mia!*, and she was nominated for a Grammy Award (her fifth nomination) for her work on the *Mamma Mia!'s* soundtrack. In 2009, Streep became the most-nominated performer in Golden Globe Awards history when her double lead actress nods for *Doubt* (2008) and *Mamma Mia!* (2008) gave her 23 in total. The following year, Streep received her seventh Globe for her performance in *Julie & Julia* (2009). In 2012, she broke her own record when she garnered her 26th nomination and overall eighth win for *The Iron Lady* at the 69th Golden Globe Awards. In 2013, she broke the record again when she received her 27th Golden Globe nomination for her performance in *Hope Springs* at the 70th Golden Globes. In 2004, Streep received the AFI Life Achievement Award. Besides, she has garnered a list of honorary awards granted by film festivals and other institutions and thus made herself one of the greatest actresses in film history.

4. Contemporary Cinema

4.1 Films Between Late 1970s and 1980s

A new era for watching movies began in the mid-1970s with the popularity of computer-made, sound-enhanced films such as *Star Wars* (1977) by George Lucas. At the same time satellites and video tape recorders initiated a wave of films viewing in homes in the United States and, increasingly, throughout the world. Similarly, recent documentaries and experimental films seem to have become video productions.

4.1.1 Technology

The advent of the videocassette recorder (VCR), as strenuously resisted by the studios as television itself had been, added yet another diversion with which movies had to compete. The VCR revolution changed the way films were made and seen. The use of widescreen processes declined severely also, and for similar reasons. Against all this was the commendable fact that in fact, the entire history of film was now at the right hand of anybody who lived near a well-stocked video store. By 1987, video rentals surpassed ticket sales as the industry's leading source of revenue. The marketing of movies attained a standard of excellence that sometimes overshadowed the film being marketed. Slick movies like *Batman* (1989) were promoted into firestorm success.

4. 1. 2 Studio System

To the independent filmmakers' displeasure, the studio system had returned in 1980s, to a degree. Organizations like Paramount once again began signing box office favorites to long-term contracts: Eddie Murphy at Paramount, Bette Midler and Tom Selleck at Disney, and so on. The top ten box-office performers of the 1980s were, in this order, Harrison Fort, Dan Aykroyd, Eddie Murphy, Bill Murray, Tom Cruise, Sylvester Stallone, Jock Nicholson, John Candy, Steve Guttenberg, and Danny DeVito. And studios again began buying into theater chains. By the end of the decade, the studios owned 3,500 of the nation's 22,000 screens, according to critic Gregg Kilday. The highly successful Disney studio was a good example of the new studio system. It constructed an efficient assembly line of modestly budgeted films.

4. 1. 3 Film Genre

In the early 1970s the film genre seemed to be a dead form in Hollywood. But an important change came in 1975 with the release of Steven Spielberg's *Jaws*. Two years later came George Lucas' *Star Wars*. The business of Hollywood production would not be the same. These classically conservative adventure tales sent producers back to make more genre films and revitalized the science fiction genre in one move. From *Jaws* came *Raiders of the Lost* Ark and the other two *Indiana Jones* films. From *Star Wars* we have gotten two Sequels and *E. T. Grease* proved the musical was a lively and healthy genre; *Beverly Hills Cop*, both parts so far, proved moviegoers still wanted detective dramas. Hollywood aimed these squarely at the teenagers who were their most faithful customers.

There was the cycle of the sequel — four *Rockys* (1976, 1979, 1982, 1985), four *Supermans* (1978, 1980, 1983, 1987), three *Halloweens* (1978, 1981 and 1983) and eight *Friday the 13ths* (1980, 1981, 1982, 1984, 1985, 1986, 1988, 1989). Other genres made their return in the late 1970s and early 1980s. The horror film was revived early on in the 1970s with *The Exorcist* (1973). Even *Jaws*, with its monster shark, must be seen as part of this wave of horror film. There were werewolves in Joe Dante's *The Howling* (1981) and John Landis' *An American Werewolf in London* (1981). Vampires also revived in John Badham's *Dracula* (1979) and Tony Scott's *The Hunger* (1983). Zombies appeared in George Romero's *Dawn of the Dead* (1979) and in *Halloween* and *The Fog* (1980), by John Carpenter, who is regarded as the best director in recent years of the horror film genre. The monster film has even been crossbred with other genres, particularly the science fiction film as in *Alien* (1979) and *Aliens* (1986). The alien becomes friendly and more popular in films like Steven Spielberg's *E. T.* (1982).

When George Lucas was working on *Star Wars*, he successfully reformulated myths from the past into what then was the highest grossing film of all time. The commercial success of his comic book fantasies spawned a whole new set genre films. There were sword-and-sorcery films like John Boorman's *Excalibur* (1981) and John Milius' *Conan the Barbarian* (1982) and its sequel *Conan the Destroyer* (1984). Indeed Lucas and Spielberg teamed together to have the twentieth-century scientist battle forces of evil in *Raiders of the Lost Ark* (1981), *Indiana Jones and the Temple of Doom* (1984), and *Indiana Jones and the Last Crusade* (1989). Comedy has also changed, redone for the teenage audience. There have been many more comic romances based on the broadest possible humor, such as *Rock "n" Roll High School* (1979), *Fast Times at Ridgemont High* (1982), and *Revenge of the Nerds* (1984).

4.1.4 Mainstream Directors

Many of the best movies of the 1980s were made by veteran directors, established artists like Bruce Beresford, Peter Weir, Milos Forman, Woody Allen, Steven Spielberg, and Paul Mazursky. Most of these filmmakers came to prominence in the 1970s. Sydney Pollack's *Tootsie* (1982) was one of the hallmarks of the feminist cinema, a witty exploration of gender roles, with a brilliant performance by Dustin Hoffman in the title part. Similarly, three of John Huston's greatest works — *Wise Blood* (1980), *Prizzi's Honor* (1985), and *The Dead* (1987) — were made when the old master was in his seventies, an extraordinary achievement in itself.

But there were also some newcomers who managed to create enduring works. Lawrence Kasdan showed a weird ability to imitate someone else's source material, and then give it a slight twist, such as in films *Body Heat* (1981), *The Big Chill* (1983), *Silverado* (1985), and *The Accidental Tourist* (1988). Barry Levinson showed that it was still possible to make quality, personal movies with remarkable profits. The first film written and directed by him, *Diner* (1982), was a Baltimore version of Fellini's *I Vitelloni*, about a bunch of young men nervously circling around adulthood by sitting around talking. It was a success. Levinson then began a habit of alternating apparently commercial projects with apparently personal ones. He followed his *Diner* with *The Natural* (1984), *Young Sherlock Holmes* (1985), *Tin Men* (1987), *Good Morning, Vietnam* (1987) and *Rain Man* (1988), the last one a painstakingly observed movie about a middle-aged autistic (by Dustin Hoffman) and his slimy, opportunistic younger brother (by Tom Cruise).

Of the commercial directors of the 1980s, few had the energy, good will or high spirits of Robert Zemeckis. Zemeckis and his writing partner Bob Gale began as disciples of Steven Spielberg. Zemeckis came into his own with *Used Cars* (1980) and encountered a box-office disappointment. Finally he got the hit with the romantic comedy/adventure film *Romancing the Stone* (1984). Since then, he has gone from strength to strength, including the adept *Back to the Future* (1985) and its two sequels. The big hit *Who Framed Roger Rabbit* (1988) is an ingenious amalgam of live action and animation, which served as both a tribute to and rebirth of classical animation. His biggest hit was *Forrest Gump* (1994), which provided Tom Hanks with one of his greatest roles.

4. 2 Films in 1990s

The American motion picture industry had no economic competition as the movies ended their first hundred years. However, the movie business no longer made a great deal of economic sense, in spite of its leading status in the world.

4. 2. 1 The Hollywood Studios

Costs at making films becoming immense and staggering, the studios sought to minimize risk by taking coproduction partners on even modestly budgeted films. For the independents, co-financing pictures with a major studio allows them to cut the risk. Co-financing also means that the studios stand to benefit far less from the occasional hit, because foreign rights are usually handed to the co-financiers in return for their investment. The tendency toward internationalization invaded the Hollywood studios. Columbia Pictures was purchased by Sony Corporation in 1989; Universal is owned by Seagram. At the end of the century, among the major Hollywood studios, only Disney was a free-standing, independent entity.

The major studios more or less opted out of the quality film business, mainly because of economics. Most of them made only one or two critic' awards-winning films each year, and designed the rest films purely and simply for box office. Even art films could be expensive. *Shakespeare in Love*, the Best Picture Oscar winner of 1998, cost nearly $40 million, too much for even a quasi-independent.

The changing nature of studio ownership changed the rules of the game. In decades past, studios lusted for Oscar recognition and made sure to produce a number of films that could bring them awards and the box-office bump that accompanied them. Most movies of this era were shot in an indistinguishable style. It would be difficult to identify the director without the credits. Contemplative long shots, crane shots, and a smooth methodical pace largely disappeared from mainstream American movies because filmmakers worried that an audience used to the luxury of the remote control would grow restless and tune out.

The apparent decline might be just a temporary calm, symptomatic of the uneasy, slightly disengaged limbo into which the post-cold war world has fallen. Perhaps the malaise is a mental retooling, stemming from the fact that the movie business has changed more in the last two decades than it had in the previous 80 years.

However, something was gained for everything that was lost. Screen acting has reached its best while skill was lost in some of moviemaking's component parts. Plenty of superlative actors spanned the generations, like Clint Eastwood, Kevin Spacey, Johnny Depp and Gwyneth Platrow. Even stars in the classic mode are making choices to realize their ambition. Among them are Tom Cruise and Leonardo DiCaprio, etc.

And animation was better and more widespread than ever too. Mainstream films like *The Lion*

King (1994) were produced by Disney, of quality and beauty with strong underlying messages. Fox and Warners also did good jobs in this field, though their animations got smaller-sized audiences than Disney. Films like *Anastasia* (1997) and television animation such as *The Simpsons*, *South Park*, and *Rugrats* furthered the acceptance of the style to the mass audience. CGI (computer graphics imaging) also made contributions to expand the animation business, with a new type of computer animation of bright, plastic sheen which is smoother, less organic, less obviously drawn than conventional animation. It made its mainstream debut in Disney's *Toy Story* (1995). It also played a leading role in the revolution of special effects in movies like *Jurassic Park* (1993).

The most impressive thing in this era is that the 1990s saw more variety in U. S. filmmaking than any previous period. Hollywood turned into a shape-shifting culture. There rose numerous gifted African American filmmakers — the Hughes brothers, Forest Whitaker, Spike Lee, and John Singleton, to name only a few. Likewise, many acting talents emerged from the expanding Hispanic population, like Jennifer Lopez, Antonio Banderas and Salma Hayek, and so do directors such as Alfonso Arau and Robert Rodrigues.

4. 2. 2 Major Filmmakers

When it comes to filmmakers in this era, the leading directors of the 1990s were those a decade ago, older, grayer, but undoubtedly still the leaders of the gang. First on the list was Steven Spielberg, who entered the 1990s as the oldest manchild in Hollywood and made the greatest commercial success in filmmaking history. He proved himself as the foremost filmmaking talent of his generation by turning out movies like *Jurassic Park* (1992), *Schindler's List* (1993), *Admistad* (1997), and the World War II epic, *Saving Private Ryan* (1998).

Besides Spielberg, some other directors were also in the leading rank, including Martin Scorsese, Woody Allen and Clint Eastwood. Martin Scorsese struggled through the decade with a succession of hit-and-miss films. His mob drama *GoodFellas* (1990) won great commercial success, followed by *Cape Fear* (1991), *The Age of Innocence* (1993), adapted from Edith Wharton's Pulitzer Prize winning novel, *Casino* (1995), starring his favorite actor Robert De Niro. Scorsese ended the decade with the respectful and arty spiritual drama, *Kundun*(1997).

Woody Allen's movies of the 1990s may not rank with his extraordinary artistic ones of the 1980s. However, no other filmmaker can match the diversity and sheer volume of his output. Among his products, some were regarded as third-rate: *Shadows and Fog* (1992), *Manhattan Murder Mystery* (1993) and *Celebrity* (1998). Luckily, his light comedies during this decade were especially appreciated and respected in Europe, like *Bullets Over Broadway* (1994), *Mighty Aphrodite* (1995) and *Everyone Says I Love You* (1996).

Among the major American filmmakers of the 1990s, Clint Eastwood is recognized as the most inconsistent one, partly as a result of his incurable habit of risk-taking. Take some of his films for instance. He gives no suspense in his manhunt movie *A Perfect World* (1993), and no real thrills in his thriller *Absolute Power* (1997). While sometimes his risks gain surprisingly success, for example in his films *In the Line of Fire* (1993) and *The Bridges of Madison County* (1995). *Unforgiven* (1992) is almost universally regarded as a masterpiece, in which Eastwood also gave one of his best performances in this film — funny, terrifying and unstoppable.

4.3 Films in the 21st Century

Featuring Change and Innovation, the new millennium to American Cinema is the era of franchise films and an age of advanced special effects (CGI and Performance Capture).

4.3.1 Major Hollywood Studios and Franchise Films

American movie industry started its rebirth of the new century as early as in 1999. Quite a few of films in this year gained both commercial success and favorable comments from critics, like M. Night Shymalan's *The Sixth Sensev*, Spike Jonze's *Being John Malkovichv*, and the Wachowski Brothers' *The Matrix*. However, the big studios diminished their accomplishment since 2000, partly as a result of the established change of the old order, especially that concerning costs and formats. There are now mainly six corporate entertainment empires that dominate the movie business: Time/Warner, Viacom, Twentieth Century Fox, NBC/Universal, Disney, and Sony. They are devoted to films that can be reliably produced for the audience without sensibility. The studios seemed to give up efforts for good movies at the beginning of the new century, with dimmer movies like *Pearl Harbor* (2001) and *Planet of the Apes* (2001).

The creation and feeding of franchises is encouraged to be sold on as many global platforms as possible, also for economic consideration. These include such family franchises as films like *Shrek* (2001) and *Harry Potter* series (2001, 2002, 2004, 2005, 2007, 2009, 2010, 2011), or more teen-oriented franchises such as *The Lord of the Rings* series (2001, 2002, 2003) and its prequel *The Hobbit* (1012), *Spider Man* series (2002, 2004, 2007), and *X-Men* series (2000, 2003, 2006, 2009, 2011, 2013).

Long runs have been rare since even hit movies may see a decrease of grosses as much as 50 percent. It is very rare to be blessed with movies like *Titanic* that keep in theaters for long run due to good reputation and box-office record. The studios have developed a skill in dealing with their films, even if they are terrible. *Planet of the Apes* (2001) is a good example. A sequel of this film was never considered in spite of its high grosses and profit.

Usually, the big studios have trouble marketing anything else when they have been specializing in one kind of movie, which makes some flexible distributors like Miramax Films get more chances of marketing. However, in the latter half of the 2000s, Hollywood studios realized that they could use social networking to market films, such as Facebook and Twitter. A great success in this way is *The Twilight Saga: New Moon* (2009). The romantic vampire *Twilight* sequel was followed by millions of Facebook and Twitter fans. *Inglorious Basterds* (2009) from

Universal Pictures and *Where the Wild Things Are* (2009) from Warner Bros. held out similar cheerful situation. The best example came from the low-budget, breakout, and independent horror film *Paranormal Activity* (2009). The studio launched a campaign with the eventful feature developed by a San Diego company known for promoting concerts. It eventually made estimated earnings of $107.9 million (to date), an almost 720K% return on investment.

4.3.2 After-Effects of 9 · 11 Terrorist Attack and the Iraq War

The first decade of the New Millennium began with fears over Y2K (Year 2000 Problem), the 9 · 11 terrorist attacks in 2001 and the following Iraq War. The latter two were soon the source of Hollywood interpretations. Movies related to 9 · 11 and its after-effect were released, including intense combat film *Black Hawk Down* (2001), action film *Collateral Damage* (2002), post-9 · 11-event Film *25th Hour* (2002), real-time drama *United 93* (2006), and Paramount's, innovative documentary film *Voices of Iraq* (2004), and Oliver Stone's *World Trade Center* (2006), etc.

However, it seemed that American audiences did not like realistic war dramas during real wartime. Considering the market and profit, most filmgoers hesitated to attend films related to the unpopular Iraq War, and so did film studios. However, there were still some bold exceptions. Director Irwin Winkler produced a R-rated war drama, *Home of the Brave* (2006), only to be faced with a huge loss at box office. Despite the lesson from *Home of the Brave*, some directors continued impassioned explorations of Iraq War-related films and again suffered box-office casualties. This is the case especially in 2007: there emerged a lot of such kind of films like Paul Haggis' *In the Valley of Elah*, Michael Winterbottom's *A Mighty Heart*, Gavin Hood's *Rendition*, Robert Redford's *Lions for Lambs*, Brian DePalma's *Redacted* and James Strouse's *Grace is Gone.* The realistic terrors of the Iraq War for a squad of bomb defusers were dealt with in Best Director-winning Kathryn Bigelow's tense war thriller *The Hurt Locker* (2009), the Best Picture of its year.

◎ Exercises

1. Explain the following terms in English.

1) the nickelodeon
2) sound film
3) film noir
4) the Red Scare
5) independent producer

2. Match the following filmmakers with their relevant information.

1) He completed the design of an electrically controlled camera and a peep-show machine called the Kinetoscope.

2) In 1903, he made *The Great Train Robbery*, which took a few more steps in evolving a film grammar.

3) Labeled as the "father of the American cinema", he was the first American director who established the cultural significance of motion pictures.

4) In 1919, he co-founded the distribution company United Artists, which gave him complete control over his films.

5) He moved to Hollywood in 1939 and made his first Hollywood try *Rebecca*.

6) His final film was *Eyes Wide Shut*, starring Tom Cruise and Nicole Kidman as a wealthy Manhattan couple.

7) She gained four Academy Awards for Best Actress—an unequaled record for any performer.

8) She is best remembered for her roles in *Casablanca*, a World War II drama co-starring Humphrey Bogart.

9) In the Italian-set *Roman Holiday*, she played her first leading role as Princess Ann who escapes the reins of royalty and falls in love with an American newsman.

10) In 2013, she received her 27th Golden Globe nomination for her performance in *Hope Springs* at the 70th Golden Globes.

11) In director Barry Levinson's *Rain Man*, his performance gained him his second Academy Award.

12) He was an activist, notably for his supporting African-American Civil Rights Movement and various American Indian Movements.

13) He collaborated with George Lucas on an action adventure film *Raiders of the Lost Ark* in 1981, the first of the Indiana Jones films.

14) In 1990, he founded The Film Foundation, a nonprofit organization dedicated to film preservation.

15) He epitomized a group of filmmakers known as the "New Hollywood" that emerged in the early 1970s with ideas that challenged conventional film-making.

a. Charlie Chaplin

b. Steven Spielberg

c. Alfred Hitchcock

d. Thomas A. Edison

e. Stanley Kubrick

f. Ingrid Bergman

g. Edwin S. Porter

h. Katharine Hepburn

i. David Wark Griffith

j. Audrey Hepburn

k. Marlon Brando

l. Meryl Streep
m. Dustin Hoffman
n. Martin Scorsese
o. Francis Ford Coppola

3. Discuss and answer the following questions.

1) Can you introduce the birth of motion pictures briefly?
2) What are new film genres which appeared in 1930s?
3) How did Hollywood develop into the center of filmmaking?
4) How many major stages could be included in the film history?
5) Can you introduce some film actors or actresses who were active in 1930s?
6) When did independent producers rise? And how?
7) What happened during the "Revival" period in the development of film industry?
8) What are the new changes in the film industry in 1990s?

Unit 2
The World of Films

1. Film Studios

A film studio (also known as movie studio or simply studio) is a major entertainment company or motion picture company that has its own privately-owned studio facility or facilities that are used to make films, which is handled by the production company. The majority of firms in entertainment industry have never owned their own studios, but have rented space from other companies. There are also independently owned studio facilities, who have never produced a motion picture of their own because they are not entertainment companies or motion picture companies; they are companies who sell only studio space.

The largest film studio in the world is Ramoji Film City, in Hyderabad, India.

1.1 Development of Film Studios

In 1893, Thomas Edison built the first movie studio in the United States when he constructed the Black Maria, a tarpaper-covered structure near his laboratories in West Orange, New Jersey, and asked circus, vaudeville, and dramatic actors to perform for the camera. In the early 1900s, companies started moving to Los Angeles, California. Early movie producers also relocated to Southern California to escape Edison's Motion Picture Patents Company, which controlled almost all the patents relevant to movie production at the time.

The Big Five/The Big 5

By the mid-1920s, the evolution of a handful of American production companies into wealthy motion picture industry conglomerates that owned their own studios, distribution divisions, and theaters, and contracted with performers and other filmmaking personnel, led to the sometimes confusing equation of "studio" with "production company" in industry slang. Five large companies, 20th Century Fox, RKO Pictures, Paramount Pictures, Warner Bros., and Metro-Goldwyn-Mayer came to be known as the "Big Five", the "Majors", or "the Studios" in trade publications such as variety, and their management structures and practices collectively came to be known as the "studio system."

The Little 3

Although they owned few or no theaters to guarantee sales of their films, Universal Pictures, Columbia Pictures, and United Artists also fell under these rubrics, making a total of eight generally recognized "major studios". United Artists, although its controlling partners owned not one but two production studios during the Golden Age, had an often-tenuous hold on the title of "major" and operated mainly as a backer and distributor of independently produced films.

The Big Five's ownership of movie theaters was eventually opposed by eight independent producers. In 1948, the federal government won a case against Paramount in the Supreme Court, which ruled that the vertically integrated structure of the movie industry constituted an illegal monopoly. This decision, reached after twelve years of litigation, hastened the end of the studio system and Hollywood's "Golden Age".

By the 1950s, the physical components of a typical major film studio had become standardized. Since then, a major film studio has usually been housed inside a physically secure compound with a high wall, which protects filmmaking operations from unwanted interference from paparazzi and crazed fans of leading movie stars.

Halfway through the 1950s, with television proving to be a lucrative enterprise not destined to disappear any time soon—as many in the film industry had once hoped—movie studios were increasingly being used to produce programming for the burgeoning medium. Some midsize film companies, such as Republic Pictures, eventually sold their studios to TV production concerns, which were eventually bought by larger studios, such as the American Broadcasting Company which was purchased by The Walt Disney Company in 1996.

With the growing diversification of studios into such fields as video games, television, theme parks, home video and publishing, they have become multi-national corporations. As the studios increased in size they began to rely on production companies, like J. J. Abrams' Bad Robot Productions, to handle many of the creative and physical production details of their feature films. Instead the studios transformed into financing and distribution entities for the films made by their affiliated production companies. With the decreasing cost of CG and visual effects, many studios sold large chunks of their once massive studio spaces or backlots to private real-estate developers. Century City in Los Angeles was once part of the 20th Century Fox backlot, which was among the largest and most famous of the studio lots. In most cases portions of the backlots were retained and are available for rental by various film and television productions. Some studios offer tours of their backlots, while Universal Pictures allows visitors to its adjacent Universal Studios Hollywood theme park to take a tram tour of the backlot where films such as *Psycho* and *Back to the Future* were once shot.

1.2 Notable Film Studios

1.2.1 Metro-Goldwyn-Mayer

Metro-Goldwyn-Mayer Studios Inc. (also known as Metro-Goldwyn-Mayer Pictures, commonly referred to as Metro-Goldwyn-Mayer, Metro or simply MGM), is an American media company, involved primarily in the production and distribution of films and television programs. Once being the largest and most glamorous of film studios, MGM was founded in 1924. MGM was the last studio to convert to sound pictures, but in spite of this fact, from the end of the silent film era through the late 1950s, Metro-Goldwyn-Mayer was the dominant motion picture studio in Hollywood. Always slow to respond to the changing legal, economic, and demographic nature of the motion picture industry during the 1950s and 1960s, and although at times its films did well at the box office, the studio lost significant amounts of money throughout the 1960s. In 1971, it was announced that MGM would merge with 20th Century Fox, a plan which never came into fruition. Over the next thirty-nine years, the studio was bought and sold at various points in its history until, on November 3, 2010.

In 2011, MGM was finalizing a distribution deal with Sony Pictures Entertainment to handle distribution of its 4,000 films and DVDs worldwide and on digital platforms, including the two upcoming Bond films: *Skyfall and Spectre*. The new MGM, under Barber and Birnbaum's control, focuses on co-investing on films made by another party, which handle all distribution and marketing for the projects. MGM handles international television distribution rights for the new films as well as its library of existing titles and also retains its in-house production service.

The studio's logo is a roaring lion surrounded by a ring of film inscribed with the studio's motto. The logo, which features Leo the Lion, was created by Dietz in 1916 for Goldwyn Pictures and updated in 1924 for MGM's use. Originally silent, the sound of Leo the Lion's roar was added to films for the first time in August 1928. In the 1930s and 1940s, the studio billed itself as having "more stars than there are in heaven", a reference to the large number of A-list movie stars under contract to the company. This second motto was also coined by Howard Dietz, the studio's chief publicist. The studio's official motto, "Ars Gratia Artis", is a Latin phrase meaning "Art for art's sake".

1.2.2 Paramount Pictures

Paramount Pictures dates its existence from the 1912 founding date of the Famous Players Film Company. Hungarian-born founder, Adolph Zukor, who had been an early investor in nickelodeons, saw that movies appealed mainly to working-class immigrants. Paramount is the fifth oldest surviving film studio in the world after the French studios Gaumont Film Company (1895) and Pathé (1896), followed by the Nordisk Film Company (1906), and Universal Studios (1912). It is the last major film studio still headquartered in the Hollywood district of Los Angeles, Paramount was the first successful nationwide distributor; until 1914, films were sold on a statewide or regional basis which had proved costly to film producers. Also, Famous Players and producers were privately owned while Paramount was a corporation.

In 1930s, Paramount could truly be described as a movie factory, turning out sixty to seventy pictures a year. While in 1940s, Paramount cut back on production, from seventy-one pictures to a more modest nineteen annually in the war years. Paramount Pictures Corporation was formed to be the production distribution company, with the 1,500-screen theater chain handed to the new United Paramount Theaters on December 31, 1949. In 1951, Paramount bought a stake in International Telemeter, an experimental pay TV service which operated with a coin inserted into a box. By the early 1960s, Paramount's future was doubtful. The high-risk movie business was wobbly; the theater chain was long gone. In 1970, Paramount teamed with Universal Studios to form Cinema International Corporation, a new company that would distribute films by the two studios outside the United States. Paramount's successful run of pictures extended into the 1980s and 1990s, generating hits like *Airplane!*, *American Gigolo*, *Ordinary People*. In 1990s, Paramount Pictures went under the guidance of Jonathan Dolgen, chairman and Sherry Lansing, president. During their administration over Paramount, the studio had an extremely successful period of films with two of Paramount's ten highest-grossing films being produced during this period. The most successful of these films was *Titanic*.

On December 11, 2005, the Paramount Motion Pictures Group announced that it had purchased DreamWorks SKG (which was co-founded by former Paramount executive Jeffrey Katzenberg) in a deal worth $1.6 billion and in 2008, DreamWorks executives announced that they were leaving Paramount and relaunching an independent DreamWorks. In March 2012, Paramount licensed their name and logo to a luxury hotel investment group which subsequently named the company Paramount Hotels and Resorts. The investors plan to build 50 hotels throughout the world based on the themes of Hollywood and the California lifestyle.

Paramount is the last major film studio located in Hollywood proper. When Paramount moved to its present home in 1927, it was in the heart of the film community. Paramount is a member of the Motion Picture Association of America (MPAA). It has distributed various commercially successful film series, such as *Shrek*, *Transformers*, *Mission: Impossible*, *Marvel Cinematic Universe* (2008-2012), *Indiana Jones*, *Star Trek*, *Madagascar*, *Kung Fu Panda*, etc.

1.2.3 Warner Bros.

Warner Bros. Entertainment Inc. —also known as Warner Bros. Pictures since 1948, formerly known as Warner Bros. Studios, commonly referred to as Warner Bros. (spelled Warner Brothers during the company's early years), or simply WB—is an American producer of film, television, and music entertainment.

One of the major film studios, it is a subsidiary of Time Warner, with its headquarters in Burbank, California and New York. Warner Bros. has several subsidiary companies, including Warner Bros. Studios, Warner Bros. Pictures, Warner Bros. Interactive Entertainment, Warner Bros. Television, Warner Bros. Animation, Warner Home Video, New Line Cinema, TheWB. com, and DC Entertainment. Warner owns half of The CW Television Network. Warner Bros. is also a member of the Motion Picture Association of America (MPAA).

1.2.4 20th Century Fox

Twentieth Century Fox Film Corporation (Twentieth Century-Fox Film Corporation, with hyphen, from 1935 to 1985)—also known as 20th Century Fox, or 20th Century Fox Pictures, is one of the six major American film studios as of 2011. Located in the Century City area of Los Angeles, just west of Beverly Hills, the studio is currently a subsidiary of 21st Century Fox.

The company was founded on May 31, 1935, as the result of the merger of Fox Film Corporation, founded by William Fox in 1915, and Twentieth Century Pictures, founded in 1933 by Darryl F. Zanuck and Joseph M. Schenck.

Twentieth Century Fox has distributed various commercially successful film series, including *Star Wars*, *Ice Age*, *X-Men*, *Die Hard*, *Planet of the Apes*, *Fantastic Four*, *Alien and Predator*. Television series produced by Fox include *The Simpsons*, *The X-Files*, *Family Guy*, *Buffy the Vampire Slayer*, *Glee*, *and 24*. Among the most famous actresses to come out of this studio were Shirley Temple, who was 20th Century Fox's first film star, Betty Grable, Gene Tierney, Marilyn

Monroe and Jayne Mansfield. The studio also contracted the first African-American cinema star, Dorothy Dandridge. 20th Century Fox is also a member of the Motion Picture Association of America (MPAA).

1.2.5 Columbia Pictures

Columbia Pictures Industries, Inc. (CPII) is an American film production and distribution studio. Columbia Pictures now forms part of the Columbia TriStar Motion Picture Group, owned by Sony Pictures Entertainment, a subsidiary of the Japanese conglomerate Sony. It is one of the leading film studios in the world, a member of the so-called Big Six. It was one of the so-called Little Three among the eight major film studios of Hollywood's Golden Age.

The studio, founded in 1918 as Cohn-Brandt-Cohn Film Sales by brothers Jack and Harry Cohn and Joe Brandt, released its first feature film in August 1922. It adopted the Columbia Pictures name in 1924 and went public two years later. The name is derived from "Columbia", a national personification of the United States, which is used as the company's logo.

In its early years a minor player in Hollywood, Columbia began to grow in the late 1920s, spurred by a successful association with director Frank Capra.

With Capra and others, Columbia became one of the primary homes of the screwball comedy. In the 1930s, Columbia's major contract stars were Jean Arthur and Cary Grant (who was shared with RKO Pictures). In the 1940s, Rita Hayworth became the studio's premier star and propelled their fortunes into the late 1950s. Rosalind Russell, Glenn Ford, and William Holden also became major stars at the studio.

In 1982, the Studio was purchased by Coca-Cola; that same year it launched TriStar Pictures as a joint venture with HBO and CBS. Five years later, Coca-Cola spun off Columbia, which merged with Tri-Star to create Columbia Pictures Entertainment. After a brief period of independence with Coca-Cola maintaining a financial interest, the combined studio was acquired by Japanese company, Sony in 1989.

1.2.6 Universal Studios

Universal Studios Inc. (also known as Universal Pictures), is an American motion picture studio, owned by Comcast through its wholly owned subsidiary NBC Universal, and is one of the six major movie studios. Its production studios are at 100 Universal City Plaza Drive in Universal City, California. Distribution and other corporate offices are in New York City.

Founded in 1912 by Carl Laemmle, Mark

Dintenfass, Charles Baumann, Adam Kessel, Pat Powers, William Swanson, David Horsley, and Jules Brulatour, it is the oldest movie studio in the United States of America. It is also the fourth oldest in the world that is still in continuous production; the first being Gaumont Pictures, the second oldest is Pathé, the third is Nordisk Film, and the fifth oldest is Paramount Pictures. On May 11, 2004, the controlling stake in the company was sold by Vivendi Universal to General Electric, parent of NBC. The resulting media super-conglomerate was renamed NBC Universal, while Universal Studios Inc. remained the name of the production subsidiary. In addition to owning a sizable film library spanning the earliest decades of cinema to more contemporary works, it also owns a sizable collection of TV shows through its subsidiary NBC Universal Television Distribution. It also acquired rights to several prominent filmmakers' works originally released by other studios through its subsidiaries over the years.

Three of Universal Studios' films—*Jaws* (1975), *E. T. The Extra-Terrestrial* (1982), and *Jurassic Park* (1993)—achieved box office records, each becoming the highest-grossing film made at the time.

1.2.7 Walt Disney Pictures

Walt Disney Pictures is an American film studio and one of several film distribution labels of The Walt Disney Studios, owned by The Walt Disney Company.

The studio's predecessor was founded as the Disney Brothers Cartoon Studio, by filmmaker Walt Disneyand his business partner and brother, Roy, in 1923. Walt Disney Productions had its first fully live-action film in 1950 with the release of Treasure Island, considered by Disney to be the official conception for what would eventually evolve into the modern-day Walt Disney Pictures.

Walt Disney Pictures had pioneered the live-action remakes of animated films created by Walt Disney Animation Studios, with a live-action adaptation of *One Hundred and One Dalmatians* released in 1996. *Pirates of the Caribbean* is the studio's most successful franchise, with two of its sequels, released in 2006 and 2011, earning over \$1 billion in worldwide box office gross. In 2010, Disney released *Alice in Wonderland*, an adaptation of the 1951 animated film of the same name that became the second \$1 billion-grossing film in the studio's history. With the success of *Maleficent* (2014) and *Cinderella* (2015), the studio announced a whole series of live-action adaptations of animated films as being in early stages. Animated features produced by Walt Disney Animation Studios, mainly by Pixar Animation Studios.

Until 1985, instead of a traditional production logo, Disney films used to feature a title card that read "Walt Disney Presents", and later, "Walt Disney Productions Presents", and introduced its fantasy castle logo. The logo was created by Walt Disney Feature Animation in traditional animation and featured a white Sleeping Beauty Castle design against a blue background, with the studio's name and underscored by "When You Wish Upon A Star".

2. Film Genres

All filmgoers are familiar with the idea of genre, even if they don't know exactly what "genre" is. The term "genre" is originally French, and it simply means "kind" or "type". When we speak of film genres, we're referring to certain types of films, such as the action film, the horror film, the musical, the Western and many others. The use of the term "genre" is convenient and it has been developing informally during the progress of film industry. Filmmakers, industry decision-makers, critics, and viewers all contribute to the formation of genres which indicate that certain films seem to resemble one another in significant ways. Genres also change over time, as filmmakers invent or create new things both in film contents and formulas. Therefore, defining the precise boundaries between genres can be difficult and tricky. Some genres are based on story content (the detective film), while others are borrowed from literature (the comedy). Some genres are budget-based (the blockbuster), while others are based on location (the Western). Even some critics challenge whether genres really exist, or whether they are merely made up by critics. In a word, Genre is always a vague term with no fixed boundaries, which arouses the intriguing question of defining just what a genre is and what places a group of films in a genre?

2.1 Defining a Genre

Most theories concerning film genre are borrowed from literary genre criticism. When it comes to genre, the examples that come to mind are usually those fictional films which were versus documentary ones. But there can be genres of other basic sorts of cinema, too. Experimental films and animated films have genres as well.

Most scholars now agree that genre cannot be defined in a single hard-and-fast way. According to critics, the genre of film can be defined in different ways. For instance, the genre of a film is identified by comparing it to a list of films already deemed to fall within a certain genre. Or the genre of a film is based on the accepted cultural consensus within society. In film theory, genre refers to the method based on similarities in the narrative elements from which films are constructed. The theme, the setting, the mood and the format are key words in defining genres. The setting is the environment where the story and action takes place. The theme (or topic or subject) indicates the issues or concepts that the film revolves around. The mood means the emotional tone of the film. The format refers to the way the film was shot or the manner of presentation. The target audience is often considered an additional way of categorizing film genres.

Take the theme as an example. Some genres stand out by their themes. A gangster film focuses on large-scale urban crime. A science-fiction film features a technology out of the reach of contemporary science. However theme is not so crucial to defining other genres. Musicals can be recognized mainly by their manner of presentation (the format): singing, dancing, or both. The war film is chiefly featured with battlefields (the setting) where battles are fought. And some genres are defined by the distinctive emotional effect they aim for (the mood): amusement in comedies, tension in suspense films.

As for the categorization of films, there is a complicated question that genres can be more or less broad. Some large, blanket genre categories fit many films. For example, thrillers may encompass horror films, detective stories, and hostage films. Suppose film genres are categorized based on the setting, films with the same settings can be very different because of different themes or moods. For example, both *The Battle of Midway* and *All Quiet on the Western Front* feature wartime context, but the former explores the themes of honor, sacrifice, and valor, and the latter is an anti-war film putting emphasis on the pain and horror of war. While film noir movies are argued that they mainly involve an urban setting, cheap hotels and underworld bars, many classic noirs take place chiefly in small towns, rural areas, or on the open road. Undoubtedly, in view of the complexity and difficulty of dividing films into genres, subgenres are devised by critics, viewers, and filmmakers to try to describe more precisely what films are like. In other words, film genres often branch out into subgenres. Nevertheless, it's also argued that animation, children's films, family films, cult films, documentary films, pornographic films and silent films are non-genre-based film categories.

There are other methods of dividing films into groups besides genre. Some groupings may be casually described as genres although the definition is questionable. For example, art films are referred to as a genre, even though an art film can be included in various genres. Independent films are similar to art films and they can belong to any genre.

Generally, genres have loyal audiences and corresponding supportive publications like magazines and websites. Those films that are difficult to categorize into a genre are often less successful.

2.2 Analyzing a Genre

A tacit agreement has been reached by filmmakers, critics and viewers on which genres are based. The films of a genre share common identity and genre conventions that reappear in film after film. For instance, certain plot elements may be the shared conventions. An investigation is always anticipated in a mystery film; singing and dancing settings will be expectedly found in a musical. The gangster's rise and fall are focused on during his struggles against police and rival gangs.

There are other genre conventions which are more thematic, concerning general meanings that are demonstrated again and again. Loyalty and obedience to one's teacher are generally advocated in the Hong Kong martial-arts film. Traditionally, a screwball comedy centers on the thematic opposition between a stiff, unyielding social environment and characters' desire for freedom and innocent stupidity. Characteristic film techniques also make a part of genre conventions. The action picture often features rapid cutting and slow-motion violence.

In addition, recurring symbolic images are viewed as conventional iconography which carries meaning from film to film such as objects and settings. If a close-up of a tommy gun lifted out of a 1920s Ford appears in a film, the film would be very possibly identified as a gangster one. Even stars can be iconographic: Judy Garland for the musical, John Wayne for the Western, Jim Carrey for comedy.

Knowing conventions enables the viewer to have a pathway into the film for conventions allow the genre films to communicate information quickly and economically. Alternatively, a film can revise or reject the conventions associated with its genre for viewers often expect some fresh variations. Thus filmmakers may seek to surprise or shock viewers by breaking certain conventions that are normally used. The interplay of convention and innovation, familiarity and novelty is central to the development of film genres. In view of this, it is less likely that genres remain unchanged for very long. The broader genres like thrillers, romances, and comedies may stay popular for decades, but a comedy in 1920s is likely to be very different from one in the 1960s. In a word, genres change over history and by mixing conventions from different genres, filmmakers create new possibilities from time to time.

As for the function of genres, they are useful in areas of marketing, criticism and consumption. Genres affect industry officials' and filmmakers' decisions about what films to make. The genre is a simple and easy way to characterize and publicize films when filmmaking is surrounded by a vast and complicated publicity system. In all aspects of the filmmaking and film-viewing processes, genres help assure that most members of a society share at least some general ideas about the types of films that compete for people's attention. On the whole, genre is best used to describe and analyze films instead of evaluating them.

2.3 Main Film Genres

Many film genres become established by borrowing existing conventions from other media. Yet the film medium always imposes its own distinctive qualities and circumstances on an adopted genre. Film genres have their own history, combining borrowings from other arts and distinctive innovations. Most cinema genres and subgenres become established when one film achieves success and is widely imitated.

Major film genres are broad enough to accommodate practically any film ever made, although film categories can never be defined precisely. By separating the various elements in a film and categorizing them in genres, there is the possibility to easily evaluate a film within its genre and allow for meaningful comparisons on which the judgments on greatness are based. Films were not really subjected to genre analysis by film historians until the 1970s. All films have at least one major genre, although there are a great many films that are regarded as crossbreeds or hybrids with three or four subgenres that identify them.

The following are some of the most common and identifiable film genre categories, with descriptions of each type or category.

Main Film Genres	
Genre Types (represented by icons)	Genre Descriptions
	Action films usually feature high energy, big-budget physical stunts and chases, possibly with fights and battles, escapes and rescues, destructive power (e. g. natural and man-made disasters), non-stop motion, spectacular rhythm and pacing, and often two-dimensional "good-guy" heroes or heroines battling "bad guys" — all designed for satisfying audience escapism. The James Bond "fantasy" spy/espionage series, martial arts films, so-called "blaxploitation" films, and some superhero films are included. A major sub-genre is the disaster film.
	Adventure films are usually exciting stories, with novel experiences or exotic locales, very similar to or often paired with the action film genre. They cover traditional swashbucklers, serialized films, and historical spectacles (similar to the epics film genre), searches or expeditions for lost continents, "jungle" and "desert" epics, treasure hunts, disaster films, or searches for the unknown.
	Comedies feature light-hearted plots which are consistently and deliberately designed to amuse and provoke laughter by exaggerating situation, character, language, action and relationship. This category involves various forms of comedy through cinematic history, including slapstick, screwball, spoofs and parodies, romantic comedies, black comedy (dark satirical comedy), and more.
	Crime (gangster) films center on the sinister actions of criminals or mobsters who operate outside the law, stealing and murdering their way through life. Criminal and gangster films are often categorized as film noir or detective-mystery films — because of underlying similarities between these cinematic forms. This category includes a description of various "serial killer" films.

续表

Main Film Genres	
Genre Types (represented by icons)	**Genre Descriptions**
	 Dramas are serious, plot-driven presentations, portraying realistic situations, characters, and stories along with intense character development and interaction. Usually, they are not focused on special effects, comic elements or action. Dramatic films are probably the largest film genre with many subgenres.
	 Epics include costume dramas, historical dramas, war films, medieval romps, or "period pictures" that often cover a large expanse of time set against a vast, panoramic backdrop. Epics often share elements of the elaborate adventure films genre. Epics take an historical or imagined event, mythic, legendary, or heroic figure, and add an extravagant setting and lavish costumes, accompanied by grandeur and spectacle, dramatic scope, high production values, and a sweeping musical score. Epics are often a more spectacular, lavish version of a biopic film. Some "sword and sandal" films (Biblical epics or films occurring during antiquity) qualify as a sub-genre.
	 Horror films are designed to frighten and to invoke our hidden worst fears, often in a terrifying, shocking finale, while captivating and entertaining us at the same time in a cathartic experience. Horror films feature a wide range of styles, from the earliest silent Nosferatu classic, to today's CGI monsters and deranged humans. They are often combined with science fiction when the menace or monster is related to a corruption of technology, or when Earth is threatened by aliens. The fantasy and supernatural film genres are not usually synonymous with the horror genre. There are many sub-genres of horror: slasher, teen terror, serial killers, Satanic, Dracula, Frankenstein, etc.
	 Musical/dance films are cinematic forms that emphasize full-scale scores or song and dance routines in a significant way (usually with a musical or dance performance integrated as part of the film narrative), or they are films that are centered on combinations of music, dance, song or choreography. Major subgenres include the musical comedy or the concert film.

续表

Main Film Genres	
Genre Types (represented by icons)	**Genre Descriptions**
	Sci-fi films are often quasi-scientific, visionary and imaginative-complete with heroes, aliens, distant planets, impossible quests, improbable settings, fantastic places, great dark and shadowy villains, futuristic technology, unknown and unknowable forces, and extraordinary monsters ("things or creatures from space"), either created by mad scientists or by nuclear havoc. They are sometimes an offshoot of fantasy films (or superhero films), or they share some similarities with action/adventure films. Science fiction often expresses the potential of technology to destroy humankind and easily overlaps with horror films, particularly when technology or alien life forms become malevolent, as in the "Atomic Age" of sci-fi films in the 1950s.
	War (and anti-war) films acknowledge the horror and heartbreak of war, letting the actual combat fighting (against nations or humankind) on land, sea, or in the air provide the primary plot or background for the action of the film. War films are often paired with other genres, such as action, adventure, drama, romance, comedy (black), suspense, and even epics and westerns, and they often take a denunciatory approach toward warfare. They may include POW tales, stories of military operations, and training.
	Westerns are the major defining genre of the American film industry — a eulogy to the early days of the expansive American frontier. They are one of the oldest, most enduring genres with very recognizable plots, elements, and characters (six-guns, horses, dusty towns and trails, cowboys, Indians, etc.). Over time, westerns have been re-defined, re-invented and expanded, dismissed, re-discovered, and spoofed.
	Animations are not a strictly-defined genre category, but rather a film technique, although they often contain genre-like elements. This section presents an historical overview of these kinds of films, noted for frame-by-frame creation. Also includes claymation (use of clay objects), anime (a style of animation with its roots in Japanese comic books, usually adult-oriented sci-fi and fantasy) or CGI (computer-generated animation). Animated films are often considered kids or family-oriented films, although they may be enjoyed by all ages.

3. Film Awards and Film Festivals

Film awards and film festivals, as a significant part of film industry, have their function in the recognition and commendation of excellent filmmakers and their masterpieces, with ceremonies held annually or periodically, which always arouse wide attention and attract film practitioners and enthusiasts from different parts of the world. Usually, film festivals consist of a series of film-related theme activities and exhibitions in which even audiences can be involved in. In this unit, there is a collection of American and British film awards and film festivals which enjoy reputation and popularity across the world, though a lot more awards and festivals should be entitled to recommendation.

3.1 Film Awards

Film awards are designed to honor filmmakers who have made contributions to the development of film industry and their films which have been widely acclaimed and exerted influence on the public and some certain culture. Film awards usually include the following: best picture, best screenplay, best director, best leading actor, best leading actress, best supporting actor, best supporting actress, best visual effects, best original score, best costume design, and others.

Film awards are usually divided into four major categories: critics' awards voted by a group of critics, such as American Film Institute Awards and Los Angeles Film Critics Association Awards; industry awards voted by professionals working in some branch of the film industry, such as British Academy Film Awards and the Oscars; audience awards voted by the general public, such as Empire Awards in Britain and MTV Movie Awards in America; and festival awards, referring to that awards are presented to the best film shown in a particular film festival, such as Seattle International Film Festival and London Film Festival.

The awards sometimes also have popular unofficial names which are mentioned if applicable, for example, the "Oscar" for Hollywood's Academy Awards. Many awards are simply identified by the name of the group presenting the award.

3.1.1 Academy Awards

The Academy Awards, now officially known as The Oscars, is a set of awards given annually for excellence of cinematic achievements. The Oscar statuette is officially named the Academy Award of Merit and is one of nine types of Academy Awards. Organized and overseen by the Academy of Motion Picture Arts and Sciences (AMPAS), the awards are given each year at a formal ceremony. The AMPAS was originally conceived by Metro-Goldwyn-Mayer studio executive Louis B. Mayer as a professional honorary organization to help improve the film industry's image and help mediate labor disputes. The awards themselves were later initiated by the Academy as awards "of merit for distinctive achievement" in the industry.

The awards were first given in 1929 at a ceremony created for the awards, at the Hollywood Roosevelt Hotel. Over the years that the award has been given, the categories presented have changed; currently Oscars are given in more than a dozen categories, and include films of various types. As one of the most prominent award ceremonies in the world, the Academy Awards ceremony is televised live in more than 100 countries annually. It is also the oldest award ceremony in the media; its equivalents, the Grammy Awards for music, the Emmy Awards for television, and the Tony Awards for theater, are all modeled after the Academy Awards. During Oscar Season, studios spend millions of dollars and hire publicists specifically to promote their films for the Academy Awards undoubtedly demonstrates its positive exposure and prestige.

On February 26, 2017, for honoring the best filmmakers and their works of 2016, the 89th Academy Awards ceremony, hosted by Jimmy Kimmel and broadcasted on ABC, was held at the Dolby Theatre, in Los Angeles, California. A total of 3,048 Oscars have been awarded from the inception of the award through the 89th.

3.1.2 Golden Globe Awards

The Golden Globe Awards is an accolade bestowed by the 93 members of the Hollywood Foreign Press Association (HFPA), which was founded by a group of writers in 1943, to recognize excellence in film and television, both domestic and foreign. The annual formal ceremony and dinner at which the awards are presented is a major part of the film industry's awards season, which culminates each year with the Academy Awards. Because of the revenues generated from the annual ceremony HFPA donates millions of dollars to entertainment-related charities, along with funding scholarships and other programs for future film and television professionals.

The 1st Golden Globe Awards was held in January 1944 at the 20th Century-Fox studios in Los Angeles. The 74th Golden Globe Awards, honoring the best in film and television for 2016, was hosted by Jimmy Fallon and presented on January 8, 2017, at the Beverly Hilton Hotel in Beverly Hills, California, where they have been held annually since 1961.

The broadcast of the Golden Globe Awards, telecast to 167 countries worldwide, generally ranks as the third most-watched awards show each year, behind only the Oscars and the Grammy Awards. Until Ricky Gervais hosted the 67th annual Golden Globe Awards Ceremony in 2010, the award ceremony was one of two major Hollywood award ceremonies (the other being the Screen Actors Guild Awards) that did not have a regular host; every year a different presenter introduced the ceremony at the beginning of the broadcast. The Golden Globe Awards' theme song, which debuted in 2012, was written by Japanese musician and songwriter Yoshiki Hayashi.

3.1.3 National Society of Film Critics Awards

The National Society of Film Critics (NSFC) is an American film critic organization in which approximately 60 members are involved, who write for a variety of weekly and daily newspapers as well as major publications and media outlets.

National Society of Film Critics was founded in 1966 in the New York City apartment of *Saturday Review* critic Hollis Alpert, one of several co-founding film critics who was refused membership to the New York Film Critics Circle, as it preferred critics who worked for mainstream newspapers. His co-founders included Pauline Kael, a writer for *The New Yorker*; Joe Morgenstern, then a movie reviewer for *Newsweek*; and Richard Schickel, a film critic for *Life* Magazine. The Society was also founded in order to counteract the influence of *New York Times* critic Bosley Crowther, who dominated the New York City film critic scene for many years. The original founding film critics, who were overwhelmingly based in New York, called their new group a "national" organization because they wrote for a number of magazines and newspapers with a national circulation.

The organization is known for their highbrow tastes, and its annual awards are one of the most prestigious film critics awards in the United States. In past years, many of their Best Picture winners have been foreign films and their choices rarely parallel the Academy Awards. They have agreed with the Oscar in five instances over the past forty years: 1977's *Annie Hall*, 1992's *Unforgiven*, 1993's *Schindler's List*, 2004's *Million Dollar Baby* and 2009's *The Hurt Locker*.

The NSFC is also the American representative of the International Federation of Film Critics (FIPRESCI), which comprises the national organizations of professional film critics and film journalists from around the world. The FIPRESCI has members in more than 50 countries worldwide.

3.1.4 Golden Raspberry Awards

A Golden Raspberry Award, or Razzie for short, is an award presented in recognition of the worst in film. Founded by American copywriter and publicist John J. B. Wilson in 1980, the annual Razzie Awards ceremony in Los Angeles precedes the corresponding Academy Awards

ceremony by one day. The term raspberry in the name is used in its irreverent sense, as in "blowing a raspberry". The awards themselves are in the form of a "golf-sized raspberry" which sits atop a Super 8 mm film reel, the whole of which is spray-painted gold. The first Golden Raspberry Awards ceremony was held on March 31, 1981, at John J. B. Wilson's living room alcove in Los Angeles to honor the worst in film of the 1980 film season. The 37th ceremony was held on February 25, 2017.

American copywriter and publicist John J. B. Wilson traditionally held potluck dinner parties at his house in Los Angeles on the night of the Academy Awards. In 1981, after the 53rd Academy Awards had completed for the evening, Wilson invited friends to give random award presentations in his living room. Wilson decided to formalize the event, after watching a double feature of *Can't Stop the Music* and *Xanadu*. He gave them ballots to vote on worst in film. Wilson stood at a podium made of cardboard in a tacky tuxedo, with a foam ball attached to a broomstick as a fake microphone, and announced *Can't Stop the Music* as the first Golden Raspberry Award for Worst Picture. The impromptu ceremony was a success and the following week a press release about his event released by Wilson was picked up by a few local newspapers, including a mention in the *Los Angeles Daily News* with the headline: "Take These Envelopes, Please."

Approximately three dozen people came to the 1st Golden Raspberry Awards. The 2nd Golden Raspberry Awards had double the attendance as the first and the 3rd awards ceremony had double this number. By the 4th Golden Raspberry Awards ceremony, CNN and two major wire services covered the event. Wilson realized that by scheduling the Golden Raspberry Awards prior to the Academy Awards, the ceremony would get more press coverage.

3.1.5 People's Choice Awards

The People's Choice Awards, voted on by the general public, is an American awards show designed to honor the people and the work of popular culture. The show has been held annually since 1975. The People's Choice Awards, broadcast on CBS, is produced by Procter & Gamble and the famous producer Mark Burnett. Apart from the required local advertising and network promotional time, all advertising during the awards show is solely by P&G brands for Procter & Gamble has been the show's only sponsor since 1982. The 43rd show, hosted by Joel McHale, was held in January 18, 2017. It is announced that E! (formerly E!: Entertainment Television) would begin airing the show and overseeing the awards' digital, social, and voting platforms in 2018.

The first award show was created by Bob Stivers in 1975. recognizing *The Sting* as Favorite Picture of 1974, Barbra Streisand as the year's Favorite Film Actress, and John Wayne as its

Favorite Film Actor. Ratings for the annual event peaked In 1977, the third People's Choice Awards attracted 35. 3 million viewers which resulted in its peak ratings. The viewers witnessed *Star Wars* win as the Favorite Picture, and Streisand and Wayne win again in the Film Actress and Actor categories. Up to now, Ellen DeGeneres is the most awarded person with a total of 20 People's Choice Awards. The winners of the 31st People's Choice Awards (on January 9, 2005) were based on online voting instead of traditional polls.

The award categories have varied over the years. For example, at the 16th People's Choice Awards, Favorite All-Around Movie (*Batman*), and both a Favorite Movie Actor (Tom Cruise) and a World Favorite Movie Actor (Dustin Hoffman) are among categories. The first ceremony in 1975 had 14 categories while currently, 65 categories are established including 15 ones presented to the public's favorite filmmakers and their works.

3. 1. 6 British Academy Film Awards

The British Academy Film Awards or BAFTA Film Awards, hosted by the British Academy of Film and Television Arts (BAFTA) which is supported by a membership of about 6,000 people from the film, television and video game industries, are presented in an annual award show to honor the best British and international contributions to film.

BAFTA was founded in 1947 as The British Film Academy by filmmakers David Lean, Alexander Korda, Carol Reed, Charles Laughton, Roger Manvell and others. In 1958, merged with The Guild of Television Producers and Directors, the Academy developed into The Society of Film and Television, which eventually became The British Academy of Film and Television Arts in 1976.

BAFTA is aimed at supporting, developing and promoting the art forms of the moving image, by identifying and rewarding excellence, inspiring practitioners and benefiting the public. Apart from high-profile awards ceremonies BAFTA runs a year-round program of educational events including film screenings and tribute evenings.

The Academy awards winners are granted a statuette, exactly, a theatrical mask designed by American sculptor Mitzi Cunliffe, which was commissioned by the Guild of Television Producers in 1955. Though there are categories of The British Short Film and British Short Animation awards which are set only for UK films, the awards are mostly open to all nationalities

The award ceremony, held in London, previously in April or May, takes place in February since 2002 in order to precede the Oscars. The Awards ceremony is delayed broadcast on British television the same evening (usually BBC One), and across the world for example it's shown on BBC America in the United States. It has been broadcast in color since 1970. The 70th British Academy Film Awards ceremony was held on 12 February 2017 at the Royal Albert Hall in

London.

3.1.7 British Independent Film Awards

In 1998, the British Independent Film Awards, a prestigious, respected and much-loved industry institution, was founded by Elliot Grove and Suzanne Ballantyne, who also founded the Raindance Film Festival in 1993. At that time, with the prize on board, Elliot and Suzanne held their first planning meeting in June 1998 by seeking the advice and help of a small group of committed founding members, thus resulting in the first BIFA a mere 13 weeks later at the Café Royal in London's West End.

The British Independent Film Awards is aimed at highlighting and rewarding the most excellent, innovative and creative independent filmmaking and filmmakers in the UK, along with identifying and encouraging emerging talent, supporting and celebrating the independent film community, and promoting British film and talent to the public.

Annually, the BIFA voters, made up of the Screening Group and Nomination Committee, are entitled to viewing more than 250 entered films before the long list and nominations, based on a rigorous discussion and selection, are decided by confidential vote. An independent jury, comprised of leading practitioners and talents from the British film industry, is newly appointed each year and not involved in the nominations process, shouldering the responsibility for watching all nominated films. They have meetings to discuss all the nominated films and decide the winners by secret ballot. Once these ballots have been counted and validated, the winners are announced at The British Independent Film Awards.

BIFA's first Board, appointed in June 2015 and enlarged in 2017, comprises filmmakers, a distributors, marketing and publicity professionals, and oversees, steers and advises the BIFA team on all aspects of BIFA's year-round activity. Having no influence on the voting process, board members will serve fixed terms, with the distributor role rotated regularly. Additionally, BIFA presents honorary awards, which are bestowed either by BIFA's Board and Nomination Committee or by its independent jury, appointed annually.

3.2 Film Festivals

A film festival, usually in a single city or region, is an organized, extended presentation of films in one or more cinemas or screening venues. Film festivals, typically annual events, introduce both domestic and international films depending upon the festivals' focus. Some festivals center on a specific film-maker or genre (e.g., film noir) or subject matter (e.g., horror film festivals); some other film festivals specialize in short films of a defined maximum length.

Currently, more films are shown at film festivals outdoors.

The best-known film festivals are the Cannes Film Festival, the Berlin International Film Festival, and the Venice Film Festival which is the oldest film festival still running. The Sundance Film Festival in the States, based on attendance, is the largest film festival worldwide. In the Southern Hemisphere, the Melbourne International Film Festival ranks the largest film festival, also one of the oldest in the world. In Europe, one of the most important and oldest film festivals is the San Sebastián International Film Festival in Spain. When it comes to film festivals in the United States, the Columbus International Film & Video Festival, also known as The Chris Awards, held in 1953, is the first film festival. In addition, Seattle International Film Festival is recognized as the largest film festival in the USA, regularly showing more than 400 films in a month across the city. In the UK, Edinburgh International Film Festival is the longest running festival.

Film festivals typically receive few donations from the general public and occasionally operate as nonprofit business associations rather than public charities. The majority of festivals are organized on a nonprofit membership-based model, and their major revenue lies in the combination of ticket sales, membership fees, and corporate sponsorship. Larger festivals maintain year-round staff who are usually engaged in community and charitable projects outside festival season.

3.2.1 London Film Festival

The London Film Festival, officially called the BFI London Film Festival, is organized annually by the British Film Institute (BFI) since 1953 when a group of film critics firmly believed that London should have its own film festival just like other major European cities such as Cannes, Venice and Berlin and called for organization of a film festival in London.

Run in the second half of October, it is the UK's largest public festival of its kind which shows the most exciting and original films by internationally established film-makers as well as the emerging ones and attracts thousands of film enthusiasts to see over 300 films, documentaries and shorts from all over the world.

As a public event which is designed to enable the British public to enjoy films that cannot be seen in British cinemas, it also awards the most original and creative film-makers and their works. Four types of awards are presented annually: Best Film Award presented to the most original, imaginative and creative motion picture; Best British Newcomer Award presented to emerging British talents; the Sutherland Trophy (named after George Sutherland-Leverson-Gower, 5th Duke of Sutherland) presented to the most original film that is screened during the Festival; and the Grierson Award presented to the best documentary screened during the Festival. In addition, it also entitles prominent individuals for their achievements to the honor of the BFI Fellowship.

The London Film Festival currently cannot be comparable to the major festivals such as those held in Cannes and Venice, for it was founded relatively late. But London Film Festival is developing rapidly in prestige and significance, which results in the growing number of film celebrities on the red carpet each year and their participation in the answers and questions sessions which enable audiences to have more insight into the screened films and the art of film making and receive excellent reception from the audiences.

3.2.2 Seattle International Film Festival

The Seattle International Film Festival (SIFF), held annually in Seattle, Washington since 1976 when it was held at a then-independent cinema named the Moore Egyptian Theater, belongs to the top film festivals in North America. Now, the festival typically takes advantage of about half a dozen cinemas including its own SIFF Cinema at Seattle Center since 2007, with the exact roster varying from year to year. The SIFF spans over three weeks (24 days) in May/June, featuring a diverse assortment of predominantly independent and foreign films, and a strong contingent of documentaries.

Generally, SIFF enjoys a reputation as an audience festival instead of an industry festival. The festival often partially overlaps the Cannes Film Festival, which is said to reduce attendance by industry VIPs. During the 1980s, SIFF audiences developed a fame for appreciating films that did not fit standard industry niches. SIFF also played an important part in the entry of Dutch films into the United States market. Since 1985, the festival has granted the Golden Space Needle Award each year to the festival's most popular film. Ballots are cast by audience members at the end of each film. These years, audiences, in an increasing number, show greater enthusiasm for attending the festival.

The festival is known for its unique component among major film festivals: a four-film "Secret Festival". Those who are involved in the Secret Festival have no idea about what they will see in advance, and they must sign an oath to promise they will not reveal anything afterwards. The SIFF Group also curates the Global Lens film series, the Screenwriters Salon, co-curates the Sci-Fi Shorts Film Festival at the Science Fiction Museum and Hall of Fame, and coordinates SIFF-A-Go-Go travel programs (organized tours to other film festivals).

3.2.3 Sundance Film Festival

The Sundance Film Festival takes place annually in Utah of the United States, and also being a program of the Sundance Institute. Held in January in Park City and Salt Lake City, Utah, as well as at the Sundance Resort, the festival serves as a showcase for American and international

independent filmmakers and their new work in an effort to honor excellence, innovation, and creativity. In 2016, it attracted more than 46,660 attendees, which made it the largest independent film festival in the United States and across the world. The 2017 Sundance Film Festival took place from January 19 to January 29, 2017.

The festival consists of competitive sections and out-of-competition sections, with the former for American and international dramatic and documentary films, both feature films and short films, and the latter including *NEXT*, *New Frontier*, *Spotlight*, *Midnight*, *Premieres and Documentary Premieres*. Sundance, founded by Sterling Van Wagenen, John Earle, and Cirina Hampton Catania, made its debut in Salt Lake City in August 1978, as the Utah/US Film Festival with the attempt to attract more filmmakers to Utah. The 1978 festival featured some excellent films such as *A Streetcar Named Desire*, *Midnight Cowboy*, *Mean Streets*, and *The Sweet Smell of Success*.

In 1979, the festival featured over 60 films and a great many well-known Hollywood filmmakers, which made it profitable for the first time. What's more, the first Frank Capra Award was given to Jimmy Stewart. The involvement of actor and Utah resident Robert Redford, who became the festival's inaugural chairman, contributed greatly to the growth and popularity of the festival. In 1981, the festival moved to Park City, Utah, and changed the dates from September to January with the consideration of drawing more attention from Hollywood because operating a film festival at a ski resort during winter was a good strategy.

Over the decades, originated as a low-profile venue for small-budget, independent creators from outside the Hollywood system, the festival has experienced a great change with now being a media extravaganza for Hollywood celebrity actors, paparazzi, and luxury lounges set up by companies not affiliated with Sundance. In recent years, the festival organizers have tried curbing these activities and have begun in 2007 with their ongoing Focus on Film campaign.

◎ Exercises

1. Explain the following terms in English.

1) Academy Awards
2) London Film Festival
3) Columbia Pictures
4) Warner Bros.
5) Westerns

2. Match the following items with their relevant information.

Section A

1) *Lincoln*	a. historical film
2) *The Sound of Music*	b. gangster film
3) *The Silence of the Lambs*	c. science fiction
4) *Saving Private Ryan*	d. action film
5) *Brokeback Mountain*	e. war film
6) *The Godfather*	f. the western
7) *Matrix*	g. comedy
8) *Forrest Gump*	h. drama
9) *The Day after Tomorrow*	i. horror film
10) *The Shawshank Redemption*	j. musical

Section B

1) It enjoys a reputation as an audience festival instead of an industry festival.

2) Its first ceremony in 1975 had 14 categories while currently, 65 categories are established.

3) It is the longest running festival in the UK.

4) The awards winners are granted a statuette, exactly, a theatrical mask designed by American sculptor Mitzi Cunliffe.

5) It was founded by American copywriter and publicist John J. B. Wilson in 1980.

6) Its first ceremony was held in January 1944 at the 20th Century-Fox studios in Los Angeles.

7) In 1981, it moved to Park City, Utah, and changed the dates from September to January.

8) Annually, its voters, made up of the Screening Group and Nomination Committee, view more than 250 entered films.

9) It has distributed various commercially successful film series, including *Star Wars*, *Ice Age*.

10) Its logo is a roaring lion surrounded by a ring of film inscribed with the studio's motto.

a. Golden Raspberry Awards
b. Edinburgh International Film Festival
c. People's Choice Awards
d. Seattle International Film Festival
e. British Academy Film Awards
f. Golden Globe Awards
g. British Independent Film Awards
h. Sundance Film Festival
i. Twentieth Century Fox
j. Metro-Goldwyn-Mayer

3. Discuss and answer the following questions.

1) Can you introduce a well-known film studio and the films made by it?

2) What genres of films do you usually like watching? Can you give examples?
3) Can you describe the characteristics of a main film genre?
4) What's your understanding of the statement "No genre can be defined in a single way."?
5) What's your favorite film award or film festival?
6) How can you define a successful film award or film festival?
7) Do you agree that a film award or film festival has its cultural limitation?
8) Why do you think the Academy Awards has made it to be one of the most important awards in the world?

Unit 3
Language of Film

There are a number of reasons why the role of films should be valued in the teaching and learning of English language. It's known that language is used to refer to any distinctive means of communication. Like English, films are human efforts designed to express ideas and make communication. In other words, a film is a whole language that can be learned including form, structure, theme, symbol, narration, shot, scene and others. For example, individual shots are the building bricks of the film language, just as words are the building bricks of a written language. Obviously, different shots are identified and employed to serve different purposes and answer different questions.

Undoubtedly, a film has an unparalleled power to transmit knowledge and thoughts. More importantly, it may illuminate the argument on the study of literature and culture. A film, as a means of communication, is both an art and a craft. Like the learning of any other language, the more thoroughly we master it, the more effectively we can communicate.

1. Film Terms

With the purpose of being knowledgeable about filmmaking and film industry, understanding the fundamental film-related terms and vocabulary is a must, and then with further insight into the film language. As a result, a part of the most basic and common terms are listed in this compendium for reference with their simple definitions provided for often complex terms as a baseline for literacy. In addition, illustrations and examples from films are presented to help describe them more fully and understand them more exactly. The listing of the terms here covers a majority of the important terms relevant to the process and various aspects of filmmaking, such as pre-production, directing, special effects, score, and box office, censorship, blockbuster, IMAX, etc.. With no doubt, this is not a complete collection of all film-related terms, for a great many terms are so obscure or technical that they cannot be defined and mastered easily.

Film Terms Glossary		
Film Terms	**Definition and Explanation**	**Example**
action	(1) any movement or series of events (usually rehearsed) that take place before the camera and propel the story forward toward its conclusion; (2) the word called out (by a megaphone) at the start of the current take during filming to alert actors to begin performing.	 Example: a megaphone to call out the word "ACTION"
adaptation	the presentation of one art form through another medium; a film based upon, derived from (or adapted from) a stage play (or from another medium such as a short story, book, article, history, novel, video game, comic strip/book, etc.) which basically preserves both the setting and dialogue of the original; can be in the form of a script (screenplay) or a proposal treatment.	 Example: *Who's Afraid of Virginia Woolf?* (1966) is a very faithful rendering or adaptation of Edward Albee's play of the same name; also, *Gone with the Wind* (1939) was adapted from Margaret Mitchell's novel, and *Apocalypse Now* (1979) was taken from Joseph Conrad's *Heart of Darkness*.
black or dark comedy	a type of comedy film, first popular during the late 1950s and early 1960s in which normally serious subjects, such as war, death, dismemberment, misery, suffering, or murder, are treated with macabre humor and satire through iconography, dialogue, and the characters; settings may include cemeteries, war rooms, funerals.	 Example: Hitchcock's *Dr. Strangelove, Or: How I Learned to Stop Worrying and Love the Bomb* (1964), Robert Altman's *Whatever Happened to Baby Jane?* (1962), and *Fargo* (1996)

续表

Film Terms Glossary		
Film Terms	**Definition and Explanation**	**Example**
box office	the measure of the total amount of money or box-office receipts paid by movie-goers to view a movie; also referred to as B. O. or gross; usually divided into domestic grosses (unadjusted and adjusted for inflation), and worldwide grosses.	 Example: *Gone with the Wind* held the record of highest-grossing film for twenty-five years and, adjusted for inflation, has earned more than any other film.
blockbuster	now in common usage, an impactful movie that is a huge financial success — usually with box office of more than \$200 million (the new benchmark by the early 2000s, after the original mark was \$100 million) upon release in North America; ticket lines for blockbusters literally go around the "block"; also known as box-office hit; the term may also refer to a costly film that must be exceptionally popular in order to recoup its expenses and make a profit.	 Example: The term was first applied to Steven Spielberg's *Jaws* (1975), often acknowledged as the first blockbuster; James Cameron's *Titanic* (1997) was also a massive blockbuster hit.

续表

Film Terms Glossary		
Film Terms	**Definition and Explanation**	**Example**
blue-screen or blue-screen shot	a special-effects process whereby actors work in front of an evenly-lit, monochromatic (usually blue or green) background, screen, or backdrop. The background is then replaced (or matted) in post-production by chroma-keying or optical printer, allowing other footage or computer-generated images (CGI) to form the background image. Since 1992, most films use a green-screen.	  Example: a bluescreen for *Jurassic Park III* (2001), or greenscreen for *Charlie's Angels* (2000)
camera angle	the point of view (POV) or perspective (including relative height or direction) chosen from which to photograph a subject. Various camera angles, compositions, or positions include: front, behind, side, top, high (looking down), low (looking up), straight-on or eye-level (standard or neutral angle), tilted (canted or oblique), or subjective, etc.	 Example: Extreme camera angles can be found in *The Third Man* (1949).
caption	the descriptive, printed line(s) of text that occasionally appears on the screen, usually at the bottom of the frame, to describe the time/place, or to translate a foreign word/phrase. different from closed-captioning (closed captions are all white uppercase (capital) letters encased in a black box that require a decoder or television with a decoder chip to be viewed) for deaf or hard-of-hearing viewers.	 Example: a caption from a foreign film, Kieslowski's *Decalogue* (1988)

续表

Film Terms Glossary		
Film Terms	**Definition and Explanation**	**Example**
cast	a collective term for all of the actors/performers (or talent) appearing in a particular film; usually broken down into two parts: the leads with speaking roles, and the seconds or supporting characters, background players or extras, and bit players.	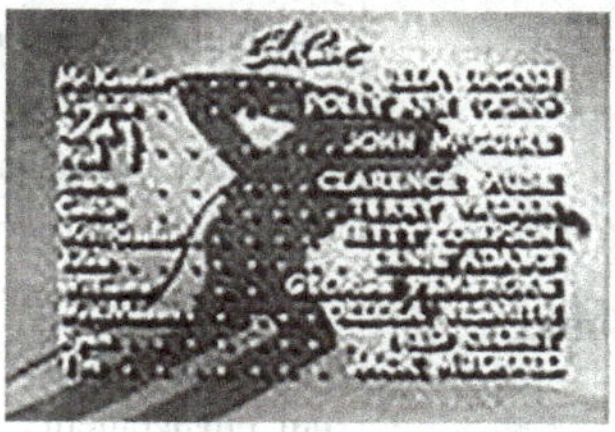 Example: typical end credits (for the major cast members) from an older film
censorship	the process of determining what can or can not be viewed by the public or depicted by the motion picture industry; also refers to changes required of a movie by some person or body (other than the studios or film-makers, such as a national or regional film classification board).	Example: The arthouse film *Last Tango in Paris* (1972) with adult-oriented sexual content, now rated NC-17, was originally rated X, and banned in various places for its "obscenity".
CGI	Computer-Generated Imagery (or Images), a term referring to the use of 3D computer graphics and technology (digital computers and specialized software) in film-making to create filmed images, special effects and the illusion of motion; often used to cut down on the cost of hiring extras.	 Example: *Jurassic Park* (1993) and its giant dinosaurs, or used in large crowd scenes in *Gladiator* (2000) or in the prologue battle scene in *The Lord of the Rings: The Fellowship of the Ring* (2001)
cinematography (also **cinematographer**)	specifically refers to the art and technique of film photography, the capture of images, and lighting effects, or to the person expert in and responsible for capturing or recording-photographing images for a film, through the selection of visual recording devices, camera angles, film stock, lenses, framing, and arrangement of lighting; the chief cinematographer responsible for a movie is called the director of photography (or D. P.), or first cameraman; one of the earliest movie-picture machines, patented by the Lumiere brothers in 1895, was termed a Cinematographe.	 Example: *Visions of Light: The Art of Cinematography* (1993) profiled a history of the art of cinematography with examples from more than 125 films from some of the greatest film-makers of all time.

续表

Film Terms Glossary		
Film Terms	**Definition and Explanation**	**Example**
climax	the highest point of anxiety or tension in a story or film in which the central character/protagonist faces, confronts, and deals with the consequence (s) of all his/her actions, or faces the antagonist in a climactic battle or final engagement; a crisis often leads to a climax; a climax may be followed by an anti-climax or denouement.	 Example: The two protagonists cling for their lives from Mount Rushmore in the climax of Hitchcock's *North by Northwest* (1959).
close-up (CU)	a shot taken from a close distance in which the scale of the object is magnified, appears relatively large and fills the entire frame to focus attention and emphasize its importance; i. e., a person's head from the shoulders or neck up is a commonly-filmed close-up; a tight shot makes the subject fill almost the entire frame; also extreme close-up (ECU or XCU) is a shot of a part of a character (e. g., face, head, hands) to emphasize detail; also known as detail shot or close on; contrast to long-shot (LS).	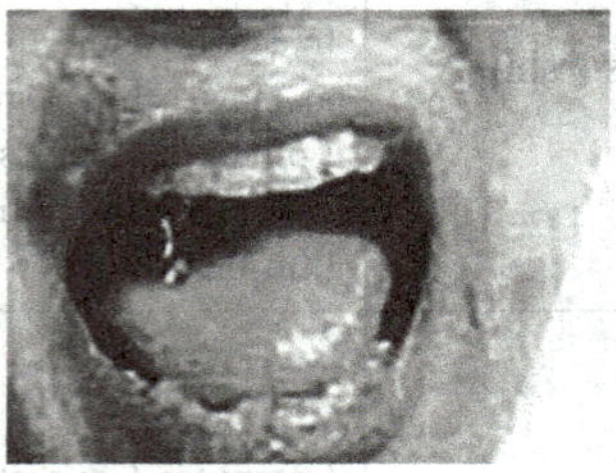 Example: an extreme close-up or tight shot from Hitchcock's *Psycho* (1960)
costume or wardrobe and costume design	refers to the garments or clothing worn by actors/performers in a film; a costume (or wardrobe) designer researches, designs, and selects the costumes to be appropriate to the film's time period, the characters, their location, and their occupations, whereas the costumer (or stylist) is responsible for acquiring, selecting, manufacturing, and/or handling the clothing and accessories; a costume drama is a film set in a particular historical time period, often with elaborate costuming.	 Example: *Superman*: *The Movie* (1978) (pictured); also films with important wardrobe elements including *Cabaret* (1972), *3 Women* (1977), *Ed Wood* (1994), and *Hedwig and the Angry Inch* (2001)

续表

Film Terms Glossary		
Film Terms	**Definition and Explanation**	**Example**
critic (**or film critic, film reviewer**)	an individual who writes and/or publishes a review of a film from either an artistic or entertainment point of view. Film reviews often analyze and discuss a film's details, its content and characters, a critique of the performances, camera work, directing, editing, production, and script; film critics are usually more philosophical and theoretical than film reviewers or commentators; film criticism refers to the analysis of the narrative, historical and stylistic characteristics of film.	 Example: one of the best known and most knowledgeable film critics of all time, *Chicago Tribune's* Roger Ebert, known for his "thumbs-up" and "thumbs-down" reviews
cut (or **cutting**)	an abrupt or sudden change or jump in camera angle, location, placement, or time, from one shot to another; consists of a transition from one scene to another (a visual cut) or from one soundtrack to another (a sound cut); cutting refers to the selection, splicing and assembly by the film editor of the various shots or sequences for a reel of film, and the process of shortening a scene; also refers to the instructional word "cut" said at the end of a take by the director to stop the action in front of the camera.	 Example: *Citizen Kane*, directed by Orson Welles, had a notable episode about the final cut privilege.
director (**and directing**)	the creative artist responsible for complete artistic control of all phases of a film's production (such as making day-to-day determinations about sound, lighting, action, casting, even editing), for translating/interpreting a script into a film, for guiding the performances of the actors in a particular role and/or scene, and for supervising the cinematography and film crew. The director is usually the single person, most responsible for the finished product.	 Example: Ingmar Bergman examines a sheet of film, during work on *Wild Strawberries*.

续表

Film Terms Glossary		
Film Terms	**Definition and Explanation**	**Example**
dub **(or dubbing)**	the act of putting a new soundtrack on a film or adding a soundtrack (of dialogue, sound effects, or music) after production, to match the action and/or lip movements of already-filmed shots; commonly used when films are shot on location in noisy environments; also refers to adding translated dialogue to a foreign-language film; as opposed to direct sound — which is sound recorded when filming a scene; contrast to looping.	 Example: a dubbing studio
editing (editor)	the process (performed by a film editor) of selecting, assembling, arranging, collating, trimming, structuring, and splicing-joining together many separate camera takes (includes sound also) of exposed footage (or daily rushes) into a complete, determined sequence or order of shots (or film) - that follows the script; an editor works in a cutting room; the choice of shots has a tremendous influence upon the film's final appearance.	 Example: the original editing machine: an upright Moviola
experiment-tal film	refers to a film, usually a low-budget or indie film not oriented toward profit-making, that challenges conventional filmmaking by using camera techniques, imagery, sound, editing, and/or acting in unusual or never-before-seen ways.	 Example: Hitchcock's *Rope* (1948)

续表

Film Terms Glossary		
Film Terms	**Definition and Explanation**	**Example**
feature (film)	a "full-length" motion picture, one greater than 60 minutes in length — but usually about 90-120 minutes on one particular topic; also known as a theatrical; contrast to shorts.	 Example: an actor playing the Australian bushranger Ned Kelly in *The Story of the Kelly Gang* (1906), the world's first dramatic feature-length film
film noir	a French phrase literally meaning "black film" that developed in the early 40s; refers to a genre of mostly black/white films that blossomed in the post-war era in American cinema, with bleak subject matter and a somber, downbeat tone; the plot (often a quest), low-key lighting (harsh shadows and chiaroscuro) often in night scenes, camera angles (often canted or high angle shots), the setting (the gloomy underworld of crime and corruption), iconography (guns, urban settings), characters (disillusioned, jaded), and other elements (voice-overs and flashbacks) combined to present a dark atmosphere of pessimism, tension, cynicism, or oppression. Film noirs, often crime films, were usually set in grim and seedy cities, with characters including criminals, anti-heroes, private detectives, and duplicitous *femme fatales*.	 Example: American films of the 1940s and early 1950s, including *The Maltese Falcon* (1941), *Double Indemnity* (1944), *Sorry, Wrong Number* (1948), and *Sunset Boulevard* (1950). Also present day noirs, such as *Body Heat* (1981) and *The Man Who Wasn't There* (2001); Carl Reiner's *Dead Men Don't Wear Plaid* (1982) was a parody of film noir (and contained excerpted footage from classic film noir films).

续表

Film Terms Glossary		
Film Terms	**Definition and Explanation**	**Example**
flashback	a filmic technique that alters the natural order of the narrative; a flashback may often be the entire film; it takes the story order back chronologically in time to a previous or past event, scene, or sequence that took place prior to the present time frame of the film; the flashbacked story that provides background on action and events is often called the backstory; contrast to flash-forward.	 Example: *Citizen Kane* (1941) is composed mostly of flashbacks and flash-forwards — i. e., Joseph Cotten in a rest home remembering the past, in a flashback; also many film noirs begin with a flashback, such as *Mildred Pierce* (1945) and *Out of the Past* (1947).
focus	refers to the degree of sharpness or distinctness of an image (or an element of an image such as a person, object, etc.); as a *verb*, it refers to the manipulation or adjustment of the lens to create a sharper image.	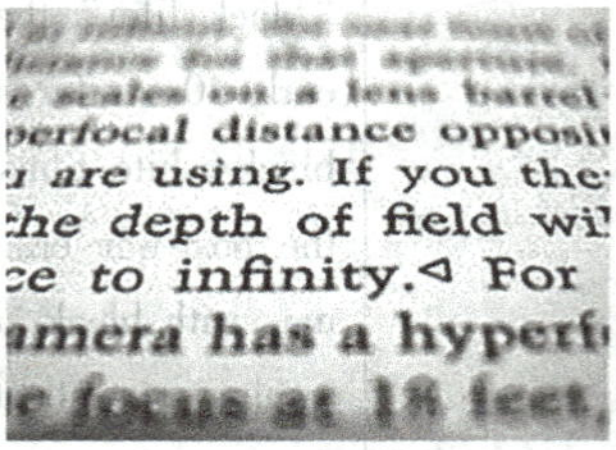 Example: an image that is partially in focus, but mostly out of focus in varying degrees
follow-up	refers to a cinematic work that comes after, regardless of whether it is a sequel or a prequel; contrast to a prequel, serial, series, sequel, spin-off or remake.	Example: *Star Wars Episode 1: The Phantom Menace* (1999) was a follow-up to the sequel, *Star Wars Episode 6: Return of the Jedi* (1983), as was *Toy Story 2* (1999) to *Toy Story* (1995).
frame	refers to a single image, the smallest compositional unit of a film's structure, captured by the camera on a strip of motion picture film — similar to an individual slide in still photography; a series of frames juxtaposed and shown in rapid succession make up a motion (or moving) picture; also refers to the rectangular area within which the film image is composed by the film-maker — in other words, a frame is what we see (within the screen).	 Example: a strip of film negative, showing a single rectangular frame or box that contains the image that is projected. There are 16 frames per foot of 35mm film.

续表

Film Terms Glossary		
Film Terms	**Definition and Explanation**	**Example**
independent films (independents andindie)	small independent, low-budget companies, mini-majors, or entities for financing, producing, and distributing films (i. e., Miramax, New Line Cinema, Polygram) working outside of the system or a major Hollywood studio; however, an indie may lose its independent status when its grows large and powerful; also refers to a movie, director, distributor or producer (sometimes unconventional) not associated with or produced by a major Hollywood film studio; often with groundbreaking subject matter designed for sophisticated audiences, and not necessarily produced with commercial success as the goal, unlike mainstream films.	Example: California-based Miramax, although the leader in the independent film movement in the early 1990s, has become so powerful and successful that it has lost most of its independent studio status; indie films include Jim Jarmusch's *Stranger Than Paradise* (1984), and Kevin Smith's *Clerks* (1994); the cable TV Independent Film Channel showcases indie films.
IMAX	a specialized, big-screen film format about ten times larger than the traditional cinema format (35mm) and three times larger than the standard 70 mm widescreen format; debuted in Osaka Japan at the 1970 Exposition; IMAX films, often short documentaries, "educational", travelogue or nature films, are shot and projected on 15 perforation/70mm gauge film — "15/70", the largest film format in existence, which produces incredible high-definition sharpness in films projected on up to eight-story high screens in theatres equipped with advanced digital surround-sound systems.	 Example: the 15 kW Xenon short-arc lamp used in IMAX projectors

续表

Film Terms Glossary		
Film Terms	**Definition and Explanation**	**Example**
makeup	refers to the materials that are used to prepare the performer for his/her respective role(s) before the camera, anywhere from facial pancake to elaborate costuming, latex masks, and other ghastly transformations.	 Example: from *Raiders of the Lost Ark* (1981)
monologue	a scene or a portion of a script in which an actor gives a lengthy, unbroken speech without interruption by another character.	 Example: Keyes' (Edward G. Robinson) long speech about suicide statistics in *Double Indemnity* (1944), or Romeo's last embrace and death scene in *Romeo and Juliet* (1968)
montage	a French word literally meaning "editing", "putting together" or "assembling shots"; refers to a filming technique, editing style, or form of movie collage consisting of a series of short shots or images that are rapidly put together into a coherent sequence to create a composite picture, or to suggest meaning or a larger idea; in simple terms, the structure of editing within a film; a montage is usually not accompanied with dialogue; dissolves, cuts, fades, super-impositions, and wipes are often used to link the images in a montage sequence.	 Example: The two montage sequences in *Holiday Inn* (1942) show the two basic montage styles.

续表

Film Terms Glossary		
Film Terms	**Definition and Explanation**	**Example**
narration	the telling of a story, and the supplemental information given to the film audience by an off-screen voice; sometimes the narrator is a character in the film, who provides information in a flashback.	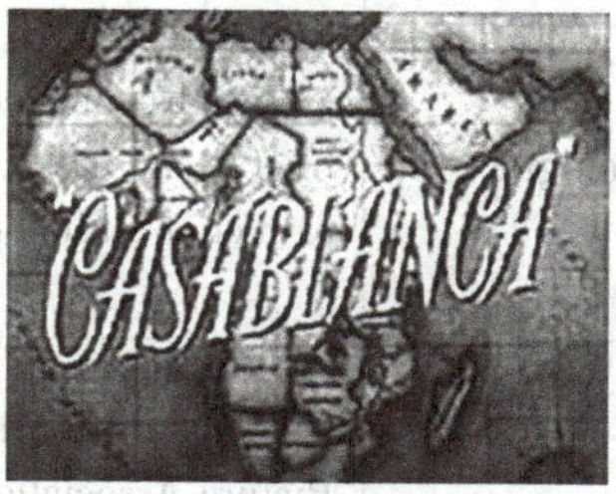 Example: during the opening credits in *Casablanca* (1942), and throughout *Letter from an Unknown Woman* (1948); also the lyrics-as-narration (by the Doors' song "The End") in the opening of *Apocalypse Now* (1979).
point of view (POV)	the perspective from which the film story is told, and to let the viewer know what the character is seeing; also refers to a shot that depicts the outlook, view, vantage point or position of a character.	 Example: an explicit POV shot from the public domain horror film *The Driller Killer*, putting the audience into the perspective of the protagonist playing pinball with the top shot coming five seconds before the below shot
post-production	the final stage in a film's production after principal photography or shooting, involving picture editing, the addition of sound/visual effects, musical scoring, mixing, dubbing, distribution, etc.; in digital post-production, can also include changing facial expressions, removing flaws or obtrusive objects (microphone, boom, etc.), enhancing the visual image, etc.	 Example: a sound control room at Tainted Blue Studios, 2010

续表

Film Terms Glossary		
Film Terms	**Definition and Explanation**	**Example**
prologue	a speech, preface, introduction, or brief scene preceding the main action or plot of a film; contrast to epilogue.	Example: *The Lord of the Rings: The Fellowship of the Ring* (2001) provided a prologue to briefly explain the essential history of Middle-Earth and its inhabitants.
rating system(s) or ratings	also known as the MPAA (Motion Picture Association of America) film rating system, first officially instituted in late 1968; it refers to the ever-evolving classification system for films usually based upon age-appropriateness, and the judgment of a film's suitability for various audiences, in terms of sexual content, offensiveness, or violence.	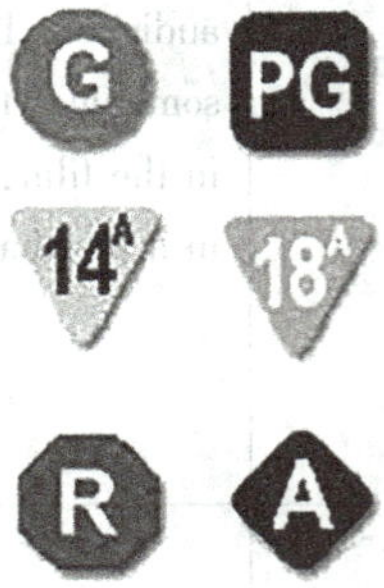 Example: Canadian rating labels used outside Québec
scene	usually a shot (or series of shots) that together comprise a single, complete and unified dramatic event, action, unit, or element of film narration, or block (segment) of storytelling within a film, much like a scene in a play; a scene normally occurs in one location and deals with one action; the end of a scene is often indicated by a change in time, action and/or location.	 Example: the classic love scene of John Wayne and Maureen O'Hara caught in a drenching rainstorm in a graveyard, and their rain-soaked embrace in *The Quiet Man* (1952)
script (also shooting script)	refers to the written text of a film — a blueprint for producing a film detailing the story, setting, dialogue, movements and gestures of actors, and the shape and sequence of all events in the film; a scenario is a script that includes camera and set direction as well as dialogue and cast direction; a shooting script is a detailed final version of the screenplay with the separate scenes arranged in proper sequence, and used by the cast during actual film-making.	 Example: shooting script for *The Shawshank Redemption* (1994)

续表

Film Terms Glossary		
Film Terms	**Definition and Explanation**	**Example**
shot	the basic building block or unit of film narrative; refers to a single, constant take made by a motion picture camera uninterrupted by editing, interruptions or cuts, in which a length of film is exposed by turning the camera on, recording, and then turning the camera off; it can also refer to a single film frame (such as a still image); shot analysis refers to the examination of individual shots.	 Example: a single film frame or shot, of Fay Wray rehearsing the moment of meeting Kong, from *King Kong* (1933)
silent film (or silents)	the term for motion pictures without sound (spoken dialogue or synchronized soundtrack), although they were often accompanied by live commentary, piano-music, sound effects, and/or orchestration; the period from about 1895 to 1927.	 Example: a scene from *The Birth of a Nation* (1915), the highest-grossing silent film in the United States
slow-motion (or slo-motion)	refers to an effect resulting from running film through a camera at faster-than-normal speed (shooting faster than 24 frames per second), and then projecting it at standard speed; if a camera runs at 60 frames per second, and captures a one-second-long event, a 24-frame playback will slow that event to two and a half seconds long; this filmic technique is usually employed to fully capture a "moment in time" or to produce a dramatic (or romantic feeling).	Example: often used in sports films in which the climactic winning catch or play is run in slow-motion

续表

Film Terms Glossary		
Film Terms	**Definition and Explanation**	**Example**
special effects	a broad, wide-ranging term used by the film industry meaning to create fantastic visual and audio illusions that cannot be accomplished by normal means, such as travel into space. Many visual (photographic) or mechanical (physical) filmic techniques or processes are used to produce special illusionary effects, such as optical and digital effects, CGI, in-camera effects, the use of miniatures/models, mattes, rear-camera projections, stop-motion animation, bluescreens, full-scale mockups, pyrotechnics (squibs (miniature explosions, i. e. a gunshot)), stunt men, animatronics (electronic puppets), rain/snow/wind machines, etc.	 Example: *King Kong* (1933) and the use of models  Example: Hitchcock's *The Birds* (1963)
studio(s)	(1) the for-profit companies that specialize in developing, financing and distributing most American commercial films; (2) also refers to the actual site for a film production, with physical sets, stages, offices, backlots (located on the outdoor grounds of a film studio and used for filming exteriors), etc.	 Example: an archival view of the front entrance to Paramount Pictures film studio
Stunt double(s)	a stunt performer(s) that take the place of an actor when the scene calls for a dangerous or risky action (car crash, fight, window jump, etc.); doubles usually have the same build or appearance as the star; not to be confused with a stand-in or a body double; stunts are supervised, conducted and planned by a stunt coordinator.	 Example: Harrison Ford with his stunt double Vic Armstrong on the set of *Indiana Jones and the Last Crusade* (1989)

续表

Film Terms Glossary		
Film Terms	**Definition and Explanation**	**Example**
talkies	The common term used for films with sound (beginning in 1927), although rarely used currently. The advent of talkies marked the dawning of the era of sound films, as opposed to silent films.	 Example: The landmark film *In Old Arizona* (1929), was advertised as "100% All-Talking", and "You Hear What You See" on its poster, because it was the first sound western from a major studio (Fox Pictures); *Singin' in the Rain* (1952) took a look back at the dawning of the talkies.
3-D	a film that has a three-dimensional, stereoscopic form or appearance, giving the life-like illusion of depth; often achieved by viewers donning special red/blue (or green) or polarized lens glasses; when 3-D images are made interactive so that users feel involved with the scene, the experience is called virtual reality; 3-D experienced a heyday in the early 1950s.	 Example: Audience wearing special glasses watch a 3D "stereoscopic film" at the Telekinema on the South Bank in London during the Festival of Britain 1951.
trailer	a short publicity film, preview, or advertisement composed of short excerpts and scenes from a forthcoming film or coming attraction, usually two-three minutes in length; often presented at the showing of another film. Historically, these advertisements were placed at the end of a newsreel or supporting feature and so "trailed" them, hence the name; also commonly known as preview(s).	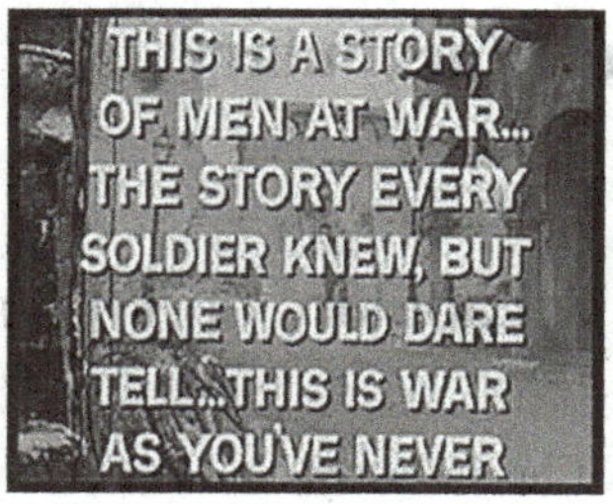 Example: screenshot, from a film trailer, for 1956 film, *Attack*!.

续表

Film Terms Glossary		
Film Terms	**Definition and Explanation**	**Example**
voice-over (or **v. o.**)	refers to recorded dialogue, usually narration, that comes from an unseen, off-screen voice, character or narrator, that can be heard by the audience but not by the film characters themselves; narration is a type of voice-over; v. o. often conveys the character's thoughts, either as a "voice" heard within one's head, or as other narrative information and commentary to explain the action or plot; often a technique in film noirs.	Example: Capt. Willard's voice-overs in *Apocalypse Now* (1979), Deckard's v. o. in Hollywood's version of Ridley Scott's *Blade Runner* (1982), the mortally wounded hero's flashback narration in *Double Indemnity* (1944), or the voice-over narrated by the dead man floating in a pool in the opening of *Sunset Boulevard* (1950) (pictured here).
widescreen	refers to projection systems in which the aspect ratio is wider than the 1.33: 1 ratio that dominated sound film before the 1950s; in the 1950s, many widescreen processes were introduced (to combat the growing popularity of television), such as CinemaScope (an anamorphic system), VistaVision (a non-anamorphic production technique in which the film is run horizontally through the camera instead of vertically), and Todd-AO and Super Panavision (that both used wider-gauge film).	 Example: *Oklahoma*! (1955) and *Around the World in Eighty Days* (1956)

2. Film Vocabulary

2.1 Vocabulary on Filmmaking and Filmmaker

cinema, film industry 电影业

screendom, moviedom 电影界

action still 电影剧照

assistant director 副导演

audience	观众
camera crew	摄制组
cameraman	摄影师
costume designer	化妆设计
composer	作曲家
credits	摄制人员名单
director	导演
film editor	电影编辑
film cutter	影片剪辑员
screenscript, scenario	电影剧本
producer	制片
recording engineer	录音师
scenarist	剧作家
script girl	场务
sound effects man	音响效果操作员
special effects man	特别效果操作员
screen	荧幕
title	片名
talent scout	星探
film critic	影评人
film fan	影迷
filmgoer	爱看电影的人
publicity officer	电影宣传员
public idol	大众偶像
usher	领座员
booth-man, projectionist	电影放映员
film projector	电影放映机
box office	电影院售票处
drive-in	免下车电影院

2.2 Vocabulary on Film Company

film distribution corporation	电影发行公司
film production corporation	电影制作公司
film studio	电影制片厂
film tycoon, film magnate	影业巨头
20th Century Fox	二十世纪福克斯电影公司
Columbia	哥伦比亚电影公司

Touchstone	试金石电影公司
Metro-Goldwin-Mayer (MGM)	米高梅电影公司
Paramount	派拉蒙电影公司
Radio-Keith-Orpheum(RKO)	雷电华电影公司
Universal	环球电影公司
United Artists	联美电影公司
Warner Bros.	华纳兄弟电影公司
DreamWorks	梦工厂电影公司
Pixar Animation	皮克斯动画电影公司
Summit	顶峰娱乐电影公司
Walt Disney	华特·迪士尼电影公司
New Line	新线电影公司
Fox Searchlight	福克斯探照灯电影公司
Miramax	米拉麦克斯电影公司
Spyglass	望远镜电影公司
Village Roadshow	威秀电影公司
Legendary	传奇电影公司
Castle Rock	城堡石电影公司

2.3 Vocabulary on Film Award

American Academy of Arts and Sciences	美国艺术与科学学院
Academy Awards	金像奖
Nominations for Academy Awards	金像奖提名
Oscar	奥斯卡奖
Golden Globe Awards	金球奖
Golden Raspberry Awards	金酸莓奖
British Academy of Film and Television Arts (BAFTA)	英国电影和电视艺术学院
British Academy Film Awards, BAFTA Film Awards	英国电影学院奖
Berlin International Film Festival	柏林国际电影节
Golden Bear	金熊奖
Venice International Film Festival	威尼斯国际电影节
Golden Lion	金狮奖
Cannes International Film Festival	戛纳国际电影节
Golden Palm	金棕榈奖
Asia-Pacific Film Festival	亚太影展
Shanghai International Film Festival	上海国际电影节
Golden Goblet Awards	金爵奖

Golden Rooster Awards	金鸡奖
Golden Horse Awards	金马奖
Hong Kong Film Awards	香港电影金像奖
Best Achievement in Directing	最佳导演
Best Actor	最佳男主角
Best Actress	最佳女主角
Best Achievement in Film Editing	最佳剪辑
Best Achievement in Cinematography	最佳摄影
Best Achievement in Art Direction	最佳艺术指导
Best Achievement in Sound	最佳音像成就
Best Achievement Award for Visual Effects	最佳视觉效果
Best Achievement in Short Subjects, Live Action	最佳实景短片
Best Achievement in Documentary Features	最佳纪录短片
Best Achievement in Costume Design	最佳服装设计
Best Achievement in Short Subjects, Animated	最佳卡通短片
Best Original Dramatic Score	最佳原配乐
Best Picture	最佳影片
Best Supporting Actor	最佳男配角
Best Supporting Actress	最佳女配角
Best Screenplay	最佳改编剧本
Best Story	最佳原著剧本
Best Scoring Adaptation	最佳改配乐
Best Foreign Language Film	最佳外语片
Best Song	最佳歌曲
Special Awards	特别奖
Life Achievement Award	终身成就奖

2.4 Vocabulary on Actor and Actress

cast	演员表
all star cast	全明星阵容
actor	男演员
actress	女演员
best actor	最佳男演员
best actress	最佳女演员
comedian	滑稽演员
co-star	共同主演
character	人物

child star	童星
character actor	性格演员
double	兼演两角色的演员
dubbing actor	配音演员
extra	临时演员
guest player	客串演员
ham	拙劣演员
heave	演庄重角色的演员
hero, heroine	主人公
leading actor, male lead	男主角
leading actress, female lead	女主角
movie king	影帝
movie queen	影后
movie star	电影明星
principal	主要演员
part, role	角色
regular player	职业演员
superstar	超级明星
second lead	第二主角
supporting actor	男配角
supporting actress	女配角
semi-star	二流演员
third lead	第三主角
tragedian	悲剧演员
stunt man, stunt woman	特技演员
stand-in, stuntman	替身
tile character, title role	剧名角色
understudy	预备演员
villain	反面角色

2.5 Vocabulary on Film Genre

motion picture, flicker, pix, cinema	电影
art film	艺术电影
black film, film noir, black cinema	黑色电影
blue film	色情电影
black-and-white film	黑白电影
technicolor film, color film	彩色电影

best seller	卖座电影
B-picture	劣等电影
serial	分集电影
stereoscopic film	立体电影
silent, silent film	无声电影
sound film, talkie, talking film	有声电影
blockbuster	热门大片
nouvelle vague	新潮派影片
adventure film	惊险片
animated cartoon, animation	卡通片
affectional film, romance, love film	爱情片
crime film	犯罪片
comedy	喜剧片
color-blind film	色盲片
costume film	古装片
documentary film	纪录片
detective film	侦探片
disaster film	灾难片
documentary film, document	纪实片
ethical film	伦理片
film d'avant-garde	前卫片
feature film	故事片
foreign version, dubbed film	译制片
gangster film	绑匪片
horror film, dracula film	恐怖片
literary film	文艺片
musical	音乐片
newsreel	新闻片
puppet film	木偶片
swordsmen film	武侠片
science film	科幻片
suspense	悬念片
tragedy	悲剧片
thriller film, blood curdler	紧张片
theatrical film	戏曲片
wild western film, western	西部片
semi-documentary	半纪录性电影
spectacular film	场面壮观的电影

short subject	正片前加演的短片
cinerama	宽银/荧幕立体电影
cinepanoramic	全景宽银/荧幕电影
cinemascope	弧形宽银幕及立体声电影

2.6 Vocabulary on Film Technique

post-production	后期制作
pre-production	前期制作
post-exposure	后期曝光
artistic effect	艺术效果
big close shot	大特写
camera, crank in	开拍
close up	特写镜头
chanted shot	倾斜镜头
cheat shot	特技镜头
contrast	对比
characterization	人物塑造
dramatic effect	舞台效果
dubbing	配音
dissolve	渐隐
extreme long shot	特远景
fast motion	快镜头
follow shot	跟镜头
full-length shot	长镜头
flip-frame	画面翻转
freeze frame	定格
floor	摄影现场
front light	顺光
flashback	倒叙
fade-out	淡出
fade -in	淡入
frame-in; frame-out	入画面，出画面
finish, end	(电影)终，完
flash-forward	提前叙述未来事件
high angle shot	高角度镜头
high-key light	高调照明
highlight	强光部分

intensity control	亮度控制
ironic	讽刺
low angle shot	低角度镜头
location	外景拍摄地
location sound recording	现场录音
light effect	灯光效果
low-key light	低调照明
medium long shot	中长镜头
Montage	蒙太奇
off-camera sound; off-camera voice; voice-over	画外音
panorama shot/panning	摇镜头
panorama	全景摇摄
rear light, back light	逆光
synthetic art	合成艺术
shooting start	开镜
screen test	试镜
shot	镜头
slow motion	慢镜头
score	配乐
sound effects	音响效果
synchronization	同期录音
sound recording	录音
side light	侧光
symbol	象征
suspense	悬念
subtitle, caption	字幕
top light, overhead light	顶光
track-shot	推拉镜头

◎ Exercises

1. Explain the following terms in English.

1) montage
2) trailer
3) editor
4) independent film
5) flashback

2. Match the following film terms with their definitions.

1) the actual site for a film production

2) the garments or clothing worn by actors/performers in a film

3) the presentation of one art form through another medium

4) the creation of fantastic visual and audio illusions that cannot be accomplished by normal means

5) the printed lines of text superimposed and displayed at the bottom of the screen frame

6) a cinematic work that comes after, regardless of whether it is a sequel or a prequel

7) a French word literally meaning "editing", "putting together" or "assembling shots"

8) a French phrase literally meaning "black film" that developed in the early 1940s

9) an abrupt or sudden change or jump in camera angle, location, placement, or time, from one shot to another

10) the perspective from which the film story is told, and to let the viewer know what the character is seeing

a. costume

b. point of view

c. cut

d. montage

e. follow-up

f. subtitles

g. film noir

h. studio

i. special effects

j. adaptation

3. Discuss and answer the following questions.

1) What do you think of the role of English films in English learning?

2) How do you define the language of films?

3) What cinematic terms are you most interested in? Can you explain them?

5) What cinematic terms do you think are the most difficult to understand?

4) Can you illustrate some film terms with more examples?

6) What films may be viewed as "blockbuster"? Can you take one as an example?

7) What are the famous studios which have impressed you? Can you list some of the films made by them?

8) How do you view the role of a director in the making of a film?

9) What does post-production include in filmmaking?

10) Can you list some films which have been adapted? How do you define a good adaptation?

Unit 4
Classic Films

There is a collection of American and British classic films introduced in this unit, which are produced in different times, from 1930s and 1940s to now. The films cover a wide range of themes focused on humanity and morality, and reflect specific social and cultural background and people's real life, or explore some unknown fields by taking advantage of human imagination. The films belong to various film genres, such as romance, comedy, thriller, science fiction, war film, biographical film, etc.

The films are all selected from AFI (American Film Institute) list of top 100 greatest films or BFI (British Film Institute) equivalent, and undoubtedly they are always among many other rankings of greatest films of all time. The reason why they are viewed as classic films lies in the combination of profound theme, skillful narration, twisted plot, memorable quotes, outstanding acting and others. It's clear that many more classic films are worth introducing and sharing, such as American film *It Happened One Night* (1934), *On the Waterfront* (1954), *Psycho* (1960), *The Graduate* (1967), 2001: *A Space Odyssey* (1968), *Jaw* (1975), *One Flew over the Cuckoo's Nest* (1975), *Annie Hall* (1977), *Saving Private Ryan* (1998), *Inception* (2010), etc. and British films *Henry V* (1944), *Brief Encounter* (1945), *Brighton Rock* (1947), *The Bridge on the River Kwai*(1957), *Get Carter* (1971), *The Long Good Friday* (1980), *The Full Monty* (1997), *The Theory of Everything* (2014), etc.

1. American Films

The American film industry, usually known as Hollywood, has exerted a profound and extensive effect on cinema all over the world since the early 20th century. Classical Hollywood Cinema, developed from 1917-1960, is recognized as the dominant style of American cinema, which characterizes most films to this day.

Although Auguste and Louis Lumière are greatly honored for their creation of modern filmmaking, and undoubtedly, American cinema soon took the leading role in the emerging industry. In 1894, the world's first commercial motion picture exhibition was held in New York City, using Thomas Edison's Kinetoscope. Since the 1920s, the American cinema has grossed more money annually than that of any other country and has always been at the forefront of film development in the following decades.

Since the early 20th century, Hollywood in Los Angeles, California has been made a major base for the U. S. film industry, and now has become the cinema center of the world where thousands of film enthusiasts rush there for fulfilling their dreams. Director D. W. Griffith is viewed as the pioneer in the development of film grammar. Orson Welles's *Citizen Kane* (1941) is frequently voted as the greatest film of all time in various rankings, particularly in critics' polls.

The major film studios of Hollywood have created most commercially successful films in the world, such as *The Birth of a Nation* (1915), *Gone with the Wind* (1939), *The Sound of Music* (1965), *Star Wars* (1977), *E. T. the Extra-Terrestrial* (1982), *Jurassic Park* (1993), *Titanic* (1997), *Avatar* (2009). Currently, American film studios collectively generate several hundred films every year, which results in one of the biggest and most prolific industry across the world.

1.1 *City Lights*

Introduction

City Lights is a 1931 American pre-Code silent romantic comedy film written, produced, directed by and starring Charlie Chaplin. In the story, a dewy-eyed tramp falls in love with a sightless flower girl and accumulates money to help her medically with the aid of a wealthy erratic tippler.

It's known that Chaplin's feature *The Circus*, released in 1928, was his last silent film before the motion picture industry embraced sound recording and brought the silent film era to a close. In Chaplin's eyes, *City Lights* was still a silent film, for technically the film demonstrates the synchronization of music, sound effects, and some unintelligible sounds that copied speech pattern films.

After almost one year's work on the script for the film, Chaplin began its filming in December, 1928. The filming was difficult with a span of three years, for Chaplin, as a perfectionist; was noted for doing many more "takes" than other directors at the time. The scene of the tramp's first meeting the flower girl was repeatedly shot, even more than 300 times. In addition, *City Lights* marked the first time Chaplin composed the film score for one of his productions

Chaplin was afraid of the film's reception because silent films were becoming obsolete by then, but unexpectedly it's reviews were mostly positive. *City Lights* became one of Chaplin's most financially successful and critically acclaimed works. The film's re-release in 1950 confirmed its popularity, as once again it was positively reviewed by audiences and critics.

Nowadays, the film is viewed by a great many critics as not only the highest accomplishment of Chaplin's career, but one of the greatest films of all time. In 1991, *City Lights* was selected by the Library of Congress for preservation in the United States National Film Registry because of its cultural, historical, and aesthetical significance. In 2007, the American Film Institute ranked it 11th on its list of the best American films ever made.

Plot

The story begins with the Tramp sleeping on a new statue unveiled by the officials of a city, only to be driven away. Afterwards, he wanders on the streets and comes across a beautiful Flower Girl. The Tramp at first is unaware of her blindness and buys a flower. Just when she is about to give him his change, she hears that a man gets into a nearby luxury car and believes that the Tramp has departed. The Tramp then tiptoes away.

Later in the evening, the Tramp runs into a drunken Millionaire who is attempting to commit suicide on the waterfront. The Tramp eventually convinces The Millionaire he should live. After taking the Tramp back to his mansion and giving him a change of clothes, they go out for a night on the town, where the Tramp inadvertently causes much havoc. Early the next morning, they back to the mansion and encounter the Flower Girl on her way to her vending spot. The Tramp uses some money that is gained from The Millionaire in order to buy all the girl's flowers and then drives her home in the Millionaire's Rolls-Royce.

After he leaves, the Flower Girl tells her Grandmother about her wealthy acquaintance. Interestingly, when being sober, The Millionaire does not recognize the Tramp and has the butler order him out. Later that day, The Millionaire meets the Tramp for the second time while intoxicated, and invites him home again for a lavish party. The next morning, the same thing happens that the Millionaire can't remember the Tramp. For a plan to leave for a cruise, the Millionaire again has the Tramp tossed out.

Deciding to find a job to earn money for helping the Flower Girl with her eye problem, he becomes a street sweeper. In the meantime, the Flower Girl and her Grandmother is noticed that they will be evicted if they cannot pay their back rent by the next day. The Tramp visits the girl, finds the eviction notice and tells the girl about the happening at her request. He reassures her that he will pay the rent. But due to his lateness back to work the Tramp is fired.

The Tramp is worried about earning money when he meets a boxer who persuades him to stage a fake fight, promising to split the $50 prize money. However, the boxer flees after he receives a warning that the police are looking for him, which leaves the Tramp a no-nonsense replacement opponent. With no doubt, the Tramp is knocked out despite a valiant effort,.

It is not long after he meets the drunken Millionaire who has just returned from Europe. On hearing the Flower Girl's plight, the Millionaire gives the Tramp $1,000. But out of their expectation, two burglars were hiding in the Millionaire's house when they entered. The burglars knock out the millionaire and take the rest of his money, and fortunately flee before the police's arrival. Consequently, the Tramp is accused of stealing the money, for the Millionaire cannot remember him, not to mention giving him the $1,000. The Tramp narrowly escapes to give the money to the girl and says he will be going away for a while. Finally, the Tramp is arrested and jailed.

Months later, the released Tramp returns to the girl's customary street corner with the purpose of searching for her, but in vain. He has not expected that the girl has opened up a flourishing flower shop with her Grandmother after she restores her sight. One more thing that he can't also expect is that the girl does not give up finding her mysterious benefactor. While retrieving a flower from the gutter outside the shop and decide to leave, he finds himself staring at the girl through the window. Seeing that he has crushed the flower he retrieved, the girl kindly offers him a fresh one and a coin. When the girl takes hold of his hand to place the coin in it, she recognizes the touch of his hand and realizes he is just the one she is looking for. "You?" she says, and he nods, asking, "You can see now?" She replies, sobbing, "Yes, I can see now." The Tramp smiles shyly at the girl as the film ends.

◎ Quotes

Scene 1

The Tramp: Be careful how you're driving.

Eccentric Millionaire: Am I driving?

Scene 2

The Tramp: You can see now?

A Blind Girl: Yes, I can see now

Scene 3

The Tramp: Tomorrow the birds will sing.

1.2 *Gone with the Wind*

Introduction

Gone with the Wind is a 1939 American epic historical romance film adapted from Margaret Mitchell's Pulitzer-winning 1936 novel and produced by David O. Selznick, of Selznick International Pictures. Set in the 19th-century American South, the film tells the story of Scarlett O'Hara, played by Vivien Leigh, and her romantic pursuit of Ashley Wilkes (Leslie Howard) who is married to his cousin, Melanie Hamilton (Olivia de Havilland), and her marriage to Rhett Butler (Clark Gable). Set against the backdrop of the American Civil War and Reconstruction era, the story is told from the perspective of white

Southerners.

The production of the film was troubled from the start. Filming was delayed for two years due to David O. Selznick's determination to secure Clark Gable for the role of Rhett Butler, and the "search for Scarlett" led to 1,400 women being interviewed for the part. The original screenplay was written by Sidney Howard, but underwent many revisions by several writers in an attempt to get it down to a suitable length. The original director, George Cukor, was fired shortly after filming had begun and was replaced by Victor Fleming, who in turn was briefly replaced by Sam Wood.

The film received good reviews upon its release in December 1939, although some reviewers found it dramatically lacking and bloated. The casting was widely praised and many reviewers found Vivien Leigh especially suited to her role as Scarlett. At the 12th Academy Awards held in 1940, it received ten Academy Awards (eight competitive, two honorary) from thirteen nominations, including wins for Best Picture, Best Director (Victor Fleming), Best Adapted Screenplay (posthumously awarded to Sidney Howard), Best Actress (Vivien Leigh) and Best Supporting Actress (Hattie McDaniel, becoming the first African-American to win an Academy Award). It set new records for the total number of wins and nominations at the time.

The film was immensely popular; becoming the highest-earning film made up to that point, and retained the record for over a quarter of a century. Adjusted for inflation, it is still the most successful film in box-office history.

The film has been criticized for its historical revisionism and glorification of slavery, but nevertheless it has been credited for triggering changes to the way African Americans are depicted on film. It was re-released periodically throughout the 20th century and became ingrained in popular culture. It has placed in the top ten of the American Film Institute's list of top 100 American films since the list's inception in 1998, and in 1989, *Gone with the Wind* was selected to be preserved by the National Film Registry.

Plot

Part 1

On the eve of the American Civil War in 1861, Scarlett O'Hara lives at Tara, her family's cotton plantation in Georgia, with her parents and two sisters. Scarlett learns that Ashley Wilkes—whom she secretly loves—is to be married to his cousin, Melanie Hamilton, and the engagement is to be announced the next day at a barbecue at Ashley's home, the nearby plantation Twelve Oaks.

At the Twelve Oaks party, Scarlett notices that she is being admired by Rhett Butler, who has been disowned by his family. Rhett finds himself in further disfavor among the male guests when, during a discussion of the probability of war, he states that the South has no chance against the superior numbers and industrial might of the North. Scarlett secretly confesses to Ashley that she loves him, but he rebuffs her by responding that he and the sweet Melanie are more compatible. Afterwards, Rhett reveals to Scarlett he has overheard their conversation, but promises to keep her secret.

The barbecue is disrupted by the declaration of war and the men rush to enlist. As Scarlett watches Ashley kiss Melanie goodbye from the upstairs window, Melanie's shy younger brother Charles asks for her hand in marriage before he goes. Though she does not love him, Scarlett consents, and they are married before he leaves to fight.

Scarlett is quickly widowed when Charles dies from a bout of pneumonia and measles while serving in the Confederate Army. Scarlett's mother sends her to the Hamilton home in Atlanta to cheer her up, although the O'Haras' outspoken housemaid Mammy tells Scarlett she knows she is going there only to wait for Ashley's return. Scarlett, who should not attend a party while in deep mourning, attends a charity bazaar in Atlanta with Melanie. There, Scarlett is the object of shocked comments on the part of the elderly women who represent proper Atlanta society.

Rhett, now a blockade runner for the Confederacy, makes a surprise appearance. To raise money for the Confederate war effort, gentlemen are invited to offer bids for ladies to dance with them. Rhett makes an inordinately large bid for Scarlett and, to the disapproval of the guests, Scarlett agrees to dance with him. As they dance, Rhett tells her he intends to win her, which she says will never happen.

The tide of war turns against the Confederacy after the Battle of Gettysburg in which many of the men of Scarlett's town are killed. Scarlett makes another unsuccessful appeal to Ashley while he is visiting on Christmas furlough, although they do share a private and passionate kiss in the parlor on Christmas Day, just before he returns to war.

Eight months later, as the city is besieged by the Union Army in the Atlanta Campaign, Melanie goes into premature and difficult labor. Keeping her promise to Ashley to take care of Melanie, Scarlett and her young house servant Prissy must deliver the child without medical assistance. Scarlett calls upon Rhett to bring her home to Tara immediately with Melanie, Prissy, and the baby. He appears with a horse and wagon and takes them out of the city through the burning depot and warehouse district. Instead of accompanying her all the way to Tara, he sends her on her way with a nearly dead horse, helplessly frail Melanie, her baby, and tearful Prissy, and with a passionate kiss as he goes off to fight.

On her journey home, Scarlett finds Twelve Oaks burned, ruined and deserted. She is relieved to find Tara still standing but deserted by all except her parents, her sisters, and two servants: Mammy and Pork. Scarlett learns that her mother has just died of typhoid fever and her father's mind has begun to fail under the strain. With Tara pillaged by Union troops and the fields untended, Scarlett vows she will do anything for the survival of her family and herself.

Part 2

Scarlett sets her family and servants to picking the cotton fields, facing many hardships along the way, including the killing of a Union deserter who attempts to rape her during a burglary. With the defeat of the Confederacy and war's end, Ashley returns, but finds he is of little help at Tara. When Scarlett begs him to run away with her, he confesses his desire for her and kisses her passionately, but says he cannot leave Melanie. Meanwhile, Scarlett's father dies after he is thrown from his horse in an attempt to chase away a scalawag from his property.

Scarlett realizes she cannot pay the rising taxes on Tara implemented by Reconstructionists, so pays a visit to Rhett in Atlanta. However, upon her visit, Rhett, now in jail, tells her his foreign bank accounts have been blocked, and that her attempt to get his money has been in vain. As Scarlett departs, she encounters her sister's fiancé, the middle-aged Frank Kennedy, who now owns a successful general store and lumber mill. Scarlett lies to Kennedy by saying Suellen got tired of waiting and married another beau, and after becoming Mrs. Frank Kennedy, Scarlett takes over his business and becomes wealthy. When Ashley is offered a job with a bank in the north, Scarlett uses emotional blackmail to persuade him to take over managing the mill.

Frank, Ashley, Rhett and several other accomplices make a night raid on a shanty town after Scarlett narrowly escapes an attempted gang rape while driving through it alone, resulting in Frank's death. With Frank's funeral barely over, Rhett visits Scarlett and proposes marriage, and she accepts. They have a daughter whom Rhett names Bonnie Blue, but Scarlett, still pining for Ashley and chagrined at the perceived ruin of her figure, lets Rhett know that she wants no more children and that they will no longer share a bed.

When visiting the mill one day, Scarlett and Ashley are spied in an embrace by two gossips, including Ashley's sister India, who dislikes Scarlett. They eagerly spread the rumor, and Scarlett's reputation is again sullied. Later that evening, Rhett, having heard the rumors, forces Scarlett to attend a birthday party for Ashley. Incapable of believing anything bad of her beloved sister-in-law, Melanie stands by Scarlett's side so that all know that she believes the gossip to be false. After returning home from the party, Scarlett finds Rhett downstairs drunk, and they argue. The argument leads to marital rape, which causes Rhett to return the following day to apologize for his behavior and offer a divorce, which Scarlett rejects saying it would be a disgrace.

Rhett takes Bonnie on an extended trip to London, but cuts the trip short after Bonnie suffers a terrible nightmare. On their return Scarlett is delighted to see him, but he rebuffs her attempts at reconciliation. She informs him that she is pregnant, but an argument ensues, and an enraged Scarlett lunges at Rhett resulting in her falling down the stairs and suffering a miscarriage. As Scarlett is recovering, Bonnie dies while attempting to jump a fence with her pony. Melanie visits their home to comfort them, but then collapses during a second pregnancy she was warned could kill her.

On her deathbed, Melanie asks Scarlett to look after Ashley for her, as Scarlett had looked after her for Ashley. With her dying breath, Melanie tells Scarlett to be kind to Rhett because he loves her. Outside, Ashley collapses in tears, forcing Scarlett to realize that Ashley only ever truly loved Melanie. Scarlett dashes home to find Rhett preparing to leave. She pleads with him, telling him she realizes now that she had loved him all along, and that she never really loved Ashley. However, he refuses; saying that with Bonnie's death went any chance of reconciliation. As Rhett is about to walk out the door, Scarlett begs him to stay but to no avail, and he walks away into the early morning fog leaving Scarlett weeping on the staircase and vowing to one day win back his love.

◎ Quotes

Scene 1

Scarlett: Rhett, Rhett... Rhett, if you go, where shall I go? What shall I do?

Rhett Butler: Frankly, my dear, I don't give a damn.

Scene 2

Scarlett: As God is my witness, as God is my witness they're not going to lick me. I'm going to live through this and when it's all over, I'll never be hungry again. No, nor any of my folk. If I have to lie, steal, cheat or kill. As God is my witness, I'll never be hungry again.

Scene 3

Scarlett: [pleads with Rhett as he is about to leave to join the Confederate Army] Oh, Rhett! Please, don't go! You can't leave me! Please! I'll never forgive you!

Rhett Butler: I'm not asking you to forgive me. I'll never understand or forgive myself. And if a bullet gets me, so help me, I'll laugh at myself for being an idiot. There's one thing I do know... and that is that I love you, Scarlett. In spite of you and me and the whole silly world going to pieces around us, I love you. Because we're alike. Bad lots, both of us. Selfish and shrewd. But able to look things in the eyes as we call them by their right names.

Scarlett: [struggles] Don't hold me like that!

Rhett Butler: [holds her tighter] Scarlett! Look at me! I've loved you more than I've ever loved any woman and I've waited for you longer than I've ever waited for any woman.

[kisses her forehead]

Scarlett: [turns her face away] Let me alone!

Rhett Butler: [forces her to look him in the eyes] Here's a soldier of the South who loves you, Scarlett. Wants to feel your arms around him, wants to carry the memory of your kisses into battle with him. Never mind about loving me, you're a woman sending a soldier to his death with a beautiful memory. Scarlett! Kiss me! Kiss me... once...

[he kisses her]

1.3 *Citizen Kane*

Introduction

Citizen Kane is a 1941 American mystery drama film which was Orson Welles's first feature film. It's co-written, produced, directed by Orson Welles and also stars him. Although nominated for Academy Awards in nine categories, it only won an Academy Award for Best Writing (Original Screenplay). *Citizen Kane* is widely accepted by critics, filmmakers, and fans as the greatest film and the most influential film of all time, and topped the 100 greatest movies voted by the

American Film Institute in 1998 and 2007 respectively. *Citizen Kane* has been acclaimed and considered innovative mainly for its cinematography, music, and narrative structure, and thus has set a precedent for the later film-making.

As a quasi-biographical film, *Citizen Kane* is inspired primarily by the American newspaper magnate William Randolph Hearst combined with aspects of Welles's own life, with its examining the life and legacy of Charles Foster Kane played by Welles. Kane's career in the publishing world is born of idealistic social service, but gradually evolves into a ruthless pursuit of power. *Citizen Kane* eschews the traditional linear, chronological narrative, and tells Kane's story entirely in flashback using different points of view, many of them from Kane's aged and forgetful associates. The most innovative technical aspect of *Citizen Kane* is the extended use of deep focus. *Citizen Kane* is viewed by film scholars and historians as Welles's attempt to create a new style of filmmaking by studying various forms of film making, and combining them all into one.

The Broadway successes of Welles's Mercury Theatre and the 1938 radio broadcast of "The War of the Worlds" caught the attention of Hollywood and he signed a contract with RKO Pictures in 1939. While making *Citizen Kane*, he was unusually given great freedom to develop his own story, to use his own cast and crew, and to have final cut privilege. *Citizen Kane* was a rare film in that its principal roles were played by actors new to motion pictures. In spite of a critical success, *Citizen Kane* failed to recoup its costs at the box office. After its release in 1941, the film faded from view but was subsequently returned to the public's attention when it was praised by French critics and given an American revival in 1956. The film was released on Blu-ray in 2011, for a special 70th anniversary edition.

Plot

It's 1941, in Florida, the elderly newspaper tycoon Charles Foster Kane dies after uttering the single word "Rosebud". A newsreel obituary tells the life story of Kane, an amazingly wealthy newspaper publisher who built a dying newspaper into a major empire, married and divorced twice, failed to run for governor and experienced the collapse of his newspaper empire during the Depression. Kane's death becomes sensational around the world, and the newsreel's producer assigns reporter Jerry Thompson to discover the meaning of Kane's last word and make sure of the essence of the controversial newspaperman.

Thompson sets out to interview Kane's friends and associates. He first approaches Kane's second wife, Susan Alexander Kane, now an alcoholic who runs her own nightclub, only to be refused. Then Thompson goes to the private archive of the late banker Walter Parks Thatcher from which Thompson learns that Kane's childhood began in poverty in Colorado.

In 1871, Kane's mother sends him away to live with Thatcher so that he would be properly educated. While Thatcher and Kane's parents discuss arrangements inside, the young Kane plays happily with a sled in the snow outside and protests being sent to live with Thatcher.

Years later, at the age of 25, after gaining full control over his trust fund, Kane enters the newspaper business and takes control of the *New York Inquirer* and starts publishing scandalous articles that attack Thatcher's business interests. After the stock market crash in 1929, Kane is forced to sell controlling interest of his newspaper empire to Thatcher.

Back in the present, Thompson continues his interviews with talking to Kane's personal business manager, Mr. Bernstein. Bernstein recalls how Kane hired the best journalists available to build the Inquirer's circulation. Kane rose to power by successfully manipulating public opinion regarding the Spanish-American War, together with marrying Emily Norton, his first wife, the niece of the President of the United States.

In a retirement home, Thompson talks with Kane's estranged best friend, Jedediah Leland who claims that Kane believed in nothing except himself, but suggests that Kane's story is about how he lost love because he had none to give. As Kane's empire expands, his marriage to Emily deteriorates. He begins an affair with amateur singer Susan Alexander while he is running for Governor of New York, which is discovered by both his wife and his political opponent. As a result, his political career is ended by the public scandal. Afterwards, Kane marries Susan and forces her into a humiliating operatic career for which she has neither the talent nor the ambition.

Back in the present, Susan now consents to an interview with Thompson, and recalls her failed opera career. Kane finally allows her to give up her singing career after she attempts to commit suicide. After years spent dominated by Kane and living in isolation, Susan leaves Kane. Kane's butler Raymond recounts that, after Susan's leaving, Kane begins violently destroying the contents of her bedroom. Then he suddenly calms down when he sees a snow globe and murmurs, "Rosebud".

Kane's belongings are being cataloged or discarded. Thompson concludes that he is unable to uncover the mystery and that the meaning of Kane's last word will forever remain an enigma. As the film ends, the camera reveals that "Rosebud" is the trade name of the sled on which the eight-year-old Kane was playing on the day that he was taken from his home in Colorado. Thought to be junk by Kane's staff, the sled is burned in a furnace.

◎ Quotes

Scene 1

Mr. Bernstein: A fellow will remember a lot of things you wouldn't think he'd remember. You take me. One day, back in 1896, I was crossing over to Jersey on the ferry, and as we pulled out, there was another ferry pulling in, and on it there was a girl waiting to get off. A white dress she had on. She was carrying a white parasol. I only saw her for one second. She didn't see me at all, but I'll bet a month hasn't gone by since that I haven't thought of that girl.

Scene 2

Charles Foster Kane: You know, Mr. Thatcher, if I hadn't been very rich, I might have been a really great man.

Walter Parks Thatcher: Don't you think you are?

Charles Foster Kane: I think I did pretty well under the circumstances.

Walter Parks Thatcher: What would you like to have been?

Charles Foster Kane: Everything you hate.

Scene 3

Charles Foster Kane: [to Thatcher] The trouble is, you don't realize you're talking to two people. As Charles Foster Kane, who has 82,634 shares of Public Transit Preferred. You see, I do have a general idea of my holdings. I sympathize with you. Charles Foster Kane is a scoundrel. His paper should be run out of town. A committee should be formed to boycott him. You may, if you can form such a committee, put me down for a contribution of $1,000 dollars. On the other hand, I am the publisher of the Inquirer! As such, it's my duty — and I'll let you in on a little secret, it's also my pleasure — to see to it that decent, hard-working people in this community aren't robbed blind by a pack of money-mad pirates just because — they haven't anybody to look after their interests.

1.4 *Casablanca*

Introduction

Casablanca is a 1942 American romantic drama film directed by Michael Curtiz and based on the unproduced stage play *Everybody Comes to Rick's* by Murray Burnett and Joan Alison. The film stars Humphrey Bogart, Ingrid Bergman, and Paul Henreid; and features Claude Rains, Conrad Veidt, Sydney Greenstreet, Peter Lorre, and Dooley Wilson. Set during World War II, it focuses on a man torn between, in the words of one character, "love and virtue". He must choose between his love for a woman and helping her Czech Resistance leader husband escape the Vichy-controlled Moroccan city of Casablanca to continue his fight against the Nazis.

Story editor Irene Diamond convinced producer Hal Wallis to purchase the film rights of the play in January 1942. Brothers Julius J. and Philip G. Epstein were initially assigned to write the script. However, despite studio resistance, they left after the attack on Pearl Harbor to work on *Frank Capra's Why We Fight* series. Howard Koch was assigned to the screenplay until the Epsteins returned. Casey Robinson assisted with three weeks of rewrites, but his work would later go uncredited. Wallis chose Curtiz to direct the film after his first choice, William Wyler, became unavailable. Filming began on May 25, 1942, and ended on August 3, and was shot entirely at Warner Bros. Studios in Burbank, and one sequence at Van Nuys Airport in Van Nuys.

Although *Casablanca* was an A-list film with established stars and first-rate writers, no one involved with its production expected it to be anything out of the ordinary. It was just one of hundreds of pictures produced by Hollywood every year. *Casablanca* had its world premiere on November 26, 1942 in New York City, and was released on January 23, 1943, in the United States. The film was a solid if unspectacular success in its initial run, rushed into release to take advantage of the publicity from the Allied invasion of North Africa a few weeks earlier.

Despite a changing assortment of screenwriters adapting an unproduced play, and Bogart attempting his first romantic leading role, *Casablanca* won three Academy Awards, including Best Picture. Its lead character, memorable lines, and pervasive theme song have all become iconic. The film has consistently ranked near the top of lists of the greatest films of all time.

Plot

It is early December 1941. American expatriate Rick Blaine is the proprietor of an upscale nightclub and gambling den in Casablanca. "Rick's Café Américain" attracts a varied clientele: Vichy French, Italian, and German officials; refugees desperate to reach the still neutral United States; and those who prey on them. Although Rick professes to be neutral in all matters, it is later revealed he ran guns to Ethiopia and fought on the Loyalist side in the Spanish Civil War.

Petty crook Ugarte shows up and boasts to Rick of "letters of transit" obtained by murdering two German couriers. The papers allow the bearer to travel freely around German-controlled Europe and to neutral Portugal, and are thus almost priceless to the refugees stranded in Casablanca. Ugarte plans to sell them at the club later that night. Before he can, however, he is arrested by the local police under the command of Vichy Captain Louis Renault, an unabashedly corrupt official. Ugarte dies in custody without revealing that he had entrusted the letters to Rick.

At this point, the reason for Rick's bitterness—his former lover, Norwegian Ilsa Lund—walks into his establishment. Upon spotting Rick's friend and house pianist, Sam, Ilsa asks him to play "As Time Goes By". Rick storms over, furious that Sam has disobeyed his order never to perform that song, and is stunned to see Ilsa. She is accompanied by her husband, Victor Laszlo, a renowned fugitive Czech Resistance leader. They need the letters to escape to America, where he can continue his work. German Major Strasser has come to Casablanca to see that Laszlo does not succeed.

When Laszlo makes inquiries, Ferrari, a major underworld figure and Rick's friendly business rival, divulges his suspicion that Rick has the letters. In private, Rick refuses to sell at any price, telling Laszlo to ask his wife the reason. They are interrupted when Strasser leads a group of officers in singing "Die Wacht am Rhein". Laszlo orders the house band to play "La Marseillaise". When the band looks to Rick, he nods his head. Laszlo starts singing, alone at first, then patriotic fervor grips the crowd and everyone join in, drowning out the Germans. In retaliation, Strasser has Renault close the club.

That night, Ilsa confronts Rick in the deserted café. When he refuses to give her the letters, she threatens him with a gun, but then confesses that she still loves him. She explains that when they first met and fell in love in Paris, she believed that her husband had been killed attempting to escape from a concentration camp. Later, while preparing to flee with Rick from the imminent fall of the city to the German army, she learned that Laszlo was alive and in hiding. She left Rick without explanation to tend her ill husband.

The lovers are reconciled. Rick agrees to help, leading her to believe that she will stay with him when Laszlo leaves. When Laszlo unexpectedly shows up, having narrowly escaped a police raid on a Resistance meeting, Rick has waiter Carl spirit Ilsa away.

Laszlo, aware of Rick's love for Ilsa, tries to persuade him to use the letters to take her to safety. When the police arrest Laszlo on a minor, trumped-up charge, Rick convinces Renault to release him by promising to set him up for a much more serious crime: possession of the letters of transit. To allay Renault's suspicions, Rick explains he and Ilsa will be leaving for America.

When Renault tries to arrest Laszlo as arranged, Rick forces him at gunpoint to assist in their escape. At the last moment, Rick makes Ilsa board the plane to Lisbon with her husband, telling her she would regret it if she stayed, "Maybe not today, maybe not tomorrow, but soon and for the rest of your life."

Strasser, tipped off by Renault, drives up alone. Rick kills him when he tries to intervene. When the police arrive, Renault pauses, and then tells them to "round up the usual suspects". Renault suggests to Rick that they join the Free French at Brazzaville as they walk away into the fog.

◎ Quotes

Scene 1

Yvonne: Where were you last night?

Rick: That's so long ago, I don't remember.

Yvonne: Will I see you tonight?

Rick: I never make plans that far ahead.

Scene 2

Rick: Last night we said a great many things. You said I was to do the thinking for both of us. Well, I've done a lot of it since then, and it all adds up to one thing: you're getting on that plane with Victor where you belong.

Ilsa: But, Richard, no, I... I...

Rick: Now, you've got to listen to me! You have any idea what you'd have to look forward to if you stayed here? Nine chances out of ten, we'd both wind up in a concentration camp. Isn't that true, Louie?

Captain Renault: I'm afraid Major Strasser would insist.

Ilsa: You're saying this only to make me go.

Rick: I'm saying it because it's true. Inside of us, we both know you belong with Victor. You're part of his work, the thing that keeps him going. If that plane leaves the ground and you're not with him, you'll regret it. Maybe not today. Maybe not tomorrow, but soon and for the rest of your life.

Ilsa: But what about us?

Rick: We'll always have Paris. We didn't have, we, we lost it until you came to Casablanca. We got it back last night.

Ilsa: When I said I would never leave you.

Rick: And you never will. But I've got a job to do, too. Where I'm going, you can't follow. What I've got to do, you can't be any part of. Ilsa, I'm no good at being noble, but it doesn't take much to see that the problems of three little people don't amount to a hill of beans in this crazy world. Someday you'll understand that.

[Ilsa lowers her head and begins to cry]

Rick: Now, now...

[Rick gently places his hand under her chin and raises it so their eyes meet]

Rick: Here's looking at you kid.

Scene 3

Rick: Of all the gin joints, in all the towns, in all the world, she walks into mine.

1.5 *Singin' in the Rain*

Introduction

Singin' in the Rain is a 1952 American musical comedy film directed by Gene Kelly and Stanley Donen, starring Gene Kelly, Donald O'Connor and Debbie Reynolds, and choreographed by Gene Kelly. It offers a lighthearted depiction of Hollywood, with the three stars portraying performers caught up in the transition from silent films to "talkies".

The film was only a modest hit when first released, with O'Connor's Best Actor win at the Golden Globes, Comden and Green's win at the Writers Guild of America Awards, and the best supporting actress Oscar nomination for Jean Hagen being the only major recognitions. However, it was accorded its legendary status by contemporary critics. It is now frequently described as one of the best musicals ever made, topping the AFI's 100 Years of Musicals list, and ranking fifth in its updated list of the greatest American films in 2007.

Plot

Don Lockwood is a popular silent film star with humble roots as a singer, dancer and stunt man. Don barely tolerates his vapid, shallow leading lady, Lina Lamont, though their studio, Monumental Pictures, links them romantically to increase their popularity. Lina herself is convinced they are in love, despite Don's protestations otherwise.

At the premiere of his newest film, The Royal Rascal, Don tells the gathered crowd an exaggerated version of his life story, including his motto, which is "Dignity. Always dignity". His words are humorously contradicted by flashbacks showing him taking on a wide range of menial and humiliating roles on stage and in film alongside his best friend Cosmo Brown.

To escape from his fans after the premiere, Don jumps into a passing car driven by Kathy Selden. She drops him off, but not before claiming to be a stage actress and sneering at his "undignified" accomplishments. Later, at a party, the head of Don's studio, R. F. Simpson, shows a short demonstration of a Vitaphone talking picture but his guests are unimpressed. To Don's amusement and Kathy's embarrassment, she pops out of a mock cake right in front of him as part of the entertainment; Kathy, it turns out, is a chorus girl. Furious at Don's teasing, she throws a real cake at him, only to hit Lina right in the face. Don is smitten with her, but she runs off into the night.

Don searches for her for weeks after discovering she was fired, believing himself to be responsible, but Lina tells him while filming a love scene that she made sure Kathy lost her job as an act of revenge and jealousy. Later, Don finds Kathy working in another Monumental Pictures production and they apologize to each other. She confesses to having been a fan of Don all along and they begin to fall in love.

After a rival studio has an enormous hit with its first talking picture, 1927's *The Jazz Singer*, R. F. decides he has no choice but to convert the next Lockwood and Lamont film, The Dueling Cavalier, into a talkie. The production is beset with difficulties in capturing sound, but by far the worst problem is Lina's grating voice. An exasperated diction coach tries to teach her how to speak properly, but to no avail. Don also takes diction lessons (albeit with much better results).

The Dueling Cavalier's test screening is a disaster; the actor's speaking is barely audible thanks to the awkward placing of the microphones, Don repeats the line "I love you" to Lina over and over, to the audience's derisive laughter, and in the middle of the film, the sound goes out of synchronization, with hilarious results.

After the premiere, Don, Kathy and Cosmo come up with the idea to turn *The Dueling Cavalier* into a musical called *The Dancing Cavalier*, complete with a modern musical number called "Broadway Melody". Don will be able to show off his natural singing and dancing talent, but are stumped when they must think about what to do with Lina. Cosmo, inspired by a scene in "The Dueling Cavalier" where Lina's voice was out-of-sync, suggests they dub Lina's voice with Kathy's.

They bring the idea to R. F., who goes ahead with it. When Lina finds out, she is infuriated. She becomes even angrier when she discovers that R. F. intends to give Kathy a screen credit and a big publicity promotion. Lina, after consulting lawyers, threatens to sue R. F. unless he cancels Kathy's buildup and orders her to continue working uncredited as Lina's voice. R. F. reluctantly agrees to her demands.

The premiere of *The Dancing Cavalier* is a tremendous success. When the audience clamors for Lina to sing live, Don, Cosmo, and R. F. improvise and get her to lip sync into the microphone while Kathy, hidden behind the stage curtain, sings into a second one. While Lina is "singing", Don, Cosmo and R. F. gleefully raise the curtain. When Cosmo replaces Kathy at the microphone, the sham becomes obvious. Lina flees in embarrassment. A distressed Kathy tries to run away as well, but not before Don proudly announces to the audience that she's "the real star of the film". The final shot shows Kathy and Don kissing in front of a billboard for their new film, *Singin' in the Rain*.

◎ Quotes

Scene 1

[Don Lockwood is being mobbed by several fans on the street]

Don Lockwood: [desperately] Hey, Cos! Do something! Call me a cab!

Cosmo Brown: OK, you're a cab.

Don Lockwood: [unimpressed] Thanks a lot!

Scene 2

Don Lockwood: [while filming a love scene] Why, you rattlesnake! You got that poor kid fired.

Lina Lamont: That's not all I'm gonna do if I ever get my hands on her.

Don Lockwood: I never heard of anything so low. Why did you do it?

Lina Lamont: Because you liked her. I could tell.

Don Lockwood: So that's it. Believe me, I don't like her half as much as I hate you, you reptile.

Lina Lamont: Sticks and stones may break my bones...

Don Lockwood: I'd like to break every bone in your body.

Lina Lamont: You and who else, you big lummox?

Scene 3

Don Lockwood: Now Lina, you've been reading all those fan magazines again! Now look Lina, you shouldn't believe all that banana oil Dora Bailey and the columnists dish out. Now try to get this straight: there is nothing between us. There has never been anything between us. Just air.

Lina: Oh, Donny, you don't mean that.

1.6 *Vertigo*

Introduction

Vertigo is a 1958 American film noir psychological thriller film directed and produced by Alfred Hitchcock, written by Alec Coppel and Samuel A. Taylor, and stars James Stewart as a private detective John "Scottie" Ferguson who is a former policeman forced into early retirement because of his acrophobia and vertigo, and is invited by his friend, Gavin Elster, to investigate Gavin's wife Madeleine played by Kim Novak.

The filming began on location in San Francisco in September 1957. In the film, the dolly zoom, an in-camera effect that distorts perspective to create disorientation, is popularized for the first time to convey Scottie's acrophobia, which results in an effect called "the Vertigo effect".

Although the film received mixed comments after initial release, it is currently recognized as a classic and typical Hitchcock film which attracts significant scholarly criticism. In 2012, it was voted as the best film ever made in the British Film Institute's Sight & Sound critics' poll. What's more, it is often placed among the greatest films in various lists, including a 2007 ranking as the ninth-greatest American film of all time.

Plot

John "Scottie" Ferguson, now a detective in San Francisco, is forced into early retirement because his acrophobia and vertigo bring about the death of a policeman.

Scottie is invited by an acquaintance Gavin Elster to follow his wife Madeleine, for Gavin claims that she is in some sort of danger. Scottie finally agrees in spite of his initial reluctance, and follows Madeleine to several places including an art museum where she gazes at the Portrait of Carlotta who is Madeleine's great-grandmother. However, Madeleine herself doesn't know it and can't remember the places she has visited. Afterwards, she is rescued by Scottie when she leaps into water in a bay.

The following day Scottie meets Madeleine and spends the day with her during which Madeleine recounts a nightmare and Scottie identifies its setting as the childhood home of Carlotta. Then they arrive there and express their love for each other. Unexpectedly, Madeleine runs into a church and up the bell tower. Scottie doesn't follow her due to his acrophobia and witnesses Madeleine plunge to her death.

Madeleine's death is declared a suicide, which results in Scottie's depression and entry into a sanatorium, almost catatonic. After release, Scottie frequently pays visits to the places that Madeleine used to visit with fancying seeing her again. One day, he comes across Judy Barton, a woman who reminds him of Madeleine in spite of her different appearance.

In fact, Judy was "Madeleine Elster" whom Scottie met and loved, for she was required to disguise Gavin's wife as part of Gavin's murder plot. In other words, Gavin had deliberately taken advantage of Scottie's acrophobia to substitute his wife's freshly killed body in the apparent "suicide jump". In a drafted letter to Scottie Judy wants to tell Scottie the truth, but she rips up the letter and continues the charade on account of her love for Scottie.

Scottie, still obsessed with "Madeleine", makes appointments with Judy and insists that Judy should dress like "Madeleine". Scottie is deeply convinced that they finally find happiness together. But then, he is shocked by the necklace Judy wears as it was portrayed in the painting of

Carlotta. Scottie comes to know the truth, and the fact that Judy had been Elster's mistress.

At the church where "Madeleine" committed her suicide, Scottie forces Judy up the bell tower and makes her admit her deceit. In order to relive the event, Scottie conquers his acrophobia by reaching the top. In the end, Scottie figures out Judy's role in Gavin's plot and the fake suicide by Gavin's throwing the body of his wife from the bell tower. Scottie embraces Judy after her begging for forgiveness when she is startled by a shadowed figure rises from the trapdoor of the tower, and she subconsciously steps backward and falls to her death.

◎ Quotes

Scene 1

Madeleine: Only one is a wanderer; two together are always going somewhere.

Scene 2

Scottie: I love you, Madeleine.

Madeleine: I love you, too. It's too late.

Scottie: No, no, we're together.

Madeleine: It's too late. There's something I must do...

Scottie: [kisses her passionately] No, there is nothing you must do. There is nothing you must do. No one possesses you. You're safe with me.

Madeleine: [frantically] No, it's too late.

[Madeleine breaks free and runs across the courtyard. Scottie trails behind her, eventually catching up to her. He holds her tightly]

Madeleine: Look, it's not fair. It's too late. It wasn't supposed to happen this way. It shouldn't have happened...

Scottie: But it had to happen. We're in love. That's all that counts!

Madeleine: [struggling] Look. Let me go! Please let me go!

Scottie: Listen to me. Listen to me.

Madeleine: [calmly] You believe I love you?

Scottie: Yes.

Madeleine: And if you lose me, then you'll know I, I loved you. And I wanted to go on loving you.

Scottie: I won't lose you.

Madeleine: Let me go into the church — alone.

Scottie: Why?

[they kiss for the last time. Scottie releases his grip and Madeleine walks away towards the bell tower.]

Scene 3

Scottie: And then what did he do? Did he train you? Did he rehearse you? Did he tell you exactly what to do, what to say? You were a very apt pupil too, weren't you? You were a very apt pupil!

Well, why did you pick on me? Why me?

1.7 *The Godfather*

Introduction

The Godfather is a 1972 American crime film directed by Francis Ford Coppola and produced by Albert S. Ruddy from a screenplay by Mario Puzo and Coppola. Based on Puzo's 1969 novel of the same name, the film stars Marlon Brando and Al Pacino played as the leaders of a fictional New York crime family. The story, spanning the years 1945 to 1955, centers on the transformation of Michael Corleone from reluctant family outsider to ruthless Mafia boss while also chronicling the family under the patriarch Vito Corleone.

The Godfather is widely regarded as one of the greatest films in world cinema—and as one of the most influential, especially in the gangster genre. Now ranked as the second greatest film in American cinema (behind *Citizen Kane*) by the American Film Institute, it was selected for preservation in the United States National Film Registry in 1990.

The film was for a time the highest grossing picture ever made, and remains the box-office leader for 1972. It won three Oscars that year: for Best Picture, for Best Actor (Brando) and in the category Best Adapted Screenplay for Puzo and Coppola. Its nominations in seven other categories included Pacino, James Caan and Robert Duvall for Best Supporting Actor and Coppola for Best Director. The success spawned two sequels: *The Godfather Part II* in 1974 and *The Godfather Part III* in 1990.

Plot

On the day of his only daughter's wedding, Vito Corleone hears requests in his role as the Godfather, the Don of a New York crime family. Vito's youngest son, Michael, in a Marine Corps uniform, introduces his girlfriend, Kay Adams, to his family at the sprawling reception. Vito's godson Johnny Fontane, a popular singer, pleads for help in securing a coveted movie role, so Vito dispatches his consigliere, Tom Hagen, to the abrasive studio head, Jack Woltz, to secure the casting. Woltz is unmoved until the morning he wakes up in bed with the severed head of his prized stallion.

Shortly before Christmas 1945, drug baron Virgil "The Turk" Sollozzo, backed by the Corleones' rivals, the Tattaglias, asks Vito for investment in the emerging drug trade and protection through his political connections. Vito disapproves of drug dealers, so he sends his enforcer, Luca Brasi, to spy on them. The family then receives two fish wrapped in Brasi's vest, imparting that he "sleeps with the fishes".

An assassination attempt by Sollozzo's men lands Vito in the hospital, so his eldest son, Sonny, takes command. Sollozzo kidnaps Hagen to pressure Sonny to accept his deal. Michael thwarts a second assassination attempt on his father at the hospital, but is accosted by corrupt police captain McCluskey, who breaks his jaw; Sonny retaliates by having Tattaglia's son killed. Michael comes up with a plan to hit Sollozzo and McCluskey that his brother approves over Hagen's objections: on the pretext of settling the dispute, Michael lures the pair to a restaurant, retrieves a planted handgun and murders them.

Despite a clampdown from the authorities, the Five Families erupt in open warfare and the brothers' fear for their safety. Michael takes refuge in Sicily, and Fredo Corleone is sheltered by associate Moe Greene in Las Vegas. Sonny attacks his brother-in-law Carlo on the street for abusing his sister Connie. When it happens again, Sonny speeds for her home but assassins ambush him at a highway toll booth and riddle him with submachine gun fire. Michael's time abroad has led to marriage to Apollonia Vitelli. Their euphoria is shattered when a car bomb intended for him takes her life.

Vito, saddened to learn that, despite his hopes, Michael has become involved in the family business, decides to end the feuds. Believing that the Tattaglias were under orders of the now dominant Don Emilio Barzini, he promises, before the heads of the Five Families, to withdraw his opposition to their heroin business and forgo revenge for Sonny's murder. His safety guaranteed, Michael returns home and over a year later marries Kay.

With his father at the end of his career and his surviving brother too weak, Michael takes the reins of the family, promising his wife to make the business legitimate within five years. He allows rival families to pressure Corleone enterprises even as he plans to move family operations to Nevada and delegates New York business to members who stay behind. Hagen, upset when Michael replaces him with Vito, is mollified by the older man's reassurance about their long-range plans for him. When Michael travels to Las Vegas to buy out Greene's stake in the family's casinos, Greene derides the Corleones as a fading power. To add injury to insult, Michael sees Fredo falling under Greene's sway.

Vito collapses and dies in his garden while playing with Michael's son, Anthony. At the funeral, caporegime Salvatore Tessio arranges a meeting between Michael and Don Barzini, signalling his treachery as Vito had warned. The meeting is set for the same day as the christening of Connie's son, to whom Michael will stand as godfather. As the christening proceeds, Corleone assassins, acting on Michael's orders, murder the other New York dons and Moe Greene. Tessio is told that Michael is aware of his betrayal and taken off to his death.

After Carlo is questioned by Michael on his involvement in setting up Sonny's murder and confesses he was contacted by Barzini, caporegime Peter Clemenza kills him with a wire garrote. Michael is confronted by Connie, who accuses him of having her husband killed. He denies killing Carlo when questioned by Kay, an answer she accepts. As Kay watches warily, Michael receives his capos, who address him as the new Don Corleone.

◎ Quotes

Scene 1

Johnny Fontane: [discussing his problems] I don't know what to do, Godfather. My voice is weak, it's weak. Anyway, if I had this part in the picture, it puts me right back on top, you know. But this... this man out there. He won't give it to me, the head of the studio.

Don Corleone: What's his name?

Don Corleone: Woltz. He said there's no chance, no chance...

[Meanwhile, Hagen finds Sonny and summons him]

Johnny Fontane: A month ago he bought the rights to this book, a best seller. The main character is a guy just like me. I wouldn't even have to act, just be myself. Oh, Godfather, I don't know what to do, I don't know what to do...

[All of a sudden, Don Corleone rises from his chair and gives Fontane a savage shake]

Don Corleone: YOU CAN ACT LIKE A MAN!

[gives a quick slap to Fontane]

Don Corleone: What's the matter with you? Is this what you've become, a Hollywood finocchio who cries like a woman? "Oh, what do I do? What do I do?" What is that nonsense? Ridiculous!

[The Don's unexpected mimicry makes Hagen and even Fontane laugh; around this time Sonny comes in]

Don Corleone: Tell me, do you spend time with your family?

Johnny Fontane: Sure I do.

Don Corleone: Good. Because a man who doesn't spend time with his family can never be a real man.

[gives a quick look at Sonny and affectionately embraces Fontane]

Don Corleone: You look terrible. I want you to eat, I want you to rest well. And a month from now this Hollywood big shot's gonna give you what you want.

Johnny Fontane: Too late. They start shooting in a week.

Don Corleone: I'm gonna make him an offer he can't refuse. Okay? I want you to leave it all to me. Go on, go back to the party.

[a gratified Fontane leaves]

Scene 2

Michael: My father is no different than any powerful man, any man with power, like a president or senator.

Kay Adams: Do you know how naive you sound, Michael? Presidents and senators don't have men killed.

Michael: Oh. Who's being naive, Kay?

Scene 3

Don Corleone: I hope you don't mind the way I keep going over this Barzini business.

Michael: No, not at all.

Don Corleone: It's an old habit. I spent my whole life trying not to be careless. Women and children can afford to be careless, but not men.

1.8 *Star Wars*

Introduction

Star Wars, later retitled *Star Wars Episode IV*: *A New Hope*, written and directed by George Lucas, is a 1977 American epic space opera film which is the first film in the original *Star Wars* trilogy, the first *Star Wars* film in general, and the beginning of the *Star Wars* franchise, starring Mark Hamill, Harrison Ford, Carrie Fisher, and others.

The story centers on the Rebel Alliance's efforts to fight against the Galactic Empire and destroy its space station, the Death Star. In 1975, Lucas formed his own visual effects company Industrial Light & Magic (ILM) which began its work on *Star Wars* in a warehouse in Van Nuys, California. Most of the visual effects used pioneering digital motion control photography was employed in most of the visual effects through creating the illusion of size by using small models and slowly moving cameras.

Released in theatres in the United States on May 25, 1977, it earned $775 million totally, including $314 million overseas, and surpassed *Jaws* (1975) to become the highest-grossing film of all time, but the record doesn't remain due to the release of *E. T.*: *the Extra-Terrestrial* (1982). Considering inflation, *Star Wars* is actually the second-highest-grossing film in North America, and the third-highest-grossing film in the world.

Apart from a huge commercial success, it was a big winner at the 50th Academy Awards, receiving seven among ten nominations, along with one Golden Globe award and two British Academy Film Awards. Selected as part of the U. S. Library of Congress' National Film Registry because of its cultural, historical, and aesthetical significance, the film is often viewed as one of the best films of all time, and one of the most important films in the history of cinema. It launched an industry of tie-in products, including TV series spinoffs, novels, comic books, and video games, and merchandise including toys, games and clothing.

The film is followed by two critically and commercially successful sequels, *The Empire Strikes Back* in 1980 and *Return of the Jedi* in 1983. In addition, there are three prequels *The Phantom Menace* in 1999, *Attack of the Clones* in 2002, and *Revenge of the Sith* in 2005, which makes a prequel trilogy. It's reported a sequel trilogy beginning with *The Force Awakens* in 2015 has been planned and the film's fourth sequel *The Last Jedi* will be released in December 2017. In fact, a direct prequel, *Rogue One* was released in 2016.

Plot

A civil war opens in the galaxy. The architectural plans for the Galactic Empire's Death Star, a heavily armed space station capable of destroying an entire planet, have been stolen. Princess Leia, the leader of the Rebel Alliance, who has the plans, is captured by Imperial Forces under the command of the evil Darth Vader. But the plans have been hidden in the memory of an astromech droid, R2-D2 which flees to the surface of the desert planet Tatooine with C-3PO, a protocol droid.

The droids are captured and sold to the farmhand Luke Skywalker who accidentally triggers part of Leia's message of requiring help from Obi-Wan Kenobi. The next morning, Luke meets Ben Kenobi, an old hermit who lives in the hills and reveals himself to be Obi-Wan. Obi-Wan tells Luke of his days as one of the Jedi Knights, former Galactic Republic peacekeepers, and the fact that Vader was his former pupil who turned to the dark side of the Force and killed Luke's father. Obi-Wan then presents to Luke his father's weapon — a lightsaber.

In Leia's complete message, she believes that the Death Star plans should be taken to her home planet of Alderaan and given to her father for analysis. Obi-Wan and Luke make up their minds to go to Alderaan and learn the ways of the Force. They hire smuggler Han Solo to transport them to Alderaan on Han's ship, the Millennium Falcon. Upon arrival, the group discovers that the planet has been destroyed by order of the Death Star's commanding officer, Grand Moff Tarkin, who shows off his power. The Falcon is captured by the Death Star's tractor beam and brought into its hangar bay.

Obi-Wan then goes to disable the tractor beam when Luke finds that Leia is imprisoned aboard, and rescues her. After several escapes, the group fights its way back to the Falcon. Eventually, Obi-Wan makes it in disabling the tractor beam. On the way back to the Falcon, he engages in a lightsaber duel with Vader, and he is sure of the others' escape before he is killed. The Falcon escapes from the Death Star without the knowledge of carrying a tracking beacon used by the Empire to follow to the Rebels' hidden base on Yavin IV.

Luke joins the Rebel assault squadron, while Han has the intension to be away after collecting his payment for the transport. In the ensuing battle, after several unsuccessful attack runs, the Rebels suffer heavy losses and Luke was one of the few surviving pilots. Vader leads a squadron of TIE fighters and prepares to attack Luke's X-wing fighter, but Han returns and fires at the Imperials, sending Vader spiraling away. Encouraged by Obi-Wan's spirit, Luke uses the Force and succeeds in destroying the Death Star seconds before it can fire on the Rebel base. Back on Yavin IV, Luke and Han are awarded with medals for their heroism.

◎ Quotes

Scene 1

Princess Leia Organa: It's not over yet.

Han Solo: It is for me, sister. Look, I ain't in this for your revolution, and I'm not in it for you, Princess. I expect to be well paid. I'm in it for the money.

Princess Leia Organa: You needn't worry about your reward. If money is all that you love, then that's what you'll receive.

[to Luke]

Princess Leia Organa: Your friend is quite the mercenary. I wonder if he really cares about anything. Or anybody.

[she stalks out]

Luke Skywalker: [calling after her] I care.

[to Han]

Luke Skywalker: So, what do you think of her, Han?

Han Solo: I'm tryin' not to, kid.

Luke Skywalker: Good.

Han Solo: [baiting him] Still, she's got a lot of spirit. I don't know, whaddya think? You think a princess and a guy like me...

Luke Skywalker: [quickly] No.

Scene 2

[Han answers the intercom after commandeering an attack station]

Han Solo: [sounding official] Uh, everything's under control. Situation normal.

Voice: What happened?

Han Solo: [getting nervous] Uh, we had a slight weapons malfunction, but uh... everything's perfectly all right now. We're fine. We're all fine here now, thank you. How are you?

Voice: We're sending a squad up.

Han Solo: Uh, uh... negative, negative. We had a reactor leak here now. Give us a few minutes to lock it down. Large leak, very dangerous.

Voice: Who is this? What's your operating number?

Han Solo: Uh...

[Han shoots the intercom]

Han Solo: [muttering] Boring conversation anyway. LUKE, WE'RE GONNA HAVE COMPANY!

Scene 3

Stormtrooper: Let me see your identification.

Ben Obi-Wan Kenobi: [with a small wave of his hand] You don't need to see his identification.

Stormtrooper: We don't need to see his identification.

Ben Obi-Wan Kenobi: These aren't the droids you're looking for.

Stormtrooper: These aren't the droids we're looking for.

Ben Obi-Wan Kenobi: He can go about his business.

Stormtrooper: You can go about your business.

Ben Obi-Wan Kenobi: Move along.
Stormtrooper: Move along... move along.

1.9 *Raging Bull*

Introduction

Raging Bull is a 1980 American biographical black-and-white sports drama film directed by Martin Scorsese, and adapted from Jake LaMotta's memoir *Raging Bull: My Story*. It stars Robert De Niro as Jake LaMotta, an Italian American middleweight boxer who was destroyed by his self-destructive and obsessive rage, sexual jealousy, and animalistic appetite along with his relationship with his wife and family. There are other two figures in the story who has great importance in Jake's life and career: Joey, Jake's well-intentioned brother and manager who tries to help Jake battle his inner demons, and his wife Vickie.

De Niro became fascinated by the character of Jake LaMotta after he read the autobiography upon which the film is based, though he was unsatisfied with the book's writing style, and then introduced the book to Martin Scorsese in the hope that he would consider the project.

Scorsese repeatedly turned down the opportunity to sit in the director's chair, claiming he had no idea what *Raging Bull* was about, but after nearly dying from a drug overdose, Scorsese agreed to make the film, to save both his own life and his career. He and De Niro together made uncredited contributions to the screenplay thereafter

The film began shooting at the Los Angeles Olympic Auditorium in April 1979. During the filming, each of the boxing scenes was choreographed for a specific visual style. It's worth mentioning that De Niro gained approximately 60 pounds to portray LaMotta in his later post-boxing years.

In spite of receiving mixed initial reviews (and criticism focused on its violent content), it gained a high critical reputation, and is now often considered Scorsese's magnum opus and one of the greatest films ever made. In 1990, it became the first film to be selected for preservation in the National Film Registry in its first year of eligibility. When it comes to awards, it was nominated for eight Academy Awards in 1981 and won two: Best Actor, for De Niro, and Best Film Editing. By the end of the 1980s, *Raging Bull* had been regarded as a modern classic with its positive reputation. Up to now, *Raging Bull* has been voted one of the best films of all time in numerous critics' polls.

Plot

The film begins with the scene in 1964 where an aging and overweight Jake LaMotta practices his stand-up comic routine before his debut at a comedy nightclub.

A flashback brings audiences back to his boxing career in 1941 against his opponent in the infamous Cleveland bout. Jake's brother, Joey LaMotta, discusses a potential shot for the middleweight title with one of his Mafia connections, Salvy Batts. Some time later, even though he is already married, after meeting a fifteen-year-old girl named Vickie at an open-air swimming pool in his neighborhood, he makes a final decision to develop a relationship with her.

In 1943, Jake defeats Sugar Ray Robinson, and has a rematch three weeks later. With the ignorance of Jake's dominating Robinson during the bout, the judges surprisingly rule in favor of Robinson. Joey believes Robinson's victory only lies in his enlistment into the Army the following week.

In 1945, Jake marries Vickie. However, Jake is constantly afraid that Vickie has feelings for other men. Jake shows evident jealousy in front of his opponent, the local Mob boss, Tommy Como, and Vickie. Joey accidentally notices that Vickie approaches a table with Salvy and his crew and he has a word with Vickie who claims she is giving up on his brother. Como later has Joey tell Jake that if he wants a chance at the championship title, which Como controls, he will have to take a dive first.

In a match, after briefly pummeling his opponent, Jake does not even bother to put up a fight, for which he is suspended shortly after from the board on suspicion of throwing the fight. But Jake is not affected by the incident in his career and eventually in 1949, wins the middleweight championship title.

Later, when Jake asks Joey if he had an affair with his wife, Joey refuses to answer, insults Jake, and leaves. Jake has no choice but to directly asks Vickie about the affair, only to prompt her to sarcastically state that she had sex with the entire neighborhood (including his brother, Salvy, and Tommy Como). Jake angrily walks to Joey's house, with Vickie following him, and assaults Joey in front of his wife and children.

In 1950, Jake defends his championship belt in a grueling fifteen-round bout, then he makes a call to his brother after the fight, which is useless in mending fences between them. Estranged from Joey, Jake encounters a slow decline in his career and is destined to lose his title to Sugar Ray Robinson in their final fight in 1951.

By 1956, Jake and his family have moved to Miami. Jakes messes up in his life, for he stays out all night at his new nightclub. As a consequence, Vickie proposes a divorce together with full custody of their kids. She also warns that Jake should not be anywhere near them otherwise she would call the police.

Misfortunes never come singly. Jake is later arrested for introducing under-age girls to men in his club. He tries to bribe his way out of his criminal case by using the jewels from his championship belt instead of selling the belt itself, but fails and in 1957, ends up in jail, sorrowfully questioning his misfortune and crying in despair. In 1958, back in New York City, Jake comes across his estranged brother Joey who forgives Jake but with his elusiveness.

Going back to the opening in 1964, Jake refers to the "I coulda' have been a contender" scene from the 1954 film *On the Waterfront* complaining that his brother should have been there for him but is also keen enough to give himself some slack. After being informed of the crowded auditorium where he is about to perform, Jake starts to chant "I'm the boss" while shadowboxing.

◎ Quotes

Scene 1

Jake La Motta: Is it done?

Irma: No, it's not done.

Jake La Motta: Don't overcook it. You overcook it, it's no good. It defeats its own purpose.

[Irma gives Jake a stern but nasty look]

Jake La Motta: What are you doin'? I just said don't overcook it. You're overcookin'it, bring it over.

Irma: You want your steak?

Jake La Motta: Bring it over. Bring it over! It's like a piece of charcoal! Bring it over here!

Irma: You want your steak?

Jake La Motta: YEAH, RIGHT NOW!

[Irma stabs the steak, exits the stove and slams the steak on his plate. She hastily pours carrots on the plate]

Irma: Okay. There's your stupid steak. Can't wait for it to be done?

Jake La Motta: No, I can't wait.

Irma: Good! Okay? Happy? Happy?

Jake La Motta: That's all I want. That's all I want!

Irma: That's... there! No, more! There!

[Jake routinely flips the table, spilling the contents all over the floor]

Jake La Motta: Bodder me abott a steak? Huh?

Irma: That's GREAT!

Jake La Motta: YOU BODDA ME ABOTT A STEAK?

Irma: YEAH!

Scene 2

Jake La Motta: Don't give me that look, Joey. I gotta accept your answer, you know? But If I hear anything, I swear on our mother I'm gonna kill somebody. I'm gonna kill somebody, Joey.

Joey LaMotta: [angrily] Well go ahead and kill if you're a tough guy, go kill people! Kill Vicki, kill Salvy, kill Tommy Como, kill me while you're at it, what do I care? You kill yourself, the way you eat! Ya fat fuck, look at you!

Jake La Motta: What do you mean — I don't understand, kill you?

Joey LaMotta: Me! Kill me, start here! Do me a fuckin' favor! Cause you're driving me crazy! You're a killer, you're a big shot, just kill. You're a killer.

Scene 3

[Sugar Ray Robinson has just battered Jake La Motta half to death, but Jake has stayed on his feet]

Jake La Motta: You didn't get me down, Ray.

1.10 *Schindler's List*

Introduction

Schindler's List, a 1993 American epic historical drama film, based on the novel *Schindler's Ark* by Australian novelist Thomas Keneally, is directed and co-produced by Steven Spielberg and scripted by Steven Zaillian. The film focuses on the hero, a German businessman, Oskar Schindler who at huge risk saved the lives of more than a thousand refugees, mostly Polish Jews during World War II. It explores the theme of good versus evil, with a "good German" Oskar Schindler symbolizing justice and nobility, a popular characterization in American cinema. The film stars Liam Neeson as Schindler, and Ralph Fiennes, Ben Kingsley.

The filming about Schindler Jews first appeared in early 1960s. Spielberg became interested in the story after reading a book review of *Schindler's Ark*, but he was not sure that he had been ready for making such a film and tried to pass the project to several other directors. Finally he made the decision to direct the film himself. As a Jew, Spielberg felt shooting *Schindler's List* was deeply emotional for him, for he was forced to confront elements of his childhood, such as the antisemitism he faced. Spielberg also commented that he felt more like a journalist than a film maker, for he just set up scenes and then watched events unfolding.

In 1993, in Kraków, Poland, the crew shot at or near the actual locations during a period of 72 days. Shooting the film in black and white contributes to the documentary style of cinematography with a sense of timelessness.

Undoubtedly, *Schindler's List* is a great success in commercial sense, earning $321.2 million worldwide on a $22 million budget. When it comes to reviews, the film is highly praised and always voted among the greatest films ever made. It received seven Academy Awards out of twelve nominations, including Best Picture, Best Director, Best Adapted Screenplay, and Best Original Score, as well as numerous other awards including seven BAFTAs and three Golden Globes. In 2007, the film was ranked the 8th on the list of the 100 best American films of all time by the American Film Institute. It is also selected for preservation in the National Film Registry by the Library of Congress in 2004.

Plot

Shortly after the outbreak of World War II, the German Army defeats the Polish Army in three weeks which leads to the relocation of Polish Jews from surrounding areas to Krakow in late 1939. Oskar Schindler, a successful businessman, an opportunistic member of the Nazi party, hopes to use the abundant cheap labor force of Jews to manufacture enamelware for the German military. By lavishing bribes upon the military and then sponsored by the military, Schindler acquires a factory for the production of army mess kits and cooking paraphernalia.

On the one hand, Schindler runs the factory with the help of Itzhak Stern, a functionary in the local Jewish Council who has contacts with the now-underground Jewish business community in the ghetto. On the other hand, he pleases the Nazis and enjoys his new-found wealth and status. For saving cost, Schindler hires Jews instead of Poles and the workers in Schindler's factory are allowed outside the ghetto. In order to save as many workers as possible from being transported to concentration camps or even being killed, Stern falsifies documents to ensure that the workers are deemed essential by the Nazi bureaucracy.

Amon Göth arrives in Krakow to initiate construction of a labor camp nearby Paszów. Soon hundreds of German troops are sent to empty the cramped rooms and shoot anyone who is not cooperative, or for no reason at all. Schindler is profoundly affected after watching the massacre, but he has to be more careful to befriend Göth and thus continues to enjoy the German support and protection. The camp is built outside the city at Paszów. Afterwards, Schindler bribes Göth into allowing him to build a sub-camp for his workers, with the purpose of keeping them safe from the depredations of the guards.

Eventually, Göth receives the order from Berlin dismantle Paszów together with shipping the remaining Jews to Auschwitz. On hearing the news, Schindler prevails upon Göth to let him keep "his" workers so that he can move them to a factory in his old home, which results in Göth's charging a certain amount for each worker. Schindler and Stern make a list of workers that should keep them off the trains to Auschwitz. "Schindler's List" comprises so-called "skilled" inmates, and it means the gulf between life and death for those who are included in the list.

All of the men on Schindler's list arrive safely at the new site, but accidentally the women and the children are redirected to Auschwitz where they have to suffer from harrowing experience. The next day, Schindler rushes immediately to Auschwitz to get the women out of Auschwitz. He bribes the camp commander with a cache of diamonds so that he is able to spare all the women and the children.

For protecting Schindler women, Schindler institutes firm controls on the Nazi guards assigned to the factory. In the meantime, he has to spend much of his fortune acquired in Poland bribing Nazi officials. Finally he runs out of money just as the German army surrenders, ending the war in Europe.

As a German Nazi and self-described profiteer, Schindler must flee the oncoming Soviet Red Army. He packs a car in the night, and bids farewell to his workers who give him a letter explaining he is not a criminal to them, along with a ring engraved with the Talmudic quotation, "He who saves the life of one man, saves the world entire." Schindler is deeply moved with the sense of guilty, feeling he could've done more to save many more lives. He leaves with his wife during the night, dressed in Polish prisoner clothes and disguised as refugees. Afterwards, the Schindler Jews are announced to be liberated by the Red Army.

The film ends with a procession of new-aged Jews who worked in Schindler's factory, each of whom reverently sets a stone on his grave. The actors walk hand-in-hand also place stones on Schindler's grave to show their great respect to Schindler. It's been reported that the survivors and descendants of the approximately 1,100 Schindler Jews now grow into the number of over 6,000.

◎ Quotes

Scene 1

Oskar Schindler: Power is when we have every justification to kill, and we don't.

Amon Goeth: You think that's power?

Oskar Schindler: That's what the Emperor said. A man steals something, he's brought in before the Emperor, he throws himself down on the ground. He begs for his life, he knows he's going to die. And the Emperor... pardons him. This worthless man, he lets him go.

Amon Goeth: I think you are drunk.

Oskar Schindler: That's power, Amon. That is power.

Scene 2

Oskar Schindler: I could have got more out. I could have got more. I don't know. If I'd just... I could have got more.

Itzhak Stern: Oskar, there are eleven hundred people who are alive because of you. Look at them.

Oskar Schindler: If I'd made more money... I threw away so much money. You have no idea. If I'd just...

Itzhak Stern: There will be generations because of what you did.

Oskar Schindler: I didn't do enough!

Itzhak Stern: You did so much.

[Schindler looks at his car]

Oskar Schindler: This car. Goeth would have bought this car. Why did I keep the car? Ten people right there. Ten people. Ten more people.

[removing Nazi pin from lapel]

Oskar Schindler: This pin. Two people. This is gold. Two more people. He would have given me two for it, at least one. One more person. A person, Stern. For this.

[sobbing]

Oskar Schindler: I could have gotten one more person... and I didn't! And I... I didn't!

Scene 3

Oskar Schindler: In every business I tried, I can see now, it wasn't me that failed. Something was missing. Even if I'd known what it was, there's nothing I could have done about it because you can't create this thing. And it makes all the difference in the world between success and failure.

Emilie Schindler: Luck?

Oskar Schindler: [Schindler kisses his wife's hand and smiles] War.

1.11 *The Lion King*

Introduction

The Lion King is a 1994 American animated epic musical film produced by Walt Disney Feature Animation and released by Walt Disney Pictures. In fact, *The Lion King*, which was conceived in late 1988, was the first Disney animated feature to be an original story instead of being based on an already existing work.

The story, directed by Roger Allers and Rob Minkoff, takes place in a kingdom of lions in Africa and centers on the lion cub and future king Simba's searching and fighting for his identity, which was inspired by the lives of Joseph and Moses, from the *Bible*, and William Shakespeare's *Hamlet*. It's worth mentioning that Elton John, one of the composers, wrote its original songs. The voice actors were chosen for how they fit and could add to the characters.

Production began in 1991 concurrently with Pocahontas which attracted most of Disney's top animators who did not have much faith in *The Lion King*. The character animators studied real-life animals for reference, as was done for the 1942 Disney film *Bambi*. In addition, computers helped the filmmakers present their vision in new ways.

Upon its release in June, 1994, *The Lion King* was widely praised for its music, story, and animation and it finished its theatrical run as the highest-grossing release of 1994 and the second highest-grossing film of all time. As for awards, the film won two Golden Globes for Best Motion Picture-Musical or Comedy and Best Original Score, as well as two Academy Awards, for Best Original Score and Best Original Song with "Can You Feel the Love Tonight" by Elton John and Tim Rice.

On Rotten Tomatoes, the film holds a rating of 91%, based on 113 reviews, with an average rating of 8.3 out of 10. In 2016, the film was selected for preservation in the United States National Film Registry by the Library of Congress because of its cultural, historical, and aesthetical significance.

Plot

The Lion King takes place in the Pride Lands of Africa, where a lion rules over the other animals as king. King Mufasa shows young Simba, his newborn son, the Pride Lands and tells him the responsibilities of kingship and the circle of life which connects all living things. Scar, Mufasa's younger brother, covets the throne so he plots to kill Mufasa and Simba in order to be the king.

Scar tricks Simba and his best friend Nala into exploring a forbidden elephants' graveyard at the cost of being attacked by three spotted hyenas who are Scar's accomplices. Mufasa is alerted to the danger rescues the cubs. Mufasa forgives Simba despite that he is angry with Simba. For the sake of Simba's growth, he further explains that the great kings of the past watch over them from the night sky, and so will he do one day in the future.

The insidious Scar plots again, to be exact, sets a trap for his brother and nephew by luring Simba into a gorge and having the hyenas drive a large herd of wildebeest into a stampede that will trample him. Being sure that Mufasa will rush to save Simba, he informs Mufasa of Simba's danger. Obviously, Mufasa saves Simba but ends up hanging perilously from the gorge's edge. Unluckily, he is betrayed and framed by Scar who sends him falling to his death.

Scar makes Simba believe that Simba should be blamed for the tragedy. Then Simba takes Scar's advice and flees. As a consequence, Scar steps forward as the new king after telling the pride that both Mufasa and Simba were killed in the stampede. He then allows a large pack of hyenas to live in the Pride Lands.

Simba collapses in a desert and is rescued by his new friends with whom Simba lives a carefree life and grows up in the jungle. Years later, Simba, now an adult, rescues his friends from a hungry lioness who turns out to be Nala. Simba and Nala reunite and fall in love, but when Nala tells him that the Pride Lands have become a drought-stricken wasteland under Scar's reign and urges him to return home, Simba feels hesitated and finally refuses, for he loses himself in the guilty over his father's death and has no courage to face what has happened.

Simba is then visited by the ghost of Mufasa in the night sky, who tells him he must claim his rightful place as king. Simba realizes he has no way to run from his past, and makes his decision to back home. With the aid of his friends, Simba now stands in front of Scar who reminds Simba of his role in Mufasa's death with evil purpose and forces him to move to the edge of the rock where Mufasa was killed. Enraged, Simba pins Scar to the ground and forces him to reveal the truth to the rest of the pride.

All Simba's friends and the lionesses fight against the hyenas while Scar, attempting to escape, is cornered by Simba at the top of Pride Rock. Scar begs for mercy but is ordered by Simba to leave the Pride Lands forever. Scar then attacks his nephew, only to find himself attacked and eaten alive by the hyenas who overheard his attempt to betray them.

With his enemies gone, Simba takes over the kingship of the Pride Lands which restore to the past glory due to the rainfall and the birth of Simba and Nala's newborn cub.

◎ Quotes

Scene 1

Adult Simba: I know what I have to do. But going back means I'll have to face my past. I've been running from it for so long.

[Rafiki hits Simba on the head with his stick]

Adult Simba: Ow! Jeez, what was that for?

Rafiki: It doesn't matter. It's in the past.

[laughs]

Adult Simba: Yeah, but it still hurts.

Rafiki: Oh yes, the past can hurt. But from the way I see it, you can either run from it, or... learn from it.

[swings his stick again at Simba, who ducks out of the way]

Rafiki: Ha. You see? So what are you going to do?

Adult Simba: First, I'm gonna take your stick.

[Simba snatches Rafiki's stick and throws it and Rafiki runs to grab it]

Rafiki: No, no, no, no, not the stick! Hey, where you going?

Adult Simba: I'm going back!

Rafiki: Good! Go on! Get out of here!

[Rafiki begins laughing and screeching loudly]

Scene 2

Mufasa: Everything you see exists together in a delicate balance. As king, you need to understand that balance and respect all the creatures, from the crawling ant to the leaping antelope.

Young Simba: But, Dad, don't we eat the antelope?

Mufasa: Yes, Simba, but let me explain. When we die, our bodies become the grass, and the antelope eat the grass. And so we are all connected in the great Circle of Life.

Scene 3

Scar: I'm surrounded by idiots.

1.12 *The Shawshank Redemption*

Introduction

The Shawshank Redemption is a 1994 American drama film written and directed by Frank Darabont and starring Tim Robbins and Morgan Freeman.

Adapted from the Stephen King novella *Rita Hayworth and Shawshank Redemption*, the film tells the story of Andy Dufresne, a banker who spends nearly two decades in Shawshank State Prison for the murder of his wife and her lover despite his claims of innocence. During his time at

the prison, he befriends a fellow inmate, Ellis Boyd "Red" Redding, and finds himself protected by the guards after the warden begins using him in his money laundering operation.

Despite a lukewarm box office reception that barely recouped its budget, the film received multiple award nominations and favorable reviews from critics for its acting and realism. It has since enjoyed a remarkable life on cable television, VHS, DVD, and Blue-ray. In 2005, the film was selected by American Library of Congress for preservation in the National Film Registry because of its cultural, historical, and aesthetical significance. In 2007, it was included in the American Film Institute's list of 100 greatest American films.

Plot

In 1947, banker Andy Dufresne is convicted of murdering his wife and her lover, based on circumstantial evidence, and is sentenced to two consecutive life sentences at Shawshank State Penitentiary. Andy quickly befriends contraband smuggler Ellis "Red" Redding, an inmate serving a life sentence. Red procures a rock hammer for Andy, allowing him to create small stone chess pieces. Red later gets him a large poster of Rita Hayworth, followed in later years by images of Marilyn Monroe and Raquel Welch. Andy works in the prison laundry, but is regularly assaulted by the "bull queer" gang "the Sisters" and their leader Bogs.

In 1949, Andy overhears the brutal chief guard Byron Hadley complaining about taxes on a forthcoming inheritance and informs him about a financial loophole. After another vicious assault by the Sisters nearly kills Andy, Hadley severely beats Bogs resulting in Bogs being sent to another prison. Andy is not attacked again. Warden Samuel Norton meets with Andy and reassigns him to the prison library to assist elderly inmate Brooks Hatlen, a pretext for Andy to manage financial duties for the prison. His advice and expertise are soon sought by other guards at Shawshank and from nearby prisons. Andy begins writing weekly letters to the state government for funds to improve the decrepit library.

In 1954, Brooks is freed on parole, but unable to adjust to the outside world after 50 years in prison, he hangs himself. Andy receives a library donation that includes a recording of The Marriage of Figaro. He plays an excerpt over the public address system, resulting in his receiving solitary confinement. After his release, Andy explains that he holds onto hope as something that the prison cannot take from him, but Red dismisses the idea. In 1963, Norton begins exploiting prison labor for public works, profiting by undercutting skilled labor costs and receiving kickbacks. He has Andy launder the money using the alias "Randall Stephens".

In 1965, Tommy Williams is incarcerated for burglary. He joins Andy's and Red's circle of friends, and Andy helps him pass his General Educational Development (G. E. D.) examinations. In 1966, after hearing the details of Andy's case, Tommy reveals that an inmate at another prison claimed responsibility for an identical murder, suggesting Andy's innocence. Andy approaches Norton with this information, but the warden refuses to listen. Norton places Andy in solitary confinement and has Hadley murder Tommy, under the guise of an escape attempt. Andy refuses to continue with the scam, but Norton threatens to destroy the library and take away his protection and preferential treatment.

After Andy is released from solitary confinement, he tells Red of his dream of living in Zihuatanejo, a Mexican Pacific coastal town. While Red shrugs it off as being unrealistic, Andy instructs him, should he ever be freed, to visit a specific hayfield near Buxton to retrieve a package.

The next day at roll call, upon finding Andy's cell empty, an irate Norton throws one of Andy's rocks at the poster of Raquel Welch hanging on the wall. The rock tears through the poster, revealing a tunnel that Andy had dug with his rock hammer over the previous two decades. The previous night, Andy escaped through the tunnel and the prison's sewage pipe with Norton's ledger, containing details of the money laundering.

While guards search for him the following morning, Andy, posing as Randall Stephens, visits several banks to withdraw the laundered money. Finally, he sends the ledger and evidence of the corruption and murders at Shawshank to a local newspaper. The police arrive at Shawshank and take Hadley into custody, while Norton commits suicide to avoid arrest.

After serving 40 years, Red receives parole. He struggles to adapt to life outside prison and fears he never will. Remembering his promise to Andy, he visits Buxton and finds a cache containing money and a letter asking him to come to Zihuatanejo. Red violates his parole and travels to Fort Hancock, Texas to cross the border to Mexico, admitting he finally feels hope. On a beach in Zihuatanejo, he finds Andy, and the two friends are happily reunited.

◎ Quotes

Scene 1

Andy Dufresne: [in letter to Red] Remember Red, hope is a good thing, may be the best of things, and no good thing ever dies.

Scene 2

1967 Parole Hearings Man: Ellis Boyd Redding, your files say you've served 40 years of a life sentence. Do you feel you've been rehabilitated?

Red: Rehabilitated? Well, now let me see. You know, I don't have any idea what that means.

1967 Parole Hearings Man: Well, it means that you're ready to rejoin society...

Red: I know what you think it means, sonny. To me, it's just a made-up word. A politician's word, so young fellas like yourself can wear a suit and a tie, and have a job. What do you really want to know? Am I sorry for what I did?

1967 Parole Hearings Man: Well, are you?

Red: There's not a day goes by I don't feel regret. Not because I'm in here, because you think I should. I look back on the way I was then: a young, stupid kid who committed that terrible crime. I want to talk to him. I want to try to talk some sense to him, tell him the way things are. But I can't. That kid's long gone, and this old man is all that's left. I got to live with that. Rehabilitated? It's just a bullshit word. So you go on and stamp your form, sonny, and stop wasting my time. Because to tell you the truth, I don't give a shit.

Scene 3

Andy Dufresne: [referring to Andy using an alias to launder money for the warden] If they ever try to trace any of those accounts, they're gonna end up chasing a figment of my imagination.

Red: Well, I'll be damned. Did I say you were good? Shit, you're a Rembrandt!

Andy Dufresne: Yeah. The funny thing is — on the outside, I was an honest man, straight as an arrow. I had to come to prison to be a crook.

1.13 *Forrest Gump*

Introduction

Forrest Gump is a 1994 American comedy-drama film based on the 1986 novel of the same name and centers on the character Forrest Gump who is regarded as a stupid man with low I. Q. but makes it to be a football player, a ping-pang player, a war hero, a runner, and a millionaire. The film is directed by Robert Zemeckis and stars Tom Hanks, Robin Wright, Gary Sinise, Mykelti Williamson, and Sally Field.

The story depicts several decades in the life of Forrest Gump, more specifically, the period between Forrest's birth in 1944 and 1982. Forrest Gump, a slow-witted but kind-hearted, good-natured and athletically prodigious man from Alabama, witnesses, and to some extent, influences some of the defining events of the latter half of the 20th century in the United States.

In late 1993, the filming of *Forrest Gump* took place mainly in South Carolina, as well as parts of coastal Virginia and North Carolina. Extensive visual effects were used to incorporate the protagonist into archived footage and to develop other scenes. Using computer-generated imagery techniques, it was possible to demonstrate Gump's meeting deceased personages and shaking their hands. The film is also featured with a comprehensive soundtrack with music intended to pinpoint specific time periods portrayed on screen.

Forrest Gump became a commercial success as the top-grossing film in North America released in that year, earning over US $677 million worldwide during its theatrical run. Since its release, the film received generally positive reviews. It won Best Picture, Best Leading Actor, Best Director, Best Visual Effects, Best Adapted Screenplay, and Best Film Editing at the 67th Academy Awards in 1995. The film was nominated for seven Golden Globe Awards, winning three of them. It also garnered multiple other awards and nominations, including People's Choice Awards, and Young Artist Awards, among others. Varying interpretations have been made of the film's protagonist and its political symbolism.

Apart from the film's multiple awards and nominations, it has also been recognized by the American Film Institute on several of its lists of the greatest films. Likewise, the film ranks among the best films on many other lists. Forrest Gump's saying "Mama always said life was like a box of chocolates. You never know what you're gonna get", has greatly impressed fans and been frequently quoted.

Plot

In 1981, Forrest Gump tells his life story to strangers who sit next to him at a bus stop in Savannah, Georgia. The listeners change regularly throughout his narration, each showing a different attitude ranging from disbelief and indifference to rapt veneration.

Back in 1950s, in Greenbow, Alabama, young Forrest lives with his mother by renting rooms to passers-by. Due to wearing leg braces, he is unable to walk properly, but fortunately convinced that he has no difference from others by his great mother who has managed to win an opportunity for young Forrest to enter a school for average children.

On his first day of school, Forrest meets a girl named Jenny Curran who shows her friendliness to young Forrest unlike other children and leaves an angel-like image on his mind. Once, his trying to escape bullies enables him to run fast and from then on he begins his running all the way into college as a football player and an American all-star team member.

After his college graduation, he enlists in the army and is sent to Vietnam, where he makes fast friends with a black man named Bubba, who convinces Forrest to go into the shrimping business with him when the war is over. Unluckily, during an ambush, Bubba is killed in action while Forrest is awarded the Congressional Medal of Honor for his heroism, exactly, his saving many of his platoon, including his Lieutenant, Dan Taylor, who loses both his legs.

When Forrest is in recovery for a bullet shot at hospital, he discovers playing ping-pong comes naturally to him, and he can play it so well that he eventually rises to celebrity status, later even playing ping-pong competitively against Chinese teams. To Forrest's pleasure, at an anti-war rally in Washington, D. C. Forrest reunites with Jenny, who admires the hippie counterculture and has a totally different lifestyle from his.

After retiring from army, Forrest backs home and endorses a company that specializing in making ping-pong paddles, which brings a large sum of money which is used to buy a shrimping boat in order to fulfil his promise to Bubba. Forrest cooperates with Lieutenant Dan in running shrimping. In spite of the initial failure, Forrest has achieved enormous success in shrimping, for his boat has been the only one that has not been destroyed by a hurricane in the area. Lt. Dan uses their money to invest in Apple Computer and Forrest is financially secure for the rest of his life. Shockingly a piece of bad news that his mother is dying brings Forrest back home.

Forrest feels greatly sad and lonely after his mother's death when Jenny returns to visit

Forrest. Forrest proposes marriage to Jenny but encounters failure and once again Jenny leaves him. On a whim, Forrest elects to go for a run. Seemingly capriciously, he decides to keep running across the country several times, over some three and a half years, becoming famous.

Back to bus stop where Forrest tells passers-by his story, he reveals that he is waiting at the bus stop because he received a letter from Jenny who invited him to visit her. For the third time, Forrest is reunited with Jenny, finding he has an adorable son with Jenny. Though Forrest is told that Jenny is suffering from a virus (probably HIV, though this is never definitively stated), he still brings Jenny and their son back to Greenbow, Alabama where Forrest and Jenny hold a wedding. Jenny dies soon. The story ends with father and son waiting for the school bus on little Forrest's first day of school.

◎ Quotes

Scene 1

Forrest Gump: You died on a Saturday morning. And I had you placed here under our tree. And I had that house of your father's bulldozed to the ground. Momma always said dyin' was a part of life. I sure wish it wasn't. Little Forrest, he's doing just fine. About to start school again soon. I make his breakfast, lunch, and dinner every day. I make sure he combs his hair and brushes his teeth every day. Teaching him how to play ping-pong. He's really good. We fish a lot. And every night, we read a book. He's so smart, Jenny. You'd be so proud of him. I am. He, uh, wrote a letter, and he says I can't read it. I'm not supposed to, so I'll just leave it here for you. Jenny, I don't know if Momma was right or if, if it's Lieutenant Dan. I don't know if we each have a destiny, or if we're all just floating around accidental-like on a breeze, but I, I think maybe it's both. Maybe both is happening at the same time. I miss you, Jenny. If there's anything you need, I won't be far away.

Scene 2

Drill Sergeant: Gump! What's your sole purpose in this army?

Forrest Gump: To do whatever you tell me, drill sergeant!

Drill Sergeant: God damn it, Gump! You're a god damn genius! This is the most outstanding answer I have ever heard. You must have a goddamn I. Q. of 160. You are goddamn gifted, Private Gump. Listen up, people...

Forrest Gump: [narrates] Now for some reason I fit in the army like one of them round pegs. It's not really hard. You just make your bed real neat and remember to stand up straight and always answer every question with "Yes, drill sergeant."

Drill Sergeant: ... Is that clear?

Forrest Gump: Yes, drill sergeant!

Scene 3

[repeated line]

Forrest Gump: My momma always said, "Life was like a box of chocolates. You never know what you're gonna get."

1.14 *Titanic*

Introduction

Titanic is a 1997 American epic romance-disaster film directed, written, co-produced and co-edited by James Cameron. It stars Leonardo DiCaprio and Kate Winslet as the hero and heroine who belong to different social classes and fall in love aboard the ship Titanic during its ill-fated maiden voyage.

James Cameron's fascination with shipwrecks inspired the making of the film in which he felt a love story interspersed with the human loss would undoubtedly convey the emotional impact of the disaster. Cameron believed that the sinking of Titanic was a mere morality tale and his film would give audiences the experience of living the history.

In 1995, Cameron began the film's production and shot the footage of the actual Titanic wreck. Principal photography for *Titanic* began in July 1996 and two months later, the production moved to the newly built Fox Baja Studios in Rosarito, Mexico, where a full-scale RMS Titanic had been constructed. It is worth mentioning that the filming itself was really difficult, with its schedule intended to last 138 days but finally 160 days. Many cast members came down with colds, flu, or kidney infections after spending hours in cold water.

The film, partially funded by Paramount Pictures and 20th Century Fox, was the most expensive film ever made at the time, with a production budget of $200 million, for scale models, computer-generated imagery, and a reconstruction of the Titanic were used to re-create the sinking. Interestingly, it was predicted to be a significant disappointment at the box office by various film critics, especially due to its production budget.

After its release in 1997, *Titanic* received positive reviews widely. *Titanic* began its awards sweep starting with the Golden Globes, winning four. The film garnered fourteen Academy Awards nominations, tying *All About Eve* (1950) for the most Oscar nominations, and won 11, including the awards for Best Picture and Best Director. It was the second film to receive eleven Academy Awards, after *Ben-Hur*.

Titanic is also a great commercial success with an initial worldwide gross of over $1.84 billion, being the first film to reach the billion-dollar mark. It became the highest-grossing film of all time worldwide in 1998, and held the record for twelve years until *Avatar* (2009), also written and directed by Cameron, surpassed it in 2010. In addition, quotes in the film contribute to its popularity. Its catchphrase "I'm the king of the world!" has become one of the most popular quotations in the film industry.

Plot

In 1996, the search of the necklace with a rare diamond, the Heart of the Ocean makes the drawing of a young woman wearing the necklace public, and Rose Dawson Calvert, the woman in the drawing, is found and tells her experiences aboard Titanic.

Back in 1912 Southampton, 17-year-old first-class passenger Rose DeWitt Bukater, her fiancé Cal Hockley, and her mother Ruth board the luxurious Titanic. Ruth is deeply convinced that Rose's marriage will solve their family's financial problems and retain their high-class status.

Rose feels disappointed with her engagement and considers suicide by jumping from the stern, but she is intervened and discouraged by Jack Dawson, a penniless artist. For saving Rose from falling, Jack is invited to dine with them in first class the following night. Following dinner, Rose secretly joins Jack at a party in third class.

Jack and Rose develop a tentative friendship despite Cal and Ruth's disapproval, and gradually Rose realizes she prefers Jack over Cal. At her request, Jack sketches nude Rose wearing Cal's engagement present, the Heart of the Ocean necklace. They feel close to each other and the love in bud between them.

On the forward deck, they witness a collision with an iceberg and overhear the officers and designer discussing its seriousness. Jack and Rose attempt to inform Cal of the collision before Cal discovers Jack's sketch of Rose and feels humiliated. Then Jack is arrested because of being accused of theft and handcuffed to a pipe.

With the ship sinking, Rose flees Cal and her mother and frees Jack. Though Rose has the chance to survive in boarding a lifeboat, she decides that she cannot leave Jack and jumps back on board. Cal takes his bodyguard's pistol and chases Rose and Jack into the flooding first-class dining saloon. After using up his ammunition, Cal suddenly realizes that the necklace has been handed over to Rose.

After braving several obstacles, Jack and Rose return to the boat deck. The lifeboats have departed and passengers are falling to their deaths as the stern rises out of the water. The ship breaks in half, lifting the stern into the air. Jack and Rose ride it into the ocean and he helps her onto a wooden panel only buoyant enough for one person. He assures her that she will die an old woman, warm in her bed. With Jack's encouragement Rose is eventually saved while Jack dies of hypothermia. Back in the present, Rose takes out the Heart of the Ocean — in her possession all along — and drops it into the sea over the wreck site.

◎ Quotes

Scene 1

Rose: [thinking both of them will die soon] I love you, Jack.

Jack: Don't you do that, don't say your good-byes. Not yet, do you understand me?

Rose: I'm so cold.

Jack: Listen, Rose. You're gonna get out of here, you're gonna go on and you're gonna make lots of babies, and you're gonna watch them grow. You're gonna die an old... an old lady warm in her bed, not here, not this night. Not like this, do you understand me?

Rose: I can't feel my body.

Jack: Winning that ticket, Rose, was the best thing that ever happened to me... it brought me to you. And I'm thankful for that, Rose. I'm thankful. You must do me this honor. Promise me you'll survive. That you won't give up, no matter what happens, no matter how hopeless. Promise me now, Rose, and never let go of that promise.

Rose: I promise.

Jack: Never let go.

Rose: I'll never let go, Jack. I'll never let go. I promise.

Scene 2

Jack: [yelling, standing on the bow with his arms stretched outwards] I'm the king of the world!

Scene 3

Jack: [to Ruth and other guests dining at their table] Well, yes, ma'am, I do... I mean, I got everything I need right here with me. I got air in my lungs, a few blank sheets of paper. I mean, I love waking up in the morning not knowing what's gonna happen or, who I'm gonna meet, where I'm gonna wind up. Just the other night I was sleeping under a bridge and now here I am on the grandest ship in the world having champagne with you fine people. I figure life's a gift and I don't intend on wasting it. You don't know what hand you're gonna get dealt next. You learn to take life as it comes at you... to make each day count.

Molly Brown: Well said, Jack.

1.15 *Avatar*

Introduction

Avatar is a 2009 American science fiction action film written and directed by James Cameron, and starring Sam Worthington, Zoe Saldana, Stephen Lang, Michelle Rodriguez, Joel David Moore, Giovanni Ribisi and Sigourney Weaver. The film is set in the mid-22nd century, when humans are mining a precious mineral called unobtanium on Pandora, a lush habitable moon of a gas giant in the Alpha Centauri star system. The expansion of the mining colony threatens the continued existence of a local tribe of Na'vi — a humanoid species indigenous to Pandora. The film's title refers to a genetically engineered Na'vi body with the mind of a remotely located human, and is used to interact with the natives of Pandora.

Development of *Avatar* began in 1994, when Cameron wrote an 80-page treatment for the film. Filming was supposed to take place after the completion of Cameron's 1997 film *Titanic*, for a planned release in 1999, but according to Cameron, the necessary technology was not yet available to achieve his vision of the film. Work on the language of the film's extraterrestrial beings began in summer 2005, and Cameron began developing the screenplay and fictional universe in early 2006.

Avatar was officially budgeted at \$237 million. Other estimates put the cost between \$280 million and \$310 million for production and at \$150 million for promotion. The film made extensive use of cutting edge motion capture filming techniques, and was released for traditional viewing, 3D viewing (using the RealD 3D, Dolby 3D, XpanD 3D, and IMAX 3D formats), and for "4D" experiences in select South Korean theaters. The stereoscopic filmmaking was touted as a breakthrough in cinematic technology.

Avatar premiered in London on December 10, 2009, and was internationally released on December 16 and in the United States and Canada on December 18, to positive critical reviews, with critics highly praising its groundbreaking visual effects. During its theatrical run, the film broke several box office records and became the highest-grossing film, as well as in the United States and Canada, surpassing *Titanic*, which had held those records for twelve years (and was also directed by Cameron). It also became the first film to gross more than \$2 billion.

Avatar was nominated for nine Academy Awards, including Best Picture and Best Director, and won three, for Best Art Direction, Best Cinematography and Best Visual Effects. The film's home media release went on to break opening sales records and became the top-selling Blu-ray of all time. Following the film's success, Cameron signed with 20th Century Fox to produce three sequels, making *Avatar* the first of a planned tetralogy.

Plot

By 2154, humans have severely depleted Earth's natural resources. The Resources Development Administration (RDA) mines for a valuable mineral — unobtanium — on Pandora, a densely forested habitable moon orbiting the gas giant Polyphemus in the Alpha Centauri star system. Pandora, whose atmosphere is poisonous to humans, is inhabited by the Na'vi, 10-foot tall (3.0 m), blue-skinned, sapient humanoids who live in harmony with nature and worship a mother goddess called Eywa.

To explore Pandora's biosphere, scientists use Na'vi-human hybrids called "avatars", operated by genetically matched humans; Jake Sully, a paraplegic former marine, replaces his deceased twin brother as an operator of one. Dr. Grace Augustine, head of the Avatar Program, considers Sully an inadequate replacement but accepts his assignment as a bodyguard. While protecting the avatars of Grace and scientist Norm Spellman as they collect biological data, Jake's avatar is attacked by a thanator and flees into the forest, where he is rescued by Neytiri, a female Na'vi. Witnessing an auspicious sign, she takes him to her clan, whereupon Neytiri's mother Mo'at, the clan's spiritual leader, orders her daughter to initiate Jake into their society.

Colonel Miles Quaritch, head of RDA's private security force, promises Jake that the company will restore his legs if he gathers intelligence about the Na'vi and the clan's gathering place, a giant arboreal called Hometree, on grounds that it stands above the richest deposit of unobtanium in the area. When Grace learns of this, she transfers herself, Jake, and Norm to an outpost. Over three months, Jake grows to sympathize with the natives.

After Jake is initiated into the tribe, he and Neytiri choose each other as mates, and soon afterward, Jake reveals his change of allegiance when he attempts to disable a bulldozer that threatens to destroy a sacred Na'vi site. When Quaritch shows a video recording of Jake's attack on the bulldozer to Administrator Parker Selfridge, and another in which Jake admits that the Na'vi will never abandon Hometree, Selfridge orders Hometree destroyed.

Despite Grace's argument that destroying Hometree could damage the biological neural network native to Pandora, Selfridge gives Jake and Grace one final chance to convince the Na'vi to evacuate before commencing the attack. While trying to warn the Na'vi, Jake confesses to being a spy and the Na'vi take him and Grace captive. Seeing this, Quaritch's men destroy Hometree, killing Neytiri's father (the clan chief) and many others. Mo'at frees Jake and Grace, but they are detached from their avatars and imprisoned by Quaritch's forces. Pilot Trudy Chacón, disgusted by Quaritch's brutality, carries them to Grace's outpost, but during the escape, Quaritch fires at them, hitting Grace.

To regain the Na'vi's trust, Jake connects his mind to that of Toruk, a dragon-like predator feared and honoured by the Na'vi. Jake finds the refugees at the sacred Tree of Souls and pleads with Mo'at to heal Grace. The clan attempts to transfer Grace from her human body into her avatar with the aid of the Tree of Souls, but she dies before the process can complete.

Supported by the new chief Tsu'tey, who acts as Jake's translator, Jake speaks to unite the clan and tells them to gather all of the clans to battle against the RDA. Noticing the impending gathering, Quaritch organizes a pre-emptive strike against the Tree of Souls, believing that its destruction will demoralize the natives. On the eve of battle, Jake prays to Eywa, via a neural connection to the Tree of Souls, to intercede on behalf of the Na'vi.

During the subsequent battle, the Na'vi suffer heavy casualties, including Tsu'tey and Trudy; but are rescued when Pandoran wildlife unexpectedly join the attack and overwhelm the humans, which Neytiri interprets as Eywa's answer to Jake's prayer. After Jake destroys a makeshift bomber before it can reach the Tree of Souls; Quaritch escapes from his own damaged aircraft, wearing an AMP suit and breaks open the avatar link unit containing Jake's human body, exposing it to Pandora's poisonous atmosphere. Quaritch then prepares to slit the throat of Jake's avatar, but Neytiri kills Quaritch and saves Jake from suffocation.

With the exceptions of Jake, Norm, Max and a few other scientists, all humans are expelled from Pandora and sent back to Earth, after which Jake is transferred permanently into his avatar with the aid of the Tree of Souls.

◎ Quotes

Scene 1

Jake Sully: [as Jake pleads for Eywa's help in attacking the "Sky People"] If Grace is there with you — look in her memories — she can show you the world we come from. There's no green there. They killed their Mother, and they're gonna do the same here. More Sky People are gonna come. They're gonna come like a rain that never ends. Unless we stop them. They chose me for something. I will stand and fight. You know I will. But I need a little help here.

Neytiri: Our great mother does not take sides, Jake; she protects the balance of life.

Jake Sully: It was worth a try.

Scene 2

[They find a Hammerhead Titanothere]

Dr. Grace Augustine: Don't shoot! Don't shoot. You'll piss him off.

Jake Sully: It's already pissed off.

Dr. Grace Augustine: Jake, that armor's too thick. Trust me. It's a territorial threat display. Do not run or he'll charge.

Jake Sully: What do I do? Dance with it?

Dr. Grace Augustine: Just hold your ground.

[the Hammerhead Titanothere charges and Jake run towards him and yells to scare him. He goes away once seeing the Thanator]

Jake Sully: Ha, ha! Yeah, come on! What you got! Oh yeah, who's bad? That's right. Yeah, that's what I'm talkin' about, bitch. That's right, get your punk ass back to mommy. Yeah? Yeah, you got nothin'. You keep runnin'. Why don't you bring some of your friends, huh?

[Turns around and sees an angry Thanator standing in front of him]

Jake Sully: [to Grace] What about this one? Run? Don't run? What?

Dr. Grace Augustine: Run! Definitely run!

Scene 3

Jake Sully: I see you.

Neytiri: I see you.

2. British Films

The British film industry and its studios have made a huge success as a part of the world's cinema, and have created a number of memorable films, many of which have won Academy Awards of America and have received positive comments worldwide. Undoubtedly, the British cinema has played a significant role over the course of film history, but it didn't embrace it "golden time" until 1940s while film production in other parts of the world reached an all-time high in late 1930s. During 1940s, the directors David Lean, Michael Powell, Carol Reed and others produced their most highly acclaimed work in the UK.

On the one hand, a great many films have been jointly produced by US and UK studios; on the other hand, the identity of the British cinema, and its relationship with the American cinema has always been widely debated. Filmmakers' attempts to compete with the American cinema have partly affected the development of film production in Britain, such as the producer Alexander Korda whose career was marked by this objective, the Rank Organisation in the 1940s, and Goldcrest in the 1980s. In reality, numerous British-born filmmakers, including Alfred Hitchcock, Ridley Scott, Charlie Chaplin and Cary Grant have achieved success and gained popularity primarily through their work in the United States.

Currently, British cinema is exerting its influence by those well-known films with a commercial and critical success, including the second and third highest-grossing film series (*Harry Potter* and *James Bond*), by those film practitioners who are entitled to international fame, including Maggie Smith, Colin Firth, Daniel-Day-Lewis, Kate Winslet, and Eddie Redmayne, and by BAFTA film awards, the British equivalent of the Academy Awards, and the BFI (British Film Institute) London Film Festival. It's worth mentioning that BFI has produced a poll ranking concerning the 100 greatest British films of all time, the BFI Top 100 British films.

2.1 *Great Expectations*

Introduction

Great Expectations, based on the novel by Charles Dickens, is a 1946 British film directed by David Lean, produced by Ronald Neame and stars John Mills, Bernard Miles, Finlay Currie, Jean Simmons, Martita Hunt, Alec Guinness and Valerie Hobson. The script, a slimmed-down version of Dickens' novel, was inspired by an abridged 1939 stage version of the novel which was written by David Lean, Ronald Neame and other three. The film, now viewed as one of Lean's best, was one of the two films directed by Lean based on Dickens' novels, the other being his 1948 adaptation of *Oliver Twist*.

The film was positively commented after its release, and considered as the finest film yet made from a Dickens novel. It won two Academy Awards (Best Art Direction and Best Cinematography) and was nominated for three others (Best Picture, Best Director and Best Screenplay). In 1999, it came fifth in a BFI (British Film Institute) poll of the top 100 British films of all time.

Plot

Phillip "Pip" Pirrip is an orphan who lives with his shrewish older sister and her kind-hearted blacksmith husband, Joe Gargery. One day, Pip comes across an escaped convict, Abel Magwitch, and is intimidated into getting him some food and a file for his chains. Later, Magwitch is caught and taken back to the prison ship.

Miss Havisham, an eccentric rich spinster, invites Pip to come to her mansion regularly to accompany her and to play with her adopted daughter, beautiful Estella. Pip quickly falls in love with Estella who is a cruel teenage girl and mocks terribly at Pip's coarse manners as possible as she can. As time flies, Pip turns 14 and he has to end his visits for starting his apprenticeship as a blacksmith. Estella also leaves for France to learn to become a lady.

Several years later Pip is found by Miss Havisham's lawyer, Mr. Jaggers, and told that a mysterious benefactor has offered to change him into a gentleman with great expectations. Pip believes it is Miss Havisham who kind-heartedly offers him the opportunity.

Pip goes to London and meets his teacher, Herbert Pocket, who is supposed to teach him how to behave like a gentleman. From Herbert, Pip shockingly learns that Miss Havisham is not what he always expects, for she is determined to avenge herself against all men by making use of Estella as her instrument to break men's hearts.

After Pip turns 21, Pip is delighted to be reunited with Estella and spends much time together with Estella. Estella tells him that she has no heart and she has absolutely no feelings for Bentley Drummle, the wealthy but unpopular man with whom she flirts. To his surprise, Pip suddenly receives another visitor from Magwitch, who reveals that he is Pip's patron. Pip falls into deep disappointment because he realizes that Miss Havisham is not the person who brings good fortune to him but the one who always makes use of him.

Again, Pip visits Estella at the old woman's house and is informed that she is going to marry Drummle. When confronted with Miss Havisham, Pip complains that he now becomes unhappy as she has expected. Miss Havisham begs Pip's forgiveness and wants to follow him as Pip leaves, only to find her dress ignited by a piece of flaming wood from the fireplace. Pip returns to save her, but in vain.

Pip is warned that Magwitch's trace has been known by someone, therefore, he makes preparations to smuggle the old man onto a packet boat and accompany him to the continent. Pip, Herbert and Magwitch are finally intercepted by the waiting police who have got the news ahead of time. Magwitch is dying due to his serious injury and he reveals to Pip that he has a lost daughter. After Pip's suspicion that the lost daughter is Estella is confirmed by Mr. Jaggers, Pip tells Magwitch of her fate, and his love for her. In the end, Magwitch passes away with great contentment.

Pip goes back home with illness and his lost expectations. After recovering, Pip revisits Miss Havisham's deserted house, where he finds Estella. Without doubt, Estella loses her engagement with Drummle because of her true parentage, and she decides to live in seclusion in the house which she has inherited. On hearing that Pip has never stopped loving her, after hesitating, she embraces him and they leave the house together.

◎ Quotes

Scene 1

[welcoming Pip to her decaying mansion]

Miss Havisham: Come nearer. Let me look at you. Come close. Look at me. You aren't afraid of a woman who has never seen the sun since before you were born?

Scene 2

Mr. Jaggers: Now, Pip: put the case that this legal advisor has often seen children tried at the criminal bar. Put the case that he has known them to be habitually imprisoned, whipped, neglected, cast out, neglected, cast out, qualified in all ways for the hangman, and growing up to be hanged. Put the case that here was one pretty little child out of the heap that could be saved. Put that last case to yourself very carefully, Pip.

Scene 3

Pip: [narrating] In trying to become a gentleman, I had succeeded in becoming a snob.

2.2 *The Red Shoes*

Introduction

The Red Shoes is a 1948 British drama film written, directed and produced by the team of Michael Powell and Emeric Pressburger, known collectively as *The Archers*. Based on the fairy tale "The Red Shoes" by Hans Christian Andersen, the film focuses on a ballerina, the lead dancer in a ballet called *The Red Shoes*, who is in a dilemma, namely, to make a choice between her dancing career and her family.

The film stars Moira Shearer, Anton Walbrook and Marius Goring and features several renowned dancers from the ballet world. It is particularly known for its cinematography, particularly its use of color. Though positively commented, it did not make much money at first in the UK, because there was no enough money spent on its promotion due to severe financial problems.

At the 21st Academy Awards, *The Red Shoes* won awards for Best Original Score and Best Art Direction, as well as three nominations: Best Picture, Best Original Screenplay and Best Film Editing. In 1999, it was voted the 8th greatest British film of all time by the British Film Institute. Currently, it is considered as one of the best British films. In 2006, digital restoration of the film was made by Warner Bros. Motion Picture Imaging.

Plot

The story is based on a Hans Christian Andersen fairy tale concerning a pair of enchanted crimson ballet slippers, The Red Shoes. There are three main roles in the story: the beautiful Vicky Page, a young socialite who loves ballet, the rising composer Julian Craster whom Vicky loves, and her dictatorial director, Boris Lermontov. Vicky and Lermontov make an agreement that Vicky concentrates on her dancing while Lermontov is responsible for anything else. Vicky rises to fame as the prima ballerina in a world-class Ballet Company, attracting wide attention and winning respect from her colleagues.

Lermontov discovers the romance between his talented composer and his beautiful protege, and he cruelly leaves Vicky in a dilemma in which she must give up Julian or the dancing, only to be shocked and hurt because Vicky marries Julian. Despite the fact that Vicky leaves the company, Lermontov still remains confident that Vicky will return to him.

Dancing is truly unforgettable to Vicky. So when offered the chance to dance "The Red Shoes" show once more, she shows her hesitation, but eventually gives in to Lermontov's alternate threatening and coaxing. At the time, Julian is preparing for the premiere of his new work in London. After knowing that Vicky has been coaxed back into dancing with the Lermontov Ballet, he is inevitably furious and arrives at her dressing room as she prepares to dance "The Red Shoes" ballet. Vicky explains to him that she has missed her dancing. By embracing him, Vicky tries to convince Julian wordlessly that she doesn't want to leave him when Lermontov breaks in. As a winner, Lermontov crows his victory over Julian by talking proudly of Vicky's apparent betrayal. Julian has no choice but to give an ultimatum, dancing or their marriage.

The rapidly escalating tension and the competition between the two men leaves Vicky distressed so much so that she can only cry broken-heartedly. Obviously, she cannot afford to lose either of them for they both play an important part in her life. Lermontov views Vicky's indecisiveness as his victory and forces Julian to leave. Lermontov then gives comfort to Vicky by promising that she will dance like never before.

Wearing the red shoes before her performance on stage, Vicky, apparently under the influence of the magic red shoes, runs out of the theatre. On the platform of the train station where Julian intends to take a train, Vicky jumps from a balcony and falls in front of an approaching train. Unfortunately, Julian catches sigh of Vicky's suicide, and he cradles her crushed body, takes off the Red Shoes at her request just as in the end of The Red Shoes ballet.

Lermontov, though shaken by the tragedy, announces that Vicky will never dance again, but that they will perform the ballet once more without her. No understudy will actually take the place of Vicky and dance her role, leaving a lone spotlight on the stage.

◎ Quotes

Scene 1

Boris Lermontov: Why do you want to dance?

[Vicky thinks for a short while]

Victoria Page: Why do you want to live?

[Lermontov is surprised at the answer]

Boris Lermontov: Well I don't know exactly why, er, but I must.

Victoria Page: That's my answer too.

Scene 2

[Describing the ballet of the Red Shoes]

Boris Lermontov: "The Ballet of The Red Shoes" is from a fairy tale by Hans Andersen. It is the story of a young girl who is devoured with an ambition to attend a dance in a pair of Red Shoes. She gets the shoes and goes to the dance. For a time, all goes well and she is very happy. At the end of the evening she is tired and wants to go home, but the Red Shoes are not tired. In fact, the Red Shoes are never tired. They dance her out into the street, they dance her over the mountains and valleys, through fields and forests, through night and day. Time rushes by, love rushes by, life rushes by, but the Red Shoes go on.

Julian Craster: What happens in the end?

Boris Lermontov: Oh, in the end, she dies.

Scene 3

Boris Lermontov: How would you define ballet, Lady Neston?

Lady Neston: Well, one might call it the poetry of motion perhaps, or...

Boris Lermontov: One might. But for me it is a great deal more. For me it is a religion. And one doesn't really care to see one's religion practiced in an atmosphere... such as this.

2.3 *The Third Man*

Introduction

The Third Man is a 1949 British film noir which centers on an American pulp writer's investigation on the mysterious death of his old friend in post-WWII Vienna, only to discover incredible dark secrets about his friend's life and death. The film is directed by Carol Reed and written by Graham Greene and stars Joseph Cotten, Alida Valli, Orson Welles, and Trevor Howard.

The film is mainly featured with of black-and-white expressionist cinematography, with harsh lighting and distorted "Dutch angle" camera technique. The style of the film demonstrates the atmosphere of an exhausted, cynical, post-war Vienna at the start of the Cold War combined with the iconic theme music, seedy locations and acclaimed performances. The title music "The Third Man Theme" topped the international music charts in 1950.

In the United Kingdom, *The Third Man* was the most popular film at the British box office for 1949. It also received overwhelmingly positive reviews in America. It is considered one of the greatest films of all time, acclaimed for its acting, musical score and atmospheric cinematography. In 1999, it was voted the greatest British film of all time by the British Film Institute.

Plot

The story happens in post-war Vienna which is divided into four sectors after World War II, with each controlled by one of the occupying forces: American, British, French, and Soviet. Opportunistic racketeering thrives in this damaged and impoverished city. Holly Martins, an American pulp Western writer, arrives at the city, looking forward to meeting his childhood friend, Harry Lime, who has offered him a job, only to discover that Lime was killed just hours earlier by a speeding truck while crossing the street.

At Lime's funeral, Martins meets two British Army Police: Sergeant Paine, a fan of Martins' pulp novels; and his superior, Major Calloway, who says Lime was a criminal and suggests Martins leave town. Martins makes the decision to stay in Vienna in order to seek an opportunity to clear his friend's name. afterwards, Martins encounters Lime's two friend, Kurtz and Popescu, who carried Lime to the side of the street after the accident. Before dying, according to Kurtz, Lime asked the two men to take care of Martins and Anna Schmidt, Lime's actress girlfriend.

With the aim of collecting more information, Martins goes to visit Anna who suggests in passing that Lime's death may not have been an accident. Martins and Anna goes to question the porter at Lime's apartment building. The porter talks of one important detail that Kurtz and Popescu did not move the body out of the street alone, instead, with the help of a third man.

It is not long before the police come to Anna's flat for evidence. find and confiscate her forged passport and detain her. Anna tells Martins that she is of Czechoslovak nationality and will be deported from Austria by the Russian occupying forces if discovered. Lime's medical adviser, Dr. Winkel, also agrees that there were only two men present at the spot where the accident occurred. Later, the porter claims secretly that he has more to offer concerning Lime's death, but he is murdered before his arranged meeting with Martins. At the book club, Martins is asked about his next book, and replies that it will be called *The Third Man*, "a murder story" inspired by facts.

The British army policeman Calloway again advises Martins to leave Vienna, only to be refused by Martins who insists that Lime's death be investigated. With reluctance, Calloway uncovers the secret that Lime had been stealing penicillin from military hospitals, and selling it on the black market diluted so much that many patients died. In postwar Vienna, antibiotics, at a very high price, were new and scarce outside military hospitals. Disillusioned, he makes up his mind to leave Vienna and when saying good-bye to Anna at her flat, surprisingly discovers that Anna has the knowledge of Lime's misdeeds but remains her loyalty to Lime. At the moment, Martins notices someone watching from a dark doorway and then realizes the man is Lime.

The next day, Martins finds Lime and is shocked at Lime's audacity and brazenness for in a monologue on the insignificance of his victims, Lime shows the full extent of his amorality. Lime sneaks out for his rendezvous with Martins, but is warned to run away by Anna in time. Lime tries again to escape through the sewers as what he did last time, but was shot by the police. Badly injured, Lime is followed by Martins who picks up a revolver. A shot is heard. Later, Martins attends Lime's funeral for the second time. At the risk of missing his flight out of Vienna, Martins waits in the cemetery to speak to Anna. The story ends with the scene where Anna approaches Martins from a distance and walks past, ignoring him.

◎ Quotes

Scene 1

Harry Lime: Don't be so gloomy. After all it's not that awful. Like the fella says, in Italy for 30 years under the Borgias they had warfare, terror, murder, and bloodshed, but they produced Michelangelo, Leonardo da Vinci, and the Renaissance. In Switzerland they had brotherly love — they had 500 years of democracy and peace, and what did that produce? The cuckoo clock. So long Holly.

Scene 2

Harry Lime: Nobody thinks in terms of human beings. Governments don't. Why should we? They talk about the people and the proletariat, I talk about the suckers and the mugs — it's the same thing. They have their five-year plans, so have I.

Martins: You used to believe in God.

Harry Lime: Oh, I still do believe in God, old man. I believe in God and Mercy and all that. But the dead are happier dead. They don't miss much here, poor devils.

Scene 3

Calloway: Go home Martins, like a sensible chap. You don't know what you're mixing in, get the next plane.

Martins: As soon as I get to the bottom of this, I'll get the next plane.

Calloway: Death's at the bottom of everything, Martins. Leave death to the professionals.

Martins: Mind if I use that line in my next Western?

2.4 *Saturday Night and Sunday Morning*

Introduction

Saturday Night and Sunday Morning, an adaptation of the 1958 novel of the same name, is a 1960 British drama film directed by Karel Reisz, produced by Tony Richardson, and written by Alan Sillitoe who is also the author of the original novel.

The film centers on a young machinist who spends his weekends drinking and partying, and has an affair with a married woman, depicting British working-class life in a serious manner for the first time and dealing realistically with sex and abortion.

At the forefront of and as a part of the British New Wave of filmmaking, the film belongs to a series of "kitchen sink drama" films which were made in the late 1950s and early 1960s, by directors such as Karel Reisz, Jack Clayton, Lindsay Anderson, John Schlesinger and Tony Richardson and adapted from the works of writers such as Alan Sillitoe, John Braine and John Osborne. The films all show a common trope that angry young man from the working-class rebel against the oppressive system of his elders.

Saturday Night and Sunday Morning received an X-rating from the British Board of Film Classification on its theatrical release, and later was submitted for re-rating for the home video release and given a PG rating. The film achieved a popular success in box-office earnings and gained favorable comments widely. In 1999, the film was placed the 14th greatest British film of all time by the British Film Institute on its Top 100 British films list.

Plot

Arthur Seaton, a young machinist at a bicycle factory in Nottingham, makes up his mind not to be tied down to living a tedious life full of domestic trifles like the people around him, including his parents, whom he describes as "dead from the neck up". Therefore, he always spends his money in drinking and seeking fun at weekends.

Arthur starts to date Doreen, a beautiful single woman closer to his age, who still lives with her mother and looks forward to marriage. In the meantime, he is having an affair with Brenda, the wife of an older colleague, who is viewed as a sexual outlet, for Doreen is a traditional girl and avoids his sexual advances.

Unexpectedly, Brenda becomes pregnant by Arthur, and asks Arthur for help in terminating the undesirable pregnancy. (At the time of the film, abortion remained illegal in Britain.) Arthur takes her to see his Aunt Ada who has Brenda sit in a hot bath and drink gin, but in vain. Arthur has no choice but to provide Brenda with the name of a doctor who performs illegal abortions. But Brenda changes her mind and decides to keep the child and accept the consequences.

Eventually, Brenda's pregnancy and her affair with Arthur is uncovered by her husband Jack. The enraged Jack chases Arthur down through a town fairground where he once dated Doreen, and beats him severely with the help of his brother and a fellow soldier. When he escapes an amusement ride where he is trapped, Arthur is caught and beaten again by the two soldiers.

It takes Arthur one-week time to recover, and during his recovery, Doreen visits him and then furthers their relationship. Later, Arthur returns to work, and is aware of the end of his affair with Brenda because of her husband's warning. Arthur makes the decision to marry Doreen. while discussing the prospect of a new home with Doreen, Arthur still has mixed feelings about settling down into domestic life and has no knowledge about what his life will be.

◎ Quotes

Scene 1

Arthur Seaton: Mam called me barmy when I told her I fell of a gasometer for a bet. But I'm not barmy, I'm a fighting pit prop that wants a pint of beer, that's me. But if any knowing bastard says that's me I'll tell them I'm a dynamite dealer waiting to blow the factory to kingdom come. I'm me and nobody else. Whatever people say I am, that's what I'm not because they don't know a bloody thing about me! God knows what I am.

Scene 2

[last lines]

Doreen: What did you do that for?

Arthur Seaton: I don't know, just felt like it I suppose.

Doreen: Maybe one of those houses will be for us.

Arthur Seaton: I know.

Doreen: You shouldn't throw things like that.

Arthur Seaton: It won't be the last one I'll throw. C'mon duck, let's go down!

Scene 3

Doreen: You know the girl at our firm?

Arthur Seaton: Which one?

Doreen: You know, Tina, the one in the photo.

Arthur Seaton: What about her?

Doreen: She got married yesterday, she looked ever so nice.

Arthur Seaton: What was the bloke like, could you smell the drink? They must've been drunk to get married.

Doreen: You're in a rotten mood today.

Arthur Seaton: I lost 5 quid at the races.

Doreen: Serves you right, you shouldn't waste your money.

Arthur Seaton: It's not wasted, I enjoy betting.

Doreen: I don't care what you do with your money, its naught to do with me.

Arthur Seaton: Well, stop telling me off then.

Doreen: I'm not telling you off, you don't think I'm bothered about you like that do you?

Arthur Seaton: That's not what you said in the pictures just now.

Doreen: You're a pig, bringing it up like that.

2.5 *Lawrence of Arabia*

Introduction

Lawrence of Arabia, based on the life of T. E. Lawrence, is a 1962 epic historical drama

film, directed by David Lean and produced by Sam Spiegel, with the screenplay by Robert Bolt and Michael Wilson. The film stars Peter O'Toole in the title role, and centers on Lawrence's experiences in the Arabian Peninsula during World War I, covering his emotional struggles with the personal violence inherent in war, his divided allegiance between his native Britain and its army, together with his own identity and his newly-established relationship with the Arabians.

The filming, frequently delayed due to the lack of a finished script, spanned from May 1961 to September 1962, with more than 1,000 people involved in making the film among whom there were over 200 crew members. Various members of the film's crew portrayed minor characters, and most of the film's characters are based on real characters to varying degrees.

In 1963, with ten nominations at the 35th Academy Awards, it won seven totally: Best Picture, Best Director, Best Original Score, Best Cinematography, Best Art Direction, Best Film Editing and Best Sound Mixing. Apart from this, it won the Golden Globe Award for Best Motion Picture — Drama and the BAFTA Awards for Best Film and Outstanding British Film.

The film is highly acclaimed, especially the dramatic score and the Super Panavision 70 cinematography, and widely considered one of the greatest and most influential films in the film history. In 1991, because of its cultural, historical, and aesthetical significance, the film was selected for preservation in the United States Library of Congress National Film Registry. In 1998, the film was placed the fifth by American Film Institute on the list of 100 greatest American films, and 7th on the 2007 updated list. Likewise, in 1999, it was ranked the third greatest British film of all time by the British Film Institute.

Plot

Part I

The film begins with a memorial service at St Paul's Cathedral in 1935 where a reporter tries to gain insights into a remarkable, enigmatic man named Lawrence from those who knew him, but with little success. Lawrence is killed in a motorcycle accident.

Backward during First World War, Lawrence is a misfit British Army lieutenant, known for his insolence and education. Lawrence is assigned to assess the prospects of Prince Faisal in his revolt against the Turks. Ignoring being warned to keep quiet, Lawrence shows his outspokenness when meeting Faisal which piques the prince's interest.

After a major defeat, instead of retreating, Lawrence proposes a daring surprise attack on Aqaba, for its capture would provide a port from which the British could offload much-needed supplies. The town is strongly fortified against a naval assault but only lightly defended on the landward side. Lawrence convinces Faisal to provide fifty men, led by a skeptical Sherif Ali.

Though considered impassable, they cross the Nefud Desert, and travel day and night on the last stage to reach water. One of Ali's men falls off his camel unnoticed on account of fatigue during the night. Without any hesitation, Lawrence decides to turn back and rescues the man, which wins over Sherif Ali. Lawrence is granted Arab robes to wear.

Lawrence persuades the leader of the powerful local Howeitat tribe to turn against the Turks. The next morning, the Arabs overrun the Turkish garrison. Lawrence heads to Cairo to inform the new commander, General Allenby, of his victory for which Lawrence is promoted to major and given arms and money for the Arabs. Lawrence is deeply disturbed, and wonders there is any basis for the Arabs' suspicions that the British have designs on Arabia, only to be given the answer "no" by Allenby.

Part II

Lawrence launches a guerrilla war, blowing up trains and harassing the Turks at every turn, which is publicized by an American war correspondent and makes Lawrence famous. Unfortunately, when Lawrence scouts the enemy-held city of Deraa with Ali, he is captured and taken to the Turkish Bey. Lawrence suffers from being severely flogged before thrown into the street. Lawrence is shaken due to the terrible experience. He returns to British headquarters in Cairo but does not fit in.

Shortly afterwards, Lawrence is urged by General Allenby to support the "big push" on Damascus. Lawrence finally compromises and agrees to return after hesitation. Lawrence recruits an army that is driven more by money rather than by the Arab cause. The sight of a column of retreating Turkish soldiers, who have just massacred the innocent residents, brings about a slaughter in which Lawrence himself participates. But he soon regrets his actions.

Lawrence's men take Damascus ahead of Allenby's forces. The Arabs set up a council to administer the city, only to be proven that the desert tribesmen are ill-suited for such a task. Failed to maintain the public utilities, the Arabs soon abandon most of the city to the British. Lawrence is promoted to colonel and immediately ordered back to England on account of his uselessness to both Faisal and the British. Lawrence, a dejected army man, is driven away in a British staff car. As he leaves the city, his automobile is passed by a motorcycle, which leaves a trail of dust in its wake.

◎ Quotes

Scene 1

[Lawrence has just extinguished a match between his thumb and forefinger. William Potter surreptitiously attempts the same]

William Potter: Ooh! It damn well 'urts!

T. E. Lawrence: Certainly it hurts.

Officer: What's the trick then?

T. E. Lawrence: The trick, William Potter, is not minding that it hurts.

Scene 2

T. E. Lawrence: I killed two people. One was... yesterday? He was just a boy and I led him into quicksand. The other was... well, before Aqaba. I had to execute him with my pistol, and there was something about it that I didn't like.

General Allenby: That's to be expected.

T. E. Lawrence: No, something else.

General Allenby: Well, then let it be a lesson.

T. E. Lawrence: No... something else.

General Allenby: What then?

T. E. Lawrence: I enjoyed it.

Scene 3

Mr. Dryden: If we've been telling lies, you've been telling half-lies. A man who tells lies, like me, merely hides the truth. But a man who tells half-lies has forgotten where he put it.

2. 6 *Gandhi*

Introduction

Gandhi, 1982 British-Indian epic biographical drama film, is written by John Briley, produced and directed by Richard Attenborough who had dreamed about the filming, but with two previous failures in his attempts. During pre-production, it was speculated as to who would play the role of Gandhi, and the final choice was Ben Kingsley who is partly of Indian heritage

The film dramatizes the life of Mohandas Karamchand Gandhi, the leader of India's non-violent, non-cooperative independence movement against the United Kingdom's rule of the country during the 20th century. The film covers Gandhi's life from his youth in 1893 when he was thrown off a South African train for being in a whites-only compartment, to his assassination and funeral in 1948.

Released in India, the United Kingdom and the United States in late 1982, the film was nominated for Academy Awards in eleven categories, winning eight, including Best Picture and Best Director, Best Actor and Best Original Screenplay. In India, it was one of the highest-grossing film of all-time and the highest for a foreign film during the time of its release. The screenplay of *Gandhi is* available as a published book. The film is widely reviewed and praised not only in India but also internationally, particularly Ben Kingsley's outstanding performance.

Plot

The film begins on the day when Gandhi was assassinated on 30 January 1948. After an evening prayer, an elderly Gandhi is out for his evening walk and meets a large number of greeters and admirers. One man among the crowd shoots him point blank in the chest. Gandhi then falls dead. Dignitaries from around the world makes a part of the huge procession at his funeral.

Back in 1893, Gandhi, a 23-year-old young man, is thrown off a South African train because he is an Indian and travels in a first-class compartment. Gandhi is aware of the discrimination against Indians and makes the decision to start a non-violent protest campaign for the rights of all Indians in South Africa.

After numerous arrests and the unexpected attention of the world, the government finally gives in by recognizing rights for Indians. Due to this victory, regarded as a national hero, Gandhi is invited back to India and urged to take up the fight for India's independence from the British Empire.

Without hesitation, Gandhi devotes himself to launching a non-violent non-cooperation campaign on an unprecedented scale, coordinating millions of Indians nationwide.

Though obstacles and frustrations are unavoidable, such as violence against the protesters and Gandhi's occasional imprisonment, the campaign arouses wide attention, and leaves Britain into a passive position in front of intense public pressure. After World War II, Britain is so weak that it can't continuously enforce its will in India, which leads to India's independence in the end.

This victory doesn't bring peace to Indians which means their troubles are far from over. Religious tensions between Hindus and Muslims erupt into nation-wide violence. Gandhi takes up a hunger strike, declaring he will not eat until the fighting stops. At last, the fighting is brought to a halt at the cost of the division of the country. It is decided that the northwest area of India and eastern part of India, both places where Muslims are in the majority, will make a new country called Pakistan, with the purpose that violence will gradually disappear by encouraging the Muslims to live in a separate country.

Gandhi is opposed to the idea, and in spite of his political compromise the Partition of India is inevitably carried out. In his last days, Gandhi makes contribution to trying to bring about peace between both nations, which results in the anger of many dissidents on both sides and furtherly, the assassination of Gandhi.

◎ Quotes

Scene 1

Gandhi: An eye for an eye only ends up making the whole world blind.

Scene 2

Nahari: I'm going to Hell! I killed a child! I smashed his head against a wall.
Gandhi: Why?
vNahari: Because they killed my son! The Muslims killed my son!
[indicates boy's height]
Gandhi: I know a way out of Hell. Find a child, a child whose mother and father have been

killed and raise him as your own.

[indicates same height]

Gandhi: Only be sure that he is a Muslim and that you raise him as one.

Scene 3

Gandhi: Whenever I despair, I remember that the way of truth and love has always won. There may be tyrants and murderers, and for a time, they may seem invincible, but in the end, they always fail. Think of it: always.

2.7 *A Room with a View*

Introduction

A Room with a View is a 1985 British romance film, based on E. M. Forster's 1908 novel of the same name, directed by James Ivory and produced by Ismail Merchant. It stars Julian Sands and Helena Bonham Carter as the hero and the heroine, and Maggie Smith, Daniel Day-Lewis, Judi Dench in supporting roles. The film focuses on a love story happened between Lucy Honeychurch, a young lady living in the restrictive and repressed England of Edwardian era, and George Emerson, a free-spirited young man. The film is sectioned into thematic parts by closely following the chapter titles of the novel. The filming took place extensively on location in Florence as the main characters meet at a hotel in Florence, Italy.

The film achieved its commercial success at the box office as well as receiving universal critical acclaim. At the 59th Academy Awards, nominated for eight awards including Best Picture, it won three: Best Adapted Screenplay, Best Art Direction and Best Costume Design. It's also the winner of five British Academy Film Awards and one Golden Globe Award. In 1999 the British Film Institute voted *A Room with a View* among its list of greatest British films of the 20th Century. Currently, the film holds a 100% rating on Rotten Tomatoes. The well-known American film reviewer Roger Ebert gave the film four out of four stars, viewing it as an intellectual film concerning emotions, and thinking highly of its significance in encouraging people to value how they feel, instead of simply acting on their feelings.

Plot

Lucy Honeychurch, a beautiful girl from an English village in Surrey is brought up in an upper-middle class but loving and easygoing household. Now she is on holiday in Italy with her much older cousin and chaperone, Charlotte Bartlett, a conservative English lady with an extremely restrictive personality. Charlotte always tends to manipulate others by expressing her emotions while Lucy has fewer inhibitions, which causes strong tension between them.

At a small guest house in Florence, Lucy meets a group of interesting people among whom Lucy develops a friendship with George, Mr. Emerson's son, a handsome, philosophical young man. To Lucy's surprise, these English people try to discard the repression and caution commonly recognized in Victorian times and demonstrate the forward-thinking ideals of the turn-of-the-century.

The Emersons look sincere but with no awareness of finer upper-class Victorian manners, which seems unfamiliar and unacceptable to Charlotte and Lucy. Lucy complains her room where she can't enjoy a view, and then offered to switch rooms by Mr. Emerson. Gradually, Lucy finds herself attracted by George due to his mysterious thinking and readily expressed emotions.

The people staying at the pension take a carriage ride in the country. The unchaperoned Lucy is misdirected to George in a barley field as he admires the view. George suddenly embraces and passionately kisses Lucy as she approaches him, which is witnessed by Charlotte who has followed Lucy, and immediately ended by Charlotte. Charlotte believes George's act is dissolute while Lucy feels there is a secret desire and romance in bud in her heart despite being shocked by George's passion.

In order to save Lucy's reputation and her own, Charlotte should have permitted the engagement between Lucy and George. Instead, she convinces Lucy that the kissing is a shame and cannot be made public. In fact, Charlotte experienced such a heart-broken affair in her youth, so she shows her disgust and anger toward George whom she considered a dishonorable man.

Back in England, Lucy pretends to forget the incident and accepts a marriage proposal from Cecil Vyse, a wealthy and respectable but snobbish and pretentious man. It seems that Cecil lacks personality or emotion, for he prefers walking around outside or reading a novel aloud to playing tennis with Lucy. Shortly afterwards, Lucy learns the Emersons will be her neighbors and sure enough, George appears in the village. Lucy feels disrupted and her suppressed feelings rekindled, but she consistently refuses George's pursuit of her for keeping secret as she promised.

Then Lucy makes a sudden decision to break off her engagement to Cecil and plans to visit Greece. Lucy accidentally encounters George's father before the Emersons are about to move. Finally, she is conscious of her escape from George by travelling to other places. The story ends with Lucy and George's marriage in the Italian pension where they met, to be exact, in the room with a view.

◎ Quotes

Scene 1

George Emerson: He's the sort who can't know anyone intimately, least of all a woman. He doesn't know what a woman is. He wants you for a possession, something to look at, like a painting or an ivory box. Something to own and to display. He doesn't want you to be real, and to think and to live. He doesn't love you. But I love you. I want you to have your own thoughts and ideas and feelings, even when I hold you in my arms.

Scene 2

Reverend Beebe: It's not coincidental that you're here now, when one comes to reflect on it.

George Emerson: I have reflected. It's fate. Everything is fate.

Reverend Beebe: You've not reflected at all. Let me cross-examine you. Where did you meet Mr. Vyse, who will marry Miss Honeychurch?

George Emerson: The National Gallery.

Reverend Beebe: Looking at Italian art! You see, you talk of coincidence and fate. You're naturally drawn to things Italian, as are we and all our friends, aren't we, Freddy? That narrows the field immeasurably.

George Emerson: It is fate. But call it Italy if it pleases you, Vicar

Scene 3

Lucy Honeychurch: Why need mother hear of it?

Charlotte Bartlett: Well, you tell her everything, don't you?

Lucy Honeychurch: I suppose I do, generally.

Charlotte Bartlett: There's such a beautiful confidence between you. One would hate to break it. And as I have said before, I am to blame.

Lucy Honeychurch: I wouldn't want mother to think so.

Charlotte Bartlett: She will think so, if you tell her.

Lucy Honeychurch: I shall never speak of it, either to mother or to anyone.

Charlotte Bartlett: We will both be as silent as the grave.

2.8 *Four Weddings and a Funeral*

Introduction

Four Weddings and a Funeral is a 1994 British romantic comedy film directed by Mike Newell, written by Richard Cutis and stars Hugh Grant and Andie MacDowell. The story depicts the adventures of Charles and his circle of friends on a number of social occasions where they each encounter romance.

Completed in six weeks, costing under £3 million, the film becomes an unexpected success and the highest-grossing British film in cinema history at the time, with worldwide box office in excess of $ 245.7 million. It won two Academy Award nominations for Best Picture and Best Original Screenplay and four BAFTA awards including Grant's BAFTA Award for Best Actor. In addition, Grant was also awarded the Golden Globe Award for Best Actor — Motion Picture Musical or Comedy.

The film was very well received with critics, currently holding a 95% "Certified Fresh" approval on reviews aggregator Rotten Tomatoes. Film critic Roger Ebert gave the film three-and-a-half stars out of four, thinking highly of its direction and Grant's performance. In 1999, Four Weddings and a Funeral placed 23rd on the British Film Institute's Top 100 British films list.

Plot

The film tells the story that Charles, a good-natured but socially awkward man living in London, becomes smitten with Carrie, an American whom Charles keeps meeting at four weddings and a funeral. At the first wedding Charles serves as the best man and he wonders whether the bride and the bridegroom will ever get married. Charles encounters Carrie with whom he spends a wonderful night. Carrie believes they will have to get married now that they have slept together. Charles endeavors to respond before realizing she is joking.

The second wedding belongs to a couple who became romantically involved at the previous one. To his pleasant surprise, Charles meets Carrie again, only to be introduced to her fiancé, a wealthy politician. At the reception, Charles finds himself seated with several ex-girlfriends who tells embarrassing stories concerning his inability to be discreet. Charles has to escape to an empty hotel suite, seeing Carrie and her fiancé leave in a taxicab. Later Charles is awkwardly confronted with one of his ex-girlfriends and is being told that he is afraid of letting anyone get too close to him. Charles then nerves himself to run into Carrie, which bring about another sweet night together.

Some time later, Charles receives an invitation to Carrie's wedding. He goes shopping for a present when he coincidentally sees Carrie again and helps her select her wedding dress. Though he feels embarrassed, Charles tries confessing his love to her and hinting that he has the willingness to have a relationship with her, but in vain.

At the third wedding, Carrie's wedding, Charles finds himself in low spirits at the prospect of Carrie marrying fiancé. As Charles watches Carrie and her newly married husband dance, Fiona, one of his ex-girlfriend, figures out his feelings for Carrie. In addition, Fiona confesses that she has loved Charles since they first met years earlier. Charles shows his appreciation and empathy without responding to her love. During the groom's toast, one of Charles's friends dies of a heart attack, which results in the funeral where Charles and his friends talk about bachelordom, true love and marriage.

Several months later, the fourth wedding appears. Charles has decided to marry Henrietta. However, Carrie's sudden coming brings Charles the news that she is now separated from her husband. During the ceremony, when the vicar asks whether Charles does love someone else, and Charles replies, "I do." Henrietta punches Charles and the wedding is halted.

Carrie apologizes to Charles for attending the wedding. Finally Charles confesses that he longs for a lady's love totally and utterly for the first time in his life and he makes a proposal of lifelong commitment without marriage to Carrie who accepts. The story ends with people's marriages and the birth of Charles and Carrie's son.

◎ Quotes

Scene 1

Charles: How do you do, my name is Charles.

Old man: Don't be ridiculous, Charles died 20 years ago!

Charles: Must be a different Charles, I think.

Old man: Are you telling me I don't know my own brother!

Charles: No, no.

Scene 2

[at Gareth's funeral]

Matthew: Gareth used to prefer funerals to weddings. He said it was easier to get enthusiastic about a ceremony one had an outside chance of eventually being involved in. In order to prepare this speech, I rang a few people, to get a general picture of how Gareth was regarded by those who met him: "Fat" seems to have been a word people most connected with him. "Terribly rude" also rang a lot of bells. So very "fat" and very "rude" seems to have been a stranger's viewpoint. On the other hand, some of you have been kind enough to ring me and let me know that you loved him, which I know he would have been thrilled to hear. You remember his fabulous hospitality, his strange experimental cooking: the recipe for "Duck à la Banana" fortunately goes with him to his grave. Most of all, you tell me of his enormous capacity for joy. When joyful, when joyful for highly vocal drunkenness. But I hope joyful is how you will remember him, not stuck in a box in a church. Pick your favorite of his waistcoats and remember him that way. The most splendid, replete, big-hearted, weak-hearted as it turned out, and jolly bugger most of us ever met. As for me, you may ask how I will remember him, what I thought of him. Unfortunately, there I run out of words. Perhaps you will forgive me if I turn from my own feelings to the words of another splendid bugger: W. H. Auden. This is actually what I want to say: "***Stop all the clocks, cut off the telephone, Prevent the dog from barking with a juicy bone. Silence the pianos and with muffled drum, Bring out the coffin, let the mourners come. Let the aeroplanes circle, moaning overhead, Scribbling on the sky the message 'He is Dead'***. Put crepe bows 'round the white necks of the public doves, Let traffic policemen wear black cotton gloves. He was my North, my South, my East and West, My working week and my Sunday rest; My noon, my midnight, my talk, my song. I thought that love would last forever; I was wrong. The stars are not wanted now; put out every one, Pack up the moon and dismantle the sun; Pour away the ocean and sweep up the wood, For nothing now can ever come to any good."

Scene 3

[Charles comes running after Carrie]

Charles: Ehm, look. Sorry, sorry. I just, ehm, well, this is a very stupid question and... particularly in view of our recent shopping excursion, but I just wondered, by any chance, ehm, eh, I mean obviously not because I guess I've only slept with 9 people, but-but I-I just wondered... ehh. I really feel, ehh, in short, to recap it slightly in a clearer version, eh, the words of David Cassidy in fact, eh, while he was still with the Partridge family, eh, "I think I love you", and eh, I—I just wondered by any chance you wouldn't like to... Eh... Eh... No, no, no of course not... I'm an idiot, he's not... Excellent, excellent, fantastic, eh, I was gonna say lovely to see you, sorry to disturb... Better get on...

Carrie: That was very romantic.

Charles: Well, I thought it over a lot, you know, I wanted to get it just right.

2.9 *Sense and Sensibility*

Introduction

Sense and Sensibility, based on Jane Austen's 1811 novel of the same name, is a 1995 British-American period drama film directed by Ang Lee, produced by Lindsay Doran and written by actress Emma Thompson who stars as Elinor Dashwood. It also stars Kate Winslet, Hugh Grant and Alan Rickman. The story focuses on the Dashwood sisters' pursuit of love and marriage, along with their financial security.

Lindsay Doran, a longtime admirer of Austen's novel, invited Thompson to write the screenplay who spent five years drafting as a first-time screenwriter. Thompson's work was not fully faithful to the original one in order to cater the taste of contemporary viewers. In addition, Doran was convinced that Ang Lee's directing would appeal to a wider audience.

After its release in December 1995 in the United States and in February 1996 in the United Kingdom, the film achieved success both in commercial sense and in critical sense. The film received three awards and eleven nominations at the 1995 British Academy Film Awards. It also earned seven Academy Awards nominations. Thompson was the winner of the Best Adapted Screenplay, becoming the only person to have won Academy Awards for both acting and screenwriting. *Sense and Sensibility* has always been recognized as one of the best Austen adaptations of all time, which contributes to the popularity of Austen's works and more productions in similar genres.

Plot

The film is an adaption of Jane Austin's book *Sense and Sensibility*. When Mr. Dashwood dies, he requires his son John, from his previous marriage, to take care of his wife and three daughters — Elinor, Marianne and Margaret who are not entitled to his inheritance except only £500 a year. By contrast, John is left with the bulk of the estate of Norland Park.

John's wife Fanny, a greedy, snobbish woman, immediately installs herself and her husband in the palatial home and forces the Dashwood ladies to look for a new home. Fanny's brother Edward Ferrars is invited to stay with them, which brings about the budding friendship between Edward and Elinor and troubles Fanny who does everything possible to prevent it from developing.

Mrs. Dashwood and her daughters move in a small cottage house which belongs to her cousin Sir John Middleton on his estate, Barton Park in Devonshire. It is here that Marianne meets the older Colonel Brandon, who falls in love with her at first sight, and who in Marianne's eyes is an old bachelor without the knowledge of romance. Instead, the dashing but deceitful John Willoughby steals Marianne's heart. What the Dashwood family cannot expect is that Brandon's ward is found to be pregnant with Willoughby's child, and Willoughby has been disinherited by his aunt Lady Allen Willoughby has no choice but to move to London, dumping Marianne and leaving her heartbroken.

The impoverished Lucy Steele is invited to stay with John and Fanny, as a way for Fanny to avoid inviting the Dashwood sisters to visit them. Lucy confides in Elinor that she and Edward have been engaged secretly for five years, thus dashing Elinor's hopes of romance with him. Edward is demanded by his mother to break off the engagement and he refuses, only to find his fortune transferred to his younger brother, Robert. On hearing this, Colonel Brandon offers Edward the parish on his estate, feeling sympathy for the unfortunate but honorable Edward.

On their way home from London to Devonshire, Elinor and Marianne stop for the night at the country estate of the Palmers, who live near Willoughby. Marianne cannot resist the temptation to go to see his estate and she walks five miles in a torrential rain. Marianne is found by Colonel Brandon in the rain and brought back. Consequently, she falls seriously ill and recovers with Elinor's careful nursing. Later, Colonel Brandon and Marianne begin spending time together, as Marianne has a new appreciation for him.

Back in Devonshire, unexpectedly Lucy has married Edward's younger brother Robert and thanks to this, Edward is released from his engagement. In the end, Edward proposes to Elinor without hesitation and becomes a vicar, while Marianne falls in love with and marries Colonel Brandon.

◎ Quotes

Scene 1

Elinor Dashwood: You talk of feeling idle and useless. Imagine how that is compounded when one has no hope and no choice of any occupation whatsoever.

Edward Ferrars: Our circumstances are therefore precisely the same.

Elinor Dashwood: Except that you will inherit your fortune. We cannot even earn ours.

Edward Ferrars: Perhaps Margaret is right.

Elinor Dashwood: Right?

Edward Ferrars: Piracy is our only option.

Scene 2

Marianne: Always resignation and acceptance. Always prudence and honour and duty. Elinor, where is your heart?

Elinor Dashwood: What do you know of my heart? What do you know of anything but your own suffering. For weeks, Marianne, I've had this pressing on me without being at liberty to speak of it to a single creature. It was forced on me by the very person whose prior claims ruined all my hope. I have endured her exultations again and again whilst knowing myself to be divided from Edward forever. Believe me, Marianne, had I not been bound to silence I could have provided proof enough of a broken heart, even for you.

Scene 3

Colonel Brandon: Your sister seems very happy.

Elinor Dashwood: Yes. Marianne does not approve of hiding her emotions. In fact, her romantic prejudices have the unfortunate tendency to set propriety at naught.

Colonel Brandon: She is wholly unspoiled.

Elinor Dashwood: Rather too unspoiled, in my view. The sooner she becomes acquainted with the ways of the world, the better.

Colonel Brandon: I knew a lady very like your sister — the same impulsive sweetness of temper — who was forced into, as you put it, a better acquaintance with the world. The result was only ruination and despair. Do not desire it, Miss Dashwood.

2.10 *The English Patient*

Introduction

The English Patient is a 1996 British-American war drama film based on the novel of the same name by Sri Lankan-Canadian writer Michael Ondaatje. The film, written for the screen and directed by Anthony Minghella, stars Ralph Fiennes, Kristin Scott Thomas, Willem Dafoe and Juliette Binoche. Ondaatje worked closely with the filmmakers. The film was shot on location in Italy. with a production budget of $31 million.

Set before and during World War II, *The English Patient* is a story of love, fate, misunderstanding and healing. Told in a series of flashbacks, the film can best be explained by unwinding it into its two chronological phases.

Received 12 nominations at the 69th Academy Awards, the film eventually won nine, including Best Picture, Best Director for Minghella, and Best Supporting Actress for Juliette Binoche. In addition, it was a major winner at other award ceremonies: 2 out of 7 nominated Golden Globe Awards categories; and 6 out of 13 nominated BAFTA Award categories. The film achieved a widely critical and commercial success.

Plot

The film is set during World War II and depicts a critically burned man, at first known only as "the English patient", who is being looked after by Hana, a French-Canadian nurse in an abandoned Italian monastery. The patient is reluctant to disclose any personal information but through a series of flashbacks, viewers are allowed into his past. It is slowly revealed that he is in fact a cartographer, Count Lúszló de Almúsy, who was making a map of the Sahara Desert, and whose affair with a married woman, Katharine Clifton, ultimately brought about his present situation.

As the patient remembers more, David Caravaggio, a Canadian intelligence operative and former thief, arrives at the monastery. Caravaggio lost his thumbs while being interrogated by a German army officer, and he gradually reveals that it was the patient's actions that had brought about his torture. In addition to the patient's story, the film devotes time to Hana and her romance with Kip, an Indian Sikh sapper in the British Army. Due to various events in her past, Hana believes that anyone who comes close to her is likely to die, and Kip's position as a bomb defuser makes their romance full of tension.

In the first phase, set in the late 1930s, the minor Hungarian noble Count Laszlo de Almúsy is co-leader of a Royal Geographical Society archeological and surveying expedition in Egypt and Libya. He and his English partner Madox are at heart academics with limited sophistication in the swirling politics of Europe and North Africa. Shortly after the film begins, both the morale and finances of their expedition are bolstered by a British couple, Geoffrey and Katherine Clifton, that joins the exploration party. The Count is taken by the gorgeous and refined Katherine. When Geoffrey is often away from the group on other matters, an affair takes wing.

The final months before the war's onset bring an archeological triumph: the Count's discovery of an ancient Saharan cave decorated with "swimming figure" paintings dating from prehistoric times, the "Cave of Swimmers". This period also sees the romance between Katherine and the Count rising to a sensuous peak and then seemingly fading. Katherine is plagued with the guilt of infidelity, while the Count shows a streak of jealousy along with an imbalance that will later haunt him.

The fall of 1939 and the war bring all excavation at the cave to a halt, and Madox and the Count go their separate ways. Geoffrey Clifton meanwhile has pieced together the outline of the affair, and seeks a sudden and dramatic revenge: crashing his plane, with Katherine aboard, into the Count's desert camp. The wreck kills Geoffrey instantly, seriously injures Katherine, and narrowly misses the Count. He manages to take Katherine into the relative shelter of the swimming figure cave, leaves her with food, water, a flashlight, and a fire, then begins his scorching three-day walk back to the nearest town to get help.

The town is held by the British Army, and the dazed and dehydrated Count, with his non-English name, is unable to coherently explain to officials the plane crash and Katherine's plight. Instead he loses his temper during questioning and is thrown into military jail. He is sent in chains on a train "north to Benghazi", escapes, finds himself behind Afrika Korps lines and trades his desert maps with the Germans for petrol for Madox's biplane, a De Havilland Tiger Moth, which he had left behind at the close of their archaeological expedition.

By the time he returns to the cave, Katherine is dead — and in all but a physical sense, so is the Count. He manages to bundle Katherine's body into the plane and takes off. Mistaking the Tiger Moth for an RAF reconnaissance aircraft, a German anti-aircraft battery shoots down the plane as Almásy pilots it over the desert. Horribly burned but alive, he is rescued by Bedouin tribesmen but Katharine's body is vaporized in the explosion.

Hana finds reconciliation at the film's end. Kip survives a brush with death on the war's last day and her hope in love is rekindled. The Count asks for, and dies of, an overdose of morphine from Hana. The last scene shows Hana getting a ride to Florence, where Kip was reassigned; we are left with the possibility they may be reunited.

◎ Quotes

Scene 1

Katharine Clifton: My darling. I'm waiting for you. How long is the day in the dark? Or a week? The fire is gone, and I'm horribly cold. I really should drag myself outside but then there'd be the sun. I'm afraid I waste the light on the paintings, not writing these words. We die. We die rich with lovers and tribes, tastes we have swallowed, bodies we've entered and swum up like rivers. Fears we've hidden in — like this wretched cave. I want all this marked on my body. We are the real countries. Not boundaries drawn on maps with the names of powerful men. I know you'll come to carry me out to the Palace of Winds. That's what I've wanted: to walk in such a place with you. With friends, on an earth without maps. The lamp has gone out and I'm writing in the darkness.

Scene 2

Katharine Clifton: This — what is this?

Almásy: It's a folk song.

Katharine Clifton: Arabic.

Almásy: No, no. It's Hungarian. My daijka sang it to me when I was a child growing up in Budapest.

Katharine Clifton: It's beautiful. What's it about?

Almásy: Szerelem means love. And the story, well, there's this Hungarian count. He's a wanderer. He's a fool. And for years he's on some kind of a quest for... who knows what. And then one day, he falls under the spell of a mysterious English woman. A harpy, who beats him, and hits him, he becomes her slave, and he sews her clothes, and worships...

[Katharine starts hitting him]

Almásy: Stop it! Stop it! You're always beating me!

Katharine Clifton: Bastard! You bastard, I believed you! You should be my slave.

Scene 3

Hana: [reads Almásy's note on the firecracker] "Betrayals in war are childlike compared with our betrayals during peace. New lovers are nervous and tender, but smash everything. For the heart is an organ of fire." For the heart is an organ of fire. I love that. I believe that. K? Who is K?

Almásy: K is for Katharine.

2.11 *Trainspotting*

Introduction

Trainspotting, a 1996 British black comedy crime film based on the novel of the same name by Irvine Welsh, is directed by Danny Boyle, and stars Ewan McGregor, Ewen Bremner, Jonny Lee Miller, Kevin McKidd, Robert Carlyle, and Kelly Macdonald in her acting debut.

The story centers on a group of heroin addicts in an economically depressed area of Edinburgh, and explores the theme "drug abuse" and the young people's experiences and sufferings in life, together with other themes like urban poverty and squalor in Edinburgh.

In the original book, there is a scene in a disused railway station where Renton and Begbie meet an old drunkard who, actually Begbie's estranged father, asks them if they are trainspotting. The film title is a reference to the scene which is not included in the film.

The filming spanned seven weeks in mid-1995 on a budget of £1.5 million with an abandoned cigarette factory in Glasgow being the shooting location. Time constraints and a tight budget result in that most scenes were done in one take.

The film's release in the United Kingdom in February 1996 exerted an immediate impact on popular culture and sparked controversy in some countries as well, including Britain, Australia and the United States, as to whether or not it promoted and romanticized drug use.

In Britain, *Trainspotting* is met with widespread acclaim from critics. ranking 10th by the British Film Institute (BFI) in its list of Top 100 British films of all time.

Plot

The films opens with the introduction to Heroin addict Mark Renton and his circle of friends: amoral con artist Simon "Sick Boy" Williamson (also an addict); slow-witted, kind-hearted Daniel "Spud" Murphy (another addict); clean-cut athlete Thomas "Tommy" MacKenzie; and the aggressive and pugnacious psychopath Francis "Franco" Begbie, who fights against anyone who stands in the way.

Renton decides to give up heroin and buys opium suppositories to ease the transition. After that, he locks himself in a cheap hotel room to endure the withdrawal period. Later at a club with his friends, he meets a girl named Diane and has sexual act with Diane in her bedroom. The next morning, to his surprise, he finds that Diane is a 15-year-old schoolgirl and tries to ignore the happening, only to be forced to remain in touch after Diane blackmails him.

Renton starts using heroin again with his friends. Tommy, whose girlfriend dumped him after a chain of events initiated by Renton, becomes an addict like them. One day, a storm comes for Allison, their friend and fellow addict, discovers that her infant daughter has died due to the group's ignoring, which causes their panic. Ridiculously, one of the guys is the infant's father but no one knows who he is.

On account of stealing from a bookshop, Renton and Spud are arrested. Spud is put into jail while Renton gets away with it by taking part in a drug interventions program, where he is given methadone. The support from his family doesn't drag Renton out of morass. Renton is so desperate for drugs that at his drug dealer's flat, he nearly dies of an overdose, only to be sent to hospital. After leaving the hospital, Renton is taken home, locked in his bedroom and compelled to go through withdrawal. Renton feels frightened because he has hallucinations of Diane singing on the bed, the infant crawling on the ceiling, and Renton's parents answering questions about HIV in an imaginary TV game show.

Renton is finally awoken from his nightmares and hallucinations by his parents. To his relief, Renton finds himself tested negative in spite of years of sharing syringes with other addicts while Tommy is now HIV positive and severely ill. Renton lives a new life in London with taking a job as a property letting agent. While enjoying sobriety, he saves money secretly and corresponds with Diane. However, good days are not long as Renton expects, for Begbie, who has committed an armed robbery, and Sick Boy, now a pimp and drug dealer, move into Renton's bedsit unannounced, to Renton's annoyance.

In Edinburgh, Tommy dies of AIDS-related illness and the three go back to attend his funeral where they meet Spud, who has been released from prison. Sick Boy suggests a lucrative yet dangerous heroin transaction which requires Renton to supply half of the initial £4,000. Renton, after testing the heroin's purity, agrees and the four sell the heroin to a dealer in London for £16,000.

The next morning, as the others sleep, Renton quietly takes the money from sleeping Begbie, which is found by Spud who wakes up just as Renton is leaving the hotel room. When Begbie awakens, he destroys the room in a violent rage. The police subsequently arrives, but Spud and Sick Boy successfully flees. By leaving Spud £4,000, Renton vows to live a stable and normal life and he embraces his new life.

◎ Quotes

Scene 1

[first lines]

Mark "Rent-boy" Renton: [narrating] Choose Life. Choose a job. Choose a career. Choose a family. Choose a fucking big television, choose washing machines, cars, compact disc players and electrical tin openers. Choose good health, low cholesterol, and dental insurance. Choose fixed interest mortgage repayments. Choose a starter home. Choose your friends. Choose leisurewear and matching luggage. Choose a three-piece suit on hire purchase in a range of fucking fabrics. Choose DIY and wondering who the fuck you are on Sunday morning. Choose sitting on that couch watching mind-numbing, spirit-crushing game shows, stuffing fucking junk food into your mouth. Choose rotting away at the end of it all, pissing your last in a miserable home, nothing more than an embarrassment to the selfish, fucked up brats you spawned to replace yourselves. Choose your future. Choose life... But why would I want to do a thing like that? I chose not to choose life. I chose somethin' else. And the reasons? There are no reasons. Who needs reasons when you've got heroin?

Scene 2

Mark "Rent-boy" Renton: Excuse me, excuse me. I don't mean to harass you, but I was very impressed with the capable and stylish manner in which you dealt with that situation. And I was thinking to myself, now this girl's special.

Diane: Thanks.

Mark "Rent-boy" Renton: What's your name?

Diane: Diane.

Mark "Rent-boy" Renton: And where are you going, Diane?

Diane: I'm going home.

Mark "Rent-boy" Renton: Well, where's that?

Diane: It's where I live.

Mark "Rent-boy" Renton: Great.

Diane: What?

Mark "Rent-boy" Renton: Well, I'll come back with you if you like, but like, I'm not promising anything, you know.

Diane: Do you find that this approach usually works? Or let me guess, you've never tried it before. In fact, you don't normally approach girls — am I right? The truth is that you're a quiet sensitive type but, if I'm prepared to take a chance, I might just get to know the inner you: witty, adventurous, passionate, loving, loyal. Taxi! A little bit crazy, a little bit bad. But hey — don't us girls just love that?

Mark "Rent-boy" Renton: Eh?

Diane: Well, what's wrong boy — cat got your tongue?

Scene 3

Mark "Rent-boy" Renton: [on a high] Take the best orgasm you've ever had... multiply it by a thousand, and you're still nowhere near it.

Allison: It beats any meat injection. That beats any fucking cock in the world.

2.12 *Elizabeth*

Introduction

Elizabeth, a 1998 British biographical film is written by Michael Hirst and directed by

Shekhar Kapur, starring Cate Blanchett in the title role of Queen Elizabeth I of England. The film centers on the early years of Elizabeth's reign, followed by the sequel, *Elizabeth: The Golden Age* (2007), which covers the later years of her reign.

The story, full of palace intrigues, attempted assassinations and executions, sees how young Elizabeth puts down the threats both internal and external, defeats all her enemies, and finally grows to be the "Virgin Queen" who initiates Golden Age in England.

Elizabeth premiered in September 1998 at the Venice Film Festival, also shown at the Toronto International Film Festival and received positive reviews from critics and the public. It was awarded the 1998 BAFTA Award for Best British Film and was nominated for seven awards at the 71st Academy Awards, including Best Picture and Best Actress, winning Best Makeup.

The Australian actress Blanchett has aroused international attention successfully by her portrayal of Elizabeth, for which she won several awards, notably a BAFTA and a Golden Globe in 1998. It's said that the director's original choice for the role was not Cate Blanchett before the chosen actress turned it down.

Plot

In 1558 when England divided by faith, Protestant vs. Catholic, the Catholic Queen Mary Tudor, who has no heir, dies of a uterine tumor. Mary's Protestant half-sister, Elizabeth, under house arrest for conspiracy charges, is freed and given the throne of the Queen of England.

What Elizabeth is confronted with and inherits is a distressed England besieged by debts, crumbling infrastructure, hostile neighbors and treasonous nobles. The Duke of Norfolk is among them. Though William Cecil, the queen's adviser, advises her to marry, produce an heir, and thus secure her rule, Elizabeth still secretly develops an affair with Lord Robert Dudley. But Cecil appoints Francis Walsingham, a Protestant exile returned from France, to act as Elizabeth's bodyguard and adviser.

When facing an additional 4,000 French troops in neighboring Scotland, unfamiliar with military strategy, Elizabeth orders a military response, which proves disastrous because the younger, ill-trained English forces fail to be comparable to the professional French soldiers.

Elizabeth is informed that Catholic lords and priests intentionally deprived her army of proper soldiers and attempted to remove her by making use of her defeat. Realizing the depth of the conspiracy against her, Elizabeth gives serious thought to her marriage.

In dealing with England's religious divisions to stabilize her rule, Elizabeth proposes the *Act of Uniformity*, which unites English Christians under the Church of England, but separates England from the Vatican. Consequently, the Vatican decides to help Norfolk overthrow Elizabeth.

After surviving an assassination attempt, Elizabeth has to meet the challenge of another plot to kill her and learns in detail that a Vatican agreement has been made to elevate Norfolk to the English crown. Walsingham arrests Norfolk, and executes him and every conspirator except Lord Robert, whom Elizabeth allows to live in order to remind herself of her blindness and the lesson.

In the end, Elizabeth cuts her hair and proclaims herself married to England, known as the "Virgin Queen".

◎ Quotes

Scene 1

Queen Mary: Why will you not confess your crimes against me?

Elizabeth: Because, Your Majesty, I have committed none.

Queen Mary: You speak with such sincerity. I see you are still a consummate actress. My husband is gone. They have poisoned my child. They say it is a tumor.

[Moans in pain]

Elizabeth: Madam, you are not well.

Queen Mary: They say this cancer will make you queen, but they are wrong. Look there, it is your death warrant. All I need do is sign it.

Elizabeth: Mary, if you sign that paper you will be murdering your own sister.

Scene 2

Lord Robert: When you are Queen...

Elizabeth: I am not...

[whispering]

Elizabeth: I am not Queen yet!

Lord Robert: You will be. Elizabeth, Queen of England. A court to worship you, a country to obey you, poems written celebrating your beauty, music composed in your honor, and they will mean nothing to you. I will mean nothing to you.

Elizabeth: [laughs gaily] How could you ever be nothing to me? Robert, you know you are everything to me.

Scene 3

[last lines]

Elizabeth: Observe, Lord Burghley, I am married... to England.

2.13 *Harry Potter and the Philosopher's Stone*

Introduction

Harry Potter and the Philosopher's Stone (released in some countries as *Harry Potter and the Sorcerer's Stone*), based on the novel of the same name by J. K. Rowling, is a 2001 British-American fantasy film written by Steve Kloves, produced by David Heyman and directed by Chris Columbus. The film stars Daniel Radcliffe as Harry Potter, with Rupert Grint as Ron Weasley,

and Emma Watson as Hermione Granger. The film, as the first part, belongs to the long-running Harry Potter film series. It tells the story of Harry Potter who begins his first-year education at Hogwarts School of Witchcraft and Wizardry, where he learns wizardry and fights against his enemies with his friends.

In 1997, producer David Heyman searched for a children's book that could be adapted into a well-received film, and then he was suggested *Harry Potter and the Philosopher's Stone*.

Director Chris Columbus was the final choice to make the film from a short list of directors that included Steven Spielberg who declined the offer though initially negotiated. Production took place in the United Kingdom in 2000, with Rowling's requirement that the entire cast should be British or Irish.

After its release in the United Kingdom and the United States in November 2001, the film succeeded in both critical and commercial sense, with it being the highest grossing film of 2001. It gained many nominations as well including the Academy Award for Best Original Score, Best Art Direction and Best Costume Design.

The film is followed by seven sequels from *Harry Potter and the Chamber of Secrets* in 2002 to *Harry Potter and the Deathly Hallows — Part 2* in 2011, which has achieved great popularity worldwide.

Plot

An orphaned infant named Harry Potter is delivered by the professors of Hogwarts School of Witchcraft and Wizardry to his only remaining relatives, the Dursleys in Little Whinging, Surrey, England. Years later, Harry has grown up but he is not living a satisfying life with the Dursleys for he is considered a big trouble in the Dursleys family.

After inadvertently causing an accident on a family outing and receiving several unsolicited letters by owl, Hagrid, the professor of Hogwarts School, appears and informs Harry that he is a wizard and is famous in the Wizarding World for being the first and only one to survive an attack by Lord Voldemort who is a once-powerful dark wizard. It's said that Voldemort terrorized the Wizarding World and killed those who stood in his way including Harry's parents.

Harry feels delighted that he will a student in Hogwarts. He then boards the train to Hogwarts via the concealed Platform 9¾ at King's Cross station after purchasing studying supplies from the hidden London street Diagon Alley. On the train, Harry encounters his new friends: Ron Weasley, a boy from a large but poor pure-blood wizarding family, and Hermione Granger, a witch born to non-magical parents.

At the great hall of Hogwarts, Harry and all the other first-year students are sorted to enter four houses: Gryffindor, Hufflepuff, Ravenclaw, and Slytherin. Harry ends up in Gryffindor along with Ron and Hermione as he wishes, for he is unwilling to be a member of Slytherin because

Slytherin is noted for cultivating darker wizards and witches. Among the first-year students, Draco Malfoy impresses Harry greatly and later becomes a rival to Harry. At Hogwarts, Harry begins his new school life, learning wizardry and discovering more about his past and his parents.

At a restricted area of the school, Harry, Ron and Hermione find Fluffy, a giant three-headed dog owned by Hagrid, guarding the Philosopher's Stone, an item that can be used to grant its owner immortality, as long as it is constantly used. Harry strongly suspects that his potions teacher, Severus Snape, is greedy to obtain the stone in order to help Voldemort back to a human form.

After knowing that Fluffy will fall asleep if music is played, Harry, Ron, and Hermione decide to find the stone ahead of Snape. However, they are confronted with a series of difficult tasks that prevent people from finding the stone, such as surviving a deadly plant known as Devil's Snare, flying amidst winged, flying keys, and winning a dangerous, life-sized game of chess.

Later, to Harry's surprise, it is Professor Quirrell, a Defense Against the Dark Arts teacher, who wants to steal the stone while Snape is protecting Harry all along. Voldemort appears, living on the back of Quirrell's head, attempts to convince Harry to give him the stone which Harry suddenly finds in his pocket as the result of an enchantment by Dumbledore, only to be refused by Harry. Harry's touch turns Quirrell into dust, but Voldemort's spirit rises from Quirrell's ashes and passes through Harry, knocking him unconscious before fleeing.

Harry wakes up at the school's hospital with the company of the headmaster Dumbledore who explains that the stone has been destroyed and thinks highly of the children's courage despite Ron nearly being killed in the chess match. It is because the death of Harry's mother provides Harry with a magical, love-based protection against Voldemort that Harry could defeat enemies.

In the end, Harry, Ron, and Hermione are rewarded with house points for their heroic deeds, winning Gryffindor the House Cup. Summer is approaching, Harry is reluctant to leave Hogwarts for he realizes it is truly his home.

◎ Quotes

Scene 1

Dumbledore: Harry, do you know why Professor Quirrell couldn't bear to have you touch him?

[Harry shakes his head]

Dumbledore: It was because of your mother. She sacrificed herself for you, and that kind of act leaves a mark.

[Harry reaches up to touch his scar]

Dumbledore: No, no. This kind of mark cannot be seen. It lives in your very skin.

Harry: What is it?

Dumbledore: Love, Harry. Love.

Scene 2

Hermione: You'll be okay, Harry. You're a great wizard. You really are.

Harry: Not as good as you.

Hermione: Me? Books and cleverness. There are more important things: friendship and bravery. And Harry, just be careful.

Scene 3

Hermione: Now if you two don't mind, I'm going to bed before either of you come up with another clever idea to get us killed — or worse, expelled.

Ron: She needs to sort out her priorities!

2.14 *Slumdog Millionaire*

Introduction

Slumdog Millionaire, loosely adapted from the novel *Q & A* (2005) by the Indian author and diplomat Vikas Swarup, is a 2008 British drama film directed by Danny Boyle, written by Simon Beaufoy, and produced by Christian Colson.

Set and filmed in India, it tells the story of Jamal Malik, an 18-year-old young man from the Juhu slums of Mumbai, who joins a TV show named Who Wants to Be a Millionaire?, and incredibly knows answers to all questions for which he is accused of cheating. Jamal recounts his life story to explain why he can answer each question.

The film had its world premiere at the Telluride Film Festival in August 2008 where it was welcomed by audiences. Later, it had a nationwide release in the United Kingdom, the United States and India respectively in January 2009.

In the same year, it achieved a great success with ten Academy Award nominations and finally made it to be the winner of eight awards including Best Picture, Best Director, and Best Adapted Screenplay. What's more, it won seven BAFTA Awards including Best Film, five Critics' Choice Awards and four Golden Globes. Slumdog Millionaire is widely acclaimed for its plot, soundtrack and direction, always named in the top ten lists of various newspapers. In India, it even becomes a subject of discussion among a variety of people.

Plot

It is the story of Jamal Malik, an 18-year-old orphan from the slums of Mumbai, who is about to embrace the most important day of his life. He is taking part in the Indian TV program called "Who Wants to Be a Millionaire?" and is just one question away from winning the grand prize: 20 million rupees.

However, shockingly, he is detained and tortured by the police for he is accused of cheating in the program. The reason lies in that Jamal, a simple "slumdog" with very little education, has no possibility to know all the answers to the questions. Therefore, in retrospect, Jamal recounts the incidents happened in his life which offered him answers.

Back to Jamal's childhood, at the age of five, he manages to obtain the autograph of a Bollywood super star. He and his brother Salim sells the picture, followed immediately by the death of his mother during the Bombay riots. On their way to flee, the brothers meet Latika, a girl also from their slum. Salim is unwilling to take her in but at last agrees for Jamal suggests that she could be the "third musketeer", a character from the Alexandre Dumas novel *The Three Musketeers*.

Unfortunately, the children encounter a gangster, Maman who tricks and then trains street children for begging. After discovering Maman's cruelty which means that he blinds the children to make them more reliable beggars, the three flee to a departing train. Latika fails to board the train as Salim lets go of her hand on purpose, which leads to her being recaptured by Maman.

In the following years, the brothers, travelling on top of trains, earn a living by selling goods, picking pockets, working as dish washers. While disguising themselves as tour guides at the Taj Mahal, they also steal people's shoes.

Jamal persists in finding Latika and they return to Mumbai. To their surprise, Latika is being raised by Maman to be a prostitute, who is about to bring a large sum of money to Maman as a virgin. The brothers rescue her, and have to shoot Maman to death. Salim then works for Javed—Maman's rival crime lord and he orders Jamal to leave him and Latika alone by drawing a gun on him. Jamal has no choice but to listen to Latika and go away.

Years later, Jamal, working at an Indian call centre as a Chaiwala searches the centre's database for Salim and Latika. He makes it in finding Salim, now a high-ranking lieutenant in Javed's crime organisation.

Jamal later bluffs his way into Javed's residence to reunite with Latika who asks him to forget about her when faced with Jamal's love. Nevertheless Jamal doesn't give up, instead, he waits for her every day at five o'clock at a train station. Latika attempts to meet him there, but fails and is recaptured by Javed's men. Again, Latika and Jamal lose touch with each other.

As he knows that Latika watches the show regularly, Jamal decides to be a contestant on Who Wants to Be a Millionaire, and becomes a wonder across India. Jamal uses the 50/50 lifeline on the penultimate question, though he is fed with a wrong answer, Jamal is smart enough to choose the other one which turns out to be the correct answer.

Back to the opening in the film, the police inspector listens to Jamal's explanation of how he knew each answer. Jamal is allowed back to the show for what he explained sounds bizarrely plausible. At Javed's safehouse, Latika watches TV and knows what Jamal is doing as Jamal has predicted. Salim feels deeply guilty and he helps Latika flee by offering her his own phone and a car key.

Jamal has no answer to the final question which is the name of the third musketeer in *The*

Three Musketeers. Then he uses his "Phone-A-Friend" lifeline to call Salim, but Latika answers the phone and tells Jamal that she is safe. Relieved, Jamal arbitrarily picks the right answer, and wins the grand prize. Salim kills Javed before he is shot. The story ends with Jamal and Latika's meeting on the platform at the railway station.

◎ Quotes

Scene 1

[Salim and Jamal are sitting on the edge of an apartment floor, under construction]

Older Salim: That... used to be our slum. Can you believe that, huh?

[pointing at something]

Older Salim: We used to live right there, man. Now, it's all business. India is at the center of the world now, bhai. And I... I am at the center... of the center. This is all Javed bhai's.

Jamal Malik: Javed Khan... the gangster from our slum? You work for him?

Older Salim: Come on, who else do you think would save us from Maman's guys, huh?

Jamal Malik: What do you do for him?

Older Salim: Anything he asks.

[pause in conversation, as Salim's phone rings]

Older Salim: He's coming. You need to go now. Take my card.

Jamal Malik: What for?

Older Salim: You think I'm gonna let you out of my sights again, huh? You stay with me now, younger brother. Now, go. My place.

Jamal Malik: Salim, where is Latika?

Older Salim: Still...? She's gone, brother. Long gone. Now, go. Go to my place.

Scene 2

Youngest Jamal: I just need Maman to like my singing, and were in the money, big money Latika.

Youngest Latika: And then what? Can we stop begging?

vYoungest Jamal: Begging? Are you kidding? We'll live in a big house on Harbor Road. You, me and Salim, the three musketeers.

Youngest Latika: Harbor Road? Really?

Youngest Jamal: Yes, in the moonlight. You and me. You'll dance with me won't you?

[dances]

Youngest Latika: [laughs] I hope you sing better than you dance.

Scene 3

Latika: You want to do something for me?

Jamal Malik: Anything.

Latika: Then forget me!

2.15 *The King's Speech*

Introduction

The King's Speech is a 2010 British historical drama film directed by Tom Hooper, written by David Seidler, and stars Colin Firth as the title role. The writer Seidler, who developed a stammer in his youth, was inspired by King George VI's success in overcoming his stammer after reading about the king's life story.

The film tells the story of King George VI who suffers from stammer, eventually defeats it and successfully makes his first wartime radio broadcast on Britain's declaration of war on Germany in 1939 with the help of Lionel Logue, an Australian speech and language therapist. The film shows the friendship between the king and his therapist as well.

The filming took place in London and around Britain from November 2009 to January 2010. Nine weeks before filming began, Logue's notebooks were discovered and quotations from them were incorporated into the script. The cinematography demonstrates its difference from that of other historical films mainly because three techniques are employed: hard light, wider lenses, and off-center framing of characters.

Released in the United Kingdom in January 2011, the film achieved a great commercial and critical success. On a budget of £8 million, it earned over £250 million worldwide. It was extensively acclaimed for its visual style, art direction, and acting. The film's representation of historical detail also aroused discussion, especially the reversal of Winston Churchill's opposition to abdication.

It's worth mentioning that Colin Firth has made it by earning himself Golden Globe Award, Academy Award, British Academy Film Award for his excellent acting as King George VI. To sum up, the film received many awards and nominations, including seven British Academy Film Awards, and four Academy Awards.

Plot

The film opens with the closing of the British Empire Exhibition at Wembley Stadium, where the Prince Albert, Duke of York, the second son of King George V, addresses people with a strong stammer.

"Bertie", as Prince Albert is called by his family, feels frustrated in the search for his treatment but his wife Elizabeth introduces a man to him who is Lionel Logue, an Australian-born, non-medically trained Harley Street speech defects therapist.

After the first session of therapy, Bertie is disappointed for he believes the first session is not going well although he manages to recite on an acetate recording, Hamlet's "To be, or not to be" soliloquy sublimely all the while hearing piped-in classical music on a pair of head phones.

King George V, Bertie's father, makes his 1934 Christmas wireless address, and emphasizes to Bertie the significance of the machine in the role of the Royal Family invading the homes of the people. Bertie returns for daily treatments of exercises and practices to overcome the rooted physical and psychological obstacles of his speaking difficulty.

After the death of George V in 1936, David, his eldest son accedes to the throne as King Edward VIII, whose perspective marriage with the twice-divorced American socialite Wallis Simpson brings a constitutional crisis. The new king, as head of the Church of England, cannot marry her simply because both her previous husbands are alive.

At an unscheduled session, Bertie is delighted with his improvement when speaking to most people, while frustrated by his stammering when talking to David for he shows great concern over David's folly with Simpson. In Lionel's eyes, Bertie has the ability to be a good king, but he accuses Lionel of speaking treason and quits Lionel. King Edward eventually steps out of his dilemma and decides to abdicate in order to marry Simpson, and hence Bertie becomes King George VI, which brings Lionel back to Bertie.

Bertie's and Lionel's relationship is made known to the King's advisors when there are preparations for his coronation in Westminster Abbey. It is uncovered that George never sought advice from his advisors about his speech defect treatment and that Lionel served as a medical doctor without any formal training. In response, Lionel explains that there was no formal training at the time when he started with speech defects and his therapy is based on his personal experience in helping Australian soldiers.

Bertie is still not sure of his suitability as king and is encouraged by Lionel to express his voice by disrespecting King Edward's Chair and the Stone of Scone. As a result, Bertie successfully completes the coronation ceremony due to his repeated rehearsal.

In 1939, Bertie encounters difficulty that he must finish his speech over the wireless concerning the Britain's declaration of World War II with Nazi Germany. Bertie summons Lionel to Buckingham Palace to prepare Bertie for his wireless address to Britain and the Empire. In what's more, the Archbishop of Canterbury, Winston Churchill and Prime Minister Neville Chamberlain are present to support Bertie.

In the broadcasting room, Bertie delivers his speech with Lionel conducting him, and gradually he speaks freely. To his relief, Bertie does a good job and receives congratulations from people in the palace, though he still has difficulty enunciating "w" from which the King thinks he could be recognized. The Royal Family step onto the balcony of the palace and are applauded by the crowd. From then on, when making speech during the war, the King is always accompanied by Lionel and they remain friends for the rest of their lives.

◎ Quotes

Scene 1

King George VI: In this grave hour, perhaps the most fateful in our history, I send to every household of my peoples, both at home and overseas, this message, spoken with the same depth of feeling for each one of you, as if I were able to cross your threshold and speak to you myself: For the second time in the lives of most of us, we are at... at war. Over and over again we have tried to find a peaceful way out of the differences between ourselves and those who are now our enemies, but it has been in vain. We have been forced into a conflict, for we are called to meet the challenge of a principle, which, if it were to prevail, would be fatal to any civilized order in the world. Such a principle, stripped of all disguise, is surely the mere primitive doctrine that "might is right". For the sake of all that we ourselves hold dear, it is unthinkable that we should refuse to meet the challenge. It is to this high purpose that I now call my people at home, and my peoples across the seas, who will make our cause their own. I ask them to stand calm and firm and united in this time of trial. The task will be hard. There may be dark days ahead, and war can no longer be confined to the battlefield, but we can only do the right as we see the right, and reverently commit our cause to God. If one and all we keep resolutely faithful to it, then, with God's help, we shall prevail.

Scene 2

King George VI: [Sees Logue is sitting on the coronation throne] What are you doing? Get up! You can't sit there! GET UP!

Lionel Logue: Why not? It's a chair.

King George VI: No, it... That is not a chair. That is... that is Saint Edward's chair.

Lionel Logue: People have carved their names on it.

King George VI: [simultaneously] That... chair... is the seat on which every king and queen...

Lionel Logue: [simultaneously] It's held in place by a large rock.

King George VI: That is the Stone of Scone. You ah—are trivializing everything. You trivialize...

Lionel Logue: I don't care about how many royal arseholes...

King George VI: Listen to me.

Lionel Logue: ... have sat in this chair.

King George VI: Listen to me. Listen to me!

Lionel Logue: Listen to you? By what right?

King George VI: By divine right, if you must. I am your king.

Lionel Logue: No, you're not. You told me so yourself. You said you didn't want it. Why should I waste my time listening...?

King George VI: Because I have a right to be heard! I have a voice!

Lionel Logue: [pauses] Yes, you do.

[Longer pause]

Lionel Logue: You have such perseverance, Bertie. You're the bravest man I know. You'll make a bloody good king.

◎ Exercises

1. Introduce the following films in English.

1) *Citizen Kane*
2) *City Lights*
3) *The Third Man*
4) *Trainspotting*
5) *Harry Potter and the Philosopher's Stone*

2. Match the actors or actresses with their films.

Section A

1) *Citizen Kane*	a. Vivien Leigh
2) *Casablanca*	b. Gene Kelly
3) *Schindler's List*	c. Marlon Brando
4) *The Shawshank Redemption*	d. Orson Welles
5) *Vertigo*	e. Kate Winslet
6) *The Godfather*	f. Robert De Niro
7) *Gone with the Wind*	g. Liam Neeson
8) *Raging Bull*	h. James Stewart
9) *Sing'in in the Rain*	i. Ingrid Bergman
10) *Titanic*	j. Morgan Freeman

Section B

1) *A Room with a View*	a. Ralph Fiennes
2) *The King's Speech*	b. Peter O'Toole
3) *Trainspotting*	c. John Mills
4) *The Third Man*	d. Orson Welles
5) *Great Expectations*	e. Ewan McGregor
6) *Four Weddings and a Funeral*	f. Maggie Smith
7) *Elizabeth*	g. Hugh Grant
8) *Sense and Sensibility*	h. Kate Blanchet
9) *Lawrence of Arabia*	i. Kate Winslet
10) *The English Patient*	j. Colin Firth

3. Discuss and answer the following questions.

1) Among the films introduced above, which one is your favorite? And why?

2) How do you interpret the humanity, love and justice exhibited in *Casablanca*?
3) Do you think what has been conveyed or reflected in the story *The Godfather*?
4) How do you define "hope" in *The Shawshank Redemption*? And how do you like Andy?
5) Do you admire the love between Jack and Rose in *Titanic*? Why or why not?
6) Do you agree that *Forrest Gump's* success is accidental? In real life, can a man like him succeed?
7) What has attracted you most in the film *Vertigo*? Have you seen other Hitchcock's films?
8) What makes *Singin' in the Rain* so great that it is the No. 1 musical on the American Film Institute's list of great musicals?
9) Why do you think King George VI could overcome his speaking problem?
10) Do you like the story *The Third Man*? Who does "the third man" refer to?
11) In your eyes, what kind of man is Lawrence? Why is he called "Lawrence of Arabia"?
12) What did "the English patient" suffer during the WWII? Do you admire his love?
13) Do you think what's the theme of the story *Great Expectations*? How do you define "great expectations"?
14) Can you tell the life story of Queen Elizabeth I? Do you know other kings or queens in British history?
15) Have you read Jane Austin's novel *Sense and Sensibility*? What do you think of the social status of women in Jane Austin's era?

Module Two
Literature in English Films

Unit 1
British Literature Overview

Often referred to as UK literature, British literature primarily refers to the body of written works produced in the English language from the 7th century to the present day by British authors from the United Kingdom, which includes England, Scotland, Northern Ireland, Wales, the Channel Islands, and Isle of Man. British literature includes works in Old, Middle, and Modern English, each of which represents a different period. British literature has come to possess different characteristics over the years. People can fully appreciate it by learning the different types of literature that came to play in its history.

1. The Old English Period and Middle English Period (450-1500)

The Old English period started in the 5th century when the Jutes, Angles and Saxons came to England from Germany, defeated the English tribes and started their reign. It ended in 1066 when Norman France, under William, conquered England. The subsequent Middle English period started with the Norman Conquest in 1066 and ended with the end of 15th century.

1.1 Old English Literature (c. 658-1066)

The Prehistoric Old English (c. 450 to c. 650) period was basically barren in literary creations since Old English in this period was mostly a reconstructed language and no literary witnesses survived (with the exception of limited epigraphic evidence). In this sense, Old English literature refers to literature written in Old English, in Anglo-Saxon England from about the 7th century to the decades after the Norman Conquest of 1066.

From the end of the 7th century, Old English flourished in substantial quantity and in a multitude of genres and forms, representing the most significant body of popular literature of any European country at that time. Its officially authorized status—its use by government and church—meant that as a language of expression, it could be employed for all kinds of writing, much of it of exceptionally high quality.

In descending order of quantity, Old English literature consists of: sermons and saints' lives; biblical translations; translated Latin works of the early Church Fathers; Anglo-Saxon chronicles and narrative history works; laws, wills and other legal works; practical works on grammar, medicine, geography; and poetry. In all there are over 400 surviving manuscripts from the period, of which about 189 are considered significant.

Poetry

Most Old English poetry is preserved in four manuscripts of the late 10th and early 11th centuries. The Beowulf Manuscript contains *Beowulf*, *Judith*, and three prose tracts; the Exeter Book includes lyrics, riddles, instructive poems, and religious narratives; the Junius Manuscript —also called the Caedmon Manuscript, even though its contents are no longer attributed to Caedmon—contains biblical paraphrases; and the Vercelli Book contains saints' lives, several short religious poems, and prose homilies.

Most Old English poems are recorded without authors, and very few names are known with any certainty; the primary are Cædmon and Cynewulf.

The Angles, Saxons, and Jutes who invaded Britain in the 5th and 6th centuries brought with them the common Germanic metre; but of their earliest oral poetry, probably used for praise, magic, and short narrative, little or none survives. For nearly a century after the conversion of King Æthelberht I of Kent to Christianity, there is no evidence that the English wrote poetry in their own language. But author and scholar, "the Father of English History" St. Bede the Venerable(672-735), in his *Historia Ecclesiastica Gentis Anglorum* (*Ecclesiastical History of the English People*), wrote that in the late 7th century Caedmon, an illiterate Northumbrian cowherd, was inspired in a dream to compose a short hymn in praise of the creation. Caedmon later composed verses based on Scripture, which was elaborated for him by monks at Streaneshalch (now called Whitby), but only *The Hymn of Creation* survives. Caedmon legitimized the native verse form by adapting it to Christian themes. Others, following his example, gave England a body of vernacular poetry unparalleled in Europe before the end of the 1st millennium.

The most important author from whom a considerable body of work survives is Cynewulf. His works include *The Fates of the Apostles*; *The Ascension* (also called *Christ II*); *Juliana*; and *Elene*, perhaps the best of his poems. Cynewulf's work is lucid and technically elegant; his theme is the continuing evangelical mission from the time of Christ to the triumph of Christianity under Constantine. Also in the "Cynewulf group" are several poems with Christ as their subject, of which the most important is *The Dream of the Rood*, in which the cross speaks of itself as Christ's loyal thane and yet the instrument of his death. This tragic paradox echoes a recurring theme of secular poetry and at the same time movingly expresses the religious paradoxes of Christ's triumph in death and humankind's redemption from sin.

Major great works of Old English poetry include *Beowulf*, *The Wanderer*, *The Seafarer*, *The Battle of Brunanburh*, *The Battle of Maldon*, *Deor*, *Judith* and so on.

Beowulf, an Old English epic poem consisting of 3,182 alliterative lines, is commonly cited as one of the most important works of Old English literature and is the first English poem still intact as a whole piece today. It was believed to have been produced between 975 and 1025. The author was an anonymous Anglo-Saxon poet, referred to by scholars as the "Beowulf poet".

The poem is set in Scandinavia. Beowulf, a hero of the Geatland in Sweden, comes to the aid of Hrothgar, the king of Denmark, whose great hall in Heorot has been under attack by a monster known as Grendel. After Beowulf kills him with his bare hands, Grendel's mother attacks the hall and is then also defeated. Victorious, Beowulf goes home to Geatland and later becomes king of the Geats. After a period of fifty years, Beowulf, aided by a young warrior Wiglaf, defeats a fire-breathing dragon that burns the royal hall, but is fatally wounded in the battle. He pronounces Wiglaf his successor. The poem ends with Beowulf's burial and a premonition that the kingdom will be overthrown.

Beowulf is considered an epic poem in that the main character is a hero who travels great distances to prove his strength at impossible odds against supernatural evils and beasts. Although the poem begins with Beowulf's arrival, Grendel's attacks have been an ongoing event. An elaborate history of characters and their ancestors is spoken of, as well as their interactions with each other, debts owed and repaid, and deeds of great courage. The warriors form a kind of brotherhood linked by loyalty to their lord.

Of several poems dealing with English history and preserved in the *Anglo-Saxon Chronicle*, the most notable is *The Battle of Brunanburh*, which celebrates the victory of King Athelstan over the Scots and Norse. *The Battle of Maldon* which describes the defeat of Aldorman Byrhtnoth and much of his army at the hands of Viking invaders in 991, discovers in defeat an occasion to celebrate the heroic ideal, contrasting the determination of many of Byrhtnoth's thanes to avenge his death or die in the attempt with the cowardice of others who left the field. *The Wanderer* is narrated by a man, deprived of lord and kinsmen, whose journeys lead him to the realization that there is stability only in heaven. *The Seafarer* is similar, but its journey theme more explicitly symbolizes the speaker's spiritual yearnings. Several others have similar themes, and three elegies—*The Husband's Message*, *The Wife's Lament*, and *Wulf and Eadwacer*—describe what appears to be a conventional situation: the separation of husband and wife by the husband's exile. *Deor* is a poet laments the loss of his position at court by alluding to sorrowful stories from Germanic legend.

Several poems of the Junius Manuscript are based on the Old Testament narratives Genesis, Exodus, and Daniel. Of these, *Exodus* is remarkable for its intricate diction and bold imagery. The fragmentary *Judith* of the Beowulf Manuscript embellishes the story from the Apocrypha of the heroine who led the Jews to victory over the Assyrians.

In addition to the poems in these books are various heroic poems inserted throughout the *Anglo-Saxon Chronicle*. The earliest from 937 is called *The Battle of Brunanburh* and there are five shorter poems: *Capture of the Five Boroughs* (942); *Coronation of King Edgar* (973);

Death of King Edgar (975); *Death of Alfred the Nobel Son of King Athelread* (1036); and *Death of King Edward the Confessor* (1065).

Prose

The amount of surviving Old English prose is much greater than the amount of poetry. Old English prose works include legal writings, medical tracts, religious texts, and translations from Latin and other languages.

The earliest English prose work, the law code of King Aethelbert I of Kent, was written within a few years of the arrival in England (597) of St. Augustine of Canterbury. Other 7th-and 8th-century prose, similarly practical in character, includes more laws, wills, and charters. According to Cuthbert, who was a monk at Jarrow, Bede at the time of his death had just finished a translation of the Gospel of St. John, though this did not survive. Two medical tracts, *Herbarium* and *Medicina de quadrupedibus*, very likely dated from the 8th century.

During the late 9th century, King Alfred (849-899) led a vigorous program to translate into English "certain books that are necessary for all men to know." Alfred himself translated the *Pastoral Care* of St. Gregory I the Great, the *Consolation of Philosophy* of Boethius, the *Soliloquies of Augustine* by St. Augustine of Hippo, and the first 50 *Psalms*. His *Pastoral Care* is a fairly literal translation, but his *Consolation of Philosophy* is extensively restructured and revised to make explicit the Christian message that medieval commentators saw in that work. He revised the *Soliloquies* even more radically, departing from his source to draw from Gregory and St. Jerome, as well as from other works by Augustine. Alfred's prefaces to these works are of great historical interest.

At King Alfred's urging, Bishop Werferth of Worcester translated the *Dialogues* of Gregory; probably Alfred also inspired anonymous scholars to translate Bede's *Historia Ecclesiastica* and Paulus Orosius's *Historiarum Adversum Paganos Libri Vii* (*Seven Books of History against the Pagans*). Both of these works are much abridged; the Bede translation followed its source strictly, but the translator of Orosius added many details of northern European geography and also accounts of the voyages.

The Anglo-Saxon Chronicle, a collection of annals in Old English chronicling the history of the Anglo-Saxons, probably originated in Alfred's reign. Its earliest annals (beginning in the reign of Julius Caesar) are concise, except the entry for 755, which records in detail a feud between the West Saxon King Cynewulf and the would-be usurper Cyneheard. The entries covering the Danish wars of the late 9th century are much fuller, and those running from the reign of Ethelred II to the Norman Conquest in 1066 contain many passages of excellent writing.

The early 10th century is not notable for literary production, but some of the homilies in the Vercelli Book and the Blickling Manuscript may belong to that period.

The prose literature of the mid- to late 10th century is associated with the Benedictine Reform, a movement that sought to impose order and discipline on a monastic establishment that was thought to have grown loose. Aethelwold, bishop of Winchester and one of the leaders of the reform, translated *The Rule of St. Benedict*. But the greatest and most prolific writer of this period was his pupil Aelfric, whose works include three cycles of 40 homilies each, as well as homilies not in these cycles; a Latin grammar; a treatise on time and natural history; pastoral letters; and several translations. His Latin *Colloquy* gives a fascinating glimpse into the Anglo-Saxon monastic classroom. Aelfric wrote with lucidity and astonishing beauty, using the rhetorical devices of Latin literature frequently; his later alliterative prose, which loosely imitates the rhythms of Old English poetry, influenced writers long after the Norman Conquest. Wulfstan, archbishop of York, wrote legal codes and a number of homilies, including *Sermo Lupi ad Anglos* ("Sermon of Wolf to the English"), a fierce denunciation of the morals of his time. Byrhtferth of Ramsey wrote several Latin works and the *Enchiridion*, a textbook on the calendar, notable for its fancy style. Numerous anonymous works, some of very high quality, were produced in this period, including homilies, saints' lives, dialogues, and translations of such works as the Gospels, several Old Testament books, monastic rules, redemptive handbooks, and the romance *Apollonius of Tyre* (translated from Latin but probably derived from a Greek original).

1.2 Middle English Literature (1100-1500)

The term Middle English literature refers to the literature written in the form of the English language known as Middle English, from the early 12th century to the beginning of 16th century.

Early Period

After the Norman Conquest of England, the written form of the Anglo-Saxon language continued in some monasteries but few literary works are known from this early period. Under the influence of the new aristocracy, Law French became the standard language of courts, parliament, and polite society.

As the invaders integrated, their language and literature mingled with that of the natives. The Norman dialects of the ruling classes became Anglo-Norman French, and Anglo-Saxon underwent a gradual transition into Middle English. Political power was no longer in English hands, so the West Saxon literary language (Old English) had no more influence than any other dialect. Middle English literature is written, then, in the many dialects that correspond to the history, culture, and background of the individual writers.

While Anglo-Norman French or Latin was preferred for high culture and administration, English literature by no means died out, and a number of important works illustrate the development of the language.

Around the turn of the 13th century, Layamon, a poet of the late 12th/early 13th century, wrote his *Brut*, a notable work that was the first to present the legends of Arthur and the Knights of the Round Table in English poetry. Layamon's language is recognisably Middle English, though his prosody shows a strong Anglo-Saxon influence remaining.

Other transitional works were preserved as popular entertainment, including a variety of romances and lyrics. With time, the English language regained prestige, and in 1362 it replaced French and Latin in Parliament and courts of law. Early examples of Middle English literature are the *Ormulum*, a 12th-century outlay of the Holy Book consisting of just under 19,000 lines of early Middle English verse written by an English monk named Orm, *Havelock the Dane*, a Middle English romance, and Thomas of Hales's *Love Rune*.

Late Period

It was with the 14th century that major works of English literature began once again to appear; these include Pearl Poet's *Pearl*, *Patience*, *Cleanness*, and *Sir Gawain and the Green Knight*; William Langland's(1332-1386) political and religious allegory *Piers Plowman*(*c. 1370-1390*); John Gower's(1330-1408) *Confessio Amantis*(1390); and the works of Geoffrey Chaucer (1343-1400), the most highly regarded English poet of the Middle Ages, who was seen by his contemporaries as an English successor to the great tradition of Virgil and Dante.

Sir Gawain and the Green Knight is a late 14th-century Middle English chivalric romance associated with legendary British leader King Arthur, with its plot combining two types of folklore themes, the beheading game and the exchange of winnings. It describes how Sir Gawain, a knight of King Arthur's Round Table, accepts a challenge from a mysterious "Green Knight" who challenges any knight to strike him with his axe if he will take a return blow in a year and a day. Gawain accepts and beheads him with his blow, at which the Green Knight stands up, picks up his head, and reminds Gawain of the appointed time. In his struggles to keep his bargain, Gawain demonstrates chivalry and loyalty until his honour is called into question by a test involving Lady Bertilak, the lady of the Green Knight's castle. *Sir Gawain and the Green Knight* is an important poem in the romance genre, which typically involves a hero who goes on a quest which tests his courage, and it remains popular to this day in modern English renderings as well as through film and stage adaptations.

Geoffrey Chaucer, known as the Father of English literature, is widely considered the greatest English poet of the Middle Ages. While he achieved fame during his lifetime as an author, philosopher, and astronomer, Chaucer also maintained an active career in the civil service as a bureaucrat, courtier and diplomat. Chaucer's work was crucial in legitimizing the literary use of the Middle English vernacular at a time when the dominant literary languages in England were French and Latin. Among Chaucer's many works are *The Canterbury Tales*(1387-1400), *The Book of the Duchess*(1386), *The House of Fame* (*1379-1380*), *The Legend of Good Women* (in the 1380s) and *Troilus and Criseyde* (during the mid 1380s).

It is believed that in the early 1380s Chaucer started the work for which he is best known — *The Canterbury Tales*, a collection of stories told by fictional pilgrims on the road to the cathedral at Canterbury; tales that would help to shape English literature. *The Canterbury Tales* contrasts with other literature of the period in the naturalism of its narrative, the variety of stories the pilgrims tell and the varied characters who are engaged in the pilgrimage. Many of the stories narrated by the pilgrims seem to fit their individual characters and social standing, although some of the stories seem ill-fitting to their narrators, perhaps as a result of the incomplete state of the work. Chaucer drew on real life for his pilgrims in *The Canterbury Tales*: the innkeeper shares the name of a contemporary keeper of an inn in Southwark, and real-life identities for the Wife of Bath, the Merchant, the Man of Law and the Student have been suggested. The many jobs that Chaucer held in medieval society—page, soldier, messenger, bureaucrat, foreman and administrator—probably exposed him to many of the types of people he described in the *Tales*. He was able to shape their speech and satirise their manners in what was to become popular literature among people of the same types.

The latter portion of the 14th century also saw not only the consolidation of English as a written language, taking over from French or Latin in certain areas, but a large shift from primarily theological or religious subject matter to also include that of a more worldly nature. Popular book production saw a growth in the amount of books being copied, both secular and religious. Thus, the latter portion of the 14th century can be seen as one of the most significant periods in the history of the English language.

The reputation of Chaucer's successors in the 15th century has suffered in comparison with him, though John Lydgate (1370-1451), Thomas Hoccleve (1368-1426), and John Skelton (1463-1529) are widely studied.

At this time the origins of Scottish poetry began with the writing of *The Kingis Quair* (*The King's Book*) by James I of Scotland (1394-1473). The main poets of this Scottish group were Robert Henryson (1425-1500), William Dunbar (1459-1520), and Gavin Douglas (1474-1522). Henryson and Douglas introduced a note of almost fierce satire, which may have owed something to the Gaelic bardic poetry, while Douglas's version of Virgil's *Aeneid* is one of the early monuments of Renaissance literary humanism in English.

It was a vibrant time for religious drama as well: many morality plays and miracle plays were produced, and some scripts survive today. The encyclopedic verse dialogue *Sidrak and Bokkus* is another example of late Middle English literature.

2. The Renaissance (1500-1660)

The literature of the Renaissance was written within the general movement of the Renaissance which arose in 14th century Italy and continued until the 16th century while being diffused into the western world. It is characterized by the adoption of a humanist philosophy, the recovery of the classical literature of Antiquity and benefited from the spread of printing in the latter part of the 15th century.

During the same period, England graduated from an overlooked "barbarian" nation to a seat of commercial power and influence. This power naturally translated into a literature that was bold, sweeping, innovative, and trend-setting. Spanning the years 1500-1660, the English Renaissance produced some of the greatest works of literature the world has known with the literary output of

Renaissance England rivals anything else of the period. Poets experimented with form, and dramatists revived and reinvented the classical traditions of the Greeks and Romans.

The dominant forms of English literature during the Renaissance were the poem and the drama. Among the many varieties of poetry one might have found in 16th-century England were the lyric, the elegy, the tragedy, and the pastoral. Near the close of the English Renaissance, John Milton composed his epic *Paradise Lost*, widely considered the grandest poem in the language. In the area of drama, no one matched William Shakespeare in terms of variety, profundity, and exquisite use of language. More than anyone else, he elevated the English language to a level of sumptuousness that previous generations would not have thought possible. In addition, the theatre in Renaissance England steadily evolved from a village festival attraction to a bona fide cultural institution.

For the writers of the Renaissance Greco-Roman inspiration was shown both in the themes of their writing and in the literary forms they used. The world was considered from an anthropocentric perspective. Platonic ideas were revived and put to the service of Christianity. The search for pleasures of the senses and a critical and rational spirit completed the ideological panorama of the period.

2.1 Elizabethan Era (1558-1603)

Elizabethan literature refers to bodies of work produced during the reign of Queen Elizabeth I (1558-1603), probably the most splendid age in the history of English literature, during which such writers as Edmund Spenser, Sir Philip Sidney, William Shakespeare, Christopher Marlowe flourished.

The Elizabethan age saw the flowering of poetry, was a golden age of drama (especially for the plays of Shakespeare), and inspired a wide variety of splendid prose including historical chronicles, versions of the Holy Scriptures, pamphlets, and literary criticism to the first English novels.

Poetry

In the late 16th century, English poetry was characterized by elaboration of language and extensive allusion to classical myths. The most important poets of this era include Edmund Spenser (1552-1999) and Sir Philip Sidney (1554-1586). Queen Elizabeth I herself, a product of Renaissance humanism, produced occasional poems such as *On Monsieur's Departure* (1582) and *The Doubt of Future Foes* (1568-1571).

Edmund Spenser was one of the most important poets of this period, author of *The Faerie Queene* (1590), an epic poem celebrating the Tudor dynasty and Elizabeth I. Edmund Spenser had a significant influence on 17th-century poetry and was the primary English influence on John Milton.

Another major figure, Sir Philip Sidney, was an English poet, courtier and soldier, and is remembered as one of the most prominent figures of the Elizabethan Age. He was a pioneer in the succession of English poets, being the first to write a continuous sequence of fourteen-line sonnets such as *Astrophel and Stella* (composed in the 1580s), *The Defence of Poetry* (1582), and *The Countess of Pembroke's Arcadia* (1590). In Sidney's works, readers are exploring the world of English-style sonnets. He is able to write in a way that is equally plain and ornamental and his use of personification in many of the poems allows him to develop his flexibility of style and make fantastic elements more accessible.

Shakespeare also popularized the English sonnet, which made significant changes to Petrarch's model.

Drama

The English playwrights of the Elizabethan Era were fascinated by Italian model: a community of Italian actors had settled in London. The linguist and lexicographer John Florio (1553-1625), whose father was Italian, was a royal language tutor at the Court of James I, and a possible friend and influence on William Shakespeare, had brought much of the Italian language and culture to England. He was also the translator of *Montaigne* into English. The earliest Elizabethan plays include *Gorboduc* (1561), by Thomas Sackville (1536-1608) and Thomas Norton (1532-1584), and Thomas Kyd's (1558-1594) revenge tragedy *The Spanish Tragedy* (1582-1592). Highly popular and influential in its time, *The Spanish Tragedy* established a new genre in English literature theatre, the revenge play or revenge tragedy. Its plot contains several violent murders and includes as one of its characters a personification of Revenge. *The Spanish Tragedy* was often referred to in works written by other Elizabethan playwrights, including William Shakespeare, Ben Jonson, and Christopher Marlowe. Many elements of *The Spanish Tragedy*, such as the play-within-a-play used to trap a murderer and a ghost intent on revenge, appear in Shakespeare's *Hamlet*. Besides, Thomas Kyd is frequently proposed as the author of the hypothetical *Ur-Hamlet* (1587) that may have been one of Shakespeare's primary sources for *Hamlet*.

William Shakespeare (1564-1616) stood out in this period both as a poet and playwright. Shakespeare wrote plays in a variety of genres, including histories, tragedies, comedies and the late romances, or tragicomedies. His early classical and Italianate comedies, like *A Comedy of Errors* (1594), contain tight double plots and precise comic sequences, gave way in the mid-1590s to the romantic atmosphere of his greatest comedies, *A Midsummer Night's Dream* (1595-1596), *Much Ado About Nothing* (1598-1599), *As You Like It* (1599), and *Twelfth Night* (1601-1602). After the lyrical *Richard II* (1595), written almost entirely in verse, Shakespeare introduced prose comedy into the histories of the late 1590s, *Henry IV*, *Parts 1* and *2*, and *Henry V*. This period began and ended with two tragedies: *Romeo and Juliet* (1595), and *Julius Caesar* (1599), based on Sir Thomas North's 1579 translation of Plutarch's *Parallel Lives*, which introduced a new kind of drama.

Other important figures in the Elizabethan theatre include Christopher Marlowe (1564-1593), Thomas Dekker (1570-1632), Robert Greene (1558-1592) and Jane Lumley (1537-1578), etc.

Christopher Marlowe's subject matter is different from Shakespeare's as it focuses more on the moral drama of the Renaissance man than any other things. Drawing on German folklore, Marlowe introduced the story of Faust to England in his play *Doctor Faustus* (1592), about a scientist and magician who, obsessed by the thirst of knowledge and the desire to push man's technological power to its limits, sells his soul to the Devil. *Faustus* makes use of the dramatic framework of the morality plays in its presentation of a story of temptation, fall, and damnation, and its free use of morality figures such as the good angel and the bad angel and the seven deadly sins, along with the devils Lucifer and Mephistopheles.

Thomas Dekker is noted for his realistic portrayal of daily London life and for his sympathy for the poor and oppressed. Dekker was, between 1598 and 1602, involved in about forty plays, usually in collaboration. He is particularly remembered for *The Shoemaker's Holiday* (1599), a work where he appears to be the sole author.

Robert Greene was another popular dramatist but he is now best-known for a posthumous pamphlet attributed to him, *Groats-Worth of Witte, Bought with a Million of Repentance* (1592), widely believed to contain an attack on William Shakespeare.

Jane Lumley was the first person to translate *Euripides* into English. Besides, her translation of *Iphigeneia at Aulis* is the first known dramatic work by a woman in English.

Prose

In terms of prose, two of the most important Elizabethan prose writers were John Lyly (1553 or 1554-1606) and Thomas Nashe (1567-1601).

John Lyly is an English writer, poet, dramatist, playwright, and politician, best known for his books *Euphues*: *The Anatomy of Wit* (1578) and *Euphues and His England* (1580). Lyly's mannered literary style, originating in his first books, is known as euphuism. Lyly must also be considered and remembered as a primary influence on the plays of William Shakespeare, and in particular the romantic comedies. Lyly's play *Love's Metamorphosis* (1600) is a large influence on Shakespeare's *Love's Labour's Lost* (written in the mild-1590s), and *Gallathea* (1584) is a possible source for other plays.

Thomas Nash, was the first husband of William Shakespeare's granddaughter Elizabeth Barnard and was the dominant male figure amongst Shakespeare's senior family line after the death of Dr. John Hall, Shakespeare's son-in-law, in 1635. Nash was a playwright, poet, and satirist, who is best known for his novel *The Unfortunate Traveller* (1594) and he is also considered the greatest of the English Elizabethan pamphleteers.

2.2 Jacobean Period (1603-1625)

English literature from 1603 to 1625 is properly called Jacobean, after the new English monarch, James I. The successor to Elizabethan literature, Jacobean literature was often dark in mood, questioning the stability of the social order or preoccupied with the problem of evil.

Drama

Shakespeare's career continued into the Jacobean period, and in the early 17th century Shakespeare wrote the so-called "problem plays": *Troilus and Cressida* (1602), *Measure for Measure* (1604), and *All's Well That Ends Well* (*1604*), as well as a number of his best known tragedies, including *Hamlet* (1602), *Othello* (1603), *Macbeth* (1606), *King Lear* (1606) and *Anthony and Cleopatra* (1606). The plots of Shakespeare's tragedies often hinge on such fatal errors or flaws, which overturn order and destroy the hero and those he loves. In his final period, Shakespeare turned to romance or tragicomedy and completed three more major plays: *Cymbeline* (1609), *The Winter's Tale* (1611) and *The Tempest* (1611), as well as the collaboration, *Pericles, Prince of Tyre* (1619). Less gloomy than the tragedies, these four plays are more solemn in tone than the comedies of the 1590s, but they end with reconciliation and the forgiveness of potentially tragic errors.

Other Jacobean dramatic writers became preoccupied with the problem of evil: the plays of John Webster (1580-1643), John Marston (1576-1634), Thomas Middleton (1580-1627), and George Chapman (1559-1634) induce all the terror of tragedy but little of its pity.

The Jacobean era's comedy includes the acid satire of Ben Jonson (1572-1637) and the varied works of Francis Beaumont (1584-1616) and John Fletcher (1579-1625).

As an English playwright, poet, actor, and literary critic, Ben Jonson exerted a lasting impact upon English poetry and stage comedy. He was classically educated, well-read and cultured, with an appetite for controversy (personal and political, artistic and intellectual) and is generally regarded as the second most important English playwright during the reign of James I after William Shakespeare. Jonson popularized the comedy of humours and is best known for the satirical plays *Every Man in His Humour* (1598), *Volpone* or *the Fox* (1605-1606), *The Alchemist*, *Catiline and Bartholomew Fair* (1614) and for his lyric poetry.

Francis Beaumont was a dramatist in the English Renaissance theatre, most famous for his collaborations with John Fletcher on comedies and tragedies between about 1606 and 1613. Of those believed to be the joint work of Beaumont and Fletcher, *The Maid's Tragedy* (1619) and *Philaster* (1610) are considered the masterpieces unmatched except by Shakespeare. As regards their respective powers, Beaumont is held to have had the more solemn, solider, and more majestic genius, while Fletcher excelled in brightness, wit, and joy.

Another feature of drama at this time, however, was the development of the extravagant courtly entertainment known as the masque, which reached its literary peak in the works of Ben Jonson and the prominent English architect Inigo Jones (1573-1652).

Poetry

Jonson's comparatively lucid and graceful verse and the writings of his Cavalier successors constituted one of the two main streams of Jacobean poetry.

Ben Jonson's poetry sheds on English literary history, such as politics, systems of patronage and intellectual attitudes. For the general reader, Jonson's reputation rests on a few lyrics that, though brief, are surpassed for grace and precision by very few Renaissance poems: *On My First Sonne* (1603); *To Celia* (1616); and *To Penshurst* (1616). Jonson is widely regarded as the pioneer of the Cavalier poetry, an influential school of English poetry of the 17th century. The Cavalier poets influenced by Johnson include Robert Herrick (1591-1674), Richard Lovelace (1617-1657), Thomas Carew (1595-1640), and Sir John Suckling (1609-1641).

The other poetic stream lay in the intellectual complexity of John Donne (1572-1631) and the Metaphysical poets.

If Ben Jonson represents the cavalier strain of poetry, emphasizing grace and clarity of expression; John Donne, the pre-eminent representative of the metaphysical poets, by contrast, represents the metaphysical school of poetry, with its reliance on strained, baroque metaphors and often vague phrasing. His poetry is noted for its vibrancy of language and inventiveness of metaphor, especially compared to that of his contemporaries, and his style is characterized by abrupt openings and various paradoxes, ironies and dislocations.

Prose

In the field of prose, writers such as Francis Bacon (1561-1626) and Robert Burton (1577-1640) showed a new toughness and flexibility of style.

Francis Bacon, 1st Viscount St Alban, an English philosopher, statesman, scientist, jurist, orator, and author, is extremely influential through his works, especially as philosophical advocate and practitioner of the scientific method during the scientific revolution. With regards to his prose, it is fresh, vigorous, powerful and aphoristic so that he was able to dominate English prose for decades from the last years of Queen Elizabeth I's reign to the end of that of James I. Bacon's *Essays* (1597) is the best embodiment his wisdom and unique style, touching upon a wide variety of subjects such as truth, love, envy, high position, good nature, riches, ambition, beauty, vainglory, learning, and politics and economy. Bacon also reveals his political concerns in essays such as *Of Counsel*, *Of Nobility*, and *Of Seditions and Troubles* and his socio-economic ideas in such essays as *Of Riches*, *Of Usury*, and *Of Building*.

Robert Burton was an English scholar at Oxford University, best known for the classic *The Anatomy of Melancholy* (1621) which focuses sharply on the self; unlike Bacon, Burton assumes that knowledge of psychology, not natural science, is humankind's greatest need.

The era's monumental prose achievement was the King James Version of the Bible, an English translation of the Christian Bible for the Church of England begun in 1604 and completed in 1611. The style of King James Bible has influenced English literature markedly and set the ultimate standard of English prose style.

2.3 Late Renaissance (1625-1660)

The Metaphysical poets John Donne and George Herbert (1593-1633) were still alive after

1625, and later in the 17th century a second generation of metaphysical poets were writing, including Richard Crashaw (1613-1649), Andrew Marvell (1621-1678), Thomas Traherne (1636 or 1637-1674) and Henry Vaughan (1622-1695). Their style was characterized by wit and metaphysical conceits—far-fetched or unusual similes or metaphors, such as in Andrew Marvell's comparison of the soul with a drop of dew; or Donne's description of the effects of absence on lovers to the action of a pair of compasses.

Another important group of poets at this time were the Cavalier poets. They were an important group of writers, who came from the classes that supported King Charles I during the Wars of the Three Kingdoms (the British Civil Wars from 1639 to 1651). They were also cavaliers in their style of life and counted the writing of polished and elegant lyrics as only one of their many accomplishments as soldiers, courtiers, lovers, and wits. The Cavalier poets were not a formal group, but all were influenced by Ben Jonson. The best-known of the cavalier poets are Robert Herrick (1591-1674), Richard Lovelace (1617-1657), Thomas Carew (1595-1640), and Sir John Suckling (1609-1641). Although Herrick, a clergyman, was detached from the court, his short, fluent, graceful lyrics on love and romance, and his carpe diem ("seize the day") philosophy ("Gather ye rose-buds while ye may") are typical of the Cavalier style. Besides writing love lyrics addressed to mistresses with fanciful names like Anthea, Althea, Lucasta, or Amarantha, the Cavaliers sometimes wrote of war, honour, and their duty to the king. Richard Lovelace's well-known poem, *To Lucasta, Going to the Wars* (1649) was a combination of all these themes.

John Milton (1608-1674) is one of the greatest English poets, who wrote at a time of religious flux and political turbulence. He is generally seen as the last major poet of the English Renaissance, though his major epic poems were written in the later Restoration period, including *Paradise Lost* (1671). Among the important poems Milton wrote during this period are *L'Allegro* (1631); *Il Penseroso* (1634); *Comus* (1634); and *Lycidas* (1638). His later major works are *Paradise Regained* (1671) and *Samson Agonistes* (1671). Milton's works reflect deep personal convictions, a passion for freedom and self-determination, and the urgent issues and political turbulence of his day. Writing in English, Latin, and Italian, he achieved international renown within his lifetime, and his celebrated *Areopagitica* (1644), written in condemnation of pre-publication censorship, is among history's most influential and passionate defences of free speech and freedom of the press.

3. The Neoclassical Period (1660-1798)

Neoclassical literature is writing from a period spanning from 1660 to 1798. Relying on the classic styles of the ancient Greeks and Romans, its main characteristic is an emphasis on logic, common sense, properness and adequate performance in society. Largely a response to the previous chaos of the Renaissance, the writings of this time included a variety of genres, including novels, diaries, essays and satires. Grammar and word study became more formalized, with authors preferring simplicity. Although writing eventually transitioned to more Romantic concepts, the influence of Neoclassical thought is still evident today.

Neoclassical literature can be divided into three major sections: Restoration, Augustan and Pre-Romanticism. The first section spans approximately 1660-1700, while the second covers 1700-1750. The generally accepted years for the Pre-Romanticism are 1750-1798.

3.1 The Restoration (1660-1700)

Restoration literature is the English literature written during the historical period commonly referred to as the English Restoration (1660-1689), which corresponds to the last years of the direct Stuart reign in England, Scotland, Wales, and Ireland. In general, the term is used to stand for roughly homogeneous styles of literature that center on a celebration of or reaction to the restored court of Charles II. It is a literature that includes extremes, for it encompasses both the English epic of *Paradise Lost*, the obscene closet drama of *Sodom*, the high-spirited sexual comedy of *The Country Wife* and the moral wisdom of *The Pilgrim's Progress*. It saw Locke's *Treatises of Government*, the founding of the Royal Society, the hysterical attacks on theaters from Jeremy Collier, and the pioneering of literary criticism from John Dryden and John Dennis. The period witnessed news become a commodity, the essay developed into a periodical art form, and the beginning of textual criticism.

Poetry

The Restoration was an age of poetry. Not only was poetry the most popular form of literature, but it was also the most significant form of literature, as poems affected political events and immediately reflected the times. Throughout the period, the lyric, historical, and epic poem was being developed.

Sir William Davenant (1606-1668) was the first Restoration poet to attempt an epic. His *Gondibert* (1651) was of epic length and the prefaces to *Gondibert* show the struggle for a formal epic structure, as well as how the early Restoration saw themselves in relation to Classical literature.

John Milton's (1608-1674) *Paradise Lost* was published during the Restoration period. Milton no less than Davenant wished to write the English epic, and chose blank verse as his form. He rejected the cause of English exceptionalism: his *Paradise Lost* seeks to tell the story of all mankind, and his pride is in Christianity rather than Englishness. Significantly, Milton began with an attempt at writing an epic on King Arthur, for that was the matter of English national founding.

While Milton rejected the cause of English exceptionalism, in the end, others made the attempt. Richard Blackmore (1654-1729) wrote both a *Prince Arthur* (1695) and *King Arthur* (1697). Both attempts were long, tedious, and failed both critically and popularly.

However, the Restoration period ended without an English epic. *Beowulf* may now be called the English epic, but the work was unknown to Restoration authors, and Old English was incomprehensible to them.

The Restoration Poets expressed their points of view in other forms, usually public or formally disguised poetic forms such as odes, pastoral poetry, and ariel verse and one of the characteristics of the period is its devaluation of individual sentiment and psychology in favour of public utterance and philosophy.

John Dryden (1631-1700), also called "Glorious John", was also a major force during Restoration, working on both plays and poetry to such a degree that the entire first section of the period sometimes is called "the Age of Dryden". Two of his most famous works are *To My Lord Chancellor* (1662) and *Marriage a la Mode* (1673). He attempted at the Jacobean pastoral along the lines of Walter Raleigh and Philip Sidney, but his greatest successes and fame came from his attempts at apologetics for the restored court and the Established Church. His *Absalom and Achitophel* (1681) and *Religio Laici* (1682) both served the King directly by making controversial royal actions seem reasonable. Dryden also pioneered the mock-heroic. His *MacFlecknoe* (1682) set up the satirical parody. Even when James II came to the throne and Roman Catholicism was on the rise, Dryden attempted to serve the court, and his *The Hind and the Panther* (1687) praised the Roman church above all others. After that point, Dryden suffered for his conversions, and he was the victim of many satires.

Dryden was attached to the court of Charles, and so were Buckingham, Dorset and Rochester. The court poets follow no one particular style, except that they all show sexual awareness, a willingness to satirize, and a dependence upon wit to dominate their opponents. Each of these poets wrote for the stage as well as the page. George Villiers, 2nd Duke of Buckingham (1628-1687), wrote some court poetry, but he, like Charles Sackville, 6th Earl of Dorset (1643-1706), was a patron of poetry more than a poet. John Wilmot, 2nd Earl of Rochester (1647-1680), meanwhile, was a prolix and outrageous poet. His *Sodom* is an obscene Restoration closet drama, published in 1684 and his poetry is almost always sexually frank and is frequently political. He also has a mock topographical poem, several mock odes and mock pastorals.

Aphra Behn and Robert Gould, by contrast, were outsiders who were profoundly royalists. Aphra Behn (1640-1689), the first professional female novelist in English, broke cultural barriers and served as a literary role model for later generations of women authors. While she was best known publicly for her drama, Behn wrote a great deal of poetry that would be the basis of her later reputation. One of the most remarkable aspects of Behn's success in court poetry, however, is that Behn was herself a commoner. As a woman, a commoner, and Kentish, she is remarkable for her success in moving in the same circles as the King himself.

If Behn is a curious exception to the rule of noble verse, Robert Gould (1660-1709) breaks that rule altogether. Gould was born of a common family and orphaned at the age of thirteen, however, he somehow learned to read and write, as well as possibly to read and write Latin. In the

1680s and 1690s, Gould's poetry was very popular and his great success came with *Love Given O'er, or A Satyr Upon ... Woman* in 1692. It was a partial adaptation of a satire by the Roman poet Juvenal, but with an immense amount of explicit attack against women. Gould also wrote *The Play House: A Satyr* (1689) with detailed descriptions of the actions and actors involved in the Restoration stage. He followed the success of *Love Given O'er* (1685) with a series of poems, all of which have specific, graphic, and witty attacks of female behavior.

The Restoration period was an age of energetic and voluminous satire, however, since there were great dangers in being associated with political satire, its publication was generally done anonymously and a great many poems, some of them of merit, are unpublished and largely unknown. Nevertheless, such poetry was a vital part of the vigorous Restoration scene.

Prose

Prose in the Restoration period was dominated by Christian religious writing, but the Restoration also saw the beginning of two genres that would dominate later periods: journalism and fiction.

The Restoration moderated most of the more violent religious writing, but radicalism persisted after the Restoration. Puritan authors such as John Milton were forced to retire from public life, and those authors who had preached against monarchy were partially suppressed. Consequently, violent religious writings were forced underground. Some made public vows of pacifism and preached a new theology of peace and love. Other Puritans contented themselves with being able to meet freely and act on local church communities. Two religious authors stood out beyond the others in this time: John Bunyan(1628-1688) and Izaak Walton(1594-1683).

Bunyan's *The Pilgrim's Progress* (1678) is an allegory of personal salvation and a guide to the Christian life. Bunyan writes about how the individual saint can prevail against the temptations of mind and body that threaten damnation. The book is written in a straightforward narrative and shows influence from both drama and biography, and yet it also shows an awareness of the allegorical tradition found in Edmund Spenser.

Izaak Walton's *The Compleat Angler* (1653) is similarly introspective. On the surface, his book is a guide to fishing, but, like *Pilgrim's Progress*, its main business is guiding the individual. Readers treasure its contents for their descriptions of nature and serenity.

More court-oriented religious prose includes sermon collections and a great literature of debate over the convention and issues before the House of Lords.

Religious writing often developed into political and economic writing, just as political and economic writing implied or directly addressed religion. Indeed, the Restoration saw the publication of a number of significant pieces of political and philosophical writing. Additionally, the court's adoption of Neoclassicism and empirical science led to receptiveness toward significant philosophical works.

Thomas Sprat (1635-1713) wrote his *History of the Royal Society* in 1667 and set forth, in a single document, the goals of empirical science ever after. He praised a spare, clean, and precise vocabulary for science and explanations that are as comprehensible as possible. Similarly, he emphasized the need for conciseness in description, as well as reproducibility of experiments.

William Temple (1628-1699), after he retired from being what today would be called Secretary of State, wrote several prose works in praise of retirement, contemplation, and direct observation of nature. He also brought the Ancients and Moderns quarrel into English with his *Reflections on Ancient and Modern Learning* (1694). The debates that followed in the wake of this quarrel would inspire many of the major authors of the first half of the 18th century.

The Restoration was also the time when John Locke (1632-1704) wrote many of his philosophical works. Locke's empiricism was an attempt at understanding the basis of human understanding itself and thereby devising a proper manner for making sound decisions. These same scientific methods led Locke to his *Two Treatises of Government* (1689), which later inspired the thinkers in the American Revolution.

Additionally, the Restoration saw the beginning of the first professional and periodical (meaning that the publication was regular) journalism in England. Journalism developed late, generally around the time of William of Orange's (1650-1702) claiming the throne in 1689. Coincidentally or by design, England began to have newspapers just when William came to court from Amsterdam, where there were already newspapers being published.

Roger L'Estrange (1616-1704) produced both *The News* and *City Mercury*, but neither of them was a sustained effort. Henry Muddiman (1629-1692) was the first to succeed in a regular newspaper with the *London Gazette*. In 1665, Muddiman produced the *Oxford Gazette* as a digest of news of the royal court, which was in Oxford to avoid the plague in London. When the court moved back to Whitehall later in the year, the title *London Gazette* was adopted. Muddiman had begun as a journalist in the Interregnum (between the execution of Charles I in 1649 and the arrival of his son Charles II in London in 1660 which marked the start of the Restoration) and had been the official journalist of the Long Parliament (in the form of *The Parliamentary Intelligencer*). Although Muddiman's productions were the first regular news accounts, they were still not the first modern newspaper, as the work was sent in manuscript by post to subscribers and was not a printed sheet for general sale to the public. That had to wait for *The Athenian Mercury*.

The Athenian Mercury was the first regularly published periodical in England. John Dunton (1659-1733) and the "Athenian Society" (actually a mathematician, minister, and philosopher paid by Dunton for their work) began publishing in 1691, just after the reign of William III and Mary II began. In addition to news reports, *The Athenian Mercury* allowed readers to send in questions anonymously and receive a printed answer. The questions mainly dealt with love and health, but there were some bizarre and intentionally amusing questions as well. The questions section allowed the journal to sell well and to be profitable. Therefore, it ran for six years, produced four books that spun off from the columns, and then received a bound publication as *The Athenian Oracle*. He also published the first periodical designed for women *The Ladies' Mercury*.

The Athenian Mercury set the stage for the later *Spectator*, *Gray's Inn Journal*, *Temple Bar Journal*, and scores of politically oriented journals, such as the original *The Guardian*, *The Observer*, *The Freeholder*, *Mist's Journal*, and many others. Meanwhile, *The Athenian Mercury* published poetry from contributors, and it was the first to publish the poetry of Jonathan Swift (1667-1745) and Elizabeth Singer Rowe (1659-1733). The trend of newspapers would similarly explode in subsequent years; a number of these later papers had runs of a single day and were composed entirely as a method of planting political attacks.

Although it is impossible to satisfactorily date the beginning of the novel in English, long fiction and fictional biographies began to distinguish themselves from other forms in England during the Restoration period. An existing tradition of Romance fiction in France and Spain was popular in England. For example, Ludovico Ariosto's *Orlando Furioso* (1516) engendered prose narratives of love, peril, and revenge, and Gauthier de Costes, seigneur de la Calprenède's novels were quite popular during the Interregnum and beyond.

The "Romance" was considered a feminine form, and there was contempt against women who read "novels". Despite that, Aphra Behn became one of the most significant figures in the rise of the novel in the Restoration period. She was not only the first professional female novelist, but she may also be among the first professional novelists of either sex in England. Her first novel was *Love-Letters Between a Nobleman and His Sister* (1684) which is highly romantic, sexually explicit, and political. Behn also wrote several "Histories" of fictional figures, such as her *The History of a Nun* (1689). As the genre of "novel" did not exist, these histories were prose fictions based on biography. However, her most famous novel was *Oroonoko* in 1688. This was a fictional biography, published as a "true history", of an African king who had been enslaved in Suriname, a colony Behn herself had visited.

Behn's novels show the influence of tragedy and her experiences as a dramatist. Later novels by Daniel Defoe (1660-1731) would adopt the same narrative framework, although his choice of biography would be tempered by his experience as a journalist writing "true histories" of criminals.

Other forms of fiction were also popular. Available to readers were versions of the stories of *Reynard the Fox*, as well as various indigenous folk tales, such as the various Dick Whittington and Tom Thumb fables. Most of these were in verse, but some circulated in prose. These largely anonymous or folk compositions circulated as chapbooks.

Theater

The return of Charles II to power in 1660 was a major event in English theatre history. As soon as the previous Puritan regime's ban on public stage representations was lifted, the drama recreated itself quickly and abundantly.

In the 1660s and 1670s, the London theater scene was vitalised by the competition between two Royal patent companies. The mid-1670s were a high point of both quantity and quality, with John Dryden's *Aureng-Zebe* (1675), William Wycherley's (1641-1716) *The Country Wife*

(1675) and *The Plain Dealer* (1676), George Etherege's (1636-1692) *The Man of Mode* (1676), and Aphra Behn's *The Rover* (1677).

From 1682 the production of new plays dropped sharply. The 1680s were especially lean years for comedy, the only exception being the remarkable career of Aphra Behn, the first professional British woman dramatist. There was a swing away from comedy to serious political drama, reflecting preoccupations and divisions following on the political crisis. The few comedies produced also tended to be political in focus, the Whig dramatist Thomas Shadwell (1642-1692) sparring with the Tories John Dryden and Aphra Behn.

In the calmer times after 1688, Londoners were again ready to be amused by stage performance, but the single "United Company" was not well prepared to offer it. Later, some dissatisfied actors set up their own co-operative company in 1695. A few years of re-invigorated two-company competition followed which allowed a brief second flowering of the drama, especially comedy. Comedies like William Congreve's (1670-1729) *Love For Love* (1695) and *The Way of the World* (1700), and John Vanbrugh's (1664-1726) *The Relapse* (1696) and *The Provoked Wife* (1697) were "softer" and more middle class in ethos, very different from the aristocratic extravaganza twenty years earlier, and aimed at a wider audience.

Drama

If "Restoration literature" is the literature that reflects and reflects upon the court of Charles II, Restoration drama arguably ended before Charles II's death, as the playhouse moved rapidly from the domain of courtiers to the domain of the city middle classes. On the other hand, Restoration drama shows altogether more fluidity and rapidity than other types of literature, and so, even more than in other types of literature, its movements should never be viewed as absolute. Each decade had brilliant exceptions to every rule and entirely forgettable confirmations of it.

Genre in Restoration drama is peculiar. Authors labelled their works according to the old tags, "comedy" and "drama" and, especially, "history", but these plays defied the old categories. From 1660 onwards, new dramatic genres arose, mutated, and intermixed very rapidly. In tragedy, the leading style in the early Restoration period was the male-dominated heroic drama, exemplified by John Dryden's *The Conquest of Granada* (1672) and *Aureng-Zebe* (1675) which celebrated powerful, aggressively masculine heroes and their pursuit of glory both as rulers and conquerors, and as lovers. These plays were sometimes called by their authors' histories or tragedies, and contemporary critics would call them after Dryden's term of "Heroic drama". Heroic dramas center on the actions of men of decisive natures, men whose physical and (sometimes) intellectual qualities make them natural leaders. In one sense, this was a reflection of an idealised king such as Charles or Charles's courtiers might have imagined. However, such dashing heroes were also seen by the audiences as occasionally standing in for noble rebels who would redress injustice with the sword. The plays are, however, tragic in the strictest definition, even though they are not necessarily sad.

In the 1670s and 1680s, a gradual shift occurred from heroic to pathetic tragedy, where the focus was on love and domestic concerns, even though the main characters might often be public figures. After the phenomenal success of Elizabeth Barry (1658-1713) in moving the audience to tears in the role of Monimia in Thomas Otway's (1652-1685) *The Orphan* (1680), "she-tragedies", which focused on the sufferings of an innocent and virtuous woman, became the dominant form of pathetic tragedy. With the conjunction of the playwright "master of pathos" Thomas Otway and the great tragedienne Elizabeth Barry in *The Orphan*, the focus shifted from hero to heroine. Prominent she-tragedies include John Banks's (1650-1706) *Virtue Betrayed, or, Anna Bullen* (1682), Thomas Southerne's (1660-1746) *The Fatal Marriage* (1694), and Nicholas Rowe's (1674-1718) *The Fair Penitent* (1702) and *Lady Jane Grey* (1715).

While she-tragedies were more comfortably tragic, in that they showed women who suffered for no fault of their own and featured tragic flaws that were emotional rather than moral or intellectual, their success did not mean that more obviously political tragedy was not staged. Thomas Otway's *Venice Preserv'd* of 1682 was a royalist political play that seemed to praise the king for his actions in the Meal Tub Plot. *Venice Preserv'd* is, in a sense, the perfect synthesis of the older politically royalist tragedies and histories of Dryden and the newer she-tragedies of feminine suffering, for, although the plot seems to be a political allegory, the action centers on a woman who cares for a man in conflict, and most of the scenes and dialogue concern her pitiable sufferings at his hands.

In the area of comedy, Restoration comedy is notorious for its sexual explicitness. The best-known plays of the early Restoration period were unsentimental or "hard" comedies of John Dryden, William Wycherley (1641-1716), and George Etherege (1636-1692), which reflected the atmosphere at Court, and celebrated an aristocratic macho lifestyle of unremitting sexual intrigue and conquest.

During the second wave of Restoration comedy in the 1690s, the "softer" comedies of William Congreve (1670-1729) and John Vanbrugh (1664-1726) reflected mutating cultural perceptions and great social change. The playwrights of the 1690s set out to appeal to more socially mixed audiences with a strong middle-class element, and to female spectators, for instance by moving the war between the sexes from the arena of intrigue into that of marriage. The focus in comedy was less on young lovers outwitting the older generation, more on marital relations after the wedding bells. In Congreve's plays, the give-and-take set pieces of couples still testing their attraction for each other have mutated into witty prenuptial debates on the eve of marriage, as in the famous "Proviso" scene in *The Way of the World* (1700).

Restoration drama had a bad reputation for three centuries. The "incongruous" mixing of comedy and tragedy beloved by Restoration audiences was criticized. The later Victorians blamed the comedy as too indecent for the stage, and the standard reference work of the early 20th century, *The Cambridge History of English and American Literature*, dismissed the tragedy as being of "a level of dulness and lubricity never surpassed before or since". Today, the Restoration total theatre experience is again valued, both by postmodern literary critics and on the stage.

One thing should not be ignored is the Restoration spectacular. The spectacular, or elaborately staged "machine play", hit the London public stage in the late 17th-century Restoration period, engaging audiences with action, music, dance, moveable scenery, baroque illusionistic painting, gorgeous costumes, and special effects such as trapdoor tricks, "flying" actors, and fireworks. From the start, these shows had ill reputations as vulgar and commercial threats to the witty, "legitimate" Restoration dramas. They drew Londoners in unprecedented numbers, however, and left them dazzled and delighted.

3.2 The Augustan Age (1700-1750)

Augustan literature (sometimes referred to misleadingly as Georgian literature) is a style of British literature produced in the first half of the 18th century during the reigns of Queen Anne, King George I, and George II. It was a literary epoch that featured the rapid development of the novel, an explosion in satire, the mutation of drama from political satire into melodrama and an evolution toward poetry of personal exploration.

Prose

The essay, satire, and dialogue (in philosophy and religion) thrived in the age, and the English novel was truly begun as a serious art form.

Literacy in the early 18th century passed into the working classes, as well as the middle and upper classes. Furthermore, literacy was not confined to men, though rates of female literacy were very difficult to establish. For those who were literate, circulating libraries in England began in the Augustan period. Libraries were open to all, but they were mainly associated with female patronage and novel reading.

In terms of essay, English essayists were aware of Continental models, but they developed their form independently from that tradition, and periodical literature grew between 1692 and 1712. Periodicals were inexpensive to produce, quick to read, and a viable way of influencing public opinion, and consequently there were many broadsheet periodicals headed by a single author and staffed by hirelings (so-called "Grub Street" authors). One periodical outsold and dominated all others, however, and that was *The Spectator*, written by Joseph Addison (1672-1719) and Richard Steele (1672-1729). The dispassionate view of the world (the pose of a spectator, rather than participant) was essential for the development of the English essay, as it set out a ground wherein Addison and Steele could comment and meditate upon manners and events.

Samuel Johnson's command of words and his practical wisdom gained a following as he published more than 200 essays offering insights into the follies of human nature and moral perseverance. Rather than being philosophers like Montesquieu, the English essayist could be an honest observer and his reader's peer. After the success of *The Spectator*, more political periodicals of comment appeared. However, the political factions and coalitions of politicians very quickly realized the power of this type of press, and they began funding newspapers to spread rumors.

Politicians wrote papers, wrote into papers, and supported papers, and it was well known that some of the periodicals, like *Mist's Journal*, were party mouthpieces.

The 18th century was a time of enlightenment progression occurring in all intellectual fields. However, the English language was deteriorating into a mess. A group of London booksellers commissioned well-known essayist Samuel Johnson (1709-1714), to compile a set of rules governing the English Language. After nine years and the help of six assistants the first edition of *A Dictionary of the English Language* was published in 1755. Johnson's great knowledge of letters, words and literature brought uniqueness to his dictionary. Each word was defined in detail, with descriptions of their various uses and numerous literary quotes as illustrations. This was the first dictionary of its kind, containing 40,000 words and nearly 114,000 quotes packed together with Johnson's personal touch. A warm reception greeted Johnson's Dictionary as it was the first dictionary that could be read with pleasure. The definitions were full of wit and depth of thought was supported by passages from beloved poets and philosophers, which a reader could be content spending an evening poring over its pages. Johnson's choice of structure and format has certainly shaped future English dictionaries and lexicons and the role they play in language development.

In terms of religious writing, the Augustan period showed less literature of controversy than the Restoration. There were Puritan authors, however, and one of the names usually associated with the novel is perhaps the most prominent in Puritan writing: Daniel Defoe (1660-1731). After the coronation of Queen Anne, dissenter literature moved from the offensive to the defensive, from revolutionary to conservative. Defoe's *The Shortest Way with the Dissenters; Or, Proposals for the Establishment of the Church* (1702) is satirical, attacking all of the worries of Establishment figures over the challenges of dissenters. It is, in other words, defensive. Later still, the most majestic work of the era, and the one most quoted and read, was William Law's (1686-1761) *A Serious Call to a Devout and Holy Life* (1729). *Some Physio-Theological Considerations about the Possibility of the Resurrection* (1675) of Robert Boyle remained popular as well. Both Law and Boyle called for revivalism, and they set the stage for the later development of Methodism and George Whitefield's (1714-1770) sermon style. However, their works aimed at the individual, rather than the community. The age of revolutionary divines and militant evangelists in literature was over for a considerable time.

Also in contrast to the Restoration, when philosophy in England was fully dominated by John Locke, the 18th century had a vigorous competition among followers of Locke. Bishop Berkeley (1685-1753) extended Locke's emphasis on perception to argue that perception entirely solves the Cartesian problem of subjective and objective knowledge by saying "to be is to be perceived". David Hume (1711-1776), on the other hand, took empiricist skepticism to its extremes, and he was the most radically empiricist philosopher of the period.

In social and political philosophy, economics underlies much of the debate. Bernard de Mandeville's (1670-1733) *The Fable of the Bees* (1705) became a center-point of controversy regarding trade, morality, and social ethics. Mandeville argued that wastefulness, lust, pride, and all the other "private" vices were good for the society at large, for each led the individual to employ others, to spend freely, and to free capital to flow through the economy. Mandeville's work is full of paradox and is meant, at least partially, to problematize what he saw as the naive philosophy of human progress and inherent virtue.

The ground for the novel had been laid by journalism, drama and satire. Long prose satires like Jonathan Swift's (1667-1745) *Gulliver's Travels* (1726) had a central character who went through adventures and might learn lessons. However, the most important single satirical source for the writing of novels came from the Spanish writer Cervantes's *Don Quixote*. In general, one can see these three axes, drama, journalism, and satire, as blending in and giving rise to three different types of novel.

Daniel Defoe's *Robinson Crusoe* (1719) was the first major novel of the new century and was published in more editions than any other works besides *Gulliver's Travels*. Defoe worked as a journalist during and after its composition, and therefore he encountered the memoirs of Alexander Selkirk, who had been stranded in South America on an island for some years. Defoe took aspects of the actual life and, from that, generated a fictional life, satisfying an essentially journalistic market with his fiction. In the 1720s, Defoe interviewed famed criminals and produced accounts of their lives. In particular, he investigated the notorious English thief and gaol-breaker Jack Sheppard and the "Thief-Taker General" Jonathan Wild and wrote true accounts of the former's escapes (and fate) and the latter's life. From his reportage on the prostitutes and criminals, Defoe may have become familiar with the real-life Mary Mollineaux, who may have been the model for Moll in *Moll Flanders* (1722). In the same year, Defoe produced *A Journal of the Plague Year* (1722), which summoned up the horrors and tribulations of 1665 for a journalistic market for memoirs, and an attempted tale of a working-class male rise in *Colonel Jack* (1722). His last novel returned to the theme of fallen women in *Roxana* (1724).

Samuel Richardson's (1689-1761) *Pamela: or, Virtue Rewarded* (1740) is the next landmark development in the English novel. Richardson's generic models were quite distinct from those of Defoe. In fact, *Pamela: or, Virtue Rewarded* is among the most famous examples of the sentimental novel. *Pamela*, like its author, presents a dissenter's and a Whig's view of the rise of the classes. The work drew a nearly instantaneous set of satires, of which Henry Fielding's (1707-1754) *Shamela*, and *An Apology for the Life of Miss Shamela Andrews* (1742) is the most memorable.

Between 1747 through 1748, Samuel Richardson published *Clarissa* in serial form. Unlike *Pamela*, it is not a tale of virtue rewarded. Instead, it is a highly tragic and affecting account of a young girl whose parents push her into the arms of a scheming rake named Lovelace. In the end, Clarissa dies by her own will. The novel is a masterpiece of psychological realism and emotional effect, and when Richardson was drawing to a close in the serial publication, even Henry Fielding wrote to him, begging him not to kill Clarissa. As with *Pamela*, Richardson emphasized the individual over the social and the personal over the class. Even as Fielding was reading and enjoying *Clarissa*, he was also writing a counter to its messages. His *Tom Jones* of 1749 offers up the other side of the argument from *Clarissa*. *Tom Jones* agrees substantially in the power of the individual to be more or less than his or her birth would indicate, but it again emphasizes the place of the individual in society and the social ramifications of individual choices. Fielding answers Richardson by featuring a similar plot device (whether a girl can choose her own mate) but showing how family and village can complicate and facilitate matches and happiness.

The Augustan era is considered a high point of British satiric writing, and its masterpieces are Swift's *Gulliver's Travels* (1726) and *A Modest Proposal* (1729), Pope's *Dunciads* (1728-1743), *Imitations of Horace* (1733-1738), and *Moral Essays* (1731-1735), Samuel Johnson's *The Vanity of Human Wishes* and *London* (1748), Henry Fielding's *Shamela* (1742) and *Jonathan Wild* (1743), and John Gay's (1685-1732) *The Beggar's Opera* (1728). There were several thousand other satirical works written during the period, which have until recently been, by widespread consensus, ignored.

Many scholars of the era argue that a single name overshadows all others in 18th-century prose satire: Jonathan Swift (1667-1745). Swift wrote poetry as well as prose, and his satires ranged over all topics. Critically, Swift's satire marked the development of prose parody away from simple satire or burlesque. What Swift did was to combine parody, with its imitation of form and style of another, and satire in prose. Swift's works would pretend to speak in the voice of an opponent and imitate the style of the opponent and have the parodic work itself be the satire. Swift's first major satire was *A Tale of a Tub* (1703-1705), which introduced an ancients/moderns division that would serve as a distinction between the old and new conception of value. The "moderns" sought trade, empirical science, the individual's reason above the society's, while the "ancients" believed in inherent and immanent value of birth, and the society over the individual's determinations of the good. In Swift's satire, the moderns come out looking insane and proud of their insanity, and dismissive of the value of history. In Swift's most significant satire, *Gulliver's Travels* (1726), autobiography, allegory, and philosophy mix together in the travels. Thematically, *Gulliver's Travels* is a critique of human vanity, of pride. Book one, the journey to Liliput, begins with the world as it is. Book two shows that the idealized nation of Brobdingnag with a philosopher king is no home for a contemporary Englishman. Book four depicts the land of the Houyhnhnms, a society of horses ruled by pure reason, where humanity itself is portrayed as a group of "yahoos" covered in filth and dominated by base desires. It shows that, indeed, the very desire for reason may be undesirable, and humans must struggle to be neither Yahoos nor Houyhnhnms, for book three shows what happens when reason is unleashed without any consideration of morality or utility (i. e. madness, ruin, and starvation).

There were other satirists who worked in a less vicious way, who took a puzzled pose and only made lighthearted fun. Tom Brown (1662-1704), Ned Ward (1667-1731), and Tom D'Urfey (1653-1723) were all satirists in prose and poetry whose works appeared in the early part of the Augustan age. Tom Brown's most famous work in this vein was *Amusements Serious and Comical, Calculated for the Meridian of London* (1700). Ned Ward's most memorable work was

The London Spy (1704-1706). *The London Spy*, before *The Spectator*, took up the position of an observer and uncomprehendingly reporting back. Tom D'Urfey's *Wit and Mirth: or Pills to Purge Melancholy* (1719) was another satire that attempted to offer entertainment, rather than a specific bit of political action, in the form of coarse and catchy songs.

Particularly after Swift's success, parodic satire had an attraction for authors throughout the 18th century. A variety of factors created a rise in political writing and political satire, and Robert Walpole's (1676-1745) success and domination of House of Commons was a very effective proximal cause for polarized literature and thereby the rise of parodic satire. The parodic satire took apart the cases and plans of policy without necessarily contrasting a normative or positive set of values. Therefore, it was an ideal method of attack for ironists and conservatives—those who would not be able to enunciate a set of values to change toward but could condemn present changes as ill-considered. Satire was present in all genres during the Augustan period. Perhaps primarily, satire was a part of political and religious debate. Every significant politician and political act had satires to attack it. Few of these were parodic satires, but parodic satires, too, emerged in political and religious debate. So omnipresent and powerful was satire in the Augustan age that more than one literary history has referred to it as the "Age of satire" in literature.

Poetry

In the Augustan era, poets wrote in direct counterpoint and direct expansion of one another, with each poet writing satire when in opposition. There was a great struggle over the nature and role of the pastoral in the early part of the century, reflecting two simultaneous movements: the invention of the subjective self as a worthy topic, with the emergence of a priority on individual psychology, against the insistence on all acts of art being performance and public gesture designed for the benefit of society at large. The development seemingly agreed upon by both sides was a gradual adaptation of all forms of poetry from their older uses. Odes would cease to be encomium, ballads cease to be narratives, elegies cease to be sincere memorials, satires no longer be specific entertainments, parodies no longer be performance pieces without sting, song no longer be pointed, and the lyric would become a celebration of the individual rather than a lover's complaint. These developments can be seen as extensions of Protestantism. It can be argued that the development of the subjective individual against the social individual was a natural reaction to trade over other methods of economic production. Whatever the prime cause, a largely conservative set of voices argued for a social person and largely emergent voices argued for the individual person.

The entire Augustan age's poetry was dominated by Alexander Pope (1688-1744). His lines were repeated often enough to lend quite a few clichés and proverbs to modern English usage. Pope had few poetic rivals, but he had many personal enemies and political, philosophical, or religious opponents, and Pope himself was quarrelsome in print. Pope and his enemies fought over central matters of the proper subject matter for poetry and the proper pose of the poetic voice.

There was a great struggle over the nature and role of the pastoral in the early part of the century. After Pope published his *Pastorals* of the four seasons in 1709, an evaluation in *The Guardian* praised Ambrose Philips's(1674-1749) pastorals above Pope's, and Pope replied with a mock praise of Philips's *Pastorals* that showed disrespect on them. Pope quoted Philips's worst lines, mocked his execution, and delighted in pointing out his empty lines. Pope later explained that any depictions of shepherds and their mistresses in the pastoral must not be updated shepherds, that they must be icons of the Golden Age. Philips's *Pastorals* were not particularly awful poems, but they did reflect his desire to "update" the pastoral. In 1724, Philips would update poetry again by writing a series of odes dedicated to all ages and characters. Henry Carey (1687-1743) was one of the best at satirizing these poems, and his *Namby Pamby* (1725) greatly downplayed Philips and Philips's endeavor.

What is notable about Philips's against Pope, however, is the fact that both poets were adapting the pastoral and the ode, both altering it. Pope's insistence upon a Golden Age pastoral was no less than Philips's desire to update it meant making a political statement. While it is easy to see in Ambrose Philips an effort at modernist triumph, it is no less the case that Pope's artificially restricted pastoral is a statement of what the ideal should be.

Pope's friend John Gay (1685-1732) also adapted the pastoral. Gay, working at Pope's suggestion, wrote a parody of the updated pastoral in *The Shepherd's Week* (1714). He also imitated *The Satires* of Juvenal with his *Trivia* (1714). In 1728, his *The Beggar's Opera* was an enormous success, running for an unheard-of eighty performances. All of these works have in common a gesture of compassion. In *Trivia*, Gay writes as if commiserating with those who live in London and are menaced by falling masonry and bedpan slops, and *The Shepherd's Week* features great detail of the follies of everyday life and eccentric character. Even *The Beggar's Opera*, which is a satire of Robert Walpole, portrays its characters with compassion: the villains have pathetic songs in their own right and are acting out of exigency rather than boundless evil.

Throughout the Augustan era the "updating" of Classical poets was a commonplace. These were not translations, but rather they were imitations of Classical models, and the imitation allowed poets to veil their responsibility for the comments they made. Alexander Pope would manage to refer to the King himself in unflattering tones by "imitating" Horace in his *Epistle to Augustus*. Similarly, Samuel Johnson wrote a poem that falls into the Augustan period in his "imitation of Juvenal" entitled *London*(1378). The imitation was inherently conservative, since it argued that all that was good was to be found in the old classical education, but these imitations were used for progressive purposes, as the poets who used them were often doing so to complain of the political situation.

In satire, Pope achieved two of the greatest poetic satires of all time in the Augustan period. *The Rape of the Lock* (1712 and 1714) was a gentle mock-heroic. Pope applied Virgil's heroic and epic structure to the story of a young woman having a lock of hair snipped by an amorous baron. A decade after the gentle, laughing satire of *The Rape of the Lock*, Pope wrote *the Dunciad* (1728). The story is that of the goddess Dulness choosing a new Avatar. She settles upon one of Pope's personal enemies, Lewis Theobald, and the poem describes the coronation and heroic games undertaken by all of the dunces of Great Britain in celebration of Theobald's ascension. When Pope's enemies responded to the *Dunciad* with attacks, Pope produced the *Dunciad Variorum* (1729), with a "learned" commentary upon the original *Dunciad*. In 1742, he added a fourth book and changed the hero from Lewis Theobald to Colley Cibber. In the fourth book of the *New Dunciad*, Pope expressed the view that, in the battle between light and dark (enlightenment and the Dark Ages), Night and Dulness were fated to win, that all things of value were soon going to be subsumed under the curtain of unknowing.

Drama

The Augustan era is difficult to define chronologically in prose and poetry, but it is very easy to date its end in drama. The Augustan era's drama ended definitively in 1737, with the Licensing Act prior to 1737, however, the English stage was changing rapidly from the Restoration comedy and Restoration drama, and their noble subjects, to the quickly developing melodrama.

George Lillo (1691-1739) and Richard Steele(1672-1729) wrote the trend-setting plays of the early Augustan period. Lillo's plays consciously turned from heroes and kings and toward shopkeepers and apprentices. Steele's *The Conscious Lovers* (1722) hinges upon his young hero avoiding fighting a duel. The plays set up a new set of values for the stage. Instead of amusing the audience or inspiring the audience, they sought to instruct the audience and to ennoble it.

Joseph Addison (1672-1719) also wrote a play, entitled *Cato*, in 1713, which concerned the Roman statesman Cato the Younger. The figure of Cato was a transparent symbol of Roman integrity, and the Whigs saw in him a champion of Whig values, and the Tories saw in him an embodiment of Tory sentiments or, like *The Examiner*, tried to claim that Cato was above political "faction".

As during the Restoration, economics drove the stage in the Augustan period. Under Charles II court patronage meant economic success and so the Restoration stage featured plays that would suit the monarch and/or court. However, after the reign of William and Mary, the court and the crown stopped taking a great interest in the playhouse. Theatres had to get their money from the audience of city dwellers, and plays that reflected city anxieties and celebrated the lives of citizens were staged.

Thus, there were quite a few plays that were not literary but were staged more often than the literary plays. John Rich (1692-1761) and Colley Cibber (1671-1757) duelled over special theatrical effects. They put on plays that were actually just spectacles, and the text of the play was almost an afterthought. Dragons, whirlwinds, thunder, ocean waves and even actual elephants were on stage. Battles, explosions and horses were put on the boards.

Additionally, opera made its way to England during this period. Inasmuch as opera combined singing with acting, it was a mixed genre, which violated all the strictures of neoclassicism. Also, high melodies would cover the singers' expressions of grief or joy, thus breaking "decorum".

3.3 The Pre-Romanticism (1750-1798)

Between the Augustan Age in the first half of the 18th century and the Romanticism in the first few decades of the 19th century, there was a transitional period also known as Pre-Romanticism in British literature. There was a reaction against classicism and reason and a search for new models of poetry taken no longer from ancient Rome and Greece but from the Middle Ages. The period was greatly affected by the French Revolution, the American Revolution and the Industrial Revolution.

There was a new interest towards the poor and the children, who lived at the margin of society during the Augustan Age. Satire and realism were respectively replaced by sentimentalism and imagination, paving the way to the flourishing of Romanticism. The Age preserved its main features with its emphasis on reason, precision, order, clarity and harmony, but some other features appeared in opposition to them: interest in country life, new way of seeing nature, different role of art, new themes based on feelings and so on.

Adam Smith (1723-1790) is remembered by lay persons as the father of capitalism, but his *Theory of Moral Sentiments* of 1759 also attempted to strike out a new ground for moral action. His emphasis on "sentiment" was in keeping with the era, as he emphasized the need for "sympathy" between individuals as the basis of fit action. These ideas, and the psychology of David Hartley (1705-1757), were influential on the sentimental novel.

The sentimental novel or "novel of sensibility" is a genre which developed during the second half of the 18th century. It celebrates the emotional and intellectual concepts of sentiment, sentimentalism, and sensibility. Sentimentalism, which is to be distinguished from sensibility, was a fashion in both poetry and prose fiction which began in the 18th century in reaction to the rationalism of the Augustan Age. Sentimental novels relied on emotional response, both from their readers and characters. They feature scenes of distress and tenderness, and the plot is arranged to advance emotions rather than action. The ability to display feelings was thought to show character and experience, and to shape social life and relations. Among the most famous sentimental novels in English are Samuel Richardson's *Pamela, or Virtue Rewarded* (1740), Oliver Goldsmith's (1728-1774) *Vicar of Wakefield* (1766), Laurence Sterne's (1713-1768) *Tristram Shandy* (1759-1767) and *Sentimental Journey* (1768), Henry Brooke's (1703-1783) *The Fool of Quality* (1765-1770), Henry Mackenzie's (1745-1831) *The Man of Feeling* (1771) and Maria Edgeworth's (1768-1849) *Castle Rackrent* (1800).

Poetry in this period was no longer concerned with "wit" but with simple feelings and nature. Poetry was pervaded by a melancholic tone and was often associated with meditation on death. This kind of poetry was remembered as Graveyard Poetry. The poets of the Graveyard Group were melancholic and sought for solitude. Their thoughts were directed towards death, or the fear of death, suicide and graves. The settings of their poems were often medieval ruins, caverns, coffins and skeletons. The most important poet of the group was Thomas Gray (1716-1771) and his most famous poem was *Elegy Written in a Country Churchyard* (1751), based on the concept of the levelling power of death. Other Churchyard poets in this period were William Cowper (1731-1800), Christopher Smart (1722-1771), Thomas Chatterton (1752-1770), and Edward Young (1683-1765).

The Graveyard poets influenced the Gothic Novel and the Ossian Poetry which became very popular literary forms especially among they who were unsatisfied with classical novel and poetry and looked for Gothicism, a mixture of both medieval features (ruins, ancient castle and so on) and supernatural. Both poems and novels of this kind were melodramatic, full of horrors and supernatural and set in a medieval context.

In the late 18th century, Horace Walpole's (1717-1797) novel *The Castle of Otranto* (1764) created the Gothic fiction genre, that combined elements of horror and romance. The pioneering gothic novelist Ann Radcliffe (1764-1823) introduced a gothic villain which developed into the Byronic hero. Her most popular and influential work *The Mysteries of Udolpho* (1795) is frequently cited as the archetypal Gothic novel. *Vathek* (1786) by William Beckford (1709-1770), and *The Monk* (1796) by Matthew George Lewis (1775-1818), were further notable early works in both the gothic and horror literary genres. The first short stories in the United Kingdom were gothic tales like Richard Cumberland's (1632-1718) "remarkable narrative" *The Poisoner of Montremos* (1791).

James Macpherson (1736-1796) was the first Scottish poet to gain an international reputation. Claiming to have found poetry written by the ancient bard Ossian, he published "translations" that acquired international popularity, being proclaimed as a Celtic equivalent of the Classical epics. *Fingal*, written in 1762, was speedily translated into many European languages, and its appreciation of natural beauty and treatment of the ancient legend have been credited, more than any single work, with bringing about the Romantic movement in European, and especially in German literature. It was also popularized in France by figures that included Napoleon. Eventually it became clear that the poems were not direct translations from the Gaelic, but flowery adaptations made to suit the aesthetic expectations of his audience.

Both Robert Burns (1759-1796) and Walter Scott (1771-1832) were highly influenced by the Ossian cycle. Robert Burns was a pioneer of the Romantic movement. As well as writing poems, Burns also collected folk songs from across Scotland, often revising or adapting them. His *Poems, Chiefly in the Scottish Dialect* was published in 1786. Among poems and songs of Burns that remain well-known across the world are, *Auld Lang Syne*, *A Red, Red Rose*, *A Man's A Man for A' That*, *To a Louse*, *To a Mouse*, *The Battle of Sherramuir*, *Tam o' Shanter* and *Ae Fond Kiss.* Sir Walter Scott, 1st Baronet was a Scottish historical novelist, playwright and poet. Many of his works remain classics of both English-language literature and of Scottish literature. Famous titles include *Ivanhoe*, *Rob Roy*, *Old Mortality*, *The Lady of the Lake*, *Waverley*, *The Heart of Midlothian* and *The Bride of Lammermoor.*

In the midst of this development of the novel, other trends were also taking place. There were utopian novels, like Sarah Scott's (1720-1795) *Millennium Hall* (1762), autobiographical women's novels like Frances Burney's (1752-1840) works, female adaptations of older, male motifs, such as Charlotte Lennox's (1730-1804) *The Female Quixote* (1752) and many others. These novels do not generally follow a strict line of development or influence.

Similarly, the later 18th century saw a ballad revival, with Thomas Percy's (1560-1605) *Reliques of Ancient English Poetry* (1765). The relics were not always very ancient, as many of the ballads dated from only the 17th century, and so what began as an antiquarian movement soon became a folk movement. When this folk-inspired impulse combined with the solitary and individualistic impulse of the Churchyard Poets, Romanticism was nearly inevitable.

4. The Romantic Period (1798-1837)

Under the impetus of the Industrial Revolution and French Revolution, romanticism appeared in England as a new trend in literature at the turn of the 18th and 19th centuries. Various dates are given for the Romantic period but here the publishing of William Wordsworth's *Lyrical Ballads* in 1798 is taken as the beginning, and the crowning of Queen Victoria in 1837 as its end.

Poetry

The landscape is often prominent in the poetry of this period, so much so that the Romantics, especially perhaps William Wordsworth (1770-1850), are often described as "nature poets". However, the longer Romantic "nature poems" have a wider concern because they are usually meditations on "an emotional problem or personal crisis".

The poet, painter, and printmaker William Blake (1757-1827) was an important early Romantic poet. Largely disconnected from the major streams of the literature of the time, Blake was generally unrecognized during his lifetime, but is now considered a influential figure in the history of both the poetry and visual arts of the Romantic Age. Among his most important works are *Songs of Innocence* (1789) and *Songs of Experience* (1794) "and profound and difficult 'prophecies'" such as *Visions of the Daughters of Albion* (1793), *The First Book of Urizen* (1794), *Milton* (1804-1810), and *Jerusalem: the Emanation of the Giant Albion* (1804).

After Blake, among the earliest Romantics were the Lake Poets, a small group of friends, including William Wordsworth (1770-1850), Samuel Taylor Coleridge (1772-1834), Robert Southey (1774-1843) and journalist Thomas de Quincey (1785-1859). However, at the time Walter Scott was the most famous poet. Scott achieved immediate success with his long narrative poem *The Lay of the Last Minstrel* in 1805, followed by the full epic poem *Marmion* in 1808. Both were set in the distant Scottish past.

The early Romantic Poets brought a new emotionalism and introspection, and their emergence is marked by the first romantic manifesto in English literature, the *Preface* to *Lyrical Ballads* (1798). It is an essay, composed by William Wordsworth, for the second edition of the poetry collection *Lyrical Ballads* which changed the course of English literature and poetry. The poems in *Lyrical Ballads* (1798) were mostly by Wordsworth, though Coleridge contributed. Among Wordsworth's most important poems, are "Michael", "Lines Composed a Few Miles Above Tintern Abbey", "Resolution and Independence", "Ode: Intimations of Immortality from Recollections of Early Childhood" and the long, autobiographical epic *The Prelude* which was begun in 1799 but published posthumously in 1850. Coleridge's longest major poem is *Rime of the Ancient Mariner in Lyrical Ballads* (1798). It is a tragic ballad relating the experiences of a sailor who has returned from a long sea voyage. Coleridge is also especially remembered for *Kubla Khan* (1797), *Frost at Midnight* (1798), *Dejection: An Ode* (1802), *Christabel* (1797), as well as the major prose work *Biographia Literaria* (1817). His critical work, especially on Shakespeare, was highly influential, and he helped introduce German idealist philosophy to English-speaking culture. Coleridge and Wordsworth, along with Carlyle, were a major influence, through Ralph Waldo Emerson, on American transcendentalism.

Robert Southey (1774-1843) was another of the so-called Lake Poets, although his fame was long overshadowed by that of his contemporaries and friends William Wordsworth and Samuel Taylor Coleridge. Thomas De Quincey (1785-1859) was an English essayist, best-known for his *Confessions of an English Opium-Eater* (1821), an autobiographical account of his laudanum use and its effect on his life. William Hazlitt (1778-1830), friend of both Coleridge and Wordsworth, was another important essayist at this time, though today he is best known for his literary criticism, especially *Characters of Shakespeare's Plays* (1817-1818).

The second generation of Romantic poets includes Lord Byron (1788-1824), Percy Bysshe Shelley (1792-1822) and John Keats (1795-1821). Byron, however, was still influenced by 18th-century satirists and was, perhaps the least "romantic" of the three. Byron achieved enormous fame and influence throughout Europe with works exploiting the violence and drama of their exotic and historical settings. A trip to Europe resulted in the first two cantos of *Childe Harold's Pilgrimage* (1812), a mock-heroic epic of a young man's adventures in Europe, but also a sharp satire against London society. The poem contains elements thought to be autobiographical, as Byron generated some of the storyline from experience gained during his travels between 1809 and 1811. However, despite the success of *Childe Harold*, the lengthy narrative poem *Don Juan* (1818-1823) and other works, Byron was forced to leave England for good in 1816 and seek shelter on the Continent, because, among other things, of his alleged affair with his half-sister Augusta Leigh. Here he joined Percy Bysshe and Mary Shelley, with his secretary John William Polidori (1795-1821) on the shores of Lake Geneva, during the "year without a summer". Polidori's *The Vampyre* was published in 1819, creating the literary vampire genre. This short-story was inspired by the life of Lord Byron and his poem *The Giaour* (1813). Between 1819 and 1824 Byron published his unfinished epic satire *Don Juan*, which, though initially condemned by the critics, "was much admired by Goethe who translated part of it".

Shelley is perhaps best-known for poems such as *Ozymandias* (1818), *Ode to the West Wind*

(1819), *To a Skylark*(1820), *Music*, *When Soft Voices Die*(1821), *The Cloud*(1820), *The Masque of Anarchy* (1819) and *Adonaïs*, *an Elegy Written on the Death of Keats*(1821). Shelley became an idol of the next three or four generations of poets, including important Victorian and Pre-Raphaelite poets such as Robert Browning (1812-1889), and Dante Gabriel Rossetti (1828-1882), as well as later William Butler Yeats (1865-1839). Shelley's influential poem *The Masque of Anarchy* (1819) calls for nonviolence in protest and political action. It is perhaps the first modern statement of the principle of nonviolent protest. The leader of the Indian independence movement Mahatma Gandhi's passive resistance was influenced and inspired by Shelley's verse, and Gandhi would often quote the poem to vast audiences.

Though John Keats shared Byron and Shelley's radical politics, "his best poetry is not political", but is especially noted for its music and imagery, along with a concern with material beauty and the transience of life. Among his most famous works are *The Eve of St Agnes*(1819), *Ode to Psyche*(1819), *La Belle Dame sans Merci*(1819), *Ode to a Nightingale*(1819), *Ode on a Grecian Urn*(1820), *Ode on Melancholy* (1819), *To Autumn* (1819) and the incomplete *Hyperion*(1819), a "philosophical" poem in blank verse, which was "conceived on the model of Milton's *Paradise Lost*". Keats' letters "are among the finest in English" and important "for their discussion of his aesthetic ideas", including "negative capability". Keats has always been regarded as a major Romantic, "and his status as a poet has grown steadily through all changes of fashion".

Other important male poets in this period include John Clare (1793-1864) and George Crabbe (1754-1832). Clare was the son of a farm labourer, who came to be known for his celebratory representations of the English countryside and his mourning over the changes taking place in rural England. He is often now considered to be among the most important 19th-century poets. Crabbe was an English poet whose poetry was admired by Lord Byron. Crabbe's works include *The Village* (1783), *Poems* (1807), *The Borough* (1810), and his poetry collections *Tales* (1812) and *Tales of the Hall* (1819).

Women writers were increasingly active in all genres throughout the 18th century, and by the 1790s women's poetry was flourishing. Notable poets later in the period include Anna Laetitia Barbauld (1743-1825), Joanna Baillie (1762-1851), Susanna Blamire (1747-1794), Hannah More (1745-1833). Other women poets include Mary Alcock (1742-1798) and Mary Robinson (1758-1800) both of whom highlighted the enormous gap between life for the rich and the poor, and Felicia Hemans (1793-1835) author of nineteen individual books during her lifetime, and who continued to be republished widely after her death in 1835. Another female poet worth mentioning in this period is Dorothy Wordsworth (1771-1855), William's sister, who was modest about her writing abilities. She produced poems of her own; and her journals and travel narratives certainly provided inspiration for her brother.

Novel

In terms of novel, the most important British novelist at the beginning of the early 19th century was Sir Walter Scott. His novel writing career was launched in 1814 with *Waverley*, often called the first historical novel, and was followed by *Ivanhoe* (1820). The Waverley Novels, including *The Antiquary* (1816), *Old Mortality* (1816), *The Heart of Midlothian* (1818), and whose subject is Scottish history, are now generally regarded as Scott's masterpieces. He was one of the most popular novelist of the era and his historical romances inspired a generation of painters, composers, and writers throughout Europe. His novels also inspired many operas, of which the most famous are *Lucia di Lammermoor* by Gaetano Donizetti and *La jolie fille de Perth*, (*The Fair Maid of Perth*) by Georges Bizet.

Mary Shelley (1797-1851) is remembered as the author of *Frankenstein* (1818). The plot of this is said to have come from a waking dream she had, in the company of Percy Shelley, Lord Byron, and John Polidori, following a conversation about galvanism and the feasibility of returning a corpse or assembled body parts to life, and on the experiments of the 18th-century natural philosopher and poet Erasmus Darwin (1731-1802), who was said to have animated dead matter. Sitting around a log fire at Byron's villa, the company also amused themselves by reading German ghost stories, prompting Byron to suggest they each write their own supernatural tale.

Jane Austen's (1775-1817) works critique the novels of sensibility of the second half of the 18th century and are part of the transition to 19th-century realism. Her plots, though fundamentally comic, highlight the dependence of women on marriage to secure social standing and economic security. Austen brings to light the hardships women faced, who usually did not inherit money, could not work and where their only chance in life depended on the man they married. She reveals not only the difficulties women faced in her day, but also what was expected of men and of the careers they had to follow. This she does with wit and humour and with endings where all characters, good or bad, receive exactly what they deserve. Her work brought her little personal fame and only a few positive reviews during her lifetime, but the publication in 1869 of her nephew's *A Memoir of Jane Austen* introduced her to a wider public, and by the 1940s she had become accepted as a major writer. Austen's works include *Sense and Sensibility* (1811), *Pride and Prejudice* (1813), *Mansfield Park* (1814), *Emma* (1815), *Northanger Abbey* (1817) and *Persuasion* (1817).

Drama

Byron, Keats and Shelley all wrote for the stage, but with little success in England, with Percy Bysshe Shelley's *The Cenci* (1819) perhaps the best work produced, though that was not played in a public theatre in England until a century after his death. Byron's plays, along with dramatizations of his poems and Scott's novels, were much more popular on the Continent, and especially in France, and through these versions several were turned into operas, many still performed today. If contemporary poets had little success on the stage, the period was a legendary one for performances of Shakespeare, and went some way to restoring his original texts and removing the Augustan "improvements" to them.

5. The Victorian Period (1837-1901)

The Victorian Period in literature covers more than 70 years from 1837 to 1901. The Victorians returned to writing which reflected the relevant concerns of the period and was generally more restrained and less sensual than that of the Romantics. In particular, the novel began to overtake poetry in importance in the Victorian period.

Novel

While in the preceding Romantic period poetry had been the dominant genre, it was the novel that was most important in the Victorian period. Charles Dickens (1812-1870) dominated the first part of Victoria's reign: his first novel, *Pickwick Papers*, was published in 1836, and his last *Our Mutual Friend* between 1864-1865. William Thackeray's (1811-1863) most famous work *Vanity Fair* appeared in 1848, and the three Brontë sisters, Charlotte (1816-1855), Emily (1818-1848) and Anne (1820-1849), also published significant works in the 1840s. A major later novel was George Eliot's (1819-1880) *Middlemarch* (1872), while the major novelist of the later part of Queen Victoria's reign was Thomas Hardy (1840-1928), whose first novel, *Under the Greenwood Tree*, appeared in 1872 and his last, *Jude the Obscure*, in 1895.

Charles Dickens is the most famous Victorian novelist. Extraordinarily popular in his day with his characters taking on a life of their own beyond the page; Dickens is still one of the most popular and read authors of the world. His first novel, *The Pickwick Papers* (1836-1837) written when he was twenty-five, was an overnight success, and all his subsequent works sold extremely well. The comedy of his first novel has a satirical edge and this pervades his writing. Dickens worked diligently and productively to produce the entertaining writing that the public wanted, but also to offer commentary on social problems and the difficulties of the poor and oppressed. His most important works include *Oliver Twist* (1837-1839), *Nicholas Nickleby* (1838-1839), *A Christmas Carol* (1843), *Dombey and Son* (1846-1848), *David Copperfield* (1849-1850), *Bleak House* (1852-1853), *Little Dorrit* (1855-1857), *A Tale of Two Cities* (1859), and *Great Expectations* (1860-1861). There is a gradual trend in his fiction towards darker themes which mirrors a tendency in much of the writing of the 19th century.

William Thackeray was Dickens' great rival in the first half of Queen Victoria's reign. He tended to depict a more middle class society than Dickens did. He is best known for his novel *Vanity Fair* (1848), subtitled *A Novel without a Hero*, which is an example of a form popular in Victorian literature: a historical novel in which recent history is depicted.

Anne, Charlotte and Emily Brontë produced notable works of the period, although these were not immediately appreciated by Victorian critics. *Wuthering Heights* (1847), Emily's only work, is an example of Gothic Romanticism from a woman's point of view, which examines class, myth, and gender. *Jane Eyre* (1847), by her sister Charlotte, is another major 19th century novel that has gothic themes. Anne's second novel *The Tenant of Wildfell Hall* (1848), written in realistic rather than romantic style, is mainly considered to be the first sustained feminist novel. Later in this period George Eliot (Mary Ann Evans), published *The Mill on the Floss* in 1860, and in 1872 her most famous work *Middlemarch*. Like the Brontës she published under a masculine pseudonym.

In the later decades of the Victorian era Thomas Hardy was the most important novelist. His works include *Under the Greenwood Tree* (1872), *Far from the Madding Crowd* (1874), *The Mayor of Casterbridge* (1886), *Tess of the d'Urbervilles* (1891), and *Jude the Obscure* (1895).

Other significant novelists of this era were Elizabeth Gaskell (1810-1865), Anthony Trollope (1815-1882), George Meredith (1828-1909), and George Gissing (1857-1903).

Poetry

In terms of poetry, Robert Browning (1812-1889) and Alfred Tennyson (1809-1892) were Victorian England's most famous poets, though more recent taste has tended to prefer the poetry of Thomas Hardy, who, though wrote poetry throughout his life, did not publish a collection until 1898, as well as that of Gerard Manley Hopkins (1844-1889), whose poetry was published posthumously in 1918. Algernon Charles Swinburne (1837-1909) is also considered an important literary figure of the period, especially his poems and critical writings. Early poetry of Irish poet William Butler Yeats was also published in Victoria's reign.

The husband and wife team of Elizabeth Barrett Browning (1806-1861) and Robert Browning (1812-1889) conducted their love affair through verse and produced many tender and passionate poems. Both Matthew Arnold(1822-1888) and Gerard Manley Hopkins(1844-1889) wrote poems which sit somewhere in between the exultation of nature of the Romantic Poetry and the Georgian Poetry of the early 20th century. However, Hopkins's poetry was not published until 1918. Arnold's works anticipated some of the themes of these later poets, while Hopkins drew inspiration from verse forms of Old English poetry such as *Beowulf*.

The reclaiming of the past was a major part of Victorian literature with an interest in both classical literature but also the medieval literature of England. The Victorians loved the heroic, chivalrous stories of knights of old and they hoped to regain some of that noble, courtly behavior and impress it upon the people both at home and in the wider empire. The best example of this is Alfred Tennyson's (1809-1892) *Idylls of the King*(1859-1885), which blended the stories of King Arthur, particularly those by Thomas Malory, with contemporary concerns and ideas. The Pre-Raphaelite Brotherhood (a group of English painters, poets, and critics, founded in 1848) also drew on myth and folklore for their art, with poet, illustrator, painter and translator Dante Gabriel Rossetti(1828-1882) contemporaneously regarded as the chief poet amongst them, although his sister Christina (1830-1894) is now held by scholars to be a stronger poet.

Drama

In drama, farces, musical burlesques, extravaganzas and comic operas competed with Shakespeare productions and serious drama by the likes of James Planché (1796-1880) and Thomas William Robertson (1829-1871). In 1855, the German Reed Entertainments began a process of elevating the level of musical theatre in Britain that finally led to the famous series of comic operas by Gilbert and Sullivan (the Victorian-era theatrical partnership of the librettist W. S. Gilbert (1836-1911) and the composer Arthur Sullivan (1842-1900)). The two men collaborated on fourteen comic operas between 1871 and 1896, of which *H. M. S. Pinafore*, *The Pirates of Penzance* and *The Mikado* are among the best known. They were followed by the 1890s with the first Edwardian musical comedies (a form of British musical theatre from the period between the early 1890s until the rise of the American musicals following the First World War). The first play to achieve 500 consecutive performances was the London comedy *Our Boys* by H. J. Byron(1835-1884), opening in 1875. Its astonishing new record of 1,362 performances was bested in 1892 by *Charley's Aunt* by Brandon Thomas(1848-1914). After W. S. Gilbert, Oscar Wilde(1854-1900) became the leading poet and dramatist of the late Victorian period. Wilde's plays, in particular, stand apart from the many now forgotten plays of Victorian times and have a closer relationship to those of the Edwardian dramatists such as George Bernard Shaw(1856-1950), whose career began in the 1890s. Wilde's 1895 comic masterpiece, *The Importance of Being Earnest*, was the greatest of the plays in which he held an ironic mirror to the aristocracy while displaying virtuosic mastery of wit and paradoxical wisdom. It has remained extremely popular.

Children's Literature

The Victorians are credited with "inventing childhood", partly via their efforts to stop child labour and the introduction of compulsory education. As children began to be able to read, literature for young people became a growth industry, with not only established writers producing works for children (such as Dickens' *A Child's History of England from 1851 to 1853*) but also a new group of dedicated children's authors. Writers like Lewis Carroll (1832-1898), R. M. Ballantyne(1825-1894) and Anna Sewell (1820-1878) wrote mainly for children, although they had an adult following. Other authors such as Anthony Hope (1863-1933) and Robert Louis Stevenson(1850-1894) wrote mainly for adults, but their adventure novels are now generally classified as for children. Other genres included nonsense verse, poetry which required a childlike interest. School stories flourished: Thomas Hughes'(1822-1896) *Tom Brown's Schooldays* (1857) and Joseph Rudyard Kipling's(1865-1936) *Stalky & Co.* (1899) are classics.

Rarely were these publications designed to capture a child's pleasure; however, with the increase in use of illustrations, children began to enjoy literature, and were able to learn morals in a more entertaining way. With the newfound acceptance of reading for pleasure, fairy tales and folk tales became popular. Compiling folk tales by many authors with different topics made it possible for children to read literature by and about lots of different things that interested them. There were different types of books and magazines written for boys and girls. Girls' stories tended to be domestic and to focus on family life, whereas boys' stories were more about adventures.

Science, Philosophy and Discovery

The Victorian era was an important time for the development of science and the Victorians had a mission to describe and classify the entire natural world. Much of this writing does not rise to the level of being regarded as literature but one book in particular, Charles Darwin's (1809-1882) *On the Origin of Species* (1859), remains famous. The theory of evolution contained within the work shook many of the ideas the Victorians had about themselves and their place in the world. Although it took a long time to be widely accepted, it would dramatically change subsequent thought and literature. Much of the work of popularizing Darwin's theories was done by his younger contemporary Thomas Henry Huxley (1825-1895), who wrote widely on the subject.

A number of other non-fiction works of the era made their mark on the literature of the period. The philosophical writings of John Stuart Mill (1806-1873) covered logic, economics, liberty and utilitarianism. The large and influential histories of Thomas Carlyle (1795-1881): *The French Revolution, A History* (1837) and *On Heroes, Hero-Worship, and The Heroic in History* (1841) were full of political thought at the time. The writings of Thomas Babington Macaulay (1800-1859) on English history helped codify the Whig narrative that dominated the historiography for many years. John Ruskin (1819-1900) wrote a number of highly influential works on art and the history of art and championed such contemporary figures as J. M. W. Turner and the Pre-Raphaelites. The religious writer John Henry Newman's (1801-1890) Oxford Movement aroused intense debate within the Church of England, exacerbated by Newman's own conversion to Catholicism, which he wrote about in his autobiography *Apologia Pro Vita Sua* (1864).

A number of monumental reference works were published in this era, most notably the *Oxford English Dictionary* which would eventually become the most important historical dictionary of the English language. Also published during the later Victorian era were *The Dictionary of National Biography* and the ninth edition of the *Encyclopedia Britannica*.

Nature Writing

In the UK, Philip Henry Gosse (1810-1888) and Sarah Bowdich Lee (1791-1866) were two of the most popular nature writers in the early part of the Victorian era. *The Illustrated London News*, founded in 1842, was the world's first illustrated weekly newspaper and often published articles and illustrations dealing with nature; in the second half of the 19th century, books, articles, and illustrations on nature became widespread and popular among an increasingly urbanized reading public.

Supernatural and Fantastic Literature

The old Gothic tales that came out of the late 19th century are the first examples of the genre of fantastic fiction. These tales often centred on larger-than-life characters such as Sherlock Holmes, famous detective of the times, Sexton Blake, Phileas Fogg, and other fictional characters of the era, such as Dracula, Edward Hyde, the Invisible Man, and many other fictional characters who often had exotic enemies to foil. Spanning the 18th and 19th centuries, there was a particular type of story-writing known as gothic. Gothic literature combines romance and horror in attempt to thrill and terrify the reader. Possible features in a gothic novel are foreign monsters, ghosts, curses, hidden rooms and witchcraft. Gothic tales usually take place in locations such as castles, monasteries, and cemeteries, although the gothic monsters sometimes cross over into the real world, making appearances in cities such as London.

6. 20th Century Literature (1900-2000)

In terms of the British literature of the 20th century, the main periods are captured in the bipartite division, modernist literature and postmodern literature, flowering from roughly 1900 to 1945 and 1945 to 2000 respectively.

6.1 Modernism (1900-1945)

Modernism is a major literary movement, of the first part of the 20th century. Early modernist writers, especially those writing after World War I and the disillusionment that followed, broke the implicit contract with the general public that artists were the reliable interpreters and representatives of mainstream ("bourgeois") culture and ideas, and, instead, developed unreliable narrators, exposing the irrationality at the roots of a supposedly rational world. They also attempted to take into account changing ideas about reality developed by Darwin, Mach, Freud, Einstein, Nietzsche, Bergson and others. From this developed innovative literary techniques such as stream of consciousness, interior monologue, as well as the use of multiple points of view.

Poetry

The career of the major modernist poet, Irishman William Butler Yeats (1865-1939), began late in the Victorian era. Yeats was one of the foremost figures of 20th-century literature. In 1923 he was awarded the Nobel Prize in Literature, the first Irishman so honored. Yeats is generally considered one of the few writers who completed their greatest works after being awarded the Nobel Prize: these works include *The Tower* (1928) and *The Winding Stair and Other Poems* (1929). The impact of modernism on his work can be seen in the increasing abandonment of the more conventionally poetic diction of his early work in favor of the more austere language and more direct approach to his themes that increasingly characterizes the poetry and plays of his middle period, comprising the volumes *In the Seven Woods* (1903), *Responsibilities* (1914) and *The Green Helmet* (1910). His later poetry and plays are written in a more personal vein, and the works written in the last twenty years of his life include mention of his son and daughter, as well as meditations on the experience of growing old.

Free verse and other stylistic innovations came to the forefront in this era, with which Thomas Stearns Eliot (1888-1965) was especially associated. T. S. Eliot was born American, migrated to England in 1914, and he was "arguably the most important English-language poet of the 20th century." He produced some of the best-known poems in the English language, including *The*

Waste Land(1922) and *Four Quartets* (1935-1942). *The Waste Land* mirrors "the futility and anarchy" in its own way, in its fragmented structure, and the absence of an obvious central, unifying narrative.

During the early decades of the 20th century the Georgian poets like Rupert Brooke (1887-1915), Walter de la Mare (1873-1956), and John Masefield (1878-1967) maintained a conservative approach to poetry by combining romanticism, sentimentality and hedonism, sandwiched as they were between the Victorian era, with its strict classicism, and Modernism, with its strong rejection of pure aestheticism.

Edward Thomas (1878-1917) is sometimes treated as another Georgian poet. Thomas enlisted in 1915 and is also one of the First World War Poets along with Hugh MacDiarmid (1892-1978), Wilfred Owen (1893-1918), Isaac Rosenberg (1890-1917), Edmund Blunden (1896-1974) and Siegfried Sassoon (1886-1967). *In Parenthesis*, a modernist epic poem by David Jones (1895-1974) first published in 1937, is probably the best known contribution from Wales to the literature of the First World War.

In the 1930s the Auden Group, sometimes called simply the Thirties Poets, was an important group of politically left-wing writers, that included Wystan Hugh Auden (1907-1973) and two Anglo-Irish writers, Cecil Day-Lewis (1904-1972) and Louis MacNeice (1907-1963). A. H. Auden was a major poet who had a similar influence on subsequent poets as W. B. Yeats and T. S. Eliot had had on earlier generations. He published about four hundred poems, including seven long poems (two of them book-length). His poetry was encyclopedic in scope and method, ranging in style from obscure 20th-century modernism to the lucid traditional forms such as ballads and limericks.

Drama

Irish playwrights George Bernard Shaw (1856-1950) and J. M. Synge (1871-1909) were influential in British drama. George Bernard Shaw turned the Edwardian theatre into an arena for debate about important political and social issues, like marriage, class, "the morality of armaments and war" and the rights of women. An important dramatist in the 1920s, and later, was Irishman Seán O'Casey (1880-1964). Also in the 1920s and later Noël Coward (1899-1973) achieved enduring success as a playwright, publishing more than 50 plays from his teens onwards. Many of his works, such as *Hay Fever* (1925), *Private Lives* (1930), *Design for Living* (1932), *Present Laughter* (1942) and *Blithe Spirit* (1941), have remained in the regular theatre repertoire.

In the 1930s W. H. Auden and English-American novelist Christopher Isherwood (1904-1986) co-authored verse dramas, of which *The Ascent of F6* (1936) is the most notable. T. S. Eliot had begun this attempt to revive poetic drama with *Sweeney Agonistes* in 1932, and this was followed by *The Rock* (1934), *Murder in the Cathedral* (1935) and *Family Reunion* (1939). There were three further plays after the war.

Novel

The Polish-British writer Joseph Conrad (1857-1924) is regarded as one of the greatest novelists to write in the English language. He is remembered for novels like *Heart of Darkness* (1899) and *Lord Jim* (1900), which drew on his experience as a mariner and addressed profound themes of nature and existence. *Lord Jim* is a good example of a modernist fiction because it constitutes elements of a modernist novel. Conrad used a lot of modernist tricks in his narratives, including stream of consciousness, unreliable and biased narrators, a focus on characters' inner lives and a fairly cynical view of the world — all of which we see in *Lord Jim* at one time or another.

Other important early modernists include Dorothy Richardson (1873-1957), whose novel *Pointed Roof* (1915), is one of the earliest examples of the stream-of-consciousness technique, and D. H. Lawrence (1885-1930), who published *The Rainbow* in 1915, though it was immediately seized by the police.

Significant modernist works continued to be created in the 1920s and 1930s. In 1922 Irishman James Joyce's (1882-1941) important modernist novel *Ulysses* appeared. *Ulysses* has been called "a demonstration and summation of the entire movement". Set during one day in Dublin, in it Joyce creates parallels with Homer's epic poem the *Odyssey*. The 1920s also witnessed the publishing of several prominent novels by Virginia Woolf (1882-1941). As an influential feminist, and a major stylistic innovator, she applied the stream-of-consciousness technique in novels like *Mrs Dalloway* (1925) and *To the Lighthouse* (1927). Then in 1928 Lawrence privately published *Lady Chatterley's Lover*, though the unexpurgated version was not published in Britain until 1959. In 1929, Virginia Woolf's essay *A Room of One's Own* containing her famous dictum "A woman must have money and a room of her own if she is to write fiction" was published. The 1930s saw the publishing of John Cowper Powys' (1872-1963) *A Glastonbury Romance* (1932), Samuel Beckett (1906-1989)'s first major work, the novel *Murphy* (1938), Graham Greene's (1904-1991) first major novel *Brighton Rock* (1938), and James Joyce's *Finnegans Wake*, in which he created a special language to express the consciousness of a dreaming character.

6.2 Postmodern Literature (1945-2000)

The term Postmodern Literature is used to describe certain tendencies in post-World War II literature. Postmodern literature is characterized by reliance on narrative techniques such as fragmentation, paradox, and the unreliable narrator. In particular, postmodern writers are seen as reacting against the precepts of modernism, and they often operate as literary "bricoleurs", parodying forms and styles associated with modernist (and other) writers and artists. Postmodern works also tend to celebrate chance over craft, and further employ metafiction to undermine the text's authority or authenticity. Another characteristic of postmodern literature is the questioning of distinctions between high and low culture through the use of pastiche, the combination of subjects and genres not previously deemed fit for literature.

Novel

In 1947 Malcolm Lowry (1909-1957) published *Under the Volcano*. George Orwell's (1903-1950) allegorical novella *Animal Farm* was published in 1945 and the dystopian novel *Nineteen Eighty-Four* in 1949. An essayist and novelist, Orwell produced works that are important social and political commentaries of the 20th century. Evelyn Waugh's (1903-1966) Second World War trilogy *Sword of Honour* (1952-1961) was published in this period.

Graham Greene's (1904-1991) works span the 1930s to the 1980s. His novels explore the puzzling moral and political issues of the modern world. Other novelists writing in the 1950s and later were Anthony Powell (1905-2000), Nobel Prize laureate Sir William Golding (1911-1993), Anglo-Irish philosopher Dame Iris Murdoch (1919-1999) and Scottish novelist Dame Muriel Spark (1918-2006). Anthony Burgess (1917-1993) is especially remembered for his dystopian novel *A Clockwork Orange* (1962). Mervyn Peake (1911-1968) published his *Gothic Fantasy Gormenghast Trilogy* between 1946 and 1959. Angela Carter (1940-1992) was a novelist and journalist, known for her feminist, magical realism, and picaresque works.

Sir Salman Rushdie (1948-) is among a number of post Second World War writers from former British colonies who permanently settled in Britain. Rushdie achieved fame with *Midnight's Children* (1981). His most controversial novel *The Satanic Verses* (1989) was inspired in part by the life of Muhammad.

Doris Lessing (1919-2003) from Southern Rhodesia (now Zimbabwe) published her first novel *The Grass is Singing* in 1950, after immigrating to England. She initially wrote about her African experiences. Lessing soon became a dominant presence in the English literary scene, publishing frequently, and won the Nobel Prize for Literature in 2007. Sir V. S. Naipaul (1932-) was another immigrant, born in Trinidad, who won the Nobel Prize in Literature. Also from the West Indies is George Lamming (1927-) who wrote *In the Castle of My Skin* (1953), while from Pakistan came Hanif Kureshi (1954-), a playwright, screenwriter, filmmaker, novelist and short-story writer. Kazuo Ishiguro (1954-) was born in Japan, but his parents immigrated to Britain when he was six. Martin Amis (1949) is one of the most prominent British novelists of the end of the 20th, beginning of the 21st century. Pat Barker (1943-) has won many awards for her fiction. English novelist and screenwriter Ian McEwan (1948-) is a highly regarded writer.

Drama

An important cultural movement in the British theatre that developed in the late 1950s and early 1960s was "kitchen sink realism" (or "kitchen sink drama"), art, novels, film, and television plays. The term "angry young men" was often applied members of this artistic movement. It used a style of social realism which depicts the domestic lives of the working class, to explore social issues and political issues. The "drawing room plays" of the post war period, typical of dramatists like Sir Terence Rattigan (1911-1977) and Sir Noël Coward (1899-1973), were challenged in the 1950s by these "angry young men", in plays like John Osborne's (1929-1994) *Look Back in Anger* (1956).

Again in the 1950s the Theatre of the Absurd profoundly affected British dramatists. The term Theatre of the Absurd is applied to plays written by primarily European playwrights, that express the belief that human existence has no meaning or purpose and therefore all communication breaks down. Logical construction and argument gives way to irrational and illogical speech and to its ultimate conclusion. The Theatre of the Absurd is generally seen as beginning in the 1950s with Samuel Beckett's (1906-1989) play *Waiting for Godot*. English playwrights who were influenced by the Theater of Absurd include Harold Pinter (1930-2008) (*The Birthday Party*, 1958), and Tom Stoppard (1937-) (*Rosencrantz and Guildenstern are Dead*, 1966).

The Theatres Act 1968 abolished the system of censorship of the stage that had existed in Great Britain since 1737. The new freedoms of the London stage were tested by Howard Brenton's (1942-) *The Romans in Britain*, first staged at the National Theatre during 1980, and subsequently the focus of an unsuccessful private prosecution in 1982.

Other playwrights whose careers began later in the century are Sir Alan Ayckbourn (1939-), Michael Frayn (1933-), David Hare (1947-) and David Edgar (1948-).

During the 1950s and 1960s many major British playwrights either effectively began their careers with the BBC, or had works adapted for radio, including Caryl Churchill (1938-) and Tom Stoppard (1937-) whose "first professional production was in the fifteen-minute *Just Before Midnight* programme on BBC Radio, which showcased new dramatists". John Mortimer (1923-2009) made his radio debut as a dramatist in 1955, with his adaptation of his own novel *Like Men Betrayed* (1953) for the BBC Light Programme. Other notable radio dramatists included Brendan Behan (1923-1964), from Ireland, and novelist Angela Carter (1940-1992).

Among the most famous works created for radio, are Dylan Thomas's (1914-1953) *Under Milk Wood* (1954), Samuel Beckett's *All That Fall* (1957), Harold Pinter's (1930-2008) *A Slight Ache* (1959) and Robert Bolt's (1924-1995) *A Man for All Seasons* (1954).

Poetry

While poets T. S. Eliot, W. H. Auden, Dylan Thomas and Basil Bunting (1900-1985) were still publishing after 1945, new poets started their careers in the 1950s and 1960s including Philip Larkin (1922-1985) (*The Whitsun Weddings*, 1964) and Ted Hughes (1930-1998) (*The Hawk in the Rain*, 1957). Northern Ireland has produced a number of significant poets, the most famous being Nobel prize winner Seamus Heaney (1939-2013) though he regarded himself as Irish and not British. Others poets from Northern Ireland include Derek Mahon (1941-), Paul Muldoon (1951-), James Fenton (1949-), Michael Longley (1939-), and Medbh McGuckian (1950-).

In the 1960s and 1970s Martian poetry aimed to break the grip of "the familiar", by describing ordinary things in unfamiliar ways, as though, for example, through the eyes of a

Martian. Poets most closely associated with it are Craig Raine (1944-) and Christopher Reid (1964-). Martin Amis (1949-), an important novelist in the late 20th and 21st centuries, carried into fiction this drive to make the familiar strange.

Another literary movement in this period was the British Poetry Revival, a wide-reaching collection of groupings and subgroupings that embraces performance, sound and concrete poetry. Leading poets associated with this movement include J. H. Prynne (1936-), Eric Mottram (1924-1995), Tom Raworth (1938-2017), Denise Riley (1948-) and Lee Harwood (1939-2015). It reacted to the more conservative group called "The Movement".

The Liverpool poets were Adrian Henri (1932-2000), Brian Patten (1946-) and Roger McGough (1937-). Their work is characterised by its directness of expression, simplicity of language, suitability for live performance and concern for contemporary subjects and references.

Geoffrey Hill (1932-2016) has been considered to be among the most distinguished English poets of his generation, Charles Tomlinson (1927-2015) is another important English poet of an older generation, though since his first publication in 1951, has built a career that has seen more notice in the international scene than in his native England.

Literature for Children and Young Adults

Roald Dahl (1916-1990) is a prominent author of children's fantasy novels, like *Charlie and the Chocolate Factory* in 1964, which are often inspired from experiences from his childhood, with often unexpected endings, and unsentimental, dark humour. Popular school stories from this period include Ronald Searle's (1920-2011) *St Trinian's* (1948).

J. K. Rowling's (1965-) *Harry Potter* (1997-2007) fantasy series is a sequence of seven novels that chronicle the adventures of the adolescent wizard Harry Potter is the best-selling book-series in history. The series has been translated into 67 languages, placing Rowling among the most translated authors in history. Cressida Cowell (1966-) wrote *How to Train Your Dragon* (2003), a series of twelve books set in a fictional Viking world.

Scottish Literature

Scotland has in the late 20th century produced several important novelists, including James Kelman (1946-) who like Samuel Beckett can create humour out of the most grim situations; A. L. Kennedy (1965-) whose 2007 novel *Day* (2007) was named Book of the Year in the Costa Book Awards; Alasdair Gray (1934-) whose *Lanark: A Life in Four Books* (1981) is a dystopian fantasy set in his home town Glasgow.

Highly anglicised Lowland Scots is often used in contemporary Scottish fiction, for example, the Edinburgh dialect of Lowland Scots used in *Trainspotting* (1966) by Irvine Welsh (1958-) to give a brutal depiction of the lives of working class Edinburgh drug users. In Northern Ireland, James Fenton's (1949-) poetry is written in contemporary Ulster Scots. The poet Michael Longley (1939-) has experimented with Ulster Scots for the translation of Classical verse, as in his 1995 collection *The Ghost Orchid*.

◎ Exercises

1. Explain the following terms in English.

1) the Cavalier poetry
2) the sentimental novel
3) the Graveyard poetry
4) the Theatre of the Absurd
5) modernism

2. Match the authors with their corresponding works.

Author	Works
1) John Bunyan	a. *As You Like It*
2) Geoffrey Chaucer	b. *Essays*
3) Johnson Swift	c. *The Pilgrim's Progress*
4) John Milton	d. *A Christmas Carol*
5) Mary Shelly	e. *The Canterbury Tales*
6) Virginia Woolf	f. *Gulliver's Travels*
7) Francis Bacon	g. *Frankenstein*
8) William Shakespeare	h. *To the Lighthouse*
9) John Locke	i. *Paradise Lost*
10) Charles Dickens	j. *Two Treatises of Government*

3. Discuss and answer the following questions.

1) What are the dominant forms of English literature during the Renaissance? Please name the great poets and their works during the period.
2) What are the characteristics of Shakespeare's plays in the Jacobean Period? Please give some examples.
3) Why is the Restoration Period called the age of poetry? Who are the leading poets and what are their masterpieces of this period?
4) Who are the leading novelists in the Victorian Period? What are their works and their characteristics?

Unit 2

British Literature and English Films

1. The Renaissance in Films

William Shakespeare: *A Midsummer Night's Dream*(1595)/ *Romeo and Juliet*(1595)

An Introduction to William Shakespeare

William Shakespeare (1564-1616) was an English playwright, actor and poet, widely regarded as the greatest writer in the English language and the world's preeminent dramatist. He is often called England's national poet, and the "Bard of Avon".

Though no birth records exist, church records indicate that William Shakespeare was baptized at Holy Trinity Church in Stratford-upon-Avon on April 26, 1564. Stratford-upon-Avon is located 103 miles west of London and during Shakespeare's time was a market town bisected with a country road and the River Avon.

William was the third child of John Shakespeare, a leather merchant, and Mary Arden, a local landed heiress. William had two older sisters, Joan and Judith, and three younger brothers, Gilbert, Richard and Edmund. Before William's birth, his father became a successful merchant and held official positions as alderman and bailiff, an office resembling a mayor. However, John's fortunes declined sometime in the late 1570s. Few records exist of William's childhood, and virtually none regarding his education. But it is inferred that he most likely attended the King's New School, in Stratford, which taught reading, writing and the classics.

William Shakespeare married Anne Hathaway on November 28, 1582, in Worcester, in Canterbury Province. Hathaway was from Shottery, a small village a mile west of Stratford. Their first child, a daughter they named Susanna, was born on May 26, 1583. Two years later, on February 2, 1585, twins Hamnet and Judith were born. Hamnet later died of unknown causes at age 11.

Sometime between 1585 and 1592, he began a successful career in London as an actor, writer, and part-owner of a playing company called the Lord Chamberlain's Men, later known as the King's Men, an acting company in London with which he was connected for most of his career. He had works published and sold as popular literature.

By 1597, Shakespeare had already written and published 15 of his 37 plays. By 1599, William Shakespeare and his business partners built their own theater on the south bank of the Thames River, which they called the Globe. In 1605, Shakespeare purchased leases of real estate near Stratford for 440 pounds, which doubled in value and earned him 60 pounds a year. This made him an entrepreneur as well as an artist, and scholars believe these investments gave him the time to write his plays uninterrupted.

While it's difficult to determine the exact chronology of William Shakespeare's plays, over the course of two decades, from about 1590 to 1613, he produced a total of 37 plays revolving around several main themes: histories, tragedies, comedies and tragicomedies.

With the exception of *Romeo and Juliet* (1595), William Shakespeare's first plays were mostly histories written in the early 1590s. *Richard II*, *Henry VI* (*Parts 1*, *2* and *3*) and *Henry V* dramatize the destructive results of weak or corrupt rulers, and have been interpreted by drama historians as Shakespeare's way of justifying the origins of the Tudor Dynasty. *Julius Caesar* (1599) portrays upheaval in Roman politics that may have resonated with viewers at a time when England's aging monarch, Queen Elizabeth I, had no legitimate heir, thus creating the potential for future power struggles.

Shakespeare also wrote several comedies during his early period: the witty romance *A Midsummer Night's Dream* (1595), the romantic *The Merchant of Venice* (1596-1597), the wit and wordplay of *Much Ado About Nothing* (1598-1599) and the charming *As You Like It* (1599).

Other plays written before 1600 include *Titus Andronicus* (1588-1593), *The Comedy of Errors* (1589-1594), *The Two Gentlemen of Verona* (1589-1593), *The Taming of the Shrew* (1590-1594), *Love's Labour's Lost* (1588-1597), *King John* (1594-1596), *The Merry Wives of Windsor* (1597) and *Henry V* (1599).

It was in William Shakespeare's later period, after 1600, that he wrote the tragedies *Hamlet* (1599-1602), *King Lear* (1605-1606), *Othello* (1603-1604) and *Macbeth* (1606-1607). In these, Shakespeare's characters present vivid impressions of human temperament that are timeless and universal. Possibly the best known of these plays is *Hamlet*, which explores betrayal, retribution, incest and moral failure. These moral failures often drive the twists and turns of Shakespeare's plots, destroying the hero and those he loves.

In William Shakespeare's final period, he wrote several tragicomedies. Among these are *Cymbeline*(1609), *The Winter's Tale*(1609-1611) and *The Tempest*(1610-1611). Though graver in tone than the comedies, they are not the dark tragedies of *King Lear* or *Macbeth* because they end with reconciliation and forgiveness.

Other plays written during this period include *All's Well That Ends Well* (1601-1605), *Measure for Measure*(1603-1604), *Timon of Athens*(1605-1608), *Coriolanus*(1605-1608) and *Henry VIII*(1613).

As for the writing style, William Shakespeare's early plays were written in the conventional style of the day, with elaborate metaphors and rhetorical phrases that didn't always align naturally with the story's plot or characters. However, Shakespeare was very innovative, adapting the traditional style to his own purposes and creating a freer flow of words. With only small degrees of variation, Shakespeare primarily used a metrical pattern consisting of lines of unrhymed iambic pentameter, or blank verse, to compose his plays. At the same time, there are passages in all the plays that are not in line with this and use forms of poetry or simple prose.

While Shakespeare was regarded as the foremost dramatist of his time, evidence indicates that both he and his contemporaries looked to poetry, not playwriting, for enduring fame. When Shakespeare experienced a pause in his theatrical career about 1592-1594, he dedicated poems *Venus and Adonis* (1593) and *The Rape of Lucrece* (1594) to Henry Wriothesley, the Earl of Southampton. Shakespeare's sonnets were composed between 1593 and 1601, though not published until 1609. That edition, *The Sonnets of Shakespeare*, consists of 154 sonnets, all written in the form of three quatrains and a couplet that is now recognized as Shakespearean. The sonnets fall into two groups: sonnets 1-126, addressed to a beloved friend, a handsome and noble young man, and sonnets 127-152, to an evil but fascinating "Dark Lady", who the poet loves in spite of himself. Nearly all of Shakespeare's sonnets examine the inevitable decay of time, and the immortalization of beauty and love in poetry.

William Shakespeare appears to have retired to Stratford around 1613, at age 49, where he died 3 years later in 1616.

Shakespeare occupies a position unique in world literature. His existing works, including collaborations, consist of approximately 38 plays, 154 sonnets, two long narrative poems, and a few other verses, some of uncertain authorship. Today, his works have been repeatedly adapted and rediscovered by new movements in scholarship and performance. His plays have been translated into every major living language and are performed more often than those of any other playwright.

An Introduction to the Film *A Midsummer Night's Dream*

Brief Information

Release year	1999
Directed by	Michael Hoffman
Production company	Regency Enterprises
Distributed by	Fox Searchlight Pictures
Country	United Kingdom; United States; Italy
Starring	Stanley Tucci as Robin Goodfellow/Puck
	Rupert Everett as Oberon
	Michelle Pfeiffer as Titania
	Anna Friel as Hermia
	Dominic West as Lysander
	Calista Flockhart as Helena
	Christian Bale as Demetrius

Plot

In 19th century Monte Athena, in the Kingdom of Italy, young lovers Lysander and Hermia are forbidden to marry by her father Egeus, who has promised Hermia to Demetrius. Lysander and Hermia make plans to flee to the forest to escape the arrangement. Demetrius follows them, having been made aware of the plan by Helena, a young woman who is desperately in love with him. Once in the forest, they wander into the fairy world, ruled by Oberon and Titania, King and Queen of the fairies. Oberon and his servant sprite Puck cause chaos among the lovers with a magic potion that causes both Lysander and Demetrius to fall in love with Helena, leading to a separation between all four that reaches a climax (famously in this adaptation) in a mud-wrestling scene. Oberon then bewitches Titania with the same potion.

Meanwhile, an acting troupe prepares a play for the entertainment of the Duke. The leader of the actors and the actors, including a weaver named Bottom, and Francis Flute take their rehearsal to the forest. The naughty Puck magically bewitches Bottom with the head of an ass and Bottom is then seen by the bewitched Titania. Titania seeks Bottom's favor in her bower, attended by fairies. Oberon tires of the sport and puts all to rights, pairing Lysander back with Hermia and Demetrius with Helena, and finally making up with his own queen, Titania.

In the final part, Bottom and his troupe of "rude Mechanicals" perform their amateur play, based on the tragedy of Pyramus and Thisbe, before Duke Theseus, his wife Hippolyta, and the court, producing a comedy by chance.

Excerpt from the Book *A Mid Summer Night's Dream*

Act 1, Scene I

SCENE I. Athens. The palace of THESEUS.

Enter THESEUS, HIPPOLYTA, PHILOSTRATE, and Attendants

THESEUS

Now, fair Hippolyta, our nuptial hour
Draws on apace; four happy days bring in
Another moon: but, O, methinks, how slow
This old moon wanes! she lingers my desires,
Like to a step-dame or a dowager
Long withering out a young man revenue.

HIPPOLYTA

Four days will quickly steep themselves in night;
Four nights will quickly dream away the time;
And then the moon, like to a silver bow
New-bent in heaven, shall behold the night
Of our solemnities.

THESEUS

Go, Philostrate,
Stir up the Athenian youth to merriments;
Awake the pert and nimble spirit of mirth;
Turn melancholy forth to funerals;
The pale companion is not for our pomp.
Exit PHILOSTRATE
Hippolyta, I woo'd thee with my sword,
And won thy love, doing thee injuries;
But I will wed thee in another key,
With pomp, with triumph and with revelling.

Enter EGEUS, HERMIA, LYSANDER, and DEMETRIUS

EGEUS

Happy be Theseus, our renowned duke!

THESEUS

Thanks, good Egeus: what's the news with thee?

EGEUS

Full of vexation come I, with complaint
Against my child, my daughter Hermia.
Stand forth, Demetrius. My noble lord,
This man hath my consent to marry her.
Stand forth, Lysander: and my gracious duke,
This man hath bewitch'd the bosom of my child;
Thou, thou, Lysander, thou hast given her rhymes,
And interchanged love-tokens with my child:
Thou hast by moonlight at her window sung,
With feigning voice verses of feigning love,
And stolen the impression of her fantasy
With bracelets of thy hair, rings, gawds, conceits,
Knacks, trifles, nosegays, sweetmeats, messengers
Of strong prevailment in unharden'd youth:
With cunning hast thou filch'd my daughter's heart,
Turn'd her obedience, which is due to me,
To stubborn harshness: and, my gracious duke,
Be it so she; will not here before your grace
Consent to marry with Demetrius,
I beg the ancient privilege of Athens,
As she is mine, I may dispose of her:
Which shall be either to this gentleman
Or to her death, according to our law
Immediately provided in that case.

THESEUS

What say you, Hermia? be advised fair maid:
To you your father should be as a god;
One that composed your beauties, yea, and one
To whom you are but as a form in wax
By him imprinted and within his power

To leave the figure or disfigure it.
Demetrius is a worthy gentleman.

HERMIA

So is Lysander.

THESEUS

In himself he is;
But in this kind, wanting your father's voice,
The other must be held the worthier.

HERMIA

I would my father look'd but with my eyes.

THESEUS

Rather your eyes must with his judgment look.

HERMIA

I do entreat your grace to pardon me.
I know not by what power I am made bold,
Nor how it may concern my modesty,
In such a presence here to plead my thoughts;
But I beseech your grace that I may know
The worst that may befall me in this case,
If I refuse to wed Demetrius.

THESEUS

Either to die the death or to abjure
For ever the society of men.
Therefore, fair Hermia, question your desires;
Know of your youth, examine well your blood,
Whether, if you yield not to your father's choice,
You can endure the livery of a nun,
For aye to be in shady cloister mew'd,
To live a barren sister all your life,
Chanting faint hymns to the cold fruitless moon.
Thrice-blessed they that master so their blood,
To undergo such maiden pilgrimage;
But earthlier happy is the rose distill'd,
Than that which withering on the virgin thorn
Grows, lives and dies in single blessedness.

An Introduction to the Film *Romeo and Juliet*

Brief Information

Release Year	2013
Directed by	Carlo Carlei
Production Companies	Echo Lake Entertainment Swarovski Entertainment Icon Productions
Distributed by	Entertainment Film Distributors (UK) Relativity Media (US)
Country	United Kingdom Italy United States

Award	Category	Nominee
IFMCA Award	Film Score of the Year, Best Original Score for a Drama Film and Film Music Composition of the Year	Abel Korzeniowski for the composition track "A Thousand Times Goodnight".

Plot

During the late Middle Ages in Verona, two wealthy families, the Montagues and Capulets, have been feuding for centuries. One day at the market place, the feuding families start a fight which makes the Prince furious and he threatens that if the peace of Verona is disturbed again, he shall take their lives. Meanwhile, Romeo, a young Montague, reveals that he is in love with Lord Capulet's niece, Rosaline. Romeo's cousin, Benvolio persuades him to forget Rosaline but Romeo rejects him fiercely.

Later that night, there is a party held by Lord Capulet. Romeo comes in secretly with Benvolio and Mercutio hoping to meet Rosaline. Instead, Romeo sees Juliet who is Lord Capulet's daughter and falls in love with her. Juliet feels the same and they share a dance. They go together to a quiet place and share a passionate kiss. Juliet's nurse interrupts and when Romeo talks to the nurse, he discovers that Juliet is a Capulet.

After the party ends, Romeo sneaks into Juliet's garden secretly where he witnesses Juliet expressing her love for Romeo. They have a romantic time and decide to get married the next day. Romeo seeks help from Friar Laurence to wed them and the Friar agrees thinking that their love may end the violent war between Capulets and Montagues. They perform the ceremony and afterwards Juliet returns home. Romeo catches up with Mercutio and Benvolio but they meet Tybalt and his men on the way. This starts another violent fight during which Tybalt kills Mercutio with a knife. Romeo is furious and runs after Tybalt seeking revenge. They fight and Romeo kills Tybalt. As the result of this loss, the Prince drives Romeo away from Verona.

Meanwhile both families are filled with grief over their losses, especially Juliet. The Friar sends Romeo to Juliet so he can spend one last night with her. Romeo goes to Juliet and they consummate their marriage. Romeo leaves in haste the next morning. But Juliet is shocked when her father brings news of planning to wed Juliet with Count Paris. Juliet is resistant but her father threatens to disown her if she does not wed Paris. Juliet goes to Friar Laurence for help, threatening to take her life if the Friar does not have a solution. The Friar in return, gives her a medicine that will put her in a deathlike sleep temporarily while he will inform Romeo about this and they shall run away together. Juliet is overjoyed and drinks the potion that night. Her parents are heartbroken and instead of her marriage, her funeral is planned. During the funeral, Benvolio sees Juliet and thinks she is dead and immediately runs off to tell Romeo.

Friar's letter however, does not reach Romeo and Benvolio tells Romeo that Juliet is dead. Romeo is shocked and devastated and plans to take his life. He buys poison and goes to Juliet. He kisses Juliet one last time, then he drinks the potion unaware that Juliet has awakened. Juliet is overjoyed to see him and they kiss but Romeo suddenly collapses and she finds out that he took poison and Romeo dies in her arms. The Friar arrives but he is too late. He hears some guards coming and goes to hold them off. While Juliet is filled with grief, she finds and stabs herself with Romeo's dagger. The Friar arrives and finds them both dead.

Their funeral is held together and the Capulets and Montagues finally reconcile, ending their feud.

Excerpt from the Book *Romeo and Juliet*

Act 2. Scene II

SCENE II. Capulet's orchard.

Enter ROMEO

ROMEO: He jests at scars that never felt a wound. [JULIET appears above at a window]
But, soft! what light through yonder window breaks?
It is the east, and Juliet is the sun.
Arise, fair sun, and kill the envious moon,
Who is already sick and pale with grief,
That thou her maid art far more fair than she:
Be not her maid, since she is envious;
Her vestal livery is but sick and green
And none but fools do wear it; cast it off.
It is my lady, O, it is my love!
O, that she knew she were!
She speaks yet she says nothing: what of that?
Her eye discourses; I will answer it.
I am too bold, 'tis not to me she speaks:
Two of the fairest stars in all the heaven,
Having some business, do entreat her eyes
To twinkle in their spheres till they return.
What if her eyes were there, they in her head?
The brightness of her cheek would shame those stars,
As daylight doth a lamp; her eyes in heaven
Would through the airy region stream so bright
That birds would sing and think it were not night.

See, how she leans her cheek upon her hand!
O, that I were a glove upon that hand,
That I might touch that cheek!

JULIET: Ay me!

ROMEO: She speaks:
O, speak again, bright angel! for thou art
As glorious to this night, being o'er my head
As is a winged messenger of heaven
Unto the white-upturned wondering eyes
Of mortals that fall back to gaze on him
When he bestrides the lazy-pacing clouds
And sails upon the bosom of the air.

JULIET: O Romeo, Romeo! wherefore art thou Romeo?
Deny thy father and refuse thy name;
Or, if thou wilt not, be but sworn my love,
And I'll no longer be a Capulet.

ROMEO: [Aside] Shall I hear more, or shall I speak at this?

JULIET: 'Tis but thy name that is my enemy;
Thou art thyself, though not a Montague.
What's Montague? it is nor hand, nor foot,
Nor arm, nor face, nor any other part
Belonging to a man. O, be some other name!
What's in a name? that which we call a rose
By any other name would smell as sweet;
So Romeo would, were he not Romeo call'd,
Retain that dear perfection which he owes
Without that title. Romeo, doff thy name,
And for that name which is no part of thee
Take all myself.

ROMEO: I take thee at thy word:
Call me but love, and I'll be new baptized;
Henceforth I never will be Romeo.

JULIET: What man art thou that thus bescreen'd in night
So stumblest on my counsel?

ROMEO: By a name
I know not how to tell thee who I am:
My name, dear saint, is hateful to myself,
Because it is an enemy to thee;

Had I it written, I would tear the word.
JULIET: My ears have not yet drunk a hundred words
Of that tongue's utterance, yet I know the sound:
Art thou not Romeo and a Montague?
ROMEO: Neither, fair saint, if either thee dislike.
JULIET: How camest thou hither, tell me, and wherefore?
The orchard walls are high and hard to climb,
And the place death, considering who thou art,
If any of my kinsmen find thee here.
ROMEO: With love's light wings did I o'er-perch these walls;
For stony limits cannot hold love out,
And what love can do that dares love attempt;
Therefore thy kinsmen are no let to me.
JULIET: If they do see thee, they will murder thee.
ROMEO: Alack, there lies more peril in thine eye
Than twenty of their swords: look thou but sweet,
And I am proof against their enmity.
JULIET: I would not for the world they saw thee here.
ROMEO: I have night's cloak to hide me from their sight;
And but thou love me, let them find me here:
My life were better ended by their hate,
Than death prorogued, wanting of thy love.

2. Neo-classical in Films

2.1 Daneil Defoe: *Robinson Crusoe* (1719)

An Introduction to Daniel Defoe

Daniel Defoe (1660-1731) was an English trader, writer, journalist, pamphleteer, and spy. He is most famous for his novel *Robinson Crusoe*, which is second only to the Bible in its number of translations.

Daniel Foe was born about 1660 in London to a poor, but hard-working butcher named James Foe, who was, in addition, a Dissenter from the Church of England. Daniel later changed his name to Daniel Defoe, wanting to sound more gentlemanly. As a Dissenter, Foe could not send his son to the University of Oxford or to Cambridge; he sent him instead to the excellent academy at Newington Green kept by the Reverend Charles Morton. There Daniel received an education in many ways better, and certainly broader, than any he would have had at an English university. Morton was an admirable teacher, later becoming first vice president of Harvard College; and the clarity, simplicity, and ease of his style of writing—together with the Bible, the works of John Bunyan, and the pulpit oratory of the day—may have helped to form Defoe's own literary style.

In the Dissenting academy, Daniel studied science and the humanities, preparing to become a Presbyterian minister. It was not long, however, before he decided against the ministry. Living for the rest of his life in the strict confines of a parish seemed hopeless. Daniel recognized his independent, ambitious nature and wanted to be a part of the rapidly growing business world of London. He dealt in many commodities, traveled widely at home and abroad, and became an acute and intelligent economic theorist, in many respects ahead of his time; but misfortune, in one form or another, fell on him continually. It was true enough. In 1692, after prospering for a while, Defoe went bankrupt for £17,000. He suffered further severe losses in 1703, when his prosperous brick-and-tile works failed during his imprisonment for political offenses, and he did not actively engage in trade after this time.

Soon after setting up in business, in 1684, Defoe married Mary Tuffley, the daughter of a well-to-do Dissenting merchant. Not much is known about her, and he mentions her little in his writings, but she seems to have been a loyal, capable, and devoted wife. She bore 8 children, of whom 6 lived to maturity, and when Defoe died the couple had been married for 48 years.

Having always been interested in politics, Defoe published his first literary piece, a political pamphlet, in 1683. He continued to write political works, working as a journalist, until the early 1700s. Many of Defoe's works during this period targeted support for King William III, also known as "William Henry of Orange." Some of his most popular works include *The True-Born Englishman* (1701), which shed light on racial prejudice in England following attacks on William for being a foreigner; and the *Review*, a serious, forceful, and long-lived periodical that was published from 1704 to 1713, during the reign of Queen Anne, King William II's successor. Political opponents of Defoe's repeatedly had him imprisoned for his writing in 1713.

Defoe is noted for being one of the earliest supporters of the novel, as he helped to popularize the form in Britain with others such as Aphra Behn and Samuel Richardson, and is among the founders of the English novel. Defoe took a new literary path in 1719, around the age of 59, when he published *Robinson Crusoe*, a long, imaginative fiction novel based on several short essays that he had composed over the years. The book is presented as an autobiography of the title character (whose birth name is Robinson Kreutznaer)—a castaway who spends twenty-eight years on a remote tropical desert island near Trinidad, encountering cannibals, captives, and mutineers, before ultimately being rescued. Despite its simple narrative style, *Robinson Crusoe* was well received in the literary world and is often credited as marking the beginning of realistic fiction as a literary genre. It is generally seen as a contender for the first English novel and has never lost its appeal to adventure and romance.

A handful of novels followed soon after—often with rogues and criminals as lead characters—including *Moll Flanders*(1722), *Colonel Jack*(1722), *Captain Singleton*(1720), *Journal of the Plague Year*(1722) and his last major fiction piece, *Roxana* (1724).

In the mid-1720s, Defoe returned to writing editorial pieces, focusing on such subjects as morality, politics and the breakdown of social order in England. Some of his later works include *Everybody's Business Is Nobody's Business* (1725); the nonfiction essay *Conjugal Lewdness: or, Matrimonial Whoredom* (1727); and a follow-up piece to the *Conjugal Lewdness* essay, entitled *A Treatise Concerning the Use and Abuse of the Marriage Bed*(1727).

But debts still plagued Defoe, and he died at 71, hiding in a boarding house, trying to evade a bill collector. However, Defoe is still remembered today as a productive and talented writer producing more than three hundred works in his life time—political pamphlets, journalistic pieces and fantasy-filled novels—on diverse topics, including politics, crime, religion, marriage, psychology, and the supernatural. The characters that Defoe created in his fiction books have been brought to life countless times over the years, in editorial works, as well as stage and screen productions.

An Introduction to the Film *Robinson Crusoe*

Brief Information

Release year	1997
Directed by	Rod Hardy George T. Miller
Production company	Touchstone Pictures
Distributed by	Buena Vista Pictures
Country	United States
Starring	Pierce Brosnan as Robinson Crusoe William Takaku as Man Friday Polly Walker as Mary McGregor

Plot

The film opens to a fictionalized Daniel Defoe being offered to read the autobiography of a survivor from a shipwreck. He reluctantly obliges and begins to get engrossed in the narrative.

Robinson Crusoe is a Scottish gentleman with experience in the Royal Navy and the British army. He accidentally kills his lifelong friend Patrick in a fight over his childhood love Mary. Patrick's brothers arrive and threaten Crusoe, but his servant manages to buy time for an escape.

Fleeing back to Mary, Crusoe subsequently ends up leaving for a year so that Mary can attempt to smooth over relations with Patrick's family.

Crusoe joins the merchant marine transporting assorted cargoes between ports in the Pacific, Indian and Atlantic oceans. He sets down the ship's journeys at the request of the captain until a typhoon destroys the ship and leaves him near the coast of New Guinea.

On his first day ashore on the island he buries other crew members who have washed up on the surrounding beaches. The next day he heads to the ship, which have beached itself on a reef. He saves tools, supplies and weapons from the ship. Crusoe also frees the captain's corgi Skipper from a supply room. Crusoe begins to acclimate himself to the island while hoping for a passing European ship. One day a ship finally appears, but Crusoe notices it too late to be rescued. Crusoe resolves to adapt himself to the island and moves inland, building a shelter and growing food.

One day he hears alarming drums and human voices. Investigating the noises he finds a tribe from a nearby island making human sacrifices. After two prisoners have been sacrificed Crusoe intervenes by firing his weapon, which allows the third prisoner to escape. Later he meets the escaped native and attempts to befriend him. Cultural and language barriers prevent them from communicating before they are attacked by a group of the tribesmen. He witnesses the native cut out the heart of a defeated enemy and calls him a savage heathen before fleeing to his shelter and preparing a defence.

Days later Crusoe falls into a trap laid by the native. Crusoe communicates the danger and power of his firearms on a bat, which allows them to begin communicating. He names the man Friday and has himself referred to as Master. Within six months Friday has learned the basics of English, but when Crusoe attempts to convert him to Christianity, Friday refuses and an argument follows. Friday separates himself from Crusoe. Missing the companionship, Crusoe attempts to make peace with Friday.

Reunited, the two set a trap for the tribe of natives who attempted to sacrifice Friday before. Once they arrive Crusoe lights a fuse leading to a load of gunpowder, but Skipper chases after the lit fuse and also dies in the explosion. At Skipper's funeral Crusoe gains a deeper appreciation for Friday's religion.

Later Crusoe decides they must leave the island due to a forthcoming attack by the native tribe. Friday mentions that he has heard of New Britain. He says he cannot take Crusoe to his home island because he is considered dead for being a sacrifice and he cannot go to New Britain because the Europeans enslave his people. Friday subsequently learns that "Master" is not Crusoe's real name, but an indicator of enslavement and once again leaves Crusoe, who subsequently attempts to build a canoe to get to New Britain by himself.

A typhoon arrives while Crusoe has nearly finished his boat. Friday returns and accepts that Crusoe has decided not to make him a slave. The two attempt to rescue their crops and wildlife, but the typhoon destroys them — as well as Crusoe's canoe. The pair set traps to defend the island, but expect to die in the defence.

The tribesmen arrive in force. Crusoe and Friday manage to defend the island, but Crusoe is shot by an arrow. Friday decides to try to save Crusoe by taking him to his home island. Upon arriving there Friday's tribe capture Crusoe, believing him to have come to enslave the people. They force Crusoe to fight Friday to the death for his freedom. After sparing Friday, Friday is about to land a killing blow when he is hit by a bullet. But Crusoe becomes upset because Friday is his friend. A European scout party rescues Crusoe and returns him to Scotland where he is reunited with Mary.

Excerpt from the Book *Robinson Crusoe*

Chapter 4

After I had been there about ten or twelve days, it came into my thoughts that I should lose my reckoning of time for want of books, and pen and ink, and should even forget the Sabbath days; but to prevent this, I cut with my knife upon a large post, in capital letters — and making it into a great cross, I set it up on the shore where I first landed — "I came on shore here on the 30th September 1659."

Upon the sides of this square post I cut every day a notch with my knife, and every seventh notch was as long again as the rest, and every first day of the month as long again as that long one; and thus I kept my calendar, or weekly, monthly, and yearly reckoning of time.

In the next place, we are to observe that among the many things which I brought out of the ship, in the several voyages which, as above mentioned, I made to it, I got several things of less value, but not at all less useful to me, which I omitted setting down before; as, in particular, pens, ink, and paper, several parcels in the captain's, mate's, gunner's and carpenter's keeping; three or four compasses, some mathematical instruments, dials, perspectives, charts, and books of navigation, all which I huddled together, whether I might want them or no; also, I found three very good Bibles, which came to me in my cargo from England, and which I had packed up among my things; some Portuguese books also; and among them two or three Popish prayer-books, and several other books, all which I carefully secured. And I must not forget that we had in the ship a dog and two cats, of whose eminent history I may have occasion to say something in its place; for I carried both the cats with me; and as for the dog, he jumped out of the ship of himself, and swam on shore to me the day after I went on shore with my first cargo, and was a trusty servant to me many years; I wanted nothing that he could fetch me, nor any company that he could make up to me; I only wanted to have him talk to me, but that would not do. As I observed before, I found pens, ink, and paper, and I husbanded them to the utmost; and I shall show that while my ink lasted, I kept things very exact, but after that was gone I could not, for I could not make any ink by any means that I could devise.

And this put me in mind that I wanted many things notwithstanding all that I had amassed together; and of these, ink was one; as also a spade, pickaxe, and shovel, to dig or remove the earth; needles, pins, and thread; as for linen, I soon learned to want that without much difficulty. This want of tools made every work I did go on heavily; and it was near a whole year before I had entirely finished my little pale, or surrounded my habitation. The piles, or stakes, which were as heavy as I could well lift, were a long time in cutting and preparing in the woods, and more, by far, in bringing home; so that I spent sometimes two days in cutting and bringing home one of those posts, and a third day in driving it into the ground; for which purpose I got a heavy piece of wood at first, but at last bethought myself of one of the iron crows; which, however, though I found it, made driving those posts or piles very laborious and tedious work. But what need I have been concerned at the tediousness of anything I had to do, seeing I had time enough to do it in? nor had I any other employment, if that had been over, at least that I could foresee, except the ranging the island to seek for food, which I did, more or less, every day.

I now began to consider seriously my condition, and the circumstances I was reduced to; and I drew up the state of my affairs in writing, not so much to leave them to any that were to come after me — for I was likely to have but few heirs — as to deliver my thoughts from daily poring over them, and afflicting my mind; and as my reason began now to master my despondency, I began to comfort myself as well as I could, and to set the good against the evil, that I might have something to distinguish my case from worse; and I stated very impartially, like debtor and creditor, the comforts I enjoyed against the miseries I suffered, thus: —

Evil: I am cast upon a horrible, desolate island, void of all hope of recovery.

Good: But I am alive; and not drowned, as all my ship's company were.

Evil: I am singled out and separated, as it were, from all the world, to be miserable.

Good: But I am singled out, too, from all the ship's crew, to be spared from death; and He that miraculously saved me from death can deliver me from this condition.

Evil: I am divided from mankind — a solitaire; one banished from human society.

Good: But I am not starved, and perishing on a barren place, affording no sustenance.

Evil: I have no clothes to cover me.

Good: But I am in a hot climate, where, if I had clothes, I could hardly wear them.

Evil: I am without any defence, or means to resist any violence of man or beast.

Good: But I am cast on an island where I see no wild beasts to hurt me, as I saw on the coast of Africa; and what if I had been shipwrecked there?

Evil: I have no soul to speak to or relieve me.

Good: But God wonderfully sent the ship in near enough to the shore, that I have got out as many necessary things as will either supply my wants or enable me to supply myself, even as long as I live.

Upon the whole, here was an undoubted testimony that there was scarce any condition in the world so miserable but there was something negative or something positive to be thankful for in it; and let this stand as a direction from the experience of the most miserable of all conditions in this world: that we may always find in it something to comfort ourselves from, and to set, in the description of good and evil, on the credit side of the account.

Having now brought my mind a little to relish my condition, and given over looking out to sea, to see if I could spy a ship — I say, giving over these things, I begun to apply myself to arrange my way of living, and to make things as easy to me as I could.

I have already described my habitation, which was a tent under the side of a rock, surrounded with a strong pale of posts and cables: but I might now rather call it a wall, for I raised a kind of wall up against it of turfs, about two feet thick on the outside; and after some time (I think it was a year and a half) I raised rafters from it, leaning to the rock, and thatched or covered it with boughs of trees, and such things as I could get, to keep out the rain; which I found at some times of the year very violent.

I have already observed how I brought all my goods into this pale, and into the cave which I had made behind me. But I must observe, too, that at first this was a confused heap of goods, which, as they lay in no order, so they took up all my place; I had no room to turn myself: so I set myself to enlarge my cave, and work farther into the earth; for it was a loose sandy rock, which yielded easily to the labour I bestowed on it: and so when I found I was pretty safe as to beasts of prey, I worked sideways, to the right hand, into the rock; and then, turning to the right again, worked quite out, and made me a door to come out on the outside of my pale or fortification. This gave me not only egress and regress, as it was a back way to my tent and to my storehouse, but gave me room to store my goods.

2.2 Jonathan Swift: *Gulliver's Travels* (1726)

An Introduction to Jonathan Swift

Jonathan Swift (1667-1745) was an Anglo-Irish essayist, political pamphleteer, and poet and is regarded as the foremost prose satirist in the English language.

Jonathan Swift was born in Dublin, Ireland on November 30, 1667. His father, an attorney, also named Jonathan Swift, died just two months before he arrived. Without steady income, his mother struggled to provide for her newborn. Moreover, Swift was a sickly child. It was later discovered that he suffered from Meniere's Disease, a condition of the inner ear that leaves the

afflicted nauseous and hard of hearing. In an effort to give her son the best upbringing possible, Swift's mother gave him over to Godwin Swift, her late husband's brother and a member of the respected professional attorney and judges group Gray's Inn. Godwin Swift enrolled his nephew in the Kilkenny Grammar School, which was perhaps the best school in Ireland at the time. Swift's transition from a life of poverty to a rigorous private school setting proved challenging. He did, however, make a fast friend with William Congreve, the future poet and playwright.

At age 14, Swift commenced his undergraduate studies at Trinity College in Dublin. In 1686, he received a Bachelor of Arts degree, and went on to pursue a master's. Not long into his research, huge unrest broke out in Ireland. The king of Ireland, England and Scotland was soon to be overthrown. What became known as the Glorious Revolution of 1688 spurred Swift to move to England and start anew. His mother found a secretary position for him under the revered English statesman, Sir William Temple. For ten years, Swift worked in Surrey's Moor Park and acted as an assistant to Temple, helping him with political errands, and also in the researching and publishing of his own essays and memoirs. Temple was impressed by Swift's abilities and after a time, entrusted him with sensitive and important tasks.

During his Moor Park years, Swift met the daughter of Temple's housekeeper, a girl just 8 years old named Esther Johnson. When they first met, she was 15 years Swift's junior, but despite the age gap, they would become lovers for the rest of their lives. When she was a child, he acted as her mentor and tutor, and gave her the nickname "Stella". When she was of age, they maintained a close but ambiguous relationship, which lasted until Johnson's death. It was rumored that they married in 1716, and that Swift kept of lock of Johnson's hair in his possession at all times.

During his decade of work for Temple, Swift returned to Ireland twice. On a trip in 1695, he took all necessary requirements to become an appointed priest in the Anglican tradition. Under Temple's influence, he also began to write, first short essays and then a manuscript for a later book. In 1699, Temple died. Swift completed the task of editing and publishing his memoirs—not without disputes by several of Temple's family members—and then, reluctantly, accepted a less prominent post as secretary and chaplain to the Earl of Berkeley. After making the long journey to the Earl's estate, Swift was informed the position had been filled. Discouraged but resourceful, he leaned on his priestly qualifications and found work ministering to a pea-sized congregation just twenty miles outside of Dublin. For the next ten years, he gardened, preached and worked on the house provided to him by the church. He also returned to writing. His first political pamphlet was titled *A Discourse on the Contests and Dissentions in Athens and Rome* (1701).

In 1704, Swift anonymously released *The Battle of the Books* and *A Tale of a Tub*. In *The Battle of the Books*, he defended Temple's contention that the ancients were superior to the moderns in literature and learning. *A Tale of a Tub*, a satire on religious excesses, although widely popular with the masses, was harshly disapproved of by the Church of England. Seemingly, it criticized religion, but Swift meant it as a parody of pride. Nonetheless, his writings earned him a reputation in London, and when the Tories came into power in 1710, they asked him to become editor of the *Examiner*, their official paper. After a time, he became fully immersed in the political landscape and began writing some of the most cutting and well-known political pamphlets of the day, including *The Conduct of the Allies* (1711), an attack on the Whigs. Privy to the inner circle of Tory government, Swift laid out his private thoughts and feelings in a stream of letters to his beloved Stella. They would later be published as *The Journal to Stella* (1766).

When he saw that the Tories would soon fall from power, Swift returned to Ireland. In 1713, he took the post of dean at St. Patrick's Cathedral in Dublin and he joined Alexander Pope, John Arbuthnot, John Gay, and others in forming the celebrated Scriblerus Club. About this time Swift became involved with another woman, Esther Vanhomrigh, the Vanessa of his poem *Cadenus and Vanessa*(1726). The intensity of his relationship with her, as with Stella, is questionable, but Vanessa died a few weeks after his final breakup with her in 1723. He is also rumored to have had a relationship with the celebrated beauty Anne Long.

Swift became a national hero of the Irish with his *Drapier Letters* (1724) and his bitterly ironical pamphlet *A Modest Proposal* (1729), which proposes that the children of the poor be sold as food for the tables of the rich. His blank, ironic writing style, particularly in *A Modest Proposal*, has led to such satire being subsequently termed "Swiftian".

While leading his congregation at St. Patrick's, Swift began to write what would become his best-known work. His satirical masterpiece *Gulliver's Travels* appeared in 1726. Written in four parts, it describes the travels of Lemuel Gulliver to Lilliput, a land inhabited by tiny people whose tiny size renders all their self-important activities absurd; to Brobdingnag, a land populated by giants who are amused when Gulliver tells them about the glories of England; to Laputa and its neighbor Lagado, peopled by fake philosophers and scientists; and to the land of the Houhynhnms, where horses behave with reason and men, called Yahoos, behave as beasts. The book was an immediate success, and hasn't been out of print since its first run. Interestingly, much of the storyline points to historical events that Swift had lived through years prior, during intense political turmoil. And ironically, this merciless satire of human foolishness subsequently was turned into a story for children after some modification.

Not long after the celebration of this work, Swift's longtime love, Esther Johnson, fell ill and died in 1728. Her life's end moved Swift to write *The Death of Mrs. Johnson*. Shortly after her death, a stream of Swift's other friends also died, including John Gay and John Arbuthnot. Swift, always supported by the people around him, was now quite troubled.

In his last years Swift was paralyzed and suffered from a brain disorder, and by 1742 he was declared unsound of mind. On October 19, 1745, Jonathan Swift died. He was laid to rest next to Esther Johnson inside Dublin's St. Patrick's Cathedral.

An Introduction to the Film *Gulliver's Travels*

Brief Information

Release date	December 22, 1939
Directed by	Dave Fleischer
Production company	Fleischer Studios
Distributed by	Paramount Pictures
Country	United States
Starring	Pinto Colvig as Gabby Jack Mercer as King Little, Twinkletoes, Sneak, Snoop, Snitch Sam Parker as Gulliver

Plot

On November 5, 1699, Lemuel Gulliver washes onto the beach of Lilliput, after a storm at sea and ultimate shipwreck. Following the calm of the storm, the Town Crier "Gabby" stumbles across Gulliver and rushes to warn King Little. But Little and King Bombo of Blefescu are signing a wedding contract between their children, Princess Glory of Lilliput and Prince David of Blefuscu. All is fine until an argument starts over which national anthem is to be played at the wedding. The argument cancels the wedding and starts a war.

After failures, Gabby tells King Little of the "giant on the beach" (i. e. Gulliver), and leads a mob to the beach to capture him. There, the Lilliputians tie Gulliver to a wagon on which they convey him to the capital. In the next morning, Gulliver awakens and breaks himself free; but when they see that the invading Blefuscuians are intimidated by his size, the Lilliputians enlist his help against their neighbor, treating him with hospitality and making him a new set of clothes.

King Bombo, who has sent three spies, Sneak, Snoop, and Snitch, into Lilliput, orders them to kill Gulliver; whereupon the spies steal Gulliver's flintlock pistol, confiscated by the Lilliputians, and prepare to use it against him. Meanwhile, Gulliver learns of the war's cause from Glory and David, and proposes a new song that combines the two proposed by their fathers.

When the spies assure King Bombo that they can kill Gulliver, Bombo announces by carrier pigeon "Twinkletoes", that he will attack at dawn. Gabby got this message and warns the Lilliputians; but is himself captured by the spies and stuffed in a sack, who prepare the pistol. As the Blefuscuian fleet approaches Lilliput, Gulliver ties them together and draws them disarmed to shore. The spies fire at Gulliver from a cliff, but Prince David diverts the shot and falls to his apparent death. Using David's body to illustrate his point, Gulliver scolds both Lilliput and Blefuscu for fighting; but when they celebrate a truce, reveals that David is unharmed, whereupon David and Glory sing their combined song for everyone to hear. The spies release Gabby. Both thereafter build a new ship for Gulliver, on which he departs.

Excerpt from the Book *Gulliver's Travels*

Chapter VI

[Of the inhabitants of Lilliput; their learning, laws, and customs; the manner of educating their children. The author's way of living in that country. His vindication of a great lady.]

Although I intend to leave the description of this empire to a particular treatise, yet, in the mean time, I am content to gratify the curious reader with some general ideas. As the common size of the natives is somewhat under six inches high, so there is an exact proportion in all other animals, as well as plants and trees: for instance, the tallest horses and oxen are between four and five inches in height, the sheep an inch and half, more or less: their geese about the bigness of a sparrow, and so the several gradations downwards till you come to the smallest, which to my sight, were almost invisible; but nature has adapted the eyes of the Lilliputians to all objects proper for their view: they see with great exactness, but at no great distance. And, to show the sharpness of their sight towards objects that are near, I have been much pleased with observing a cook pulling a lark, which was not so large as a common fly; and a young girl threading an invisible needle with invisible silk. Their tallest trees are about seven feet high: I mean some of those in the great royal park, the tops whereof I could but just reach with my fist clenched. The other vegetables are in the same proportion; but this I leave to the reader's imagination.

I shall say but little at present of their learning, which, for many ages, has flourished in all its branches among them: but their manner of writing is very peculiar, being neither from the left to the right, like the Europeans, nor from the right to the left, like the Arabians, nor from up to down, like the Chinese, but aslant, from one corner of the paper to the other, like ladies in England.

They bury their dead with their heads directly downward, because they hold an opinion, that in eleven thousand moons they are all to rise again; in which period the earth (which they conceive to be flat) will turn upside down, and by this means they shall, at their resurrection, be found ready standing on their feet. The learned among them confess the absurdity of this doctrine; but the practice still continues, in compliance to the vulgar.

There are some laws and customs in this empire very peculiar; and if they were not so directly contrary to those of my own dear country, I should be tempted to say a little in their justification. It is only to be wished they were as well executed. The first I shall mention, relates to informers. All crimes against the state, are punished here with the utmost severity; but, if the person accused makes his innocence plainly to appear upon his trial, the accuser is immediately put to an ignominious death; and out of his goods or lands the innocent person is quadruply recompensed for the loss of his time, for the danger he underwent, for the hardship of his imprisonment, and for all the charges he has been at in making his defence; or, if that fund be deficient, it is largely supplied by the crown. The emperor also confers on him some public mark of his favour, and proclamation is made of his innocence through the whole city.

They look upon fraud as a greater crime than theft, and therefore seldom fail to punish it with death; for they allege, that care and vigilance, with a very common understanding, may preserve a man's goods from thieves, but honesty has no defence against superior cunning; and, since it is necessary that there should be a perpetual intercourse of buying and selling, and dealing upon credit, where fraud is permitted and connived at, or has no law to punish it, the honest dealer is always undone, and the knave gets the advantage. I remember, when I was once interceding with the emperor for a criminal who had wronged his master of a great sum of money, which he had received by order and ran away with; and happening to tell his majesty, by way of extenuation, that it was only a breach of trust, the emperor thought it monstrous in me to offer as a defence the greatest aggravation of the crime; and truly I had little to say in return, farther than the common answer, that different nations had different customs; for, I confess, I was heartily ashamed.

Although we usually call reward and punishment the two hinges upon which all government turns, yet I could never observe this maxim to be put in practice by any nation except that of Lilliput. Whoever can there bring sufficient proof, that he has strictly observed the laws of his country for seventy-three moons, has a claim to certain privileges, according to his quality or condition of life, with a proportionable sum of money out of a fund appropriated for that use: he likewise acquires the title of SNILPALL, or legal, which is added to his name, but does not descend to his posterity. And these people thought it a prodigious defect of policy among us, when I told them that our laws were enforced only by penalties, without any mention of reward. It is upon this account that the image of Justice, in their courts of judicature, is formed with six eyes, two before, as many behind, and on each side one, to signify circumspection; with a bag of gold open in her right hand, and a sword sheathed in her left, to show she is more disposed to reward than to punish.

In choosing persons for all employments, they have more regard to good morals than to great abilities; for, since government is necessary to mankind, they believe, that the common size of human understanding is fitted to some station or other; and that Providence never intended to make the management of public affairs a mystery to be comprehended only by a few persons of sublime genius, of which there seldom are three born in an age: but they suppose truth, justice, temperance, and the like, to be in every man's power; the practice of which virtues, assisted by experience and a good intention, would qualify any man for the service of his country, except where a course of study is required. But they thought the want of moral virtues was so far from being supplied by superior endowments of the mind, that employments could never be put into such dangerous hands as those of persons so qualified; and, at least, that the mistakes committed by ignorance, in a virtuous disposition, would never be of such fatal consequence to the public weal, as the practices of a man, whose inclinations led him to be corrupt, and who had great abilities to manage, to multiply, and defend his corruptions.

In like manner, the disbelief of a Divine Providence renders a man incapable of holding any public station; for, since kings avow themselves to be the deputies of Providence, the Lilliputians think nothing can be more absurd than for a prince to employ such men as disown the authority under which he acts.

In relating these and the following laws, I would only be understood to mean the original institutions, and not the most scandalous corruptions, into which these people are fallen by the degenerate nature of man. For, as to that infamous practice of acquiring great employments by dancing on the ropes, or badges of favor and distinction by leaping over sticks and creeping under them, the reader is to observe, that they were first introduced by the grandfather of the emperor now reigning, and grew to the present height by the gradual increase of party and faction.

3. Romanticism in Films

3.1 Lord Byron: *Don Juan* (1818-1823)

An Introduction to Lord Byron

George Gordon Byron, 6th Baron Byron, FRS (1788-1824), commonly known simply as Lord Byron, was one of the greatest British poets and a leading figure in the Romantic Movement.

Born George Gordon Byron (he later added "Noel" to his name) to Captain John Byron and Catherine Gordon on January 22, 1788, Lord Byron was the sixth Baron Byron of a rapidly fading aristocratic family. A clubfoot from birth left him self-conscious most of his life. As a boy, young George endured the father who abandoned him, the schizophrenic mother and a nurse who abused him. As a result he lacked discipline and a sense of moderation, traits he held on to his entire life.

In 1798, at age 10, George inherited the title of his great-uncle, William Byron, and was officially recognized as Lord Byron. In 1803, Byron fell deeply in love with his distant cousin, Mary Chaworth, and this unrequited passion found expression in several poems, including *Hills of Annesley* and *The Adieu*.

From 1805 to 1808, Byron attended Trinity College irregularly, engaged in many sexual escapades and fell deep into debt. During this time, he found diversion from school and partying with boxing, horse riding and gambling. In June 1807, he formed an enduring friendship with John Cam Hobhouse and was initiated into liberal politics, joining the Cambridge Whig Club.

After receiving a severe review of his first volume of poetry, *Hours of Idleness*, in 1808, Byron retaliated with the satirical poem *English Bards and Scotch Reviewers* (1809). The poem attacked the literary community with wit and satire, and gained him his first literary recognition. Upon turning 21, Byron took his seat in the House of Lords. A year later, with John Hobhouse, he embarked on a grand tour through the Mediterranean and Aegean seas, visiting Portugal, Spain, Malta, Albania, Greece and Turkey. It was during his journey, filled with inspiration, he began writing *Childe Harold's Pilgrimage* (1812-1818), a poem of a young man's reflections on travel in foreign lands.

In July 1811, Byron returned to London after the death of his mother, and in spite of all her failings, her passing plunged him into a deep mourning. High praise by London society pulled him out of his depression, as did a series of love affairs, first with the passionate and odd Lady Caroline Lamb, who described Byron as "mad, bad and dangerous to know", and then with Lady Oxford, who encouraged Byron's radicalism. Then, in the summer of 1813, Byron apparently entered into an intimate relationship with his half sister, Augusta, then married. The trouble and guilt he experienced as a result of these love affairs were reflected in a series of dark and repentant poems, *The Giaour* (1813), *The Bride of Abydos* (1813) and *The Corsair* (1814).

In September 1814, seeking to escape the pressures of his amorous entanglements, Byron proposed to the educated and intellectual Anne Isabella Milbanke (also known as Annabella Milbanke). They married in January 1815, and in December of that year, their daughter, Augusta Ada, better known as Ada Lovelace, was born. However, by January the ill-fated union broke up, and Annabella left Byron amid his drinking, increased debt, and rumors of his relations with his half sister and of his bisexuality. He never saw his wife or daughter again.

In April 1816, Byron left England, never to return. He traveled to Geneva, Switzerland, befriending Percy Bysshe Shelley, his wife Mary and her stepsister, Claire Clairmont. While in Geneva, Byron wrote the third canto to *Childe Harold*, depicting his travels from Belgium up the Rhine to Switzerland. On a trip to the Bernese Oberland, Byron was inspired to write the Faustian poetic-drama *Manfred* (1816-1817). By the end of that summer the Shelleys departed for England, where Claire gave birth to Byron's daughter Allegra in January 1817.

In October 1816, Byron and John Hobhouse sailed for Italy. Along the way he continued his lustful ways with several women and portrayed these experiences in his greatest poem, *Don Juan* (1818-1823). The poem was a witty and satirical change from the melancholy of *Childe Harold* and revealed other sides of Byron's personality. He would go on to write 16 cantos before his death and leave the poem unfinished.

By 1818, Byron's life of self-indulgence had aged him well beyond his 30 years. He then met 19-year-old Teresa Guiccioli, a married countess. The pair were immediately attracted to each other and carried on an unconsummated relationship until she separated from her husband. Byron soon won the admiration of Teresa's father, who had him initiated into the secret Carbonari society dedicated to freeing Italy from Austrian rule. Between 1821 and 1822, Byron edited the society's short-lived newspaper, *The Liberal*.

In 1823, a restless Byron accepted an invitation to support Greek independence from the Ottoman Empire. Byron spent 4,000 pounds of his own money to refit the Greek naval fleet and took personal command of a Greek unit of elite fighters. On February 15, 1824, he fell ill. Doctors bled him, which weakened his condition further and likely gave him an infection.

After leading an unconventional lifestyle and producing a massive amount of emotion-stirring literary works, Byron died in 1824 at a young age of 36. He was deeply mourned in England and became a hero in Greece. His body was brought back to England, but the clergy refused to bury him at Westminster Abbey, as was the custom for individuals of great stature. Instead, he was buried in the family vault near Newstead. In 1969, a memorial to Byron was finally placed on the floor of Westminster Abbey.

An Introduction to the Film *Don Juan*

Brief Information

Release year	1926
Directed by	Alan Crosland
Production company	Warner Bros. Pictures
Distributed by	Warner Bros. Pictures
Country	United States
Starring	John Barrymore as Don Jose de Marana/ Don Juan de Marana Jane Winton as Donna Isobel John Roche as Leandro Warner Oland as Cesare Borgia Estelle Taylor as Lucrezia Borgia

Plot

In the prologue, Don José, warned of his wife's disloyalty, seals his wife's lover alive in his hiding place and drives her from the castle; abandoned to his lust, he is stabbed by his last mistress, and with his dying words he begs his son, Don Juan, to take all from women but yield nothing. Ten years later, young Don Juan, a graduate of the University of Pisa, is famous as a lover and pursued by many women, including the powerful Lucrezia Borgia, who invites him to her ball. His contempt for her caused her hatred of Adriana, the daughter of the Duke Della Varnese, with whom he is fascinated; and Lucrezia plots to marry her to Count Giano Donati, one of the Borgia henchmen, and poison the duke. Don Juan intervenes and destorys the scheme, winning the love of Adriana, but the Borgia declare war on the duke's kinsmen, offering them safety if Adriana marries Donati; Don Juan is summoned to the wedding, but he prefers death to marriage with Lucrezia. He escapes and kills Donati in a duel. The lovers are led to the death-tower, but while Adriana pretends suicide, he escapes; and following a series of battles, he defeats his pursuers and is united with Adriana.

Excerpt from the Book *Don Juan*

CANTO THE SECOND. [96]

I.

OH ye! who teach the ingenuous youth of nations,
  Holland, France, England, Germany, or Spain,
I pray ye flog them upon all occasions—
  It mends their morals, never mind the pain:
The best of mothers and of educations
  In Juan's case were but employed in vain,
Since, in a way that's rather of the oddest, he
Became divested of his native modesty. [ay]

II.

Had he but been placed at a public school,
  In the third form, or even in the fourth,
His daily task had kept his fancy cool,
  At least, had he been nurtured in the North;
Spain may prove an exception to the rule,
  But then exceptions always prove its worth—

A lad of sixteen causing a divorce
Puzzled his tutors very much, of course.

III.

I can't say that it puzzles me at all,
  If all things be considered: first, there was
His lady-mother, mathematical,
  A—never mind; —his tutor, an old ass;
A pretty woman—(that's quite natural,
  Or else the thing had hardly come to pass)
A husband rather old, not much in unity
With his young wife—a time, and opportunity.

IV.

Well—well; the World must turn upon its axis,
  And all Mankind turn with it, heads or tails,
And live and die, make love and pay our taxes,
  And as the veering wind shifts, shift our sails;
The King commands us, and the Doctor quacks us,
  The Priest instructs, and so our life exhales,
A little breath, love, wine, ambition, fame,
Fighting, devotion, dust, —perhaps a name.

V.

I said that Juan had been sent to Cadiz—
  A pretty town, I recollect it well—
'Tis there the mart of the colonial trade is,
  (Or was, before Peru learned to rebel),
And such sweet girls! [97]—I mean, such graceful ladies,
  Their very walk would make your bosom swell;
I can't describe it, though so much it strike,
Nor liken it—I never saw the like: [az]

VI.

An Arab horse, a stately stag, a barb
  New broke, a camelopard, a gazelle,
No—none of these will do; —and then their garb,
  Their veil and petticoat—Alas! to dwell
Upon such things would very near absorb
  A canto—then their feet and ankles, —well,
Thank Heaven I've got no metaphor quite ready,

(And so, my sober Muse—come, let's be steady—

VII.

Chaste Muse! —well, —if you must, you must)—the veil
  Thrown back a moment with the glancing hand,
While the o'erpowering eye, that turns you pale,
  Flashes into the heart: —All sunny land
Of Love! when I forget you, may I fail
  To—say my prayers—but never was there planned
A dress through which the eyes give such a volley,
Excepting the Venetian Fazzioli. [98]

VIII.

But to our tale: the Donna Inez sent
  Her son to Cadiz only to embark;
To stay there had not answered her intent,
  But why? —we leave the reader in the dark—
'T was for a voyage the young man was meant,
  As if a Spanish ship were Noah's ark,
To wean him from the wickedness of earth,
And send him like a Dove of Promise forth.

IX.

Don Juan bade his valet pack his things
  According to direction, then received
A lecture and some money: for four springs
  He was to travel; and though Inez grieved
(As every kind of parting has its stings),
  She hoped he would improve—perhaps believed:
A letter, too, she gave (he never read it)
Of good advice—and two or three of credit.

3.2 Jane Austen: *Pride and Prejudice* (1813)

An Introduction to Jane Austen

Jane Austen (1775-1817) was an English novelist known primarily for her six major novels, which interpret, critique and comment upon the British landed gentry at the end of the 18th century. Her novels, including *Pride and Prejudice* (1813) and *Sense and Sensibility* (1811), are considered literary classics, bridging the gap between romance and realism.

The seventh child and second daughter of Cassandra and George Austen, Jane Austen was born on December 16, 1775, in Steventon, Hampshire, England. Jane's parents were well-respected community members. Her father served as the Oxford-educated rector for a nearby Anglican parish. The family was close and the children grew up in an environment that stressed learning and creative thinking. When Jane was young, she and her siblings were encouraged to read from their father's extensive library. The children also authored and put on plays and charades. Over the span of her life, Jane would become especially close to her father and older sister, Cassandra. Indeed, she and Cassandra would one day collaborate on a published work. In order to acquire a more formal education, Jane and Cassandra were sent to boarding schools during Jane's pre-adolescence. After a short period of formal education cut short by financial constraints, they returned home and lived with the family from that time forward.

Ever fascinated by the world of stories, Jane began to write in bound notebooks. In the 1790s, during her adolescence, she started to craft her own novels and wrote *Love and Freindship* (1790), a parody of romantic fiction organized as a series of love letters. Using that framework, she unveiled her wit and dislike of sensibility, or romantic hysteria, a distinct perspective that would eventually characterize much of her later writing. The next year she wrote *The History of England* (1791), a 34-page parody of historical writing that included illustrations drawn by Cassandra. These notebooks, encompassing the novels as well as short stories, poems and plays, are now referred to as Jane's *Juvenilia*.

Jane spent much of her early adulthood helping run the family home, playing piano, attending church, and socializing with neighbors. Her nights and weekends often involved cotillions (balls at which young ladies are presented to society), and as a result, she became an accomplished dancer. On other evenings, she would choose a novel from the shelf and read it aloud to her family, occasionally one she had written herself. She continued to write, developing her style in more ambitious works such as *Lady Susan* (1794), another epistolary story about a manipulative woman who uses her sexuality, intelligence and charm to have her way with others. Jane also started to write some of her future major works, the first called *Elinor and Marianne* (1811), another story told as a series of letters, which would eventually be published as *Sense and Sensibility* (1811). She began drafts of *First Impressions*, which would later be published as *Pride and Prejudice* (1813), and *Susan*, later published as *Northanger Abbey* (1817) by Jane's brother, Henry, following Jane's death.

In 1801, Jane moved to Bath with her father, mother and Cassandra. Then, in 1805, her father died after a short illness. As a result, the family was thrust into tough financial situations;

the three women moved from place to place, skipping between the homes of various family members to rented flats. It was not until 1809 that they were able to settle into a stable living situation at Jane's brother Edward's cottage in Chawton.

Then in her 30s, Jane started to anonymously publish her works. In the period spanning 1811-1816, she pseudonymously published *Sense and Sensibility*, *Pride and Prejudice* (a work she referred to as her "darling child", which also received critical acclaim), *Mansfield Park* (1814) and *Emma*(1815).

In 1816, at the age of 41, Jane started to become ill with what some say might have been Addison's disease. She made impressive efforts to continue working at a normal pace, editing older works as well as starting a new novel called *The Brothers* (1817), which would be published after her death as *Sanditon* (1817). Another novel, *Persuasion* (1818), would also be published posthumously. At some point, Jane's condition deteriorated to such a degree that she ceased writing. She died on July 18, 1817, in Winchester, Hampshire, England.

Jane Austen's use of biting irony, along with her realism and social commentary has earned her great and historical importance to critics and scholars. Austen's plots often explore the dependence of women on marriage in the pursuit of favorable social standing and economic security. Her works critique the novels of sensibility of the second half of the 18th century and are part of the transition to 19th-century literary realism. Her novels have rarely been out of print, although they were published anonymously and brought her little fame during her lifetime. A significant transition in her posthumous reputation occurred in 1869, 52 years after her death, when her nephew's publication of *A Memoir of Jane Austen* introduced her to a wider audience.

Today, Austen is considered one of the greatest writers in English history, both by academics and the general public. In 2002, as part of a BBC poll, the British public voted her No. 70 on a list of "100 Most Famous Britons of All Time". Austen's transformation from little-known to internationally renowned author began in the 1920s, when scholars began to recognize her works as masterpieces, thus increasing her general popularity. The Janeites, a Jane Austen fan club, eventually began to take on wider significance, similar to the Trekkie phenomenon that characterizes fans of the Star Trek franchise. The popularity of her work is also evident in the many film and TV adaptations of *Emma*, *Mansfield Park*, *Pride and Prejudice*, and *Sense and Sensibility*, as well as the TV series and film *Clueless*, which was based on *Emma*.

Austen was in the worldwide news in 2007, when author David Lassman submitted to several publishing houses a few of her manuscripts with slight revisions under a different name, and they were routinely rejected. He chronicled the experience in an article titled "Rejecting Jane", a fitting tribute to an author who could appreciate humor and wit.

An Introduction to the Film *Pride & Prejudice*

Brief Information

Release year	2005
Directed by	Joe Wright
Production company	Studio Canal Working Title Films
Distributed by	Focus Features
Country	France United Kingdom United States
Starring	Keira Knightley as Elizabeth Bennet Matthew Macfadyen as Mr Fitzwilliam Darcy Brenda Blethyn as Mrs. Bennet Rosamund Pike as Jane Bennet

Award	Category	Recipients and nominees
Boston Society of Film Critics	Best New Filmmaker	Joe Wright
British Academy Film Awards	Most Promising Newcomer	Joe Wright
Empire Awards	Best British Film	*Pride & Prejudice*
	Best Newcomer	Kelly Reilly
London Film Critics' Circle	British Director of the Year	Joe Wright
	British Supporting Actor of the Year	Tom Hollander

Plot

During the late 18th century, the Bennet family, consisting of Mr. and Mrs. Bennet and their five daughters—Jane, Elizabeth, Mary, Kitty and Lydia—live in comparative financial independence as gentry at Longbourn, a working farm in rural England. As the Bennet's have no sons, Longbourn is destined to be inherited by Mr. Bennet's cousin, Mr. Collins, and so Mrs. Bennet is anxious to marry off her five daughters before Mr. Bennet dies, in order to secure herself in her widowhood.

Wealthy bachelor Charles Bingley has recently moved into Netherfield, a large, nearby estate. He is introduced to local society at an assembly ball, along with his arrogant sister Caroline and reserved friend, Mr. Darcy, who "owns half of Derbyshire". Bingley is enchanted with the gentle and beautiful Jane, while Elizabeth takes an instant dislike to Darcy after he coldly rejects her attempts at conversation and after she later overhears him insulting her. When Jane becomes sick on a visit to Netherfield, Elizabeth goes to stay with her, quarreling with both Caroline and Darcy.

Later the Bennets are visited by Mr. Collins, a vain clergyman who talks of little but his patroness, Lady Catherine de Bourgh. After learning from Mrs. Bennet that Jane is expected to become engaged soon, Collins decides to pursue Elizabeth, completely neglecting her lack of receptivity towards himself. Meanwhile, the easy-going and charming Lieutenant Wickham of the newly-arrived militia captures the girls' attention; he wins Elizabeth's sympathy by telling her that Darcy has cheated him of his inheritance. At a ball at Netherfield, Elizabeth, startled by Darcy's sudden appearance and request, accepts a dance with him before realizing it, but vows to her best friend Charlotte Lucas that she has "sworn to hate him forever". During the dance, she attacks him with witty sarcasm and Darcy responds in kind. At the same ball, Charlotte expresses concern to Elizabeth that Jane's behaviour towards Mr. Bingley is too reserved, and that Bingley may not realise that she loves him.

The next day, at Longbourn, Collins proposes to Elizabeth, but she strongly declines. When Bingley unexpectedly returns to London, Elizabeth sends a heartbroken Jane to the city to stay with their aunt and uncle, the Gardiners, in hopes of re-establishing contact between Jane and Bingley. Later, Elizabeth is surprised to learn that her friend Charlotte will marry Collins to gain financial security and avoid remaining a spinster.

Months later, Elizabeth visits the newly-wed Mr. and Mrs. Collins at Rosings, Lady Catherine's manor estate; they are invited to dine there, and meet Darcy and Colonel Fitzwilliam, who are Lady Catherine's nephews. Here Darcy shows greater interest in Elizabeth, especially when she replies to Lady Catherine's insult with spirited wit. The next day, not realizing that Jane is Elizabeth's sister, Colonel Fitzwilliam lets slip to Elizabeth that Darcy has separated Bingley from Jane. Distressed, she flees outside, but Darcy chooses that moment to track her down and propose marriage.

He says that he loves her "most passionately", despite her "lower rank". Elizabeth refuses him, citing his treatment of Jane and Bingley and of Wickham; they argue fiercely, with Darcy explaining that he has been convinced that Jane did not return Bingley's love. Darcy leaves angry and heartbroken. He finds Elizabeth later and presents her with a letter, which explains that Wickham is a gambler who demanded and received £30,000 in cash in-lieu of the clergy position intended for him by Darcy's father; upon being refused more money, after having squandered it all a few years later, Wickham had attempted to seduce and elope with Darcy's 15-year-old sister, Georgiana, in order to obtain her £30,000 inheritance, but abandoned her upon learning that he would never receive the money.

A couple of months later, the Gardiners take Elizabeth on a trip to the Peak District; their visit also includes Darcy's estate, Pemberley; Elizabeth agrees to go with them, believing that he is away travelling. Elizabeth is stunned by its wealth and beauty, and hears nothing but good things about Darcy from his housekeeper. There, she accidentally runs into Darcy, who has arrived home early. He invites her and the Gardiners to meet his sister. His manners have softened considerably, and Georgiana takes an instant liking to Elizabeth. When Elizabeth learns that her immature and flirtatious youngest sister Lydia has run away with Wickham, she tearfully blurts out the news to Darcy and the Gardiners before returning home. Her family expects social ruin for having a disgraced daughter, but over a week later they are relieved to hear that Mr. Gardiner has discovered the pair in London and that they have married. Lydia later tells Elizabeth that Darcy was the one who found them and paid for the marriage.

When Bingley and Darcy suddenly return to Netherfield, Jane accepts Bingley's proposal. The same evening, Lady Catherine unexpectedly visits Elizabeth, insisting that she give up Darcy, as he is supposedly to marry her own daughter, Anne. Elizabeth refuses and, unable to sleep, walks on the moor at dawn. There, she meets Darcy, also unable to sleep after hearing of his aunt's behaviour. He admits his continued love and Elizabeth accepts his proposal. Mr. Bennet gives his consent after Elizabeth assures him of her love for Darcy. In the U. S. release of the film, an additional last scene shows the newlyweds outside of Pemberley, happy together.

Except from the Book *Pride and Prejudice*

Chapter 1

It is a truth universally acknowledged, that a single man in possession of a good fortune must be in want of a wife.

However little known the feelings or views of such a man may be on his first entering a neighbourhood, this truth is so well fixed in the minds of the surrounding families, that he is considered as the rightful property of some one or other of their daughters.

"My dear Mr. Bennet", said his lady to him one day, "have you heard that Netherfield Park is let at last?"

Mr. Bennet replied that he had not.

"But it is", returned she; "for Mrs. Long has just been here, and she told me all about it."

Mr. Bennet made no answer.

"Do not you want to know who has taken it?" cried his wife impatiently.

"You want to tell me, and I have no objection to hearing it."

This was invitation enough.

"Why, my dear, you must know, Mrs. Long says that Netherfield is taken by a young man of large fortune from the north of England; that he came down on Monday in a chaise and four to see the place, and was so much delighted with it that he agreed with Mr. Morris immediately; that he is to take possession before Michaelmas, and some of his servants are to be in the house by the end of next week."

"What is his name?"

"Bingley."

"Is he married or single?"

"Oh! single, my dear, to be sure! A single man of large fortune; four or five thousand a year. What a fine thing for our girls!"

"How so? how can it affect them?"

"My dear Mr. Bennet", replied his wife, "how can you be so tiresome! You must know that I am thinking of his marrying one of them."

"Is that his design in settling here?"

"Design! nonsense, how can you talk so! But it is very likely that he may fall in love with one of them, and therefore you must visit him as soon as he comes."

"I see no occasion for that. You and the girls may go, or you may send them by themselves, which perhaps will be still better; for, as you are as handsome as any of them, Mr. Bingley might like you the best of the party."

"My dear, you flatter me. I certainly have had my share of beauty, but I do not pretend to be any thing extraordinary now. When a woman has five grown up daughters, she ought to give over thinking of her own beauty."

"In such cases, a woman has not often much beauty to think of."

"But, my dear, you must indeed go and see Mr. Bingley when he comes into the neighbourhood."

"It is more than I engage for, I assure you."

"But consider your daughters. Only think what an establishment it would be for one of them. Sir William and Lady Lucas are determined to go, merely on that account, for in general, you know they visit no new comers. Indeed you must go, for it will be impossible for us to visit him, if you do not."

"You are over-scrupulous, surely. I dare say Mr. Bingley will be very glad to see you; and I will send a few lines by you to assure him of my hearty consent to his marrying which ever he chuses of the girls; though I must throw in a good word for my little Lizzy."

"I desire you will do no such thing. Lizzy is not a bit better than the others; and I am sure she is not half so handsome as Jane, nor half so good humoured as Lydia. But you are always giving her the preference."

"They have none of them much to recommend them", replied he; "they are all silly and ignorant like other girls; but Lizzy has something more of quickness than her sisters."

"Mr. Bennet, how can you abuse your own children in such way? You take delight in vexing me. You have no compassion on my poor nerves."

"You mistake me, my dear. I have a high respect for your nerves. They are my old friends. I have heard you mention them with consideration these twenty years at least."

"Ah! you do not know what I suffer."

"But I hope you will get over it, and live to see many young men of four thousand a year come into the neighbourhood."

"It will be no use to us if twenty such should come, since you will not visit them."

"Depend upon it, my dear, that when there are twenty I will visit them all."

Mr. Bennet was so odd a mixture of quick parts, sarcastic humour, reserve, and caprice, that the experience of three and twenty years had been insufficient to make his wife understand his character. Her mind was less difficult to develope. She was a woman of mean understanding, little information, and uncertain temper. When she was discontented, she fancied herself nervous. The business of her life was to get her daughters married; its solace was visiting and news.

4. Realism in Films

4.1 Charles Dickens: *Oliver Twist* (1818-1823)

An Introduction to Charles Dickens

Charles Dickens (1812-1870) was an English writer and social critic. He created some of the world's best-known fictional characters and is regarded by many as the greatest novelist of the Victorian era.

Charles Dickens was born Charles John Huffam Dickens on February 7, 1812, in Portsmouth, on the southern coast of England. He was the second of eight children. His father, John Dickens, was a naval clerk who dreamed of striking it rich. Charles Dickens' mother, Elizabeth Barrow, aspired to be a teacher and school director. Despite his parents' best efforts, the family remained poor. Nevertheless, they were happy in the early days. In 1816, they moved to Chatham, Kent, where young Charles and his siblings were free to roam the countryside and explore the old castle at Rochester.

In 1822, the Dickens family moved to Camden Town, a poor neighborhood in London. By then the family's financial situation had grown worse, as John Dickens had a dangerous habit of living beyond the family's means. Eventually, John was sent to prison for debt in 1824, when Charles was just 12 years old. Following his father's imprisonment, Charles Dickens was forced to leave school to work at a boot-blacking factory alongside the River Thames. At the rundown, rodent-ridden factory, Dickens earned six shillings a week labeling pots of "blacking", a substance used to clean fireplaces. It was the best he could do to help support his family. Looking back on the experience, Dickens saw it as the moment he said goodbye to his youthful innocence, stating that he wondered "how [he] could be so easily cast away at such a young age". He felt abandoned and betrayed by the adults who were supposed to take care of him. These sentiments would later become a recurring theme in his writing.

Much to his relief, Dickens was permitted to go back to school when his father received a family inheritance and used it to pay off his debts. But when Dickens was 15, his education was pulled out from under him once again. In 1827, he had to drop out of school and work as an office boy to contribute to his family's income. As it turned out, the job became an early launching point for his writing career.

Within a year of being hired, Dickens began freelance reporting at the law courts of London. Just a few years later, he was reporting for two major London newspapers. In 1833, he began submitting sketches to various magazines and newspapers under the pseudonym "Boz". In 1836, his clippings were published in his first book, *Sketches by Boz.* Dickens' first success caught the eye of Catherine Hogarth, whom he soon married. Catherine would grace Charles with a brood of 10 children before the couple separated in 1858.

Dickens's literary success began with the 1836 serial publication of *The Posthumous Papers of the Pickwick Club* (commonly known as *The Pickwick Papers*) which was wildly popular with readers. His series of sketches, originally written as captions for artist Robert Seymour's humorous sports-themed illustrations, took the form of monthly serial installments. His novels, most published in monthly or weekly instalments, pioneered the serial publication of narrative fiction, which became the dominant Victorian mode for novel publication. The instalment format allowed Dickens to evaluate his audience's reaction, and he often modified his plot and character development based on such feedback.

Around this time, Dickens had also become publisher of a magazine called *Bentley's Miscellany.* In it he started publishing his first novel, *Oliver Twist* (1838), which follows the life of an orphan living in the streets. The story was inspired by how Dickens felt as an impoverished child forced to get by on his wits and earn his own keep. Dickens continued showcasing *Oliver Twist* in the magazines he later edited, including *Household Words* and *All the Year Round*, the latter of which he founded. The novel was extremely well received in both England and America. Dedicated readers of *Oliver Twist* eagerly anticipated the next monthly installment.

Over the next few years, Dickens struggled to match the level of *Oliver Twist*'s success. From 1838 to 1841, he published *The Life and Adventures of Nicholas Nickleby*, *The Old Curiosity Shop* and *Barnaby Rudge*.

In 1842, Dickens and his wife, Kate, embarked on a five-month lecture tour of the United States. Upon their return, Dickens penned *American Notes for General Circulation*, a sarcastic travelogue criticizing American culture and materialism. In 1843, Dickens wrote his novel *The Life and Adventures of Martin Chuzzlewit*, a story about a man's struggle to survive on the ruthless American frontier. The book was published the following year.

Over the next couple of years, Dickens published two Christmas stories. One was the classic *A Christmas Carol* (1843), which features the timeless protagonist Ebenezer Scrooge, an old miser, who, with the help of a ghost, finds the Christmas spirit.

In 1845, Dickens spent a year in Italy writing *Pictures from Italy*. Over the next two years he published, in installments, his next novel, *Dealings with the Firm of Dombey and Son*. The novel's main theme is how business tactics affect a family's personal finances. It takes a dark view of England and is critical to Dickens' body of work in that it set the tone for his other novels.

From 1849 to 1850, Dickens worked on *David Copperfield*, the first work of its kind; no one had ever written a novel that simply followed a character through his everyday life. In writing it, Dickens tapped into his own personal experiences, from his difficult childhood to his work as a journalist. Although *David Copperfield* is not considered Dickens' best work, it was his personal favorite. It also helped define the public's expectations of a Dickensian novel.

During the 1850s, Dickens suffered two devastating losses: the deaths of his daughter and father. He also separated from his wife during that decade, with Dickens attacking Kate publicly. He had also met a young actress named Ellen "Nelly" Ternan, with whom he had an intimate relationship. It is also believed that he went to great lengths to erase any documentation alluding to Ternan's presence in his life.

His novels also began to express a darkened worldview. In *Bleak House*, published in installments from 1852 to 1853, he deals with the hypocrisy of British society. It was considered his most complex novel to date. *Hard Times* (1854) takes place in an industrial town at the peak of economic expansion. In it, Dickens focuses on the shortcomings of employers as well as those who seek change. Also among Dickens' darker novels is *Little Dorrit* (1857), a fictional study of how human values come in conflict with the world's brutality.

Coming out of his "dark novel" period, in 1859 Dickens published *A Tale of Two Cities*, a historical novel that takes place during the French Revolution. He published it in a periodical he founded, *All the Year Round*. His next novel, *Great Expectations* (1860-1861), focuses on the protagonist's lifelong journey of moral development. It is widely considered his greatest literary accomplishment. A few years later, Dickens produced *Our Mutual Friend* (1865), a novel that analyzes the psychological impact of wealth on London society.

In 1865, Dickens was in a train accident and never fully recovered. Despite his fragile condition, he continued to tour until 1870. On June 9, 1870, Dickens had a stroke and, at age 58, died at Gad's Hill Place, his country home in Kent, England. He was buried in Poet's Corner at Westminster Abbey, with thousands of mourners gathering at the beloved author's gravesite. Scottish satirical writer Thomas Carlyle described Dickens' passing as "an event worldwide, a unique of talents suddenly extinct". At the time of Dickens' death, his final novel, *The Mystery of Edwin Drood*, was left unfinished.

Dickens' novels and short stories enjoyed unprecedented and lasting popularity during his lifetime, and by the 20th century critics and scholars had recognized him as a literary genius.

An Introduction to the Film *Oliver Twist*

Brief Information

Release year	2005
Directed by	Roman Polanski
Distributed by	TriStar Pictures
Country	United Kingdom Czech Republic France Italy
Starring	Barney Clark as Oliver Twist Ben Kingsley as Fagin Jamie Foreman as Bill Sikes Leanne Rowe as Nancy

Plot

In the 1800s, young orphan (Oliver Twist) is forcibly brought to a workhouse in an unidentified town In England on his ninth birthday. He and the other resident children are treated poorly and given very little food. Facing starvation, the boys select Oliver through a lottery to ask for more food at the next meal, which he does. This results in Oliver being punished, and the workhouse officials, who are wealthy, well-fed, hypocritical men, decide to get rid of him. After nearly being sold as an apprentice to a cruel chimney sweep, Oliver is sent to Mr. Sowerberry, a coffin-maker, whose wife and senior apprentice take an instant dislike to the newcomer. After more poor treatment, Oliver snaps and attacks Noah, the arrogant older apprentice, for having insulted his mother. Noah howls instantly and bring Mrs. Sowerberry and Charlotte rushing in to drag Oliver away and lock him in the cold dark cellar. The violent behavior of the orphan is duly brought to the notice of Mr. Sowerberry and also Mr. Bumble. Oliver is beaten, and knowing his life with the Sowerberrys will only get worse, he escapes on foot early the next morning.

With little food, Oliver determines to walk 70 miles to London. After he collapses from hunger and exhaustion, a kindly old woman gives him food and lodgings for the night. After a week of travel, he arrives at the city, barefoot and penniless. He meets Jack Dawkins, or "The Artful Dodger", a boy-thief who takes Oliver to his home and hideout at Saffron Hill that he shares with many other young pickpockets and their odd elderly leader, Fagin. Soon, Oliver is being trained to join their gang. On his first outing with the pickpockets, two of the boys steal a man's handkerchief and Oliver is framed. However he is proven innocent by an eyewitness, and the owner of the handkerchief (the wealthy Mr. Brownlow) takes pity on Oliver, who has collapsed from a fever in the courtroom. Brownlow, believing that Oliver is innocent, informally adopts him, giving him new clothes and the promise of a good education. However, while out running an errand for Brownlow, Oliver is forcibly returned to the pickpocket gang by Fagin's associate, the evil Bill Sikes, and the young prostitute Nancy (who is in a complex and abusive relationship with Sikes). Fagin and Sikes worry that Oliver would "peach", and tell the authorities about their criminal activity. Oliver is put under supervision until Bill Sikes discovers the boy's connection to the rich Mr. Brownlow. During midnight, Sikes and his accomplice, Toby Crackit, force Oliver to aid them in robbing Brownlow's house. They are discovered and Oliver is wounded in a brief gunfight between Brownlow and Sikes. As the three escape, Bill decides to murder Oliver to ensure his silence, but falls into a nearby river before he can take action.

Sikes survives his near-drowning, but is confined to bed with a heavy fever. Fagin, despite treating Oliver kindly, remains crime-focused and plots with Sikes to kill Oliver when Sikes has recovered. Nancy has a maternal love for Oliver and does not want to see him hurt, but she is controlled by the abusive Sikes. She drugs Bill, and goes to Brownlow's house where she arranges to have him meet her on London Bridge at midnight so she can provide information about Oliver. At the meeting, Nancy cautiously reveals that Oliver is staying with Fagin, and that the authorities will easily find them. Brownlow leaves to call the police. The Artful Dodger, who has been sent by a suspicious Fagin to spy on Nancy, has heard everything and is bullied by Bill Sikes to give up the information. Sikes is furious at Nancy's betrayal, and brutally beats her to death in their apartment.

The next day, information about Oliver and Fagin appears in the newspaper, along with Nancy's murder and Sikes is a suspect. Sikes's ever-present dog, Bullseye, is a dead giveaway to his identity. After unsuccessfully trying to kill the dog, Sikes takes up residence with Toby Crackit. Fagin, Oliver, and the boys are hiding there too, after escaping their previous location before the police could find it. Bullseye escapes his master's cruelty, and leads a group of police and locals to the group's hideout. Eventually, Dodger, outraged at Sikes for killing the good-hearted Nancy, reveals their location to authorities. Bill Sikes takes Oliver onto the roof, knowing they won't shoot if the boy is with him. When trying to scale the building using a rope, Sikes, distracted by his dog, loses his footing and accidentally hangs himself to death.

Some time later, Oliver is living comfortably with Mr. Brownlow again. Fagin is arrested for his pick pocketing actions, and Oliver wishes to visit him in jail. Brownlow takes him to the prison, where they find Fagin shouting and wailing in his cell. Oliver is upset at Fagin's fate, as he has been something of a father figure to him. Oliver tells Fagin "You were kind to me", but soon, their bond breaks when a policeman initially tells Oliver to leave, thinking that Fagin can play tricks on the boy's innocent mind, and wanting to escape execution. As Mr. Brownlow escorts a tearful Oliver to his own carriage, gallows are being set up in the courtyard. Townspeople begin to gather to watch Fagin's execution, while Mr. Brownlow and Oliver leave to start their new lives afresh.

Excerpt from the Book *Oliver Twist*

The members of this board were very sage, deep, philosophical men; and when they came to turn their attention to the workhouse, they found out at once, what ordinary folks would never have discovered— the poor people liked it! It was a regular place of public entertainment for the poorer classes; a tavern where there was nothing to pay; a public breakfast, dinner, tea, and supper all the year round; a brick and mortar elysium, where it was all play and no work. "Oho!" said the board, looking very knowing; "we are the fellows to set this to rights; we'll stop it all, in no time." So, they established the rule, that all poor people should have the alternative (for they would compel nobody, not they), of being starved by a gradual process in the house, or by a quick one out of it. With this view, they contracted with the water-works to lay on an unlimited supply of water; and with a corn-factor to supply periodically small quantities of oatmeal; and issued three meals of thin gruel a day, with an onion twice a week, and half a roll on Sundays. They made a great many other wise and humane regulations, having reference to the ladies, which it is not necessary to repeat; kindly undertook to divorce poor married people, in consequence of the great expense of a suit in Doctors' Commons; and, instead of compelling a man to support his family, as they had theretofore done, took his family away from him, and made him a bachelor! There is no saying how many applicants for relief, under these last two heads, might have started up in all classes of society, if it had not been coupled with the workhouse; but the board were long-headed men, and had provided for this difficulty. The relief was inseparable from the workhouse and the gruel; and that frightened people.

For the first six months after Oliver Twist was removed, the system was in full operation. It was rather expensive at first, in consequence of the increase in the undertaker's bill, and the necessity of taking in the clothes of all the paupers, which fluttered loosely on their wasted, shrunken forms, after a week or two's gruel. But the number of workhouse inmates got thin as well as the paupers; and the board were in ecstasies.

The room in which the boys were fed, was a large stone hall, with a copper at one end: out of which the master, dressed in an apron for the purpose, and assisted by one or two women, ladled the gruel at meal-times. Of this festive composition each boy had one porringer, and no more— except on occasions of great public rejoicing, when he had two ounces and a quarter of bread besides. The bowls never wanted washing. The boys polished them with their spoons till they shone again; and when they had performed this operation (which never took very long, the spoons being nearly as large as the bowls), they would sit staring at the copper, with such eager eyes, as if they could have devoured the very bricks of which it was composed; employing themselves, meanwhile, in sucking their fingers most assiduously, with the view of catching up any stray splashes of gruel that might have been cast thereon. Boys have generally excellent appetites. Oliver Twist and his companions suffered the tortures of slow starvation for three months: at last they got so voracious and wild with hunger, that one boy, who was tall for his age, and hadn't been used to that sort of thing (for his father had kept a small cookshop), hinted darkly to his companions, that unless he had another basin of gruel(r)per diem, he was afraid he might some night happen to eat the boy who slept next him, who happened to be a weakly youth of tender age. He had a wild, hungry eye; and they implicitly believed him. A council was held; lots were cast who should walk up to the master after supper that evening, and ask for more; and it fell to Oliver Twist.

The evening arrived; the boys took their places. The master, in his cook's uniform, stationed himself at the copper; his pauper assistants ranged themselves behind him; the gruel was served out; and a long grace was said over the short commons. The gruel disappeared; the boys whispered each other, and winked at Oliver; while his next neighbours nudged him. Child as he was, he was desperate with hunger, and reckless with misery. He rose from the table; and advancing to the master, basin and spoon in hand, said: somewhat alarmed at his own temerity:

"Please, sir, I want some more."

The master was a fat, healthy man; but he turned very pale. He gazed in stupefied astonishment on the small rebel for some seconds, and then clung for support to the copper. The assistants were paralysed with wonder; the boys with fear.

"What!" said the master at length, in a faint voice.

"Please, sir," replied Oliver, "I want some more."

The master aimed a blow at Oliver's head with the ladle; pinioned him in his arms; and shrieked aloud for the beadle.

The board were sitting in solemn conclave, when Mr. Bumble rushed into the room in great excitement, and addressing the gentleman in the high chair, said,

"Mr. Limbkins, I beg your pardon, sir! Oliver Twist has asked for more!"

There was a general start. Horror was depicted on every countenance.

"For more!" said Mr. Limbkins. "Compose yourself, Bumble, and answer me distinctly. Do I understand that he asked for more, after he had eaten the supper allotted by the dietary?"

"He did, sir," replied Bumble.

"That boy will be hung," said the gentleman in the white waistcoat. "I know that boy will be hung."

Nobody controverted the prophetic gentleman's opinion. An animated discussion took place. Oliver was ordered into instant confinement; and a bill was next morning pasted on the outside of the gate, offering a reward of five pounds to anybody who would take Oliver Twist off the hands of the parish. In other words, five pounds and Oliver Twist were offered to any man or woman who wanted an apprentice to any trade, business, or calling.

"I never was more convinced of anything in my life," said the gentleman in the white waistcoat, as he knocked at the gate and read the bill next morning: "I never was more convinced of anything in my life, than I am that that boy will come to be hung."

As I purpose to show in the sequel whether the white-waistcoated gentleman was right or not, I should perhaps mar the interest of this narrative (supposing it to possess any at all), if I ventured to hint just yet, whether the life of Oliver Twist had this violent termination or no.

4.2 Brontë Sisters: *Jane Eyre* (1847) / *Wuthering Heights* (1847)

The Brontës were a 19th-century literary family associated with the village of Haworth in the West Riding of Yorkshire, England. The Brontë sisters, Charlotte (1816-1855), Emily (1818-1848), and Anne (1820-1849), are well-known as poets and novelists.

Like many contemporary female writers, they originally published their poems and novels under male pseudonyms: Currer, Ellis, and Acton Bell. Their stories immediately attracted attention for their passion and originality. Charlotte's *Jane Eyre* was the first to know success, while Emily's *Wuthering Heights*, Anne's *The Tenant of Wildfell Hall* and other works were later to be accepted as masterpieces of literature.

An Introduction to Charlotte Brontë

Charlotte Brontë (1816-1855) was an English novelist and poet, the eldest of the three Brontë sisters who survived into adulthood and whose novels have become classics of English literature.

Charlotte Brontë was born in 1816 as the third daughter of the Rev. Patrick Brontë and his wife Maria. In 1824 she was enrolled as a pupil at the Clergy Daughter's School at Cowan Bridge but was brought home the next year due to the death of Maria and Elizabeth, the two eldest daughters of the Brontë family.

In 1826 Mr. Brontë brought home a box of wooden soldiers for Branwell, the only son of the Brontë family, to play with. Charlotte, Emily, Branwell, and Ann, playing with the soldiers, conceived of and began to write in great detail about an imaginary world which they called Angria.

In 1831 Charlotte became a pupil at the school at Roe Head, but she left school the following year to teach her sisters at home. She returned to Roe Head School in 1835 as a governess. For a time her sister Emily attended the same school as a pupil, but became homesick and returned to Haworth. Ann took her place from 1836 to 1837.

In 1838, Charlotte left Roe Head School. In 1839 she accepted a position as governess in the Sidgewick family, but left after three months and returned to Haworth. In 1841 she became governess in the White family, but left, once again, after nine months.

Upon her return to Haworth, the three sisters, led by Charlotte, decided to open their own school after the necessary preparations had been completed. In 1842 Charlotte and Emily went to Brussels to complete their studies. After a trip home to Haworth, Charlotte returned alone to Brussels, where she remained until 1844.

Upon her return home the sisters embarked upon their project for founding a school, which proved to be a failure unfortunately: their advertisements did not bring about a single response from the public. The following year Charlotte discovered Emily's poems, and decided to publish a selection of the poems of all three sisters: 1846 brought the publication of their poems, written under the pseudonyms of Currer, Ellis and Acton Bell. Charlotte also completed *The Professor*, which was rejected for publication. The following year, however, Charlotte's *Jane Eyre*, Emily's *Wuthering Heights*, and Ann's *Agnes Grey* were all published, still under the Bell pseudonyms.

In 1848 Charlotte and Ann visited their publishers in London, and revealed the true identities of the "Bells". In the same year Branwell died of alcoholism and drug abuse, and Emily died shortly thereafter. Ann died the following year.

In 1849 Charlotte, visiting London, began to move in literary circles, making the acquaintance, for example, of William Thackeray, a prominent British novelist, writer and author of the *Vanity Fair*. In 1850 Charlotte edited her sister's various works, and met Elizabeth Gaskell (often referred to as Mrs. Gaskell), an English novelist, biographer, and short story writer. In 1851 she visited the Great Exhibition in London, and attended a series of lectures given by William Thackeray.

The Rev. A. B. Nicholls, curate of Haworth since 1845, proposed marriage to Charlotte in 1852. The Rev. Mr. Brontë objected violently, and Charlotte, who, though she may have pitied him, was in any case not in love with him, refused him. Nicholls left Haworth in the following year, the same in which Charlotte's *Villette* was published. By 1854, however, Mr. Brontë's opposition to the proposed marriage had weakened, and Charlotte and Nicholls became engaged. Nicholls returned as curate at Haworth, and they were married, though it seems clear that Charlotte, though she admired him, still did not love him.

In 1854 Charlotte, expecting a child, caught pneumonia. It was an illness which could have been cured, but she seemed to have seized upon it (consciously or unconsciously) as an opportunity of ending her life, and after a lengthy and painful illness, she died, probably of dehydration.

1857 saw the posthumous publication of *The Professor*, which had been written in 1845-1846, and in that same year Mrs. Gaskell's *Life of Charlotte Brontë* was published.

An Introduction to the Film *Jane Eyre*

Brief Information

Release year	2011
Directed by	Cary Joji Fukunaga
Production company	BBC Films Ruby Films
Distributed by	Universal Pictures (UK) Focus Features (US)
Country	United Kingdom United States

Starring	Mia Wasikowska as Jane Eyre Michael Fassbender as Edward Fairfax Rochester Jamie Bell as St. John Rivers Judi Dench as Mrs. Fairfax Sally Hawkins as Mrs. Reed	

Award	Category	Recipient(s)
National Board of Review Awards	Spotlight Award	Michael Fassbender (Also for Shame, A Dangerous Method, and X-Men: First Class)
Los Angeles Film Critics Association Awards	Best Actor	Michael Fassbender (Also for Shame, A Dangerous Method, and X-Men: First Class)
Evening Standard British Film Awards	Best Actor	Michael Fassbender (Also for Shame)
Sant Jordi Award	Best Foreign Actor	Michael Fassbender (Also for A Dangerous Method and X-Men: First Class)

Plot

The film begins with Jane Eyre running away from Thornfield Hall in the middle of the night and finding herself alone on the moors, in the pouring rain. She manages to reach the doorstep of Moor House, the home of Mr. St. John Rivers, a clergyman, and his two sisters. They take Jane in, saving her life.

There follows a flashback, to the 10-year-old Jane Eyre, an orphan, living with her maternal uncle's family, the Reeds, at Gateshead Hall. Jane's aunt, Sarah Reed, doesn't like Jane and is very cruel to her; Mrs. Reed's three children are also abusive towards her. One day, Jane is locked in the Red Room, where her uncle died, and which Jane believes is haunted. She knocks herself unconscious on the door, after a huge puff of smoke comes down the chimney.

Jane's aunt sends her to Lowood School for Girls, which is run by a cruel clergyman, Mr. Brocklehurst. Mrs. Reed tells him that Jane is a dishonest child and is not to be trusted. Jane tells her aunt how much she hates her and that she is a hard-hearted woman. At Lowood, while another pupil, Helen Burns, is being beaten, Jane accidentally drops her slate. Mr. Brocklehurst brands her a liar and makes her stand on a chair all day. Jane and Helen become close friends, but Helen later dies of consumption (tuberculosis).

Eight years later, Jane leaves Lowood and takes up a post with Alice Fairfax of Thornfield Hall. She will be a governess to Adèle Varens, a young French girl who is Mr. Rochester's ward. When she first arrives at Thornfield, a gloomy, isolated mansion, Jane mistakes Mrs. Fairfax for her employer, but she finds out that she is only the housekeeper for her absent master. While Jane is walking into town to post a letter, a horse passes her and throws its rider. Jane helps the gentleman to his horse. Later, back at the mansion, she learns that the horse rider is Edward Rochester, master of the house. He jokingly tells her that she must have bewitched his horse to make him fall. They gradually fall in love with one another.

One night, Jane is awoken by a strange noise at her door, only to find that Mr. Rochester's room is on fire, which the two of them manage to extinguish. He thanks her for saving his life and holds her hand affectionately. The next day, Rochester leaves Thornfield to visit Lady Blanche Ingram, his future wife; he brings her back to Thornfield with him a few weeks later. When a man named Richard Mason of Spanish Town, Jamaica, shows up, Jane can see that Rochester is disturbed. That night, a scream awakens everyone. Rochester assures his guests it is just a servant's reaction to a nightmare, but after they go back to their rooms, he secretly has Jane tend to a bleeding Mason while he fetches a doctor. Rochester has the doctor take Mason away.

Jane receives a letter from her old nurse, Bessie. Jane's cousin, John Reed, has committed suicide, the news of which has so shocked his mother, Sarah Reed, that it has brought on a stroke. Apparently, Mrs. Reed has been asking to see Jane. Jane returns to Gateshead, where her dying aunt shows her a letter from Jane's paternal uncle, John Eyre, asking for her to go to live with him in Madeira. He wants to adopt Jane and bequeath her at his death. Jane notices that the letter was dated three years ago. Mrs. Reed admits to telling her uncle that Jane had died of typhus at Lowood School. She tells Jane that she (Mrs. Reed) has been cursed by her. Jane forgives her aunt and returns to Thornfield, having begun a correspondence with John Eyre.

Jane informs Rochester that she must leave Thornfield because of his forthcoming marriage to Blanche Ingram. However, Rochester suddenly proclaims his love for Jane and proposes to her; they kiss passionately. During the wedding ceremony, Mr. Mason appears, along with a lawyer, declaring that Mr. Rochester cannot marry Jane because he is still married to Mr. Mason's sister, Bertha; he adds that his sister is still living at Thornfield Hall. Mr. Rochester admits this is true and takes Jane to meet his wife, calling her his own demon; they find her locked away in a room at Thornfield. Rochester tells Jane that his father wanted him to marry Bertha for her money. Once they were married, he discovered that she was rapidly descending into madness and was forced to lock her away in Thornfield; she was the one responsible for the strange happenings in the house. Refusing to act against her principles, and despite her love for Rochester, Jane leaves Thornfield in the middle of the night.

After Jane regains her health, St. John finds her a teaching position at a nearby charity school. One night, she hears knocking at her door and imagines it to be Rochester, but it turns out to be St. John at the door informing her that her uncle, John Eyre, has died, leaving her all his property and that she is rich, to the tune of £20,000 (equivalent to £1,600,000 in 2015). Jane offers to share the money with St. John and his sisters, suggesting that they live together at Moor house; they agree to the offer. St. John asks Jane to marry him and go with him to India. Jane agrees to go to India with him, but rejects the marriage proposal, suggesting that they travel as brother and sister, as that's how she sees their relationship. On the moor, Jane suddenly hears Rochester's voice calling her name.

Jane returns to Thornfield, only to find the house a blackened ruin. She learns from Mrs. Fairfax that Rochester's wife set the house on fire and died, jumping from the roof. Jane finds Rochester, who has lost his eyesight in the fire. Jane reunites with him and they embrace.

Excerpt from the Book *Jane Eyre*

I was a discord in Gateshead Hall: I was like nobody there; I had nothing in harmony with Mrs. Reed or her children, or her chosen vassalage. If they did not love me, in fact, as little did I love them. They were not bound to regard with affection a thing that could not sympathise with one amongst them; a heterogeneous thing, opposed to them in temperament, in capacity, in propensities; a useless thing, incapable of serving their interest, or adding to their pleasure; a noxious thing, cherishing the germs of indignation at their treatment, of contempt of their judgment. I know that had I been a sanguine, brilliant, careless, exacting, handsome, romping child—though equally dependent and friendless—Mrs. Reed would have endured my presence more complacently; her children would have entertained for me more of the cordiality of fellow-feeling; the servants would have been less prone to make me the scapegoat of the nursery.

Daylight began to forsake the red-room; it was past four o'clock, and the beclouded afternoon was tending to drear twilight. I heard the rain still beating continuously on the staircase window, and the wind howling in the grove behind the hall; I grew by degrees cold as a stone, and then my courage sank. My habitual mood of humiliation, self-doubt, forlorn depression, fell damp on the embers of my decaying ire. All said I was wicked, and perhaps I might be so; what thought had I been but just conceiving of starving myself to death? That certainly was a crime; and was I fit to die? Or was the vault under the chancel of Gateshead Church an inviting bourne? In such vault I had been told did Mr. Reed lie buried; and led by this thought to recall his idea, I dwelt on it with gathering dread. I could not remember him; but I knew that he was my own uncle—my mother's brother—that he had taken me when a parentless infant to his house; and that in his last moments he had required a promise of Mrs. Reed that she would rear and maintain me as one of her own children. Mrs. Reed probably considered she had kept this promise; and so she had, I dare say, as well as her nature would permit her; but how could she really like an interloper not of her race, and unconnected with her, after her husband's death, by any tie? It must have been most irksome to find herself bound by a hard-wrung pledge to stand in the stead of a parent to a strange child she could not love, and to see an uncongenial alien permanently intruded on her own family group.

A singular notion dawned upon me. I doubted not—never doubted— that if Mr. Reed had been alive he would have treated me kindly; and now, as I sat looking at the white bed and overshadowed walls—occasionally also turning a fascinated eye towards the dimly gleaning mirror—I began to recall what I had heard of dead men, troubled in their graves by the violation of their last wishes, revisiting the earth to punish the perjured and avenge the oppressed; and I thought Mr. Reed's spirit, harassed by the wrongs of his sister's child, might quit its abode—whether in the church vault or in the unknown world of the departed—and rise before me in this chamber. I wiped my tears and hushed my sobs, fearful lest any sign of violent grief might waken a preternatural voice to comfort me, or elicit from the gloom some haloed face, bending over me with strange pity. This idea, consolatory in theory, I felt would be terrible if realised: with all my might I endeavoured to stifle it—I endeavoured to be firm. Shaking my hair from my eyes, I lifted my head and tried to look boldly round the dark room; at this moment a light gleamed on the wall. Was it, I asked myself, a ray from the moon penetrating some aperture in the blind? No; moonlight was still, and this stirred; while I gazed, it glided up to the ceiling and quivered over my head. I can now conjecture readily that this streak of light was, in all likelihood, a gleam from a lantern carried by some one across the lawn: but then, prepared as my mind was for horror, shaken as my nerves were by agitation, I thought the swift darting beam was a herald of some coming vision from another world. My heart beat thick, my head grew hot; a sound filled my ears, which I deemed the rushing of wings; something seemed near me; I was oppressed, suffocated: endurance broke down; I rushed to the door and shook the lock in desperate effort. Steps came running along the outer passage; the key turned, Bessie and Abbot entered.

"Miss Eyre, are you ill?" said Bessie.

"What a dreadful noise! it went quite through me!" exclaimed Abbot.

"Take me out! Let me go into the nursery!" was my cry.

"What for? Are you hurt? Have you seen something?" again demanded Bessie.

"Oh! I saw a light, and I thought a ghost would come." I had now got hold of Bessie's hand, and she did not snatch it from me.

"She has screamed out on purpose," declared Abbot, in some disgust.

"And what a scream! If she had been in great pain one would have excused it, but she only wanted to bring us all here: I know her naughty tricks."

"What is all this?" demanded another voice peremptorily; and Mrs. Reed came along the corridor, her cap flying wide, her gown rustling stormily. "Abbot and Bessie, I believe I gave orders that Jane Eyre should be left in the red-room till I came to her myself."

"Miss Jane screamed so loud, ma'am," pleaded Bessie.

"Let her go," was the only answer. "Loose Bessie's hand, child: you cannot succeed in getting out by these means, be assured. I abhor artifice, particularly in children; it is my duty to show you that tricks will not answer: you will now stay here an hour longer, and it is only on condition of perfect submission and stillness that I shall liberate you then."

"O aunt! have pity! Forgive me! I cannot endure it—let me be punished some other way! I shall be killed if—"

"Silence! This violence is all most repulsive:" and so, no doubt, she felt it. I was a precocious actress in her eyes; she sincerely looked on me as a compound of virulent passions, mean spirit, and dangerous duplicity.

Bessie and Abbot having retreated, Mrs. Reed, impatient of my now frantic anguish and wild sobs, abruptly thrust me back and locked me in, without farther parley. I heard her sweeping away; and soon after she was gone, I suppose I had a species of fit: unconsciousness closed the scene.

An Introduction to Emily Brontë

Emily Brontë, in full Emily Jane Brontë, pseudonym Ellis Bell (1818-1848), English novelist and poet who produced but one novel, *Wuthering Heights*, a classic of English literature.

Born in 1818, in Thornton, Yorkshire, England, Emily Brontë was the fifth child of Reverend Patrick Brontë and his wife, Maria Branwell Brontë.

At the age of 6, Emily was sent to the Clergy Daughters' School at Cowan Bridge with Charlotte and her two oldest sisters, Elizabeth and Maria. Both Elizabeth and Maria became seriously ill at school and returned home, where they died of tuberculosis in 1825. Brontë's father removed both Emily and Charlotte from the school as well.

At home in Haworth, Emily enjoyed her quiet life. She read extensively and began to make up stories with her siblings. The Brontë children, which included brother Branwell, had strong imaginations. They created tales inspired by toy soldiers given to Branwell by their father. In 1835, the shy Emily tried leaving home for school. She went with Charlotte to Miss Wooler's school in Roe Head where Charlotte worked as a teacher. But she stayed only a few months before heading back to Haworth.

Coming from a poor family, Emily tried to find work. She became a teacher at the Law Hill School in September 1837, but she left her position the following March. Emily and her sister Charlotte traveled to Brussels in 1842 to study, but the death of their aunt Elizabeth forced them to return home.

Some of Emily's earliest known works involve a fictional world called Gondal, which she created with her sister Anne. She wrote both prose and poems about this imaginary place and its inhabitants. Emily also wrote other poems as well. Her sister Charlotte discovered some of Emily's poems and sought to publish them along with her own work and some by Anne. Published in 1846 under the pen name of Ellis Bell, the book only sold a few copies and gained little attention.

Again publishing as Ellis Bell, Emily published her defining work, *Wuthering Heights* in 1847. She may well have spent a long time on this intense, solidly imagined novel. *Wuthering Heights* is distinguished from other novels of the period by its dramatic and poetic presentation, its abstention from all comment by the author, and its unusual structure. It recounts in the retrospective narrative of an onlooker, which in turn includes shorter narratives, the impact of

Heathcliff on the two families of Earnshaw and Linton in a remote Yorkshire district at the end of the 18th century. Embittered by abuse and by the marriage of Cathy Earnshaw—who shares his stormy nature and whom he loves—to the gentle and prosperous Edgar Linton, Heathcliff plans a revenge on both families, extending into the second generation. Cathy's death in childbirth fails to set him free from his love-hate relationship with her, and the obsessive haunting persists until his death; the marriage of the surviving heirs of Earnshaw and Linton restores peace.

At first, reviewers did not know what to make of *Wuthering Heights*. It was only after Brontë's death that the book developed its reputation as a literary masterwork. Sharing her sisters' dry humour and Charlotte's violent imagination, Emily diverges from them in making no use of the events of her own life and showing no preoccupation with a spinster's state or a governess's position. Working, like them, within a confined scene and with a small group of characters, she constructs an action, based on profound and primitive energies of love and hate, which proceeds logically and economically, making no use of such coincidences as Charlotte relies on, requiring no rich romantic similes or rhetorical patterns, and confining the superb dialogue to what is immediately relevant to the subject. The somber power of the book and the elements of brutality in the characters offended some 19th-century opinion.

Emily Brontë died in Haworth, Yorkshire, England, on December 19, 1848, nearly two months after her brother, Branwell, fell victim to the same disease. She never knew the extent of fame she achieved with her only novel, as she died a year after its publication, aged 30. However, interest in Emily Brontë's work and life remains strong today and the parsonage where Brontë spent much of her life has now been turned into a museum.

An Introduction to the Film *Wuthering Heights* (*Hills*)

Brief Information

Release year	1939
Directed by	William Wyler
Production company	Samuel Goldwyn Productions
Distributed by	United Artists
Country	United States
Starring	Laurence Olivier as Heathcliff Merle Oberon as Catherine Earnshaw Linton David Niven as Edgar Linton Flora Robson as Ellen Dean

Plot

A traveller named Lockwood is caught in the snow and stays at the estate of Wuthering Heights, despite the cold behaviour of his aged host, Heathcliff. Late that night, after being shown into an upstairs room that was once a bridal chamber, Lockwood is awakened by a cold wind and finds the window shutter flapping back and forth. Just as he is about to close it, he feels an icy hand clutching his and sees a woman outside calling, "Heathcliff, let me in! I'm out on the moors. It's Cathy!" Lockwood calls Heathcliff and tells him what he saw, whereupon the angered Heathcliff throws him out of the room. As soon as Lockwood is gone, Heathcliff frantically calls out to Cathy, runs down the stairs and out of the house, into the snowstorm.

Ellen, the housekeeper, tells the amazed Lockwood that he has seen the ghost of Cathy Earnshaw, Heathcliff's great love, who died years before. When Lockwood says that he doesn't believe in ghosts, Ellen tells him that he might if she told him the story of Cathy. And so the main plot begins as a long flashback.

The plot then flashes back 40 years. As a boy, Heathcliff is found on the streets by Mr. Earnshaw, who brings him home to live with his two children, Cathy and Hindley. At first reluctant, Cathy eventually welcomes Heathcliff and they become very close, but Hindley treats him as an outcast, especially after Mr. Earnshaw dies. About ten years later, the now-grown Heathcliff and Cathy have fallen in love and are meeting secretly on Peniston Crag, which leads to Hindley's hatred of Heathcliff. One night, as Cathy and Heathcliff are out together, they hear music and realize that their neighbors, the Lintons, are giving a party. Cathy and Heathcliff sneak to the Lintons and climb over their garden wall, but the dogs are alerted and Cathy is injured. Heathcliff is forced to leave Cathy in their care. Enraged that Cathy would be so fascinated by the Linton's glamor and wealth, he blames them for her injury and curses them.

Months later, Cathy is fully recovered but still living at the Lintons. Edgar Linton has fallen in love with Cathy and soon proposes, and after Edgar takes her back to Wuthering Heights, she tells Ellen what has happened. Ellen reminds her about Heathcliff, but Cathy remarks that it would degrade her to marry him. Heathcliff overhears and leaves. Cathy realizes that Heathcliff has overheard, is overcome by guilt and runs out after him into a strong storm. Edgar finds her and nurses her back to health once again, and soon he and Cathy marry.

Heathcliff is thought to have disappeared forever but returns two years later, now wealthy and elegant. He has refined his appearance and manners in order to both impress and bother Cathy and secretly buys Wuthering Heights from Hindley, who has become an alcoholic. In order to further trouble Cathy, Heathcliff begins courting Edgar's naive sister, Isabella, and eventually marries her. The brokenhearted Cathy soon falls seriously ill. Heathcliff rushes to her side against the wishes of the now disappointed and bitter Isabella, and Cathy dies in Heathcliff's arms.

The flashback ends and we return to Ellen finishing her story. The family doctor, Dr. Kenneth, bursts in, saying that he (Dr. Kenneth) must be mad, having seen Heathcliff in the snow, walking with his arm around a woman. Ellen exclaims, "It was Cathy!" and Dr. Kenneth says, "No, I don't know who it was", and tells them that he was then thrown from his horse. As he draws closer, he finds Heathcliff lying in the snow. The woman has disappeared and there is no sign of her, and only Heathcliff's footprints appear in the snow, not hers. Lockwood asks, "Is he dead?", and Dr. Kenneth nods, but Ellen says, "No, not dead, Dr. Kenneth. And not alone. He's with her. They've only just begun to live."

The last thing seen in the film is the ghosts of Heathcliff and Cathy, walking in the snow, superimposed over a shot of Peniston Crag.

Excerpt from the Book *Wuthering Heights*

Chapter 34

For some days after that evening Mr. Heathcliff shunned meeting us at meals; yet he would not consent formally to exclude Hareton and Cathy. He had an aversion to yielding so completely to his feelings, choosing rather to absent himself; and eating once in twenty-four hours seemed sufficient sustenance for him.

One night, after the family were in bed, I heard him go downstairs, and out at the front door. I did not hear him re-enter, and in the morning I found he was still away. We were in April then: the weather was sweet and warm, the grass as green as showers and sun could make it, and the two dwarf apple-trees near the southern wall in full bloom. After breakfast, Catherine insisted on my bringing a chair and sitting with my work under the fir-trees at the end of the house; and she beguiled Hareton, who had perfectly recovered from his accident, to dig and arrange her little garden, which was shifted to that corner by the influence of Joseph's complaints. I was comfortably revelling in the spring fragrance around, and the beautiful soft blue overhead, when my young lady, who had run down near the gate to procure some primrose roots for a border, returned only half laden, and informed us that Mr. Heathcliff was coming in. "And he spoke to me", she added, with a perplexed countenance.

"What did he say?" asked Hareton.

"He told me to begone as fast as I could," she answered. "But he looked so different from his usual look that I stopped a moment to stare at him."

"How?" he inquired.

"Why, almost bright and cheerful. No, almost nothing — very much excited, and wild, and glad!" she replied.

"Night-walking amuses him, then," I remarked, affecting a careless manner: in reality as surprised as she was, and anxious to ascertain the truth of her statement; for to see the master looking glad would not be an every-day spectacle. I framed an excuse to go in. Heathcliff stood at the open door; he was pale, and he trembled: yet, certainly, he had a strange joyful glitter in his eyes, that altered the aspect of his whole face.

"Will you have some breakfast?" I said. "You must be hungry, rambling about all night!" I wanted to discover where he had been, but I did not like to ask directly.

"No, I'm not hungry," he answered, averting his head, and speaking rather contemptuously, as if he guessed I was trying to divine the occasion of his good humour.

I felt perplexed: I didn't know whether it were not a proper opportunity to offer a bit of admonition.

"I don't think it right to wander out of doors," I observed, "instead of being in bed: it is not wise, at any rate this moist season. I daresay you'll catch a bad cold or a fever: you have something the matter with you now!"

"Nothing but what I can bear," he replied; "and with the greatest pleasure, provided you'll leave me alone: get in, and don't annoy me."

I obeyed: and, in passing, I noticed he breathed as fast as a cat.

"Yes!" I reflected to myself, "we shall have a fit of illness. I cannot conceive what he has been doing."

That noon he sat down to dinner with us, and received a heaped-up plate from my hands, as if he intended to make amends for previous fasting.

"I've neither cold nor fever, Nelly," he remarked, in allusion to my morning's speech; "and I'm ready to do justice to the food you give me."

He took his knife and fork, and was going to commence eating, when the inclination appeared to become suddenly extinct. He laid them on the table, looked eagerly towards the window, then rose and went out. We saw him walking to and fro in the garden while we concluded our meal, and Earnshaw said he'd go and ask why he would not dine: he thought we had grieved him some way. "Well, is he coming?" cried Catherine, when her cousin returned.

"Nay," he answered; "but he's not angry: he seemed rarely pleased indeed; only I made him impatient by speaking to him twice; and then he bid me be off to you: he wondered how I could want the company of anybody else."

I set his plate to keep warm on the fender; and after an hour or two he re-entered, when the room was clear, in no degree calmer: the same unnatural — it was unnatural — appearance of joy under his black brows; the same bloodless hue, and his teeth visible, now and then, in a kind of smile; his frame shivering, not as one shivers with chill or weakness, but as a tight-stretched cord vibrates — a strong thrilling, rather than trembling.

I will ask what is the matter, I thought; or who should? And I exclaimed — "Have you heard any good news, Mr. Heathcliff? You look uncommonly animated."

"Where should good news come from to me?" he said. "I'm animated with hunger; and, seemingly, I must not eat."

"Your dinner is here," I returned; "why won't you get it?"

"I don't want it now," he muttered, hastily: "I'll wait till supper. And, Nelly, once for all, let me beg you to warn Hareton and the other away from me. I wish to be troubled by nobody: I wish to have this place to myself."

"Is there some new reason for this banishment?" I inquired. "Tell me why you are so queer, Mr. Heathcliff? Where were you last night? I'm not putting the question through idle curiosity, but — " "You are putting the question through very idle curiosity," he interrupted, with a laugh. "Yet I'll answer it. Last night I was on the threshold of hell. To-day, I am within sight of my heaven. I have my eyes on it: hardly three feet to sever me! And now you'd better go! You'll neither see nor hear anything to frighten you, if you refrain from prying."

Having swept the hearth and wiped the table, I departed; more perplexed than ever.

He did not quit the house again that afternoon, and no one intruded on his solitude; till, at eight o'clock, I deemed it proper, though unsummoned, to carry a candle and his supper to him. He was leaning against the ledge of an open lattice, but not looking out: his face was turned to the interior gloom. The fire had smouldered to ashes; the room was filled with the damp, mild air of the cloudy evening; and so still, that not only the murmur of the beck down Gimmerton was distinguishable, but its ripples and its gurgling over the pebbles, or through the large stones which it could not cover. I uttered an ejaculation of discontent at seeing the dismal grate, and commenced shutting the casements, one after another, till I came to his.

4.3 Robert Louis Stevenson: *Treasure Island* (1882)

An Introduction to Robert Louis Stevenson

Robert Louis Stevenson (1850-1894) was a 19th century Scottish literary celebrity, ranking as the 26th most translated author in the world.

Robert Louis Balfour Stevenson was born in Edinburgh, Scotland, on November 13, 1850, to Thomas and Margaret Stevenson. Lighthouse design was his father's and his family's profession, and so at the age 17, he enrolled at Edinburgh University to study engineering, with the goal of following his father in the family business. Lighthouse design never appealed to Stevenson, though, and he began studying law instead. His spirit of adventure truly began to appear at this stage, and during his summer vacations he traveled to France to be around young artists, both writers and painters. He emerged from law school in 1875, but did not practice, as, by this point, he felt that his calling was to be a writer.

In 1878, Robert Louis Stevenson saw the publication of his first volume of work, *An Inland*

Voyage; the book provides an account of his trip from Antwerp to northern France, which he made in a canoe via the river Oise. A companion work, *Travels with a Donkey in the Cevennes* (1879), continues in the introspective vein of *Inland Voyage* and also focuses on the voice and character of the narrator, beyond simply telling a tale. Also from this period are the humorous essays of *Virginibus Puerisque: And Other Papers* (1881), which were originally published from 1876 to 1879 in various magazines, and Stevenson's first book of short fiction, *New Arabian Nights* (1882). The stories marked the United Kingdom's emergence into the realm of the short story, which had previously been dominated by Russians, Americans and the French. These stories also marked the beginning of Stevenson's adventure fiction, which would come to be his calling card.

A turning point in Stevenson's personal life came during this period, when he met the woman who would become his wife, Fanny Osbourne, in September 1876. She was a 36-year-old American who was married (although separated) and had two children. Stevenson and Osbourne began to see each other romantically while she remained in France. In 1878, she divorced her husband, and Stevenson set out to meet her in California (the account of his voyage would later be captured in *The Amateur Emigrant* published in 1895). The two married in 1880, and remained together until Stevenson's death in 1894. After they were married, the Stevensons took a three-week honeymoon at an abandoned silver mine in Napa Valley, California, and it was from this trip that *The Silverado Squatters* (1883) emerged. Also appearing in the early 1880s were Stevenson's short stories *Thrawn Janet* (1881), *The Treasure of Franchard* (1883) and *Markheim* (1885), the latter two having certain connections with *Treasure Island* and *Strange Case of Dr. Jekyll and Mr Hyde* (both of which would be published by 1886), respectively.

The 1880s were notable for both Stevenson's declining health and his amazing literary output. He suffered from hemorrhaging lungs (likely caused by undiagnosed tuberculosis), and writing was one of the few activities he could do while confined to bed. While in this bedridden state, he wrote some of his most popular fiction, most notably *Treasure Island* (1883), *Kidnapped* (1886), *Strange Case of Dr. Jekyll and Mr. Hyde* (1886), and *The Black Arrow* (1888).

The idea for *Treasure Island* was ignited by a map that Stevenson had drawn for his 12-year-old stepson; Stevenson had come up with a pirate adventure story to accompany the drawing, and it was serialized in the boys' magazine *Young Folks* from October 1881 to January 1882. When *Treasure Island* was published in book form in 1883, Stevenson got his first real taste of widespread popularity, and his career as a profitable writer had finally begun. The book was Stevenson's first volume-length fictional work, as well as the first of his writings that would be dubbed "for children". By the end of the 1880s, it was one of the period's most popular and widely read books.

The year 1886 saw the publication of what would be another enduring work, *Strange Case of Dr. Jekyll and Mr. Hyde*, which was an immediate success and helped consolidate Stevenson's reputation. The work is decidedly of the "adult" classification, as it presents a jarring and horrific exploration of various conflicting traits hidden within a single person. The book went on to international acclaim, inspiring countless stage productions and more than 100 motion pictures.

In June 1888, Stevenson and his family set sail from San Francisco, California, to travel the islands of the Pacific Ocean, stopping for stays at the Hawaiian Islands, where he became good friends with King Kalākaua. In 1889, they arrived in the Samoan islands, where they decided to build a house and settle. The island setting stimulated Stevenson's imagination, and, subsequently, influenced his writing during this time: Several of his later works are about the Pacific isles, including *The Wrecker* (1892), *Island Nights' Entertainments* (1893), *The Ebb-Tide* (1894) and *In the South Seas* (1896).

Toward the end of his life, Stevenson's South Seas writing included more of the everyday world, and both his nonfiction and fiction became more powerful than his earlier works. These more mature works not only brought Stevenson lasting fame, they helped to enhance his status with the literary establishment when his work was re-evaluated in the late 20th century, and his abilities were embraced by critics as much as his storytelling had always been by readers.

Robert Louis Stevenson died of a stroke on December 3, 1894, at his home in Vailima, Samoa. He was buried at the top of Mount Vaea, overlooking the sea.

An Introduction to the Film *Treasure Island*

Brief Information

Release year	1950
Directed by	Byron Haskin
Production company	Walt Disney Productions
Distributed by	RKO Pictures Buena Vista Pictures
Country	United States
Starring	Bobby Driscoll as Jim Hawkins Robert Newton as Long John Silver Basil Sydney as Captain Smollett Denis O'Dea as Dr. Livesey Geoffrey Wilkinson as Ben Gunn

Plot

In the West Coast of England in 1765, a young boy called Jim Hawkins lives with his mother in a tiny country inn which they run. Captain William Bones, a sickly lodger, gives Hawkins a treasure map after being visited by two pirates, the second of whom gives the captain a note marked with the black spot. That same night Bones is found dead at the inn, and Jim shows Squire Trelawney the map. Trelawney recognizes the map as belonging to the buccaneer Captain

Flint and sponsors a voyage to discover the pirate's lost treasure. Trelawney hires Captain Smollett and his ship, the Hispaniola, bringing along his friend Dr. Livesey as the ship's doctor and Jim as the cabin boy.

Before departure Trelawney is taken in by Long John Silver, a one-legged inn-keeper, who agrees to gather a crew. Silver strikes up a friendship with Jim and joins the expedition as the ship's cook. Smollett is concerned about the crew, especially when he reveals to Trelawney that the nature of their journey is common knowledge.

At sea Jim overhears Silver and the crew's plan to rebel, discovering that the seamen hired by Silver are Captain Flint's old crew. Jim reveals the betrayal to Smollett who asks Jim to stay friends with Silver to learn more. Upon reaching Treasure Island, Silver offers to tow the ship to a safer anchorage, using two of the ship's row boats. While the ship is being towed, one of Silver's men, Merry, leads a rebellion on the ship. Smollett, having been forewarned of the plot by Jim, is able to hold them off with the few men loyal to him and imprisons the betrayers below decks. Silver cuts the row boats from the Hispaniola and heads for shore with the rest of his men, taking Jim as a hostage. Smollett, Trelawney, and Livesey go ashore after them, leaving two guards on the ship.

On the island, Jim escapes and meets Ben Gunn, isolated by Flint five years ago. Gunn shows Jim the boat he's built, then leads him to Flint's stockade, where he meets up with Smollett and the others. Meanwhile, Merry escapes, takes the ship and raises the Jolly Roger. Silver returns to the Hispaniola, arms his men with muskets and makes plans to take the stockade. Short of men, Silver attempts to cooperate with Smollett, but when he is refused, Silver calls his men to attack. The attack on the stockade fails, but Silver wounds Smollett. Although seemingly protected by the stockade, Smollett suspects that, with the morning tide, Silver could move the Hispaniola into cannon range and level the fort.

Jim takes Gunn's boat and cuts the Hispaniola's anchor rope. The pirate Israel Hands discovers Jim and chases him up into the ship's rigging. Hands injures Jim arm with a throwing knife but is killed by the boy's pistol. Jim strikes the Jolly Roger and raises the Union Jack. Slowed by his wound, it takes him all night to get back to the stockade, which is unguarded. Inside, Jim searches for the doctor to tend his wound, but the man asleep under Livesey's coat is Long John Silver. Jim faints on the spot. Silver finds the map on him as his men wake up. Merry wants Jim dead, but Silver states he wants to trade him for the map, which his men believe is with Smollett. The men go outside to vote, pirate-style. From the stockade's lookout, Silver sees that the ship's aground, flying the Union Jack. The men give Silver the black spot, but he objects. Panicked, they let him bargain with Livesey for the map. Silver returns with Jim, waving the map. The pirates are overjoyed until they find out that the treasure — 700,000 pounds sterling — isn't there. The pirates turn on Silver, who manages to kill three of them before Smollett's men appear to defeat the rest. Greeting Silver, Gunn reveals that he's the one who dug up Flint's treasure and has hidden it in a cave.

Captain Smollett still wants Silver taken back for trial in England. Hawkins, Trelawney and two others take Silver to the Hispaniola aboard a rowboat loaded with a chest of treasure. Silver snatches Jim's pistol and forces Trelawney and the others out of the boat. He wants Hawkins to steer while he rows, but Jim beaches them instead. Silver orders Hawkins to push him off, but Jim refuses and Silver threatens to shoot him. Silver is unable to carry out his threat and drops the pistol, attempting to push the boat off himself. Seeing Silver struggle, Jim helps him, waving a hesitant farewell as Silver rows away.

Excerpt from the Book *Treasure Island*

How that personage haunted my dreams, I need scarcely tell you. On stormy nights, when the wind shook the four corners of the house and the surf roared along the cove and up the cliffs, I would see him in a thousand forms, and with a thousand diabolical expressions. Now the leg would be cut off at the knee, now at the hip; now he was a monstrous kind of a creature who had never had but the one leg, and that in the middle of his body. To see him leap and run and pursue me over hedge and ditch was the worst of nightmares. And altogether I paid pretty dear for my monthly fourpenny piece, in the shape of these abominable fancies.

But though I was so terrified by the idea of the seafaring man with one leg, I was far less afraid of the captain himself than anybody else who knew him. There were nights when he took a deal more rum and water than his head would carry; and then he would sometimes sit and sing his wicked, old, wild sea-songs, minding nobody; but sometimes he would call for glasses round and force all the trembling company to listen to his stories or bear a chorus to his singing. Often I have heard the house shaking with "Yo-ho-ho, and a bottle of rum", all the neighbours joining in for dear life, with the fear of death upon them, and each singing louder than the other to avoid remark. For in these fits he was the most overriding companion ever known; he would slap his hand on the table for silence all round; he would fly up in a passion of anger at a question, or sometimes because none was put, and so he judged the company was not following his story. Nor would he allow anyone to leave the inn till he had drunk himself sleepy and reeled off to bed.

His stories were what frightened people worst of all. Dreadful stories they were—about hanging, and walking the plank, and storms at sea, and the Dry Tortugas, and wild deeds and places on the Spanish Main. By his own account he must have lived his life among some of the wickedest men that God ever allowed upon the sea, and the language in which he told these stories shocked our plain country people almost as much as the crimes that he described. My father was always saying the inn would be ruined, for people would soon cease coming there to be tyrannized over and put down, and sent shivering to their beds; but I really believe his presence did us good. People were frightened at the time, but on looking back they rather liked it; it was a fine excitement in a quiet country life, and there was even a party of the younger men who pretended to admire him, calling him a "true sea-dog" and a "real old salt" and such like names, and saying there was the sort of man that made England terrible at sea.

In one way, indeed, he bade fair to ruin us, for he kept on staying week after week, and at last month after month, so that all the money had been long exhausted, and still my father never plucked up the heart to insist on having more. If ever he mentioned it, the captain blew through his nose so loudly that you might say he roared, and stared my poor father out of the room. I have seen him wringing his hands after such a rebuff, and I am sure the annoyance and the terror he lived in must have greatly hastened his early and unhappy death.

All the time he lived with us the captain made no change whatever in his dress but to buy some stockings from a hawker. One of the cocks of his hat having fallen down, he let it hang from that day forth, though it was a great annoyance when it blew. I remember the appearance of his coat, which he patched himself upstairs in his room, and which, before the end, was nothing but patches. He never wrote or received a letter, and he never spoke with any but the neighbours, and with these, for the most part, only when drunk on rum. The great sea-chest none of us had ever seen open.

He was only once crossed, and that was towards the end, when my poor father was far gone in a decline that took him off. Dr. Livesey came late one afternoon to see the patient, took a bit of dinner from my mother, and went into the parlour to smoke a pipe until his horse should come down from the hamlet, for we had no stabling at the old Benbow. I followed him in, and I remember observing the contrast the neat, bright doctor, with his powder as white as snow and his bright, black eyes and pleasant manners, made with the coltish country folk, and above all, with that filthy, heavy, bleared scarecrow of a pirate of ours, sitting, far gone in rum, with his arms on the table. Suddenly he—the captain, that is—began to pipe up his eternal song:

"Fifteen men on the dead man's chest—
Yo-ho-ho, and a bottle of rum!
Drink and the devil had done for the rest—
Yo-ho-ho, and a bottle of rum!"

At first I had supposed "the dead man's chest" to be that identical big box of his upstairs in the front room, and the thought had been mingled in my nightmares with that of the one-legged seafaring man. But by this time we had all long ceased to pay any particular notice to the song; it was new, that night, to nobody but Dr. Livesey, and on him I observed it did not produce an agreeable effect, for he looked up for a moment quite angrily before he went on with his talk to old Taylor, the gardener, on a new cure for the rheumatics. In the meantime, the captain gradually brightened up at his own music, and at last flapped his hand upon the table before him in a way we all knew to mean silence. The voices stopped at once, all but Dr. Livesey's; he went on as before speaking clear and kind and drawing briskly at his pipe between every word or two. The captain glared at him for a while, flapped his hand again, glared still harder, and at last broke out with a villainous, low oath, "Silence, there, between decks!"

"Were you addressing me, sir?" says the doctor; and when the ruffian had told him, with another oath, that this was so, "I have only one thing to say to you, sir," replies the doctor, "that if you keep on drinking rum, the world will soon be quit of a very dirty scoundrel!"

The old fellow's fury was awful. He sprang to his feet, drew and opened a sailor's clasp-knife, and balancing it open on the palm of his hand, threatened to pin the doctor to the wall.

The doctor never so much as moved. He spoke to him as before, over his shoulder and in the same tone of voice, rather high, so that all the room might hear, but perfectly calm and steady: "If you do not put that knife this instant in your pocket, I promise, upon my honour, you shall hang at the next assizes."

4.4 Thomas Hardy: *Tess of d'Urbervilles* (1891)

A Brief Introduction to Thomas Hardy

Thomas Hardy (1840-1928) was one of the most renowned English literary figures and is universally recognized as a major 20th-century poet as well as a major 19th-century novelist.

Thomas Hardy was born in Higher Bockhampton, Dorset, England on June 2, 1840, the eldest son of Thomas Hardy and Jemima (Hand) Hardy. His father was a stonemason and builder; his mother passed on her love of reading and books to her son. He grew up in an isolated cottage on the edge of open heathland. Though he was often ill as a child, his early experience of rural life, with its seasonal rhythms and oral culture, was fundamental to much of his later writing. He spent a year at the village school at age eight and then moved on to schools in Dorchester, the nearby county town, where he received a good instruction in mathematics and Latin. In 1856 he was apprenticed to John Hicks, a local architect, and in 1862, shortly before his 22nd birthday, he moved to London and became a draftsman in the busy office of Arthur Blomfield, a leading ecclesiastical architect. Driven back to Dorset by ill health in 1867, he worked for Hicks again and then for the Weymouth architect G. R. Crickmay.

Though architecture brought Hardy both social and economic advancement, it was only in the mid-1860s that lack of funds and declining religious faith forced him to abandon his early ambitions of a university education and eventual position as an Anglican priest. His habits of intensive private study were then redirected toward the reading of poetry and the systematic development of his own poetic skills. The verses he wrote in the 1860s would emerge in revised form in later volumes, but when none of them achieved immediate publication, Hardy reluctantly turned to prose.

In 1867 he wrote the class-conscious novel *The Poor Man and The Lady*, which was sympathetically considered by three London publishers but never published. George Meredith, as a publisher's reader, advised Hardy to write a shapelier and less opinionated novel. The result was the densely plotted *Desperate Remedies* (1871), which was influenced by the contemporary "sensation" fiction of Wilkie Collins. In his next novel, however, the brief and affectionately humorous idyll *Under the Greenwood Tree* (1872), Hardy found a voice much more distinctively his own. In this book he evoked, within the simplest of marriage plots, an episode of social change that was a direct reflection of events involving his own father shortly before Hardy's own birth.

In March 1870 Hardy was sent to make an architectural assessment of the lonely and rundown Church of St. Juliot in Cornwall. There—in romantic circumstances later strongly recalled in prose and verse—he first met the rector's lovely sister-in-law, Emma Lavinia Gifford, who became his wife four years later. She actively encouraged and assisted him in his literary endeavors, and his next novel, *A Pair of Blue Eyes* (1873), drew heavily upon the circumstances of their courtship for its wild Cornish setting and its melodramatic story of a young woman (somewhat resembling Emma Gifford) and the two men, friends become rivals, who successively pursue, misunderstand, and fail her.

Hardy's break with architecture occurred in the summer of 1872, when he undertook to supply *Tinsley's Magazine* with the 11 monthly installments of *A Pair of Blue Eyes*—an initially risky commitment to a literary career that was soon validated by an invitation to contribute a serial to the far more prestigious *The Cornhill Magazine*. The resulting novel, *Far from the Madding Crowd* (1874), introduced Wessex for the first time and made Hardy famous by its agricultural settings and its distinctive blend of humorous, melodramatic, pastoral, and tragic elements. The book is a vigorous portrayal of the beautiful and impulsive Bathsheba Everdene and her marital choices among Sergeant Troy, the dashing but irresponsible soldier; William Boldwood, the deeply obsessive farmer; and Gabriel Oak, her loyal and resourceful shepherd.

Hardy and Emma Gifford were married, against the wishes of both their families, in September 1874. At first they moved rather restlessly about, living sometimes in London, sometimes in Dorset. His record as a novelist during this period was somewhat mixed. *The Hand of Ethelberta* (1876), an artificial social comedy turning on versions and inversions of the British class system, was poorly received and has never been widely popular. *The Return of the Native* (1878), on the other hand, was increasingly admired for its powerfully evoked setting of Egdon Heath, which was based on the somber countryside Hardy had known as a child. Hardy's next works were *The Trumpet-Major* (1880), set in the Napoleonic period, and two more novels generally considered "minor"—*A Laodicean* (1881) and *Two on a Tower* (1882). The serious illness which hampered completion of *A Laodicean* decided the Hardys to move to Wimborne in 1881 and to Dorchester in 1883.

It was not easy for Hardy to establish himself as a member of the professional middle class in a town where his humbler background was well known. He signaled his determination to stay by accepting an appointment as a local magistrate and by designing and building Max Gate, the house just outside Dorchester in which he lived until his death. Hardy's novel *The Mayor of Casterbridge* (1886) incorporates recognizable details of Dorchester's history and topography. In his next novel, *The Woodlanders* (1887), socioeconomic issues again become central as the permutations of sexual advance and retreat are played out.

Wessex Tales (1888) was the first collection of the short stories that Hardy had long been publishing in magazines. His subsequent short-story collections are *A Group of Noble Dames* (1891), *Life's Little Ironies* (1894), and *A Changed Man* (1913). Hardy's short novel *The Well-Beloved* (serialized 1892, revised for volume publication 1897) displays a hostility to marriage that was related to increasing frictions within his own marriage.

The closing phase of Hardy's career in fiction was marked by the publication of *Tess of the d'Urbervilles* (1891) and *Jude the Obscure* (1895), which are generally considered his finest novels. Though *Tess* is the most richly "poetic" of Hardy's novels, and *Jude* the most bleakly written, both books offer deeply sympathetic representations of working-class figures: Tess Durbeyfield, the erring milkmaid, and Jude Fawley, the studious stonemason. In powerful, implicitly moralized narratives, Hardy traces these characters' initially hopeful, momentarily joyful, but persistently troubled journeys toward eventual deprivation and death.

Hardy seemed always to have valued poetry more than fiction, and *Wessex Poems* (1898), his first significant public appearance as a poet, included verse written during his years as a novelist as well as revised versions of poems dating from the 1860s. *Poems of the Past and the Present* (1901) contained nearly twice as many poems as its predecessor, most of them newly written. Some of the poems are explicitly or implicitly grouped by subject or theme. In *Time's Laughingstocks* (1909), the poems are again arranged under headings, but on principles that often remain elusive. Indeed, there is no clear line of development in Hardy's poetry from immaturity to maturity; his style undergoes no significant change over time. The range of poems within any particular volume is also extremely broad—from lyric to meditation to ballad to satirical vignette to dramatic monologue or dialogue—and Hardy persistently experiments with different, often invented, stanza forms and metres.

In 1903, 1905, and 1908 Hardy successively published the three volumes of *The Dynasts*, a huge poetic drama that is written mostly in blank verse and subtitled "an epic-drama of the War with Napoleon"—though it was not intended for actual performance. The sequence of major historical events—Trafalgar, Austerlitz, Waterloo, and so on—is diversified by prose episodes involving ordinary soldiers and civilians and by an ongoing commentary from such personified

"Intelligences" as the "Spirit of the Years" and the "Spirit of the Pities". Though subsequent criticism has tended to find its structures cumbersome and its verse inert, *The Dynasts* remains an impressive—and highly readable—achievement, and its publication certainly reinforced both Hardy's "national" image (he was appointed to the Order of Merit in 1910) and his enormous fame worldwide.

The sudden death of Emma Hardy in 1912 brought to an end some 20 years of domestic discord. It also stirred Hardy to profundities of regret and remorse and to the composition of *After a Journey*, *The Voice*, and the other *Poems of 1912-1913*, which are by general consent regarded as the peak of his poetic achievement. In 1914 Hardy married Florence Emily Dugdale, who was 38 years his junior. While his second wife sometimes found her situation difficult—as when the inclusion of *Poems of 1912-1913* in the collection *Satires of Circumstance* (1914) publicly proclaimed her husband's continuing devotion to her predecessor—her attention to Hardy's health, comfort, and privacy made a crucial contribution to his remarkable productivity in old age. Late in his eighth decade he published a fifth volume of verse, *Moments of Vision* (1917), and wrote in secret an official "life" of himself for posthumous publication under the name of his widow. In his ninth decade Hardy published two more poetry collections, *Late Lyrics and Earlier* (1922) and *Human Shows* (1925), and put together the posthumously published *Winter Words* (1928).

Hardy died in 1928 at Max Gate, a house he built for himself and his first wife, Emma Lavinia Gifford, in Dorchester, a few miles from his birthplace.

An Introduction to the Film *Tess*

Brief Information

Release year	1979
Directed by	Roman Polanski
Production company	Renn Productions

	Timothy Burrill Productions
	SFP
Distributed by	Columbia Pictures
Country	France
	United Kingdom
Starring	Nastassja Kinski as Tess Durbeyfield
	Peter Firth as Angel Clare
	Leigh Lawson as Alec Stokes-d'Urberville

Awards

Award	Category	Winner(s) and Nominee(s)
53rd Academy Awards	Best Art Direction	Pierre Guffroy and Jack Stephens
	Best Cinematography	Geoffrey Unsworth and Ghislain Cloquet
	Best Costume Design	Anthony Powell
35th BAFTA Film Awards	Best Cinematography	Geoffrey Unsworth and Ghislain Cloquet
5th César Awards	Best Film	Roman Polanski
	Best Director	Roman Polanski
	Best Cinematography	Ghislain Cloquet
38th Golden Globe Awards	Best Foreign Film	France
	New Star of the Year — Female	Nastassja Kinski

Plot

The story takes place in Thomas Hardy's Wessex during the Victorian period.

The events of the story are set in motion when a clergyman, Parson Tringham, has a chance conversation with John Durbeyfield, a simple farmer. Tringham is a local historian, and in the course of his research he has discovered the "Durbeyfields" are descended from the d'Urbervilles, a noble family whose family line extends to the time of William the Conqueror. The family lost its land and influence when the male heirs died out. The parson thinks Durbeyfield might like to know his origins as a passing historical curiosity.

Durbeyfield soon holds the idea of using his noble lineage to better his family's fortunes. Finding a noble family named d'Urberville living nearby, he and his wife send their daughter Tess to call on his presumed relations, and seek employment at the manor house. At the manor house lives Alec d'Urberville and his mother. Tess is a beautiful girl, and Alec d'Urberville has an appetite for women. Alec and his mother know they are no relation to Tess, for their family name and coat of arms have been purchased. Finding her naive, penniless and attractive, he sets about taking advantage of the situation. He tries to get her alone, and attempts to seduce her with strawberries and roses, but in vain. In time he rapes her.

Tess returns home and soon discovers she is pregnant. She is angry with her mother for placing her at risk when she knew so little of the cruelness of the world. The baby is born sickly and dies. Some time later, Tess goes to a dairy farm to work as a milkmaid. She meets Angel Clare, an aspiring young farmer from a respectable family. He believes Tess to be an unspoiled country girl, and completely innocent. The two fall in love, but Tess does not reveal her previous relationship with Alec until their wedding night. Disappointed and heartbroken by the news, Angel rejects her.

Deserted by her husband, Tess meets Alec d'Urberville again. She at first angrily rejects his advances, but the death of her father puts the family in extremely hard times. Facing starvation, eviction and homelessness, Tess is compelled to resume her relationship with Alec as his mistress to support her mother and siblings.

Shortly afterwards, Angel Clare returns from travelling abroad. A disastrous missionary tour in Brazil has ruined his health. Humbled, and having had plenty of time to think, he feels regretful for his treatment of Tess. He succeeds in tracking her down but leaves heartbroken when he finds her living with Alec. Tess realizes that going back to Alec has ruined her chances of happiness with Angel, and murders Alec.

Running away to find Angel, Tess is reconciled with him; he can finally accept and embrace her as his wife without passing moral judgment on her actions. They consummate their marriage, spending two nights of happiness together on the run from the law before Tess is captured sleeping at Stonehenge. An ending summary tells that she is convicted and hanged for murder.

Excerpt from the Book *Tess of the d'Urbervilles*

Phase the Seventh: Fulfilment

Chapter LVIII

The night was strangely solemn and still. In the small hours she whispered to him the whole story of how he had walked in his sleep with her in his arms across the Froom stream, at the imminent risk of both their lives, and laid her down in the stone coffin at the ruined abbey. He had never known of that till now.

"Why didn't you tell me next day?" he said. "It might have prevented much misunderstanding and woe."

"Don't think of what's past!" said she. "I am not going to think outside of now. Why should we! Who knows what tomorrow has in store?"

But it apparently had no sorrow. The morning was wet and foggy, and Clare, rightly informed that the caretaker only opened the windows on fine days, ventured to creep out of their chamber, and explore the house, leaving Tess asleep. There was no food on the premises, but there was water, and he took advantage of the fog to emerge from the mansion, and fetch tea, bread, and butter from a shop in a little place two miles beyond, as also a small tin kettle and spirit-lamp, that they might get fire without smoke. His re-entry awoke her; and they breakfasted on what he had brought.

They were indisposed to stir abroad, and the day passed, and the night following, and the next, and next; till, almost without their being aware, five days had slipped by in absolute seclusion, not a sight or sound of a human being disturbing their peacefulness, such as it was. The changes of the weather were their only events, the birds of the New Forest their only company. By tacit consent they hardly once spoke of any incident of the past subsequent to their wedding-day. The gloomy intervening time seemed to sink into chaos, over which the present and prior times closed as if it never had been. Whenever he suggested that they should leave their shelter, and go forwards towards Southampton or London, she showed a strange unwillingness to move.

"Why should we put an end to all that's sweet and lovely!" she deprecated. "What must come will come." And, looking through the shutter-chink: "All is trouble outside there; inside here content."

He peeped out also. It was quite true; within was affection, union, error forgiven: outside was the inexorable.

"And—and," she said, pressing her cheek against his, "I fear that what you think of me now may not last. I do not wish to outlive your present feeling for me. I would rather not. I would rather be dead and buried when the time comes for you to despise me, so that it may never be known to me that you despised me."

"I cannot ever despise you."

"I also hope that. But considering what my life had been I cannot see why any man should, sooner or later, be able to help despising me.... How wickedly mad I was! Yet formerly I never could bear to hurt a fly or a worm, and the sight of a bird in a cage used often to make me cry."

They remained yet another day. In the night the dull sky cleared, and the result was that the old caretaker at the cottage awoke early. The brilliant sunrise made her unusually brisk; she decided to open the contiguous mansion immediately, and to air it thoroughly on such a day. Thus it occurred that, having arrived and opened the lower rooms before six o'clock, she ascended to the bedchambers, and was about to turn the handle of the one wherein they lay. At that moment she fancied she could hear the breathing of persons within. Her slippers and her antiquity had rendered her progress a noiseless one so far, and she made for instant retreat; then, deeming that her hearing might have deceived her, she turned anew to the door and softly tried the handle. The lock was out of order, but a piece of furniture had been moved forward on the inside, which prevented her opening the door more than an inch or two. A stream of morning light through the shutter-chink fell upon the faces of the pair, wrapped in profound slumber, Tess's lips being parted like a half-opened flower near his cheek. The caretaker was so struck with their innocent appearance, and with the elegance of Tess's gown hanging across a chair, her silk stockings beside it, the pretty parasol, and the other habits in which she had arrived because she had none else, that her first indignation at the effrontery of tramps and vagabonds gave way to a momentary sentimentality over this genteel elopement, as it seemed. She closed the door, and withdrew as softly as she had come, to go and consult with her neighbors on the odd discovery.

Not more than a minute had elapsed after her withdrawal when Tess woke, and then Clare. Both had a sense that something had disturbed them, though they could not say what; and the uneasy feeling which it engendered grew stronger. As soon as he was dressed he narrowly scanned the lawn through the two or three inches of shutter-chink.

"I think we will leave at once," said he. "It is a fine day. And I cannot help fancying somebody is about the house. At any rate, the woman will be sure to come today."

She passively assented, and putting the room in order they took up the few articles that belonged to them, and departed noiselessly. When they had got into the Forest she turned to take a last look at the house.

"Ah, happy house—goodbye!" she said. "My life can only be a question of a few weeks. Why should we not have stayed there?"

"Don't say it, Tess! We shall soon get out of this district altogether. We'll continue our course as we've begun it, and keep straight north. Nobody will think of looking for us there. We shall be looked for at the Wessex ports if we are sought at all. When we are in the north we will get to a port and away."

Having thus persuaded her the plan was pursued, and they kept a bee-line northward. Their long repose at the manor-house lent them walking power now; and towards mid-day they found that they were approaching the steepled city of Melchester, which lay directly in their way. He decided to rest her in a clump of trees during the afternoon, and push onward under cover of darkness. At dusk Clare purchased food as usual, and their night march began, the boundary between Upper and Mid-Wessex being crossed about eight o'clock.

To walk across country without much regard to roads was not new to Tess, and she showed her old agility in the performance. The intercepting city, ancient Melchester, they were obliged to pass through in order to take advantage of the town bridge for crossing a large river that obstructed them. It was about midnight when they went along the deserted streets, lighted fitfully by the few lamps, keeping off the pavement that it might not echo their footsteps. The graceful pile of cathedral architecture rose dimly on their left hand, but it was lost upon them now. Once out of the town they followed the turnpike-road, which after a few miles plunged across an open plain.

Though the sky was dense with cloud a diffused light from some fragment of a moon had hitherto helped them a little. But the moon had now sunk, the clouds seemed to settle almost on their heads, and the night grew as dark as a cave. However, they found their way along, keeping as much on the turf as possible that their tread might not resound, which it was easy to do, there being no hedge or fence of any kind. All around was open loneliness and black solitude, over which a stiff breeze blew.

5. 20th Century Literature in Films

5.1 Virginia Woolf: *Orlando* (1928)

An Introduction to Virginia Woolf

Adeline Virginia Woolf (1882-1941) was an English writer who is considered one of the foremost modernists of the 20th century, and a pioneer in the use of stream of consciousness as a narrative device.

Born on January 25, 1882, Adeline Virginia Stephen was raised in a remarkable household. Her father, Sir Leslie Stephen, and her mother, Julia Prinsep Stephen (née Jackson), were extremely well connected, both socially and artistically. Woolf and her full siblings and four half-siblings lived under one roof at 22 Hyde Park Gate, Kensington.

From the time of her birth until 1895, Woolf spent her summers in St. Ives, a beach town at the very southwestern tip of England. The Stephens' summer home, Talland House, which is still standing today, looks out at the dramatic Porthminster Bay and has a view of the Godrevy Lighthouse, which inspired her writing. In her later memoirs, Woolf recalled St. Ives with a great fondness. In fact, she incorporated scenes from those early summers into her modernist novel, *To the Lighthouse* (1927).

Virginia and other the girls in the family were taught at home and utilized the splendid confines of the family's lush Victorian library.

As a young girl, Virginia was curious, light-hearted and playful. She started a family newspaper, the *Hyde Park Gate News*, to document her family's humorous anecdotes. However, early emotional wounds darkened her childhood, including being sexually abused by her half-brothers George and Gerald Duckworth, which she wrote about in her later essays *A Sketch of the Past* and *22 Hyde Park Gate*. In 1895, at the age of 13, she also had to cope with the sudden death of her mother, which led to her first mental breakdown, and the loss of her half-sister Stella, who had become the head of the household, two years later.

While dealing with her personal losses, Woolf continued her studies in German, Greek and Latin at the Ladies' Department of King's College London. Her four years of study introduced her to a handful of radical feminists leading educational reforms. In 1904, her father died from stomach cancer, which contributed to another emotional setback that led to Woolf being institutionalized for a brief period. Virginia Woolf's dance between literary expression and personal loneliness would continue for the rest of her life. In 1905, she began writing professionally as a contributor for *The Times Literary Supplement*.

After their father's death, Woolf's sister Vanessa and brother Adrian sold the family home in Hyde Park Gate, and purchased a house in the Bloomsbury area of London. During this period, Virginia met several members of the Bloomsbury Group, a circle of prominent intellectuals and artists including her future husband, essayist Leonard Woolf, among others. The two shared a passionate love for one another for the rest of their lives.

Several years before marrying Leonard, Virginia had begun working on her first novel. The original title was *Melymbrosia*. After nine years and innumerable drafts, it was released in 1915 as *The Voyage Out*. Woolf used the book to experiment with several literary tools, including compelling and unusual narrative perspectives, dream-states and free association prose. Two years later, the Woolfs bought a used printing press and established Hogarth Press, their own publishing house operated out of their home, Hogarth House. Virginia and Leonard published some of their writing, as well as the work of Sigmund Freud, Katharine Mansfield and T. S. Eliot.

A year after the end of World War I, the Woolfs purchased Monk's House, a cottage in the village of Rodmell in 1919, and that same year Virginia published *Night and Day*, a novel set in Edwardian England. Her third novel *Jacob's Room* was published by Hogarth in 1922. Based on her brother Thoby, it was considered a significant departure from her earlier novels with its modernist elements. That year, she met author, poet and landscape gardener Vita Sackville-West, the wife of English diplomat Harold Nicolson. Virginia and Vita began a friendship that developed into a romantic affair. Although their affair eventually ended, they remained friends until Virginia Woolf's death.

In 1925, Woolf received extremely enthusiastic reviews for *Mrs. Dalloway*, her fourth novel. The fascinating story interweaved interior monologues and raised issues of feminism, mental illness and homosexuality in post-World War I England. *Mrs. Dalloway* was adapted into a 1997 film and inspired *The Hours*, a 1998 novel by Michael Cunningham and a 2002 film adaptation. Her 1928 novel, *To the Lighthouse*, was another critical success and considered revolutionary for its stream of consciousness storytelling. The modernist classic examines the subtext of human relationships through the lives of the Ramsay family as they vacation on the Isle of Skye in Scotland.

Woolf found a literary muse in Sackville-West, the inspiration for Woolf's 1928 novel *Orlando*, which follows an English nobleman who mysteriously becomes a woman at the age of 30 and lives on for over three centuries of English history. The novel was a breakthrough for Woolf who received critical praise for the groundbreaking work, as well as a newfound level of popularity.

In 1929, Woolf published *A Room of One's Own*, a feminist essay based on lectures she had given at women's colleges, in which she examines women's role in literature. In the work, she sets forth the idea that "A woman must have money and a room of her own if she is to write fiction." Woolf pushed narrative boundaries in her next work, *The Waves* (1931), which she described as "a play-poem" written in the voices of six different characters. Woolf published *The Years*, the final novel published in her lifetime in 1937, about a family's history over the course of a generation. The following year she published *Three Guineas*, an essay which continued the feminist themes of *A Room of One's Own* and addressed fascism and war.

Throughout her career, Woolf spoke regularly at colleges and universities, penned dramatic letters, wrote moving essays and self-published a long list of short stories. By her mid-forties, she had established herself as an intellectual, an innovative and influential writer and pioneering feminist. Her ability to balance dream-like scenes with deeply tense plot lines earned her incredible respect from peers and the public alike.

Despite her outward success, Virginia Woolf suffered from severe bouts of mental illness throughout her life. She took her own life by drowning in 1941 at the age of 59.

An Introduction to the Film *Orlando*

Brief Information

Release year	1992
Directed by	Sally Potter
Distributed by	Sony Pictures Classics
Country	United Kingdom
Starring	Tilda Swinton as Orlando
	Quentin Crisp as Elizabeth I
	Jimmy Somerville as Falsetto/Angel
	John Wood as Archduke Harry
	Billy Zane as Shelmerdine

Plot

The film begins in the Elizabethan Age shortly before the death of Queen Elizabeth I. On her deathbed, Elizabeth promises an androgynous young nobleman named Orlando a large tract of land and a castle built on it along with a generous monetary gift which she will only bequeath to him if he consents to her command, "Do not fade. Do not wither. Do not grow old." Both he and his heirs will keep the land and inheritance forever. Orlando agrees reluctantly and lives in splendid isolation in the castle for a couple of centuries or so during which time he indulges himself in poetry and art. His attempts to befriend a celebrated poet, however, backfire when the poet writes a devastating comment of his poetry. Orlando then travels to Constantinople as British ambassador to the Turks, but he is almost killed in a diplomatic disturbance there. Waking up the next morning, however, he learns something even more startling: he has physically transformed into a woman overnight.

The now "Lady" Orlando comes home to her estate in Middle Eastern outfit, only to learn that she faces several impending lawsuits arguing that Orlando was a woman to begin with and therefore has no right to the land or any of her/his royal inheritance.

The succeeding two centuries tire her out; the court case, bad luck in love and the wars of British history eventually bring her up to the 1990s with a young daughter to look after and a book in search of a publisher. The editor who judges the work as "quite good" is, ironically, portrayed by Heathcoate Williams — the same actor who degraded her poetry as a different character 200 years earlier. Having lived a most odd existence, Orlando finally finds a tranquil niche within it.

Excerpt from the Book *Orlando*

He—for there could be no doubt of his sex, though the fashion of the time did something to disguise it — was in the act of slicing at the head of a Moor which swung from the rafters. It was the colour of an old football, and more or less the shape of one, save for the sunken cheeks and a strand or two of coarse, dry hair, like the hair on a cocoanut. Orlando's father, or perhaps his grandfather, had struck it from the shoulders of a vast Pagan who had started up under the moon in the barbarian fields of Africa; and now it swung, gently, perpetually, in the breeze which never ceased blowing through the attic rooms of the gigantic house of the lord who had slain him.

Orlando's fathers had ridden in fields of asphodel, and stony fields, and fields watered by strange rivers, and they had struck many heads of many colours off many shoulders, and brought them back to hang from the rafters. So too would Orlando, he vowed. But since he was sixteen only, and too young to ride with them in Africa or France, he would steal away from his mother and the peacocks in the garden and go to his attic room and there lunge and plunge and slice the air with his blade. Sometimes he cut the cord so that the skull bumped on the floor and he had to string it up again, fastening it with some chivalry almost out of reach so that his enemy grinned at him through shrunk, black lips triumphantly. The skull swung to and fro, for the house, at the top of which he lived, was so vast that there seemed trapped in it the wind itself, blowing this way, blowing that way, winter and summer. The green arras with the hunters on it moved perpetually. His fathers had been noble since they had been at all. They came out of the northern mists wearing coronets on their heads. Were not the bars of darkness in the room, and the yellow pools which chequered the floor, made by the sun falling through the stained glass of a vast coat of arms in the window? Orlando stood now in the midst of the yellow body of an heraldic leopard. When he put his hand on the window-sill to push the window open, it was instantly coloured red, blue, and yellow like a butterfly's wing. Thus, those who like symbols, and have a turn for the deciphering of them, might observe that though the shapely legs, the handsome body, and the well-set shoulders were all of them decorated with various tints of heraldic light, Orlando's face, as he threw the window open, was lit solely by the sun itself. A more candid, sullen face it would be impossible to find. Happy the mother who bears, happier still the biographer who records the life of such a one! Never need she vex herself, nor he invoke the help of novelist or poet. From deed to deed, from glory to glory, from office to office he must go, his scribe following after, till they reach whatever seat it may be that is the height of their desire. Orlando, to look at, was cut out precisely for some such career. The red of the cheeks was covered with peach down; the down on the lips was only a little thicker than the down on the cheeks. The lips themselves were short and slightly drawn back over teeth of an exquisite and almond whiteness. Nothing disturbed the arrowy nose in its short, tense flight; the hair was dark, the ears small, and fitted closely to the head. But, alas, that these catalogues of youthful beauty cannot end without mentioning forehead and eyes. Alas, that people are seldom born devoid of all three; for directly we glance at Orlando standing by the window, we must admit that he had eyes like drenched violets, so large that the water seemed to have brimmed in them and widened them; and a brow like the swelling of a marble dome pressed between the two blank medallions which were his temples. Directly we glance at eyes and forehead, thus do we rhapsodize. Directly we glance at eyes and forehead, we have to admit a thousand disagreeables which it is the aim of every good biographer to ignore. Sights disturbed him, like that of his mother, a very beautiful lady in green walking out to feed the peacocks with Twitchett, her maid, behind her; sights exalted him — the birds and the trees; and made him in love with death — the evening sky, the homing rooks; and so, mounting up the spiral stairway into his brain — which was a roomy one — all these sights, and the garden sounds too, the hammer beating, the wood chopping, began that riot and confusion of the passions and emotions which every good biographer detests, But to continue — Orlando slowly drew in his head, sat down at the table, and, with the half-conscious air of one doing what they do every day of their lives at this hour, took out a writing book labelled "Aethelbert: A Tragedy in Five Acts", and dipped an old stained goose quill in the ink.

Soon he had covered ten pages and more with poetry. He was fluent, evidently, but he was abstract. Vice, Crime, Misery were the personages of his drama; there were Kings and Queens of impossible territories; horrid plots confounded them; noble sentiments suffused them; there was never a word said as he himself would have said it, but all was turned with a fluency and sweetness which, considering his age — he was not yet seventeen — and that the sixteenth century had still some years of its course to run, were remarkable enough. At last, however, he came to a halt. He was describing, as all young poets are for ever describing, nature, and in order to match the shade of green precisely he looked (and here he showed more audacity than most) at the thing itself, which happened to be a laurel bush growing beneath the window. After that, of course, he could write no more. Green in nature is one thing, green in literature another. Nature and letters seem to have a natural antipathy; bring them together and they tear each other to pieces. The shade of green Orlando now saw spoilt his rhyme and split his metre. Moreover, nature has tricks of her own. Once look out of a window at bees among flowers, at a yawning dog, at the sun setting, once think "how many more suns shall I see set", etc. etc. (the thought is too well known to be worth writing out) and one drops the pen, takes one's cloak, strides out of the room, and catches one's foot on a painted chest as one does so. For Orlando was a trifle clumsy.

5.2 George Orwell: *Animal Farm* (1945) / *1984* (1949)

An Introduction to George Orwell

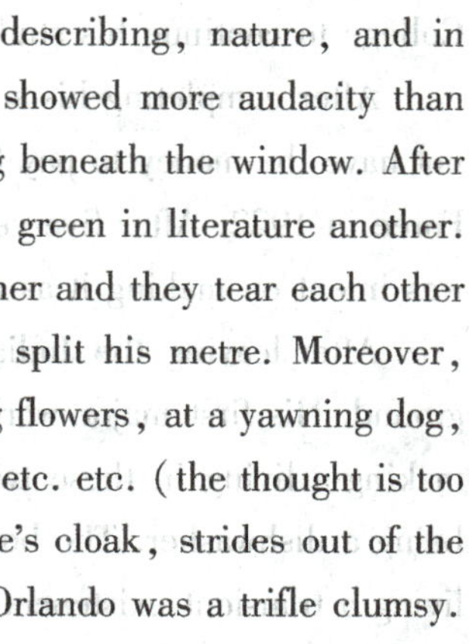

George Orwell (1903-1950) is a British journalist and author who created some of the sharpest satirical fiction of the 20th century with such works as *Animal Farm* and *Nineteen Eighty-Four*. He was also a man of strong opinions who addressed some of the major political movements of his times, including imperialism, fascism and communism.

Orwell was born Eric Arthur Blair on 25 June 1903 in eastern India, the son of a British colonial civil servant. His mother brought him and his older sister, Marjorie, to England about a year after his birth and settled in Henley-on-Thames. His father stayed behind in India and rarely visited. Orwell didn't really know his father until he retired from the service in 1912. And even after that, the pair never formed a strong bond. He found his father to be dull and conservative.

Orwell was a writing prodigy at an early age, reportedly composing his first poem around the age of four. He later wrote, "I had the lonely child's habit of making up stories and holding conversations with imaginary persons, and I think from the very start my literary ambitions were mixed up with the feeling of being isolated and undervalued." One of his first literary successes came at the age of 11 when he had a poem published in the local newspaper.

Like many other boys in England, Orwell was sent to boarding school. In 1911 he went to St. Cyprian's in the coastal town of Eastbourne, where he got his first taste of England's class system. On a partial scholarship, Orwell noticed that the school treated the richer students better than the poorer ones. He wasn't popular with his peers, and in books he found comfort from his difficult situation. He read works by Rudyard Kipling and H. G. Wells, among others. What he lacked in personality, he made up for in smarts. Orwell won scholarships to Wellington College and Eton College to continue his studies.

After completing his schooling at Eton, Orwell found himself at a dead end. His family did not have the money to pay for a university education. Instead he joined the India Imperial Police Force in 1922. After five years in Burma, Orwell resigned his post and returned to England. He was intent on making it as a writer.

After leaving the India Imperial Force, Orwell struggled to get his writing career off the ground. His first major work, *Down and Out in Paris and London*, (1933) explored his time making a living in these two cities. Orwell took all sorts of jobs to make ends meet, including being a dishwasher. The book provided a brutal look at the lives of the working poor and of those living a transient existence. Not wishing to embarrass his family, the author published the book under the pseudonym George Orwell.

Sometimes called the conscience of a generation, Orwell next explored his overseas experiences in *Burmese Days*, published in 1934. The novel offered a dark look at British colonialism in Burma, then part of the country's Indian empire. Orwell's interest in political matters grew rapidly after this novel was published. Also around this time, he met Eileen O'Shaughnessy. The pair married in June 1936, and Eileen supported and assisted Orwell in his career.

In December 1936, Orwell traveled to Spain, where he joined one of the groups fighting against General Francisco Franco in the Spanish Civil War. Orwell was badly injured during his time with a militia, getting shot in the throat and arm. For several weeks, he was unable to speak. Orwell and his wife, Eileen, were indicted on treason charges in Spain. Fortunately, the charges were brought after the couple had left the country.

Other health problems plagued the talented writer not long after his return to England. For years, Orwell had periods of sickness, and he was diagnosed with tuberculosis which he had to battle with for the rest of his life.

To support himself, Orwell took on various writing assignments. He wrote numerous essays and reviews over the years, developing a reputation for producing well-crafted literary criticism. In 1941, Orwell landed a job with the BBC as a producer. He developed news commentary and shows for audiences in the eastern part of the British Empire. Orwell drew such literary greats as T. S. Eliot and E. M. Forster to appear on his programs. With World War II raging on, Orwell found himself acting as a propagandist to advance the country's national interest. He hated this part of his job, describing the company's atmosphere in his diary as "something halfway between a girls' school and a lunatic asylum, and all we are doing at present is useless, or slightly worse than useless." Orwell resigned in 1943 saying "I was wasting my own time and the public money on doing work that produces no result. I believe that in the present political situation the broadcasting of British propaganda to India is an almost hopeless task." Around this time, Orwell became the literary editor for a socialist newspaper.

Orwell is best known for two novels, *Animal Farm* (1945) and *Nineteen Eighty-Four* (1949), both of which were published toward the end of his life. *Animal Farm* was an anti-Soviet satire in a pastoral setting featuring two pigs as its main protagonists. These pigs were said to represent Josef Stalin and Leon Trotsky. The novel brought Orwell great acclaim and financial rewards. Four years later, Orwell published another masterwork, *Nineteen Eighty-Four*. Set in an imaginary totalitarian future, the book made a deep impression, with its title and many phrases — such as "Big Brother is watching you", "newspeak" and "doublethink" — entering popular use. This bleak vision of the world divided into three oppressive nations stirred up controversy among reviewers, who found this fictional future too despairing.

By this time *Nineteen Eighty-Four* proved to be another huge success, Orwell was in the late stages of his battle with tuberculosis. He died on January 21, 1950, in a London hospital. He may have passed away all too soon, but his ideas and opinions have lived on through his work. Both *Animal Farm* and *Nineteen Eighty-Four* have been turned into films and have enjoyed tremendous popularity over the years.

An Introduction to the film *Animal Farm*

Brief Information

Release year 1999
Directed by John Stephenson
Distributor Hallmark Films
Country United States
United Kingdom
Starring Pete Postlethwaite — Farmer Jones, of Manor Farm.
Caroline Gray — Mrs. Jones
Alan Stanford — Farmer Pilkington, of Foxwood Farm.
Gail Fitzpatrick — Mrs. Pilkington
Gerard Walsh — Farmer Frederick, of Pinchfield Farm
Voices Julia Ormond — Jessie, a wise old border collie.
Patrick Stewart — Napoleon, the leader of the pigs.
Ian Holm — Squealer, the 2nd in command pig.
Julia Louis-Dreyfus — Mollie, a dapple-grey mare who likes looking pretty

Plot

As a bleak, dark scene unfolds, animals are seen struggling through the mud as Jessie, an old, nearly blind border collie reflects on the events that led them to their current situation. The film flashes back years earlier.

As the rarely sober and abusive farmer, Mr. Jones, struggles with debt to neighbor farmer Mr. Pilkington, Old Major, the aged prize Middle White boar at Manor Farm, holds a meeting with the animals in the barn. Old Major tells the animals that mankind is their enemy, for they serve and provide for mankind without reward. Old Major teaches the animals the song, "Beasts of the World", which declares that animals must overthrow man in order to be free and equal. The meeting is interrupted when Jones, after having an affair with Mr. Pilkington's wife, stumbles outside the barn and accidentally fires his gun, killing Old Major. Jones later then uses Old Major for meat, which his butcher then tries to feed to Jessie. When Jones neglects to feed the animals, Boxer, the shire horse, leads the animals to the food shed, and the pigs lead a revolution against Jones, his wife, and the farm workers, forcing them off the property.

Under the rule of animals, Manor Farm is renamed Animal Farm by Snowball, a pig who has learned to read and write. Snowball paints on the barn doors what he calls the seven commandments of Animalism, which, in accordance with Old Major's views, forbid animals from behaving like humans or killing other animals. The final commandment reads, "All animals are equal." Snowball teaches the animals to chant, "Four legs good, two legs bad" and also reveals the "Hoof and Horn", a flag that represents Animal Farm. Napoleon, another pig, declares that the farmhouse is to be preserved as a museum, and the three pigs (Snowball, Napoleon, and Squealer oversee the farm's operation. Napoleon also takes Jessie's puppies from her, claiming that it is best for them to receive an education from him. Snowball, when questioned by the farm animals, confesses that he and the other pigs have taken the farm's milk and apples for themselves. Squealer explains that the pigs' well-being takes priority because they are the brains of the farm. Jessie is the only one unconvinced.

Having learned that Jones has lost control of his farm, Pilkington leads an invasion into Animal Farm with other local farm workers. Snowball has planned for such an invasion and leads the animals to victory, causing the humans to retreat. In his defeat, Pilkington considers working with the animals instead.

Snowball proposes that the animals build a windmill to improve their operations, but Napoleon opposes the plan. When the animals show support for Snowball, Napoleon calls Jessie's puppies, now grown dogs trained as his private army, to chase Snowball out of Animal Farm and leaving his fate unknown. Napoleon declares Snowball a "traitor and a criminal", and Squealer claims that the windmill was Napoleon's plan all along; leaving the animals unaware that Napoleon is evil and therefore the real betrayer, with Squealer secretly working as Napoleon's accomplice. Napoleon declares the pigs will now "decide all aspects of the farm". When Pilkington begins to trade with the pigs, Boxer remembers Old Major mentioning that animals were not to engage in trade. Napoleon explains that "Animal Farm cannot exist in isolation." Napoleon has the skull of Old Major placed in front of the barn to oversee the farm's progress, and has a statue of himself erected nearby. Jessie confesses to the other animals that she witnessed the pigs living in the house and sleeping in the beds. Squealer explains that no commandment has been broken. He had, in fact, altered the commandment, "No animal shall sleep in a bed" to, "No animal shall sleep in a bed with sheets."

Jones and his wife disrupt Animal Farm by blowing up the almost-complete windmill with dynamite. Napoleon blames Snowball for the sabotage, and the windmill's reconstruction begins under strict supervision by Napoleon's army, the Animal Guard. Squealer announces that "Beasts of the World" no longer has meaning since Animal Farm's establishment, and he replaces it with a new song called "Glorious Leader, Napoleon". The pigs consume more food, leaving the other animals with little to eat. Napoleon declares that Snowball is causing the food shortage and that the hens will have to surrender their eggs to the market. When the hens oppose, Napoleon declares that the hens are all criminals and that no food will be given to them. The pigs produce propaganda films using Jones' filming equipment. While celebrating Napoleon as a leader, the films show the deaths of animals that have broken Napoleon's rules. It is revealed that the commandment, "No animal shall kill any other animal" has been changed to, "No animal shall kill any other animal without cause." The commandment, "No animal shall drink alcohol," is also changed to, "No animal shall drink alcohol to excess," after the pigs begin to buy whiskey from Pilkington.

After Boxer collapses from being overworked, Squealer informs Jessie that Napoleon will be sending Boxer to the hospital. Benjamin notices that the van that comes for Boxer is marked with the words "Horse Slaughterer", but Boxer is taken to his death before the other animals can intervene. As Jessie and Benjamin plan to flee from Animal Farm, Napoleon is paid for selling Boxer to the glue factory, and Squealer's latest propaganda film assures the animals that the van was from the hospital, but had been previously been the property of a horse slaughterer. Pilkington and his wife dine with the pigs in the farmhouse, where Napoleon announces that the farm's name will be changed back to Manor Farm. Watching through a glass window, Jessie sees the faces of Pilkington and Napoleon distorted in such a way that she can't tell the difference between them, and Pilkington is overheard boasting to his wife that he made money selling second-rate farm equipment to Napoleon. Muriel and Benjamin notice that the commandment "All animals are equal" has been extended to include, "but some animals are more equal than others." As Jessie, Benjamin, and Muriel escape the farm with a small group of animals, a propaganda film displays a performance of a new song dedicated to Napoleon. The performance features Napoleon wearing clothes and standing on two legs, as the Animal Guard chants, "Four legs good, two legs better!" The performance ends with a speech from Napoleon, who announces plans to make weapons and build walls to preserve the farm. He declares the revolution over and announces, "All animals are now free!"

The film returns to the present, where Jessie returns to find Manor Farm unattended. All the animals have died, but Jessie finds some dogs who survive and realizes they are her own puppies. Jessie sees Napoleon's statue now collapsed, and remarks she knew one day Napoleon's evil, cruelty, and greed would bring about his ruin. A motorcar arrives with a farmer, his wife and children; the new owners of Manor Farm. Jessie remarks she will not let this family "make the same mistakes" of the neglect of Jones or the abuse of Napoleon, and is aware the small remnant of animals will now to have work along their new masters to restore the farm.

Excerpt from the Book *Animal Farm*

ALL ANIMALS ARE EQUAL BUT SOME ANIMALS ARE MORE EQUAL THAN OTHERS

After that it did not seem strange when next day the pigs who were supervising the work of the farm all carried whips in their trotters. It did not seem strange to learn that the pigs had bought themselves a wireless set, were arranging to install a telephone, and had taken out subscriptions to John Bull, TitBits, and the *Daily Mirror*. It did not seem strange when Napoleon was seen strolling in the farmhouse garden with a pipe in his mouth — no, not even when the pigs took Mr. Jones's clothes out of the wardrobes and put them on, Napoleon himself appearing in a black coat, ratcatcher breeches, and leather leggings, while his favorite sow appeared in the watered silk dress which Mrs. Jones had been used to wear on Sundays.

A week later, in the afternoon, a number of dogcarts drove up to the farm. A deputation of neighboring farmers had been invited to make a tour of inspection. They were shown all over the farm, and expressed great admiration for everything they saw, especially the windmill. The animals were weeding the turnip field. They worked diligently hardly raising their faces from the ground, and not knowing whether to be more frightened of the pigs or of the human visitors.

That evening loud laughter and bursts of singing came from the farmhouse. And suddenly, at the sound of the mingled voices, the animals were stricken with curiosity. What could be happening in there, now that for the first time animals and human beings were meeting on terms of equality? With one accord they began to creep as quietly as possible into the farmhouse garden.

At the gate they paused, half frightened to go on but Clover led the way in. They tiptoed up to the house, and such animals as were tall enough peered in at the dining-room window. There, round the long table, sat half a dozen farmers and half a dozen of the more eminent pigs, Napoleon himself occupying the seat of honor at the head of the table. The pigs appeared completely at ease in their chairs The company had been enjoying a game of cards but had broken off for the moment, evidently in order to drink a toast. A large jug was circulating, and the mugs were being refilled with beer. No one noticed the wondering faces of the animals that gazed in at the window.

Mr. Pilkington, of Foxwood, had stood up, his mug in his hand. In a moment, he said, he would ask the present company to drink a toast. But before doing so, there were a few words that he felt it incumbent upon him to say.

It was a source of great satisfaction to him, he said — and, he was sure, to all others present — to feel that a long period of mistrust and misunderstanding had now come to an end. There had been a time — not that he, or any of the present company, had shared such sentiments — but there had been a time when the respected proprietors of Animal Farm had been regarded, he would not say with hostility, but perhaps with a certain measure of misgiving, by their human neighbors. Unfortunate incidents had occurred, mistaken ideas had been current. It had been felt that the existence of a farm owned and operated by pigs was somehow abnormal and was liable to have an unsettling effect in the neighborhood. Too many farmers had assumed, without due enquiry, that on such a farm a spirit of license and indiscipline would prevail. They had been nervous about the effects upon their own animals, or even upon their human employees. But all such doubts were now dispelled. Today he and his friends had visited Animal Farm and inspected every inch of it with their own eyes, and what did they find? Not only the most up-to-date methods, but a discipline and an orderliness which should be an example to all farmers everywhere. He believed that he was right in saying that the lower animals on Animal Farm did more work and received less food than any animals in the county. Indeed, he and his fellow-visitors today had observed many features which they intended to introduce on their own farms immediately.

He would end his remarks, he said, by emphasizing once again the friendly feelings that subsisted, and ought to subsist, between Animal Farm and its neighbors. Between pigs and human beings there was not, and there need not be, any clash of interests whatever. Their struggles and their difficulties were one. Was not the labor problem the same everywhere? Here it became apparent that Mr. Pilkington was about to spring some carefully prepared witticism on the company, but for a moment he was too overcome by amusement to be able to utter it. After much choking, during which his various chins turned purple, he managed to get it out: "If you have your lower animals to contend with," he said, "we have our lower classes!" This bon mot set the table in a roar; and Mr. Pilkington once again congratulated the pigs on the low rations, the long working hours, and the general absence of pampering which he had observed on Animal Farm.

And now, he said finally, he would ask the company to rise to their feet and make certain that their glasses were full. "Gentlemen", concluded Mr. Pilkington, "gentlemen, I give you a toast: To the prosperity of Animal Farm!"

There was enthusiastic cheering and stamping of feet. Napoleon was so gratified that he left his place and came round the table to clink his mug against Mr. Pilkington's before emptying it. When the cheering had died down, Napoleon, who had remained on his feet, intimated that he too had a few words to say.

Like all of Napoleon's speeches, it was short and to the point. He too, he said, was happy that the period of misunderstanding was at an end. For a long time there had been rumors — circulated, he had reason to think, by some malignant enemy — that there was something subversive and even revolutionary in the outlook of himself and his colleagues. They had been credited with attempting to stir up rebellion among the animals on neighboring farms. Nothing could be further from the truth! Their sole wish, now and in the past, was to live at peace and in normal business relations with their neighbors. This farm which he had the honor to control, he added, was a co-operative enterprise. The title-deeds, which were in his own possession, were owned by the pigs jointly.

He did not believe, he said, that any of the old suspicions still lingered, but certain changes had been made recently in the routine of the farm which should have the effect of promoting confidence stiff further. Hitherto the animals on the farm had had a rather foolish custom of addressing one another as "Comrade". This was to be suppressed. There had also been a very strange custom, whose origin was unknown, of marching every Sunday morning past a boar's skull which was nailed to a post in the garden. This, too, would be suppressed, and the skull had already been buried. His visitors might have observed, too, the green flag which flew from the masthead. If so, they would perhaps have noted that the white hoof and horn with which it had previously been marked had now been removed. It would be a plain green flag from now onwards.

An Introduction to the Film *Nineteen Eighty-Four/1984*

Brief Introduction

Release year	1984
Directed by	Michael Radford

Produced by	Simon Perry
Production company	Virgin Films
	Umbrella-Rosenblum Films
Distributed by	20th Century Fox
Country	United Kingdom
Starring	John Hurt as Winston Smith
	Richard Burton as O'Brien
	Suzanna Hamilton as Julia

Award	Category	Recipients
Evening Standard British Film Awards	The Best British Film of the Year	*Nineteen Eighty-Four*
Istanbul International Film Festival	The Golden Tulip Award	*Nineteen Eighty-Four*

Plot

In a dystopian 1984, Winston Smith endures a miserable existence in the totalitarian superstate of Oceania under the constant surveillance of the Thought Police. The story takes place in London, the capital city of the territory of Airstrip One (formerly "either England or Britain").

Winston works in a small office cubicle at the Ministry of Truth, rewriting history in accordance with the commands of the Party and its supreme figurehead, Big Brother. A man haunted by painful memories and restless desires, Winston is an everyman who keeps a secret diary of his private thoughts, thus creating evidence of his thoughtcrime.

His life takes a major turn when he is approached by a fellow Outer Party worker — a mysterious, bold-looking girl named Julia and they begin an affair. Their first meeting takes place in the remote countryside where they exchange revolutionary ideas before having sex. Shortly after, Winston rents a room above a pawn shop (in the supposedly safe proletarian area) where they continue their liaison. Julia—a sensual, free-spirited young woman—buys smuggled food and clothing on the black market, and for a brief few months they secretly meet and enjoy an idyllic life of relative freedom and contentment together.

It comes to an end one evening, with the sudden attack of the Thought Police. They are both arrested and it's revealed that there is a telescreen hidden behind a picture on the wall in their room, and that the charmingly old-fashioned and seemingly sensitive boss of the pawn shop, Mr. Charrington, is a secret agent of the Thought Police. Winston and Julia are taken away to the Ministry of Love to be detained, questioned and "rehabilitated" separately. There O'Brien, a high-ranking member of the Inner Party whom Winston had previously believed to be a fellow thought criminal and agent of the resistance movement led by the chief enemy of the Party, Emmanuel Goldstein, systematically tortures him.

O'Brien instructs Winston about the state's true purpose and schools him in a kind of catechism on the principles of doublethink — the practice of holding two contradictory thoughts in the mind simultaneously. For his final rehabilitation, Winston is brought to Room 101, where

O'Brien tells him, he will be subjected to the "worst thing in the world", designed specifically around Smith's personal phobias. When confronted with this unbearable horror which turns out to be a cage filled with wild rats Winston's psychological resistance finally breaks down, and he hysterically denies his devotion to Julia. Now completely subdued and removed of any rebellious thoughts, impulses, or personal attachments, Winston is restored to physical health and released.

In the final scene, Winston returns to the Chestnut Tree Café, where he has previously seen the rehabilitated thought criminals Jones, Aaronson and Rutherford (themselves once influential but later disgraced members of the Inner Party) who have since been "vaporized" and rendered unpersons. While sitting at the chess table, Winston is approached by Julia, who is similarly "rehabilitated". They share a bottle of Victory Gin and impassively exchange a few words about how they have betrayed each other. They act indifferently towards each other. After she leaves, Winston watches a broadcast of himself on the large telescreen confessing his "crimes" against the state and begging for forgiveness from the public.

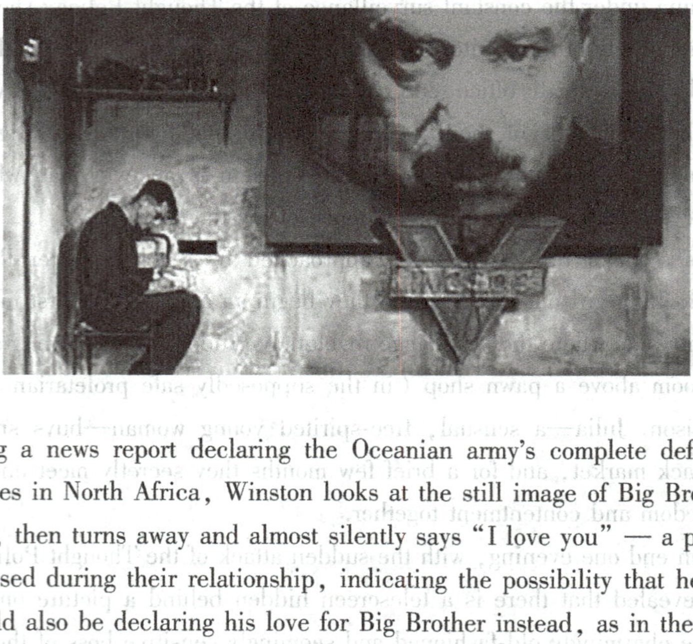

Upon hearing a news report declaring the Oceanian army's complete defeat of the enemy (Eurasian)'s forces in North Africa, Winston looks at the still image of Big Brother that appears on the telescreen, then turns away and almost silently says "I love you" — a phrase that he and Julia repeatedly used during their relationship, indicating the possibility that he still loves Julia. However, he could also be declaring his love for Big Brother instead, as in the book.

Excerpt from the Book *1984*

Part 1, Chapter 1

It was a bright cold day in April, and the clocks were striking thirteen. Winston Smith, his chin nuzzled into his breast in an effort to escape the vile wind, slipped quickly through the glass doors of Victory Mansions, though not quickly enough to prevent a swirl of gritty dust from entering along with him.

The hallway smelt of boiled cabbage and old rag mats. At one end of it a colored poster, too large for indoor display, had been tacked to the wall. It depicted simply an enormous face, more than a metre wide: the face of a man of about forty-five, with a heavy black moustache and ruggedly handsome features. Winston made for the stairs. It was no use trying the lift. Even at the best of times it was seldom working, and at present the electric current was cut off during daylight hours. It was part of the economy drive in preparation for Hate Week. The flat was seven flights up, and Winston, who was thirty-nine and had a varicose ulcer above his right ankle, went slowly, resting several times on the way. On each landing, opposite the lift-shaft, the poster with the enormous face gazed from the wall. It was one of those pictures which are so contrived that the eyes follow you about when you move. BIG BROTHER IS WATCHING YOU, the caption beneath it ran.

Inside the flat a fruity voice was reading out a list of figures which had something to do with the production of pig-iron. The voice came from an oblong metal plaque like a dulled mirror which formed part of the surface of the right-hand wall. Winston turned a switch and the voice sank somewhat, though the words were still distinguishable. The instrument (the telescreen, it was called) could be dimmed, but there was no way of shutting it off completely. He moved over to the window: a smallish, frail figure, the meagreness of his body merely emphasized by the blue overalls which were the uniform of the party. His hair was very fair, his face naturally sanguine, his skin roughened by coarse soap and blunt razor blades and the cold of the winter that had just ended.

Outside, even through the shut window-pane, the world looked cold. Down in the street little eddies of wind were whirling dust and torn paper into spirals, and though the sun was shining and the sky a harsh blue, there seemed to be no colour in anything, except the posters that were plastered everywhere. The blackmoustachio'd face gazed down from every commanding corner. There was one on the house-front immediately opposite. BIG BROTHER IS WATCHING YOU, the caption said, while the dark eyes looked deep into Winston's own. Down at streetlevel another poster, torn at one corner, flapped fitfully in the wind, alternately covering and uncovering the single word INGSOC. In the far distance a helicopter skimmed down between the roofs, hovered for an instant like a bluebottle, and darted away again with a curving flight. It was the police patrol, snooping into people's windows. The patrols did not matter, however. Only the Thought Police mattered.

Behind Winston's back the voice from the telescreen was still babbling away about pig-iron and the overfulfilment of the Ninth Three-Year Plan. The telescreen received and transmitted simultaneously. Any sound that Winston made, above the level of a very low whisper, would be picked up by it, moreover, so long as he remained within the field of vision which the metal plaque commanded, he could be seen as well as heard. There was of course no way of knowing whether you were being watched at any given moment. How often, or on what system, the Thought Police plugged in on any individual wire was guesswork. It was even conceivable that they watched everybody all the time. But at any rate they could plug in your wire whenever they wanted to. You had to live — did live, from habit that became instinct — in the assumption that every sound you made was overheard, and, except in darkness, every movement scrutinized.

Winston kept his back turned to the telescreen. It was safer, though, as he well knew, even a back can be revealing. A kilometre away the Ministry of Truth, his place of work, towered vast and white above the grimy landscape. This, he thought with a sort of vague distaste — this was London, chief city of Airstrip One, itself the third most populous of the provinces of Oceania. He tried to squeeze out some childhood memory that should tell him whether London had always been quite like this. Were there always these vistas of rotting nineteenth-century houses, their sides shored up with baulks of timber, their windows patched with cardboard and their roofs with corrugated iron, their crazy garden walls sagging in all directions? And the bombed sites where the plaster dust swirled in the air and the willow-herb straggled over the heaps of rubble; and the places where the bombs had cleared a larger patch and there had sprung up sordid colonies of wooden dwellings like chicken-houses? But it was no use, he could not remember: nothing remained of his childhood except a series of bright-lit tableaux occurring against no background and mostly unintelligible.

The Ministry of Truth — Minitrue, in Newspeak — was startlingly different from any other object in sight. It was an enormous pyramidal structure of glittering white concrete, soaring up, terrace after terrace, 300 metres into the air. From where Winston stood it was just possible to read, picked out on its white face in elegant lettering, the three slogans of the Party:

WAR IS PEACE

FREEDOM IS SLAVERY

IGNORANCE IS STRENGTH

The Ministry of Truth contained, it was said, three thousand rooms above ground level, and corresponding ramifications below. Scattered about London there were just three other buildings of similar appearance and size. So completely did they dwarf the surrounding architecture that from the roof of Victory Mansions you could see all four of them simultaneously. They were the homes of the four Ministries between which the entire apparatus of government was divided. The Ministry of Truth, which concerned itself with news, entertainment, education, and the fine arts. The Ministry of Peace, which concerned itself with war. The Ministry of Love, which maintained law and order. And the Ministry of Plenty, which was responsible for economic affairs. Their names, in Newspeak: Minitrue, Minipax, Miniluv, and Miniplenty.

The Ministry of Love was the really frightening one. There were no windows in it at all. Winston had never been inside the Ministry of Love, nor within half a kilometre of it. It was a place impossible to enter except on official business, and then only by penetrating through a maze of barbed-wire entanglements, steel doors, and hidden machine-gun nests. Even the streets leading up to its outer barriers were roamed by gorilla-faced guards in black uniforms, armed with jointed truncheons.

◎ Exercises

1. Match the following films with their relevant information.

1) *Pride and Prejudice*
2) *Jane Eyre*
3) *Wuthering Heights*
4) *Oliver Twist*
5) *Robinson Crusoe*
6) *Tess*
7) *Treasure Island*
8) *Animal Farm*
9) *Romeo and Juliet*
10) *Gulliver's Travels*

a. It was released in 1939 and tells the story of unfortunate lovers Heathcliff and Cathy who, despite a deep affection for one another, are forced by circumstance and prejudice to live their apart.

b. The story took place in the Wessex County, England during the Victorian era and the protagonist is a young, pure, innocent peasant girl who becomes a victim of fate.

c. It was produced by Walt Disney Productions and tells the treasure seeking adventures of young Jim Hawkins and pirate captain Long John Silver.

d. It tells the story of farm animals successfully revolting against their human owner, only to slide into a more brutal tyranny among themselves.

e. It is an adventure film starring Pierce Brosnan as a Scottish castaway who spends twenty-eight years on a remote tropical desert island near Trinidad, encountering unimaginable hardships and befriending an escaped prisoner Friday, before ultimately being rescued.

f. It is a 2005 British-American romantic drama which depicts five sisters from an English family of landed gentry as they deal with issues of marriage, morality and misconceptions.

g. It is an animated feature film distributed by Paramount Pictures and tells the story of an explorer who helps a small kingdom which declared war after an argument over a wedding song.

h. It is a romantic drama based on William Shakespeare's tragedy of two lovers who take their lives for each other when their love is hindered by their feuding parents.

i. It is a 2005 drama film adaptation of the classic Dickens tale depicting the sordid lives of criminals and exposing the cruel treatment of the many orphans in London in the mid-19th century.

j. It is 2011 British romantic drama film featuring a poor but aspiring, small in body but huge in soul, obscure but self-respecting girl.

2. Discuss and answer the following questions.

1) Does the movie *A Midsummer Night's Dream* end the way you expected? How? Why?

2) What can you learn from the protagonist in the film *Robinson Crusoe*?

3) What kind of women is Elizabeth Bennet in the film *Pride and Prejudice*?

4) What social issues is the film *Oliver Twist* concerned about?

5) How do you comment on the protagonist in the film *Tess*?

6) How do you comment on Heathcliff, the protagonist in the film *Wuthering Heights*?

7) What themes does the film *Orlando* try to present?

8) Who is your favorite British author among those introduced in this unit? Why?

9) Which is your favorite film among those introduced in this unit? Why?

Unit 3
American Literature Overview

1. Colonial Period and Revolutionary Period

The settlement of North America 1607—the independence war 1783

1.1 Colonial Period (1620s-1776)

The colonial period covers almost the entire 17th century and a large portion of 18th century. The year 1620 saw the pilgrims settling in the tiny colony of Plymouth in Massachusetts which is now regarded as a symbol for puritan culture during colonial settlement and Puritanism was a major influence in that period. Though the settlement in Jamestown, Virginia had already existed 13 years earlier than this, the year 1620 is still regarded as the beginning of colonial period of America.

During the colonial period, the literature of America was mainly the works of immigrants, a kind of writing of discovery or an interesting mixture of travel accounts and religious writings. The earliest colonial travel accounts are records of the perils and frustrations that challenged the courage of America's first settlers. It was neither American nor really literature in terms of content and form. It was not American because it was the work mainly of immigrants from England. It was not literature as we know it the form of poetry, essays, fiction but rather an interesting mixture of travel accounts and religious writings. The earliest American literature can be called a kind of writing of discovery—first, a hopeful discovery of the potentialities of the New World, and later, a disillusioning discovery of the harsh reality. Puritans experienced grim struggle for survival that followed immediately after their arrival in America and later became more and more practical as they moved further and further westward. Literature of the New England settlements is mainly a literary expression of the Puritan idealism. It is based on the Biblical myth of the Garden of Eden. The pious and self-disciplined Puritans worked with courage and hope toward building a new

Garden of Eden in America. The Puritan belies helped shape the colonial life. The Puritan optimism has exerted enormous impact on American literature.

1. 1. 1 Genres of Colonial Period

American Literature, defined here as it traditionally has been to be the literature of the United States, or as written on land that would one day become the United States, has as its beginning date 1583, the year the earliest English writing explorers started to write about the new continent. Some date the end of the Colonial Period as early as 1763, the start of the French and Indian War, the results of which set in motion a chain of events that led the colonies to seek independence from Great Britain. Others set it as late as 1789, the year the U. S. Constitution went into effect. This text splits the difference by using 1776, the year the Declaration of Independence was signed, as the cutoff year for the period. This year is a guideline not a rigidly held cutoff.

The writing of the period varied greatly in terms of quality and subject, but less so in terms of genre. For the sake of classification, in fact, all of the literature of the period can be broken down into just ten genres:

1) Travel writing, most often written by the explorers themselves to describe the land, indigenous peoples, and log the exploration, starting with preparations for the journey, the voyage, arrival and explorations in the territory and interactions with natives, and the return to Great Britain, if one was made;

2) Historical writing; historians have written in every age since the Hebrews wrote the *Old Testament*; these consist of long essays or narratives and relate tell a non-fiction account of what transpired; usually written in the third person, and covering significant events of general interest;

3) Religious writing, usually written by clergy in the form of journals, sermons, or commentaries on the Bible and religious experiences;

4) Philosophy, a genre that ranges from pure metaphysical speculation, to early sociology, to transcendentalism; written in the form of long essays;

5) Natural science writings;

6) Newspaper, journalism, and political essay writing, covering most recent events to essays and pamphlets written to persuade others to the author's opinion;

7) Poetry;

8) Drama;

9) Humor;

10 Fiction in the form of short stories, or sketches, and novels.

Not all of these genres span the entire period, although a few do. Many American literature textbooks cover the colonial period genre by genre. The danger in doing this is time distortion. This period of literature spans almost 300 years, longer by far than all of the other periods of literature put together. The other problem with covering this period by genre is that many of its most famous writers wrote in more than one genre, so the same writer must be considered multiple times. A final disadvantage is the proximity of many of the genres to another genre. For example, how different can a work in philosophy be from a religious tract when a religious background is assumed by the author? Many political writers touch heavily on history, and vice versa. Given these considerations, it is more fruitful to cover this period diachronically while keeping possible genres in mind.

Aside from span of time, another consideration that makes this period unique from all the others is that the writers in this period had no idea they were writing anything that could be classified as American literature. These writers were mostly British, and all were heavily indebted to British literature writing conventions long since established in the motherland. No other period of American literature is as derivative of English literature as the colonial period.

1.1.2 Colonial Period's Relation to English Literature

The British claimed most of the Atlantic seaboard north of Florida as belonging to Britain soon after Columbus discovered land across the Atlantic Ocean. Henry VII sent John Cabot to chart out the "regions or provinces of the heathen and infidel, whatsoever they may be" as early as 1497. However, circumstances never arose for England to make good on her claims until late during Elizabeth's reign. When England finally did establish her first permanent settlement in 1607 in Jamestown, Virginia, and a few years later in Massachusetts, her primary motives were:

1) The monarchical desire to expand the empire;

2) The people's longing for land to cultivate;

3) Treasure and adventure;

4) A nation's desire to be rid of excess populations, such as debtors, prisoners, and unemployed youths;

5) Expand commerce through trade, and

6) Freedom of religious practice.

The literature produced in the part of America known as the United States did not begin as an independent literature. England bestowed on the earliest settlers the English language, books, and modes of thought. England had an established literature long before the first permanent settlement across the Atlantic was considered. Shakespeare, for example, had died only four years before the Pilgrims landed at Plymouth.

For nearly two hundred years after the first English settlements in America, the majority of the works read there were written by English authors. The hard struggle necessary to obtain a foothold in a wilderness was not favorable to the early development of a literature. Those who remained in England could not clear away the forest, till the soil, and contend with Indians, but they could write the books and send them across the ocean. The early settlers were for the most part content to allow English authors to do this. For these reasons it is unsurprising that early American literature does not match in quality that produced in England during the same period.

When Americans began to write in larger numbers, there was at first close adherence to English models. For a while it seemed as if American literature would be only a feeble imitation of these models. Beginning in the eighteenth century, that started to change and some colonial writing was considered to have merit in its own right. The literature of England gained something from America as well. As early as the nineteenth century, English critics, like John Addington Symonds, Robert Louis Stevenson, and Edward Dowden, have testified to the power of the democratic element in American literature and willingly admitted that without a study of Cooper, Poe, and Hawthorne no one could give an adequate account of the landmarks of achievement in fiction written in English. French critics too have always admired Poe. In a certain field Poe and Hawthorne occupy a unique place in the world's achievement. Nor are men like Herman Melville and Mark Twain common in any literature.

Some of the reasons why American literature developed along original lines and thus conveyed a message of its own to the world are to be found in the changed environment and the varying problems and ideals of American life. Even more important than the changed ways of earning a living and the difference in climate, animals, and scenery were the struggles leading to the Revolutionary War, the formation and guidance of the Republic, and the Civil War. All these combined to give individuality to American thought and literature.

1.1.3 Representative Writers and Their Works

➢ **Captain John Smith (1579-1631)**

American literature is widely considered to begin with Captain John Smith, the hero of the Jamestown colony, and its savior during the first two years, born in Willoughby, Lincolnshire, in 1579, twenty-four years before the death of Elizabeth and thirty-seven before the death of Shakespeare. Smith was a man of Elizabethan stamp: active, ingenious, imaginative, craving new experiences.

He soon became president of the Jamestown colony and labored strenuously for its preservation. The first product of his pen in America was *A True Relation of Virginia*, written in 1608, the year in which John Milton was born. The last work written by Smith in America is entitled: *A Map of Virginia, with a Description of the Country, the Commodities, People, Government, and Religion*.

1.2 Revolutionary Period

The 18th century in America is known as the Age of Reason and Enlightenment. Rationalism was the dominant spirit. The America in 18 century witnessed two great revolutions. One was American Revolution which led to the independence of the nation; the other was the Enlightenment Movement which brought Americans a new horizon beyond the limitation of the prevailing Puritanism.

During this period, writers focused on explaining and justifying the American Revolution. This period becomes known as Early Nationalism. Writers begin to ponder what it really means to be an American. After the War of 1812, which removed the last British troops from North America, there was an even greater focus on nationalism, patriotism, and American identity. Writers emphasized on reason as opposed to faith alone, on empirical science, philosophy, theology.

1.2.1 Genres of Revolutionary Period

The revolutionary period also contained political writings, including those by colonists Samuel Adams, Josiah Quincy, John Dickinson, and Joseph Galloway, the last being a loyalist to the crown. Two key figures were Benjamin Franklin and Thomas Paine. Franklin's *Poor Richard's Almanac* and *The Autobiography of Benjamin Franklin* are esteemed works with their wit and influence toward the formation of a budding American identity. Paine's pamphlet *Common Sense* and *The American Crisis* writings are seen as playing a key role in influencing the political tone of the time.

During the revolution itself, poems and songs such as *Yankee Doodle* and *Nathan Hale* were popular. Major satirists included John Trumbull and Francis Hopkinson. Philip Morin Freneau also wrote poems about the war's course.

During the 18th century, writing shifted focus from the Puritanical ideals of Winthrop and Bradford to the power of the human mind and rational thought. The belief that human and natural occurrences were messages from God no longer fit with the new human centered world. Many intellectuals believed that the human mind could comprehend the universe through the laws of physics as described by Isaac Newton. One of these was Cotton Mather. The first book published in North America that promoted Newton and natural theology was Mather's *The Christian Philosopher* (1721). The enormous scientific, economic, social, and philosophical changes of the 18th century, called the Enlightenment, impacted the authority of clergyman and scripture, making way for democratic principles. The increase in population helped account for the greater diversity of opinion in religious and political life as seen in the literature of this time. In 1670, the population of the colonies numbered approximately 111,000. Thirty years later it was more than 250,000. By 1760, it reached 1,600,000. The growth of communities and therefore social life led people to become more interested in the progress of individuals and their shared experience in the colonies. These new ideals are accounted for in the widespread popularity of Benjamin Franklin's *Autobiography*.

Even earlier than Franklin was Cadwallader Colden (1689-1776), whose book *The History of the Five Indian Nations*, published in 1727 was one of the first texts critical of the treatment of the Iroquois in upstate New York by the English. Colden also wrote a book on botany, which attracted the attention of Linnaeus, and he maintained a long term correspondence with Benjamin Franklin.

1. 2. 2 Representative Writers and Their Works

➤ **Thomas Jefferson (1743-1826)**

He was the third President of the United States, but a literary figure in his own right as well. He wrote much political prose and many letters, which have been gathered into ten large volumes. Ignoring these, he left directions that the words, "Author of the Declaration of American Independence," should immediately follow his name on his monument. No other American prose writer has, in an equal number of words, yet surpassed this *Declaration of Independence*. Its influence has encircled the world and modified the opinions of nations as widely separated as the French and the Japanese.

Jefferson may have borrowed some of his ideas from *Magna Charta* (1215) and the *Petition of Right* (1628); he may have incorporated in this *Declaration* the yearnings that thousands of human souls had already felt, but he voiced those yearnings so well that his utterances have become classic. It has been said that he "poured the soul of the continent" into that *Declaration*, but he did more than that. He poured into it the soul of all freedom-loving humanity, and he was accepted as the spokesman of the dweller on the Seine as enthusiastically as of the revolutionists in America. Those who have misconstrued the meaning of his famous expression, "All men are created equal" have been met with the adequate reply, "No intelligent man has ever misconstrued it except intentionally."

➤ **Alexander Hamilton (1757-1804)**

Because of his wonderful youthful precocity, he reminds us of Jonathan Edwards. A student of American constitutional history says of Hamilton's pamphlets: "They show great maturity, a more remarkable maturity than has ever been exhibited by any other person, at so early an age, in the same department of thought."

After the Americans were victorious in the war, Hamilton suggested that a constitutional convention be called. For seven years this suggestion was not followed, but in 1787 delegates met from various states and framed a federal constitution to be submitted to the states for ratification. Hamilton was one of the leading delegates. After the convention had completed its work, it seemed probable that the states would reject the proposed constitution. To win its acceptance, Hamilton, in collaboration with James Madison (1751-1836) and John Jay (1745-1829), wrote the famous Federalist papers. There were eighty-five of these, but Hamilton wrote more than both of his associates together. These papers have been collected into a volume, and to this day they form a standard commentary on Constitution. This work and Hamilton's eloquence before the New York convention for ratification helped to carry the day for the Constitution and to terminate a period of dissension which was tending toward anarchy.

2. Romanticism

Romantic Period is one of the most important periods in the history of American literature. When Americans were constructing their country, they also began to realize their differences from their European counterparts. They began to hope to see an entirely different literature model which expressed American cultures. Great writers of that period captured on their pages the enthusiasm and the optimism of that dream.

Romanticism refers to an artistic and intellectual movement originating in Europe in the late 18th century and characterized by a heightened interest in nature, emphasis on the individual's experience of emotion and imagination, departure from the attitudes and forms of classicism, and rebellion against established social rules and conventions. The romantic period of American literature stretches from the end of the 18th century to the outbreak of the Civil War. It was an age of westward expansion, of the increasing gravity of the slavery question, of an intensification of the spirit of embattled sectionalism in the South, and of a powerful impulse to reform in the North. In literature it was America's first great creative period, a full flowering of the romantic impulse on American soil.

2.1 Influence of European Romanticism on American Writers

The European Romantic movement reached America in the early 19th century. American Romanticism was just as multifaceted and individualistic as it was in Europe. Like the Europeans, the American Romantics demonstrated a high level of moral enthusiasm, commitment to individualism and the unfolding of the self, an emphasis on intuitive perception, and the assumption that the natural world was inherently good, while human society was filled with corruption.

Romanticism became popular in American politics, philosophy and art. The movement appealed to the revolutionary spirit of America as well as to those longing to break free of the strict religious traditions of early settlement. The Romantics rejected rationalism and religious intellect. It appealed to those in opposition of Calvinism, which includes the belief that the destiny of each individual is preordained. The Romantic movement gave rise to New England Transcendentalism, which portrayed a less restrictive relationship between God and Universe. The new philosophy presented the individual with a more personal relationship with God. Transcendentalism and Romanticism appealed to Americans in a similar fashion, for both privileged feeling over reason, individual freedom of expression over the restraints of tradition and custom. It often involved a rapturous response to nature. It encouraged the rejection of harsh, rigid Calvinism, and promised a new blossoming of American culture.

American Romanticism embraced the individual and rebelled against the confinement of neoclassicism and religious tradition. The Romantic movement in America created a new literary genre that continues to influence American writers. Novels, short stories, and poems replaced the sermons and manifestos of yore. Romantic literature was personal, intense, and portrayed more emotion than ever seen in neoclassical literature. America's preoccupation with freedom became a great source of motivation for Romantic writers as many were delighted in free expression and emotion without so much fear of ridicule and controversy. They also put more effort into the psychological development of their characters, and the main characters typically displayed extremes of sensitivity and excitement.

The works of the Romantic Era also differed from preceding works in that they spoke to a wider audience, partly reflecting the greater distribution of books as costs came down during the period.

2.2 The Unique Characteristics of American Romanticism

Although greatly influenced by their English counterparts, the American romantic writers revealed unique characteristics of their own in their works and they grew on the native lands. For example,

(1) The American national experience of "pioneering into the west" proved to be a rich source of material for American writers to draw upon. They celebrated America's landscape with its virgin forests, meadows, groves, endless prairies, streams, and vast oceans. The wilderness came to function almost as a dramatic character that symbolized moral law.

(2) The desire for an escape from society and a return to nature became a permanent convention of American literature. Such a desire is particularly evident in Cooper's *Leather Stocking Tales*, in Thoreau's *Walden* and, later, in Mark Twain's *Adventures of Huckleberry Finn.*

(3) With the growth of American national consciousness, American character types speaking local dialects appeared in poetry and fiction with increasing frequency.

(4) Then the American Puritanism as a cultural heritage exerted great influences over American moral values and American Romanticism. One of the manifestations is the fact that American romantic writers tended more to moralize than their English and European counterparts.

(5) Besides, a preoccupation with the Calvinistic view of original sin and the mystery of evil marked the works of Hawthorne, Melville and a host of lesser writers.

2.3 Representative Writers and Their Works

➢ Washington Irving (1783-1859)

Washington Irving was the first American storyteller to be internationally recognized as a man of letters and the first great prose stylist of American romanticism, and his familiar style was destined to provide a model for the prevailing prose narrative of the future. His first book *A History of New York from the Beginning of the World to the End of the Dutch Dynasty* (1809), written under the name of Diedrich Knickerbocker, was a great success and won him wide popularity.

He is best-known for his *The Sketch Book of Geoffrey Crayon, Gent* (1819-1820), especially in which two short stories *Rip Van Winkle* and *The Legend of Sleepy Hollow* have become American classics. Later he wrote works of history and biographies, such as *The History of Life and Voyages of Christobra Columbus* (*1828*), *A Chronicle of the Conquest of Granada* and *The Alhambra* (*1832*). After that, he spent the rest of his life living a life of leisure and comfort, and writing. *The Life of Goldsmith* (*1840*) and a five-volume *Life of Washington* (*1855-1859*).

➢ James Fenimore Cooper (1789-1851)

James Fenimore Cooper is respectfully remembered as a master of adventurous narrative and as the creator of an American hero-myth. According to a charming legend, Cooper's first novel *Precaution* (*1820*) was a response to his wife's challenge to improve on the current British society fiction, and the failure of this work turned him to historical novels. Later, *The Spy*, a tale he wrote, became a great success in America and Europe. In 1823, Cooper published *The Pioneers* (1823), which together with other 4 novels *The Deer Slayer* (1841), *The Last of the Mohicans* (1826), *The Pathfinder* (1840) and *The Prairie* (1827) became his well-known Leather-stocking Tales. Cooper went on to write over thirty novels, including exciting adventures of the sea like *The Pilot*. Cooper created the American historical novel using authentic American subject.

In general, American Romanticism was a kind of imitation as well as innovation because it appeared under the Western Europe Romanticism and finally it created a unique style of fiction and poetry. American Romanticism embraced the individual and rebelled against the confinement of neoclassicism and religious tradition. American Romanticism created a new literary genre that continued to influence American writers.

➢ Romantic Poet: Walt Whitman

Whitman is a giant of American letters. His *Leaves of Grass* has always been considered a monumental work which commands great attention because of its uniquely poetic embodiment of American democratic ideals. He is the poet of the common people and the prophet and singer of democracy.

Contrary to the rhetoric of traditional poetry, Whitman's is relatively simple and even rather crude. Most of the pictures he painted with words are honest, undistorted images of different aspects of America of the day. The particularity about these images is that they are unconventional in the way they break down the social division based on religion, gender, class, and race. One of the most often-used methods in Whitman's poems is to make colors and images fleet past the mind's eye of the reader. Another characteristic in Whitman's language is his strong tendency to use oral English. Whitman's vocabulary is amazing. He would use powerful, colorful, as well as rarely-used words, words of foreign origin and sometimes even wrong words. Walt Whitman has proved a great figure in the literary history of the United States because he embodies a new ideal, a new world and a new life-style, and his influence over the following generations is significant and incredible.

➤ **Romantic Poet: Emily Dickinson**

Emily Dickinson was one of the rare greatest and profound poets in the world. She was claimed as the founder of Imagism after death. Having nothing in common with the leading writers of the time, Dickinson seems to be wholly original, taking the stuff of her poetry merely form here personal experiences in order to express what she felt about love, nature, friendship, death, and immorality, and developing her own poetic form with many peculiar features. In addition to such characteristics as the abundant use of dashes, and irregular and often idiosyncratic punctuations and capitalization, her mode of expression is characterized by clear-cut and delicately original imagery, precise diction, and fragmentary and enigmatic metrical pattern. Despite its ostensible formal irregularity and simplicity, Dickinson's poetry is remarkable for its uncommon variety, original subtlety, and unusual richness. Dickinson's profound inspiration and emotion were expressed in here remarkably poetic indirection. Her poetry exerted a great impact upon the so-called "new poetry" of the early twentieth century.

3. Realism (1860s-1890s)

Broadly defined as "the faithful representation of reality" or "verisimilitude", realism is a literary technique practiced by many schools of writing. Although strictly speaking, realism is a technique, it also denotes a particular kind of subject matter, especially the representation of middle-class life. A reaction against romanticism, an interest in scientific method, the systematizing of the study of documentary history, and the influence of rational philosophy all affected the rise of realism. According to William Harmon and Hugh Holman, "Where romanticists transcend the immediate to find the ideal, and naturalists plumb the actual or superficial to find the scientific laws that control its actions, realists center their attention to a remarkable degree on the immediate, the here and now, the specific action, and the verifiable consequence".

3.1 Realism in American Literature

Many critics have suggested that there is no clear distinction between realism and its related late nineteenth-century movement, naturalism. As Donald Pizer notes in his introduction to *The Cambridge Companion to American Realism and Naturalism: Howells to London*, the term "realism" is difficult to define, in part because it is used differently in European contexts than in American literature. Pizer suggests that "whatever was being produced in fiction during the 1870s and 1880s that was new, interesting, and roughly similar in a number of ways can be designated as realism, and that an equally new, interesting, and roughly similar body of writing produced at the turn of the century can be designated as naturalism". Put rather too simplistically, one rough distinction made by critics is that realism espousing a deterministic philosophy and focusing on the lower classes is considered naturalism.

In American literature, the term "realism" encompasses the period of time from the Civil War to the turn of the century during which William Dean Howells, Rebecca Harding Davis, Henry James, Mark Twain, and others wrote fiction devoted to accurate representation and an exploration of American lives in various contexts. As the United States grew rapidly after the Civil War, the increasing rates of democracy and literacy, the rapid growth in industrialism and urbanization, an expanding population base due to immigration, and a relative rise in middle-class affluence provided a fertile literary environment for readers interested in understanding these rapid shifts in culture. In drawing attention to this connection, Amy Kaplan has called realism a "strategy for imagining and managing the threats of social change".

Realism was a movement that encompassed the entire country, or at least the Midwest and South, although many of the writers and critics associated with realism (notably W. D. Howells) were based in New England. Among the Midwestern writers considered realists would be Joseph Kirkland, E. W. Howe, and Hamlin Garland; the Southern writer John W. DeForest's *Miss Ravenal's Conversion from Secession to Loyalty* is often considered a realist novel, too.

3.2 Representative Writers and Their Works

In America, Samuel Clemens was the early pioneer of Realism. Writing under the pen name Mark Twain, he was noteworthy for his faithful reproduction of vernacular speech patterns and vocabulary. He more or less gave birth to "local color", a sub-genre of the novel that still enjoys wide appeal today. Replicating natural speech required not just great listening skills, but a sense of how the written version sounds to the imagination. In addition to the use of vernacular, Twain was an innovator in focusing on middle and lower class characters. Previously, novels had concentrated on the experiences of the elite. Presumably, the upper crust enjoyed seeing their lives of privilege reflected back to them in art, while salt of the earth readers had something to aspire to and fantasize about. It was a revolutionary concept to incorporate unremarkable characters into an art form as serious as the novel. In a development that continues to bewilder, *The Adventures of Huckleberry Finn* is one of the most frequently banned books in the public school system. One imagines that certain language is indeed offensive; however Twain was doing nothing other than representing honest speech. Huck Finn was in all reality an astonishing leap forward in racial awareness — Jim, the freed slave, is as fully realized a character as Tom or Huck.

A great friend of Mark Twain, and an eminent American realist in his own right, was the magazine editor William Dean Howells. In charge of the *Atlantic Monthly* for several years, Howells exercised a lot of authority over the currents of taste on his side of the ocean. In his role as editor, he was instrumental in promoting the fame of literary rising stars, such as Frank Norris,

Stephen Crane, and Sarah Orne Jewett. Howells wrote copious volumes of fiction of his own, and was an unqualified success in that regard. For a time, he was widely considered the most accomplished of all American Realists. That reputation faded somewhat and today Howells's work as an editor is held up as his most important contribution. That being said, several of his novels are in the first rank of American Realism. Published in 1885, the ironically titled *The Rise of Silas Lapham* tells the story of an ambitious businessman who tumbles out of fortune through his own mistakes and poor judgment. It is an anti-success story, and illustrates one of the central ideas of Realism, that of crafting honest narratives rather than feel-good sentimental fantasies. In short, there is a kind of grimness to Realism that many readers have found unappealing. *A Modern Instance* highlights this same principle in detailing the steady disintegration of a seemingly happy marriage.

Without a doubt, American expatriate Henry James represents the most skilled and accomplished practitioner of Realism in fiction. He was fascinated by encounters between representatives of the New World, America, with members of the Old World, or Europe. He observed a distinct set of traits that permeated each of these groups. With Americans, he witnessed vigor, innocence, and strict moral righteousness. Europeans, on the other hand, represented decadence, lax morality, and deviousness. With such seeming prejudices built into his aesthetics, one is surprised to learn that James renounced his American citizenship and became a British subject. Nevertheless, James made a cottage industry out of examining what happened when these two worlds collided. Arguably his most famous work was the novella *Daisy Miller*, which relates how a young and rich American girl touring Europe is victimized by sophisticated schemers, with no compunctions about right or wrong.

At the height of his powers, Henry James crafted intricate novels that featured completely realized characters. He was remarkable for his ability to dispense with commentary or subjectivity within his narratives. The reader sees the events through the eyes of the characters; James the author makes himself as invisible as possible. In terms of prose style, he was admired for the simplicity and directness of his language, a quality not generally noted during the Victorian Period. His most successful novel was *The Portrait of a Lady*, published as one volume in 1881. With *Portrait* he expands upon many of the themes one finds in *Daisy Miller* — greed, power, and the exploitation of the New World by the Old. Revealingly, film adaptations of the novel have generally not made good impressions. As with the bulk of fiction that earns the title of Realist, the narrative simply does not lend itself to visual reproduction.

Realism came under attack largely because it represented such a bold departure from what readers had come to expect from the novel. The fascination with things falling apart was unpleasant to many, and critics sometimes accused the practitioners of Realism of focusing only on the negative aspects of life. Additionally, the intense focus on the minutiae of character was seen as unwillingness to actually tell a story. Readers complained that very little happened in realistic fiction, that they were all talk and little payoff. Henry James in particular was criticized for his verbosity, especially in his later years. By the end of the nineteenth century, Realism in the pure sense had given way to another form called Naturalism. With Naturalism, authors looked to heredity and history to define character. Ironically, many of the qualities that people found distasteful in realism — the obsession with character, the superficially mundane plots — were all intensified in Naturalism.

4. Modernism in American Literature (1914-1915)

Modernism was a set of cultural movements in all creative arts: painting, novel, poem and play, originally arising as the whole world was being reshaped by a series of profound changes occurred in almost every field of Western society and later spreading through the whole Europe and America in the late 19th century and early 20th century.

As the world underwent great revolutions of economy, politics and ideology, people realized the traditional idea, value and authority were outdated and they tried to find a new way to react to the profound changes of modern society. In this period, modernist literature came into being in response to the stimulation of modernity, which marked by a strong and conscious break with traditional forms and techniques of expression, innovative writing techniques, new ideas and a wider range of themes.

Influenced by social upheaval, economic and political transformation and European modernism, America also saw the rise of its own modernism from 1914 to 1945. American modernism is a trend of thought that either affirms the power of human beings to create, improve, and reshape their environment with the aid of scientific knowledge, technology and practical experimentation, or fears for the possible catastrophe brought by transformations of the society. Both are in its essence progressive. With a greater number of great writers producing a voluminous amount of distinguished literary works, this period is also termed the second renaissance in the history of American literature. American Modernism covered a wide variety of topics including race relations, gender roles, and sexuality. It began with the rebellion of naturalists before 1917, thrived along with the rise of the Lost Generation in the 1920, attained the zenith of prosperity in the 1930s, and ended with the second world war.

4.1 Background of Modernism

Having undergone the second industrial revolution and world war one, America gradually progressed to modernity and went on the stage of the world as a great power. With economy and science and technology speedily developed, various new machines of transportation and communication invented, America enjoyed an unbalanced prosperity in 1920s, which was known as the roaring twentieth or the jazz age. The world war one had destroyed many young people's heroic dreams and left them only with a disillusioned life. In this period, the Lost Generation emerged with Ernest Hemingway as its representative. Meanwhile, prohibition was issued, which also led to more organized crime and the gangster phenomenon. However, in 1930s, economic crisis erupted and America suffered from the great depression, to deal with which president Roosevelt went onto stage with his policy named new deal. During the depression, people who suffered from unemployment and hunger naturally sought comfort from the communism. Thus communism was prevailed through working class and left wing activities. The economic crisis left a mark on the literary creations of the period and 1930s was regarded as red decade in history of American literature. In 1941, America declared war after the Pearl Harbor Event. The war removed a large portion of the young male population, which greatly influenced economic and social life of America.

Influenced by irrational philosophy and Freudianism, modernism in literature mainly revolves on several ideas.

1) It is believed that the world is created in the act of perceiving it; that is, the world is what we say it is.

2) Modernists feel no connection with history or institutions. Their experience is that of alienation, loss, and despair.

3) Since the psychologies of Freud and Jung are influential in modernist literature, Modernists more and more concern themselves with the sub-conscious and try to explore the sub-conscious world of human being.

4) It doesn't subscribe to absolute truth. All things are relative.

5) It believes life is unordered.

6) Modernist tried stylistic innovations and experiments with language, form, symbol and myth.

New trends of literature also emerged: symbolism, expressionism, surrealism, futurism, dadaism, imagism and streams of consciousness.

4.2 Modernism in Literature

Modernism has a great influence in American literature. In response to changes of society, each field of American literature was swept by the wind of modernism.

4.2.1 Lost Generation Literature

Lost Generation literature is an important part of American modernist literature, which had an positive effect on American modernism and was regarded as the second prosperity in American literature.

Having experienced the World War I, American young people returned to their country with physical or mental wounds and a disillusion of heroism. With a rejection against mainstream values of materialism prevailed in American society, some intellectuals, poets, artists and writers fled to

Paris or London where they may enjoy freedom and a diversity of cultures there. The generation was "lost" in the sense that their inherited values were no longer relevant in the postwar world and they are thus spiritually alienated from a country that seemed to be hopelessly provincial, materialistic, and emotionally barren. Although they were unhappy with American culture, the writers were instrumental in changing their country's style of writing from Victorian to modern. In aspect of artistic style, they were influenced by French modernism, while their ideas were affected by existentialism. Having inherited American exploring spirit, they chose new themes and tried to innovate and experiment a diversity of new writing skills and styles.

Several literary figures are involved in lost generation: F. Scott Fitzgerald, Ernest Hemingway, John Dos Passos, Ezra Pound, Sherwood Anderson, Waldo Peirce, Erich Maria Remarque and Cole Porter.

4. 2. 2 Modernism in American Poetry

In this period, poetry rejected traditional poetic form, meter and Victorian diction and steered American poetry toward greater density, difficulty, and obscurity, with an emphasis on techniques such as fragmentation, ellipsis, allusion, juxtaposition, ironic and shifting personae, and mythic parallelism. However, they are innovative in different ways, which leads to two divergent ranges of modern poetic styles. One is represented by Pound, William Carlos Williams and H. D; the other is led by Eliot, followed by Ramson and Allen Tate. The conflict of those two poetic lines threads through the whole development of modern American poetry.

As for the form of the poetry, some modern American poets were highly experimental and radical, of whom Marianne Moor(1887-1972) and E. E. Cummings are two representatives.

4. 2. 3 Modernism in American Drama

Modern American drama refers to a period (1910-1945) during which American playwrights sought to overrun 19th century formal constraints, Victorian melodramas, and outdated styles of performance. In place of the bland moral certainty that characterized the 19th century drama, American dramatists of the modern era examined human relationships with ruthless candor, portraying moral ambivalence that challenged the status quo. Invigorated by August Strindberg's theatre of psychological nuance and dream-like symbolism, O'Geill, as well as other playwrights, gorged a new kind of drama.

4. 3 Representative Writers and Their Works

➢ F. Scott Fitzgerald

F. Scott Fitzgerald was one of the greatest American writers of the 20th century and also one of the most well-known authors of the Jazz Age. Many of his fictions are half autobiographical which based on his own wild, tragic life experiences and struggles. In his works, Fitzgerald exposed what he saw as the flaws of the "American Dream" and how it led to self-indulgence, greed, and ultimately disillusionment and self-destruction. His writing style is a combination of impressionism and symbolic narrative. (See details in Unit 4)

➢ **Ernest Hemingway**

Ernest Hemingway was both an author and journalist. His distinctive writing style, characterized by economy and understatement, influenced 20th-century fiction, as did his life of adventure and public image. Through his works, he created the Hemingway hero. The Hemingway hero is a man whose concepts are shaped by his view of death. He will not talk about his concepts and tend to expressed them through his own actions. He is a man of intense loyalty to a small group because he can't accept abstract things. His great works include *The Sun Also Rises*, *A Fare Well to Arms*, *For Whom the Bell Tolls*, *Old Man and Sea*. (See details in Unit 4)

➢ **John Dos Passos**

John Dos Passos is one of the major novelists of the Lost Generation, a social historian and a radical critic of the quality of American life.

His major work is the USA trilogy including *The 42nd Parallel* (1930), *1919* (1932), and *The Big Money* (1936). In these novels Dos Passos painted a vast landscape of American culture during the first decades of the twentieth century. Dos Passos's political and social reflections in the novel are deeply pessimistic of the United States, and few of the characters manage to hold onto their ideals through the First World War.

He developed kaleidoscopic technique which was employed in trilogy USA. By skillfully weaving together narration, stream of consciousness, biographies of representative figures, and quotations from newspapers and magazines, Dos Passos portrayed the first three decades of the 20th century in America. Such experimental writing technique influence many writers.

➢ **William Faulkner**

Faulkner is considered one of the most important writers of American Southern literature and made a great contribution to American modernist literature. In his fictional writings, Faulkner made an epic portrayal of the tragic conflict between the old south and the new south set in a fictional country—Yoknapatawpha which is based on his hometown. Many of his novels are based on this setting and through them he created his own southern world. In his novels, he discussed various topics. Such as the moral crisis which led to old south' destruction, conflict between races and the relationship between new south and its past.

➢ **Ezra Pound**

Ezra Pound was an American expatriate poet and critic, and a major figure in the early modernist movement in poetry. His early literary career was closely associated with imagism, a movement in poetry which against Victorian poetry stresses clarity, precision, concision and breaking with traditional rhyme and meter. He defines an image as that which presents an intellectual and emotional complex in an instant of time. He also laid down three imagist poetic principles. Later he evolved imagism to vorticism, in which he redefined image as Vortex. Vorticist images are "swirl, whirl, flutter, strike, fall, move, clash and leap, with a new emphasis on conflict and distortion". He not only modernized poetry, but also encouraged many other poets, especially Eliot, William Carlos Williams and so on.

➢ **T. S. Eliot**

Though Eliot was an English poet, he still greatly influenced the development of American modernist poetry. T. S. Eliot was an American-born English poet, playwright, and literary critic, perhaps the most important English-language poet of the 20th century. As a daring innovator and never compromising either with the public or with language itself, he has followed his belief that poetry should represents the complexities of modern civilization in language and that such representation necessarily leads to difficult poetry. He believed that poet should become more and more comprehensive, more allusive, more indirect, in order to force language into its meaning. Against 20th century romantic poet, he expressed that the poetry should be irrelative to the poet himself and the world in which the poet lives. Using the term "objective correlative", he expressed that "The only way of expressing emotion in the form of art is by finding an "objective correlative"; his great work was *The Waste Land*.

➢ **Eugene O'Neill**

Eugene O'Neill was considered as the most important playwright of American modern drama. Most of his plays involve some degree of tragedy and personal pessimism. In his plays, he represented the life of people in America during world wars: the fragmentation of family life, the alienation of the sensitive individual facing increasingly regimented and materialistic society, and the inability of human beings to sustain close relationships and live harmoniously with the communities. Against melodramas, he tried to make reformations and using drama as a medium to reflect human life, social problems and human history from physical, psychological and spiritual perspectives. As to the form of drama he was also very innovative. His plays are among the first to introduce into American drama the techniques of realism and to include speeches in American vernacular. Influence by European philosophy and psychology, he also adopted expressionism in a period of his literary career. Eugene O'Neill modernized American drama and lifted it to a world level. He also had great influence on dramatists of the later generation and the whole American culture.

5. The Contemporary American Literature (1945-)

Contemporary Literature in the United States is likewise dazzlingly diverse, exciting, and evolving. New voices have arisen from many quarters, challenging old ideas and adapting literary traditions to suit changing conditions of the national life.

5.1 American Poetry since 1945: the Anti-tradition

Poetry after the Second World War flourished in various forms for poetry itself is such a sensitive and flexible genre that it always has reverberations to the immediate social changes. Poets urged by upheavals of the post-war period participated actively all kinds of political or literary movement with their pens, to express their views, to utter their uneasiness about the uses of social power and industrial power, in poems. Theodore Roethke, Robert Lowell, Richard Wilbur, Richard Eberhart, Allen Ginsberg, Gary Snyder, Sylvia Plath, and Delmore Schwartz are among the most extraordinary. Most of the poets are grouped under such poetical schools as Black Mountain, the Beat Generation, New York Poets, Black Poets, Confessional Poets, and West Coast School. Experimentation is one aspect of all Modernist and Postmodernist poetry, but experimental poetry makes a special point of innovation. Experimental poetry can be intriguing and pleasing, but it is not poetry as commonly understood by the term, and has therefore to be judged on different grounds, most commonly those of the visual arts, which it increasingly resembles. Inspired by jazz and abstract expressionist painting, most of the experimental writers are a generation younger than Lowell. They have tended to be bohemian, counter-culture intellectuals who disassociated themselves from universities and outspokenly criticized "bourgeois" American society. Their poetry is daring, original, and sometimes shocking. In its search for new values, it claims affinity with the archaic world of myth, legend, and traditional societies such as those of the American Indian. The forms are looser, more spontaneous, organic; they arise from the subject matter and the feeling of the poet as the poem is written, and from the natural pauses of the spoken language.

Robert Lowell (1917-1977) is one of the most brilliant poets after the war. Throughout his life he loved peace and fought for it with all he might. His poetical style was always changing. In his poems he reflects the changing of his world outlook. The break form tradition gathered momentum during the 1957 obscenity trial of Allen Ginsberg's poem *Howl*. Allen Ginsberg is a name that associates itself with the Beat Generation, for this, Howl is considered masterpiece of the Beats. This best-known poem "*Howl* (1956) shows Ginsberg's anger at the society and the government. Like Lowell and Berryman, Ginsberg embodied the chaos of civilization in his own chaos.

5.2 Postmodern Literature

Postmodernism is literature characterized by reliance on narrative techniques such as fragmentation, paradox, and the unreliable narrator; and often is defined as a style or a trend which emerged in the post-World War II era. Postmodern works are seen as a response against dogmatic following of Enlightenment thinking and Modernist approaches to literature.

Postmodern literature, like postmodernism as a whole, tends to resist definition or classification as a "movement". Indeed, the convergence of postmodern literature with various modes of critical theory, particularly reader-response and deconstructionist approaches, and the subversions of the implicit contract between author, text and reader by which its works are often characterised, have led to pre-modern fictions such as *Cervantes' Don Quixote* (*1605*, *1615*).

While there is little consensus on the precise characteristics, scope, and importance of postmodern literature, as is often the case with artistic movements, postmodern literature is commonly defined in relation to a precursor. In particular, postmodern writers are seen as reacting against the precepts of modernism, and they often operate as literary "bricoleurs", parodying forms and styles associated with modernist (and other) writers and artists. Postmodern works also tend to celebrate chance over craft, and further employ meta-fiction to undermine the text's authority or authenticity. Another characteristic of postmodern literature is the questioning of distinctions between high and low culture through the use of pastiche, the combination of subjects and genres not previously deemed fit for literature.

5.3 Beat Generation

The Beat Generation is a literary movement started by a group of authors whose work explored and influenced American culture and politics in the post-World War II era. The bulk of their work was published and popularized throughout the 1950s. Central elements of Beat culture are rejection of standard narrative values, spiritual quest, exploration of American and Eastern religions, rejection of materialism, explicit portrayals of the human condition, experimentation with psychedelic drugs, and sexual liberation and exploration.

Allen Ginsberg's *Howl* (*1956*), William S. Burroughs's *Naked Lunch* (*1959*) and Jack Kerouac's *On the Road* (*1957*) are among the best known examples of Beat Literature. Both Howl and Naked Lunch were the focus of obscenity trials that ultimately helped to liberalize publishing in the United States. The members of the Beat Generation developed a reputation as new bohemian hedonists, who celebrated non-conformity and spontaneous creativity.

The core group of Beat Generation authors — Herbert Huncke, Allen Ginsberg, William S. Burroughs, Lucien Carr, and Jack Kerouac — met in 1944 in and around the Columbia University campus in New York City. Later, in the mid-1950s, the central figures (with the exception of Burroughs and Carr) ended up together in San Francisco where they met and became friends of figures associated with the San Francisco Renaissance.

In the 1960s, elements of the expanding Beat movement were incorporated into the hippie and larger counterculture movements. Neal Cassady, the driver for Ken Kesey's bus, further, was the primary bridge between these two generations. Allen Ginsberg's work also became an integral element of early 1960s hippie culture

5.4 Minority Literature

One of the key developments in late-20th-century American literature was the rise to prominence of literature written by and about ethnic minorities beyond African Americans and Jewish Americans, who had already established their literary inheritances. This development came alongside the growth of the Civil Rights movements and its corollary, the Ethnic Pride movement, which led to the creation of Ethnic Studies programs in most major universities. These programs helped establish the new ethnic literature as worthy objects of academic study, alongside such other new areas of literary study as women's literature, gay and lesbian literature, working-class literature, postcolonial literature, and the rise of literary theory as a key component of academic literary study.

5.5 Representative Writers and Their Works

➢ Irwin Allen Ginsberg

Irwin Allen Ginsberg was an American poet and one of the leading figures of the Beat Generation in the 1950s. He vigorously opposed militarism, economic materialism and sexual repression. Ginsberg is best-known for his epic poem "*Howl*", in which he celebrated his fellow "angel-headed hipsters" and harshly denounced what he saw as the destructive forces of capitalism and conformity in the United States. It is one of the classic poems of the Beat Generation.

➢ Jerome David "J. D." Salinger

Jerome David "J. D." Salinger was an American writer. His last published original work was in 1965, and his last interview in 1980. In 1951 his novel *The Catcher in the Rye* was an immediate popular success. His depiction of adolescent alienation and loss of innocence in the protagonist Holden Caulfield was influential, especially among adolescent readers.

➢ Navarre Scott Momaday

Navarre Scott Momaday is a Native American author of Kiowa descent. His work *House Made of Dawn* was awarded the Pulitzer Prize for Fiction in 1969. Momaday is considered the founding author in what critic Kenneth Lincoln has coined the Native American Renaissance. *House Made of Dawn* is considered a classic in Native American Literature.

➢ Toni Morrison

Toni Morrison is an American novelist, editor, and professor. Her novels are known for their epic themes, vivid dialogue, and richly detailed characters. Among her best-known novels are *The Bluest Eye*, *Sula*, *Song of Solomon and Beloved.* She won the Nobel Prize in 1993 and the Pulitzer Prize in 1988 for Beloved. On 29 May 2012, she received the Presidential Medal of Freedom

> **Alice Malsenior Walker**

Alice Malsenior Walke is an American author, poet, feminist, and activist. She is best-known for the critically acclaimed novel *The Color Purple* (1982) for which she won the National Book Award and the Pulitzer Prize. (See details in Unit 4)

> **Amy Tan**

Amy Tan is an American writer whose works explore mother-daughter relationships. Her most well-known work is *The Joy Luck Club*, which has been translated into 35 languages. In 1993, the book was adapted into a commercially successful film. (See details in Unit 4)

◎ Exercises

1. Explain the following terms in English.

1) Romanticism
2) Realism
3) modernism
4) Postmodern literature

2. Match the following representatives and their works.

1) Thomas Jefferson
2) Washington Irving
3) Ernest Hemingway
4) Toni Morrison
5) T. S. Eliot
6) Amy Tan
7) Mark Twain
8) John Dos Passos
9) James Fenimore Cooper
10) Alice Malsenior Walker

a. *The Joy Luck Club*
b. *The Bluest Eye*
c. *The Color Purple*
d. *The Waste Land.*
e. *The Sun Also Rises*
f. *The Big Money The Adventures of Huckleberry Finn*
g. *The Big Money*
h. *The Pioneers*

i. *The History of Life*

j. *Declaration of Independence*

3. Discuss and answer the following questions.

1) Please list 5 main genres in colonial period and explain them.

2) How can European Romanticism influence American writers?

3) Influenced by irrational philosophy and Freudianism, modernism in American literature mainly revolves on some topics. Please illustrate them in your own words.

4) What is your understanding of "Lost Generation Literature"?

Unit 4
American Literature in English Films

1. Romanticism

Romanticism was an artistic, literary, musical and intellectual movement that originated in Europe toward the end of the 18th century, and in most areas was at its peak in the approximate period from 1800 to 1850. Romanticism was characterized by its emphasis on emotion and individualism as well as glorification of all the past and nature, preferring the medieval rather than the classical. The European Romantic movement reached America in the early 19th century. American Romanticism was just as multifaceted and individualistic as it was in Europe. Like the Europeans, the American Romantics demonstrated a high level of moral enthusiasm, commitment to individualism and the unfolding of the self, an emphasis on intuitive perception, and the assumption that the natural world was inherently good, while human society was filled with corruption. There are a number of classical literal works have been adapted to films.

1.1 Nathaniel Hawthorne: *The Scarlet Letter*

An Introduction to Nathaniel Hawthorne

Nathaniel Hawthorne (July 4, 1804-May 19, 1864) was an American novelist, dark romantic, and short-story writer. He was born in 1804 in Salem, Massachusetts to Nathaniel Hathorne and the former Elizabeth Clarke Manning. His ancestors include John Hathorne, the only judge involved in the Salem witch trials who never repented of his actions. Nathaniel later added a "w" to make his name "Hawthorne" in order to hide this relation. He entered Bowdoin College in 1821, was elected to *Phi Beta Kappa* in 1824, and graduated in 1825. He published his first work in 1828, the novel *Fanshawe*; he later tried to suppress it, feeling that it was not equal to the standard of his later work. He published several short stories in periodicals, which he collected in 1837 as *Twice-Told Tales*.

The Scarlet Letter was published in 1850, followed by a succession of other novels. A political appointment as consul took Hawthorne and family to Europe before their return to Concord in 1860.

Much of Hawthorne's writing centers on New England, many works featuring moral metaphors with an anti-Puritaninspiration. His fiction works are considered part of the Romantic movement and, more specifically, dark romanticism. His themes often center on the inherent evil and sin of humanity, and his works often have moral messages and deep psychological complexity. His published works include novels, short stories, and a biography of his college friend Franklin Pierce, the 14th President of the United States.

An Introduction to the film *The Scarlet Letter*

The Scarlet Letter (1995) is a film adaptation of the Nathaniel Hawthorne novel of the same name. It was directed by Roland Joffé and stars Demi Moore, Gary Oldman, and Robert Duvall. This version was "freely adapted" from Hawthorne and deviated from the original story. It was nominated for seven Golden Raspberry Awards at the 1995 ceremony, winning "Worst Remake or Sequel".

Plot

It is 1667 in the Massachusetts Bay Colony, and an uneasy truce exists between local Puritans and their neighbours, the Algonquian. Chief Metacomet (Eric Schweig) succeeds his father Massasoit as head of the latter just as a new colonist, Hester Prynne (Demi Moore) arrives overseas from England. As Hester waits for her husband — who is due to follow shortly after — she falls for a young minister, Arthur Dimmesdale (Gary Oldman). When it emerges that Roger Prynne has likely been killed by Native Americans, they become inseparable lovers.

Finding herself pregnant with Dimmesdale's child, Hester is imprisoned for her indiscretion. The minister intends to declare his sin and face execution, but Hester convinces him otherwise. Sentenced to wear a scarlet "A" for adultery, Prynne is ostracized by the public, and a drummer boy charged to follow her whenever she comes to town. Meanwhile, Hester's husband (Robert Duvall) resurfaces, having spent his absence in captivity as a prisoner of war. Learning of the scandal, he adopts the fictitious guise of "Dr. Roger Chillingworth" and begins seeking out her paramour.

The physician eventually murders a male settler leaving Hester's home and scalps him in an effort to implicate Algonquian warriors. Infuriated by this atrocity, the colonists declare war on the Indians and Roger, distraught by the severe consequences of his action, promptly commits suicide. Hester is nearly hanged with other undesirables in the ensuing outrage, but Dimmesdale saves her neck by confessing that he is the father of her child. As he takes her place on the gallows, the Algonquian attack Massachusetts Bay; both sides sustain heavy casualties. The Puritans are more concerned with concealing the conflict from England than harassing Hester any further; she finally abandons her scarlet letter.

Excerpt from the Book *The Scarlet Letter*

The scene was not without a mixture of awe, such as must always invest the spectacle of guilt and shame in a fellow-creature, before society shall have grown corrupt enough to smile, instead of shuddering at it. The witnesses of Hester Prynne's disgrace had not yet passed beyond their simplicity. They were stern enough to look upon her death, had that been the sentence, without a murmur at its severity, but had none of the heartlessness of another social state, which would find only a theme for jest in an exhibition like the present. Even had there been a disposition to turn the matter into ridicule, it must have been repressed and overpowered by the solemn presence of men no less dignified than the governor, and several of his counsellors, a judge, a general, and the ministers of the town, all of whom sat or stood in a balcony of the meeting-house, looking down upon the platform. When such personages could constitute a part of the spectacle, without risking the majesty, or reverence of rank and office, it was safely to be inferred that the infliction of a legal sentence would have an earnest and effectual meaning. Accordingly, the crowd was sombre and grave. The unhappy culprit sustained herself as best a woman might, under the heavy weight of a thousand unrelenting eyes, all fastened upon her, and concentrated at her bosom. It was almost intolerable to be borne. Of an impulsive and passionate nature, she had fortified herself to encounter the stings and venomous stabs of public contumely, wreaking itself in every variety of insult; but there was a quality so much more terrible in the solemn mood of the popular mind, that she longed rather to behold all those rigid countenances contorted with scornful merriment, and herself the object. Had a roar of laughter burst from the multitude—each man, each woman, each little shrill-voiced child, contributing their individual parts—Hester Prynne might have repaid them all with a bitter and disdainful smile. But, under the leaden infliction which it was her doom to endure, she felt, at moments, as if she must shriek out with the full power of her lungs, and cast herself from the scaffold down upon the ground, or else go mad at once.

Yet there were intervals when the whole scene, in which she was the most conspicuous object, seemed to vanish from her eyes, or, at least, glimmered indistinctly before them, like a mass of imperfectly shaped and spectral images. Her mind, and especially her memory, was preternaturally active, and kept bringing up other scenes than this roughly hewn street of a little town, on the edge of the western wilderness: other faces than were lowering upon her from beneath the brims of those steeple-crowned hats. Reminiscences, the most trifling and immaterial, passages of infancy and school-days, sports, childish quarrels, and the little domestic traits of her maiden years, came swarming back upon her, intermingled with recollections of whatever was gravest in her subsequent life; one picture precisely as vivid as another; as if all were of similar importance, or all alike a play. Possibly, it was an instinctive device of her spirit to relieve itself by the exhibition of these phantasmagoric forms, from the cruel weight and hardness of the reality.

Be that as it might, the scaffold of the pillory was a point of view that revealed to Hester Prynne the entire track along which she had been treading, since her happy infancy. Standing on that miserable eminence, she saw again her native village, in Old England, and her paternal home: a decayed house of grey stone, with a poverty-stricken aspect, but retaining a half obliterated shield of arms over the portal, in token of antique gentility. She saw her father's face, with its bold brow, and reverend white beard that flowed over the old-fashioned Elizabethan ruff; her mother's, too, with the look of heedful and anxious love which it always wore in her remembrance, and which, even since her death, had so often laid the impediment of a gentle remonstrance in her daughter's pathway. She saw her own face, glowing with girlish beauty, and illuminating all the interior of the dusky mirror in which she had been wont to gaze at it. There she beheld another countenance, of a man well stricken in years, a pale, thin, scholar-like visage, with eyes dim and bleared by the lamp-light that had served them to pore over many ponderous books. Yet those same bleared optics had a strange, penetrating power, when it was their owner's purpose to read the human soul. This figure of the study and the cloister, as Hester Prynne's womanly fancy failed not to recall, was slightly deformed, with the left shoulder a trifle higher than the right. Next rose before her in memory's picture-gallery, the intricate and narrow thoroughfares, the tall, grey houses, the huge cathedrals, and the public edifices, ancient in date and quaint in architecture, of a continental city; where new life had awaited her, still in connexion with the misshapen scholar: a new life, but feeding itself on time-worn materials, like a tuft of green moss on a crumbling wall. Lastly, in lieu of these shifting scenes, came back the rude market-place of the Puritan, settlement, with all the townspeople assembled, and levelling their stern regards at Hester Prynne—yes, at herself—who stood on the scaffold of the pillory, an infant on her arm, and the letter A, in scarlet, fantastically embroidered with gold thread, upon her bosom.

Could it be true? She clutched the child so fiercely to her breast that it sent forth a cry; she turned her eyes downward at the scarlet letter, and even touched it with her finger, to assure herself that the infant and the shame were real. Yes these were her realities—all else had vanished!

1.2 Herman Melville: *Moby Dick/Moby-Dick*

An Introduction to Herman Melville

Herman Melville (August 1, 1819-September 28, 1891) was an American novelist, short-story writer, and poet of the American Renaissance Period. His best-known works include *Typee* (1846), a romantic account of his experiences in Polynesian life, and his whaling novel *Moby-Dick* (1851). His work was almost forgotten during his last thirty years. His writing draws on his experience at sea as a common sailor, exploration of literature and philosophy, and engagement in the contradictions of American society in a period of rapid change. He developed a complex, baroque style: the vocabulary is rich and original, a strong sense of rhythm infuses the elaborate sentences, the imagery is often mystical or ironic, and the abundance of allusion extends to biblical Scripture, myth, philosophy, literature, and the visual arts.

Moby Dick is now considered one of the greatest novels in the English language and has secured Melville's place among America's greatest writers. Written in 1851, it is the story of Ishmael's whaling voyage. It contains many examples of alliteration, allusion, similes, and metaphors; it also presents an ironic argument against Transcendentalism and the power of man. This book contains reflections of Melville's own whaling voyages and many collections of compiled whaling knowledge: the history of whaling, scientific whale groups, usage of whaling tools, etc. Altogether this book is a literary masterpiece.

An Introduction to the film *Moby Dick*

Moby Dick is a 2010 film adaptation of Herman Melville's novel *Moby-Dick*. The film is an Asylum production, and stars Barry Bostwick as Captain Ahab. It also stars Renee O'Connor, Michael B. Teh, and Adam Grimes and is directed by Trey Stokes.

Plot

On November 20, 1969, 50 miles off Soviet waters, the USS Acushnet dives under the ice. A young Ahab listens to sonar for enemy subs when suddenly he detects an unknown target. When the captain listens, he hears nothing, but Ahab insists in the presence of an emptiness. The target dives into a trench, but the captain abandons his search in favor of photographing the target. The target attacks the submarine as Ahab hears a roar. The sub is brought to the icy surface, and the target identifies itself as a gigantic, white, whale-like creature. Ahab survives, but loses his left leg to the beast when it hauls the other half of the sub back underwater.

In the present day, Dr. Michelle Herman and her assistant Pip test a whale song generator when the USS Pequod surfaces behind them and Lieutenant Commander Starbuck, the executive officer, persuades them to come aboard. In the sub, Starbuck tells them about several attacks in which eyewitnesses all report seeing an enormous whale. Although Michelle explains that the whale song generator needs a recorded whale vocalization, Captain Ahab comes to the deck and gives her the recording he took of Moby Dick back in 1969. Although Michelle disagrees on joining a Navy sub with the intent of killing an animal, she has no choice.

In San Diego, Captain Boomer (another survivor of the attack of '69) is told by his superiors of suspicious activity revolving around the Pequod. He is assigned to investigate, and thanks to a survivor from a recent attack by the White Whale, he comes to the conclusion that Ahab is on the hunt for Moby Dick.

A helicopter in search of the Pequod encounters it while the sub is following a 600-foot target. As the helicopter engages them, the sub fires a nuke at the unknown target, but the confused helicopter crew tell them they shot a school of giant squid just before they are swallowed alive by Moby Dick.

This, however, causes the whale to attack them, subsequently destroying a fin on the Pequod. The sub fires a harpoon made from the Acushnet's hull on top of Moby Dick's eye, which forces him to dive deeper, dragging the Pequod with it. As the water pressure begins to damage the hull, the line snaps and Starbuck forces the ship to surface.

Moby-Dick destroys two of the boats and forces the survivors onto the island's shores. The whale attacks them again, resulting in the death of Queequeg. Ahab takes the last boat and fires his harpoon at the whale's other eye. Moby Dick destroys the boat, killing Ahab. The remaining crew of the Pequod, including Starbuck, and Pip, follow Ahab's orders and fire nukes at the island. Moby Dick dodges the nukes and crushes the Pequod just as the island explodes. The White Whale survives to wreak havoc another day; Michelle swims to the surface just as a rescue helicopter arrives.

Excerpt from the Book *Moby Dick*

What the white whale was to Ahab, has been hinted; what, at times, he was to me, as yet remains unsaid.

Aside from those more obvious considerations touching Moby Dick, which could not but occasionally awaken in any man's soul some alarm, there was another thought, or rather vague, nameless horror concerning him, which at times by its intensity completely overpowered all the rest; and yet so mystical and well nigh ineffable was it, that I almost despair of putting it in a comprehensible form. It was the whiteness of the whale that above all things appalled me. But how can I hope to explain myself here; and yet, in some dim, random way, explain myself I must, else all these chapters might be naught.

"Both jaws, like enormous shears, bit the craft completely in twain."

—Page 510.

Though in many natural objects, whiteness refiningly enhances beauty, as if imparting some special virtue of its own, as in marbles, japonicas, and pearls; and though various nations have in some way recognised a certain royal preeminence in this hue; even the barbaric, grand old kings of Pegu placing the title "Lord of the White Elephants" above all their other magniloquent ascriptions of dominion; and the modern kings of Siam unfurling the same snow-white quadruped in the royal standard; and the Hanoverian flag bearing the one figure of a snow-white charger; and the great Austrian Empire, Caesarian, heir to overlording Rome, having for the imperial color the same imperial hue; and though this pre-eminence in it applies to the human race itself, giving the white man ideal mastership over every dusky tribe; and though, besides, all this, whiteness has been even made significant of gladness, for among the Romans a white stone marked a joyful day; and though in other mortal sympathies and symbolizings, this same hue is made the emblem of many touching, noble things — the innocence of brides, the benignity of age; though among the Red Men of America the giving of the white belt of wampum was the deepest pledge of honor; though in many climes, whiteness typifies the majesty of Justice in the ermine of the Judge, and contributes to the daily state of kings and queens drawn by milk-white steeds; though even in the higher mysteries of the most august religions it has been made the symbol of the divine spotlessness and power; by the Persian fire worshippers, the white forked flame being held the holiest on the altar; and in the Greek mythologies, Great Jove himself being made incarnate in a snow-white bull; and though to the noble Iroquois, the midwinter sacrifice of the sacred White Dog was by far the holiest festival of their theology, that spotless, faithful creature being held the purest envoy they could send to the Great Spirit with the annual tidings of their own fidelity; and though directly from the Latin word for white, all Christian priests derive the name of one part of their sacred vesture, the alb or tunic, worn beneath the cassock; and though among the holy pomps of the Romish faith, white is specially employed in the celebration of the passion of our Lord; though in the Vision of St. John, white robes are given to the redeemed, and the four-and-twenty elders stand clothed in white before the great-white throne, and the Holy One that sitteth there white like wool; yet for all these accumulated associations, with whatever is sweet, and honorable, and sublime, there yet lurks an elusive something in the innermost idea of this hue, which strikes more of panic to the soul than that redness which affrights in blood.

2. Realism

Realism is a literary doctrine that called for "reality and truth" in the depiction of ordinary life. It had originated in France, popular in 19th century. The American writers sought to portray American life as it really was, insisting that the ordinary and the local were as suitable for artistic portrayal as the magnificent and the remote.

2.1 Henry James: *The Wings of the Dove*

An Introduction to Henry James

Henry James, (15 April 1843-28 February 1916) was an American author, who largely relocated to Europe as a young man and acquired British citizenship near the end of his life. James is regarded as a key transitional figure between literary realism and literary modernism, and is considered by many to be among the greatest novelists in the English language.

He is best-known for a number of novels dealing with the social and marital interplay between Emigre Americans, English people, and continental Europeans—examples of such novels include *The Portrait of a Lady*, *The Ambassadors*, and *The Wings of the Dove*. His later works were increasingly experimental. In describing the internal states of mind and social dynamics of his characters, James often made use of a personal style in which ambiguous or contradictory motivations and impressions were overlaid or closely juxtaposed in the discussion of a single character's psyche. For their unique ambiguity, as well as for other aspects of their composition, his late works have been compared to impressionist painting.

In addition to voluminous works of fiction, James published articles and books of criticism, travel, biography, autobiography, and plays. Born in the United States, James eventually settled in England, becoming a British subject in 1915, one year before his death. James was nominated for the Nobel Prize in Literature in 1911, 1912, and 1916.

An Introduction to the film *The Wings of the Dove*

The Wings of the Dove is a 1997 British-American romantic drama film directed by Iain Softley and starring Helena Bonham Carter, Linus Roache, and Alison Elliott. The screenplay by Hossein Amini is based on the 1902 novel of the same name by Henry James. The film was nominated for four Academy Awards and five BAFTAs, recognizing Bonham Carter's performance, the screenplay, costume design and the cinematography. The film received mostly favorable reviews, and fared well at the box office. Bonham Carter received an Academy Award nomination for Best Actress.

Plot

Kate Croy and Merton Densher are two betrothed Londoners who desperately want to marry but have very little money. Kate is constantly put upon by family troubles, and is now living with her domineering aunt, Maud Lowder. Into their world comes Milly Theale, an enormously rich young American woman who had previously met and fallen in love with Densher, although she has never revealed her feelings. Her travelling companion and confidante, Mrs. Stringham, is an old friend of Maud. Kate and Aunt Maud welcome Milly to London, and the American heiress enjoys great social success.

With Kate as a companion, Milly goes to see an eminent physician, Sir Luke Strett, because she worries that she is suffering from an incurable disease. The doctor is noncommittal but Milly fears the worst. Kate suspects that Milly is deathly ill. After the trip to America where he had met Milly, Densher returns to find the heiress in London. Kate wants Densher to pay as much attention as possible to Milly, though at first he doesn't quite know why. Kate has been careful to conceal from Milly (and everybody else) that she and Densher are engaged.

With the threat of serious illness hanging over her, Milly decides to travel to Venice with Mrs. Stringham. Aunt Maud, Kate and Densher follow her. At a party Milly gives in her Venice palazzo (the older Palazzo Barbaro, called "Palazzo Leporelli" in the novel), Kate finally reveals her complete plan to Densher: he is to marry Milly so that, after her presumably soon-to-occur death, he will inherit the money they can marry on. Densher had suspected this was Kate's idea, and he demands that she consummate their affair before he will go along with her plan.

Aunt Maud and Kate return to London while Densher remains with Milly. Unfortunately, the dying girl learns from a former suitor of Kate's about the plot to get her money. She withdraws from Densher and her condition deteriorates. Densher sees her one last time before he leaves for London, where he eventually receives news of Milly's death. Milly does leave him a large amount of money despite everything. But Densher does not accept the money, and he will not marry Kate unless she also refuses the bequest. Conversely, if Kate chooses the money instead of him, Densher offers to make the bequest over to her in full. The lovers part on the novel's final page with a cryptic exclamation from Kate: "We shall never be again as we were!"

Excerpt from the Book *The Wings of the Dove*

Book First, Chapter 1

She waited, Kate Croy, for her father to come in, but he kept her unconscionably, and there were moments at which she showed herself, in the glass over the mantel, a face positively pale with the irritation that had brought her to the point of going away without sight of him. It was at this point, however, that she remained; changing her place, moving from the shabby sofa to the armchair upholstered in a glazed cloth that gave at once—she had tried it—the sense of the slippery and of the sticky. She had looked at the sallow prints on the walls and at the lonely magazine, a year old, that combined, with a small lamp in coloured glass and a knitted white centre-piece wanting in freshness, to enhance the effect of the purplish cloth on the principal table; she had above all from time to time taken a brief stand on the small balcony to which the pair of long windows gave access. The vulgar little street, in this view, offered scant relief from the vulgar little room; its main office was to suggest to her that the narrow black house-fronts, adjusted to a standard that would have been low even for backs, constituted quite the publicity implied by such privacies. One felt them in the room exactly as one felt the room—the hundred like it or worse—in the street. Each time she turned in again, each time, in her impatience, she gave him up, it was to sound to a deeper depth, while she tasted the faint flat emanation of things, the failure of fortune and of honour. If she continued to wait it was really in a manner that she mightn't add the shame of fear, of individual, of personal collapse, to all the other shames. To feel the street, to feel the room, to feel the table-cloth and the centre-piece and the lamp, gave her a small salutary sense at least of neither shirking nor lying. This whole vision was the worst thing yet—as including in particular the interview to which she had braced herself; and for what had she come but for the worst? She tried to be sad so as not to be angry, but it made her angry that she couldn't be sad. And yet where was misery, misery too beaten for blame and chalk-marked by fate like a "lot" at a common auction, if not in these merciless signs of mere mean stale feelings?

Her father's life, her sister's, her own, that of her two lost brothers—the whole history of their house had the effect of some fine florid voluminous phrase, say even a musical, that dropped first into words and notes without sense and then, hanging unfinished, into no words nor any notes at all. Why should a set of people have been put in motion, on such a scale and with such an air of being equipped for a profitable journey, only to break down without an accident, to stretch themselves in the wayside dust without a reason? The answer to these questions was not in Chirk Street, but the questions themselves bristled there, and the girl's repeated pause before the mirror and the chimney-place might have represented her nearest approach to an escape from them.

Wasn't it in fact the partial escape from this "worst" in which she was steeped to be able to make herself out again as agreeable to see? She stared into the tarnished glass too hard indeed to be staring at her beauty alone. She readjusted the poise of her black closely-feathered hat; retouched, beneath it, the thick fall of her dusky hair; kept her eyes aslant no less on her beautiful averted than on her beautiful presented oval. She was dressed altogether in black, which gave an even tone, by contrast, to her clear face and made her hair more harmoniously dark. Outside, on the balcony, her eyes showed as blue; within, at the mirror, they showed almost as black. She was handsome, but the degree of it was not sustained by items and aids; a circumstance moreover playing its part at almost any time in the impression she produced. The impression was one that remained, but as regards the sources of it no sum in addition would have made up the total. She had stature without height, grace without motion, presence without mass. Slender and simple, frequently soundless, she was somehow always in the line of the eye—she counted singularly for its pleasure. More "dressed", often, with fewer accessories, than other women, or less dressed, should occasion require, with more, she probably couldn't have given the key to these felicities. They were mysteries of which her friends were conscious—those friends whose general explanation was to say that she was clever, whether or no it were taken by the world as the cause or as the effect of her charm. If she saw more things than her fine face in the dull glass of her father's lodgings she might have seen that after all she was not herself a fact in the collapse. She didn't hold herself cheap, she didn't make for misery. Personally, no, she wasn't chalk-marked for auction. She hadn't given up yet, and the broken sentence, if she was the last word, WOULD end with a sort of meaning. There was a minute during which, though her eyes were fixed, she quite visibly lost herself in the thought of the way she might still pull things round had she only been a man. It was the name, above all, she would take in hand—the precious name she so liked and that, in spite of the harm her wretched father had done it, wasn't yet past praying for. She loved it in fact the more tenderly for that bleeding wound. But what could a penniless girl do with it but let it go?

2.2 Mark Twain: *The Million Pound Note*

An Introduction to Mark Twain

Samuel Langhorne Clemens (November 30, 1835-April 21, 1910), better known by his pen name Mark Twain, was an American writer, humorist, entrepreneur, publisher, and lecturer. Among his novels are *The Adventures of Tom Sawyer* (*1876*) and its sequel, *The Adventures of Huckleberry Finn* (*1885*), the latter often called "The Great American Novel".

Twain was raised in Hannibal, Missouri, which later provided the setting for *Tom Sawyer and Huckleberry Finn.* He served an apprenticeship with a printer and then worked as a typesetter, contributing articles to the newspaper of his older brother Orion Clemens. He later became a riverboat pilot on the Mississippi River before heading west to join Orion in Nevada. He referred humorously to his lack of success at mining, turning to journalism for the *Virginia City Territorial Enterprise*. His humorous story, "*The Celebrated Jumping Frog of Calaveras County*", was published in 1865, based on a story that he heard at Angels Hotel in Angels Camp, California where he had spent some time as a miner. The short-story brought international attention and was even translated into French. His wit and satire, in prose and in speech, earned praise from critics and peers, and he was a friend to presidents, artists, industrialists, and European royalty.

Twain was born shortly after an appearance of Halley's Comet, and he predicted that he would "go out with it" as well; he died the day after the comet returned. He was lauded as the "greatest humorist this country has produced", and William Faulkner called him "the father of American literature".

An Introduction to the film *The Million Pound Note*

The Million Pound Note is a 1954 British comedy, directed by Ronald Neame and starring Gregory Peck. It is based on the Mark Twain short-story, "*The Million Pound Bank Note*".

Plot

In 1903, American seaman Henry Adams (Gregory Peck) is stranded penniless in Britain and gets caught up in an unusual wager between two wealthy, eccentric brothers, Oliver and Roderick Montpelier. They persuade the Bank of England to issue a one million pound banknote, which they present to Adams in an envelope, only telling him that it contains some money. The reason for this is that Oliver believes that the mere existence of the note will enable the possessor to obtain whatever he needs, while Roderick insists that it would actually have to be spent for it to be of any use.

Once Adams gets over the shock of discovering how much the note is worth, he tries to return it to the brothers, but is told that they have left for a month. He then finds a letter in the envelope, explaining the wager and promising him a job if he can avoid spending the note for the month.

At first, everything goes as Oliver had predicted. Adams is mistaken for an eccentric millionaire and has no trouble getting food, clothes, and a hotel suite on credit, just by showing his note. The story of the note is reported in the newspapers. Adams is welcomed into exclusive social circles, meeting the American ambassador and English aristocracy. He becomes very friendly with Portia Lansdowne, the niece of the Duchess of Cromarty. Then fellow American

Lloyd Hastings asks him to back a business venture. Hastings tells Adams that he does not have to put up any money himself; the mere association will allow Hastings to raise the money that he needs to start up a gold mine by selling shares.

Trouble arises when the Duke of Frognal, who had been unceremoniously evicted from the suite Adams now occupies, hides the note as a joke. When Adams is unable to produce the note, panic breaks out amongst the shareholders and Adams' creditors. All is straightened out in the end, and Adams is able to return the note to the Montpelier brothers at the end of the month.

Excerpt from the Book *The Million Pound Bank Note*

Maybe those men mean me well, maybe they mean me ill; no way to decide that—let it go. They've got a game, or a scheme, or an experiment, of some kind on hand; no way to determine what it is—let it go. There's a bet on me; no way to find out what it is—let it go. That disposes of the indeterminable quantities; the remainder of the matter is tangible, solid, and may be classed and labeled with certainty. If I ask the Bank of England to place this bill to the credit of the man it belongs to, they'll do it, for they know him, although I don't; but they will ask me how I came in possession of it, and if I tell the truth, they'll put me in the asylum, naturally, and a lie will land me in jail. The same result would follow if I tried to bank the bill anywhere or to borrow money on it. I have got to carry this immense burden around until those men come back, whether I want to or not. It is useless to me, as useless as a handful of ashes, and yet I must take care of it, and watch over it, while I beg my living. I couldn't give it away, if I should try, for neither honest citizen nor highwayman would accept it or meddle with it for anything. Those brothers are safe. Even if I lose their bill, or burn it, they are still safe, because they can stop payment, and the Bank will make them whole; but meantime I've got to do a month's suffering without wages or profit—unless I help win that bet, whatever it may be, and get that situation that I am promised. I should like to get that; men of their sort have situations in their gift that are worth having.

I got to thinking a good deal about that situation. My hopes began to rise high.

Without doubt the salary would be large. It would begin in a month; after that I should be all right. Pretty soon I was feeling first-rate. By this time I was tramping the streets again. The sight of a tailor-shop gave me a sharp longing to shed my rags, and to clothe myself decently once more. Could I afford it? No; I had nothing in the world but a million pounds. So I forced myself to go on by. But soon I was drifting back again. The temptation persecuted me cruelly. I must have passed that shop back and forth six times during that manful struggle. At last I gave in; I had to. I asked if they had a misfit suit that had been thrown on their hands. The fellow I spoke to nodded his head towards another fellow, and gave me no answer. I went to the indicated fellow, and he indicated another fellow with his head, and no words. I went to him, and he said:

"'Tend to you presently."

I waited till he was done with what he was at, then he took me into a back room, and overhauled a pile of rejected suits, and selected the rattiest one for me. I put it on. It didn't fit, and wasn't in any way attractive, but it was new, and I was anxious to have it; so I didn't find any fault, but said, with some diffidence:

"It would be an accommodation to me if you could wait some days for the money. I haven't any small change about me."

The fellow worked up a most sarcastic expression of countenance, and said:

"Oh, you haven't? Well, of course, I didn't expect it. I'd only expect gentlemen like you to carry large change."

I was nettled, and said:

"My friend, you shouldn't judge a stranger always by the clothes he wears. I am quite able to pay for this suit; I simply didn't wish to put you to the trouble of changing a large note."

He modified his style a little at that, and said, though still with something of an air:

"I didn't mean any particular harm, but as long as rebukes are going, I might say it wasn't quite your affair to jump to the conclusion that we couldn't change any note that you might happen to be carrying around. On the contrary, we can."

I handed the note to him, and said:

"Oh, very well; I apologize."

He received it with a smile, one of those large smiles which goes all around over, and has folds in it, and wrinkles, and spirals, and looks like the place where you have thrown a brick in a pond; and then in the act of his taking a glimpse of the bill this smile froze solid, and turned yellow, and looked like those wavy, wormy spreads of lava which you find hardened on little levels on the side of Vesuvius. I never before saw a smile caught like that, and perpetuated. The man stood there holding the bill, and looking like that, and the proprietor hustled up to see what was the matter, and said, briskly:

"Well, what's up? what's the trouble? what's wanting?"

I said: "There isn't any trouble. I'm waiting for my change."

"Come, come; get him his change, Tod; get him his change."

Tod retorted: "Get him his change! It's easy to say, sir; but look at the bill yourself."

The proprietor took a look, gave a low, eloquent whistle, then made a dive for the pile of rejected clothing, and began to snatch it this way and that, talking all the time excitedly, and as if to himself:

"Sell an eccentric millionaire such an unspeakable suit as that! Tod's a fool—a born fool. Always doing something like this. Drives every millionaire away from this place, because he can't tell a millionaire from a tramp, and never could. Ah, here's the thing I am after. Please get those things off, sir, and throw them in the fire. Do me the favor to put on this shirt and this suit; it's just the thing, the very thing—plain, rich, modest, and just ducally nobby; made to order for a foreign prince—you may know him, sir, his Serene Highness the Hospodar of Halifax; had to leave it with us and take a mourning-suit because his mother was going to die — which she didn't. But that's all right; we can't always have things the way we—that is, the way they—there! trousers all right, they fit you to a charm, sir; now the waistcoat; aha, right again! now the coat—lord! look at that, now! Perfect—the whole thing! I never saw such a triumph in all my experience."

I expressed my satisfaction.

"Quite right, sir, quite right; it'll do for a makeshift, I'm bound to say. But wait till you see what we'll get up for you on your own measure. Come, Tod, book and pen; get at it. Length of leg, 32"—and so on. Before I could get in a word he had measured me, and was giving orders for dress-suits, morning suits, shirts, and all sorts of things. When I got a chance I said:

"But, my dear sir, I can't give these orders, unless you can wait indefinitely, or change the bill."

"Indefinitely! It's a weak word, sir, a weak word. Eternally—that's the word, sir. Tod, rush these things through, and send them to the gentleman's address without any waste of time. Let the minor customers wait. Set down the gentleman's address and—"

"I'm changing my quarters. I will drop in and leave the new address."

"Quite right, sir, quite right. One moment—let me show you out, sir. There—good day, sir, good day."

3. Naturalism

At the end of the 19th century, monopoly capitalism came into being, the conflicts in society became more and more intense, naturalism came upon the American literary stage. The naturalistic writers attempted to achieve extreme objectivity and frankness, presenting characters of low social and economic classes who were dominated by their environment and heredity. Naturalism presents a new and harsher realism.

3.1 John Griffith London: *The Call of the Wild*

An Introduction to John Griffith London

John Griffith London (January 12, 1876-November 22, 1916) was an American novelist, journalist, and social activist. A pioneer in the then-burgeoning world of commercial magazine fiction, he was one of the first fiction writers to obtain worldwide celebrity and a large fortune from his fiction alone, including science fiction.

Some of his most famous works include *The Call of the Wild* and *White Fang*, both set in the Klondike Gold Rush, as well as the short stories "*To Build a Fire*", "*An Odyssey of the North*", and "*Love of Life*". He also wrote about the South Pacific in stories such as "*The Pearls of Parlay*" and "*The Heathen*", and of the San Francisco Bay area in *The Sea Wolf*.

London was part of the radical literary group "The Crowd" in San Francisco and a passionate advocate of unionization, socialism, and the rights of workers. He wrote several powerful works dealing with these topics, such as his dystopian novel *The Iron Heel*, his non-fiction exposé *The People of the Abyss*, and *The War of the Classes*.

An Introduction to the Film *The Call of the Wild*

The Call of the Wild: Dog of the Yukon is a 1997 movie. The screenplay by Graham Ludlow is based on Jack London's classic novel *The Call of the Wild* (1903), is narrated by Richard Dreyfuss, and stars Rutger Hauer. The Hollywood Reporter said it was, "… a pleasant surprise. Much more faithful to Jack London's 1903 classic than the two Hollywood versions." The New York Post claimed Ludlow's adaptation was the "best version yet of Jack London's classic story of survival."

Plot

Jack London's classic story from 1903 about Buck, a dog kidnapped from his home in California and taken to the Yukon where he is mistreated until a prospector discovers him and relates to his situation. Although the two are bonded, Buck yearns to run free with the wild dogs in the wilderness.

Excerpt from the Book *The Call of the Wild*

Chapter 1

I. Into the Primitive

"Old longings nomadic leap,
Chafing at custom's chain;
Again from its brumal sleep
Wakens the ferine strain."

Buck did not read the newspapers, or he would have known that trouble was brewing, not alone for himself, but for every tide-water dog, strong of muscle and with warm, long hair, from

Puget Sound to San Diego. Because men, groping in the Arctic darkness, had found a yellow metal, and because steamship and transportation companies were booming the find, thousands of men were rushing into the Northland. These men wanted dogs, and the dogs they wanted were heavy dogs, with strong muscles by which to toil, and furry coats to protect them from the frost.

Buck lived at a big house in the sun-kissed Santa Clara Valley. Judge Miller's place, it was called. It stood back from the road, half hidden among the trees, through which glimpses could be caught of the wide cool veranda that ran around its four sides. The house was approached by gravelled driveways which wound about through wide-spreading lawns and under the interlacing boughs of tall poplars. At the rear things were on even a more spacious scale than at the front. There were great stables, where a dozen grooms and boys held forth, rows of vine-clad servants' cottages, an endless and orderly array of outhouses, long grape arbors, green pastures, orchards, and berry patches. Then there was the pumping plant for the artesian well, and the big cement tank where Judge Miller's boys took their morning plunge and kept cool in the hot afternoon.

And over this great demesne Buck ruled. Here he was born, and here he had lived the four years of his life. It was true, there were other dogs. There could not but be other dogs on so vast a place, but they did not count. They came and went, resided in the populous kennels, or lived obscurely in the recesses of the house after the fashion of Toots, the Japanese pug, or Ysabel, the Mexican hairless, — strange creatures that rarely put nose out of doors or set foot to ground. On the other hand, there were the fox terriers, a score of them at least, who yelped fearful promises at Toots and Ysabel looking out of the windows at them and protected by a legion of housemaids armed with brooms and mops.

But Buck was neither house-dog nor kennel-dog. The whole realm was his. He plunged into the swimming tank or went hunting with the Judge's sons; he escorted Mollie and Alice, the Judge's daughters, on long twilight or early morning rambles; on wintry nights he lay at the Judge's feet before the roaring library fire; he carried the Judge's grandsons on his back, or rolled them in the grass, and guarded their footsteps through wild adventures down to the fountain in the stable yard, and even beyond, where the paddocks were, and the berry patches. Among the terriers he stalked imperiously, and Toots and Ysabel he utterly ignored, for he was king, — king over all creeping, crawling, flying things of Judge Miller's place, humans included.

His father, Elmo, a huge St. Bernard, had been the Judge's inseparable companion, and Buck bid fair to follow in the way of his father. He was not so large, — he weighed only one hundred and forty pounds, — for his mother, Shep, had been a Scotch shepherd dog. Nevertheless, one hundred and forty pounds, to which was added the dignity that comes of good living and universal respect, enabled him to carry himself in right royal fashion. During the four years since his puppyhood he had lived the life of a sated aristocrat; he had a fine pride in himself, was even a trifle egotistical, as country gentlemen sometimes become because of their insular situation. But he had saved himself by not becoming a mere pampered house-dog. Hunting and kindred outdoor delights had kept down the fat and hardened his muscles; and to him, as to the cold-tubbing races, the love of water had been a tonic and a health preserver.

And this was the manner of dog Buck in the fall of 1897, when the Klondike strike dragged men from all the world into the frozen North. But Buck did not read the newspapers, and he did not know that Manuel, one of the gardener's helpers, was an undesirable acquaintance. Manuel had one besetting sin. He loved to play Chinese lottery. Also, in his gambling, he had one besetting weakness — faith in a system; and this made his damnation certain. For to play a system requires money, while the wages of a gardener's helper do not lap over the needs of a wife and numerous progeny.

3. 2 Theodore Dreiser: *Sister Carrie*

An Introduction to Theodore Dreiser

Theodore Herman Albert Dreiser (August 27, 1871-December 28, 1945) was an American novelist and journalist of the naturalist school. His novels often featured main characters who succeeded at their objectives despite a lack of a firm moral code, and literary situations that more closely resemble studies of nature than tales of choice and agency. Dreiser's best-known novels include *Sister Carrie* (1900) and *An American Tragedy* (1925). In 1930 he was nominated to the Nobel Prize in Literature.

An Introduction to the film *Carrie*

Carrie is a 1952 feature film based on the novel *Sister Carrie* by Theodore Dreiser. It was directed by William Wyler, the film stars Jennifer Jones in the title role and Laurence Olivier as Hurstwood. Eddie Albert played Charles Drouet.

Carrie received two Academy Award nominations: Costume Design, and Best Art Direction.

Plot

Carrie Meeber (Jennifer Jones) leaves her family in a small rural town and heads to Chicago. On the train to Chicago, Charles Drouet (Eddie Albert) approaches her. In South Chicago, Carrie stays with her sister and her husband Sven who have one child. Carrie loses her sweatshop sewing job after injuring her hand.

Carrie heads to Fitzgerald's to return the money to Drouet. While there she meets George Hurstwood (Laurence Olivier), the manager of the restaurant, who is immediately smitten with her. Hurstwood and Carrie end up spending every free minute together, and the two fall in love. Just before she is about to run off with Hurstwood, she finds out that he is married.

When Carrie finds out that she is pregnant, the two think that things might take a turn for the better. But Hurstwood's wife shows up, wanting his signature and his agreement to sell the house they own jointly. Hurstwood wants his share of the proceeds but she says she will press charges against him for bigamy if he insists. Carrie is devastated. Hurstwood's wife refused to consent to a divorce and Hurstwood didn't know how to tell Carrie. She is distraught and confronts Hurstwood, who admits that he is married although terribly unhappy. Carrie is torn, but does love Hurstwood, so she decides to stay with him.

The first few days are blissful, but then reality catches up with them. Hurstwood's boss sends an officer from the bond company after Hurstwood to collect the money Hurstwood took. Hurstwood, who has already been looking for work, finds out quickly that word of him stealing the money has gotten around. Unable to find a job, Hurstwood and Carrie soon find themselves living in poverty.

Excerpt from the Book *Sister Carrie*

When Caroline Meeber boarded the afternoon train for Chicago, her total outfit consisted of a small trunk, a cheap imitation alligator-skin satchel, a small lunch in a paper box, and a yellow leather snap purse, containing her ticket, a scrap of paper with her sister's address in Van Buren Street, and four dollars in money. It was in August, 1889. She was eighteen years of age, bright, timid, and full of the illusions of ignorance and youth. Whatever touch of regret at parting characterised her thoughts, it was certainly not for advantages now being given up. A gush of tears at her mother's farewell kiss, a touch in her throat when the cars clacked by the flour mill where her father worked by the day, a pathetic sigh as the familiar green environs of the village passed in review, and the threads which bound her so lightly to girlhood and home were irretrievably broken.

To be sure there was always the next station, where one might descend and return. There was the great city, bound more closely by these very trains which came up daily. Columbia City was not so very far away, even once she was in Chicago. What, pray, is a few hours—a few hundred miles? She looked at the little slip bearing her sister's address and wondered. She gazed at the green landscape, now passing in swift review, until her swifter thoughts replaced its impression with vague conjectures of what Chicago might be.

When a girl leaves her home at eighteen, she does one of two things. Either she falls into saving hands and becomes better, or she rapidly assumes the cosmopolitan standard of virtue and becomes worse. Of an intermediate balance, under the circumstances, there is no possibility. The city has its cunning wiles, no less than the infinitely smaller and more human tempter. There are large forces which allure with all the soulfulness of expression possible in the most cultured human. The gleam of a thousand lights is often as effective as the persuasive light in a wooing and fascinating eye. Half the undoing of the unsophisticated and natural mind is accomplished by forces wholly superhuman. A blare of sound, a roar of life, a vast array of human hives, appeal to the astonished senses in equivocal terms. Without a counsellor at hand to whisper cautious interpretations, what falsehoods may not these things breathe into the unguarded ear! Unrecognised for what they are, their beauty, like music, too often relaxes, then weakens, then perverts the simpler human perceptions.

Caroline, or Sister Carrie, as she had been half affectionately termed by the family, was possessed of a mind rudimentary in its power of observation and analysis. Self-interest with her was high, but not strong. It was, nevertheless, her guiding characteristic. Warm with the fancies of youth, pretty with the insipid prettiness of the formative period, possessed of a figure promising eventual shapeliness and an eye alight with certain native intelligence, she was a fair example of the middle American class—two generations removed from the emigrant. Books were beyond her interest—knowledge a sealed book. In the intuitive graces she was still crude. She could scarcely toss her head gracefully. Her hands were almost ineffectual. The feet, though small, were set flatly. And yet she was interested in her charms, quick to understand the keener pleasures of life, ambitious to gain in material things. A half-equipped little knight she was, venturing to reconnoitre the mysterious city and dreaming wild dreams of some vague, far-off supremacy, which should make it prey and subject—the proper penitent, groveling at a woman's slipper.

"That," said a voice in her ear, "is one of the prettiest little resorts in Wisconsin."

"Is it?" she answered nervously.

The train was just pulling out of Waukesha. For some time she had been conscious of a man behind. She felt him observing her mass of hair. He had been fidgetting, and with natural intuition she felt a certain interest growing in that quarter. Her maidenly reserve, and a certain sense of what was conventional under the circumstances, called her to forestall and deny this familiarity, but the daring and magnetism of the individual, born of past experiences and triumphs, prevailed. She answered.

He leaned forward to put his elbows upon the back of her seat and proceeded to make himself volubly agreeable.

"Yes, that is a great resort for Chicago people. The hotels are swell. You are not familiar with this part of the country, are you?"

"Oh, yes, I am," answered Carrie. "That is, I live at Columbia City. I have never been through here, though."

"And so this is your first visit to Chicago," he observed.

All the time she was conscious of certain features out of the side of her eye. Flush, colourful cheeks, a light moustache, a grey fedora hat. She now turned and looked upon him in full, the instincts of self-protection and coquetry mingling confusedly in her brain.

"I didn't say that," she said.

"Oh," he answered, in a very pleasing way and with an assumed air of mistake, "I thought you did."

Here was a type of the travelling canvasser for a manufacturing house—a class which at that time was first being dubbed by the slang of the day "drummers". He came within the meaning of a still newer term, which had sprung into general use among Americans in 1880, and which concisely expressed the thought of one whose dress or manners are calculated to elicit the admiration of susceptible young women—a "masher". His suit was of a striped and crossed pattern of brown wool, new at that time, but since become familiar as a business suit. The low crotch of the vest revealed a stiff shirt bosom of white and pink stripes. From his coat sleeves protruded a pair of linen cuffs of the same pattern, fastened with large, gold plate buttons, set with the common yellow agates known as "cat's-eyes". His fingers bore several rings—one, the ever-enduring heavy seal—and from his vest dangled a neat gold watch chain, from which was suspended the secret insignia of the Order of Elks. The whole suit was rather tight-fitting, and was finished off with heavy-soled tan shoes, highly polished, and the grey fedora hat. He was, for the order of intellect represented, attractive, and whatever he had to recommend him, you may be sure was not lost upon Carrie, in this, her first glance.

4. Modernism

Literary modernism has its origins in the late 19th and early 20th centuries, mainly in Europe and North America, and is characterized by a self-conscious break with traditional ways of writing, in both poetry and prose fiction. Modernists experimented with literary form and expression, adhering to Ezra Pound's maxim to "Make it new". This literary movement was driven by a conscious desire to overturn traditional modes of representation and express the new sensibilities of their time. The horrors of the First World War saw the prevailing assumptions about society reassessed, and modernist writers were influenced by such thinkers as Sigmund Freud and Karl Marx, amongst others, who raised questions about the rationality of the human mind.

4.1 Lost Generation

This term the lost generation was created by Gertrude Stein, it was applied to the disillusioned intellectuals and aesthetes of the years following the First World War, who rebelled against former ideals and values, but could replace them only by despair or a cynical hedonism. The lost generation is as a literary genre after the First World War in the United States.

The term originates from the American writer living in Paris, Gertrude Stein. On one occasion she and others pointed to Hemingway: "You are the Lost Generation." Hemingway later made this sentence as part of his novel "*The Sun Also Rises*", so "the lost generation" has become a literary name. Lost Generation writers all hate the anti-imperialist wars, but cannot find a way out.

Ernest Hemingway: *The Old Man and the Sea*

An Introduction to Ernest Hemingway

Ernest Miller Hemingway (July 21, 1899-July 2, 1961) was an American novelist, short-story writer, and journalist. His economical and understated style had a strong influence on 20th-century fiction, while his life of adventure and his public image influenced later generations. Hemingway produced most of his work between the mid-1920s and the mid-1950s, and won the Nobel Prize in Literature in 1954. He published seven novels, six short story collections, and two non-fiction works. Additional works, including three novels, four short story collections, and three non-fiction works, were published posthumously. Many of his works are considered classics of American literature.

Hemingway left for the Italian Front to enlist with the World War I ambulance drivers. In 1918, he was seriously wounded and returned home. His wartime experiences formed the basis for his novel *A Farewell to Arms* (1929). In 1921, he moved to Paris, where he worked as a foreign correspondent and fell under the influence of the modernist writers and artists of the 1920s "Lost Generation" expatriate community. He published his debut novel, *The Sun Also Rises*. He attended the Spanish Civil War, where he had been a journalist, and after which he wrote *For Whom the Bell Tolls* (1940). He also was present at the Normandy landings and the liberation of Paris during World War II.

Shortly after the publication of *The Old Man and the Sea* (*1952*), Hemingway went on safari to Africa, where he was almost killed in two successive plane crashes that left him in pain or ill health for much of his remaining life. Hemingway maintained permanent residences in *Key West, Florida*, (1930s) and *Cuba* (1940s and 1950s), and in 1959, he bought a house in Ketchum, Idaho, where he killed himself in mid-1961.

An Introduction to the film *The Old Man and the Sea*

The Old Man and the Sea is a 1958 American adventure drama film directed by John Sturges with uncredited direction from Henry King and Fred Zinnemann. The screenplay (the "most literal, word-for-word rendition of a written story ever filmed") was adapted by Peter Viertel from the novella of the same name by Ernest Hemingway.

Dimitri Tiomkin won the Academy Award for Best Original Score for his work on the film, which was also nominated for best color cinematography. The same year, Spencer Tracy was nominated for the Academy Award for Best Actor.

Plot

The Old Man in the film is a Cuban fisherman who has gone 84 days without a catch. His only friend is a young teenager whose name is Jabby who has been barred by his father from accompanying the Old Man out to sea. On the Old Man's 85th day out, he finally hooks a huge marlin, which he then tries to bring in and haul in from far out from shore. For three days and nights he battles the fish, which is portrayed in the film (as it had been in Hemingway's novella) as a trial of mental and physical courage that becomes the ultimate test for him of his worth as a man.

Excerpt from the Book *The Old Man and the Sea*

He saw him first as a dark shadow that took so long to pass under the boat that he could not believe its length.

"No," he said. "He can't be that big."

But he was that big and at the end of this circle he came to the surface only thirty yards away and the man saw his tail out of water. It was higher than a big scythe blade and a very pale lavender above the dark blue water. It raked back and as the fish swam just below the surface the old man could see his huge bulk and the purple stripes that banded him. His dorsal fin was down

and his huge pectorals were spread wide.

On this circle the old man could see the fish's eye and the two gray sucking fish that swam around him. Sometimes they attached themselves to him. Sometimes they darted off. Sometimes they would swim easily in his shadow. They were each over three feet long and when they swam fast they lashed their whole bodies like eels.

The old man was sweating now but from something else besides the sun. On each calm placid turn the fish made he was gaining line and he was sure that in two turns more he would have a chance to get the harpoon in.

But I must get him close, close, close, he thought. I mustn't try for the head. I must get the heart.

"Be calm and strong, old man," he said.

On the next circle the fish's back was out but he was a little too far from the boat. On the next circle he was still too far away but he was higher out of water and the old man was sure that by gaining some more line he could have him alongside.

He had rigged his harpoon long before and its coil of light rope was in a round basket and the end was made fast to the bitt in the bow.

The fish was coming in on his circle now calm and beautiful looking and only his great tail moving. The old man pulled on him all that he could to bring him closer. For just a moment the fish turned a little on his side. Then he straightened himself and began another circle.

"I moved him," the old man said. "I moved him then."

He felt faint again now but he held on the great fish all the strain that he could. I moved him, he thought. Maybe this time I can get him over. Pull, hands, he thought. Hold up, legs. Last for me, head. Last for me. You never went. This time I'll pull him over.

But when he put all of his effort on, starting it well out before the fish came alongside and pulling with all his strength, the fish pulled part way over and then righted himself and swam away.

"Fish," the old man said. "Fish, you are going to have to die anyway. Do you have to kill me too?"

That way nothing is accomplished, he thought. His mouth was too dry to speak but he could not reach for the water now. I must get him alongside this time, he thought. I am not good for many more turns. Yes you are, he told himself. You're good for ever. On the next turn, he nearly had him. But again the fish righted himself and swam slowly away.

4.2 The Jazz Age

The Jazz Age describes the period after the end of World War I, through the Roaring Twenties, ending with the onset of the Great Depression. The spirit of the Roaring Twenties was marked by a general feeling of discontinuity associated with modernity, a break with traditions. Jazz and dancing rose in popularity, in opposition to the mood of the specter of World War I. As such, the period is also often referred to as the Jazz Age. It is a time marked by frivolity, carelessness, hedonism and excitement in the life of the flaming youth. Fitzgerald is largely responsible for the term and many of his literary works portray it.

Francis Scott Key Fitzgerald: *The Great Gatsby*

An Introduction to Francis Scott Key Fitzgerald

Francis Scott Key Fitzgerald (September 24, 1896-December 21, 1940), known professionally as F. Scott Fitzgerald, was an American novelist and short-story writer, whose works illustrate the Jazz Age. While he achieved limited success in his lifetime, he is now widely regarded as one of the greatest American writers of the 20th century. Fitzgerald is considered a member of the "Lost Generation" of the 1920s. He finished four novels: *This Side of Paradise*, *The Beautiful and Damned*, *The Great Gatsby*, and *Tender Is the Night*. A fifth, unfinished novel, *The Last Tycoon*, was published posthumously.

Fitzgerald also authored 4 collections of short stories, as well as 164 short stories in magazines during his lifetime. Into the 21st century, millions of copies of *The Great Gatsby* and his other works have been sold, and Gatsby, a constant best-seller, is required reading in many high school and college classes.

An Introduction to the Film *The Great Gatsby*

The Great Gatsby is a 2013 period drama film based on F. Scott Fitzgerald's 1925 novel of the same name. The film was co-written and directed by Baz Luhrmann and stars Leonardo DiCaprio as the eponymous Jay Gatsby, with Tobey Maguire, Carey Mulligan, Joel Edgerton and Elizabeth Debicki in supporting roles. Production began in 2011 and took place in Australia, with $190 million budget.

The film follows the life and times of millionaire Jay Gatsby and his neighbor Nick (Maguire), who recounts his encounter with Gatsby at the height of the Roaring Twenties in New York state. The film polarized critics, receiving both praise and criticism for its acting performances, soundtrack, visual style, and direction. Audiences responded much more positively, and F. Scott Fitzgerald's granddaughter praised the film, stating "Scott would have been proud." As of 2016, it is Baz Luhrmann's highest-grossing film, having earned over $ 350 million worldwide. At the 86th Academy Awards, the film won in both of its nominated categories: Best Production Design and Best Costume Design.

Plot

In 1929, Nick Carraway, a World War I veteran, is receiving treatment for alcoholism at a psychiatric hospital. He talks about Jay Gatsby, the most hopeful man he had ever met. Nick's doctor suggests that he writes his thoughts down, since writing is Nick's passion.

In the summer of 1922, Nick moves from the Midwest to New York after abandoning writing. He rents a small house in the North Shore village of West Egg, next to the mansion of Gatsby, a mysterious business magnate who often holds extravagant parties. One day, while Nick has dinner with his cousin, Daisy Buchanan, and her husband, Tom, he is introduced to Jordan Baker by Daisy, who hopes to make a match between them. When Nick returns home, he sees Gatsby standing on the dock, reaching towards the green light coming from the Buchanan dock.

Jordan tells Nick that Tom has a mistress who lives in the "valley of ashes", an industrial dumping site between West Egg and New York City. Nick and Tom visit the valley and stop at a garage owned by George Wilson and his wife, Myrtle, Tom's mistress. Later, Nick receives an invitation to one of Gatsby's parties. Upon arrival, Nick learns he is the only one to receive an invitation and none of the guests have ever met Gatsby. Nick encounters Jordan, and both meet Gatsby. Gatsby offers Nick a ride to town for lunch. On the way, Gatsby tells Nick he is an Oxford graduate and war hero from a wealthy Midwestern family. They go to a speakeasy, where Gatsby introduces Nick to his business partner, Meyer Wolfsheim.

Jordan tells Nick that Gatsby had a relationship with Daisy years ago and is still in love with her, and that Gatsby threw parties in the hopes that Daisy would attend. Gatsby asks Nick to invite Daisy to tea. After an awkward reunion, Gatsby and Daisy begin an affair. Gatsby is dismayed when Daisy wants to run away with him and wants her to get a divorce. He asks Nick and Jordan to accompany him to the Buchanan home, where he and Daisy plan to tell Tom that Daisy is leaving him. During the luncheon, Tom becomes suspicious of Gatsby and Daisy, but Daisy stops Gatsby from revealing anything to Tom and suggests they all go to the Plaza Hotel.

Tom drives Nick and Jordan in Gatsby's car, while Gatsby drives Daisy in Tom's car. Tom stops for gas at George's garage, where George tells him that he and Myrtle are moving and that he suspects Myrtle is unfaithful.

At the Plaza, Gatsby tells Tom of his affair with Daisy. Tom accuses Gatsby of having never attended Oxford and having made his fortune through bootlegging with mobsters. Daisy says she loves Gatsby but cannot bring herself to say she never loved Tom. Eventually, both Gatsby and Daisy leave. After a fight with George over her infidelity, Myrtle runs into the street and is fatally struck by Gatsby's car after mistaking it for Tom's. After learning about Myrtle's death, Tom tells George that the car belongs to Gatsby and that he suspects Gatsby was Myrtle's lover. Nick deduces Daisy was the driver, though Gatsby intends to take the blame. Nick overhears Daisy accepting Tom's promise to take care of everything, but he does not tell Gatsby. Gatsby admits to Nick that he was born penniless; his real name is James Gatz, and he had asked Daisy to wait for him until he had made something of himself.

The next day, Gatsby hears the phone ringing and thinks it is Daisy. Before he can answer it, he is shot and killed by George, who then kills himself. Nick is the only person other than reporters to attend Gatsby's funeral, as Daisy and Tom are leaving New York. The media paints Gatsby as Myrtle's lover and killer. Disgusted with both the city and its inhabitants, Nick leaves after taking a final walk through Gatsby's deserted mansion and reflecting on Gatsby's ability to hope. In the sanatorium, Nick finishes typing his memoir, titling it *The Great Gatsby*.

Excerpt from the Book *The Great Gatsby*

Chapter 1

In my younger and more vulnerable years my father gave me some advice that I've been turning over in my mind ever since.

"Whenever you feel like criticizing any one," he told me, "just remember that all the people in this world haven't had the advantages that you've had."

He didn't say any more but we've always been unusually communicative in a reserved way, and I understood that he meant a great deal more than that. In consequence I'm inclined to reserve all judgments, a habit that has opened up many curious natures to me and also made me the victim of not a few veteran bores. The abnormal mind is quick to detect and attach itself to this quality when it appears in a normal person, and so it came about that in college I was unjustly accused of being a politician, because I was privy to the secret griefs of wild, unknown men. Most of the confidences were unsought—frequently I have feigned sleep, preoccupation, or a hostile levity when I realized by some unmistakable sign that an intimate revelation was quivering on the horizon—for the intimate revelations of young men or at least the terms in which they express them are usually plagiaristic and marred by obvious suppressions. Reserving judgments is a matter of infinite hope. I am still a little afraid of missing something if I forget that, as my father snobbishly suggested, and I snobbishly repeat a sense of the fundamental decencies is parcelled out unequally at birth.

And, after boasting this way of my tolerance, I come to the admission that it has a limit. Conduct may be founded on the hard rock or the wet marshes but after a certain point I don't care what it's founded on.

When I came back from the East last autumn I felt that I wanted the world to be in uniform and at a sort of moral attention forever; I wanted no more riotous excursions with privileged glimpses into the human heart. Only Gatsby, the man who gives his name to this book, was exempt from my reaction—Gatsby who represented everything for which I have an unaffected scorn. If personality is an unbroken series of successful gestures, then there was something gorgeous about him, some heightened sensitivity to the promises of life, as if he were related to one of those intricate machines that register earthquakes ten thousand miles away. This responsiveness had nothing to do with that flabby impressionability which is dignified under the name of the "creative temperament"—it was an extraordinary gift for hope, a romantic readiness such as I have never found in any other person and which it is not likely I shall ever find again. No—Gatsby turned out all right at the end; it is what preyed on Gatsby, what foul dust floated in the wake of his dreams that temporarily closed out my interest in the abortive sorrows and short-winded elations of men.

My family have been prominent, well-to-do people in this middle-western city for three generations. The Carraways are something of a clan and we have a tradition that we're descended from the Dukes of Buccleuch, but the actual founder of my line was my grandfather's brother who came here in fifty-one, sent a substitute to the Civil War and started the wholesale hardware business that my father carries on today.

I never saw this great-uncle but I'm supposed to look like him—with special reference to the rather hard-boiled painting that hangs in Father's office. I graduated from New Haven in 1915, just a quarter of a century after my father, and a little later I participated in that delayed Teutonic migration known as the Great War. I enjoyed the counter-raid so thoroughly that I came back restless. Instead of being the warm center of the world the middle-west now seemed like the ragged edge of the universe—so I decided to go east and learn the bond business. Everybody I knew was in the bond business so I supposed it could support one more single man. All my aunts and uncles talked it over as if they were choosing a prep-school for me and finally said, "Why—yees" with very grave, hesitant faces. Father agreed to finance me for a year and after various delays I came east, permanently, I thought, in the spring of twenty-two.

The practical thing was to find rooms in the city but it was a warm season and I had just left a country of wide lawns and friendly trees, so when a young man at the office suggested that we take a house together in a commuting town it sounded like a great idea. He found the house, a weather beaten cardboard bungalow at eighty a month, but at the last minute the firm ordered him to Washington and I went out to the country alone. I had a dog, at least I had him for a few days until he ran away, and an old Dodge and a Finnish woman who made my bed and cooked breakfast and muttered Finnish wisdom to herself over the electric stove.

It was lonely for a day or so until one morning some man, more recently arrived than I, stopped me on the road.

"How do you get to West Egg village?" he asked helplessly.

I told him. And as I walked on I was lonely no longer. I was a guide, a pathfinder, an original settler. He had casually conferred on me the freedom of the neighborhood. And so with the sunshine and the great bursts of leaves growing on the trees—just as things grow in fast movies—I had that familiar conviction that life was beginning over again with the summer.

There was so much to read for one thing and so much fine health to be pulled down out of the young breath-giving air. I bought a dozen volumes on banking and credit and investment securities and they stood on my shelf in red and gold like new money from the mint, promising to unfold the shining secrets that only Midas and Morgan and Maecenas knew. And I had the high intention of reading many other books besides.

I was rather literary in college—one year I wrote a series of very solemn and obvious editorials for the "Yale News"—and now I was going to bring back all such things into my life and become again that most limited of all specialists, the "well-rounded man." This isn't just an epigram—life is much more successfully looked at from a single window, after all.

It was a matter of chance that I should have rented a house in one of the strangest communities in North America. It was on that slender riotous island which extends itself due east of New York and where there are, among other natural curiosities, two unusual formations of land. Twenty miles from the city a pair of enormous eggs, identical in contour and separated only by a courtesy bay, jut out into the most domesticated body of salt water in the Western Hemisphere, the great wet barnyard of Long Island Sound. They are not perfect ovals—like the egg in the Columbus story they are both crushed flat at the contact end—but their physical resemblance must be a source of perpetual confusion to the gulls that fly overhead. To the wingless a more arresting phenomenon is their dissimilarity in every particular except shape and size.

4.3 The Great Depression

The Great Depression was a severe worldwide economic depression that took place during the 1930s. The timing of the Great Depression varied across nations; in most countries it started in 1929 and lasted until 1941. It was the longest, deepest, and most widespread depression of the 20th century. The Great Depression has been the subject of much writing, as authors have sought to evaluate an era that caused both financial and emotional trauma. Perhaps the most noteworthy and famous novel written on the subject is *The Grapes of Wrath*.

John Steinbeck: *The Grapes of Wrath*

An Introduction to John Steinbeck

John Ernst Steinbeck, Jr. (February 27, 1902-December 20, 1968) was an American author who won the 1962 Nobel Prize in Literature "for his realistic and imaginative writings, combining as they do sympathetic humor and keen social perception". He has been called "a giant of American letters", and many of his works are considered classics of Western literature.

During his writing career, he authored 27 books, including 16 novels, six non-fiction books, and two collections of short stories. He is widely known for the comic novels *Tortilla Flat* (*1935*) and *Cannery Row* (*1945*), the multi-generation epic *East of Eden* (*1952*), and the novellas *Of Mice and Men* (*1937*) and *The Red Pony* (*1937*). The Pulitzer Prize-winning *The Grapes of Wrath* (*1939*) is considered Steinbeck's masterpiece and part of the American literary canon. In the first 75 years after it was published, it sold 14 million copies.

Most of Steinbeck's work is set in central California, particularly in the Salinas Valley and the California Coast Ranges region. His works frequently explored the themes of fate and injustice, especially as applied to downtrodden or everyman protagonists.

An Introduction to the Film *The Grapes of Wrath*

The Grapes of Wrath is a 1940 drama film directed by John Ford. It was based on John

Steinbeck's 1939 Pulitzer Prize-winning novel of the same name. The screenplay was written by Nunnally Johnson and the executive producer was Darryl F. Zanuck.

The film tells the story of the Joads, an Oklahoma family, who, after losing their farm during the Great Depression in the 1930s, become migrant workers and end up in California. The motion picture details their arduous journey across the United States as they travel to California in search of work and opportunities for the family members.

The film is widely considered as one of the greatest American films of all time. In 1989, this film was one of the first 25 films to be selected for preservation in the United States National Film Registry by the Library of Congress as being "culturally, historically, or aesthetically significant".

Plot

The film opens with Tom Joad, released from prison and hitchhiking his way back to his parents' family farm in Oklahoma. Tom finds an itinerant ex-preacher named Jim Casy sitting under a tree by the side of the road. Casy was the preacher who baptized Tom, but now Casy has "lost the spirit" and his faith (presaging his imminent conversion to communism). Casy goes with Tom to the Joad property only to find it deserted. There, they meet Muley Graves who is hiding out. In a flashback, he describes how farmers all over the area were forced from their farms by the deed holders of the land. A local boy, hired for the purpose, is shown knocking down Muley's house with a Caterpillar tractor. The large Joad family of twelve leaves at daybreak, along with Casy, who decides to accompany them. They pack everything into a dilapidated 1926 Hudson "Super Six" sedan adapted to serve as a truck in order to make the long journey to the promised land of California.

The trip along Highway 66 is arduous, and it soon takes a toll on the Joad family. The elderly Grandpa dies along the way. Tom writes the circumstances surrounding the death on a page from the family *Bible* and places it on the body before they bury it so that if his remains were found, his death would not be investigated as a possible homicide. They park in a camp and meet a man, a migrant returning from California, who laughs at Pa's optimism about conditions in California. He speaks bitterly about his experiences in the West.

The family arrives at the first transient migrant campground for workers and finds the camp is crowded with other starving, jobless and desperate travelers. Their truck slowly makes its way through the dirt road between the shanty houses and around the camp's hungry-faced inhabitants. Tom says, "Sure don't look none too prosperous."

After some trouble with a so-called "agitator", the Joads leave the camp in a hurry. The Joads make their way to another migrant camp, the Keene Ranch. After doing some work in the fields, they discover the high food prices in the company store for meat and other products. The store is the only one in the area, by a long shot. Later they find a group of migrant workers are striking, and Tom wants to find out all about it. He goes to a secret meeting in the dark woods. When the meeting is discovered, Casy is killed by one of the camp guards. As Tom tries to defend Casy from the attack, he inadvertently kills the guard.

Tom suffers a serious wound on his cheek, and the camp guards realize it will not be difficult to identify him. That evening the family hides Tom under the mattresses of the truck just as guards arrive to question them; they are searching for the man who killed the guard. Tom avoids being spotted and the family leaves the Keene Ranch without further incident. After driving for a while, they have to stop at the top of a hill when the engine overheats due to a broken fan belt; they have little gas, but decide to try coasting down the hill to some lights. The lights are from a third type of camp: Farmworkers' Wheat Patch Camp (Weedpatch in the book), a clean camp run by the Department of Agriculture, complete with indoor toilets and showers, which the Joad children had never seen before.

Tom is moved to work for change by what he has witnessed in the various camps. He tells his family that he plans to carry on Casy's mission in the world by fighting for social reform. He leaves to seek a new world and to join the movement committed to social justice.

Excerpt from the Book *The Grapes of Wrath*

A HUGE RED TRANSPORT truck stood in front of the little roadside restaurant. The vertical exhaust pipe muttered softly, and an almost invisible haze of steel-blue smoke hovered over its end. It was a new truck, shining red, and in twelve-inch letters on its sides —OKLAHOMA CITY TRANSPORT COMPANY. —Its double tires were new, and a brass padlock stood straight out from the hasp on the big back doors. Inside the screened restaurant a radio played, quiet dance music turned low the way it is when no one is listening. A small outlet fan turned silently in its circular hole over the entrance, and flies buzzed excitedly about the doors and windows, butting the screens. Inside, one man, the truck driver, sat on a stool and rested his elbows on the counter and looked over his coffee at the lean and lonely waitress. He talked the smart listless language of the roadsides to her. "I seen him about three months ago. He had an operation. Cut somepin out. I forget what." And she—"Doesn't seem no longer than a week I seen him myself. Looked fine then. He's a nice sort of a guy when he ain't stinko." Now and then the flies roared softly at the screen door. The coffee machine spurted steam, and the waitress, without looking, reached behind her and shut it off.

Outside, a man walking along the edge of the highway crossed over and approached the truck. He walked slowly to the front of it, put his hand on the shiny fender, and looked at the "No Riders" sticker on the windshield. For a moment he side away from the restaurant. He was not over thirty. His eyes were very dark brown and there was a hint of brown pigment in his eyeballs. His cheek bones were high and wide, and strong deep lines cut down his cheeks, in curves beside his mouth. His upper lip was long, and since his teeth protruded, the lips stretched to cover them, for this man kept his lips closed. His hands were hard, with broad fingers and nails as thick and ridged as little clam shells. The space between thumb and forefinger and the hams of his hands were shiny with callus.

The man's clothes were new—all of them, cheap and new. His gray cap was so new that the visor was still stiff and the button still on, not shapeless and bulged as it would be when it had served for a while all the various purposes of a cap—carrying sack, towel, handkerchief. His suit was of cheap gray hard cloth and so new that there were creases in the trousers. His blue chambray shirt was stiff and smooth with filler. The coat was too big, the trousers too short, for he was a tall man. The coat shoulder peaks hung down on his arms, and even then the sleeves were too short and the front of the coat flapped loosely over his stomach. He wore a pair of new tan shoes of the kind called "army last", hob-nailed and with half-circles like horseshoes to protect the edges of the heels from wear. This man sat on the running board and took off his cap and mopped his face with it. Then he put on the cap, and by pulling started the future ruin of the visor. His feet caught his attention. He leaned down and loosened the shoelaces, and did not tie the ends again. Over his head the exhaust of the Diesel engine whispered in quick puffs of blue smoke.

The music stopped in the restaurant and a man's voice spoke from the loudspeaker, but the waitress did not turn him off, for she didn't know the music had stopped. Her exploring fingers had found a lump under her ear. She was trying to see it in a mirror behind the counter without letting the truck driver know, and so she pretended to push a bit of hair to neatness. The truck driver said, "They was a big dance in Shawnee. I heard somebody got killed or somepin. You hear anything?" "No," said the waitress, and she lovingly fingered the lump under her ear.

5. Contemporary Works

Though its exact parameters remain debatable, from the early 1970s to the present day the most salient literary movement has been postmodernism.

One of the key developments in late-20th-century American literature was the rise to prominence of literature written by and about ethnic minorities beyond African Americans and Jewish Americans, who had already established their literary inheritances. This development came alongside the growth of the Civil Rights movements and its corollary, the Ethnic Pride movement, which led to the creation of Ethnic Studies programs in most major universities.

5.1 Alice Walker: *The Color Purple*

An Introduction to Alice Walker

Alice Malsenior Walker (born February 9, 1944) is an American novelist, short-story writer, poet, and activist.

She wrote the critically acclaimed novel *The Color Purple* (1982) for which she won the National Book Award and the Pulitzer Prize for Fiction. She also wrote the novels *Meridian* (*1976*) and *The Third Life of Grange Copeland* (1970), among other works.

Walker became interested in the Civil Rights Movement in part due to the influence of activist Howard Zinn, who was one of her professors at Spelman College. To continue the activism of her college years, Walker returned to the South from New York. She participated in voter registration drives, campaigns for welfare rights, and children's programs in Mississippi.

An Introduction to the Film *The Color Purple*

The Color Purple is a 1985 American period drama film directed by Steven Spielberg and written by Menno Meyjes, based on the Pulitzer Prize-winning novel of the same name by Alice Walker.

It was Spielberg's eighth film as a director, and was a change from the summer blockbusters for which he had become famous. The film was also the first feature-length film directed by Spielberg for which John Williams did not compose the music. The film starred Danny Glover, Desreta Jackson, Margaret Avery, Oprah Winfrey (in her film debut), Adolph Caesar, Rae Dawn Chong, and featured Whoopi Goldberg (also in her film debut) as Celie Harris-Johnson.

Filmed in Anson and Union counties in North Carolina, the film tells the story of a young African American girl named Celie Harris and shows the problems African American women faced during the early 20th century, including domestic violence, incest, pedophilia, poverty, racism, and sexism. Celie is transformed as she finds her self-worth through the help of two strong female companions.

Plot

Set in rural Georgia during the first 40 years of the twentieth century, the film centers on the life of a fictional character named Celie, an oppressed black woman. In the film, Celie endures rape, sexism, the loss of her children at birth, a tyrannical husband, domestic violence, chauvinism, the loss of her sister, and the demoralization of her friend (Sofia), who also loses her freedom to the law.

Celie and the other characters tell a story of overcoming racism and misogyny in the rural south during this time period, depicting a struggle for equality. Celie maintains her resolve throughout the story. By the end of the film, the characters have undergone remarkable changes and relationships have begun to heal.

Excerpt from the Book *The Color Purple*

Samuel asked if they'd ever seen the white woman missionary twenty miles farther on, and he said no. Twenty miles through the jungle is a very long trip. The men might hunt up to ten miles around the village, but the women stayed close to their huts and fields.

Then one of the women asked a question. We looked at Joseph. He said the woman wanted to know if the children belonged to me or to Corrine or to both of us. Joseph said they belonged to Corrine. The woman looked us both over, and said something else. We looked at Joseph. He said the woman said they both looked like me. We all laughed politely.

Then another woman had a question. She wanted to know if I was also Samuel's wife. Joseph said no, that I was a missionary just like Samuel and Corrine. Then someone said they never suspected missionaries could have children. Then another said he never dreamed missionaries could be black.

Then someone said, that the new missionaries would be black and two of them women was exactly what he had dreamed, and just last night, too.

By now there was a lot of commotion. Little heads began to pop from behind mothers' skirts and over big sisters' shoulders. And we were sort of swept along among the villagers, about three hundred of them, to a place without walls but with a leaf roof, where we all sat down on the ground, men in front, women and children behind. Then there was loud whispering among some very old men who looked like the church elders back home? With their baggy trousers and shiny, ill-fitting coats? Did black missionaries drink palm wine?

Corrine looked at Samuel and Samuel looked at Corrine. But me and the children were already drinking it, because someone had already put the little brown clay glasses in our hands and we were too nervous not to start sipping.

We got there around four o'clock, and sat under the leaf canopy until nine. We had our first meal there, a chicken and groundnut (peanut) stew which we ate with our fingers. But mostly we listened to songs and watched dances that raised lots of dust. The biggest part of the welcoming ceremony was about the roofleaf, which Joseph interpreted for us as one of the villagers recited the story that it is based upon. The people of this village think they have always lived on the exact spot where then; village now stands. And this spot has been good to them, they plant cassava fields that yield huge crops. They plant ground nuts that do the same. They plant yam and cotton and millet. All kinds of things. But once, a long time ago, one man in the village wanted more than his share of land to plant. He wanted to make more crops so as to use his surplus for trade with the white men on the coast. Because he was chief at the time, he gradually took more and more of the common land, and took more and more wives to work it. As his greed increased he also began to cultivate the land on which the roofleaf grew. Even his wives were upset by this and tried to complain, but they were lazy women and no one paid any attention to them. Nobody could remember a time when roofleaf did not exist in overabundant amounts. But eventually, the greedy chief took so much of this land that even the elders were disturbed. So he simply bought them off? with axes and cloth and cooking pots that he got from the coast traders.

But then there came a great storm during the rainy season that destroyed all the roofs on all the huts in the village, and the people discovered to their dismay that there was no longer any roofleaf to be found. Where roofleaf had flourished from time's beginning, there was Cassava. Millet. Groundnuts.

5.2 Amy Tan: *The Joy Luck Club*

An Introduction to Amy Tan

Amy Tan (born February 19, 1952) is an American writer whose works explore mother-daughter relationships and the Chinese American experience. Her novel *The Joy Luck Club* was adapted into a film in 1993 by director Wayne Wang.

Tan has written several other novels, including *The Kitchen God's Wife*, *The Hundred Secret Senses*, *The Bonesetter's Daughter*, *Saving Fish from Drowning*, and *The Valley of Amazement*. She also wrote a collection of non-fiction essays entitled The *Opposite of Fate: A Book of Musings*. In addition to these, Tan has written two children's books: *The Moon Lady* (1992) and *Sagwa*, *the Chinese Siamese Cat* (1994), which was turned into an animated series that aired on PBS.

Though she has won several awards for her work, Tan has also received substantial criticism for her "complicity in perpetuating racial stereotypes and misrepresentations as well as gross inaccuracies in recalling details of the Chinese cultural heritage". This, along with her frequently negative depiction of Chinese culture in her work, has led several writers and scholars to accuse Tan of pandering to Western presumptions and prejudices about Chinese people.

An Introduction to the Film *The Joy Luck Club*

The Joy Luck Club is a 1993 American film about the relationships between Chinese-American women and their Chinese mothers. It was directed by Wayne Wangand stars Ming-Na Wen, Rosalind Chao, Lauren Tom, Tamlyn Tomita, France Nguyen, Kieu Chinh, Lisa Lu, and Tsai Chin.

The film is based on the eponymous 1989 novel by Amy Tan, who co-wrote the screenplay with Ronald Bass. The film was produced by Bass, Tan, Wang and Patrick Markey while Oliver Stone served as an executive producer. Four older women, all Chinese immigrants living in San Francisco, meet regularly to play mahjong, eat, and tell stories. Each of these women has an adult Chinese-American daughter. The film reveals the hidden pasts of the older women and their daughters and how their lives are shaped by the clash of Chinese and American cultures as they strive to understand their family bonds and one another.

The film was privately screened in sneak previews in spring 1993 and film festivals in August and September 1993. It premiered in Los Angeles, New York City, and San Francisco on September 8, 1993. With the film's $10.5 million budget, it was moderately successful in the box office. It received positive critical reactions but also criticism of its perceived stereotypical presentation of Asian American male characters.

Plot

The Joy Luck Club was formed by four women in San Francisco: Lindo Jong, Ying-Ying St. Clair, An-Mei Hsu, and Suyuan Woo. The members have mainly played mahjong and told each other's stories over the years. They emigrated from their native country, China, remarried, and gave birth to children in America. Suyuan's daughter June replaced her when Suyuan died four months before the time the film is set. The mothers have high hopes for their daughters' success, but the daughters struggle through "anxieties, feelings of inadequacy, and failures". Throughout the film, the mothers and daughters bond by learning to understand each other and by overcoming their conflicts.

The film begins with June's prologue tale. In the prologue, a woman (presumably Suyuan) bought a swan in China from a market vendor who was selling it as "a duck that stretched its neck (to become) a goose". She kept it as her pet and brought it to the United States. When the immigration officials took it away from her, she plucked out only a swan feather instead while she struggled to grab the swan away. For a long time, the woman had kept the feather, planning to someday give the feather to her daughter.

Then the film transits to June's farewell surprise party in San Francisco for her upcoming reunion with her long-lost twin sisters in China. Among the guests are members of The Joy Luck Club, their daughters, other relatives, and friends. The following characters below narrate their journeys to the audience while they reflect upon their pasts.

Excerpt from the Book *The Joy luck Club*

When I was a young girl in China, my grandmother told me my mother was a ghost. This did not mean my mother was dead. In those days, a ghost was anything we were forbidden to talk about. So I knew Popo wanted me to forget my mother on purpose, and this is how I came to remember nothing of her. The life that I knew began in the large house in Ningpo with the cold hallways and tall stairs. This was my uncle and auntie's family house, where I lived with Popo and my little brother.

But I often heard stories of a ghost who tried to take children away, especially strong-willed little girls who were disobedient. Many times Popo said aloud to all who could hear that my brother and I had fallen out of the bowels of a stupid goose, two eggs that nobody wanted, not even good enough to crack over rice porridge. She said this so that the ghosts would not steal us away. So you see, to Popo we were also very precious.

All my life, Popo scared me. I became even more scared when she grew sick. This was in 1923, when I was nine years old. Popo had swollen up like an overripe squash, so full her flesh had gone soft and rotten with a bad smell. She would call me into her room with the terrible stink and tell me stories. "An-mei", she said, calling me by my school name. "Listen carefully." She told me stories I could not understand.

One was about a greedy girl whose belly grew fatter and fatter. This girl poisoned herself after refusing to say whose child she carried. When the monks cut open her body, they found inside a large white winter melon.

"If you are greedy, what is inside you is what makes you always hungry," said Popo.

Another time, Popo told me about a girl who refused to listen to her elders. One day this bad girl shook her head so vigorously to refuse her auntie's simple request that a little white ball fell from her ear and out poured all her brains, as clear as chicken broth.

"Your own thoughts are so busy swimming inside that everything else gets pushed out," Popo told me.

Right before Popo became so sick she could no longer speak, she pulled me close and talked to me about my mother. "Never say her name," she warned. "To say her name is to spit on your father's grave."

The only father I knew was a big painting that hung in the main hall. He was a large, unsmiling man, unhappy to be so still on the wall. His restless eyes followed me around the house. Even from my room at the end of the hall, I could see my father's watching eyes. Popo said he watched me for any signs of disrespect. So sometimes, when I had thrown pebbles at other children at school, or had lost a book through carelessness, I would quickly walk by my father with a know-nothing look and hide in a corner of my room where he could not see my face.

I felt our house was so unhappy, but my little brother did not seem to think so. He rode his bicycle through the courtyard, chasing chickens and other children, laughing over which ones shrieked the loudest. Inside the quiet house, he jumped up and down on Uncle and Auntie's best feather sofas when they were away visiting village friends.

But even my brother's happiness went away. One hot summer day when Popo was already very sick, we stood outside watching a village funeral procession marching by our courtyard. Just as it passed our gate, the heavy framed picture of the dead man toppled from its stand and fell to the dusty ground. An old lady screamed and fainted. My brother laughed and Auntie slapped him.

My auntie, who had a very bad temper with children, told him he had no *shou*, no respect for ancestors or family, just like our mother. Auntie had a tongue like hungry scissors eating silk cloth. So when my brother gave her a sour look, Auntie said our mother was so thoughtless she had fled north in a big hurry, without taking the dowry furniture from her marriage to my father, without bringing her ten pairs of silver chopsticks, without paying respect to my father's grave and those of our ancestors. When my brother accused Auntie of frightening our mother away, Auntie shouted that our mother had married a man named Wu Tsing who already had a wife, two concubines, and other bad children.

And when my brother shouted that Auntie was a talking chicken without a head, she pushed my brother against the gate and spat on his face.

"You throw strong words at me, but you are nothing," Auntie said. "You are the son of a mother who has so little respect she has become *ni*, a traitor to our ancestors. She is so beneath others that even the devil must look down to see her."

That is when I began to understand the stories Popo taught me, the lessons I had to learn for my mother. "When you lose your face, An-mei," Popo often said, "it is like dropping your necklace down a well. The only way you can get it back is to fall in after it."

Now I could imagine my mother, a thoughtless woman who laughed and shook her head, who dipped her chopsticks many times to eat another piece of sweet fruit, happy to be free of Popo, her unhappy husband on the wall, and her two disobedient children. I felt unlucky that she was my mother and unlucky that she had left us. These were the thoughts I had while hiding in the corner of my room where my father could not watch me.

◎ Exercises

1. Explain the following terms in English.

1) The Jazz Age

2) Naturalism

3) Lost Generation

4) The Great Depression

2. Match the following representatives and their works.

1) Herman Melville

2) Henry James

3) Mark Twain

4) John Griffith London

5) Theodore Dreiser

6) Ernest Hemingway

7) Francis Scott Key Fitzgerald

8) John Steinbeck

9) Nathaniel Hawthorne

a. *The Old Man and the Sea*

b. *The Wings of the Dove*

c. *The Million Pound Note*

d. *The Grapes of Wrath*

e. *Moby Dick*

f. *The Scarlet Letter*

g. *The Call of the Wild*

h. *The Great Gatsby*

i. *Sister Carrie*

3. Discuss and answer the following questions.

1) Who has been called "a giant of American letters"? Can you explain the writing style of him after reading excerpt from his works?

2) Please list some representative writers of "Lost Generation" and their famous masterpiece.

3) Mark Twain was lauded as the "greatest humorist this country has produced". Can you explain the humor writing way in *The Million Pound Note*?

Module Three

Culture in English Films

Unit 1
Introduction

It may be undeniable that the pleasure of watching a film is somewhat fleeting, but it is also widely acceptable that the impression of a good one could be ingrained and indelible, inspiring relentless pursuit of appreciation and study. Here comes the question: what makes a film triumphant, and so absorbing— spectacular or subtle, exotic but accessible? Attempting to unravel the answer as a goal comes to this module.

1. Culture in Films

Are you familiar with the culture in your favorite film? Many of you would say "no" or "maybe". Some would insist that to touch the culture should be the duty of film critics, while some others would say it's simple: "culture" equals to "theme" in film study. Actually, however, the appreciation of culture in films are more associated with every viewer than just film makers or critics. And it would be wrong to assume that there is only one theme in every film. It is quite possible that the scriptwriter/director has intentionally allowed for the coexistence of more than one theme. It is also possible that different viewers will have different ideas as to what constitutes the theme(s), and both theme and film critics are involved in the understanding of culture in films.

1.1 Theme

Stated simply, the theme of a film is its main point; it is what the scriptwriter and director want to tell us. In more precise terms, theme is the controlling idea of the film. This idea takes the form of a generalized comment about life — a special understanding of human experience that has significance beyond the specific narrative and the individual lives of the character who act within it. In addition to constituting a general comment about life, the theme is also the central and controlling idea; it unifies the film and makes it intellectually and emotionally coherent. Theme is not a peripheral or momentary observation cast off by one of the characters, nor is it a side effect of the narrative. It is that center of gravity around which all the other elements of the film (genre, character, narrative, style) imperceptibly revolve. Take the genre of science fiction for example, the theme of *Avatar* is "the conflict between modern human and nature", while the theme explored in *Star Wars* is "moral ambiguity" or "the conflict between technology and nature".

Nevertheless, a film cannot be reduced to its theme. A film is a work of art, not a philosophical treatise or speculative essay. A work of art, when it conveys an idea, must convey that idea artistically. This means that we should not expect to find a film's theme spelt out to us unambiguously in the form of a statement or argument. Instead, theme will emerge gradually from, and be expressed through, the film's genre, characters, narrative, and style. Theme only properly exists when it is fully integrated into the film as a whole.

1.2 Film Criticism

Film criticism is the analysis and evaluation of films, individually and collectively. In general, this can be divided into journalistic criticism that appears regularly in newspapers and other popular, mass-media outlets and academic criticism by film scholars that is informed by film theory and published in academic journals.

We characterize film criticism as a form of writing which addresses films as potential achievements and wishes to convey their distinctiveness and quality. For many people film criticism is something by an opinionated journalist, a film critic, who tells you whether a film is worth seeing. The most characteristic trait of a newspaper or web review is the announcement of judgments on the acting, story and cinematography.

Whether a film is a rotten tomato or a brilliant work of art, if people are watching it, it's worth critiquing. A good film review should entertain, persuade and inform, providing an original opinion without giving away too much of the plot. A great film review can be a work of art in its own right.

1.3 Film Appreciation

Firstly, you need to study Your Source Material, that is, how to appreciate a film.

Step 1: *Gather basic facts about the film.* You can do this before or after you watch the film, but you should definitely do it before you write the review, because you'll need to weave the facts into your review as you write. Here's what you need to know:

- The title of the film, and the year it came out.
- The director's name.
- The names of the leading actors.
- The genre.

Step 2: *Take notes on the film as you watch it.* Before you sit down to watch a film, get out a notepad or a laptop to take notes. Films are long, and you can easily forget details or major plot points. Taking notes allows you to jot down little things you can return to later.

- Make a note every time something sticks out to you, whether it's good or bad. This could be costuming, makeup, set design, music, etc. Think about how this detail relates to the rest of the film and what it means in the context of your review.
- Take note of patterns you begin to notice as the film unfolds.
- Use the pause button frequently so you make sure not to miss anything, and rewind as necessary.

Step 3: *Analyze the mechanics of the film.* Analyze the different components that came together in the film as you watch. During or after your viewing, ask yourself what impression the film left with you in these areas:

- Direction. Consider the director and how he or she chooses to portray/explain the events in the story. If the film was slow, or didn't include things you thought were necessary, you can attribute this to the director. If you've seen other films directed by the same person, compare them and determine which you like the most.
- Cinematography. What techniques were used to film the film? What setting and background elements helped to create a certain tone?
- Writing. Evaluate the script, including dialogue and characterization. Did you feel like the plot was inventive and unpredictable or boring and weak? Did the characters' words seem credible to you?
- Editing. Was the film choppy or did it flow smoothly from scene to scene? Take note of the use of lighting and other ambient effects. If the move has computer-generated graphics, think about whether or not they looked realistic/fit in with the rest of the film.
- Costume design. Did the clothing choices fit the style of the film? Did they contribute to the overall tone, rather than digressing from it?
- Set design. Consider how the setting of the film influenced its other elements. Did it add or subtract from the experience for you? If the film was filmed in a real place, was this location well-chosen?
- Score or soundtrack. Did it work with the scenes? Was it over/under-used? Was it suspenseful? Amusing? Irritating? A soundtrack can make or break a film, especially if the songs have a particular message or meaning to them.

Step 4: *Watch it one more time.* It's impossible to fully understand a film you've only seen one time, especially if you're pausing it often to take notes. Watch it at least once more before you compose your review. Pay attention to details you might have missed the first time around. Pick new points of focus again; if you took a lot of notes on the acting the first time you watched the film, focus on the cinematography the second time around.

Secondly, you will start to compose your review:

Step 1: *Create an original thesis based on your analysis.* Now that you've thoroughly studied the film, what unique insights can you bring to the table? Come up with a thesis, a central idea to discuss and back up with your observations on the various elements of the film. Your thesis should be discussed in the first paragraph of your review. Having a thesis will take your review beyond the plot summary stage and into the realm of film criticism, which is rightfully its own art form. Ask yourself the following questions to come up with a compelling thesis for your review:

- Does the film reflect on a current event or contemporary issue? It could be the director's way of engaging in a bigger conversation. Look for ways to relate the content of the film to the "real" world.
- Does the film seem to have a message, or does it attempt to elicit a specific response or emotion from the audience? You could discuss whether or not it achieves its own goals.
- Does the film connect with you on a personal level? You could write a review stemming from your own feelings and weave in some personal stories to make it interesting for your readers.

Step 2: *Follow your thesis paragraph with a short plot summary.* It's good to give readers an idea of what they'll be in for if they decide to see the film you're reviewing. Give a brief summary of the plot in which you identify the main characters, describe the setting, and give a sense of the central conflict or point of the film. Never break the number one rule of film reviews: don't give too much away. Don't ruin the film for your readers!

- When you name characters in your plot summary, list the actors' names directly afterward in parenthesis.
- Find a place to mention the director's name and the full film title.
- If you feel you must discuss information that might "spoil" things for readers, warn them first.

Step 3: *Move into your analysis of the film.* Write several paragraphs discussing interesting elements of the film that support your thesis. Discuss the acting, the direction, the cinematography, the setting, and so on, using clear, entertaining prose that keeps your readers engaged.

- Keep your writing clear and easy to understand. Don't use too much technical filmmaking jargon, and make your language crisp and accessible.
- Present both the facts and your opinion. For example, you might state something such as, "The Baroque background music was a jarring contrast to the 20th century setting". This is a lot more informative then simply saying, "The music was a strange choice for the film."

Step 4: *Use plenty of examples to back up your points.* If you make a statement about the film, back it up with a descriptive example. Describe the way scenes look, the way a certain person acted, camera angles, and so on. You can quote dialogue to help you make your points as well. In this way you are giving your readers a feel for the film and continuing to express your critique of the film at the same time.

***Step 5**: Give it some personality.* You could treat your review like a formal college essay, but it's more interesting if you make it your own. If your writing style is usually witty and funny, your review should be no exception. If you're serious and dramatic, that works, too. Let your language and writing style reflect your unique perspective and personality — it's much more entertaining for the reader.

***Step 6**: Wrap up your review with a conclusion.* It should tie back to your original thesis and provide some guidance as to whether the audience should go see the film. Your conclusion should also be compelling or entertaining on its own, since it's the end of your piece of writing.

Now you have already finished your review. Finally, you might polish your piece.

***Step 1**: Edit your review.* Once you've finished the first draft, read it through and decide whether it flows well and has the right structure. You may need to shift paragraphs around, delete sentences, or add more materials here and there to fill out parts that are stunted. Give your review at least one editorial pass, and maybe two or three, before you consider it to be editorially sound.

- Ask yourself whether your review stayed true to your thesis. Did your conclusion tie back in with the initial ideas you proposed?
- Decide whether your review contains enough details about the film. You may need to go back and add more description here and there to give readers a better sense of what the film's about.
- Decide whether your review is interesting enough as a stand-alone piece of writing. Did you contribute something original to this discussion? What will readers gain from reading your review that they couldn't from simply watching the film?

***Step 2**: Proofread your review.* Make sure you've spelled all the actors' names correctly and that you got all the dates right. Clean up typos, grammatical errors, and other spelling errors as well. A clean, proofread review will seem much more professional than (one that's full of) silly mistakes.

***Step 3**: Publish or share your review.* Post it on your blog, share it in a film discussion forum, put it up on Facebook, or email it to your friends and family. Films are the quintessential art form of our time, and like all art, they spark controversy, provide a venue for self-reflection, and greatly influence our culture. All this means they're worth discussing, whether they're flops or works of pure genius. Congratulations for contributing your valuable opinion to the discussion.

1.4 Cultural Concerns in Films

Since themes, obscure or unambiguous expressed in films, are worthy of being tasted, appreciated, and interpreted as a cultural phenomenon, and the traditional way of film criticism seems too academic to be tackled by regular viewers, the cultural analysis and demonstration of English films in the module would be multidimensionally delved from typical cultural concerns rather than evaluated as complicated journalistic criticism that appears regularly in newspapers and other popular, mass-media outlets and academic criticism by film scholars.

Typical Cultural Concerns in Hollywood Films:

1) Broad Human Concerns. They commonly reflect the most basic and universal human concerns such as love, the nature of humanity, ethical concerns, the meaning of human existence, and the possibility of a divine force guiding human affairs. For an example, *The Shawshank Redemption*, touches the nature of humanity—to be free from captivity. Chicago Sun-Times film reviewer Roger Ebert argued that *The Shawshank Redemption* is an allegory for maintaining one's feeling of self-worth when placed in a hopeless position. Andy Dufresne's integrity is the essence of the story line, especially in prison, where integrity is lacking.

2) Life Philosophies. This concern is a "generalized comment on life", but it is rarely expressed as a statement of that kind. More commonly, films will present a protagonist whose lifestyle is, at the same time, a life philosophy; and, through the relative success or failure of that character, we assess the validity of that philosophy. Conversely, we may observe the validity of the opposing life philosophy by watching the fortunes of the antagonist.

   For the fans of *Forrest Gump*, the feather present at the opening and conclusion of the film would be unforgettable. Various interpretations have been suggested for this symbolic image. Sarah Lyall of *The New York Times* noted several suggestions made about the feather: "Does the white feather symbolize the unbearable lightness of being? Forrest Gump's impaired intellect? the randomness of experience?" Hanks interpreted the feather as: "Our destiny is only defined by how we deal with the chance elements to our life and that's kind of the embodiment of the feather as it comes in. Here is this thing that can land anywhere and that it lands at your feet."

3) Religious and Ethical Concerns. The West is a fundamentally Christian culture, and although the influence of formal religion and the established Churches has declined over recent decades, the power of the Christian faith to determine the shape of one's spirituality and ethical values remains strong. Some films focus on the spiritual aspects of religion while others focus on the ethical values that derive from religion. For an example, *The Matrix* reflects a Christian ideal of transcendence (the desire to transcend the everyday world).

4) Historical Issues. These concerns commonly emerge as responses to specific historical periods or events, especially if they are foundational and /or controversial and / or have a continuing relevance today. In the West, the history of the Roman Empire has been a regular topic because it brought the West into being as a coherent political and geographical entity (e. g. *The Rise and Fall of the Roman Empire*, *Gladiator*).

5) Social/Cultural/Technological Changes. Cinema is a living art form, about as well as above life, so that it tends to respond rapidly to social, cultural, and technological changes. Films concerned with "change" provide the audience with a pace in which to visualize and adapt to its consequences (e. g. the idea of "hyperreality(超真实)" underlies *The Matrix*; the effects

of the media on human emotions is an obivious concern in *American Beauty*).

6) Social Problems. Films sometimes provide a forum in which certain pressing social problems can be presented. In part it is a "consciousness-raising" activity that brings social problems to light. In part, it is a way for the audience to deal imaginatively with the problems — to consider possible causes, to imagine possible consequences, and to hypothesize possible solutions (e. g. the enviromental problem and how far we can go in dealing with it are both tackled in *Erin Brockovich*).

The units following will specifically appreciate and analyse classical English films from typical cultural perspectives.

◎ Exercises

1. Explain the following terms in English.

1) theme
2) film criticism
3) broad human concerns in films

2. Discuss and answer the following questions.

1) Please try to introduce the theme of your favorite English film.
2) What do you think the significance of a good film is determined by, and why?
3) What are the cultural concerns in the study of Hollywood films?
4) How do you understand the symbolic image of the feather present at the opening and conclusion of *Forrest Gump*?

Unit 2
Historical Perspective

Western civilization traces its roots back to Western Europe and the Western Mediterranean. It is linked to the Roman Empire and with Medieval Western Christendom which emerged from the Middle Ages to experience such transformative episodes as the Renaissance, the Reformation, the Enlightenment, the Industrial Revolution, scientific revolution, and the development of liberal democracy.

1. Brief Introduction to British History

The history of the United Kingdom as a unified sovereign state began in 1707 with the political union of the kingdoms of England and Scotland, into a united kingdom called Great Britain. Of this new state the historian Simon Schama said "What began as a hostile merger would end in a full partnership in the most powerful going concern in the world... it was one of the most astonishing transformations in European history." A further *Act of Union* in 1800 added the Kingdom of Ireland to create the United Kingdom of Great Britain and Ireland.

The first decades were marked by Jacobite risings which ended with defeat for the Stuart cause at Culloden in 1746. In 1763, victory in the Seven Years' War led to the dominance of the British Empire, which was to be the foremost global power for over a century and grew to become the largest empire in history. As a result, the culture of the United Kingdom, and its industrial, political, constitutional, educational and linguistic influence, became worldwide.

In 1922, following the Anglo-Irish Treaty, most of Ireland seceded to become the Irish Free State; a day later, Northern Ireland seceded from the Free State and returned to the United Kingdom. As a result, in 1927 the United Kingdom changed its formal title to the "United Kingdom of Great Britain and Northern Ireland", usually shortened to "Britain" and (after 1945) to the "United Kingdom" or "UK".

In the Second World War, in which the Soviet Union and the US joined Britain as Allied Powers, Britain and its Empire fought a successful war against Germany, Italy and Japan. The cost was high and Britain no longer had the wealth to maintain an empire, so it granted independence to most of the Empire. The new states typically joined the Commonwealth of Nations. The United Kingdom has been a leading member of the United Nations, the European Unionand NATO. Since the 1990s large-scale devolution movements in Northern Ireland, Scotland and Wales have changed the political structure of the country.

Epics-historical Film— *Brave Heart*

Brave Heart/Braveheart is a 1995 American epic war film directed by and starring Mel Gibson. Gibson portrays William Wallace, a late 13th-century Scottish warrior who led the Scots in the First War of Scottish Independence against King Edward I of England. The story is inspired by Blind Harry's epic poem *The Actes and Deidis of the Illustre and Vallyeant Campioun Schir William Wallace* and was adapted for the screen by Randall Wallace.

The film was nominated for ten Academy Awards at the 68th Academy Awards and won five: Best Picture, Best Director, Best Cinematography, Best Makeup, and Best Sound Editing.

Panoramic View of *Braveheart*

In 1280, King Edward "Longshanks" invades and conquers Scotland following the death of Alexander III of Scotland, who left no heir to the throne. Young William Wallace witnesses Longshanks' treachery, survives the deaths of his father and brother, and is taken abroad on a pilgrimage throughout Europe by his paternal Uncle Argyle, where he is educated. Years later, Longshanks grants his noblemen land and privileges in Scotland, including Prima Nocte. Meanwhile, a grown Wallace returns to Scotland and falls in love with his childhood friend Murron MacClannough, and the two marry in secret. Wallace rescues Murron from being raped by English soldiers, but as she fights off their second attempt, Murron is captured and publicly executed. In retribution, Wallace leads his clan to slaughter the English garrison in his hometown and send the occupying garrison at Lanark back to England.

Longshanks orders his son Prince Edward to stop Wallace by any means necessary. Wallace rebels against the English, and as his legend spreads, hundreds of Scots from the surrounding clans join him. Wallace leads his army to victory at the Battle of Stirling Bridge and then destroys the city of York, killing Longshanks' nephew and sending his severed head to the king. Wallace seeks the assistance of Robert the Bruce, the son of nobleman Robert the Elder and a contender for the Scottish crown. Robert is dominated by his father, who wishes to secure the throne for his son by submitting to the English. Worried by the threat of the rebellion, Longshanks sends his son's wife Isabella of France to try to negotiate with Wallace. After meeting him in person, Isabella becomes enamored of Wallace.

Warned of the coming invasion by Isabella, Wallace implores the Scottish nobility to take immediate action to counter the threat and take back the country. Leading the English army himself, Longshanks confronts the Scots at Falkirk where noblemen Lochlan and Mornay, having been bribed by Longshanks, betray Wallace, causing the Scots to lose the battle. As Wallace charges toward the departing Longshanks on horseback, he is intercepted by one of the king's lancers, who turns out to be Robert the Bruce. Remorseful, he gets Wallace to safety before the English can capture him. Wallace kills Lochlan and Mornay for their betrayal, and wages a guerrilla war against the English for the next seven years, assisted by Isabella, with whom he eventually has an affair. Robert sets up a meeting with Wallace in Edinburgh, but Robert's father has conspired with other nobles to capture and hand over Wallace to the English. Learning of his treachery, Robert disowns his father. Isabella exacts revenge on the now terminally ill Longshanks by telling him that his bloodline will be destroyed upon his death as she is now pregnant with Wallace's child.

In London, Wallace is brought before an English magistrate, tried for high treason, and condemned to public torture and beheading. Even whilst being hanged, drawn and quartered, Wallace refuses to submit to the king. As cries for mercy come from the watching crowd deeply moved by the Scotsman's valor, the magistrate offers him one final chance, asking him only to utter the word, "Mercy", and be granted a quick death. Wallace instead shouts, "Freedom!", and the judge orders his death. Moments before being decapitated, Wallace sees a vision of Murron in the crowd, smiling at him.

In 1314, Robert, now Scotland's king, leads a Scottish army before a ceremonial line of English troops on the fields of Bannockburn, where he is to formally accept English rule. As he begins to ride toward the English, he stops and invokes Wallace's memory, imploring his men to fight with him as they did with Wallace. Robert then leads his army into battle against the stunned English, winning the Scots their freedom.

Historical Inaccuracy in *Brave Heart*

(1) Occupation and independence

The film suggests Scotland had been under English occupation for some time, at least during Wallace's childhood, and in the run-up to the Battle of Falkirk Wallace says to the younger Bruce, "We'll have what none of us have ever had before, a country of our own." In fact Scotland had been invaded by England only the year before Wallace's rebellion; prior to the death of King Alexander III it had been a fully separate kingdom.

(2) Portrayal of William Wallace

As John Shelton Lawrence and Robert Jewett write, "Because [William] Wallace is one of Scotland's most important national heroes and because he lived in the very distant past, much that is believed about him is probably the stuff of legend. But there is a factual strand that historians agree to", summarized from Scots scholar Matt Ewart:

> Wallace was born into the gentry of Scotland; his father lived until he was 18, his mother until his 24th year; he killed the sheriff of Lanark when he was 27, apparently after the murder of his wife; he led a group of commoners against the English in a very successful battle at Stirling in 1297, temporarily receiving appointment as guardian; Wallace's reputation as a military leader was ruined in the same year of 1297, leading to his resignation as guardian; he spent several years of exile in France before being captured by the English at Glasgow, this resulting in his trial for treason and his cruel execution.

A. E. Christa Canitz writes about the historical William Wallace further: "[He] was a younger son of the Scottish gentry, usually accompanied by his own chaplain, well-educated, and eventually, having been appointed Guardian of the Kingdom of Scotland, engaged in diplomatic correspondence with the Hanseatic cities of Lübeck and Hamburg." She finds that in *Braveheart*, "any hint of his descent from the lowland gentry (i. e., the lesser nobility) is erased, and he is presented as an economically and politically marginalized Highlander and 'a farmer'—as one with the common peasant, and with a strong spiritual connection to the land which he is destined to liberate".

2. Brief Introduction to American History

The date of the start of the history of the United States is a subject of debate among historians. Older textbooks start with the arrival of Christopher Columbus on October 12, 1492 and emphasize the European background of the colonization of the Americas, or they start around 1600 and emphasize the American frontier. In recent decades American schools and universities typically have shifted back in time to include more on the colonial period and much more on the prehistory of the Native Americans.

(1) Pre-Colonial American

Archaeological evidence suggests that the present-day United States was originally populated by people migrating from Asia via the Bering Land Bridge starting some 20,000 years ago. These people became the indigenous people who inhabited the Americans before the arrival of European explorers and who are now called Native Americans.

After a period of exploration by various European countries, Dutch, Spanish, English, French, Swedish, and Portuguese settlements were established. Christopher Columbus1 was the first European to set foot on what would one day become US territory when he came to Puerto Rico in 1492. He thought he had reached India, so he named the local people Indians, not knowing that he had discovered a new continent. Amerigo Vespucci, another navigator, proved that the land was not India; therefore the land was named America after him.

(2) English Colonial America (1607-1776)

The first English colony in America was founded at Jamestown, Virginia in 1607. Between 1607 and 1733 the British established 13 colonies along the east coast of North America. By 1750, nearly 2 million people were living in these colonies, many of whom were Puritans who left their own countries in search of religious freedom. The most typical example was the voyage of the Mayflower ship, which carried the pilgrims across the Atlantic Ocean and arrived at Plymouth on American east coast in 1620, thus building the Plymouth colony. From 1630 to 1643, the great Puritan migration brought about 20,000 Englishmen to the Massachusetts Bay colony.

(3) Forming of the USA (1776-1849)

With the rapid economic development, people of the 13 colonies desired more power to determine their own business, while the British government wanted to bring the development under control and to collect more taxes from the colonies. In order to help the British East India Company out of difficulty, the British government allowed the company to sell tea at a lower price in the colonies through its own people. This took away the tea business from American tea merchants. This unfair treatment led to the War of Independence.

In September 1774, the First Continental Congress was held in Philadelphia, which encouraged Americans to refuse to buy British goods. Colonial militia units were organized. The shot at Lexington on April 19, 1775 started the War of Independence. Three weeks later, at the Second Continental Congress the delegates agreed to support the war. A Continental Army and Navy under the command of George Washington were founded. Thomas Jefferson of Virginia drafted the Declaration of Independence which was adopted on July 4, 1776. In 1783, the British army was defeated and the British government recognized the independence of the United States of America.

The new United States Constitution favoured representative and elective government to replace the existing monarchical structures. George Washington became the first President of the United States.

After the War of Independence, the Unites States began its territorial expansion. It forced England to give up Old Northwest, and Spain to open the Mississippi River. It bought Louisiana from Napoleon, almost doubling its territory. As a result of the War with Mexico, Mexico was forced to give up California and New Mexico. In 1830, the *India Removal Act* authorized the President to negotiate treaties that exchanged India tribal lands in the eastern states for lands to the west of the Mississippi River. The act resulted in the forced migration of several native tribes to the West, with several thousand Indians dying en route. From 1789 to 1849, the territory of the United States was greatly enlarged.

(4) The Civil War (1861-1865)

In the middle of the 19th century, white Americans of the North and South were unable to reconcile fundamental difference in their approach to government, economy, society and African

American slavery. Public feeling against slavery was increased by Harriet Beecher Stowe's novel *Uncle Tom's Cabin*.

When Abraham Lincoln was elected President, the Southern states broke away and established a rebel government, the Confederate States of American, on February 9, 1861. The Civil War broke out on April 12, 1861. President Abraham Lincoln won support for Union at home and abroad by making the war a just war against slavery. He issued the famous *Emancipation Proclamation*. Thus England and France stood by the Union's side, and many blacks joined the Union army. On November 19, 1863, Lincoln made another famous speech at Gettysburg, which was ended with these memorable words: "... that government of the people, by the people, for the people, shall not perish from the earth."

After a series of battles, the Confederate army surrendered on April 9, 1865, and five days later Lincoln was shot dead. In December of that year, *The Thirteenth Amendment*, which banned slavery, was added to *the Constitution*.

(5) Rapid Growth of Economy (1865-1918)

After the Civil War, the United States experienced a tremendous growth in industry, agriculture, science, technology and population. This is because, firstly the political environment was stable; secondly the free slaves together with the immigrants from Europe and Asia offered a strong labour force; thirdly science and invention played a very important role in America's industrial development. By 1900, the production of steel and coal of the USA ranked the first in the world.

With the development of the economy, there also arose a number of social problems, which drew more and more attention of the middle-class population. Their concerns led to the Progressive Movement, demanding government regulation of the economic, social and political conditions, such as improving the living conditions for the poor, carrying out industrial accident insurance, reforming the government and ending corruption, etc. President Theodore Roosevelt strengthened federal regulation of the railroads and enforced the *Sherman Antitrust Act* against several large corporations including Rockefeller's Standard Oil Company. He also promoted conservation, with large reserves of forest land, coal, oil, mineral and water saved for future generations.

During the First World War which lasted from 1914 to 1918, the United States stood neutral in name while selling large quantities of arms and offering bank loans to Britain and France. The United States declared war on Germany on April 6, 1917. When the war ended on November 11, 1918, the US was one of the Big Four (the US, Britain, France and Italy) to enjoy the interest division of the defeated countries.

(6) Post-WWI and Great Depression (1918-1940)

Many historians had described the 1920s in the US as a period of material success and spiritual frustration and confusion. Following World War I, the US grew steadily in stature as an economic and military word power. However, it enjoyed a period of unbalanced prosperity: farm prices and wages fell while industrial profits grew. The crash of the stock market was the beginning of the Great Depression. Banks went bankrupt, young people hunted for jobs aimlessly, farmers lost their lands, and millions of homeless people slept in parks or subways.

In 1932, President Franklin D. Roosevelt passed a number of acts to prevent the possible collapse of the American economic and political system. He successfully got America out of depression during his tenure of office.

(7) World War II (1939-1945)

As with World War I, the United States had stayed neutral until Japan's surprise attack on Pearl Harbour on December 7, 1941. Four days after the attack on Pearl Harbour, on December 11, Nazi Germany declared war on the United States. There were two guiding principles of the wartime American diplomacy: to win the war, to establish a postwar political structure in accord with American interests and to prevent the Soviet Union from over-expansion.

(8) American Society During Postwar Boom

After WWII, the United States entered a period of economic boom. The cornerstones were the automobile, housing, and defense industries. Its economy grew at an average rate of 3.5% per year. The nation's GNP rose from just over $200 billion in 1946 to about $1 trillion in 1970. The postwar baby boom was both a cause and an effect of prosperity. From 1946 to 1961, over 63.5 million babies were born, making the baby boom generation the largest by far in the nation's history. Of the three cornerstones of the postwar economic boom, two were related to the upsurge in births. The first was a construction boom to provide houses and schools for all these children; and the second was automobile manufacturing for the growing new communities. The third was military spending. When the Defense Department was established in 1949, the nation spent about $13 billion a year on defense. By 1951, the Defense Department's budget was over $22 billon, and it has been going up ever since.

Epics-historical Film— *Gone with the Wind*

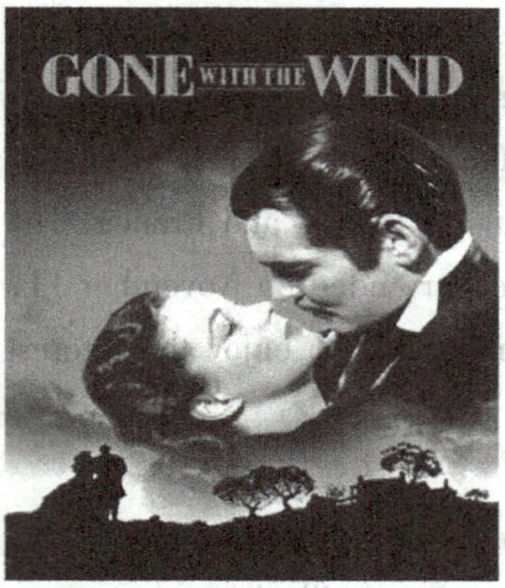

Gone with the Wind is a 1939 American epic historical romance film adapted from Margaret Mitchell's 1936 novel of the same name. The film was produced by David O. Selznick of Selznick International Pictures and directed by Victor Fleming.

Set in the American South against the backdrop of the American Civil War and Reconstruction era, the film tells the story of Scarlett O'Hara, the strong-willed daughter of a Georgia plantation owner, from her romantic pursuit of Ashley Wilkes, who is married to his cousin, Melanie Hamilton, to her marriage to Rhett Butler. The leading roles are portrayed by Vivien Leigh (Scarlett), Clark Gable (Rhett), Leslie Howard (Ashley), and Olivia de Havilland (Melanie).

Panoramic View of *Gone with the Wind*

Part 1

On the eve of the American Civil War in 1861, Scarlett O'Hara lives at Tara, her family's cotton plantation in Georgia, with her parents and two sisters. Scarlett learns that Ashley Wilkes—whom she secretly loves—is to be married to his cousin, Melanie Hamilton, and the engagement is to be announced the next day at a barbecue at Ashley's home, the nearby plantation Twelve Oaks.

At the Twelve Oaks party, Scarlett privately declares her feelings to Ashley, but he rebuffs her by responding that he and Melanie are more compatible. Scarlett is incensed when she discovers another guest, Rhett Butler, has overheard their conversation. The barbecue is disrupted by the declaration of war and the men rush to enlist. As Scarlett watches Ashley kiss Melanie goodbye, Melanie's younger brother Charles proposes to her. Although she does not love him, Scarlett consents and they are married before he leaves to fight.

Scarlett is widowed when Charles dies from a bout of pneumonia and measles while serving in the Confederate Army. Scarlett's mother sends her to the Hamilton home in Atlanta to cheer her up, although the O'Haras' outspoken housemaid Mammy tells Scarlett she knows she is going there only to wait for Ashley's return. Scarlett, who should not attend a party while in mourning, attends a charity bazaar in Atlanta with Melanie where she meets Rhett again, now a blockade runner for the Confederacy. Celebrating a Confederate victory and to raise money for the Confederate war effort, gentlemen are invited to bid for ladies to dance with them. Rhett makes an inordinately large bid for Scarlett and, to the disapproval of the guests, she agrees to dance with him.

The tide of war turns against the Confederacy after the Battle of Gettysburg in which many of the men of Scarlett's town are killed. Scarlett makes another unsuccessful appeal to Ashley while he is visiting on Christmas furlough, although they do share a private and passionate kiss in the parlor on Christmas Day, just before he returns to war.

Eight months later, as the city is besieged by the Union Army in the Atlanta Campaign, Scarlett and her young house servant Prissy must deliver Melanie's baby without medical assistance after she goes into premature labor. Afterwards, Scarlett calls upon Rhett to take her home to Tara with Melanie, her baby, and Prissy; he collects them in a horse and wagon, but once out of the city chooses to go off to fight, leaving Scarlett and the group to make their own way back to Tara. Upon her return home, Scarlett finds Tara deserted, except for her father, her sisters, and two former slaves: Mammy and Pork. Scarlett learns that her mother has just died of typhoid fever and her father has become incompetent. With Tara pillaged by Union troops and the fields untended, Scarlett vows she will do anything for the survival of her family and herself.

Part 2

As the O'Haras work in the cotton fields, Scarlett's father is killed after he is thrown from his horse in an attempt to chase away a scalawag from his land. With the defeat of the Confederacy Ashley also returns, but finds he is of little help at Tara. When Scarlett begs him to run away with her, he confesses his desire for her and kisses her passionately, but says he cannot leave Melanie. Unable to pay the taxes on Tara implemented by Reconstructionists, Scarlett dupes her younger sister Suellen's fiancé, the middle-aged and wealthy mill owner Frank Kennedy, into marrying her, by saying Suellen got tired of waiting and married another beau.

Frank, Ashley, Rhett and several other accomplices make a night raid on a shanty town after Scarlett is attacked while driving through it alone, resulting in Frank's death. With Frank's funeral barely over, Rhett proposes to Scarlett and she accepts. They have a daughter whom Rhett names Bonnie Blue, but Scarlett, still pining for Ashley and chagrined at the perceived ruin of her figure, lets Rhett know that she wants no more children and that they will no longer share a bed.

One day at Frank's mill, Scarlett and Ashley are seen embracing by Ashley's sister, India, and harboring an intense dislike of Scarlett she eagerly spreads rumors. Later that evening, Rhett, having heard the rumors, forces Scarlett to attend a birthday party for Ashley; incapable of believing anything bad of her beloved sister-in-law, Melanie stands by Scarlett's side so that all know that she believes the gossip to be false. After returning home from the party, Scarlett finds Rhett downstairs drunk, and they argue about Ashley. Rhett kisses Scarlett against her will, stating his intent to have sex with her that night, and carries the struggling Scarlett to the bedroom. The next day, Rhett apologizes for his behavior and offers Scarlett a divorce, which she rejects, saying that it would be a disgrace. When Rhett returns from an extended trip to London Scarlett informs him that she is pregnant, but an argument ensues which results in her falling down a flight of stairs and suffering a miscarriage. As she is recovering, tragedy strikes when Bonnie dies while attempting to jump a fence with her pony.

Scarlett and Rhett visit Melanie, who has suffered complications arising from a new pregnancy, on her deathbed. As Scarlett consoles Ashley, Rhett returns to their home in Atlanta; realizing that Ashley only ever truly loved Melanie. Scarlett dashes after Rhett to find him preparing to leave for good. She pleads with him, telling him she realizes now that she has loved him all along and that she never really loved Ashley, but Rhett says that with Bonnie's death went any chance of reconciliation. Scarlett begs him to stay but Rhett rebuffs her and walks out the door and into the early morning fog, leaving her weeping on the staircase and vowing to one day win back his love.

Critical Response of *Gone with the Wind*

- Cultural significance of "Miss Scarlett O'Hara"

Gone with the Wind presents a sentimental view of the Civil War, in which the "Old South" takes the place of Camelot and the war was fought not so much to defeat the Confederacy and free the slaves as to give Miss Scarlett O'Hara her comeuppance. But we've known that for years; the tainted nostalgia comes with the territory. Yet as "GWTW" approaches its 80th anniversary, it is still a towering landmark of film, quite simply because it tells a good story, and tells it wonderfully well.

For the story it wanted to tell, it was the right film at the right time. Scarlett O'Hara is not a creature of the 1860s but of the 1930s: a free-spirited, willful modern woman. The way was prepared for her by the flappers of Fitzgerald's jazz age, by the bold movie actresses of the period, and by the economic reality of the Depression, which for the first time put lots of women to work outside their homes.

Scarlett's lusts and headstrong passions have little to do with myths of delicate Southern flowers, and everything to do with the sex symbols of the movies that shaped her creator, Margaret Mitchell: actresses such as Clara Bow, Jean Harlow, Louise Brooks and Mae West. She was a woman who wanted to control her own sexual adventures, and that is the key element in her appeal. She also sought to control her economic destiny in the years after the South collapsed, first by planting cotton and later by running a successful lumber business. She was the symbol the nation needed as it headed into World War II; the spiritual sister of Rosie the Riveter.

Of course, she could not quite be allowed to get away with marrying three times, coveting sweet Melanie's husband Ashley, shooting a plundering Yankee, and banning her third husband from the marital bed in order to protect her petite waistline from the toll of childbearing. It fascinated audiences (it fascinates us still) to see her high-wire defiance in a male chauvinist world, but eventually such behavior had to be punished, and that is what "Frankly, my dear, I don't give a damn" is all about. If "GWTW" had ended with Scarlett's unquestioned triumph, it might not have been nearly as successful. Its original audiences (women, I suspect, even more than men) wanted to see her swatted down—even though, of course, tomorrow would be another day.

If the central drama of *Gone with the Wind* is the rise and fall of a sexual adventuress, the counterpoint is a slanted but passionate view of the Old South. Unlike most historical epics, "GWTW" has a genuine sweep, a convincing feel for the passage of time. It shows the South before, during and after the war, all seen through Scarlett's eyes. And Scarlett is a Southerner. So was Margaret Mitchell. The movie signals its values in the printed narration that opens the film, in language that seems astonishing in its bland, unquestioned assumptions:

"There was a land of Cavaliers and Cotton Fields called the Old South. Here in this pretty world, Gallantry took its last bow. Here was the last ever to be seen of Knights and their Ladies Fair, of Master and of Slave. Look for it only in books, for it is no more than a dream remembered, a Civilization gone with the wind."

Historical reflection on *Gone with the Wind*

Gone with the Wind has been criticized for its historical revisionism and glorification of slavery, but nevertheless it has been credited for triggering changes to the way African Americans are depicted on film. It was re-released periodically throughout the 20th century and became ingrained in popular culture. It has placed in the top ten of the American Film Institute's list of top 100 American films since the list's inception in 1998, and in 1989, *Gone with the Wind* was selected to be preserved by the National Film Registry.

Gone with the Wind has also been criticized as having perpetuated Civil War myths and black stereotypes. David Reynolds writes that "The white women are elegant, their menfolk noble or at least dashing. And, in the background, the black slaves are mostly dutiful and content, clearly incapable of an independent existence." Reynolds likened *Gone with the Wind* to *The Birth of a Nation* and other re-imaginings of the South during the era of segregation, in which white Southerners are portrayed as defending traditional values and the issue of slavery is largely ignored. From 1972 to 1996, the Atlanta Historical Society held a number of *Gone with the Wind* exhibits, among them a 1994 exhibit titled, "Disputed Territories: *Gone with the Wind* and Southern Myths". One of the questions explored by the exhibit was "How True to Life Were the Slaves in GWTW?" This section showed slave experiences were diverse and concluded that the "happy darky" was a myth, as was the belief that all slaves experienced violence and brutality.

3. Recommendation — List of Historical Films

Title	Release date	Time period	Notes
The Adventures of Robin Hood	1938	1190s	During the life of Richard the Lionheart after his release from captivity in 1194.
The Merchant of Venice	2004	1596	Set in the Republic of Venice. The film focuses on the Venetian Ghetto.
The Three Musketeers	Several adaptations (1903-2014)	1625-1673	Based on the novels ("The Three Musketeers" and its sequels) by Alexandre Dumas. The protagonists are loosely based on historical figures Charles de Batz-Castelmore d'Artagnan, Armand d'Athos, Isaac de Porthau, and Henri d'Aramitz.
A Tale of Two Cities	1989	1755-1792	England and France prior and during the French Revolution.
12 Years a Slave	2013	1841-1853	The story of free African American Solomon Northup after he was abducted and sold into slavery. Based on the autobiography of the same name.
Dances with Wolves	1990	c. 1865-1870	The American Civil War and its aftermath in the American West, interaction with the Lakota Sioux.
Pearl Harbor	2001	December 1941-April 1942	The Japanese attack on Pearl Harbor, and the subsequent American retaliation in the Doolittle Raid.
Schindler's List	1993	1939-1945	German industrialist Oskar Schindler's efforts to keep Jewish people from being interred in Nazi concentration camps during World War II.

◎ Exercises

1. Explain the following terms in English.

1) Western civilization
2) English colonial America
3) the Civil War
4) Great Depression

2. Discuss and answer the following questions.

1) What did the United States experience after the Civil War, and why?
2) As a hero, what historical values does William Wallace have towards the United Kingdom?
3) Can you illustrate the cultural significance of "Miss Scarlett O'Hara"?

Unit 3
Religious Perspective

Christianity is an Abrahamic monotheistic religion based on the life and teachings of Jesus Christ, who serves as the focal point of the Christian faith. It is the world's largest religion, with over 2. 4 billion followers, or 33% of the global population, known as Christians. Christians make up a majority of the population in 158 countries and territories. They believe that Jesus is the Son of God and the savior of humanity whose coming as the Messiah (the Christ) was prophesied in the *Old Testament*.

Christian theology is summarized in creeds such as the Apostles' Creed and Nicene Creed. These professions of faith state that Jesus suffered, died, was buried, descended into hell, and rose from the dead, in order to grant eternal life to those who believe in him and trust in him for the remission of their sins. The creeds further maintain that Jesus physically ascended into heaven, where he reigns with God the Father in the unity of the Holy Spirit, and that he will return to judge the living and the dead and grant eternal life to his followers. His incarnation, earthly ministry, crucifixion and resurrection are often referred to as "the gospel", meaning "good news". The term gospel also refers to written accounts of Jesus' life and teaching, four of which—Matthew, Mark, Luke, and John—are considered canonical and included in the Christian *Bible*.

Christianity has played a prominent role in the shaping of Western civilization. Throughout its history, Christianity has weathered schisms and theological disputes that have resulted in many distinct churches and denominations. Worldwide, the three largest branches of Christianity are the Catholic Church, the Eastern Orthodox Church and the various denominations of Protestantism. The Catholic and Eastern Orthodox churches broke communion with each other in the East-West Schism of 1054; Protestantism came into existence in the Reformation of the 16th century, splitting from the Catholic Church.

1. Brief Introduction to Faith in Christianity

Faith in Christianity is a central idea taught by Jesus himself in reference to the gospel (Good News). In the understanding of Jesus it was an act of trust and self-abandonment in which people no longer rely on their own strength and policies but commit themselves to the power and guiding word of him in whom they believe. Since the Protestant Reformation the meaning of this term has been an object of major theological disagreement in Western Christianity. The differences have been largely overcome in the Joint Declaration on the Doctrine of Justification (1999).

Some of the definitions in the history of Christian theology have followed the biblical formulation in Hebrews 11 : 1: "the assurance of things hoped for, the conviction of things not seen". As in other Abrahamic religions, it includes a belief in the existence of God, in the reality of a transcendent domain that God administers as his kingdom and in the benevolence of the will of God or God's plan for humankind.

Christianity differs from other Abrahamic religions in that it focuses on the teachings of Jesus, and on his place as the prophesied Christ. It also includes a belief in the New Covenant. According to most Christian traditions, Christian faith requires a belief in Jesus' resurrection from the dead, which he states is the plan of God the Father.

The precise understanding of the term "faith" differs among the various Christian traditions. Despite these differences, Christians generally agree that faith in Jesus lies at the core of the Christian tradition, and that such faith is required in order to be a Christian.

1.1 Faith in Jesus as Belief, Trust and Reliance

In the Protestant tradition, faith is generally understood to be closely associated with ideas of belief, trust, and reliance. This understanding is founded in the doctrinal statements of the Reformers. One of their confessional statements explains: "the principle acts of saving faith are accepting, receiving, and resting upon Christ alone for justification, sanctification, and eternal life." The Reformers contrasted faith with human efforts to do good works as a means of justification. This understanding of saving faith has remained within the Protestant tradition. Saving faith is generally understood in terms of a belief of, trust in, and reliance on the person of Jesus and his work of atonement accomplished through his death on the cross.

In a more everyday sense, faith is often discussed in terms of believing God's promises, trusting in his faithfulness, and relying on God's character and faithfulness to act. Yet, many Protestants stress that genuine faith is also acted on, and thus it brings about different behaviour or action and does not consist merely of mental belief, trust or confidence or outright antinomianism. Hence, having authentic "faith in Jesus" is generally understood to lead to changes in how one thinks and lives. However, the Protestant tradition holds that these changes in character and conduct do not have any value for obtaining a positive final judgment, but that a positive final judgment depends on faith alone (sola fide).

1.2 Faith in Jesus as Faithfulness, Loyalty and Commitment

In recent decades, scholars have researched what Pistis meant in the social context of the New Testament writers. Several scholars who have studied the usage of Pistis in both early Greek manuscripts and the *New Testament* have concluded that "faithfulness" is the most satisfactory English translation in many instances. This recent research has prompted some to argue that *New Testament* faith and belief in Jesus should be understood in terms of faithfulness, loyalty, and commitment to him and his teachings, rather than in terms of belief, trust and reliance. Such an understanding of faith can be integrated well with the moral influence theory of atonement.

1.3 Essential Elements in Christian Faith

In the Christian faith there are six component elements.

1) Belief in God as The Spirit, "infinite, eternal, and unchangeable in His being, wisdom and power, holiness, justice, goodness and truth" (John 4:24; Exodus 20:2-7; Deuteronomy 6:4; Isaiah 44:6; John 17:3; 1 Corinthians 8:4,6; Psalm 19; 104:24).
2) Belief in man, as a child of God, whose spirit is destined to live forever (Genesis 2:7; 2 Corinthians 5:1; Ecclesiastes 12:7; Matthew 6:25; 5:29,30).
3) Belief in sin which taints and corrupts the heart of man, making it finally, if unchecked, the dwelling place of all evil. The effects of sin are everywhere plainly manifest. Men not only sin through ignorance and carelessly but willfully. The worst sins are those which are of the spirit, anger, pride, malice and envy (Isaiah 53:6; 64:6; Romans 3:23; 1 John 1:8; Romans 1:18-3:23; 8:7).
4) Belief in Jesus Christ, the Son of God and the Saviour of men, who can cleanse the heart of man and save him from his sins. Jesus Christ came not only to reveal God the Father, to man but also to purge his heart from evil. "He is the propitiation for our sins" (1 John 2:1,2; Romans 8:34; Hebrews 7:24,25; Matthew 20:28; Romans 3:24,25; 5:8; 8:3; Galatians 3:13; 2 Corinthians 5:21; 1 Corinthians 1:30; Matthew 9:2-6).
5) Belief in the sanctifying power of the Holy Spirit (1 Corinthians 6:11; Ephesians 3:16; Galatians 5:22) who "testifies of Christ, as the Saviour of sinners, unites us to Him by faith, and makes us partakers of all His benefits." Jesus said, "When the Comforter is come, whom I will send unto you from the Father, even the Spirit of truth, which proceedeth from the Father, He shall testify of Me" (John 15:26). "The Spirit of truth ... will guide you into all truth.... He shall glorify Me: for He shall receive of Mine and shall show it unto you" (John 16:13,14; 14:26; 1 Corinthians 12:3; Titus 3:5,6; Matthew 28:19; John 3:5,6).

6) Belief in the resurrection and the life to come, the issues of which are declared to be eternal. "The hour is coming in which all that are in the graves shall hear His voice, and shall come forth; they that have done good, unto the resurrection of life; and they that have done evil, unto the resurrection of damnation" (John 5:28,29; Matthew 25:31-46; 25:1-13). The great rainbow of promise that spans the future, for those who trust in Christ, is in the fact that He said, "I am the resurrection and the life: he that believeth in Me, though he were dead, yet shall he live. And whosoever liveth and believeth in Me shall never die" (John 11:25,26; I Thessalonians 5:23; John 6:47; 14:2,19). The resurrection body "will be spiritual, immortal, incorruptible, and like unto the glorious body of Jesus Christ" (Philippians 3:20, 21; 1 Corinthians 15:20-23,35-57).

2. Film Appreciation— *The Man from Earth*

The Man from Earth is a 2007 American drama science fiction film written by Jerome Bixby and directed by Richard Schenkman. It stars David Lee Smith as John Oldman, the protagonist. The screenplay was conceived by Jerome Bixby in the early 1960s and completed on his deathbed in April 1998. The film gained recognition in part for being widely distributed through Internet peer-to-peer networks, which raised its profile. The film was later adapted by Schenkman into a stage play of the same name.

The plot focuses on John Oldman, a departing university professor, who claims to be a Cro-Magnon (or Magdalenian caveman) who has secretly survived for more than 14,000 years. The entire film is set in and around Oldman's house during his farewell party and is composed almost entirely of dialogue. The plot advances through intellectual arguments between Oldman and his fellow faculty members.

2.1 Panoramic View of *The Man from Earth*

The film begins with Professor John Oldman (David Lee Smith) packing his belongings onto his truck, preparing to move to a new home. His colleagues show up to give him an impromptu farewell party: Harry (John Billingsley), a biologist; Edith (Ellen Crawford), an art history professor and devout Christian; Dan (Tony Todd), an anthropologist; Sandy (Annika Peterson), a historian who is in love with John; Dr. Will Gruber (Richard Riehle), a psychiatrist; Art (William Katt), an archaeologist; and his student Linda (Alexis Thorpe).

As John's colleagues press him to explain the reason for his departure, he slowly, and somewhat reluctantly, reveals that he is a prehistoric caveman who has lived for more than 14 millennia, and that he relocates every ten years to keep others from realizing that he does not age. He begins his tale under the guise of a possible science-fiction story, but eventually stops speaking in hypotheticals and begins answering questions from a first-person perspective. His colleagues refuse to believe his story. John continues his tale, relating how he was a Sumerian for 2,000 years, a Babylonian, and eventually went east to become a disciple of Gautama Buddha. He claims to have been given a chance to sail with Christopher Columbus (admitting that at the time he still believed the earth was flat) and to have befriended Van Gogh (one of whose original paintings he apparently owns, a gift from the artist himself).

In the course of the conversation, each of John's colleagues questions his story based on knowledge from his or her own academic specialty. Harry, the biologist, struggles with how biology could allow for the possibility of a human being living for so long. Art, the archaeologist, questions John about events in prehistory. He exclaims that John's answers, though correct, could have come from any textbook. Will, the psychiatrist, questions if John feels guilt for outliving everyone he has ever known and loved, and threatens John with a gun (which is later revealed to have been unloaded) before temporarily leaving. John then learns from the group that Will's wife had died the previous day after a long illness.

The discussion turns to the topic of religion. John mentions that he is not a follower of a particular religion; though he does not necessarily believe in an omnipotent God, he does not discount the possibility of such a being's existence. Pressed by the group, John reluctantly reveals that in trying to take Buddha's teachings to the west, into the eastern Roman Empire, he became the inspiration for the Jesus story. After this revelation, emotions in the room run high. Edith begins crying. Will demands that John end his tale and give the group a sense of closure by admitting it was all a hoax, and threatens to have John involuntarily committed for psychiatric evaluation should he refuse to do so. John appears to ruminate over his response before finally "confessing" to everyone that his story was a prank.

John's friends leave the party with various reactions: Edith is relieved; Harry indicates an open mind. After everyone but Will and Sandy has left, Will overhears John and Sandy's conversation, which suggests the story was true after all. John mentions some of the pseudonyms he has used over the years, and Will realizes one was his father's name. Shocked to realize the ageless man is his own father, Will suffers a heart attack and dies. After Will's body has been taken away, Sandy realizes this is the first time John has seen one of his grown children die. John wordlessly gets in his truck and starts to drive to an unknown destination. Then he stops and waits for Sandy, who walks over to the truck.

2.2 Religious Reflections on *The Man from Earth*

2.2.1 The Historical Jesus

The climax of the story is reached when John finally reveals that he was Jesus Christ. This comes as a serious emotional challenge to one of the friends visiting him as she is a committed Christian. This revelation, of course, devastates her faith and nearly destroys her life. While the others are not as devastated as the Christian lady, only two of the visiting friends handle John's fantastic claims well. So to save his friends from more truth than they can handle (and especially the poor little Christian lady) he finally "admits" he made the whole thing up.

But we, the audience at home, soon see that he didn't make any of it up and he was telling the truth all along. But since the skeptics do not know this they are all able to go home and go back to their mundane lives in peace.

One man in the group is a bit less skeptical then the rest and he finds it marvelous that perhaps the laws of nature are not as confining as he thought they were. He decides to believe our Cro-Magnon hero, though he refuses to force him into a final admission because he'd rather just believe on faith. The other non-skeptic is a woman in love with John and eventually they drive off into the sunset together to start a new life that they know will end with him leaving her once she gets to old for him to avoid being detected.

2.2.2 Secular Liberalism and Christianity

The most troubling point of the story is where our hero admits he's Jesus Christ. His story is that he, centuries before, had met the Buddha. John admits that the Buddha is the most amazing man he had ever met. (Secular Liberals like Buddha it would appear.) John learned directly from Buddha. Centuries later, John decided to help out the poor misguided Jews by trying to teach them the teachings of Buddha. He taught them that there was one greater than he was (Buddha) but they mixed up the message and thought he was claiming to be the Son of God instead. Then John's teachings riled people up so much that they crucified him. Using his knowledge of meditation from Buddha, he slowed his body down until it seemed dead. They then buried him in the tomb and he healed and came back out. He tried to leave town but some of his followers saw him and it started a massive rumor about him having been resurrected. He tried to correct them, but having been impacted by this miracle of the return from the dead, they wouldn't listen to him. Christianity then emerged as a twisted view of the original (and correct) teachings of Buddha based on this unfortunate incident.

There is no doubt whatsoever that we are getting to the heart of Jerome Bixby's own feelings about Christianity in this part of the story.

2.2.3 Bigotry Towards Christians Is Now Socially Accepted

For almost the entire movie, the "skeptics" hang together, working against our hero to try to punch holes in his story. Only when he gets to his story of being Jesus does the Christian woman find herself frightfully alone. The other skeptics easily, and rather completely, turn on her, shooting holes in the Christian story and (in my opinion) gleefully agreeing with our hero that Christianity is a twisted version of Christ's original teachings. This is the only part of the story where the skeptics almost entirely agree with our hero, though they do not accept that he personally was Jesus. Our lone Christian finds her faith shattered and her life devastated, yet the skeptics — all really the voice of Jerome Bixby — pile it on without the slightest concern for her well-being. This questionable behavior continues for quite a while until finally, as mentioned above, the poor little Christian lady breaks into tears. Only at this point does John finally back off smashing her life apart. The skeptics (i. e. Jerome Bixby), of course, never recant a word.

The Christian woman is hardly a Bible thumping fundamentalist either. She is essentially a liberal Christian — though a believing one. God is no mere metaphor to her and Jesus is in some sense really and truly God. But she does not take the Bible literally and does not believe it is infallible. She is portrayed as intelligent and capable right up until her faith is put on trial. Then there is something pathetic about her compared to the other skeptics. She desperately clings to her religion, unable to face reality head on like our other skeptics are able to do (on this point at least) since they don't believe in God.

The spirit of meanness she is subjected to by the others made my heart ache. At first I tried to shrug this off as "it's just fiction" and "she's not real". But I finally had to admit that the bigotry she faces was our new reality.

I don't think I realized before this movie just how far bigotry towards Christians and their beliefs has solidified as part of secular liberal culture. Yes, I knew that the media portrays fundamentalist Christians in a negative light with just perhaps a bit too much glee, but I honestly did not know that even a liberal Christian like this woman has long since come to be derided by secularists.

But the thing that bothered me the most was the fact that people no longer see the characters in this movie for what they are: bigots. Instead it seems natural to have all these secular skeptics suddenly dog pile the lone Christian and temporarily turn their skepticism jointly on her cherished beliefs without regard for her feelings. Or even without regard for all the facts.

3. Recommendation List — Religious Perspectives

Title	Director	Genre	Plot
Beyond the Mask	Chad Burns	Drama, Inspirational, Apologetics & Faith, Patriotic	After a failed attempt on his life, British mercenary Will Reynolds is on the run in the American Colonies. As his past life closes in on him, Will must help his new friends unravel a plot of historical proportions to save his new home and leave his failures behind him.

续表

Title	Director	Genre	Plot
Do You Believe?	Jonathan M Gunn	Drama, Inspirational, Faith	When a local pastor is shaken to the core by the visible faith of an old street-corner preacher, he is reminded that true belief always requires action. His response ignites a faith-fueled journey that powerfully impacts everyone it touches in ways that only God could orchestrate.
God's Not Dead 2	Harold Cronk	Drama, Inspirational, Faith	When a devout Christian and high school teacher Grace Wesley (Melissa Joan Hart) is asked a question in class about faith, her response lands her in a battle of choice. In the sequel to the award-winning film God's Not Dead, see why she concludes, "I would rather stand with God and be judged by the world than stand with the world and be judged by God."
Amazing Love	Kevin Downes	Drama, Inspirational, Faith	When conflict erupts during a youth group camping trip, a pastor shares the story of *Old Testament* prophet, Hosea, to calm the waters. A beautiful tale with flashbacks to the ancient story, "Amazing Love" is a modern rendition of a Bible story your whole family will enjoy.

◎ Exercises

1. Explain the following terms in English.

1) Christianity
2) essential elements in Christian faith
3) faith in Christianity

2. Discuss and answer the following questions.

1) What is the climax of the story in *The Man from Earth*, and can you try to illustrate the possible intention of the director?
2) What are the six component elements in the Christian faith ?
3) What's role does Christianity play in the shaping of Western civilization?

Unit 4
Educational Perspective

Education is the process of facilitating learning, or the acquisition of knowledge, skills, values, beliefs, and habits. Education frequently takes place under the guidance of educators, but learners may also educate themselves. Education can take place in formal or informal settings and any experience that has a formative effect on the way one thinks, feels, or acts may be considered educational.

There is no broad consensus as to what education's chief aim or aims are or should be. Some authors stress its value to the individual, emphasizing its potential for positively influencing students' personal development, promoting autonomy, forming a cultural identity or establishing a career or occupation. Other authors emphasize education's contributions to societal purposes, including good citizenship, shaping students into productive members of society, thereby promoting society's general economic development, and preserving cultural values.

1. Essential Functions of Education

Education is essential for every society and individual. It is life itself but not a preparation for life. Man has various qualities. These qualities of the individual should be developed for the improvement of the country. So education plays a complementary role for overall individual, social and national development. It enables an individual to realize his highest self and goal. The key functions and roles of education towards individual, society and country are listed below.

1.1 Functions of Education Towards Individual

- Development of inborn potentialities — Education helps the child to develop the inborn potentialities of child providing scope to develop.
- Modifying behavior — Education helps to modify the past behavior through learning and through different agencies of education.

- All-round development — Education aims at the all round development of child-physical, mental, social, emotional, and spiritual.
- Preparing for the future — After completion of education the child can earn its livelihood getting proper education, which has productivity. The education should be imparted according to the own interest of the child.
- Developing personality — The whole personality of the child is developed physically, intellectually, morally, socially, aesthetically and spiritually. He is recognized in the society.
- Helping for adjustability — Man differs from beast. Man has reasoning and thinking power. Man tries his best to adjust with his own environment through education.

1.2 Functions of Education Towards Society

- Social change and control

The society is never station. It is progressive and dynamic. The child lives in society. It is the social environment where the personality of the child can be developed. The old traditions, customs are preserved and transmitted with the situations, which are ever changing. We should not think or believe in the blind beliefs, which are hindrances towards our development. Education helps to walk with the development of science and technology.

- Reconstruction of experiences

Education is life-long process. Life is education and education is life. Life is full of experiences. One cannot live with his past experiences which are unable to adjust in the society. So education helps the individual to reconstruct the experience and adjust with the environment.

- Development of social and moral value

Society is always in tension with narrowism. There is no social or moral value. Now the man is behaving like an animal. Animality can be changed with moral education. Education teaches the moral value and social value like co-operation, tolerance, sympathy, fellow feelings, love affection, respect towards elder, helping the poor and needy persons.

- Providing opportunity or equality

Education teaches us to give equal opportunities in all aspects irrespective of caste, creed, color, sex and religion.

1.3 Functions of Education Towards Nation

- Inculcation of civic and social responsibility — Education helps to make rising generation to understand its rights and duties as citizens of a democratic country.
- Training for leadership — The leadership quality of the individual is developed when he participates in all spheres of social, political, religious and educational activities.

- National integration — We are living in one country having diversities in respect of color, caste, language, diet, dress, habits and physical environment.
- Educational integration leads to emotional integration. Education trains people for unity, not for locality, for democracy and not for dictatorship. Education serves the most important end of educating the man.
- Total national development — Education helps for bringing about total national development by developing its all aspects i. e. social, economic, cultural, spiritual, moral, educational, etc.

Therefore, really education is an essential ingredient for all ages and stages of the life of an individual, society as well as the nation. Education can be a real panacea for all social evils.

2. Film Appreciation— *Good Will Hunting*

Good Will Hunting is a 1997 American drama film, directed by Gus Van Sant, and starring Robin Williams, Matt Damon, Ben Affleck, Minnie Driver and Stellan Skarsgard. Written by Affleck and Damon (and with Damon in the title role), the film follows 20-year-old South Boston laborer Will Hunting, an unrecognized genius who, as part of a deferred prosecution agreement after assaulting a police officer, becomes a client of a therapist and studies advanced mathematics with a renowned professor. Through his therapy sessions, Will re-evaluates his relationships with his best friend, his girlfriend and himself, facing the significant task of confronting his past and thinking about his future.

The film received positive reviews and was a financial success. It grossed over US $225 million during its theatrical run with only a modest $10 million budget. It was nominated for nine Academy Awards, including the Academy Award for Best Picture, and won two: Best Supporting Actor for Williams and Best Original Screenplay for Affleck and Damon.

After Williams' death in 2014, it was ranked at number 53 in The Hollywood Reporter's "100 Favorite Films" list.

2.1 Panoramic View of *Good Will Hunting*

Twenty-year-old Will Hunting of South Boston is a self-taught, genius-level intellect, though he works as a janitor at MIT and spends his free time drinking with his friends, Chuckie, Billy, and Morgan. When Professor Gerald Lambeau posts a difficult math problem as a challenge for his graduate students, Will solves the problem anonymously, stunning both the students and

Lambeau. As a challenge to the unknown genius, Lambeau posts an even more difficult problem. Will solves the problem, but then flees the scene when Lambeau catches him. At a bar, Will meets Skylar, a British student about to graduate from Harvard, who plans on attending medical school at Stanford.

The next day, as Will and his friends fight a gang at the basketball court, police arrive and arrest Will. Lambeau visits his court appearance and notices Will's intellect in defending himself. He arranges for him to forgo jail time if he agrees to study mathematics under Lambeau's supervision and participate in therapy sessions. Will tentatively agrees, but treats his first few therapists with mockery. In desperation, Lambeau calls on Dr. Sean Maguire, his estranged college roommate, who now teaches psychology at Bunker Hill Community College. Unlike other therapists, Sean actually challenges Will's defense mechanisms, and after a few unproductive sessions, Will begins to open up.

Will is particularly struck by Sean's story of how he met his wife by giving up his ticket to the historic game six of the 1975 World Series, after falling in love at first sight. Sean neither regrets his decision, nor does he regret the final years of his marriage, after which his wife died of cancer. This encourages Will to build a relationship with Skylar, though he lies to her about his past and is reluctant to introduce her to his friends or show her his rundown neighborhood. Will also challenges Sean to take an objective look at his own life, since Sean cannot move on from his wife's death.

Lambeau sets up a number of job interviews for Will, but Will scorns them by sending Chuckie as his "chief negotiator", and by turning down a position at the NSA with a scathing critique of the agency's moral position. Skylar asks Will to move to California with her, but he refuses and tells her he is an orphan, and that his foster father physically abused him. Will breaks up with Skylar and later storms out on Lambeau, dismissing the mathematical research he has been doing. Sean points out that Will is so adept at anticipating future failure in his interpersonal relationships that he deliberately sabotages them in order to avoid emotional pain.

Will walks in on a heated argument between Sean and Lambeau over his potential. Sean and Will share and find out that they were both victims of child abuse. Sean helps Will to see that he is a victim of his own inner demons and to accept that it is not his fault, causing him to break down in tears. Will accepts one of the job offers arranged by Lambeau. Having helped Will overcome his problems, Sean reconciles with Lambeau and takes a sabbatical to travel the world. When Will's friends present him with a rebuilt Chevrolet Nova for his twenty-first birthday, he decides to pass on his job offers and drive to California to reunite with Skylar. Sometime later, Chuckie goes to Will's house to pick him up, only to find that he is not there, much to his happiness. Sean finds a letter from Will in his mailbox, which tells him that Will is going to see Skylar.

2.2 Appreciation of *Good Will Hunting*— Theme of Education

Will in the film is the classic self-educated dude, or an autodidact if you want to be really fancy about it. But his biggest problem is that all of his good education is intellectual and all of his bad education is emotional.

For example, Will is a super smart guy who's learned a ton of stuff about math, economics, chemistry, and literature from books. But he's also learned a lot of bad emotional lessons from his abusive upbringing. He's learned not to trust anyone or love anyone... because that person might hurt him if he lets them in.

In *Good Will Hunting*, we learn that education means a whole lot more than just book-learning, and sometimes, we're not even aware of how much we're holding ourselves back in life.

Education: Instant Therapy

Good Will Hunting feels like instant therapy. It is about society's inclination to push people who maybe aren't ready to be pushed. And it's for those who believe they are academic underachievers. It does not realize how much it flirts with the "person who doesn't want to be helped" scenario. That is a powerful theme, used to devastating effect in films such as "Leaving Las Vegas" and "Taxi Driver." Matt Damon and Ben Affleck are happier than that. Where others see reality, they see hope. And so they won't quite go there.

Strictly on the facts, one has to wonder if Will truly wants the intervention he is receiving. But the cheeriness and brightness of most of the scenes suggest early on, they're going to get to Will Hunting, one way or another. The filmmakers were either so self-conscious of this angle — or just wanted to keep everyone hanging for as long as possible — that they didn't even give Will the opportunity to say "thanks", merely having Sean cut him off with "You're welcome".

The script was famously penned by Damon and Affleck, who readily admit they received guidance during the process. Skeptics questioned whether the two could've written such an engaging movie so early in their careers, but in fact the script is flawed and probably has the feel of an amateur.

Is Damon himself a closet genius? He went to the public school Cambridge Rindge & Latin, got into Harvard, studied English for a year or so, then dropped out once Hollywood noticed him. Not a bad reason for quitting Harvard. So it's doubtful this script reflects personal demons, but perhaps is based on people Damon knows.

Presumably, the protagonist is Will Hunting, a 20-year-old disenfranchised genius. Sometimes, though, it tends to be a movie about his therapist, Sean Maguire. By the end, it's not fully clear which one needed the other more, or which one has gained the most.

This dual approach has been done exceptionally well (for example, the first two "Godfather" movies comparing Michael Corleone with Vito Corleone), but is tricky. "Prince of Tides" also tried this structure, and the results were dubious, the Barbra Streisand character, Lowenstein, ultimately violating every personal and professional vow on her way to becoming liberated. "Good Will Hunting" has a different problem in that Robin Williams, as the therapist, is too good, appearing with actors not (yet) at his level, and his supplemental performance tends to be more appealing than the story of the protagonist.

3. Recommendation List — Educational Perspectives

Title	Release date	Director	Notes
WALL-E	2008	Andrew Stanton	This touching animated film envisions a future that could be where modern culture takes itself without restraint.
Up	2009	Pete Docter, Bob Peterson (co-director)	This animated film deals with issues of urban sprawl, ecology, and responsible stewardship in the midst of a touching story about unexpected friendships.
The Cove	2009	Louie Psihoyos	This documentary takes a look at both the massive slaughter of dolphins that occurs annually in a small Japanese fishing village and the dangerous health impact of mercury poisoning.
Dead Poets Society	1989	Peter Weir	English teacher John Keating inspires his students to look at poetry with a different perspective of authentic knowledge and feelings.
Race to Nowhere	2010	Vicki Abeles	This film is a close-up look at the pressures on today's students, offering an intimate view of lives packed with activities, leaving little room for down-time or family time. Parents today are expected to raise high-achieving children, who are good at everything: academics, sports, the arts, community-service. The film tackles the tragic side of our often achievement-obsessed culture, with interviews that explore the hidden world of over-burdened schedules, student suicide, academic cheating, young people who have checked out.

◎ Exercises

1. Explain the following terms in English.

1) Education

2) Essential functions of education

3) *Good Will Hunting*

2. Discuss and answer the following questions.

1) What are the functions of education towards individual?

2) What are the functions of education towards society?

3) What are the functions of education towards nation?

4) In the film *Good Will Hunting*, how does the protagonist face the significant task of confronting his past and thinking about his future?

Unit 5

Technological Changes

Technological change, technological development, technological achievement, or technological progress is the overall process of invention, innovation and diffusion of technology or processes. In essence technological change is the invention of technologies (including processes) and their commercialization via research and development (producing emerging technologies), the continual improvement of technologies (in which they often become less expensive), and the diffusion of technologies throughout industry or society (which sometimes involves disruption and convergence). In short, technological change is based on both better and more technology.

1. History of Technological Changes

The most known example of technological revolution was the Industrial revolution in the 19th century, the scientific-technical revolution about 1950-1960, the Neolithic revolution, the Digital revolution, etc. The notion of "technological revolution" is frequently overused. Therefore, it is not easy to define which technological revolutions having occurred during world history were really crucial and influenced not only one segment of human activity but had a universal impact. One universal technological revolution should be composed from several sectoral technological revolutions (in science, industry, transport, etc.).

We can identify several universal technological revolutions which occurred during the modern era in Western culture:

1. (1600-1740) Financial-agricultural revolution
2. (1780-1840) Industrial revolution
3. (1870-1920) Technical revolution (or Second Industrial Revolution)
4. (1940-1970) Scientific-technical revolution
5. (1985-present) Information and telecommunications revolution

Attempts to find comparable periods of well defined technological revolutions in the pre-modern era are highly speculative. Probably one of the most systematic attempts to suggest a timeline of technological revolutions in pre-modern Europe was done by Daniel Šmihula:

A. (1900-1100 BC) Indo-European technological revolution

B. (700-200 BC) Celtic and Greek technological revolution

C. (300-700 AD) Germano-Slavic technological revolution

D. (930-1200 AD) Medieval technological revolution

E. (1340-1470 AD) Renaissance technological revolution

1.1 The Potential Future of Technological Revolution

After 2000 there became popular the idea that a sequence of technological revolutions is not over and in the forthcoming future we will witness the dawn of a new universal technological revolution. The main innovations should develop in the fields of nanotechnologies, alternative fuel and energy systems, biotechnologies, genetic engineering, new materials technologies, etc.

1.2 Relation to "Technological Revolution" and "Technical Revolution"

Sometimes the notion of "Technological Revolution" is used for the Second Industrial Revolution in the period about 1900. But in this case the designation "Technical Revolution" would be more proper. When the notion of technical revolution is used in more general meaning it is almost identical with technological revolution but technological revolution requires material changes in used tools, machines, energy sources, production processes. Technical revolution can be restricted to changes in management, organisation and so-called non-material technologies (e.g. a progress in mathematics or accounting).

2. Film Appreciation—*A.I. Artificial Intelligence*

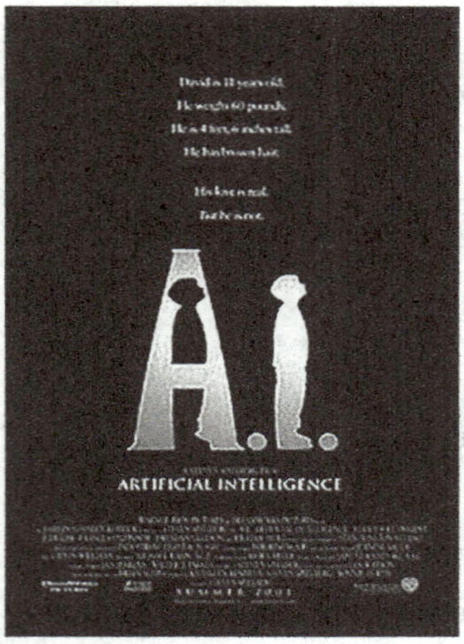

A.I. Artificial Intelligence, also known as *A.I.*, is a 2001 American science fiction drama film directed by Steven Spielberg. The screenplay by Spielberg was based on a screen story by Ian Watson and the 1969 short-story "Super-Toys Last All Summer Long" by Brian Aldiss. The film was produced by Kathleen Kennedy, Spielberg and Bonnie Curtis. It stars Haley Joel Osment, Jude Law, Frances O'Connor, Brendan Gleeson and William Hurt. Set in a futuristic post-climate change society, *A.I.* tells the story of David (Osment), a childlike android uniquely programmed with the ability to love.

Development of *A.I.* originally began with producer-director Stanley Kubrick, after he acquired the rights to Aldiss' story in the early 1970s. Kubrick hired a series of writers until the mid-1990s, including Brian Aldiss, Bob Shaw, Ian Watson, and Sara Maitland. The film languished in protracted development for years, partly because Kubrick felt computer-generated imagery was not advanced enough to create the David character, whom he believed no child actor would convincingly portray. In 1995, Kubrick handed *A. I.* to Spielberg, but the film did not gain momentum until Kubrick's death in 1999. Spielberg remained close to Watson's film treatment for the screenplay.

The film divided critics, with the overall balance being positive, and grossed approximately $235 million. The film was nominated for two Academy Awards at the 74th Academy Awards, for Best Visual Effects and Best Original Score (by John Williams). In a 2016 BBC poll of 177 critics around the world, Steven Spielberg's *A. I. Artificial Intelligence* was voted the eighty-third greatest film since 2000.

Panoramic View of *A. I. Artificial Intelligence*

In the late 22nd century, rising sea levels from global warming have wiped out coastal cities such as Amsterdam, Veniceand New York, and drastically reduced the population. A new type of robots called Mecha, advanced humanoids capable of thoughts and emotions, have been created.

David, a Mecha that resembles a human child and is programmed to display love for its owners, is sent to Henry Swinton and his wife Monica as a replacement for their son Martin, who has been placed in suspended animation until he can be cured of a rare disease. Monica warms to David and activates his imprinting protocol, causing him to have an enduring childlike love for her. David is befriended by Teddy, a robotic teddy bear who cares for David's well-being.

Martin is cured of his disease and brought home; as he recovers, he grows jealous of David. He makes David go to Monica in the night and cut off a lock of her hair. This upsets the parents, particularly Henry, who fears the scissors are a weapon.

At a pool party, one of Martin's friends accidentally pokes David with a knife, activating his self-protection programming. David grabs Martin and they fall into the pool. Martin is saved from drowning, but Henry persuades Monica to return David to his creator for destruction. However, Monica instead abandons both David and Teddy in the forest to hide as an unregistered Mecha.

David is captured for an anti-Mecha "Flesh Fair", where obsolete and unlicensed Mecha are destroyed before cheering crowds. David is nearly killed, but tricks the crowd into thinking he is human and escapes with Gigolo Joe, a male prostitute Mecha who is on the run after being framed for murder. The two set out to find the *Blue Fairy*, whom David remembers from *The Adventures of Pinocchio* and believes can turn him into a human, allowing Monica to love him and take him home.

Joe and David make their way to the resort town Rouge City, where "Dr. Know", a holographic answer engine, leads them to the top of Rockefeller Center in the flooded ruins of Manhattan. There, David meets a copy of himself and destroys it. David then meets his creator Professor Hobby, who tells David that he was built in the image of the professor's dead son David, and that more copies, including female versions called Darlene, are being manufactured.

Disheartened, David falls from a ledge, but is rescued by Joe using their amphibicopter. David tells Joe he saw the Blue Fairy underwater and wants to go down to meet her. Joe is captured by the authorities using an electromagnet. David and Teddy use the amphibicopter to go to the Fairy, which turns out to be a statue at Coney Island. The two become trapped when the Wonder Wheel falls on their vehicle. David asks repeatedly to be turned into a real boy until the ocean freezes and is deactivated once his power source is drained.

Two thousands years later, humans have become extinct and Manhattan is buried under glacial ice. The Mecha have evolved into an advanced, intelligent, silicon-based form. They find David and Teddy and discover they are original Mecha that knew living humans, making them special.

David is revived and walks to the frozen Fairy statue, which collapses when he touches it. The Mecha use David's memories to reconstruct the Swinton home and explain to him that they cannot make him human. However, David insists that they recreate Monica from DNA in the lock of hair. The Mecha warn David that the clone can only live for a day, and that the process cannot be repeated. David spends the next day with Monica and Teddy. Before she drifts off to sleep, Monica tells David she has always loved him. Teddy climbs onto the bed and watches the two lie peacefully together.

Technological Revolution and Its Conflicts— *A. I. Artificial Intelligence*

Stanley Kubrick always referred to the story as "Pinocchio". It mirrored the tale of a puppet who dreams of becoming a real boy. And what, after all, is an android but a puppet with a computer program pulling its strings? The project that eventually became Steven Spielberg's *A. I. Artificial Intelligence* (2001) was abandoned by Kubrick because he wasn't satisfied with his approaches to its central character, David, an android who appears to be a real little boy. Believing special effects wouldn't be adequate and a human actor would seem too human, he turned the project over to his friend Spielberg. Legend has it he made that decision after being impressed by Spielberg's special effects in *Jurassic Park*, but perhaps *E. T.* was also an influence: If Spielberg could create an alien who evoked human emotions, could he do the same with an android?

"We are expert at projecting human emotions into non-human subjects, from animals to clouds to computer games," Roger Ebert wrote in 1991, "but the emotions reside only in our minds. *A. I.* evades its responsibility to deal rigorously with this trait and goes for an ending that wants us to cry, but had me asking questions just when I should have been finding answers."

That is true enough on the principal level of the film, which tells David's story. Watching it again, you may be aware of something more: *A. I.* is not about humans at all. It is about the dilemma of artificial intelligence. A thinking machine cannot think. All it can do is run programs that may be sophisticated enough for it to fool us by seeming to think. A computer that passes the

Turing Test is not thinking. All it is doing is passing the Turing Test.

3. Film Appreciation — *Interstellar*

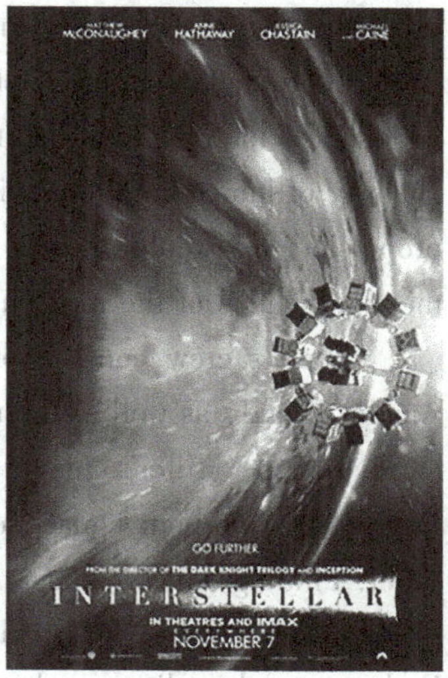

Interstellar is a 2014 epic science fiction film directed, co-written and co-produced by Christopher Nolan. The movie stars Matthew McConaughey, Anne Hathaway, Jessica Chastain, Bill Irwin, Casey Affleck, Ellen Burstyn, John Lithgow and Michael Caine. Set in a dystopian future where humanity is struggling to survive, it follows a group of astronauts who travel through a wormhole in search of a new home for humanity.

Brothers Christopher and Jonathan Nolan wrote the screenplay, which has its origins in a script Jonathan developed in 2007. Nolan produced the film with his wife, Emma Thomas, through their production company Syncopy and with Lynda Obst through Lynda Obst Productions. Caltech theoretical physicist Kip Thorne was an executive producer, acted as scientific consultant, and wrote a tie-in book (*The Science of Interstellar*). Paramount Pictures, Warner Bros. and Legendary Pictures co-financed the film. Cinematographer Hoyte van Hoytema shot the film on 35 mm in anamorphic format and IMAX 70 mm. Principal photography commenced in late 2013 in Alberta, Iceland and Los Angeles. The film utilized extensive practical and miniature effects, while the company Double Negative created additional digital effects.

Interstellar premiered on October 26, 2014 in Los Angeles. In the United States, it was first released on film stock, expanding to venues using digital projectors. The film was successful at the box office, with a worldwide gross of over \$675 million, and received positive reviews, particularly in regard to its science fiction themes, visual effects, musical score and the cast's performances. It received several awards and nominations; at the 87th Academy Awards, the film won the Academy Award for Best Visual Effects, and was nominated for Best Original Score, Best Sound Mixing, Best Sound Editing and Best Production Design.

Panoramic View of *Interstellar*

Sometime in the 21st century, a series of crop blights on Earth threatens humanity's survival. Joseph Cooper, a widowed former NASA pilot, runs a farm with his father-in-law, son Tom, and daughter Murphy. Living in a post-truthsociety (Cooper is reprimanded at school for telling Murphy that the Apollo missions did indeed happen), Cooper encourages Murphy to carefully observe and record what she sees. They realize that a pattern of dust on the floor is created by gravity variations and not — as Murphy first believed — by apoltergeist. Decoding it as a set of geographic coordinates, Cooper and Murphy follow them to a secret NASA facility, where they are met by Cooper's former professor, Dr. Brand.

Brand reveals that a wormhole mysteriously appeared near Saturn 48 years earlier, opening a pathway to a distant galaxy with potentially-habitable planets. Twelve volunteers traveled through it, each assessing the suitability of a planet as humanity's new home. Volunteers Miller, Edmunds and Mann have sent back encouraging data from planets near a black hole called Gargantua. Brand recruits Cooper to pilot the spaceship Endurance, carrying 5,000 frozen embryos for a "Plan B": to colonize a habitable planet to ensure humanity's survival. The only option for the majority of humankind to survive is his continued work on a "Plan A" — a gravitational theory for propulsion that would allow a mass exodus from Earth. Cooper agrees to go, but does not explain the significance of the mission to Murphy. His departure devastates her.

Cooper's crew consists of the scientists Romilly, Doyle, and Prof. Brand's daughter Dr. Amelia Brand, as well as the robots TARS and CASE. Traversing the wormhole, they use a lander to investigate Miller's planet, where time is severely dilated (because of its proximity to Gargantua, one hour equals seven years on Earth), and the surface is covered in knee-high deep water. Finding only wreckage from Miller's expedition, Brand retrieves Miller's data just before a gigantic tidal wave hits, killing Doyle and water-logging the engines. After returning to Endurance, they discover that 23 years have elapsed on Earth. With limited fuel to travel to only one planet, the crew chooses Mann's planet over Edmunds', since Mann is still transmitting, despite Edmunds' more promising data.

On Earth, Murphy Cooper is now a scientist and assisting Prof. Brand. On his deathbed, Prof. Brand admits that he never considered Plan A feasible and that Plan B was the only plan. In a recorded video session, Murphy Cooper notifies the crew of the death, accusing Prof. Brand's daughter and her own father of abandoning Earth. Despite Prof. Brand's assessment, she continues working on Plan A, knowing she needs more data on gravitational singularities.

Meanwhile, Mann assures the crew that the frozen planet is habitable despite its ammonia-laden atmosphere. While surveying the planet, Mann attempts to kill Cooper, revealing that he falsified the data in the hope of being rescued. He steals Cooper's Ranger and heads for Endurance. While Romilly is killed by a booby trap set by Mann, Brand rescues Cooper with a lander and they race to Endurance. Mann is killed in a failed manual docking operation, severely damaging the Endurance in the process. Cooper and Brand use their lander to stabilize the ship.

CASE warns Cooper that Endurance is slipping toward Gargantua's pull. Cooper decides to use Gargantua as a gravitational slingshot to propel the ship toward Edmunds' planet, but their proximity to Gargantua means more time will elapse on Earth. To shed weight, Cooper and TARS jettison themselves toward the black hole, so that Brand can complete the journey. Slipping past the event horizon, Cooper and TARS eject from their respective spacecraft and find themselves inside a tesseract, which resembles streams of bookshelves capable of peering into Murphy's bedroom at different periods in her life. Cooper surmises that the tesseract and wormhole were created by humans of the future to enable communication with Murphy, and that he was her "ghost" all along. Using the second hand on the watch he gave her before he left, Cooper relays the quantum data Murphy needs to solve the gravitational equation.

Following a turbulent ejection from the tesseract, Cooper awakens in a space habitat orbiting Saturn. He reunites with his daughter, now an elderly woman nearing death, who has discovered a solution to plan A. At his daughter's behest, Cooper and TARS leave to rejoin Brand and CASE who are preparing a new human colony on Edmunds' planet, which was found to be habitable.

Blessed or Doomed— *Interstellar*

Christopher Nolan's *Interstellar*, about astronauts traveling to the other end of the galaxy to find a new home to replace humanity's despoiled home-world, is frantically busy and earsplittingly loud. It uses booming music to jack up the excitement level of scenes that might not otherwise excite. It features characters shoveling exposition at each other for almost three hours, and a few of those characters have no character to speak of: they're mouthpieces for techno-babble and philosophical debate. And for all of the director's activism on behalf of shooting on film, the tactile beauty of the movie's 35mm and 65mm textures isn't matched by a sense of composition. The camera rarely tells the story in Nolan's movies. More often it illustrates the screenplay, and there are points in this one where as if you were watching the most expensive NBC pilot ever made.

Interstellar never entirely commits to the idea of a non-rational, uncanny world, it nevertheless has a mystical strain, one that's unusually pronounced for a director whose storytelling has the right-brained sensibility of an engineer, logician, or accountant. There's a ghost in this film, writing out messages to the living in dust. Characters strain to interpret distant radio messages as if they were ancient texts written in a dead language, and stare through red-rimmed eyes at video messages sent years ago, by people on the other side of the cosmos. *Interstellar* features a family haunted by the memory of a dead mother and then an absent father; a woman haunted by the memory of a missing father, and another woman who's separated from her own dad (and mentor), and driven to reunite with a lover separated from her by so many millions of miles that he might as well be dead.

With the possible exception of the last act of "Memento" and the pit sequence in "The Dark Knight Rises"—a knife-twisting hour that was all about suffering and transcendence—you can't think of a Nolan film that ladles on misery and valorizes gut feeling (faith) the way this one does; not from start to finish, anyway. The most stirring sequences are less about driving the plot forward than contemplating what the characters' actions mean to them, and to us. The best of these is the lift-off sequence, which starts with a countdown heard over images of Cooper leaving his family. It continues in space, with Caine reading passages from Dylan Thomas's villanelle "Do Not Go Gentle into that Good Night": "Old age should burn and rave at close of day; Rage, rage against the dying of the light." (If it wasn't already obvious, this sequence certifies Nolan as the most death-and-control obsessed major American filmmaker, along with Wes Anderson.)

The movie's storytelling masterstroke comes from adherence to principles of relativity: the astronauts perceive time differently depending on where Endurance is, which means that when they go down onto a prospective habitable world, a few minutes there equal weeks or months back on the ship. Meanwhile, on Earth, everyone is aging and losing hope. Under such circumstances, even tedious housekeeping-type exchanges become momentous: one has to think twice before arguing about what to do next, because while the argument is happening, people elsewhere are going grey, or suffering depression from being alone, or withering and dying. Here, more so than in any other Nolan film (and that's saying a lot), time is everything. "I'm an old physicist," Brand tells Cooper early in the film. "I'm afraid of time." Time is something we all fear. There's a ticking clock governing every aspect of existence, from the global to the familial.

4. Recommendation List — Technological Perspectives

Title	Release date	Director	Notes
The Matrix	1999	Lana Wachowski, Lilly Wachowski	A computer hacker learns from mysterious rebels about the true nature of his reality and his role in the war against its controllers.
Inception	2010	Christopher Nolan	Inception raises a tantalizing question: What if we could convince a person of something by infiltrating their dreams? A thief, who steals corporate secrets through use of dream-sharing technology, is given the inverse task of planting an idea into the mind of a CEO.
Her	2013	Spike Jonze	A lonely writer develops an unlikely relationship with an operating system designed to meet his every need.
Avatar	2009	James Cameron	A paraplegic marine dispatched to the moon Pandora on a unique mission becomes torn between following his orders and protecting the world he feels is his home.
Gravity	2013	Alfonso Cuarón	Two astronauts work together to survive after an accident which leaves them alone in space.
Transcendence	2014	Wally Pfister	A scientist's drive for artificial intelligence, takes on dangerous implications when his consciousness is uploaded into one such program.

◎ Exercises

1. Explain the following terms in English.

1) technological change

2) the potential future of technological revolution

3) relation to "technological revolution" and "technical revolution"

2. Discuss and answer the following questions.

1) What's your favorite Steven Spielberg's film? And please illustrate your understanding on it.

2) Why did Stanley Kubrick always refer to the story of *A. I. Artificial Intelligence* as "Pinocchio"?

3) In the film *Her*, a lonely writer develops an unlikely relationship with an operating system designed to meet his every need. What's your expectation on the relationship of mankind and android in the future?

Unit 6
Social Issues

A social issue is a problem that influences a considerable number of the individuals within a society. It is often the consequence of factors extending beyond an individual's social issue is the source of a conflicting opinion on the grounds of what is perceived as a morally just personal life or societal order. Social issues are distinguished from economic issues; however, some issues (such as immigration) have both social and economic aspects. There are also issues that don't fall into either category, such as warfare.

1. Social Issues Worth Solving

There can be disagreements about what social issues are worth solving, or which should take precedence. Different individuals and different societies have different perceptions.

In Rights of Man and Common Sense, Thomas Paine addresses individual's duty to "allow the same rights to others as we allow ourselves". The failure to do so caused the birth of a social issue.

There are a variety of methods people use to combat social issues. Some people vote for leaders in a democracy to advance their ideals. Outside the political process, people donate or share their time, money, energy, or other resources. This often takes the form of volunteering. Nonprofit organizations are often formed for the sole purpose of solving a social issue. Community organizing involves gathering people together for a common purpose.

A distinct but related meaning of the term "social issue" (used particularly in the United States) refers to topics of national political interest, over which the public is deeply divided and which are the subject of intense partisan advocacy, debate, and voting. Examples include same-sex marriage and abortion. In this case "social issue" does not necessarily refer to an ill to be solved, but rather to a topic to be discussed.

2. Film Appreciation— *American Beauty*

American Beauty is a 1999 American drama film directed by Sam Mendes and written by Alan Ball which won numerous awards including five Academy Awards in the United States. Kevin Spacey stars as Lester Burnham, a 42-year-old advertising executive who has a midlife crisis when he becomes infatuated with his teenage daughter's best friend, Angela (Mena Suvari). Annette Bening co-stars as Lester's materialistic wife, Carolyn, and Thora Birch plays their insecure daughter, Jane. Wes Bentley, Chris Cooper, and Allison Janney also feature. The film is described by academics as a satire of American middle-class notions of beauty and personal satisfaction; analysis has focused on the film's explorations of romantic, and paternal love, sexuality, beauty, materialism, self-liberation, and redemption.

Ball began writing *American Beauty* as a play in the early 1990s, partly inspired by the media circus around the Amy Fisher trial in 1992. He shelved the play after realizing the story would not work on stage. After several years as a television screenwriter, Ball revived the idea in 1997 when attempting to break into the film industry. The modified script had a cynical outlook that was influenced by Ball's frustrating tenures writing for several sitcoms. Producers Dan Jinks and Bruce Cohen took *American Beauty* to DreamWorks; the then-fledgling film studio bought Ball's script for $250,000, outbidding several other production bodies. DreamWorks financed the $15 million production and served as its North American distributor. *American Beauty* marked acclaimed theater director Mendes' film debut; courted after his successful productions of the musicals Oliver! and Cabaret, Mendes was, nevertheless, only given the job after 20 others were considered and several "A-list" directors turned down the opportunity.

Spacey was Mendes' first choice for the role of Lester, though DreamWorks had urged the director to consider better-known actors; similarly, the studio suggested several actors for the role of Carolyn until Mendes offered the part to Bening without DreamWorks' knowledge. Principal photography took place between December 1998 and February 1999 on soundstages at the Warner Bros. backlot in Burbank, California, and on location in Los Angeles. Mendes' dominant style was deliberate and composed; he made extensive use of static shots and slow pans and zooms to generate tension. Cinematographer Conrad Hall complemented Mendes' style with peaceful shot compositions to contrast with the turbulent on-screen events. During editing, Mendes made several changes that gave the film a less cynical tone than the script.

Released in North America on September 17, 1999, *American Beauty* was positively received by critics and grossed over $356 million worldwide. Reviewers praised most aspects of the production, with particular emphasis on Mendes, Spacey, and Ball; criticism focused on the familiarity of the characters and setting. DreamWorks launched a major campaign to increase the film's chances of Academy Award success; at the 72nd Academy Awards the following year, the film won Best Picture, Best Director, Best Actor (for Spacey), Best Original Screenplay, and Best Cinematography. It was nominated for and won many other awards and honors, mainly for the direction, writing, and acting.

Panoramic View of *American Beauty*

Lester Burnham is a middle-aged advertising executive and magazine writer who despises his job. He is unhappily married to Carolyn, a neurotic yet fiercely ambitious real estate broker who grows red roses in their yard; their teenage daughter, Jane, abhors her parents and has low self-esteem. The Burnhams' new neighbors are the Fitts family, consisting of a homophobic retired U. S. Marine Corps Colonel Frank Fitts, his near-catatonic wife, Barbara, and their teenage son, Ricky, who constantly films his surroundings with a camcorder, collecting hundreds of recordings on videotapes in his bedroom. His part-time job as a bar caterer and waiter serves as a front for his secret marijuana dealings. Frank is a strict disciplinarian who previously sent Ricky to a military school and briefly committed him to a psychiatric hospital. Jim Olmeyer and Jim Berkley, a gay couple who live nearby, welcome the Fitts family to the neighborhood. On the way to school, Frank reveals his homophobia while he angrily discusses the incident with Ricky.

Lester becomes infatuated with Jane's vain cheerleader friend, Angela Hayes, after seeing her perform a half-time dance routine at a high school basketball game with Jane. He starts having sexual fantasies about Angela, in which red rose petals are a recurring motif. Carolyn begins an affair with her married business rival, Buddy Kane. When Lester's boss and efficiency expert, Brad, tells him that he is to be laid off, Lester instead blackmails him for $60,000 and quits his job. Lester continues his liberation by taking a minimum-wage job at a fast-food restaurant, trading his Toyota Camry for a 1970 Pontiac Firebird, and starts working out after he overhears Angela tell Jane that she would find him sexually attractive if he got in shape. He begins smoking marijuana supplied by Ricky. The girls' friendship wanes after Jane starts a relationship with Ricky. Jane and Ricky bond over what Ricky considers the most beautiful imagery he has filmed: a plastic bag being blown in the wind.

Lester discovers Carolyn's infidelity, but reacts indifferently. Buddy ends the affair, fearing an expensive divorce. Frank becomes suspicious of Lester and Ricky's friendship when he finds his son's footage of a nude Lester lifting weights, which Ricky captured by chance, leading him to believe that Ricky is gay. After spying on Ricky and Lester through Lester's garage window, Frank mistakenly concludes the pair is sexually involved. He later confronts and beats Ricky for the supposed affair and accuses him of being gay. Ricky falsely admits the charges and goads his father into expelling him from their home. Meanwhile, Carolyn is sitting in her car in the rain, removing a handgun from the glove box while listening to a positive "don't be a victim" motivational speech on the radio. Jane argues with Angela about the latter's flirtation with Lester. In the midst of their argument, Ricky appears and convinces Jane to flee with him to New York City and assures Angela that she is ugly, boring, and ordinary.

Frank confronts Lester and attempts to kiss him; Lester rebuffs the colonel, who tearfully flees. Carolyn puts the gun in her handbag, shouting, "I refuse to be a victim!" Lester finds a distraught Angela sitting alone in their darkened living room; she asks him to tell her she is beautiful. He does, and they kiss.

Carolyn drives through the rain, rehearsing a confession to Lester. Just as Lester and Angela are about to have sex, Angela admits her virginity, prompting Lester to change his mind. He instead comforts her and the pair bond over their shared frustrations. Angela goes to the bathroom and Lester smiles at a family photograph in his kitchen, before being shot in the back of the head by an unseen intruder. Ricky and Jane find Lester's body, while Carolyn breaks down crying in the closet. A bloodied Frank returns home, where a gun is shown to be missing from his collection. Lester's closing narration describes meaningful experiences during his life; he says that, despite his death, he is happy because there is "so much beauty" in the world.

A Bitter Comedy on the Middle-age Crisis— *American Beauty*

American Beauty is a comedy because we laugh at the absurdity of the hero's problems. And a tragedy because we can identify with his failure—not the specific details, but the general outline.

The movie is about a man who fears growing older, losing the hope of true love and not being respected by those who know him best. Lester Burnham, the hero of *American Beauty*, is played by Kevin Spaceyas a man who is unloved by his daughter, ignored by his wife and unnecessary at work. "I'll be dead in a year," he tells us in almost the first words of the movie. "In a way, I'm dead already." The movie is the story of his rebellion.

"Both my wife and daughter think I'm this chronic loser," Lester complains. He is right. But they are not without their reasons. At an agonizing family dinner, Carolyn plays Mantovanian music that mocks every mouthful; the music is lush and reassuring, and the family is angry and silent. When Lester criticizes his daughter's attitude, she points out correctly that he has hardly spoken to her in months.

American Beauty is not about a Lolita relationship, anyway. It's about yearning after youth, respect, power and, of course, beauty. The moment a man stops dreaming is the moment he petrifies inside and starts writing snarfy letters disapproving of paragraphs like the one above. Lester's thoughts about Angela are impure, but not perverted; he wants to do what men are programmed to do, with the most beautiful woman he has ever seen.

Angela is not Lester's highway to bliss, but she is at least a catalyst for his freedom. His thoughts, and the discontent they engender, blast him free from years of emotional paralysis, and soon he makes a cheerful announcement at the funereal dinner table: "I quit my job, told my boss to— himself and blackmailed him for $60,000." Has he lost his mind? Not at all. The first thing he spends money on is perfectly reasonable: a bright red 1970 Pontiac Firebird.

This film is more about sadness and loneliness than about cruelty or inhumanity. Nobody is really bad in this movie, just shaped by society in such a way they can't be themselves, or feel joy.

3. Film Appreciation— *Erin Brockovich*

Erin Brockovich is a 2000 American biographical film directed by Steven Soderbergh and written by Susannah Grant. The film is a dramatization of the true story of Erin Brockovich, portrayed by Julia Roberts, who fought against the energy corporation Pacific Gas and Electric Company (PG&E). The film was a box office success, and critical reaction was positive.

Roberts won the Academy Award, BAFTA, Golden Globe Award, Screen Actors Guild Award, and various critics awards for Best Actress. The film itself was also nominated for Best Picture and Best Director for Steven Soderbergh at the 73rd Academy Awards. He won that year, but for directing the film *Traffic*. Early in the film the real Erin Brockovich has a cameo appearance as a waitress named Julia.

Panoramic View of *Erin Brockovich*

In 1993, Erin Brockovich is an unemployed single mother of three children, who has recently been injured in a traffic accident with a doctor and is suing him. Her lawyer, Ed Masry, expects to win, but Erin's explosive courtroom behavior under cross-examination loses her the case, and Ed will not return her phone calls afterwards. One day, he arrives at work to find her in the office, apparently working. She says that he told her things would work out and they did not, and that she needed a job. Ed takes pity on Erin, and she gets a paid job at the office.

Erin is given files for a real estate case where the Pacific Gas and Electric Company (PG&E) is offering to purchase the home of Donna Jensen, a resident of Hinkley, California. Erin is surprised to see medical records in the file and visits Donna, who explains that she had simply kept all her PG&E correspondence together. Donna appreciates PG&E's help: she has had several tumors and her husband has Hodgkin's lymphoma, but PG&E has always supplied a doctor at their own expense. Erin asks why they would do that, and Donna replies, "because of the chromium". Erin begins digging into the case and finds evidence that the groundwater in Hinkley is seriously contaminated with carcinogenic hexavalent chromium (六价铬), but PG&E has been telling Hinkley residents that they use a safer form of chromium. After several days away from the office doing this research, she is fired by Ed until he realizes that she was working all the time, and sees what she has found out.

Rehired, she continues her research, and over time, visits many Hinkley residents and wins their trust. She finds many cases of tumors and other medical problems in Hinkley. Everyone has been treated by PG&E's doctors and thinks the cluster of cases is just a coincidence, unrelated to the "safe" chromium. The Jensens' claim for compensation grows into a major class action lawsuit, but the direct evidence only relates to PG&E's Hinkley plant, not to the senior management.

Knowing that PG&E could slow any settlement for years through delays and appeals, Ed takes the opportunity to arrange for disposition by binding arbitration, but a large majority of the plaintiffs must agree to this. Erin returns to Hinkley and persuades all 634 plaintiffs to go along. While she is there, a man named Charles Embry approaches her to say that he and his cousin were PG&E employees, but his cousin recently died from the poison. The man says he was tasked with destroying documents at PG&E, but, "as it turns out", he "wasn't a very good employee".

Embry gives Erin the documents, which include a 1966 memo proving corporate headquarters knew the water was contaminated with hexavalent chromium, did nothing about it, and advised the Hinkley operation to keep this secret. The judge orders PG&E to pay a settlement amount of $333 million to be distributed among the plaintiffs.

In the aftermath, Ed hands Erin her bonus payment for the case but warns her he has changed the amount. She explodes into a complaint that she deserves more respect, but is astonished to find that he has increased it—to $2 million.

Fight for a Better Life— *Erin Brockovich*

Erin Brockovich is a nicely done story of the modern woman struggling to make her own in a man's world, using god-given assets to her best advantage.

Erin (Julia Roberts) is a single mother without a job. She convinces Ed Masry (Albert Finney), a lawyer with a low-profile practice, to hire her as an assistant. Inquisitive and curious, she runs into a peculiar situation of people in a small California desert town called Hinkely facing a abnormally high risk of a carcinogenic disease. She discovers a connection between the disease and the use of hexavalent chromium in the local Pacific Gas and Electric (PG&E) company's power plants, thus contaminating the town water supply. This leads to a David vs. Goliath legal fight with PG&E and Erin makes a name for herself as a non-conventional defender of the public interest. Based on a true story, this law suit with the real Erin Brockovich apparently ended up being one of the largest settlements ever paid in a direct-action suit ($330 million, the same as the number of gods in the Hindu mythology).

Roberts puts in a great performance as a hot-headed legal secretary, complementing the feel-good nature of this film which relies on sentimentality to drive its message about the evils of faceless corporations home. The supporting cast, including Finney as Erin's boss, and Aaron

Eckhart as her love-interest, also do a good job. The pacing is tight and the effectiveness in being a bit of a rebel is illustrated well, as is the non-effectiveness of being too stubborn and uncompromising (a lot of Erin's predicaments could be avoided by her being a bit more rational). *Erin Brockovich* is a compelling movie definitely worth checking out.

4. Recommendation List — Social Perspectives

Title	Release date	Director	Notes
12 Angry Men	1957	Sidney Lumet	A jury holdout attempts to prevent a miscarriage of justice by forcing his colleagues to reconsider the evidence.
Capitalism: A Love Story	2009	Michael Moore	An examination of the social costs of corporate interests pursuing profits at the expense of the public good.
Crash	2004	Paul Haggis	Los Angeles citizens with vastly separate lives collide in interweaving stories of race, loss and redemption.
Made in Dagenham	2010	Nigel Cole	A dramatization of the 1968 strike at the Ford Dagenham car plant, where female workers walked out in protest against sexual discrimination.
Waiting for "Superman"	2010	Davis Guggenheim	The film criticizes the American public education system by following several students as they strive to be accepted into a charter school.
An Inconvenient Truth	2006	Davis Guggenheim	Filmmaker Davis Guggenheim follows Al Gore on the lecture circuit, as the former presidential candidate campaigns to raise public awareness of the dangers of global warming and calls for immediate action to curb its destructive effects on the environment.

◎ Exercises

1. Explain the following terms in English.

1) social issue
2) *12 Angry Men*
3) individual's duty

2. Discuss and answer the following questions.

1) What do you think is the most dramatic issue relevant to our time, and which film has actually

illustrated such issue? Describe the presentation of one such issue and show how it relates to the times in which we now live.

2) An allusion(典故) is a reference to something outside of the story about which the audience will be familiar. Cinematic stories often include allusions to historical, religious, educational or technological points of interest. Describe an allusion that you noticed in a film and explain its relationship to the story as a whole.

3) Why *American Beauty* is described by academics as a satire of American middle-class?

References

1. Andrew Lynn. Appreciating Cinema. Beijing: Foreign Language Teaching and Research Press, 2009.
2. Cooke, Paul. World Cinema's "Dialogues" with Hollywood. Basingstoke: Palgrave Macmillan, 2007.
3. Corrigan, Timothy. American Cinema of the 2000s (Electronic Resource): Themes and Variations. New Brunswick, N. J.: Rutgers University Press, 2012.
4. Curran, Daniel. Guide to American Cinema, 1965-1995. Westport, Conn.: Greenwood Press, 1998.
5. Gamm, Kate. Teaching World Cinema. London: BFI Education, 2004.
6. Gazetas, Aristides. An Introduction to World Cinema. Jefferson, N. C.: McFarland, 2008.
7. Gomery, Douglas. Movie History: A survey. New York, NY: Routledge, 2011.
8. Hill, John and Gibson, P. Ch. World Cinema: Critical Approaches. Oxford; New York: Oxford University Press, 2000.
9. Hill, John and Gibson, P. Ch. American Cinema and Hollywood: Critical Approaches. Oxford: Oxford University Press, 2000.
10. Rommel-Ruiz, W. Bryan. American History Goes to the Movies: Hollywood and the American Experience. New York: Routledge, 2011.
11. Sklar, Robert. Movie-made America: A Cultural History of American Movies. New York: Vintage Books, 1994.
12. Whissen, Thomas R. Guide to American Cinema, 1930-1965. Westport, Conn.: Greenwood Press, 1998.
13. Barrett, Pam. "A Brief History of Britain", in Roger Williams, ed. Insight Guide: Great Britain (Singapore: Apa Publications, 1996).
14. Lyall, Sarah (July 31, 1994). "It's 'Forrest Gump' vs. Harrumph". *The New York Times*, Archived from the Original on October 22, 2010.
15. Ebert, Roger (1994-09-23). "Review: The Shawshank Redemption". Chicago Sun-Times, Archived from the Original on 2010-04-13, Retrieved 2010-04-13.
16. [美]大卫·波德维尔，克里丝汀·汤普森著．电影艺术：形式与风格(影印第 8 版)．曾伟祯，译. 世界图书出版公司·后浪出版公司，2012.

17. [美]约瑟夫·M·博格斯，丹尼斯·W·皮特里著. 看电影的艺术(影印第7版). 世界图书出版公司·后浪出版公司，2012.
18. 常耀信. 英国文学简史. 天津：南开大学出版社，2006.
19. 陈文玉. 英美文学与电影教程. 南京：南京大学出版社，2016.
20. 韩晓玲、张弘. 电影欣赏与英语学习. 青岛：中国海洋大学出版社，2002.
21. 胡荫桐、刘树森. 美国文学教程. 天津：南开大学出版社，2001.
22. 刘炳善. 英国文学简史. 郑州：河南人民出版社，2007.
23. 吕丽塔、张葳、史宝辉. 看电影学英美文学. 北京：外语教学与研究出版社，2014.
24. 吴伟仁. 美国文学史及选读. 北京：外语教学与研究出版社，2007.
25. 张军. 英美电影赏析. 武汉：武汉大学出版社，2014.
26. 尹鸿. 当代电影艺术导论. 北京：高等教育出版社，2007.

Website:

http://www.filmsite.org
http://en.wikipedia.org
http://www.imdb.com
http://www.afi.com
http://www.bfi.org.uk
https://www.bifa.film
https://movie.douban.com
http://www.online-literature.com/
https://www.wikipedia.org/
https://www.britannica.com/
http://en.wikipedia.org/wiki/Google
http://vc.ws.edu/engl2265/unit4/Modernism/all.htm
http://users.rowan.edu/~lindman/lost_generation.html
http://nobelprize.org/nobel_prizes/literature/laureates/1949/faulkner-bio.html
https://usa.usembassy.de/etexts/oal/lit5.htm
http://www.online-literature.com/periods/modernism.php
http://www2.sdfi.edu.cn/netclass/jiaoan/englit/amlit/romanticism.htm
http://universalium.academic.ru/256606/American_literature
http://archive.vcu.edu/english/engweb/eng372/intro.htm
https://en.wikipedia.org/wiki/Theme_(arts)
http://hist.ucalgary.ca/atimm/writing-advice/what-historical-perspective
https://en.wikipedia.org/wiki/Forrest_Gump
http://www.filmsite.org/epicsfilms.html
https://en.wikipedia.org/wiki/History_of_Western_civilization
https://en.wikipedia.org/wiki/History_of_the_United_Kingdom

https://en.wikipedia.org/wiki/Braveheart
https://en.wikipedia.org/wiki/History_of_the_United_States
https://wenku.baidu.com/view/74a5c5f0f61fb7360b4c656d.html
https://en.wikipedia.org/wiki/Gone_with_the_Wind_(film)
http://www.rogerebert.com/reviews/great-movie-gone-with-the-wind-1939
https://en.wikipedia.org/wiki/Christianity
http://biblehub.com/library/sell/studies_in_the_life_of_the_christian/study_v_the_christian_faith.htm
https://en.wikipedia.org/wiki/The_Man_from_Earth
https://www.millennialstar.org/review-of-the-man-from-earth-treatment-of-christians-considered/
https://en.wikipedia.org/wiki/Education
http://www.preservearticles.com/201102244178/what-are-the-functions-of-education-towards-individual-society-and-country.html
https://en.wikipedia.org/wiki/Good_Will_Hunting
https://www.shmoop.com/good-will-hunting/education-theme.html
http://www.widescreenings.com/hunting.html
https://en.wikipedia.org/wiki/Technological_change
https://en.wikipedia.org/wiki/Technological_revolution
https://en.wikipedia.org/wiki/A. I._Artificial_Intelligence
http://www.rogerebert.com/reviews/great-movie-ai-artificial-intelligence-2001
https://en.wikipedia.org/wiki/Interstellar_(film)
http://www.rogerebert.com/reviews/interstellar-2014
https://en.wikipedia.org/wiki/American_Beauty_(1999_film)
http://www.rogerebert.com/reviews/american-beauty-1999
https://en.wikipedia.org/wiki/Erin_Brockovich_(film)
http://www.ram.org/ramblings/movies/erin_brockovich.html